John Bartholomew Roberts
The Most Successful Pirate of ALL Time!

Blood and Swash
The Unvarnished Life (& afterlife) Story of Pirate Captain, Bartholomew Roberts

SECOND EDITION
PUBLISHED DECEMBER 2023

This edition is the result of painstaking search to correct all mistakes, including typos with specific emphasis with regard to punctuation & grammar.

Also, after locating a Treasure Trove of information that had been unobtainable when the First Edition was released, the author spent 8 months sifting through every scrap, which includes numerous references to the Trial Transcript that has been added to the Bibliography.

With both the Punctuation & Grammar corrections, and the additions to the Reference Section, the author added 45 pages to the book, 35 of which were added to the reference section.

Copyright © V'léOnica Roberts ~ 'The Captain's Champion'

'EBOOK VERSION': ISBN: 9780985749255

Enquire: mrscapnbr@gmail.com

BOOK COVER
Oil on canvas by LOUIS AMBROISE GAMERAY - 1827
Part of the National Historical Museum of Greece exhibited at the Voltaire Institute & Museum in Geneva (Switzerland).

Additional Graphics and Lettering by V'léOnica Roberts

PUBLISHED BY DOME PROPERTY MANAGEMENT
EDITED BY V'léOnica Roberts

THE MAJORITY of the INTERIOR ILLUSTRATIONS, DRAWINGS, MAPS, & OTHER IMAGES were created by V'léOnica Roberts. All others, used with permission, except those in Public Domain, are duly noted on or near the illustration; a few are given Special Thanks.

First Edition was Originally Published on May 17, 2018

Also Available in:
'BLACK & WHITE VERSION'   ISBN - 10: 0985749237 --- ISBN - 13: 9780985749231
AND
'DELUXE COLOR VERSION' ISBN - 10: 0985749245 --- ISBN 13: 9780985749248

ALL RIGHTS RESERVED. Excepting the needs by a Teacher or Scholar for the purpose to further the truth regarding Captain Bartholomew Roberts, No part of this book may be reproduced or transmitted in any form whatsoever without permission from the copyright holder.

'Tis to thee, my Stalwart Seaman,
whom I Dedicate these writings.

Thou art the abiding air in which I breathe; thus, 'tis to thee whom I wish to express not only profound recognition, but my eternal gratitude, for without the lingering mettle of thy greatness inhaled into the very fibers of my being, ne'er could I have written all that follows; what's more, the honour, bestowed me by the Almighty, that has permitted me to know and love thee, is too grand for mere words, for thou art the holder of my heart, the very essence that gives me life; moreover, this dedication, as were a portion of these writings, was conceived within the deep recesses of my heart. The rest, John Roberts, belongs to thee.

To thee, sir,
I humbly kneel.

— WITH SPECIAL THANKS TO —

In regard to the 1st half of this book, 'Bolt of Fruition,' which takes place in *'Present Time,'* I wish to thank Miss Keneta, whose charming little pirate story perfectly characterized the Captain's persona, & also Revsueca, whose interesting method of resurgence breathed life in to my original character. Lastly, the enchanting preformce by the charismatic gentleman, Edward Mulhare, and the ever lovely, Hope Lange, may they rest in peace, who magnificently delivered to television the most enchanting one minute piece of celluloid of all time, 'Their Waltz,' 'twas these elements combined that inspired my original story; however, & without detracting from those mentioned above, 'twas the motivational character, a real-life sea captain who changed the first story to reflect his own aspirations, rewriting the story, if you will, & the characters to revolve about the attributes reflected by his aura; moreover, his use of truth and deep feeling, whilst forever maintaining the persona conceived by Miss Keneta, for she, though unknowingly, captured in her story, & with great insight, the very soul of the man we know as Bartholomew Roberts, aka John Robert, 'That Great Pyrate.'

The reader needs to bear in mind that the events pertaining to Captain Roberts taking place within the times of yore, (as backed up by letters, ship's logs, news clippings, & other reports of the period, of which a facsimile of each depicted herein) are absolutely true, expanded into what began, or so I assumed, to be a Historical Fiction Novel built around fact, turned out to be more reality that fiction, meaning that the majority that pertains to Aspasia Rebekah Jourdain, la Marquise d'Éperon noire, myself being the 7th Great granddaughter of Marie Hywel, is also true, as well as having 2 lines to the Great Pirate Roberts' family. This reality also applies to my own personal history, for the historical recounts of my life as described herein that predates the birth of the 1st half of this book: my relationship with Keith McClure & all immediate family mentioned within is also true. The only fiction within Bolt Of Fruition, aside from the addition of a handful of characters, is the story itself, all the historical references are true.

Ericka Blue (née Baque) - thefairygodfather.com for her permission to use her creation, Eric the Pirate. SEE page 198.

Reverend Richard Davies (7th Great Nephew of Cap'n Roberts) for his invaluable contributions: tour of Little Newcastle & St. Peter's Church, copies of several documents, and both his, & his late Aunt Nancy, for their gracious hospitality.

John Mark Ockerbloom (Editor of The Online Books Page) for his great help in my research. https://onlinebooks.lobrary.upenn.edu

Laura Jaramillo (née Smith) & Sue Montgomery for their drawing of Cap'n Roberts throwing Keith McClure out of the window. SEE page 87.

Mark Kehoe (www.piratesurgeon.com): Having learned that my copy of the original handwritten copy of the Trial I got whilst visiting the PRO in Kew, England, had been pinched, he put me onto a typed copy.

FOREWARD
A little about the author

V'lé, being an avid student of the history that intrigues her, is like a bulldog hunting for answers, & being taught to never assume anything, & suspect everything, she's tenacious as hell. Rarely does she takes things she hears, or reads, at face value, not unless she trusts the source implicitly, otherwise she First wants to know the source of the information, & Secondly, if at all possible, she wants to see it for herself, if not then she requires more proof that the source is valid. This aspect, with regard to Captain Roberts, took her to the Caribbean, Ireland, Wales, & England where she hunted for, & found, numerous records within Churches, Public Record Offices (PRO,) Ship's Logs, Letters, Personal Collections, Old Newspapers, etc. Everything in her book regarding Captain Roberts' practical activities, & brief accountings of his life beforehand, has been researched to the nth degree; the nigh on 80 pages of reference material, coupled with more than 100 pictures &/or recreations of newspapers, letters, maps, drawings, book pages, etc, show the immense research she painstaking undertook. The overwhelming records & details found is why she has presented the book in epistolary format; with hopes that in this fashion, the reader can achieve a full understanding, & perhaps even relate to when, where, with whom, how, & why in relation to what happened. With regard to the obvious fiction showcasing Captain Roberts in Bolt Of Fruition, altho' containing numerous accountings regarding his piratical activities, Book One, of this 2 volume set, is merely the author telling a tale of the way she wishes things could be. Book Two, on the other hand; transcribed from a dream of the author's, began as a 6,500 word dream within book one, but as time went on, she has since discovered quite a few facts (both real-life people & events, happening in real places) many of which being within her own family tree, gives her cause to now hold what she previously believed with regard to the relationship betwixt la Marquise d'Éperon-noire & Captain Roberts in Book Two to be false, now to be relatively true. With regard to her own family tree, as people & events in the past were discovered, the author was taken aback by how it connected her to Book Two. For starters, the author has traced her maternal side back to Anséric de Saxe born 30 B.C. (forefather of Charlemagne) where within rests a few persons who are not only of great interest to her, but is proud to state that her lineage includes a kinship to The Great Pirate, Bartholomew Roberts, twice, one couple being Robert Roberts of Little Newcastle, Wales who married Hanna Howell of Letterston, Wales in the 17th century & later, in the 19th century, another of George Robert's (father of Bartholomew Roberts) descendants residing in Little Newcastle took another one of the author's ancestors for a wife. The author is a direct descendant of both of the Howell women. As it happens, as did several other members of the Howell family during the Stuart Restoration period, one other couple being, Hugh Howell[see page 487]*, born 17 Apr 1658 or 9 in Wales died 14 Sep 1745 in*

Babtisttown, Sussex, New Jersey, USA.) married Margaret Howell (née Middleton[1] of Cambridgeshire, England,) in Saint James, Barbados, Caribbean on 10 July 1698. Both couples migrated to the American Colonies, & while Hanna & Robert eventually settled in Massachusetts, it should be noted that long before the newlyweds set sail, other direct ancestor's within the author's lineage, on both sides, had already ventured to the New World via the Roanoke Expedition, which accounts for the modicum amount of Potawatomi Indian ancestry in her DNA; moreover, the author is also a direct descendant of Philippe II, Regent of France.

 As an added thought... In regard to the Stuart Restoration period, V'lé, always feeling a tugging at her heart, homesick as it is called, despite trying desperately to make a life for herself in the states, never having felt at home in the U.S.A.., & thus moved to Ireland in 2002, it wasn't until she stepped foot in Pembrokeshire, Wales on her way to Ireland that she realized her mistake. Committed, she resided in Ireland for 2 years before being able to relocate to Pembrokeshire, where she finally felt like she was home. Shortly after meeting her husband, they planned what they believed would be a quick trip to the states to sell their land there, & return immediately to Wales & buy a little home. Unfortunately, the Real Estate market crashed & they got stuck. In the winter of 2013, they had finally gathered enough assets to make the return possible, tragedy struck yet again; V'lé's mother took ill & died, & not long after, her beloved husband, Bart, died as well. In spite of these heartbreaking events, V'lé, with her memories of both, will never she never give up on the hope that one day she will get back home to her beloved Pembrokeshire, Wales.

Continued on page 488

Sue Montgomery
A portion of the above was added by the author after Mrs. Montgomery's passing.

---

[1] *Kin to Kate, Princess of Wales, wife of Prince William, son of Charles III.* SEE page 488

ALLOW ME THE ESTEEM PLEASURE OF INTRODUCING YOU TO

Captain Bartholomew Roberts, The Man

In my own way, altho' not as Eloquently & Concisely as 'That Great Pyrate' would hath spoketh to ye, I shall, for I believe I know him well, convey those thoughts, reasons and principles that governed the man, known as Bartholomew Roberts.

Unfortunately most people think of the good Captain as only being a pirate, and technically, he was, but it's the reasons for this piracy are what makes him different from the rest, & not only his counterparts, but others in general, & it was this philosophy that placed him in a class, almost by himself, not literally, but into the realm of those who sought to correct an appalling situation as opposed to tamely submitting to the injustice of tyranny; meaning, he was not only the most successful pirate of All-Time, but also a defender of the people, who ever they were, including a freer of slaves; an iconoclastic insurrectionist who sought to bring down the oppressors by striking deep into the very heart of the destructive force, in this case, the pockets of the arrogant class, those who reaped ALL of the rewards while sucking the life's blood out of them who toil. In this, he does not stand alone. To list but a few others: Sir Robin of Locksley, Robert Fitzooth, Earl of Huntingdon, aka Robin Hood; Sir William Wallace; & Pancho Villa.

One instance, which lasted quite a spell, & for no other reason than to amuse himself & his crew, he wreaked such havoc with one of the British Isle Governors, forcing him to beef up his fortifications, again & again, that the Governor was forced to not only get aid get aid from the King, but from France as well. Another was the famed Trepassey. Unbeknownst to most, the crown wanted to get rid of Trepassey as a fishing industry altogether, but while negotiations of how this was to go down dragged on, in came Captain Roberts, who for his own reasons, saved them the trouble. But was the government pleased, No! Instead they were in an uproar. Go figure! Both of these incidents can be found within the Calendar of State Papers Colonial Series, America & West Indies, 1720. The 1st one I mentioned is quite an amusing read! You might ask why Captain Roberts would toil with them. Well, in my opinion, it was a clear case of retribution, to prove to those who considered themselves his betters were mistaken, & he drove his point home so well, that it were those so-called betters who dubbed him, "That Great Pyrate!."

Before these hullabaloos occurred, Bartholomew Roberts, before being taken upon the Rover (a Sloop of War) by Captain Hywel Davies, was known as John Robert, who didn't bandy about his middle name, 'Bartholomew' anymore than most do today, & like most people, he was just moving along, almost unaware of his mundane way of life, just doing what we do today; going to work, paying the bills, the usual day to day, boring existence, when suddenly, after he was on board the Rover, when he realized the Despotic relationship existing betwixt the Common man and his oppressors, he did not like what he saw, being that of the Degenerate Aristocracy, who, possessing wealth and social position, used their high and mighty status to increase their own selves whilst trampling upon those, who, without recourse, reluctantly maintained them in their exalted rank. The main difference betwixt he & most others who felt thus, is that he set out to do something about it. A small revolution you might say, with a small, yet formidable army, & one other very powerful drive which propelled him forward; the need to prove himself worthy of a captaincy which had been overlooked in his case, as it was for the majority, simply because he was not a man of wealth or social standing. For this he wanted revenge, & in this, he demonstrated quite efficiently to those with the power to grant such placements, what a grave mistake they had made.

Captain Roberts knew of these people well, & altho' he was not a poor man, his family owning land, the were not among the rich either; what we, today, would call the Middle Class. As an officer (3rd Mate aboard the Princess, by way of the ship's masters and higher ranking officers than himself, John Robert was occasionally privy to some of the dealings with these high & mighties; what's more, altho' never being the sort to think of himself, as better, he was Forever bettering himself, & from this vantage point, it was easy for him to see the ways of those who did and thought ill of them for their arrogance, but not being in the position to criticize, being that a Naval Vessel is a military dictatorship and the Captain's have, quite literally, the power of life and death, and the Merchants who wielded somewhat less power, were pretty much the same, could easily strip a man of a lifetimes effort. When you consider these factors you must, providing you're aim is to understand how he felt and why, you must. first take into account the strong moral character of the man, for it is the backbone of everything he did in life; never deviating from what he believed to be either correct or unjust. In actuality, his career upon the high seas thrived because of his beliefs, & these convictions; so strong were they, they were the essence of that made him the most successful pirate of All-Time. The fact that he was successful, most everyone who reads about him knows & comprehends, but the why is what most never venture to consider.

CONTINUING... Captain Roberts was not a pirate for the purpose of robbing the rich to line his own pockets. The ships under his command were filled with 2 tons of Gold-Dust each, plus a personal share, which for the duration was mostly unspent, was equal to the 2 tons stowed upon his flagship. Any person, like the majority of pirates, who come into hordes of cash, tend to spend recklessly, yet the very existence of this overwhelming amount, especially in regard to his personal shore, more than suggests Captain Roberts to be of a much different ilk. His crew on the other hand, spent as much time ashore as possible, whooping it up as they say, whenever time permitted, but they never just spent all their coin thinking, easy come easy go. As for Bartholomew Roberts, he rarely went ashore, & when he did, reckless spending simply did not go hand in hand with our teetotaling sabbatarian's values; what's more, the fact that it was stipulated in his Articles that when each man, by ledger, had earned $1,000.00, they would disband. And as for him being called 'That Great Pyrate,' that was coined by the hierarchies of the day, i.e., his enemies. It is all these things & more that gives credence that the he was on a level so different from the rest that he not only shined like a beacon in his own time, & still does today. Think of him as you would a handful of people living today who are revered, e.g., I, myself, have seen loads of talk shows, but in the 1000's of guests over the last 40 some years, I have only seen 2 (both of whom are living today,) William Shatner & Johnny Depp, & most recently, President Trump, that reap such applause on a par with a standing ovation, the instant they walk out onto the stage. The only other time I saw something similar was in a rerun of an old T.V. skit. It guest starred Errol Flynn who did the 'Niagara Falls,' skit (originally aired back in the 1952) with Abbot & Costello. The minute the audience recognized him, they went wild! Being so loved must be a wonderful feeling, but all in all, the repercussions by over zealous fans can be equally frightening.

BUT BACK TO CAPTAIN BARTHOLOMEW ROBERTS...

What his men thought of him. For the most part, Bartholomew Roberts crew loved him, that's not to say there weren't occasional problems (but what chain of command has such not occurred) but generally it was with the fresh men who were new to both piracy, vigilantism, not to mention the unique Mister Roberts, whom most no doubt found to be odd, at least at first, thinking, who ever heard of a pirate who preferred tea to hard liquor, held church services aboard his ship(s), Never pressed men into his service, & was more interested in grain & cattle than he was in swag; what is more, he kept a ledger, & except in rare instances, clearly Paid for necessities, provisions, & services rendered. These are not the actions we think of when we hear the word pirate, nor did they in his time. Captain Roberts was indeed, unique, but then you must remember that what Captain Roberts lived for was justice; & he rendered it in the form of Vigilantism & the act of piracy afforded him the ability to serve justice in his own way while providing an income to rig and provision his ships, and pay his men.

Captain Roberts is also famous for something else. He not Only ALWAYS kept his word, but, unless some force prevented it, he Always did exactly what he said he would do. When he promised, Henry Fowle, (Cap'n of the Mary) that he would return his ship if he secured him the provisions he asked for, the promise was kept.^{CSP CS9 251.v (b)} With regard to the ill treatment of an innocent man (Cap'n Robert Dunn, a smuggler,) when he warned Lieutenant General Mathew that he'd lay waste to the island of Saint Christophers if he did not treat Cap'n Dunn like an honest man, that is also, Exactly what he did! And in one more example, he told the Governor of Martinique he hang him for his unwarranted attack if he got the chance. Again, that's Exactly what he did; after which, he kept the ship (the Onslow,) making her his 5th Royal Fortune, but so many others he let go, for it was not ships or gold he was after or lives either, taking as few as possible, using scare tactics instead of violence making for both minimum loss of life while also enhancing his reputation, always dressing his finest when going into battle, presenting a bold demeanor coupled with outlandish style and flare with his musicians playing loudly, beating drums and sounding trumpets, was enough to frighten the majority and he banked on this very aspect and then brazenly sailing in to their harbor like he was a God or the Devil himself, but he was neither, but rather a very intelligent man, possessing uncommon valor and a flare for the dramatic whose crew would & often did, follow him right into the lions den and come away victorious. This is called faith; faith in yourself and in your Captain, & this to was another reason for Captain Roberts' success. He, himself, was a master seaman & he trained his crew to such a degree, that even when drunk, they were 10 fold of any other, frequently going up against seemingly impossible odds. It was not until they were without their Captain that his crew lost, & as it was, the crew of The Great Ranger made a good fight of it for more than 2 1/2 hours before she called for quarters. Knowing what you now know, do you not believe in your heart that if Captain Roberts had been aboard the Great Ranger the outcome would have been just the opposite? I'd be surprised if you don't. Not to say it's a given, heavens no, Captain Roberts was never cocky, just a determined warrior. Never losing his head or reasoning power.

Aside from being a man of his word, Captain Roberts also Loved company, & whenever he was in port, on business, he issued a command performance that required all the ship's captain's in port, as well as other high ranking officials, to dine with wine aboard his flagship. And heaven help them if they didn't show up.

I have heard or read others, in their narrow mindedness, blame Captain Roberts for the weather and current, as if sailing a vessel was as easy as driving a car in a parking lot. They should try it sometime, out there when mother nature unleashes her fury with a force 10 wind and the swells being 30 plus feet, as if it has to be that nasty to wreak havoc upon a ship. Talk about a grand time, you do the best you can to sail, tho' sails must be furled, leaving little to make your course while you find yourself at the mercy of the wind and the current. Just surviving the conditions at all is the mark of superior seamanship, and of course luck. One day you should, just to add to you own knowledge, look up the number of ships lost at sea do to storms. The figure is staggering.

When Captain Roberts entered Whydah Road aka Ouidah Road, he did not know what he would find, but when he came across a dozen ships dealing in the slave trade, and this was the last of these episodes, not the first, did Captain Roberts turn his face like everyone else and not give a damn, saying they're Negroes like the majority of the Caucasians did then? No he did not! Captain Roberts had many Negroes aboard his vessels. To him they were men. Captain Roberts, not the least bit prejudice, judged each man on an individual basis, & when it came to his crew, the only thing he cared about was whether they were the crème de la crème. Any who did not measure up to his Very High standards were sent off with another ship or put ashore in a favorable place of their choice, & even given a paper, should they so desire, stating that they were not a pirate by choice, but forced was Captain Roberts own version of an insurance policy so the man, not meeting his specs would not be punished.

With regard to Captain Roberts Articles, tho' seemingly harsh, were not to restrict freedoms, but rather to maintain order. His reasoning for not wanting women on aboard should be obvious; not only would a woman be a distraction, but could also instill arguments among the crew, again an article to maintain order; & there was also the little matter regarding the lack of privacy aboard ships, which were not designed for co-habitation.

So to sum up; Just who was this man, this Captain Bartholomew Roberts?

In Short, he was a highly proficient navigator and master seaman. A man with conscience, compassion and conviction, who possessed uncommon valor. A great leader of men who chose to free from oppression those he could using the only methods that were available to him.

It's very important to me, that those who seek the knowledge of his life understand him. Because of this, I was saddened when I learned just how many facts the average reader missed, or failed to retain from the books they read, especially with regard to biographies, but after considerable research, & being fairly certain such occurs because the book(s), &/or other material or sources, was not presented in a way that caught the readers interest strongly enough to implant what they read firmly into their mind, I decided to use all of the printed information I could find to create an Epistolary Biodrama, together with a Narrator, Author's Notes, Trial Tidbits, & Historical Narratives to help clarify certain situations. I was especially keen on this format with regard to using letters, news clippings, logs, diary pages, maps, pictures (drawings, paintings & woodcuts &c) within the 2nd half of this book, & also the Biography. To help involve the reader, I not only wrote this book with 2 protagonists, but in 1st person (present tense,) verses 3rd person (past tense.) But most importantly, it's the getting to know, & understanding of both Bartholomew Roberts, & the times in which he lived, is what I did my best to convey. In that, I hope succeeded.

Dear Reader: With regard to what I have written above, I beseech you to take time to pause & reflect upon the snippet below.

> The test of the heroic Alexander's honesty is given in the answer he received on questioning a captive pirate, as to what right he had to infest the seas. "The same that thou hast to infest the universe; but because I do this in a small ship, I am called a robber; and because thou actest the same part with a great fleet thou art entitled a conqueror."

Sometime after Alexander III, son of Philip II, died, he was entitled, Alexander The Great, but have you ever asked why? Perhaps you should. If you're so inclined, find out; afterwards; after reading the above snippet again, ask yourself the question again. You may find yourself agreeing with the pirate that made the above statement.

The above snippet can be found within several notable works, including: The United Service Magazine - Part 2 (1834), and The Museum of Foreign Literature, Science, & Art.

Blood and Swash
The Unvarnished Life (& afterlife)
Story of Pirate Captain, Bartholomew Roberts

by V'léOnica Roberts
CD-eBooks

Table Of Contents

PRECEDING BIODRAMA
Dedication
Special Thanks To
Forward
Author's Introduction
A Snippet regarding to Alexander III, aka Alexander the Great

BOOK 1 - Bolt Of Fruition	1
BOOK 2 - Willing Captive	182
REFERENCE PAGES & a BIT MORE	412
AFTERMATH	413
STATEMENT BY AUTHOR	414
NOTES ON TREPASSEY & FERRYLAND HARBOR, AND BELL TIME	416
TYPES OF SHIPS	417
COINAGE	418
LOCATIONS	419
USEFUL TERMINOLOGY	420
PERSONAL OBSERVATIONS BY THE AUTHOR	421
THE JOLLY ROGER	423
BIBLIOGRAPHY (Numbered References):	424
SPECIAL NOTATIONS (Numbered References):	425
SOLOMON GUNDIE	426
OFFICIAL PUBLIC RECORDS (Numbered References):	427
NOREWORTHY FACYS & COMMENTS	433
THE ORIGIN OF THE NAME BARTI DDU AKA BLACK BART	435
TIMELINE	436
DISPOSITION OF CAPTAIN ROBERTS' CREW	441
SUPPLEMENTAL INFO REGARDING CAPTAIN ROBERTS' CREW, INCLUDING THAT SOD, WALTER KENNEDY	443
WELSH & FOREIGN WORDS & MOST OF THE PHRASES IN THIS BOOK	444
A LETTER REGARDING CAP'N ROBERTS PREFERRED "BLACK BOHEA" TEA	445
SIX DOCUMENTS RE CAPTAIN ROBERTS LINEAGE & SIBLINGS	446
ORIGINAL DEATH SENTENCES	453
COPY OF A THE PARTIAL LETTER WRITTEN BY CAP'N ROBERTS	454
PAINTING OF CAP'N ROBERTS' HOME, CHURCH & MONUMENT IN LITTLE NEWCASTLE	455
17 PAGES TAKEN FROM THE CALENDAR OF STATE PAPERS CONTAING INFOMATION ON CAP'N ROBERTS	458
A PAGE TAKEN FROM A BOOK BY REGARDING AN AMUSING INCIDENT TWIXT CAP'N ROBERTS & GOV PLUNKETT [B7]	475
ILLUSTRATIONS within BOOK 2 & ALSO within the REFERENCE SECTION	476
HISTORICAL NARRATIVES within BOOK 2	480
LOCATION OF TALL SHIPS within BOOK 2 (minus reference section & crews list)	481
SUMMING UP	484
LINEAGE: ASPASIA JOURDAIN, MARQUISE d'EPERON-NOIRE, et al.	487
THE AUTHOR'S FAMILY TREE CONTINUED FROM THE FORWARD	488
ABOUT THE AUTHOR	490
Books by V'léOnica Roberts aka V'lé Onica & Thank Yous by other authors	492

AND TRIAL TIDBITS:
PAGES: 389, 395, 480 & 486

BOOK 1

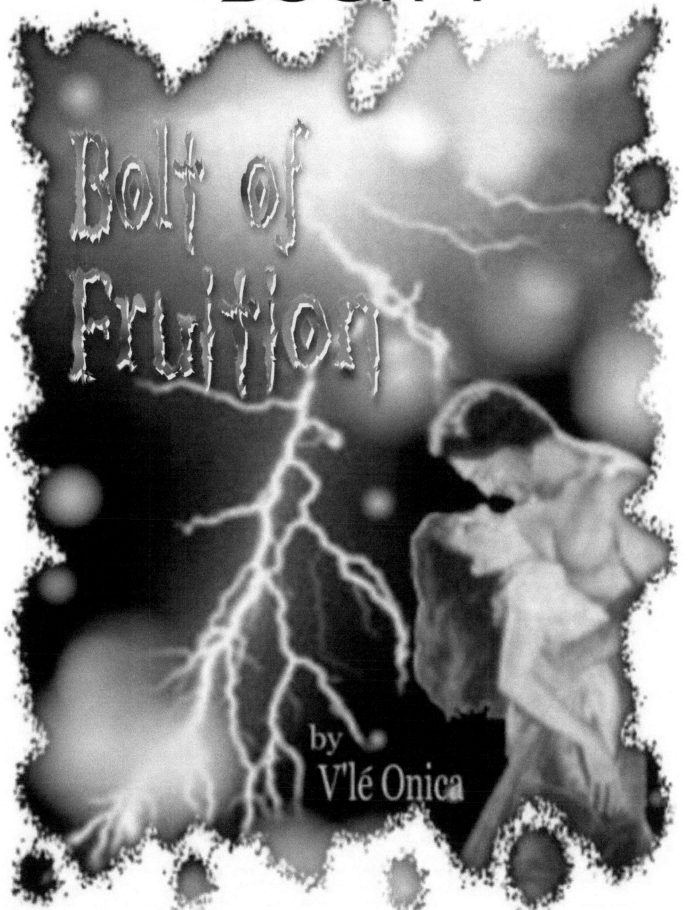

Bolt of Fruition

by V'lé Onica

BOOK 1 - Bolt Of Fruition

Chapter		Page
01	A Special Guest	1
02	A Silken Kiss	10
03	A Carnal Rendezvous	24
04	Remembrance Day	38
05	The Surreptitious Dissembler	48
06	The Proposal	59
07	Alone, At Last	81
08	Returning Home	89
09	The Captain's Out & About	91
10	One Too Many	113
11	The Morning After	126
12	Lucifer's Playground	132
13	A Dream Come True	146
14	The Ultimate Surprise	155
15	The Storm	166
16	Jubilation	175

Chapter One

A Special Guest

Ominous clouds, having unleashed their wrath upon the Western shores of Wales, have bestowed us a thunderstorm of such ferocity that the road upon which I live, it having become a muddy wallow, makes this night a particularly bad time for sightseers, especially upon the narrow roads so prevalent throughout Pembrokeshire. Because of this, I am happy not to be expecting any new visitors before weeks end.

Some years ago, centuries in fact, my domicile, '*Inn Finistère,*' now a Bed and Breakfast, with its eleven guest rooms and sprawling grounds, rests upon a jagged cliff just a stones throw from Saint George's Channel, and although it has been only a little more than a year since I moved here, while bringing to life a realistic transitional period of the Medieval and Gothic eras, I have restored my home to its original grandeur, right down to torches on the walls, period furnishings, and rug covered stone floors. In essence, except for the major appliances, shower bath and lavatory facilities, as required by law, very little modernization can be found within the imposing 14th century edifice.

For the past eleven months, I have had the ghost of an exceedingly handsome Welshman, a pirate captain named Bartholomew Roberts, residing in my home. Throughout the evening, as he often does, the Captain, to take on the likeness of his favorite Frigate, *Royal Fortune*,[1] has been hard at work redesigning the exceptionally well detailed model of the USS Constitution that I gave him some months back. This night, however, the pundit mariner, finding himself rising from his workstation with great regularity as he keeps an ever-watchful eye on the storm, has, to his chagrin, found his solitude laden with much distraction. On this occasion, from one of the many windows of his room[2] as he infrequently espies lights flickering through the flora belonging to the passing motor vehicles, one in particular has captured his attention.

> *At the very heart of what is to come, although Miss V'lé was not aware of it, there were looming forces outside that, whilst marking a bizarre turning point in her already unusual life, would intrude significantly upon the very essence of her keepings.*

Only a smudged glow of lights can be seen coming from the great house, and increasing the speed of the windshield wipers does little to clear away the annoying onslaught of rain that has mixed with the oily road grime on the windshield belonging to the vehicle parked along the cliff side of the road. Although observation is difficult for the occupant of the driver's seat, he becomes unnerved upon seeing who he believes to be Captain Roberts in the window, and believing he's been spotted, he strikes the cold steering wheel sharply with the palm of his hand in frustration whilst cursing, "Damn!" Moments later, when this egotistical dissembler turns the ignition key with haste, the engine roars to life, but as he begins to reverse his vehicle, the tires, slipping in the sludge, serves only to throw more mud out onto the already sloppy, muck and mire steeped road, until suddenly, as the tires find sufficient traction, the driver, obviously well adept in horrid driving conditions, quickly taking advantage of the

---

[1] aka the Onslow. See pages 387, 397 & 437, B2 pg 48, & HCA 8.

[2] The uppermost section of the westerly turret.

cooperative circumstance, maneuvers the vehicle in to a well executed, three-point turn.

"No matter," states the portentous figure in the passenger seat whilst flicking his thumb beneath the forefinger of his fist to ignite it, "for I have laid the plans, and the games a foot." Content as the vehicle speeds towards town; he uses his flame tipped appendage to light his cigar, whilst calmly adding, "'Tis only a matter of time before their well-hidden concupiscence for one another will surface uncontrollably."

MEANWHILE→

Within the stone blocks that make up *Inn Finistère*, all is peaceful. My mother, who spent the day working on her new book, *"Terror in Hidden Springs,"* is sleeping soundly, and Katie, my domestic and friend, having finished with her daily duties, is getting herself ready for bed, and apart from the storm raging outside, and the almost noiseless sounds of my fingernails typing ceaselessly upon the keys of my laptop, not a sound can be heard.

Suddenly, and without warning, which is rare considering the late hour, my rather unusual guest materializes behind me.

"Is it not somewhat late in the evening for work, madam, even for thee?" asks he.

Although I jump a trifle bit when he speaks, I try not to look at him, for his striking good looks and piercing sable eyes will be, as always, too distracting; therefore, as I make every effort to finish my work, although considerably slower, I continue to type whilst acknowledging his presence. "You'll have to excuse me Captain, I promised my client I'd have this online by morning."

Despite my effort to dissuade him, Captain Roberts, possessing an inquisitive nature, chooses to move closer still, and peering over my left shoulder, "Thee works too hard, madam, especially on a night such as this one be. The smaller boats in yon harbour, they will have a rough time of it."

His melodious voice is of exceptional quality, and although he possesses a thick Welsh accent, his enunciation, no doubt cultivated with great attention, makes it difficult to ignore his presence; ergo, despite my efforts to the contrary, I cannot resist the urge to twist in my chair and gaze upon him for a few moments. After which, in spite of the impressive eye candy, I remain strong, and resisting the desire that usually allows him to distract me further, my typing grows back to full speed. "Please, Captain, would you be good enough to return a little later when I'm through."

Appearing mildly dejected, Captain Roberts backs up a few steps whilst saying, "As thou wills, madam," and dematerializes.

Just about finished with the website I've spent the past couple of days working on, I continue to type feverously for another ten minutes or so before reading over my work. Satisfied the wordage and format is correct, and free of typos, I upload the new website to the internet and shutdown my computer. During the course of my activity, I totally forget that I invited the Captain to return, and as my computer shuts down, its usual *'beep'* sound alerts him that I have finished for the evening.

> *Knowing it would take his hostess a few minutes to put away papers & such, the Captain, whilst leisurely finishing his cup of black Bohea tea[1], continued to work on his model.*

---

[1] Oolong. Wuyishan.* China. 'Twas not green, but a rather dark, semi-fermented infusion, that were left to wilt & oxidize prior to firing.

*Bohea tea came from the Wuyl mountain region of Fujian & was pioneered by Monks.

BLOOD and SWASH, The Unvarnished Life (& afterlife) Story of Pirate Captain, Bartholomew Roberts.........pt.1 "BOLT OF FRUITION"

My workspace, an 18th century French Provincial writing desk situated within the sprawling design of my boudoir, rests adjacent to the French doors leading out onto the turret's balcony, wherefrom, although some distance away, I have a superb view of Saint Bride's Bay; therefore, knowing the lightning that abounds within this storm will keep me awake, I close the lid to my computer as I arise from my seat and walk over to the balcony. Looking out momentarily, I am reminded briefly of far worse storms spouting hail, lightning and tornados, and as I put them out of my mind, grateful that I no longer live in that part of the world, I slowly draw the heavy drapes that cover the French doors. Crossing the room to my wardrobe, I change in to the floor length, snow white Pompeian styled nightgown I fashioned from silk chiffon, and taking the candle snuffer with me, and leaving only the red glow of the specially made votive light[①] on the bedside table, I extinguish each of the 24 tapers burning in the massive chandelier that hangs in the center of the room. As I sit on the bed, the satin sheets having already been turned down by Katie, I slide beneath the bedclothes with ease, but just as I am to lie down, Captain Roberts materializes near the hearth.

Taking notice of my scanty attire, the well-bred gentleman turns 'round.

"My apologies, madam." Whilst giving me the moments needed to don the silk peignoir he gave me, he says, "I bring news, and altho' 'tis late, I thought 'twas best thee be inform'd."

After slipping the delicate garment onto my shoulders; wrapping it around me the best I can whilst sitting, and knowing that by his morals my attire amply meets proprieties guidelines, "You may turn around now, Captain."

Noting the remnants of a faint grin as he turns, "You should've knocked."

Whilst making a grand effort to restrain his rather pleased expression regarding my nightgown, "The news that warranted my earlier visit, does still, but be that as it may, I would not have come unannounced, this occasion, had it not been for thine earlier invitation. Did I misunderstand?"

Gesturing no with a slight nod of my head, " 'Twas I who forgot, Captain, and for that, I do apologize; however," demonstrating modesty as I reply, "in the future, when there's a possibility I may be changing my attire, I must insist upon a few moments of privacy."

With a slight nod, "As it should be, madam. And now, if thou art not too tired, may I tell the Châtelaine of *Inn Finistère* the news that induced my coming to thy room earlier?"

"Certainly, Captain."

"Someone hath been watching the gwesty from one of those infernal motor cars. Fortunately, the tempest having succeeded in overwhelming the lubber, he depart'd."

"Watching?" Curious, I guide my feet into my up market, French heel slippers, and fastening the frog closure of my décolleté fashioned peignoir as I arise, I state, "Being a rather imposing edifice, *Inn Finistère* must look foreboding as hell in this squall to strangers. It's a shame they didn't come in. The doing would've put their fears to rest."

"To say in truth, madam, with the rain being decidedly heavy, I fear'd the dolt was going to drop anchor."

"Do you think our drive will be impassable come morning?"

"Unquestionably."

With only the red flamed votive light upon my night stand to see by as I slowly make my way to the French doors, I pass before Captain Roberts, who, although looking upon me with concern, shows no outward traces of illicit desire that I can discern, and even though I wish it

---

① The red flame is produced by a specially made wick containing strontium chloride.

were otherwise, I am grateful to know he is concerned for the safety of my household. Turning my attention back to the matter at hand, "The motorist could've been in search of impromptu lodgings." Pulling back the drapes and sheers a mite to peer out, I sharply quip, "I can't see a damn thing in this fog." Letting loose of the fabric, and seeing his scowling face silently reprimanding me as I turn to face him, "Please forgive my choice of words."

Seeing the sincere look upon my face, Captain Roberts' expression softens. Obviously concerned for my safety as the Captain continues, "To return to the reason for my late call, if this person came in search of lodgings, why be it he lurk'd just beyond the entrance of the drive when the door lyes but a few steps further?"

"I'm sure that, whomever it was, would have, Captain, if the storm had not freshened." Once more taking the draperies in my hand to peer out, "Perhaps the occupants, whilst en route to their destination, just stopped to admire the place, after all, this gothic edifice is rather entrancing. Alternatively, Captain, if our access road is washed out, no one would be able to drive onto the property."

"Nay," raising his voice just a mite, " 'Twas obvious the oaf wished not to be seene."

After a few moments more, confident that no one is outside, I let loose of the heavy fabric. Turning from the window to return to my bed, all the while delighted that I am fortunate to have such a charming spirit for a permanent guest in my home, and with whom I spend a great deal of my time, I find this charismatic, gentleman pirate, to be everything a woman could possibly want in a man, and yet, even though he remains the object of my desires, knowing that ne'er shall I want any other, I still find myself in want of the physical aspects associated with a typical man woman relationship.

Continuing on my way, as I once again pass before the Captain, I stop to face him in the near darkness. Only just, can I see the outline of his face; his abundant, long sable hair; and the sheen of his damask jacket. As I look up at him, noting his face to be more or less expressionless, I find myself consumed by melancholy. Without speaking, I continue back to my bed, but after a couple steps I stop once more, turn, and as a slight smile emerges whilst looking into his eyes, I softly tell him, "I am not the least bit worried."

"Why not, pray tell?" he asks.

"Knowing that the foremost pirate in history watches over my household, how could I not feel perfectly safe." Looking up at him for a few moments longer before continuing on my way, his expression, however slightly, changes to that of a proud protector.

> *After she turned, his slight, closed-mouth smile grew somewhat larger as his eyes twinkled. He knew she was sincere, & such, her comment delighted him, for the chivalrous part of his persona, necessitating that he fulfill the need within himself to be gallant, was such that not only did he seize every opportunity, he did so with an enthralling flare.*

Sitting on the side of my bed, I lean forward to remove my slippers. "Personally, I think they were just lost, but in any event, should they return, *Inn Finistère* shall welcome them."

With his usual style, the good Captain changes moods as he brusquely states, "Nay, says I! For anny man who skulks about, doth not warrant welcoming into thine home!"

"Our home, Captain." Snuggling against the comforter as I lay down, I bid him my desire to turn in. "Good night, Captain."

"Good night, madam!" and dematerializes.

Annoyed, Captain Roberts, storms about his room for several minutes whilst muttering, "Blasted woman! 'Tis determined, she is, to allow access even to those who tarry deceptively."

> *Captain Roberts, having felt the harbinger of ill will, believing his hostess should've expressed more concern, took it upon himself, & standing ready, would repel all borders should the intruder return, & quite handily.*

Noticing that I am still wearing my peignoir, I get back up, slip it off, and after laying it near the foot of the bed, I return to the warmth of my down comforter, but after half an hour, despite my efforts to fall asleep, my mind races on. Not only am I consumed with erotic thoughts of Captain Roberts, him never seeing me in a nightgown before, but also the idea of someone watching our home. The latter suddenly striking me queer, I find myself wondering why anyone would be out at this hour, it being well after midnight, in this horrid weather. Why would anyone be out here at any time, except to pass by, sightsee, or come as a guest; furthermore, my gwesty sits back quite a ways on a private drive; a passing motorist would've never seen *Inn Finistère's* antiquated lighting on a night as gloomy as this one be, especially through such dense fog. As my mind carries on, my curiosity piques me to the point of distraction, and this not be all, for I find myself wondering why I did not consider these aspects a few minutes ago. Captain Roberts must be fuming, and as odd as it may sound, it's the thought of incurring his displeasure over my lack of logic and concern in this matter that aggravates me the most. As it is, being that I am not able to fall asleep anyway, I decide to have another look, and donning my peignoir and slippers, I, again, head for the French doors.

Except for my bedside candle and the intermittent lightning in the distance streaming through the narrow windows (formerly arrow slits now covered with glass,) it's dark as pitch. Reaching for the drapes, I find I am more than just a little apprehensive, but despite my fears, and taking advantage of the light created by nature's fury to give me courage, I pull back the drapes gingerly in my effort to peep through the sheers that cling to the glass doors.

Generally, the weather on a gloomy night such as this frightens me, but on very rare occasions, like now, as it illuminates the night sky, I am thankful, for the lightning makes it possible for me to see in the near darkness, and in this particular instance, with the fog now lifting, both the curvature of our road and the walk that leads up to *Inn Finistère's* main entrance can be seen, but beyond the dim light of the antique lamppost at the entrance of the drive, although I can see little, it's enough to assure me that no one is lurking about, neither in a car, nor on foot.

Thinking aloud as I pull on the cord to open the drapes, "Methinks my over active imagination was working overtime," and although not conscience of the doing, I turn the latch and open the French doors. Stepping out onto the balcony, I thankfully observe that the storm, having moved out to sea, has left in its wake, a gentle breeze that oddly invigorates me as its feathery mist wispily bursts from around the edge of the stone building.

> *From within his quarters, Captain Roberts, hearing the balcony doors within V'lé's bedchamber open, materialized in the center of her room. At first, his presence was only to be sure that she was safe, but when he espied his hostess on the balcony, noting that when the lightning flashed she lit up like an angel, he opted to remain, & as he gazed upon her, the flash illuminating the bareness of her form beneath her silk attire, his thoughts, however unintentional, took an unseemly turn as he imagined her not only in his arms, but in his bed.*

Although scantily clad, the nippy night air is delightfully refreshing, and as I look about, I notice that the oil fuelled sconce by the door that Katie always lights in the evening has gone out. Suddenly cold and shivering from a burst of frigid wind whisking around the corner, Captain Roberts magically positions his imposing physique on the balcony to shelter me from the draft.

"Thee must go in now, madam, or thou wilt catch thy death of cold," and placing his hands upon the ornate levers behind him, he moves slowly forward while closing the doors.

Maintaining eye contact with him as I slowly back up into the room, his electrified sable eyes fixed upon my person, seemingly to disrobe me, fills my being with a wonderful feeling of sensualism, and yet, as if we were being watched by a predacious animal, I find myself so consumed by a compelling sense of dread that I am unable to speak; concurrently, whilst being assailed by the powerful lust filled emotions taking hold of him, Captain Roberts, as he instinctively engages the latch, securing the French doors as they close behind him, says, "By this hour, madam, I thought surely thou wouldst bin sleeping."

Noting the absence of the Captain's characteristic comportment as he slowly enters the room makes me feel uneasy; nevertheless, my breathing becomes increasingly deeper as the overwhelming passion continues to surge throughout my veins; what's more, is even though my luxuria for him is nothing new, this is different, for tonight is not a superficial daydream, and despite my intense longings, my uneasiness behooves me to make every effort possible to maintain a dignified posture while offering a reasonable reply.

"I tried to go to sleep, Captain, but umm, I started thinking about what you said with regard to someone watching the house, and well, I decided to look around once more just to put my mind at ease."

Strangely detached from his entrancing gaze, he asks, "And?"

"I did not see anything out of the norm, but as you said, why come at this hour, and in this weather. And why didn't they ring first?"

"Thou hath no more neede to worry this night, fy annwyl, for the knave hath long since depart'd."

Even though nothing he says is unusual, his deportment suggests sexual desire, and although I do not know if the cause of such is new to him with regard to me, it is the first time he has openly revealed them to me, and perhaps, if this side of him is how he normally behaves when his passion is aroused, it puts another light on the matter. What a breakthrough! Until now, believing that passion was the one aspect of our relationship that would forever remain unfulfilled, and believing also that I was resigned to this, it seems only reasonable to broach the subject.

"Captain, are you consciously aware of the uncharacteristic change in your mannerisms?"

Suddenly conscious of the fact that his feelings, which he has so elegantly kept at bay, have surpassed his ability to control, and knowing that of all things, this is the one he can not allow, he attempts a gracious departure.

"Once more, madam, 'tis time thee retired for the evening. I shall stand watch whilst thee sleeps."

Again beset with confused feelings, thinking 'tis best not to press the subject just now, I respond gratefully to my protector. "Thank you, Captain. Just knowing you're in the house will permit me to sleep peacefully." But as I spoke, another force, unbeknownst to either of us, again dispels the Captain's usual care to observe propriety, and instead of dematerializing as I expected, he again begins to move towards me.

Not feeling I am in danger, yet certain something's amiss, I make my best effort to redirect his thinking. "I am sorry for ignoring your concerns earlier, Captain, and then, afterwards, to seemingly take you for granted. I..."

His gaze is intense to say the least, but managing to stay in possession of his words, "There is no neede to apologize, fy annwyl, for 'twas I who interrupt'd thee."

Noting that each step I take is followed by one of his own, I again, in an effort to distract him from thoughts that I do not believe are his own, I make a big show by deliberately stepping on my peignoir whilst stating, "In my effort to peep out, I didn't think to bring a candle with me."

In response to my statement, Captain Roberts, with a slight gesture of his hand, lights one of the candles on the mantle.

"Thank you, Captain," says I, while managing a modest smile before turning to take the last few steps to my bed.

Despite being flustered as I sit down, I indicate where I wish for him to sit by gesturing to the chair before my vanity table, and thus, as he passes the fireplace, he picks up the lighted candle with his right hand. Continuing a few steps more, he picks up the chair with his left, and turning it around, altho' 'twas not my intention for him to do so, he comes nearer still, and as he places the candle upon my bedside table, he seats himself.

As the Captain and I sit quietly, I find myself mesmerized by the small, unconscious movements of his thumb and forefinger as they glide over his profuse, sable moustache to the slight tapering on the ends before the knuckle of his forefinger eventually comes to rest momentarily on the dense tuft of hair just beneath his lower lip, throughout which, the look on his face is that of an intense stare.

Under normal circumstances he possesses more suavity than the law allows, but this look is compellingly erotic. His little movements enhance his already entrancing sex appeal, and the effect is thought-provoking, yet all the while I find myself wondering if he has any idea how these small actions effect me, or how desperately I wish he would take me in his arms if he could, but not when his actions are inspired by what my senses tell me is an evil force; ergo, in yet another attempt to change the mood, I tell him, "You're staring at me you know."

Speaking serenely, "Am I?" After a brief moment, as his eyes brighten, "Forgive me, fy annwyl, such was not my intention."

Being that this evenings atmosphere has been rather disconcerting, and sensing my unrest, he quietly asks, "What be wrong, madam?"

Not wanting to reveal my true reason, I voice a complaint. "Madam is what's wrong." Before continuing, I take a moment to be certain that my wordage and manner is in keeping with his 'Olde World' sense of propriety. "Our relationship, Captain, has long since progressed beyond the constraints regarding mere acquaintances where such formal mannerisms would be obligatory."

Captain Roberts' mind, obviously elsewhere, unconsciously utters, "Within the dim glow of the candlelight, thy dark auburn hair has glints of newly mined copper, and thy complexion, the hew of pearls."

Touched, by his words, I instinctively reach out my hand.

My action, it seems, jolts him back to reality, and suddenly realizing that his words and manner have been all too familiar, and needing time to bethink, he takes his leave. "Being thou art tired, Miss V'lé, I shall say good night."

The sound of him speaking my name, enhanced by his delicious accent, sounded beautiful, and knowing that he is again himself, well, as my heart melted, I do not want to bid him good night. "Captain…"

Whilst gazing fondly into my eyes, " 'Tis thou who art being formal now, Miss V'lé, but before thee speaks," rising from his seat, "As thou stood before me wearing onely thy nightgown and peignoir, thine appearance was intoxicating. My onely defence being that even a spirit hath just so much control, I hope thou wilt forgive me."

Before tonight, aside from knowing I was a female, I wasn't sure if the man of my hearts desire took much notice of my gender until he spoke of my appearance in a manner that ventured beyond the realm of idle friendship, and aside from society's rules of conduct that lie 'twixt ladies and gentlemen, especially with regard to his lifetime, and also that deviation of such is not permitted within his stern code of ethics, and further knowing that he himself spurned demimondaines whilst he lived, I have always taken great care not to appear wantonly in his eyes, but now, thinking that perhaps he feels the same as I, and believing there's a chance that he'll be granted a new wonder if I tell him that I'm in love with him, that's exactly what I'm gonna do, and right now! "There's nothing to forgive, Bartholomew, for I too have longed to express my feelings, and— "

Rebuking me sharply, "Avast!"

Shattered, I bow my head a moment to hide from him the anguished look on my face.

After a couple of moments, Captain Roberts, in an effort to regain his composure, picks up the candle, and after returning it to whence it came, he moseys over to the large detachable spyglass that I had installed in my expansive room; not only because its placement is ideally suited for him to teach me about ships, navigation, and the sea, but also because it makes way for us to share each others company more often.

Looking out into the dark, storm filled sky whilst trying to grasp why we are both expressing such deep emotions openly, he lingers for a long moment before slowly turning, and speaking to me in a meaningful tone, "Please forgive me, Miss V'lé. 'Twas not my intention to sound cross, but after a lifetime of scouring the globe for the woman of my most searching dreams, and not to find her until long after I have ceased to be amongst the living is a difficult reality. My one comfort be thy companionship, and that being said, 'tis this alone which alleviates the void of what would otherwise be an empty existence."

Again, without thinking, I reach out as if to touch him as I softly utter, "My dear Bartholomew—"

Sounding angst-ridden, "Please do not torture me with thy feminine charms."

Lowering my arm. "Ne'er would I purposely do any such thing. I was just hoping that perhaps—" On the verge of tears, I stop talking, and when I begin speaking again, a noticeable quiver of unhappiness can be heard in my voice. "I guess I just don't know how to properly express myself, and umm, being overly tired I'm unable to think clearly. But, at a later date, tomorrow perhaps, when I can compose both myself and my thoughts, providing you're willing of course, I would like to continue this conversation. And now," as a tear rolls down my cheek, "my most revered Captain, I would like to turn in."

Standing quietly for a moment, Captain Roberts, in his effort to console me, reluctantly replies, "Of course, Miss V'lé. Sleep well."

"Good night, Bartholomew."

Extinguishing the candle's flame 'twixt his thumb and forefinger, he dematerializes.

Removing my silk peignoir and lying it near the foot of my bed, I again slide myself beneath the bedclothes, where, burying my head in my pillow, I cry myself to sleep.

> *As the sound of V'lé's tears wrenched his heart as they flowed onto her pillow, wishing he could take her in his arms & comfort her, Captain Roberts, with all his ghostly powers, was unable to help either himself, or the woman he loved. Nonetheless, knowing that should he become physically involved his tenure could be jeopardized, his love for her compelled him, unbeknownst to her, to remain at her side until long after she had fallen asleep.*

Chapter Two
A Silken Kiss

As it does each day at *Inn Finistère*, my alarm clock sounds at 8 a.m., and as I slide out of bed, I reach for my cherished peignoir. Exquisite by all accounts, the more than three hundred year old garment consisting of various shades of pink and dark reds, has an elaborate Bird of Paradise, the Bird of Ultimate Freedom & Joy, embroidered onto the back of the luxurious Peau de Soie silk bodice. Beneath the elbow length sleeves, drapes 2 tiers of Brabant lace. The glistening skirt, decorated with a pattern of starbursts created with magenta colored mica that has been carefully placed upon the Syrian silk chiffon with mucilage, is generously full. Finishing the décolleté révélant fashioned garment is a strong frog closure attached to a pastel pink satin ribbon that serves to close the front of the peignoir at the waist.

As part of his leave to reside at *Inn Finistère*, Captain Roberts was permitted to take his most prized possessions with him in his sea chest, amongst which laid the peignoir. When he gave it to me as a gift the night we met, I felt deeply honored. I remember it so vividly in my mind, such a personal gift I thought, especially considering the era in which he lived. When I asked how he came by the garment he was rather vague, saying only that he was permitted to bring with him a few treasured items: his tools, which are part and parcel in relation to navigation; his pocket chart book containing works by Ptolemy; his Medieval sword; pistols; 3 changes of clothing; a quantity of coinage; and the peignoir, the latter being the only article of clothing he still possessed that belonged to him before his piratical activities.

Being inquisitive by nature, I asked who granted this permission, and speaking with reverence, he told me he believed such to be a gift from the Almighty. I was also curious as to why a man would own such a garment, and when I again inquired about its origin, he told me that near the beginning of, *Queen Anne's War*, he had engaged a well known seamstress, who, after working the whole of her life in London, returned to Hwlffordd, the place of her birth, and being an old family friend, she created the à la mode garment as a wedding gift for his intended. Having the garment with him when sailing out of London on the *Princess* (captured by the well-known pirate, Captain Hywel Davies a couple months later,) Captain Roberts, who loved adventure, travel, and the novelty of change, believed that one day he would find his paragon of virtue, and as they sailed the seas, he knew that one day he would lay at her feet, all the wonders of the world. Even though I knew I could never equal such perfection as what he longed for in a woman, it was touching to hear him speak with such beautiful sentiment, and thus, feeling truly privileged to be so bestowed, I accepted his gift with appreciation and joviality.

Slipping into what I consider to be among my prized possessions, I wrap my arms about myself while allowing my inner thoughts to get a firm hold of my feelings of love for the man who gave it to me. It's hard to put in to words, but the more time I spend with him, the more I feel lonely when we're apart. From the first moment I saw a picture of Bartholomew Roberts in a book when I was a teenager, I was impressed, and I remember thinking what a stately looking, as well as incredibly handsome man he was. Intrigued, I was compelled to learn more about him, and the more I learned, the more I admired him; in truth, I am deeply in love with him, and now, having enjoyed the presence of his spirit for almost a year, our relationship, should I succeed, will reach the greatest of heights.

Whilst moseying over to my wardrobe and opening the mirrored doors, I'm not only thinking about the conversation the Captain and I had last evening, but I'm ready, emotionally speaking that is, to continue that discussion. In the hopes that he'll be more receptive if I appear delicately feminine, I decide on my Tahitian style wrap skirt, and a frilly white peasant blouse. Opening 1 of the 2 small drawers affixed atop my dressing table, lies the silk chiffon scarf Captain Roberts gave me on my last birthday, but as I tuck it in at my waist, something is missing. Reaching for my Frigate shaped trinket box, which sits atop my mirrored dressing table, I remove the tall lid exposing the a pair of 17th century pierced pearl drop earrings, and a gold vanity Châtelaine given to me by the Captain. Both are exquisite, but when my eyes fall upon the scrimshaw hair comb he carved out of raw whale ivory by hand, and this being what I hope will mark a special occasion, I use the comb to secure my hair to the left side, and wear just one of the earrings in my right ear. Applying a little make-up, I give myself the once over in the full length mirror, and feeling confident my subtle allure will help make the Captain more amenable, I leave the room.

Despite the tears upon my pillow last night, the little talk I just had with myself has put me in an increasingly happy mood as I cheerfully trot down the stairs and into the kitchen.

Seeing Katie whipping up breakfast, I greet her smiling. "Good morning, Katie."

Katie O'Shannon, my housekeeper, cook, and friend, is a capable spinster woman from Ireland, and I am pleased to state that I receive a great deal of pleasure in both her delightfully free spirited, matter-of-fact attitude and bubbly personality.

Wearing a broad a smile, Katie returns my greeting. "Good morning, Miss." And being ever perceptive as she hands me the cup and saucer she has just taken down from the cupboard, knowing that my cheery mood manifests from within, adds, "You're looking rather fetching this morning. Any special occasion?"

"Thank you, Katie." Taking the cup and saucer from her hand, "Yes, I have an appointment." While filling my coffee cup from the pot on the stove, the radio announcer reports the weekend will be a wet one. "Just what we need, more rain. At this rate, *Inn Finistère* will float out to sea."

"That would please Captain Roberts, if only *Inn Finistère* were a ship," remarks Katie with a chuckle after taking a sip of her coffee.

Giggling as I sit down at the breakfast nook, "Yes, I suppose it would at that, Katie, but then I too have dreamt of living aboard a tall ship."

Replying with a positive attitude, "Maybe one day you will."

"Maybe I will at that." While Katie studiously prepares breakfast, I ask, "Are our guests down yet?"

"I haven't seen them, Miss. At the moment I am preparing your waffle and your mum's splatter dabs and Canadian bacon."

"Did young Michael manage to get the paper to us again this morning?"

Using Ireland's charming response to most everything, Katie replies, "Yup. That makes three days in a row. If he keeps this up, I'll have to make him a Bara brith loaf this Christmas."

Dabbing a little butter onto a scone, "No one really likes fruitcake, do they, Katie?"

Chuckling a mite as she shrugs whilst taking the newspaper off the counter, Katie takes a seat across from me at the table to drink some of her coffee while my waffle browns. "I do not wish to alarm you, Miss, but when I went out to get the paper this morning I noticed huge muddy footprints leading up to, and on the verandah." After taking another sip from her cup, she adds, "They're still there if you want to see them."

"As a matter of fact I do." Although hoping my trepidation doesn't show, I utter, "I didn't think there would be any."

Not quite following my statement as she rises to get the waffle, "Any what, miss?"

"Footprints. The Captain told me he saw a car parked across the road late last night."

"Well," surmises Katie, whilst bringing me the waffle on a plate, "the footprints couldn't be Michael's, he always throws the morning paper, and despite the fact that our service road is not presently drivable, ne'er," amid a mite of snickering, "thinking *Inn Finistère* is haunted, would he step foot on the verandah."

Eating my lemon cake waffle as I would a slice of toasted bread, and giggling a mite myself, "Imagine thinking such a thing."

"His car, still being in the garage, it couldn't have been Karl either."

"How about Mister Johnston?"

"I don't think so, Miss. He always enters through the mud room." Pausing a moment, she adds, " 'Tis a good mystery."

"In regard to Mister Johnston, did you remember to add cottage cheese with pineapple to the list of bi-weekly dairy products he delivers us?"

"Yes, Miss, I did."

Setting my empty coffee cup on the table as I arise from my seat, "Thanks, Katie."

"If you see your mum, will you let her know her breakfast is about ready?"

"Yes, Katie, I will." On my way to the front of the house, my mom, whose cane makes a thumping sound as she makes her way down the hall from her rooms (one of the two bedrooms situated on the ground floor,) bids me good morning as I cross into the foyer.

"Good morning, mom. Katie asked me to tell you your breakfast is just about ready."

"Thank you, V'lé." Seeing me grab for my shawl, my mom asks, "Goin' somewhere?"

"Just out front, mom." Throwing my shawl about my shoulders, "Captain Roberts saw headlights out front early this morning, and now, Katie, having just told me she saw muddy footprints on the verandah when she brought in the paper, I thought I'd have a look."

Speaking with obvious contempt for the weather, "Not only is it still raining, the barometer in the hall has been moving towards 'stormy' all morning. Perhaps the Captain's in a bad mood." Adding a light amount of laughter in her voice, she adds, "It always stormy when he's upset."

Replying to what I considered a derogatory remark, " 'Tis more likely, mom, that foul weather tends to upset him, but either way, considering how infrequently we have storms, I'd like to point out that should it be the reverse, such speaks well of his character."

Replying with a smile, "Yes, V'lé, I know, he's a saint."

"He is that." Still smiling as I open the front door, I walk outside onto the covered verandah. Closing the door behind me, I begin to look around, and sure enough, there are several large, muddy footprints on the wood decking in front of the door leading to the road, and more coming from around the corner.

Walking around the side of the house, hoping to find out from whence they came, I see a trail leading to the road. Just as I turn to walk back towards the front door, Captain Roberts materializes beside me.

As soon as I look at him, although I would not have believed such to be possible, the Captain seems to be just a tad better groomed this morning, and although more than a little curious, thinking such tedious chores would not be a factor on his plane of existence, I would never venture to ask such a personal question.

"Good morrow, Bart."

"Good morrow, Miss V'lé." Continuing in his ever present serene voice, adds, " 'Tis a most becoming outfit thou art wearing."

Pleased by his comment, I reply with a happy smile. "Thank you, Bart. You also look exceptionally nice this morning."

"Thank you. I observe thee also to be in a cheery mood, in fact, thou art beaming."

"Am I?" Grinning widely.

"Aye, fy annwyl."

Pointing to the footprints, "Katie and I, already having deduced that they did not come from any of the delivery people that came today, makes it apparent that these belong to the car you saw late last night."

Displaying concern, "Obviously the lout ventured outside his motor and was lurking about the house; furthermore, I do not believe him to be a simple prowler."

"Nor I."

Being caught by a funny, I started to laugh.

"What dost thou find so amusing?"

Laughing, "Maybe he was afraid that if he had knocked on the door, Vincent Price would answer."

"Vincent Price?"

Laughing a bit more, "Perhaps we can find time to watch a couple of his movies this week; afterwards you'll understand the reference." Pausing briefly, "Well, I have editing to do, and hopefully that tedious task will keep my mind occupied."

"Fret no more, Miss V'lé, for I shall keep watch whilst thee works on thine writings."

Just hearing his comforting voice using my given name this morning, calms me down considerably. "Thank you, Bart." Turning around, I go back inside where it is both warm and dry.

Throughout the course of the day, the barometer's needle slowly moves from **rain** to **much rain** to **stormy**, and by late afternoon the house shakes with clapping thunder.

The remaining daylight hours pass quickly, and before I know it, it is six o'clock. As expected, the storm, causing the electricity to cease functioning, brings my mother out of her room; furthermore, judging by the darkness engulfing the Havens, the power outage is fairly widespread.

> *Fortunately, during V'lé's restoration efforts, she replaced most of the electrical fixtures with torches, oil burners, candles, & excepting the private bedchambers, kitchen, laundry, & audio and video equipment, which is located behind a sliding panel in the music room, no other electricity exists. In regard to the baths, there's both a copper tub, & shower stall in each the 6 lavatories. Otherwise the Inn is nigh on authentic.*

Firelight always lends a sort of mesmerizing air to a room, and the repetitive lightning flashes piercing through the sheers enhance the effect. With the sun going down, my mom lights various lamps and torches located downstairs, while Katie, having already lit the kitchen candles, is lighting the tapers within the reception room's massive chandeliers.

Whilst walking towards the French doors within my boudoir, taking my shawl from the back of the chair where I had tossed it earlier, Captain Roberts, materializing before me at the same moment a bolt of lightning strikes violently just outside, causes me to jump like a scared rabbit.

"Me sees thou art battening down the hatches to guard against the new tempest which be abreast us."

With my left hand across my chest, I find myself taking several deep breaths while trying to regain my composure.

Remembering my fear of storms, he speaks in a comforting tone. "Have no fear, fy annwyl, for ne'er shall *Inn Finistère* suffer an ill fate under nature's fury."

With my breathing returning to normal, I continue over to the French Doors. "I was just about to make my rounds of the doors and windows when you came in." Closing the drapes, "Shall I see you down stairs later?"

"Aye."

As I depart, "I suppose there's no need to suggest you check the upper turret's windows and skylights."

"None whatsoever."

Smiling in the knowledge that all is taken care of, I head downstairs. Feeling fortunate that our guests left around noon and none are expected for several days, I see Katie bringing out more candles, and joining her, the lot of us prepare for the worst.

As the lightning strikes steadily, it causes an eerie reverberation of thunder that rolls in stereophonic quality throughout the Gothic manor. The storm is also keeping my mom from both her computer and consequently her novel, and as a result she is a little put off, but as usual, she consoles herself with the knowledge that she and Katie will either play cards or a board game until the storm passes, and maybe even Captain Roberts, who occasionally joins in if I do, will play also.

I too, whilst awaiting the opportunity to speak, uninterrupted, to the Captain, confident that I can snag some serious discussion time with him, am putting my work on his memoirs aside for the evening, but first, the current torrent must be prepared for, after which, I shall ask to speak with him privately.

When Katie ambles into the reception room and stands next to the hearth, "If it's not too early in the year for one, Miss, I thought a fire would be nice."

" 'Tis never too early for a warming fire on a damp night, Katie," comes the Captain's opinion as he materializes beside her. Adroitly, the Captain, pointing a finger toward the fireplace, opening the damper, offers his services. "Allow me, Katie."

Unlike myself, my mom and Katie are never startled by the good Captain's sudden appearances.

Taking a commanding stance before the hearth, Captain Roberts slowly outspreads his hands, and as he does, a blazing fire begins to crackle within the massive rock fireplace.

Undisturbed by the weather, "Oooo... that's nice," coos Katie amid the claps of thunder, "and so romantic."

" 'Tis that to be sure," agrees Captain Roberts. As he observes me, it is apparent to him that I seem a bit flustered, and remembering that I said I wanted to continue last nights conversation at a later date, and concerned such will be libidinous in nature, he promptly changes the subject.

"How is the hot cocoa coming, Katie?"

Just as I open my mouth to talk to him, not only does my mom enter the room, but the whistle on the tea kettle sounds off as well.

"The Captain, Miss V'lé, and I are having hot cocoa, Madam. Will you join us?"

"Definitely," replies my mom.

"Marshmallows anyone?" asks Katie.

"Most assuredly," states the Captain smiling, adding, "a heap of 'em," amid a wink.

"Me too," states my mom.

"Coming right up." Having replied in her usual bubbly tone, it's obvious, as Katie dashes off towards the kitchen, that the storm doesn't bother her in the least.

"Katie," speaking somewhat loudly as she exit's the room, "the Captain and I shall return in a few minutes. Will you be good enough to set our cocoa on the mantle."

"That I shall, Miss."

Arising from the sofa, I gesture for the Captain to follow me as I walk by the chair where he is sitting.

Wishing he could avoid this conversation, the Captain sighs slightly, but knowing I'll continue to pursue the matter, he reluctantly rises from the chair and follows me upstairs.

Walking slowly, I endeavor to gather my thoughts, as well as my courage. Upon reaching the top of the stairs, Captain Roberts walks beside me on my left as we move along the hall leading to my bed chamber. Always the gentleman, Captain Roberts has taught me to forever yield to a man's desire to be gallant, and thus, I stop just to the right of the door. Having opened the door to my boudoir for me, I proceed through, whilst saying, "Thank you." Next, stepping over to the door that opens to reveal the spiral staircase leading to his room, I ask, "May I?"

Being ever gallant, despite his presentiment, he grants entry by way of opening the door for me.

The V shaped room, some 24 feet in diameter, hosts a row of glass panels (formerly arches slits,) one within each of the 12 segments that define the architect's affection for curvature, and my fondness for both late 20th century French Provincial and late Victorian furnishings. In the center of the room, which effectively separates the sleeping area from the sitting room, is a see-thru fireplace built from stone containing several cubby holes. Twixt each segment is a coal burning torch, 6 1/2 feet from the floor, and 2 feet beneath the dome roof, which contains 3 large skylights, which surround the chimney. All about the room are convenient ledges alternating betwixt the torches where Captain Roberts has placed several books, a few plants, and his nautical equipment. Immediately upon entering, the first items that attract the eye is the Bureau à Gradin desk and chair, both of which have been refinished in French Provincial coloration & ornamentation. The writing tools and paper upon and within the desk, as he requested, conform to those that were available during his lifetime. Adorning the walls is a wide variety of maps and charts he brought with him, many of which he has been updating using the modern maps and other detailed information I brought home from the library, as well as still more reference information we located on the internet. Atop the elevated section of his desk sits the 3 1/2 foot model of the tall ship he is building. Twixt the desk and a wine red velvet settee, is a 6 foot tall, antique oil lamp, before which, yet some distance away, against the wall, rests 2 arm chairs matching the settee placed on either side of a seated dragon holding a glass game table, atop which currently rests a pirate themed chess set. From the ceiling is hung a massive, 24 taper chandelier matching the 1 in my room, as well as the 2 located within the easterly turret. Within the sleeping area, sitting at the foot of the king-sized, 4-poster bed, rests his sea chest. Behind and alongside, there's an ornate headboard, a nightstand on the left, and a gentlemen's valet on its right, all of which is shrouded behind various shades of red and black coffin draped curtains that open and close horizontally. Completing the striking room, opposite the spiral staircase, is found a large mirrored wardrobe, all of which I hope helps Captain Roberts to feel relaxed and at home.

Walking inside, I stop in front of the settee and wait for him to enter. It is here where we have shared a glass of Sambucka, or enjoyed our afternoon refreshments many times in the past while enjoying both quiet times amid a game of chess or salvo, as well as long talks, but only rarely did we discuss his past, those talks generally take place in my room while my genuine Ghost writer dictates to me, his memoirs. Our talks here, in his room, generally deal with history; a subject that interests both of us profoundly. This night, however, the topic is to be of a different sort, and although he hasn't actually said so, it's clear to me he'd rather not discuss the events that transpired last night at all.

After entering the room the Captain closes the door, but unlike our previous friendly get-togethers, he does not come further into the room, and although I feel that the feelings engulfing his being are making him uncomfortable, I try to persuade him to sit on the settee next to me by way of a polite gesture, but he begs off.

"I would prefer to stand." After a moments pause, "I am not sure the conversation thee proposes, Miss V'lé, is a good idea."

"Why is that, Captain?"

"I wish not to endanger our relationship."

But unknowingly, as I begin, myself having no way of knowing that what truly worries him is his tenure and the rules governing nonconformity in relations thereto, "Bartholomew, there's no power in the universe capable of harming our relationship."

> *Knowing his objections shan't be heeded, Captain Roberts puts his faith in the aspect that all shall turn out well.*

Continuing, "I have something I wish to tell you, but I'm not quite sure just how to say it."

"Since thou art determined to proceed, 'tis best to be forthright as agreed the night I arriv'd."

"Thank you, Bartholomew." Taking a deep breath to muster my courage, "As you know, we share many common interests, as well as a common problem. Nonetheless—"

Interrupting me, "I do not understand, I thought it was thine wish to continue our discussion from last evening, such, however, not being the case, what is it that weighs so heavily upon thy mind?"

Looking up at him, "But that is what I wish to talk to you about."

Noting my disquiet timidity as I look at him, "Thou ought ne'er feel fearful nor shy when speaking to me, for have wee not always bin able to talk plainly?"

Knowing him to be the perfect gentleman with an exceptionally strong moral code, and thinking of little else as I take a deep breath before looking into his eyes, "I want to tell you how I feel, but I don't know how."

"I knows thy feelings, fy annwyl, and I cherish our special friendship."

Quite nervously, twisting the chiffon scarf as my hands lay in my lap, "I… " then suddenly, at the risk of sounding licentious in his eyes, I blurt out, "My feelings for you go well beyond the realm of friendship. I…, I want to be with you, Bartholomew."

Finding himself somewhat baffled, "Forgive me for sounding naïve, fy annwyl, but we are together, are we not. Wee live under the same roof and share many happy times, and despite its limitations, our relationship has more rewards than most, and yet, I find thy present attitude most apprehensive."

After a few moments I again try to express my feelings, and taking another deep breath and letting it out, "Despite the fact that we only met a year ago, are you aware that you've been the only man in my life for a good many years longer?"

Seating himself beside me, he replies, "Aye."

"Well, even though I want you to know that's how I want it to be, I nonetheless hunger to be held, and—"

Interrupting me, "Art thou trying to tell me thee intends to pursue a romantic escapade?"

After pausing a moment to get my courage in high gear, "A few minutes ago you mentioned limitations within our relationship; am I correct in assuming you were referring to a lack of amorous involvement—"

Interrupting me again, he speaks slowly, "Such, Miss V'lé, is not a fitting topic for ladies and gentlemen."

Still fondling the silk scarf lying in my lap, "Understanding your reluctance to have a discussion of an intimate nature, is, I'm sure, the reason there's no mention of such activities, in regard to you personally, that is, within the history books."

"Quite, for such a subject is best left private."

"I agree wholeheartedly, Bartholomew, except when it's being discussed between those involved."

"My point exactly, and such, I wish to remind thee that our relationship does not extend to physical involvement. As for past liaisons, they should not be discussed at all."

Despite being aware of his unease, "It is not about the past that I wish to speak—"

Again interrupting me, "Even so, this is a subject best left to those who be, at the very least, promised to each other."

"But this is very important to me." Trying to hold back a tear, "Can't you throw propriety to the wind, just once?"

Raising an eyebrow whilst scrutinizing my face, "Art thou suggesting I cease to treat thee as a lady and more like a strumpet?"

"Yes! I mean No. Ah hell!" Taking a deep breath and letting out a heavy sigh, "Damn it, Captain, don't you understand what I'm trying to tell you?"

My tone, altho' harsh, is sad, and after a few moments of consideration, realizing that I am not being flippant, he says, "Just say it straight out, Miss V'lé, but in the doing, do not again ask me to dismiss my morals, for that I can not do."

"Please forgive me, Bartholomew, I didn't mean it to sound that way at all."

Gesturing for him to remain seated, I arise, and turning to face him, I gaze into his eyes, and although no longer able to hold back a tear or two, I find the strength I need.

"Your morals and ideals are the very foundation of the love I feel for you." Realizing what I had just said, and wanting to be sure he is in complete understanding, "There, I said it. I'm in love with you." Although only a glimpse of a smile shows upon his face, I get the feeling it's because he knows more about my feelings than I do myself. Sitting back down, only this time on the arm of the sofa next to him, consciously aware that I can feel his upper body against my thigh, "And because of the nature of my love is the reason I want to discuss the limits in our relationship."

As he turns to look in my eyes, I can see that he is about to say something. "Please Bart, let me finish. I want you to know that I ache inside for your touch every time you're near me, and find myself pining for you when you're not."

"But thee said that ne'er again wouldst thou be tied to a man."

"What I meant was that ne'er would I want, nor have any other man in my life except you. That's what I meant when I said I would never leave you, and a few minutes ago, when I said I wanted to be with you, I meant romantically. I hunger to feel the strength of your arms about me; I hunger for your touch, and even though you're not in love with me, I got the impression last night that you too were beset with romantic longings."

Standing abruptly, the Captain speaks somewhat critically as he turns to face me. "By what deductive means did thee come to the conclusion that thou art the onely one within this room to be in love. 'Tis my love for thee that makes it possible for me to be here." Stopping a moment to regain his composer, he softens, and looking at me with fondness, "Fy anwylaf, V'lé, 'fore thou took pride in being my champion, my existence was concluded. Then, as a result of the feelings that brim within thine heart, my ability to come here was sanctioned, and those within mine, is what made it permissible for me to remain. I fell in love with thee during our first conversation. The love thou possesses for me was and is obvious, and 'fore wee had finish'd our supper, I knew 'twas thee for whom I had search'd for in vain. 'Tis why I gave to thee the peignoir, in my heart, 'twas created for thee. All that be lacking in our relationship is physical closeness, and altho' I am very aware of thy desires, for they exist within me as well, I ask thee to recognize the precious gift wee have bin bestowed; that being to find and share ones life with their soul mate, and henceforth, being that wee already have all of the other elements that most other couples only dream of, let us not dwell upon the one that is unobtainable."

Starting a sentence as I begin to stand, "I understand— "

Before I can rise off the arm of the chair, he stops me. " 'Tis I who now requests the luxury of finishing ones thoughts."

As I settle back down he retakes his seat.

"Although I said the past ne'er should be spoke of, I wish to state that whilst I lived, excepting the one to whom I was betrothed, ne'er have I shared anny more than that of an empty encounter with any woman; such places were reserv'd for the woman I was to love. After my relationship with Rebekah was dissolved, how was I to know the woman I dreamt of had not yet bin born. I wish wee could 'ave lived in my century; what a grand time wee could 'ave had sailing the world over, but alas we can not, wee can not even touch one another, and such being the case, we must therefore find our happiness in what we do have, and thus, ecstasy of another sort shall be our reward."

"But only a few moments ago I felt the presence of your body against my thigh when I leaned next to you. Why must it stop there?"

His voice becomes solemn as he explains. "Fy annwyl arglwyddes, 'twas not thee and I that touched, but rather the man-made object betwixt us."

"But it was solid."

As do all things, I possess substance, and thereby occupy space, but 'tis not the same as flesh and bone."

As I try to understand, "Are you saying that you can hold the peignoir and place it upon my shoulders like you did on the night you gave it to me, and other solid objects such as your astrolabe and books, but you can't touch a living being."

"Well, almost." Explaining further, "Hast thou e'er felt like thee had bin kissed, or felt the eyes of another upon thy back onely to turn and find no one."

"Yes to both of those and more. In other words, you're telling me that you can touch living beings, but they cannot touch you."

"Actually spirits can be touch'd, or rather the ectoplasm that lingers about their souls canne be, but not being visible, as am I, and then onely when wishing to be seen, a person wouldst know not where a spirit lurked; be that as it may, as I said, 'tis not the same as flesh and bone, understand?"

"Perfectly." And as my mind begins to search for a resolution, I recall an incident in my past. "Something of that nature happened to my brother's girlfriend many years ago. I saw it. She flopped on the arm of the sofa, but instead of landing on it, no doubt catching the fiend off guard, it appeared to those looking on as if she hovered above it."

"Fiend?"

"We had a dangerous poltergeist, and when she landed on him it was pretty obvious. It was difficult, but with the help of a psychic, my brother exorcised it from the house."

The Captain's eyes widen as he asks with a measure of hesitation, "Thy brother, he be an exorcist?"

"Of a sort, yes, but please, Bart, dwell on that no more. You said that providing there's a barrier between us, like our clothing, we can touch, correct?"

"Aye."

Giggling, "Does that mean that you could kiss me if I were wearing cellophane lips?"

Musing briefly, "Cellophane?"

"Cellophane is a thin, transparent cellulose material that is not only pliable, but impervious to moisture. It's primarily used for wrapping candy and other food stuffs, and unlike the plastic bags used for food storage and refuse collection, which is a petroleum by-product, cellophane is made from plant life. The waxed paper that your paints and glue sits on is made out of cellophane and paraffin."

"Hmm…" Mulling over what I had said, he begins speaking with not only a hint of gleam in his eyes, but the glimmer of a smile on his face. "I know not if such would be possible, fy annwyl, but if thou art willing, the cellophane lips thou spoke of would make for an interesting experiment."

With a smile, "You keep that thought, but first I have a couple questions." After several moments pause. "Umm… am I safe in assuming that this inability to touch living beings is why you have never tried to kiss me?"

"But I have kissed you."

Smiling, "You have?"

Seeing my eyes light up the Captain quickly injects, "But except to respectfully let the woman know he's interested, ne'er would a gentleman make the first move, neither verbally, nor in his manner. He waits until he's invited."

Clearing my throat. "Obviously my manner served as an invitation."

"Aye, fy annwyl, it did, and has, frequently."

"Umm… I've tried to conduct myself respectfully."

"And splendidly, but a man can tell just by the way a woman looks at him, as well as by her little gestures."

"Why Captain, that's arrogant presumption."

"Art thou stating I read thy feelings wrongly?"

Replying amid a slight chuckle & a blushing smile, "No, Captain, you were not wrong, but most men do not have you fantastic insight." Putting on my come hither look, "So in the future, that's if I could, and I kissed you, brazen as that might be, that would be a pretty straightforward gesture, would it not?"

Chuckling, "Definitely."

"And if I did kiss you, supposing that I could, that is, would you be displeased?"

"Displeased?"

"I wouldn't want to do anything that might make me appear a wanton in your eyes."

Speaking amid a smile, "I canne think of nothing that would bring me more joy than to be kissed by you, but to delve somewhat farther, if we did attempt to engage in such an embrace, such would require us to be done fully cloath'd, and well, I am sure thou art able to grasp the rest."

"Yes, Bartholomew, I think I do. You said that providing there is a man-made barrier between us, we can touch each other, meaning we could hug each other's clothing, but not kiss, at least not without some type of barrier, although you're not sure about the last part."

"Aye, but dost thou not comprehend the ramifications of such an act, Miss V'lé, and the tension created by the unfulfilled longings that would surely follow."

As a plan formulates in my mind, I find myself needing to ask a rather sticky question before attempting an experiment; ergo, taking a moment to, again, muster my courage, I reply to his statement. "Above all else, a pirate needs faith." After a moments pause, "Although hoping not to sound impertinent, my next question is rather delicate, but I assure you, I'm asking on a strictly, need-to-know basis."

Musing a mite, his curiosity getting the better of him, says, "Ask your question?"

"Am I correct in assuming that there is more to you than what meets the eye?"

Not understanding my question, he gives me a quizzical look.

Smiling slightly, "What I mean is — um, I see your hands, neck, face and hair; am I correct in assuming that there's more?"

Laughing boisterously he replies, "Aye, fy annwyl. I am as I was whilst in the prime of life, 'tis God's gift to those who have not fallen out of favour once they pass to the next plain of existence."

Whilst pleased to hear him truly laugh for the first time, I can not hide my rather lustful smile after concurrently being made aware that my dreams of this majestically handsome man, who is the object of my desire, is all that I have dreamt of, I blurt out, "I've been robbed."

"How so?"

"Well," speaking with a smile, "first of all, that was the first time I've ever heard you laugh, I am mean really laugh. Secondly, your attire, altho' 'tis beautiful, it deprives women of enjoying a little beefcake."

"Beefcake?"

"That means to show an alluring amount of skin, as does this blouse. You never wear any attire that would give a woman a nice view."

Seeing that what I am trying to say is not obvious to him, and concerned he may find my suggestion insulting. "It's not that I do not find you attractive in your magnificent wardrobe, it's just that I think a little variety would be nice."

"What wouldst thou suggest?"

"Well, if you were to wear the vest I bought you with no shirt underneath, that would be a tasteful amount of beefcake, and those loose fitting, knee length britches I bought you, the ones that buckle on the sides, they would show off your calves, and no doubt muscular thighs quite nicely."

"Would these changes not make our limitations more difficult to withstand?"

"Not if I get my way," I reply smiling.

"And if thou dost not, what then?"

"Being pessimistic only hinder ones chances of winning, Captain, and besides, I would think a Pirate would be an optimist."

Returning my smile, "I am, fy annwyl, but I am also a realist; nevertheless, I shall henceforth, in my endeavour to correct that which thou deems an oversight concerning my choice of attire, there shall be variations in my wardrobe."

Happy to know he will start wearing the clothing I had made for him, I remain quiet as I absorb all we have said to each other, until suddenly one of the things he had said becomes affixed in my mind. "Did you say you love me?"

The Captain, looking deep into my eyes, replies, "Aye, fy nghariad, to distraction."

Knowing he's speaking more seriously to me at this moment than ever before, I am the happiest woman on earth. I am also thinking that providing there's a manmade barrier between us, we can touch each other. After a few moments of contemplation I decide to perform an experiment. Looking around for something flimsy, I remember the silk chiffon scarf I tucked in the waistband of my skirt, and clenching it within my fingers, I am hoping it will provide the needed barrier. Holding the silk chiffon fabric in front of my face, I say to him, "Would you be good enough to close your eyes and arise? I have a magic trick I would like to perform."

Within a questioning chuckle, "How dost thou expect me to see if mine eyes are closed?"

Returning his smile, whilst breathing deeply, "You won't have to keep them closed for long, Bartholomew, I promise."

As he rises to his feet and closes his eyes, I quickly drape the scarf over my head and gently kiss his lips. Even though the Captain is somewhat startled by my behavior, he is not totally surprised, and not only does he welcome my expression of love, he turns what I thought would be a simple test kiss in to one of incredible passion as he embraces me for the first time.

Notwithstanding the delicate silk barrier, the sensitivity of his lips upon mine was not only truly delectable, it was ten-fold of any other I have ever experienced.

Holding me for a few more moments before releasing me, "Thy kiss, fy nghariad, was as welcome as it was overdue. I am delightfully pleas'd thou remained steadfast."

> *Being in love with the object of his lust, and even though he would not permit himself to believe that such a feat could be accomplished as easily as a kiss, if at all, Captain Roberts' desire for copulation, being stronger than ever before, allowed his mind to relish the enchantment of the moment.*

With our hands entwined about the scarf, "As much as I would like to remain here with thee for all eternity, 'tis time, methinks, to join, thy mum and Katie before they come in search of us."

"You're quite right, Bartholomew, but first, wilt thou kiss me once more?"

"A pleasurable idea to be sure," and as he drapes the scarf over my head, he speaks with deep emotion. " 'Tis thankful I am for the ability, at last, to be able to caress thy lips with mine owne," and taking me into his loving embrace, only this time whilst placing his left hand upon my breast, fondling it tenderly, he kisses me ardently, and as my mind floods with possibilities, the fervency of his embrace causes me to melt against his damask coat.

A minute or two later, removing the scarf from my head as we part, I know that whatever the remainder of the day brings, my mind will be in deep thought as I contemplate just how I am to succeed with regard to consummating our relationship. Moments later, whilst looking into the mirror to fix my hair, "You know, Bartholomew, there's a few things I know about that you are perhaps unfamiliar."

"And what might those be, fy Melys?"

My eyes resplendent with anticipation, "You'll find out soon enough." But despite my efforts to be mysterious, the hint of blushed cheeks betray my thoughts.

Never before have I planned an interlude of a carnal nature, and although I am not aware of it, the ideas running through my mind are making me glow with a radiant sex appeal that is decidedly thought provoking to Captain Roberts.

Satisfied that my hair is presentable, "I'm ready to return to the reception room now." Whilst walking to the door, I turn to him and ask, "Seeing that we have not only kissed, but also confessed our love for one another, do you think it would be possible for you to call me V'lé, without the Miss, at least in private."

Replying with a nodding smile, "Not only possible, fy nghariad, but proper; furthermore, being so privileged, such shall be my delight."

Making our way downstairs to the reception room, my mind is whirling like that of a princess in a fairy tale. For years I have had dreams of being in the Captain's arms and aboard his ship, but ne'er did I ever imagine that out of all the women he had to choose from, that I would be the one to capture his heart.

Entering the reception room, the fireplace still a blaze, we see our mugs of cocoa are keeping warm on the mantle as requested. Speaking to both my mom and Katie, "Sorry to have taken so long, but Captain Roberts and I were discussing a little matter that came up last night."

"Aye," remarks Captain Roberts, " 'Twas most illuminating."

Assuming such was the topic of our conversation this morning over breakfast, Katie asks, "What's your opinion of the footprints, Captain?"

As he stands beside the mantle, picking up the mugs of cocoa and handing me one, the Captain replies, "I have none to offer."

As I speak, I am delighting still in the touch of Captain Roberts' lips upon mine. "Seeing how this stormy weather is suppose to last through the weekend, let's make plans now to have another round here tomorrow evening."

"Aye," replies, the Captain, "lets."

"A wonderful idea," my mom agrees smiling, adding, "Shall we play cards now?"

"By all means," replies Katie.

"Will you sit in too, Captain?" inquires my mom.

"Aye, Mrs Montgomery, I shall. What are we playing?"

"Mille Bournes."

"Sounds great," says I, smiling.

For about 3 hours, until just past 10 p.m., the lot of us enjoy cards and conversation, after which, growing tired, we decide to turn in, and saying our 'Good Nights,' we depart.

Walking me to the stairs, " 'Twas indeed an illuminating evening, Bartholomew, I look forward to tomorrow. Good night."

Captain Roberts knowing from my statement that I did not wish to be disturbed, bids me good night. "Sleep well, V'lé," but as I turn and begin to climb the stairs, he says, "No good night kiss?"

Stopping, I turn and smile, and positioning the scarf once more over my head, I dash down the steps, and leaping into his arms, my Captain holds me securely while he not only kisses me, but fondles me as well. Minutes later, releasing his hold, and as he watches me go up to my bedchamber, he says, "My fondest hope is that thou wilt find a way to realize the dreams that lye within our hearts."

Feeling happier than my conscience mind can remember, I am thinking about the various items I need for our heart felt dreams, as Captain Roberts stated so beautifully, to become a reality. What he does not know is that my dream includes unbridled fornication; then again, maybe he does, in fact, I'm sure of it, but in order for that dream to become a reality, I must find ways to provide manmade barriers that will not hinder the sense of touch. I also need to convince the shy part of my persona to become uninhibited, and for that element, I am counting on passion.

For just under an hour while laying in bed with my antique writing slope resting upon my thighs, I diligently make a list of all the items I need to buy in order to fulfill our romantic longings, and looking through the phone book I locate several shops in Cardiff that may carry the items I need. The place most familiar to me is the costume shop where I have purchased several items in the past. While looking at the map online, I make a list of each shop. Cardiff is about a 90 minute drive, so in an effort to spend my time as efficiently as possible, I list the shops in the order I will visit them. Returning my laptop and writing slope to their respective places, and with the list safely tucked away in my purse, I get into bed. Needing an early start in the morning, I reach for the alarm clock on my night stand and set it for 5 a.m.

Chapter Three

A Carnal Rendezvous

Morning came quickly. By dawn I was up, dressed, and whilst quietly having coffee and toast in the kitchen while writing a note to let my household know where I'm going, my mind still filled with the dreams I had throughout the night, and thinking of how very special they were, I am hoping that they were not merely dreams, but actual bits of precognition, and in that hope, I cling to the belief that life will be as I have always hoped it could be if I continue to make every conceivable effort to make it a reality.

Starting the engine, not having seen anyone since I retired last evening, I can only assume that no one, not even the Captain, is aware that I have left the house, but unbeknownst to me, my fearless protector, who is on the verandah working on his model, watches me drive away.

⊗⊙⊰⊱⊷⊶⊱⊗⊙

Taking note of the time, " Just past Three-Bells," says I, speaking to myself aloud whilst looking towards the morning sun. "Where could she be off to at such an hour?" Knowing her as I do, I do not belieeve she would leave the house without leaving word. The kitchen seemes the most likely place, methinks, and therefore, I make my way there. Entering the house thro' the front door, Katie, I be thinking, will be in the kitchen soon, and V'lé surely would 'ave left a note for her and her mother.

Passing thro' the dining room, I notice a sheet of V'lé's note size stationery lying on the table. Picking it up, I read it.

Wednesday June 11, 2014

To those of my household, I have gone to Cardiff and have every intention of being home in time for Dinner.

V'lé

Returning the note to the table, I venture into the kitchen, and finding the kettle still hot, I make for myself a cup of Bohea. With cup and saucer in hand, I amble up to my room.

Upon opening the door and finding a note lying on the floor with my name on it, I carry it to my writing table, whereupon, using the letter opener graciously provided by my hostess, I carefully dislodge the wax seal. Removing the paper, I am delighted to find that the personal note Miss V'lé hath written me is upon her cherished linen stationary bearing a picture of a fine Brig.

> My Dearest Bartholomew,
>
> I have gone to purchase some special items that, as I said last night, will make our heavenly relationship even more wonderful than it is now.
>
> These items are not available locally. I am therefore traveling to Cardiff with every intention of returning home in time for tea.
>
> I hope that my actions this evening will not not shock you too greatly, for I plan to act outrageously.
>
> My Undying Love,
> V'lé

"She loves me," says I amid a modest smile. 'Twas a beautiful letter; and being 'tis the first my woman hath written me,. I shall cherish it always.

Looking at the letter once more, I says aloud, "Outrageously, says she. Just what canne she be up to?"

Feeling I should reassure her, I sit before my writing desk, and taking from its holder, the exceptionally nice pheasant quill given me as a gift by V'lé's mother, I write my woman a note. Entering her bedchamber, I tie one of the delicate ribbons that lay atop her dressing table about the scroll and set it before her fregate shaped trinket box.

Returning to the verandah, cup and saucer in hand, I continue working on the model of me ship, *Royal Fortune*.

MEANWHILE →

After a 90 minute drive, listening to my favorite audio cassette along the way, I arrive in Cardiff. Leaving early in the morning as I did, it was nice not having to deal with any commuter traffic; but regardless, no journey in the midst of Wales' lush scenery is ever less than enjoyable.

Taking my folding cart from the boot, I am grateful that two of the shops I plan to visit are within easy walking distance from the car park. Heading up town, my first stop is a lingerie shop.

I've chosen the first shop because not only do they specialize in both the unusual and vintage apparel, they also have an enormous variety of body stockings, and the type I need must not only be ultra lightweight, seamless, and sheer, the garment must be crotchless. Looking through the various styles and colors, I find one perfectly suited to both my needs and skin tone. Taking it with me to the dressing room, I strip to my ninies, and like a girdle, I wiggle into the bodysuit. Surprisingly, altho' covered from high on my neck to my toes, the spandex content, as pleasing to the touch as pure nylon, feels like a layer of skin. Grabbing a fist full, my next task is to find a vintage nightgown that will harmonize with the peignoir Captain Roberts gave me. After about 10 minutes of searching I take one off the rack. Holding it up and away from the other garments, I utter, "Perfect."

On my way to the cashier I pick up a dozen pairs of delicately embroidered, sheer black silk stockings with seams in the back, and 3 satin garter belts, both of which are just the ticket to make a lady feel like a sensuous woman. Placing my purchases on the counter, I hand the cashier the tag for one of the bodysuits, whilst stating, "I'm wearing it."

"Very good, Miss."

BACK AT INN FINISTÈRE ⇁

Reaching into the cupboard, "No need, madam," Katie says to my mom, whilst taking down the serving tray. " 'Tis such a lovely day, I thought we would eat on the verandah."

Taking a seat while waiting for Katie to head outside, Sue smiles. "I'd like that. By the way, where's V'lé? I haven't seen her today."

After placing the sandwiches, crisps, and soup tureen on the tray, Katie picks it up and starts towards the kitchen door as she replies. "She left a note saying she was going to Cardiff. It's sitting on the counter by the kettle."

Rising from her seat, Sue, as hurriedly as she can, walks to the door and opens it.

As Katie passes by her, "Thank you, madam."

Following her outside, "Did she say when she'd be home?"

"Only that she expects to be home in time for tea."

"I haven't seen, Captain Roberts all day either," states my mom, "Have you?"

"No, but he was in Miss V'lé's room earlier; I heard the T.V. whilst changing the towels on the first floor bath. I think he's watching some program on dancing."

"Really? That's interesting."

STILL SHOPPING IN CARDIFF ⇁

Walking briskly, I head for the costume shop where I have purchased items several times in the past for both Captain Roberts and myself. Entering the shop, I browse through the catalog while waiting for the clerk to come out from the back room.

Greeting her cheerfully when she appears, "Hi Peggy."

"And isn't it a lovely day, Miss," replies the Irish costumer with a happy smile.

"It is Indeed."

Peggy, who is very knowledgeable in authentic costuming from the more popular eras, is attending, Coleg Glan-Hafren, Cardiff's College, and when not attending classes, or studying for her Holistic Therapy Certificate and Diploma, she works in the costume shop.

Continuing to browse through the book, I pick out several outfits dating from the days of

Troy through the Gay Nineties.

"And what will it be today, Miss, another damask suit?"

"Not this time, Peggy," and continuing with a smile, "What I am in need of is feminine attire, an entire wardrobe."

Flipping through to the few pages I have marked, showing her several outfits, "I want to be authentically dressed from the skin out, with all the trimmings."

"Surely not."

"I'm serious, Peggy."

Pulling my measurement card from her file box, she scurries into the back room whilst saying, "I'll be back in two ticks. In the meantime," pointing to the dressing screen in the corner, "you can start to get undressed."

Appearing to be wearing only my ninies by the time she returns, Peggy hands me a shift to put on while she loosens the strings on an elegant steel boned corset.

Slipping on the shift, I step out from behind the screen.

Reaching around me, Peggy slips the corset behind my back, and while I hold it in place, she fastens the hooks in front.

"Turn 'round, Miss." While she takes up the slack by pulling on the strings in back, I hang on to the front until the corset is snug as she says, "Until recently corsets were called stays."

"Then that's what I'll call my corset from now on." Flinching a mite as Peggy snugs up the restrictive garment, "Not too tight around the ribs, Peggy. The last time I wore stays, if you recall, I passed out."

"I remember," she says. "Now grab that bar so I can tighten you up," and whilst pulling on the lower strings as tightly as she can, "Stand tall, suck in your tummy, and take the deepest breath you can."

"Oh my word!"

"You're the one that wants to dress in authentic garb," replies, Peggy, with a modest snicker. "If you intend to dress in these fashions from now on, I suggest that you wear your new stays, night and day for waist training, removing it only when you bathe until you achieve the waist size you want, tightening it a little every few days as you get accustomed to it. After a couple inches disappear, and stay off for a couple months, I'll be happy to alter your new outfits, gratis. Umm, have you anyone at home who can help you?"

"My housekeeper I suppose."

Thumbing through the morning delivery manifest, "The 1880 Parisian tea gown you ordered came in this morning."

Buttoning up the camisole she handed me, "Great! I can hardly wait to try it on."

Meanwhile, at Inn Finistère →

My mom and Katie, having finished their midday meal, are enjoying a board game in the game room."

"What's on tonight's dinner menu, Katie?"

"I'm preparing Scalloped Potatoes and Pork Chops from your recipe, Dinner Rolls, Mushy Peas, and Peach Cobbler for dessert."

Smiling large, "Sounds like a great meal to be served on my Blue Willow dinner service."

"It is indeed, madam."

BLOOD and SWASH, The Unvarnished Life (& afterlife) Story of Pirate Captain, Bartholomew Roberts.........pt.1 "BOLT OF FRUITION"

TAKING PLACE AT THE COSTUME SHOP→

After a little effort, complete with its hair ornament, fan, and parasol, I am finally decked out in the scrumptious cathedral trained French fashion. "This dress will be perfect for the first of many special occasions I have planned."

Looking in the full length, 3-way mirror, "I have wanted this gown ever since I first saw Greer Garson wearing it in the last scene of, *'That Forsythe Woman,'* many years ago." Turning this way and that, having had the garment altered from an afternoon tea dress to an evening gown by switching its original high neck collar to this lovely sweetheart neckline, I am very pleased with the requested changes. "What more can I say, Katie, it's perfect. I'll wear it home."

"Why wear it now, Miss? Can your housekeeper not help you dress for the affair?"

"Not this occasion, Peggy."

"Why not, Miss?"

"Because an affair is exactly what it is. As for the period attire, let's just say that my gallant, being rather, *'Olde World'*, prefers to see his lady adorned in the more feminine fashions from past eras."

"Speaking with a smile, "It wouldn't be that gentleman you purchased those other outfits for?"

"He's the one, Peggy," I reply smiling, "but keep it to yourself."

Grinning whilst thumbing through the catalog, "I see two new women pirate costumes," and pointing to the sexy breeches, the above the knee boots, and the Gothic coat, "This little number just might be the ticket to drive him wild. Do you have these in my size?"

Dashing off, "Yup, I believe so."

Returning with the whole ensemble, "I hope these boots fit."

Sitting down and slipping them on, I walk around a minute. "They're perfect, I'll take these ensembles with me too."

"Is there anything else I can do for you today, Miss?"

Handing her the boots. "Nope, that's everything this visit, but if all goes well tonight, I'll ring come morn and let you know when to start working on the other outfits for me." Placing the packages in my cart, "It's a long drive home and it looks as if another storm is brewing, so I best be on my way." Dashing out the door, "Thanks, Peggy."

Returning to her clerical duties, Peggy murmurs, "She must really love that man."

En route to the rare record shop to pick up an array of sensual Latin and Kizomba melodies, and the three delicate waltzes I ordered for my gramophone, all of which I also have on a flash drive, I stop in the chemists shop to pick up my order comprised of surgical gloves and prophylactics. As I continue to stroll down the street, completing my errands, my attire is complimented by several people whose comments will not only increase the enjoyment of my long drive home, but will also aid me in my endeavor.

With my business in Cardiff concluded, I'm on the road home. All the way, listening to my favorite music, I am thinking of how I want our lovemaking to begin with a dance, and being the modern waltz was not introduced until more than a century after Captain Roberts died, and that he mastered it easily enough a year ago, altho' neither my mom, nor Katie are not aware that fact, I am hoping he'll be willing to learn the Kizomba.

BLOOD and SWASH, The Unvarnished Life (& afterlife) Story of Pirate Captain, Bartholomew Roberts.........pt.1 "BOLT OF FRUITION"

> *Almost the entire time Miss V'lé was gone from the house, Captain Roberts, discovering he's able to hold his woman, spent the day rehearsing the 2 modern dances she loved, the Waltz & the Kizomba, & whilst viewing her dance contests & film clips on DVDs, as well as listening to her mp3s, he gave himself a bit of insight on how to dance in the fashion that he knew would please his woman. With regard to the Kizomba, he thought it extremely seductive, but learning the dance to be completely acceptable within current propriety's limits, it quickly became his favorite.*

Seeing the Captain outside on the verandah when I arrive home, it's to my delight to see him dressed quite differently than his usual garb. The first thing I notice is that his crimson colored Boléro jacket exposes a goodly amount of his muscular torso, and the open sided, long sleeves, shows off his well-developed biceps.

What a gracious and accommodating gentleman he is to honor my request, thinks I, and as always, in grand style, and although I must admit I'm already drooling, I am eagerly waiting for him to come nearer so I can have a better look.

To match his jacket, the Captain's loose fitting knee britches with split, outside side seams held in place by metal frog like closures, shows more than just a wee bit of his muscular thighs, and although somewhat difficult to see from this angle, I am making an effort. Adding to this picture are his thigh high boots, which, when worn in pirate fashion, as are his, the upper portion of the boot is allowed to drape inside out about the calf at a jaunty angle. Lastly, off his left side, hangs his jewel encrusted, Medieval sword.

Turning off the engine, I reach down to my train, and finding the wrist loop, I slide it over my right hand. Being that the ground is still drenched from last nights storm, I am forced to step directly onto the elevated walk when getting out of my 1938 Jaguar SS convertible; after which, taking care not to spoil my gown while I put the top up, I drape my train behind my back, and over my shoulder. Finally, as I reach down to pick up my packages, Captain Roberts materializes behind me.

Whispering in my ear, "Thou art a vision of loveliness." And reaching for my packages he adds, "Permit me."

Being ever observant, he notices the sheer, skin tone garment being worn beneath my dress, and taking a chance, shivers surge up my spine as he gently kisses the nape of my neck, and while my breathes betray the emotions that flood my being as my eyes close for a moment, I lean against him; an action that pleases him greatly.

Learning that the body stocking provides the barrier needed for him to touch what appears to be my bare skin, we are both instilled with so much confidence, it's all we can do to compose ourselves as I turn and gaze upon him with a demure smile, even so, myself being determined not to spoil my surprise, it requires all my inner strength not to kiss his lips.

After parting, "My thanks, kind sir, and for thine approval, for such fills my being with boundless joy." My words, serving a dual purpose, lets him know not only that I appreciate his helpfulness, but welcome his familiarity, and by implementing the most basic of feminine devices by way of the of twirling my parasol as I seductively stroll down the walk towards the house, tells him that he is free to kiss me whenever it pleases him to do so.

> *Hearing a car pull up, Katie went to look, & when she opened the front door she could see that the Captain's eyes, clearly fixed upon Miss V'lé, were drinking in her every move as the tightness of her gown accentuated the natural sashay of her hips.*

"Welcome home, Miss."

Handing her my parasol as I walk in, "Thank you, Katie."

"What a beautiful gown. Any special occasion?"

Hearing Katie's question as he enters, the Captain replies to her himself. "Ne'er should things of joy and beauty be questioned, Katie, onely appreciat'd."

Noting that my Captain's arms are bulging with packages, "Thank you, Captain. Just set them on the secretary."

Doing as I ask, my Captain, observing my jubilant demeanor, "Thou appears cheery."

Beaming with enthusiasm, "I am, Captain. I am."

Curious to know what I have purchased, he peeks in one of the bags.

To distract him from his curiosity, "Wilt thou place the green package on the buffet under the stereo, please? It contains records for the gramophone."

"Dost thou wish me to bring the machine downstairs, fy melys?"

Smiling at him. "Yes, please. That would be wonderful."

Returning my smile with a slight nod, he carries the green package to the buffet, and having sat it down, he heads for his room.

For several months now, ever since he made his presence known to Katie and Sue, being there's little need for him to dematerialize, the Captain, wearing his period clothing, remains visible most of the time, even in the presence of guests, and not merely visible, but occasionally he socializes with them as well.

Katie's uniform is a traditional 18th Century maids outfit, and my mom usually wears a simple chemise with both a fichu and waist sash, all of which adds to the atmosphere and charm of this old place. As for myself, already having an array of period attire, one never ventures to predict what I might wear.

In preparing for what I hope will be a magical evening, knowing the gramophone is a windup machine, and therefore, like my new stereo system, which also does not depend on electricity due to the solar I have discretely installed, I am undeterred by the ever nearing storm.

Katie, bringing in a large tray and setting it on the coffee table in the conversation section of the reception room, "I thought you'd appreciate some refreshments after your trip to town, Miss."

"Thank you, Katie." Helping myself to a cup of coffee, a couple hors d'oeuvres, and a apéritif of Sambucka, "I've wanted this dress ever since I saw it in a movie more than 30 years ago, so when I was in Cardiff a couple months back, I had the visiting couture for period attire fashion it for me. It arrived from Paris this morning."

Having poured a cup of tea for the Captain, who will be down directly, Katie places it on the mantle for him like she does most every evening. "Looks like you'll be needing my help to get undressed this evening, Miss."

"No need, Katie, but I may need your help getting dressed in the morning."

While awaiting my beloved's return, I am still a little fearful that he may not approve of my amorous plans; after all, I am a lady, and last night, having to pull teeth just to get him to skirt the subject, I figure I might have to seduce him, and being that in my case that shoe has always been on another's foot, my skills in the art of seduction are rather limited; however, with passion as my guiding force, I intend to make every conceivable effort.

Returning with the gramophone, hoping one of the records I purchased will be suitable for the Kizomba, Captain Roberts, with aspirations, places it on the buffet before the stereo.

"Katie, how long before dinner is ready?"

"Perhaps a quarter hour, Miss. I was beginning to think I would need to reheat yours, although how you expect to eat much with that tight dress on is bewildering to me. I'll say one thing though, it does wonders for your figure."

Although he is not aware of it, I know that Captain Roberts is only a few steps behind me, and fairly sure that two or three promiscuous comments will create a few sparks within the fibers of my paragon of virtue, along with any other feminine wiles I can dream up, I reply, "Oh, it isn't the dress, Katie," giving her a wink whilst indicating to her that I know the Captain's right behind me, "it's my steel boned stays."

As I turn, seeing his faint, yet readable expression, pleased to see I'm succeeding, I act surprised. "Oh, you've returned, Captain," and looking past him and into the music room, "Thank you for bringing down the gramophone." Looking at him again, it's pretty clear as he looks upon me, that at this moment he's looking past my dress. Good, thinks I, smiling a mite, the remark about my steel boned stays was an attention getter, but then, just as he said last night, a woman lets a man know when she's interested. Well, I've let him know, and although he may be unaware of just how far my plans dare to venture, he lets me know he got the message with a subtle grin.

Moving past me slowly, he says, "I shall get a cloth to wipe away the dust."

Entering the kitchen he finds my mother. "Good evening, Mrs Montgomery."

"Good evening, Captain. Is there something I can get for you?"

"I am in neede of a cloth to wipe the dust from the gramophone."

"I'll take care of that chore for you," and taking a dust cloth from one of the drawers, "Where is it?"

"On the buffet before the stereo."

"I'll see to it immediately."

"Thank you, madam." Dazzled by the attire worn by his hostess, "And now, if you will excuse me, I must change, as my attire is not befitting Miss V'lé's gown."

Smiling broadly as my mom eyes him up and down, "I think she'd prefer you dressed as you are now."

With a mild chuckle, "Then I shall dress thus to-morrow." And without further discussion, he departs.

Seeing my gallant as he enters the foyer, I accost him, and implementing another seductive tactic, I rise to my tip toes, and whispering into his ear, "I intend to run my fingers through that glorious mane of yours, Captain."

Noting his expression to be one of both doubt and desire, I add, "As I pointed out yesterday, Captain, a pirate needs faith, above all else," and in my continual effort to make full use of my female devices, I dash off before he can reply.

All through dinner, both Katie and my mom ramble on about how sexy Captain Roberts looked in his new outfit.

"Yes, very becoming," I reply, speaking with a gleam of desire in my eyes.

"Makes one wish he were alive and available," remarks, Katie.

Smiling, "I know exactly what you mean, Katie, but then he has always defined the phrase 'eye candy.'"

"He certainly does," my mom agrees. "And the outfit he was wearing today was scrumptious."

Reaching for another helping of scalloped potatoes, Katie again remarks on the Captain's magnetism. "I dare say that in his day he would 'ave been impossible to resist."

Smiling as I take a sip of my coffee, "Yes, men like him, meaning he has strength and vigor, as well as being daring and handsome, they are the ones that make it difficult for a woman to remain a lady, if you get my meaning."

Pouring for herself another cup of tea, "I am sure he had them lining up," states Katie.

"Perhaps that's why he went to sea," states my mom while taking another dinner roll from the bun warmer. "Being not only handsome, but also a man possessing idealistic morals, it might've been his only way to escape the hoard of promiscuously females trying to catch him."

Giggling at her comment, "Mom, he'll hear you."

Moments later, just as I am finishing my coffee, Captain Roberts materializes beside me. Wearing another of the several outfits I had custom made for him some months back, he is carefully groomed. His stylish crimson damask, 17th century Gentleman's knee length coat, worn atop both a matching waistcoat and a white silk pirate shirt with ruffled cuffs, is trimmed with a white Venetian Lace jabot. The coat itself, with its gold Doubloon buttons and gold edging, is secured by a broad leather belt sporting a large bronze buckle in the shape of a frigate. His billowing black, knee length trousers, fashioned from broadcloth, make way for the cut of his boots. The black tricorne that rests upon a crimson and white bandana tied around his head; covering the top of his ears, is adorned with two curled ostrich plumes: one crimson, one black. About his neck, is his famous multi-colored diamond cross hanging on a multi-strand, heavy gold chain. Completing the ensemble, is a pair of finely woven, white cotton gloves, and a leather frog on his belt supporting the scabbard that holds his bejeweled medieval sword. Even though I had bought this outfit for him months ago, he has not worn it until this night. The Captain always dresses well, but even so, I have not seen him in such elegant finery since the night he first appeared to me many months ago; 'twas also the only time I have ever seen him wearing his red silk bandoleer with his two pairs of elegant flintlock pistols, and tonight, as he stands before me, his imposing posture denotes the great pride he takes in his appearance.

"You look magnificent Captain," says I.

My mom, smiling, "Indeed you do."

"Very handsome," says Katie.

"Thank you ladies," says he, offering a moderate bow. Turning to speak to me, "I felt the beauty of thy gown required my dress to be equally fashionable."

"I hoped you'd feel that way, Captain, although I must admit," as my cheeks blush, "the outfit you had on earlier complemented your physique deliciously."

If my words were not sufficient, the gleam in my eyes, whilst verbalizing such a daring statement, coupled with my little mannerisms, spoke quite clearly to Captain Roberts, and thus, as he looks deep into my eyes, "Such being the case I shall be pleas'd to wear it often."

Speaking amid an inviting smile whilst pulling out my chair, he asks, while extending his hand, "May I escort thee thither?" As I place my hand atop his, he says, "Excuse us ladies."

Exiting the dining room, "I gather from the array of thy seductive statements, thou hast plans for the evening."

"Yes, Bartholomew, I do, but I am worried thou may not approve."

In an attempt to put my fears at ease as we pass thro' the conversation area en route to the music section of the massive reception room, he assuringly states, "Nothing thou art capable of could possibly sully thy reputation, nor give me cause to think less of thee."

"Even if amatory?"

Stopping to face me, "Altho' I have no idea how thee intends to accomplish such remarkable feats, mine eyes should tell thee that not onely have I no objections to thy plans, but also that the ability for us to make sweet love would be my greatest joy."

Thinking that lovemaking with him would be anything but 'sweet;' more a kin to dynamically assertive, I would think. Nevertheless, in the midst of a demur smile with regard to his statement, I am somewhat troubled. "My dearest Bartholomew, my love and need of you is beyond words or measure, but—"

"But what?"

"I'm scared."

"Of what?"

"That things won't work out right, and—"

Shushing me, he interrupts. "Let us just give way for the night to unfold as God and nature tends."

Smiling, I gesture for him to escort me to the buffet, and opening the green bag containing the records I purchased in Cardiff, upon which I wrote the type of dance each is best suited, the first record is the haunting waltz from *'Edward Scissorshands.'* Having placed the record on the gramophone, clearly seeing in my mind all the times I have dreamt of this evening, I wind up the mechanism by turning the crank.

Extending his hand amid a seductively piercing look, I readily place mine atop his, and escorting me to the middle of the room, he says, "I've been practicing."

As we gradually begin to moving in a circular pattern, adding a few subtle variations to his movements, he begins leading me in the waltz, "Practicing, huh. You have the advantage sir, for we have not danced together since the night we met." As we travel about the room, all that comes to mind is the belief that both of us professing our love for one another has opened a new and wonderful world for us.

"Whyfor didst thou decide to wear a gown of such fashion today?"

"I remembered thee saying how beautifully feminine the fashions were in previous centuries, and being in complete agreement, I decided to increase my wardrobe."

"I am aware of thy diverse fashions, but dare I hope thou hast plans to wear more such garments so richly elegant?"

Smiling as we move jauntily about the room, "Yes. I plan to outfit an entire wardrobe from several eras."

"Art thou not concerned with what the townspeople's reaction might be?"

Shrugging, "Altho' only seldom here, I often wore outfits from different eras when living in the U.S., and no found it particularly hinky, in fact, I was, and am, frequently complemented."

"When dost thou plan to begin designing thy new ensembles?"

"I'll look at some old movies and the period fashion books I picked up at the library in the morning, but for the most part, I pretty much know what I want."

Escorting me to the gramophone as the record finishes, "Just the same, may I offer my humble suggestions?"

Beaming, "I was hoping thee would, fy Nghapten, for thine opinion is very important to me."

"A charming address, fy nghariad."

Flashing him a modest smile, I continue looking thro' the records. "Any preference?"

"Aye," replying jovially. "Didst thou purchase anny Latin or Kizomba melodies?"

"Funny thou should ask that, because in hoping thou wouldst not be opposed to learning the more modern, and dare I say, erotic dances, I bought several."

Replying, "I spent the better part of the day studying thy dance videos. The Kizomba, although I found it to be quite seductive, methinks it will my favourite."

Smiling, "Mine too. Of course we would both need to be wearing less restrictive attire.

"If it pleases thee, fy annwyl, would to-morrow's eve be too soon?"

Whilst my head nods slightly, I reply, "Perfect!" amid a slight smile.

While deciding which record to play, Katie enters the room carrying a heavy tray with a pot of hot cocoa, four mugs, and a large bowl of mini marshmallows.

Gallant as always, the Captain walks over to her, and taking the tray, "Allow me, Katie."

"Thank you, Captain. You are, without question, God's own gallant."

Giving her a slight nod as he takes the tray from her hands, Katie heads for the gramophone. "Any preference, Miss?"

"Yes, I'd like to hear either, *'Remember,'* from the film Troy, or the love song from Titanic, both of which always make me think of you, fy Nghapten."

Setting the tray on the coffee table, whilst Katie opts to play the mp3 recording of *'Remember'* on the built in stereo, I ask, "May I pour you a mug, fy Nghapten?" But when I look at him, it's clear to see that he's listening to the lyrics with great interest, and thus I remain quiet, as does, Katie.

As Katie's next choice, the haunting melody from Edward Scissorshands begins to play again, this time the mp3 version, my Captain, taking me firmly in his arms, we gently sway for a few moments before we begin to waltz.

Having filled the mugs with hot cocoa, Katie, quietly leaving the room, makes her way to the doorway of my mom's rooms. Finding her in her sitting room, "Your cocoa is waiting for you in the music room, madam."

"Thanks, Katie," replies my mom in a cheerful voice as she gets up from her computer table, and turning off the wall speaker, "It's nice to hear music playing on the Bose® stereo system V'lé had wired throughout the house.

"They're doing a lot more than listening, madam," declares Katie, grinning. "They're dancing."

Hobbling to the archway leading to the music room, my mom is surprised to find her daughter and Captain Roberts waltzing. "Do you get the impression something has changed, Katie?"

"Yes, madam," replies Katie, cheerfully. "From my perspective, it looks like they have found a way to increase their happiness."

When the music ends, I curtsy as Captain Roberts bows. Escorting me to the mantle where Katie had placed our 2 mugs of hot cocoa, my mother and Katie enter the room.

As Nights In White Satin begins, "Good evening, V'lé. Captain," begins my mom, "How is it you two are able to dance with each other all of a sudden?"

Katie, also curious. "Yes, I would like to know that one myself."

Keeping our secret, Captain Roberts explains. "It seemes that all we needed was some sort of man-made barrier, like these gloves."

"How come it took this long to find out, Captain?" asks my mom.

"Being that gloves are worn onely on formal occasions, the situation never came up before."

"I think it's wonderful, and now, thinking you two would prefer to be alone, I think I'll turn in. We can meet for cards tomorrow, instead." Setting her empty mug on the tray, she bids us, "Goodnight," and as she departs, we in turn, wish her a good night.

Noting the subtle look on the Captain's face, and understanding its meaning perfectly, "If there's nothing else, Miss, I too shall retire for the evening."

"There's nothing, Katie. Goodnight, and thank you for the hot cocoa."

Picking up the serving tray, "I'll just drop this off in the kitchen on my way to bed."

A couple moments later, when she disappears from view, "I'll be right back, fy Nghapten, I forgot to speak to Katie about tomorrow nights dinner."

Captain Roberts, having graciously giving me a slight nod of approval, I dash off.

Entering the foyer, I pick up both the garment bag, and the small box resting on the table, and lifting the front of my gown, I proceed upstairs and into my room to arrange a few details. After placing two items under my pillow, I step up to my bureau in order to put the bag containing the rest of the goodies I purchased in the top drawer, upon which, I

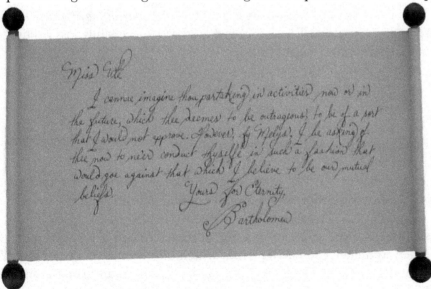

find a letter from my beloved Captain. Untying the scroll, I read the note he obviously wrote in response to the one I wrote him this morning.

As I place the scroll in the top drawer of my vanity, I remind myself that there's no getting around the fact that he's an apparition, and perhaps there are rules; therefore, if the transparent surgical gloves I bought will not allow me to run my fingers through his hair, I shan't proceed further, and taking a pair of the smaller size with me whilst exiting my room, I put them on. Heading down the hall, I glance into the music room where I see Captain Roberts patiently awaiting my return.

Noting my presence on the upper landing, Captain Roberts, lowering the needle onto the record, plays the beautiful music I snagged out of the episode of *'Madrid,'* from the TV series, *'Outlaws,'* and walking to the foot of the staircase he waits. Gazing up at me with an entrancing expression, he admires the feminine veil of chiffon, noting not only its subtle beauty, but recognizes its dual purpose in providing the needed man-made barrier, and, should it be sufficient, he'll be free to kiss me.

Bowing to me as I step on the floor of the foyer, I return my gallants gesture by making the lowest curtsy possible in my gown.

Captain Roberts, a man who possesses immense perception, extends his hand downward, palm up, and as I place my hand atop his, he draws me upright. Once fully erect, my gallant Captain, as he slowly positions the veil in front of my face, gazes upon me with incredible bedroom eyes before drawing me tightly into his embrace; whereby, taking my face gently within his hands, he oh so deliciously kisses me.

After which, "The piece of music you chose, was it by design?"

"Aye. I recognized the name."

"Then let us truly hear it," and walking over to the buffet, I turn off the gramophone, and using the stereo's control panel, I make three selections beginning with *Madrid*, to which I add an excerpt from *'Beethoven's 7th,'* and excerpts of Hans Zimmer's, *'The Kraken.'*

Strangely, the storm outside adds a mysterious air to the already present ambiance created by the crackling fire and candles that softly illuminate the room.

"This, fy Ngariad, shall be an enchanted evening."

After a few moments as we begin to dance in keeping with his times, I am doing my best to follow him. "I see thou art fond of this piece, fy Nghapten." Indicating my desire to stop as we approach the fireplace, my gallant, ever so gracefully, slows until we are positioned before the hearth. Lifting the veil out of the way, praying that the *'stay-all-day*®*'* lipstick will be enough of a barrier, my heart pounds, I lean forward, and as I successfully kiss his lips, I almost swoon as all of my uncertainties simply vanish.

In obvious amazement, the look on his face tells a world of thoughts as he quietly asks, "How—"

"One should never question a miracle, fy Nghapten, even when such is a man-made invention."

"When one knows that what they want and what can be atchiev'd is rarely realiz'd, yet still reaches beyond rational thinking, I must venture to ask why."

"An interesting statement for the world's most successful pirate. Was it not thee who time and again rushed in against impossible odds, always coming out the victor?"

"Aye, 'twas indeed, fy annwyl."

"Then I say to thee that in most cases, providing a great enough effort is made to discover the secrets needed to unlock the barriers, that which one wants *can* be achieved," and at that moment, with what appears to be my bare hand, I reach up and run my fingers through his long, curly hair.

To ease his bewilderment, altho' with no malice intended, the Captain is a little rough as he grasps my wrist. "Where didst thou find gloves such as these?"

Speaking tenderly, "At the chemist's shop, but as palavering will only spoil the mood, let us not concern ourselves with details."

Given courage by the pleasure-seeking smile that appears on his face whilst gently kissing my wrist, I speak bluntly. "And wilt the man of my dreams make sweet love to me?"

Before the echo of my question dies, the man I have been in love with most of my life lifts me into the cradle of his strong, muscular arms and carries me up the stairs and into my bed chamber.

Slowly turning my back to him when he sets me down, "Wilt thou be good enough?"

Wearing a romantically roguish expression, he unfastens the row of closely spaced hooks, and feeling the material covering the nape of my neck, "This material, what is it?"

Realizing he's asking about my body stocking, I reply, "It's a mixture of nylon and spandex. While great men of the sea were discovering new lands, others contributed many fine inventions, and altho' some, like my body stocking, may seem trivial by comparison, it, and others that we shall utilize this evening, will be as divine to us as was manna from heaven."

Nibbling on my neck, "I am, without question, grateful to the inventor, but 'twas thee who cleverly thought of wearing it, as are the other ways thou hast bested the barriers which have kept us apart."

When the last hook is undone, he slowly turns me around, and gently slipping the gown off my shoulders, letting it fall to the floor, he notes my breathing has become slow and deep, but even tho' he is aware that I find his touch intoxicating, it is also obvious that even though I have gone to a great deal of effort to create this night, I am as nervous as an untried bride. Fortunately, my ever observant sea Captain, reaching over to the bed, picks up the peignoir ensemble that lies there, and taking me by the arm, knowing that when I am ready in both body and spirit that I will come to him, he escorts me over to the dressing screen.

Speaking in a soft tone, as I take the ensemble from him, "Thank you, fy Nghapten."

Once behind the screen, I reproach myself silently, 'Here I am realizing my life's dream and I acted like a nervous virgin.' Having removed my camisole cover and petticoat, I start to slip my new sheer nightgown over my head, when I stop short. Determined to conduct myself as a lover worthy of his attentions, I don my cherished peignoir directly over my stays, and whilst fastening the closure about my waist, I notice that my hair is all wrong. Chiding myself again, I utter, "I am not to be handled with care, I should have an alluring, come ravish me appearance, not look like I oughta be put under glass," and quickly rearranging my tresses into All-Over curls with my fingers until I have a nice disheveled look, "Well, I'm as ready as I'll ever be," and as I take a deep breath whilst slowly emerging from behind the dressing screen, I am pleased to see that the man of my hearts desire has removed some of his attire, for the doing tells me he is confident in our ability to make love.

"Of the ensemble thou handed me, I decided to wear only the peignoir."

Drinking in my form, "Thine attire, tho' lovely, is merely a frame on a work of art."

His soothing compliment helps me to feel at ease, and as I slowly walk over to him, observing his hunger for me, "Sit down, fy Nghapten, and I'll remove your boots." Whilst kneeling, I reach under my pillow, and retrieving the surgical gloves I placed there earlier, "Put these on."

Whilst removing his white gloves, "I trust that when the time comes, thou hast for me, a magical way to gain entry into thy most divine orifice."

Amid a seductive grin, I reply, "But of course."

Chapter Four

Remembrance Day

After a restful night's sleep, my eyes open around nine o'clock in the morning. At first, I am feeling quite cozy under the warm covers when I suddenly find myself grow disheartened. It's not only that I hoped to find myself entwined within my lover's embrace, but the room, it's neat and tidy; where are the clothes, mine and the Captain's? Last night our clothes were strewn hither and yon.

Knowing that short of a disaster, Katie would never enter my room as I slept, tears well up within my eyes. Unable to bear such a lonely existence, believing all that I thought to be reality over the past two days, perhaps even the past year, has only been a vivid dream, I begin to sob, and as the overwhelming sadness engulfs me, I pull the covers up over my head.

From within the upper room of the turret, I hear my woman crying, and being concerned, I materialize in her room just below to find her beneath the bedclothes. Touching her shoulder gently, I ask, "Whyfor the tears, fy annwyl?"

Seeing my beloved wearing nothing more than the rich brocaded robe I made for him for the first time as I emerge from beneath the covers, and noticing the body stocking covering my arm, I am replete with happiness as I remember the passion of last nights interlude, and as a peaceful smile of fulfillment appears on my face, I gently bite on the corner of my lip. "When I woke, I believed our passionate encounter was but a mere dream."

Pulling the covers down and away from my body, my forthright Captain assures me, "'Twas no dream, fy Ngariad." Continuing as he looks upon me, "Both the nights, and dayes henceforth, shall bring forth much enjoyment." Affectionately taking a hank of my hair within his hand, he bends down, and inhaling its fragrance, he speaks in a soft, warm tone, "Wee be as one in all things now."

Returning to his usual commanding mannerisms upon rising, that when worn by my lusty sea captain are most becoming, "And now, fy melys, I shall leave thee to dress and tend our home," and having declared us to be a couple, he dematerializes.

Delighted to find him to be both an attentive, as well as a deliciously rambunctious lover, I find myself remembering how it was before he came. For seven years, ever since my hapless relationship which occurred about a year after my divorce, I spurned romance, choosing instead, aside from Katie and my mother who needs looking after, and our guests, occasional errands, and Sunday services in Little Newcastle, I have kept pretty much to myself. Even so, I must admit that within the deep recesses of my heart, I always hoped that one day I would meet the man of my dreams, then, on one magical night, appearing quite literally out of thin air, the last thing I expected is exactly what happened.

I was in my 7th year of schooling when I first read about pirate Captain, Bartholomew Roberts, and his daring adventures. So captivated was I, that I wrote a book report about 65 pirate Captains, but none of the others could hold a candle to Bartholomew Roberts. Many years later, in 1996, the very day I got on the internet for the first time, and using the same book report, I began designing a website about pirates with Captain Roberts as the centerpiece. Going further, I took it upon myself to become his champion; leaping to his defense should anyone dare to vilify his honor. How was I to know that my boundless admiration and unyielding devotion would evoke his spirit, and when he told me the upper section of the turret directly above my room would suit him perfectly, blissfully knowing he would forever be with me, I remember thinking that such an occurrence was surely unprecedented, but to start at the beginning, I remember, quite vividly, the night my deliciously urbane guest arrived. It was almost midnight, and being I had just finished the Website I had been working on for a client, I was free to check my E-mail. With the only light sources being the moon shining through the glass doors, my computer screen, and the small oil lamp on the desk that illuminated little more than the keyboard, my room was fairly dark. The first letter I was answering was from yet another pirate enthusiast who asked why I write about Captain Roberts in such a manner. In my response, my innermost feelings graced my reply. "I'm in love with his spirit," I told him. "Who he was, and what he stood for; that part of him that will never die, and I shall defend him with all that I am to my dying breath." And as my heartfelt words departed in the E-mail when I clicked send, I noticed a man standing in the shadows near the French doors leading onto my balcony. Naturally I was startled. Okay, I was understandably frightened. Even though I recognized his attire, my first thought was that I either had a rather interestingly dressed guest who was in the wrong room, or a robber with an unusual sense of humor.

Observing my tense demeanor, the stranger elegantly removed his ostrich plume adorned tricorne hat with his right hand, and bowed gracefully. As he stood erect, he introduced himself. " 'Tis no neede to be frighten'd, madam, for I am Bartholomew Roberts."

Although his speech, grace and manner was the epitome of a well-bred man from an era long since gone, I was apprehensive, and even though I had neither stood nor uttered a word, Captain Roberts sensed my skepticism; after all, spirits just don't go around materializing into people's bedrooms.

Dismayed, the man spoke once more. "Alas, madam, for I perceive thee to doubt my words. Until thou dost not, I cannae stay." Looking forlorn whilst placing his hat atop his head, he dematerialized.

His ability to vanish convinced me that he was in fact, exactly who he said he claimed to be, and in that realization, I found myself considerable more terrified by his departure than I was by his sudden appearance, and fearful that he was gone forever, I not only became frantic, I almost fell as I stood up abruptly, as I called out, "Come back, Captain!" Overwhelmed with profound sadness, I slowly walked to the area where I believed I had seen him, and again repeating my plea, this time in a gentle, tear filled tone, I uttered, "Come back, Captain. Please come back."

To my delight, not more than 2 feet from me, the spirit of, *'the Great Pirate Roberts,'* magically re-materialized in the same spot he had previously stood.

"As thou wills, madam, and with the greatest of pleasure."

Stammering, I asked, "It's not that I am not overjoyed that you have come, but how—"

Interrupting me, " 'Twas thy kind thoughts and verbal expressions desiring my companionship that brought me forth."

His courtly manners were soothing, and within the moments required by my psyche to digest his presence, I felt my body relax. Smiling at him, "You truly are, Captain

Bartholomew Roberts, the legendary pirate of the early seventeen hundreds."

As he looked upon me, his perceptive prowess being keenly aware of the amorous longing that flowed through my veins, he smiled ever so faintly as he replied, "Aye, madam, that I am."

As I gazed upon this incredibly handsome man, wishing that he could forever be at my side, I drank in every aspect of his appearance beginning with his piercing sable eyes. His attire was truly impressive. Upon his comely face he wore a full mustache and a delicious royale magnificently framed by his well groomed, curly sable colored hair, which was, and is always worn freely about his shoulders. As my eyes moved over him, I was impressed by his commanding presence. "You look exactly like your portrait, Captain." Then thinking for a moment, as he had introduced himself as Bartholomew Roberts, I asked, "Would you prefer I address you as Mister Roberts, John, Bartholomew, or Captain?"

Musing a moment, he replied, "Thou may address me in whichever respectful manner pleases thee."

Even though he had graciously given me permission to be less than formal, I felt obliged by my own sense of propriety to address him as Captain, which in my opinion, is his due. "Thank you, Captain. Henceforth, I shall allow both the situation, and those present, dictate my choice."

Acknowledging my reply with a modest nod, he turned slightly towards the window, and whilst motioning towards the French doors with his right hand, "Being the evening is warm, shall we not continue our conversation on the balcony?"

"I think that would be very nice." As we walked to the French doors, I return his courtesy. "My name is V'lé, Captain."

Whilst picking up one of the two chairs from against the wall, and placing it on the balcony, "Aye, madam, of this I be quite aware."

Holding my chair for me as I sit, "Thank you, Captain."

Whilst bringing for himself the remaining chair, setting it opposite mine, he continues, "Decorum, dictates I address thee more respectfully."

Being acquainted with the proprieties from his era, and knowing they are very important to him, holding them close myself, I am perfectly willing to observe them. "As you prefer, Captain, but then I knew you would."

As the Captain seats himself, he asks, "How did thee know?"

After a brief pause, "You've been a large part of my life for many years."

Speaking with an approving smile, "I gather thou knows my history well then."

Returning his smile, "You're not only remembered in the history books, there have been a goodly number of biographies written about you. On a personal note, I have done quite a lot of research on my own, and to be frank, the majority of those books, not having done you justice, I took it upon myself to become your Champion and am well versed in both your vigilante and piratical activities, but in regard to your personal life, except for me, who knows about Rebekah, history knows very little about you. That aside, and more important, I, unlike my contemporaries, know what you hold most dear."

"Indeed, and just what wouldst thou surmise that to be?"

"Why your morals and principles, Captain, and the personal integrity within you that adheres to them, the lot of which has brought you great honor," Aware that my statement pleased him, knowing that these are also the things I consider to be the greatest of treasures, "but even so, it's not only that I know about you, Captain, but that I understand you. I've read your ship's Articles, Newspaper Accounts, Reports by Others, including passengers, and most importantly, some of your own writings. All these, especially your writings, they told me what kind of man you were, and will always be."

Intrigued by my statement, "Indeed, and just how dost thou perceive me?"

Proud of that which was to be my next statement, I took a deep breath, and smiling, I spoke emphatically. "Well, first I must say that I know as much about you as anyone, living or dead, and a great deal more than most, but it's not only knowing what you did, Captain, but understanding why, and in this will lie my answer." Calming as I continued, "I know of your high standards; that you're strong in your convictions; possess impeccable morals; are deeply religious; and have only the highest regard for well-bred, prudent ladies, never taking advantage of one yourself, nor allowing one to be taken by force. I also know of your fondness for music, and that you had a number of musicians aboard your ships. In regard to your so-called crimes; most of which being not only justified, but generally provoked by the arrogance of others, who, although greatly less qualified, held the position you once sought, that being a Captaincy within her majesties navy. I am also quite aware of your quick temper, and regardless of how you're generally perceived, I do not believe such would flare without just provocation. You might as well know from the start, Captain, that I do not consider your piracy a crime, but more along the lines of subversive vigilantism, on a par if you will, with the legends of the true-life Robin Hood and the fictionalized Zorro, as you furthered the cause of justice that most men, regardless of how badly needed, would be unable to do, and in the doing, many lives were saved or improved, together with a goodly number of slaves who were freed. In short, you did not merely kick tyranny in the teeth, you struck a powerful blow for justice and freedom." Pausing a moment before delivering a rather large smile as I chuckled, "You're remembered as the most successful pirate of all time; nonetheless, there are always those, who being either ignorant, stupid or jealous, venture to destroy what's good by way of scurrilous statements and sordid or otherwise contemptible writings, generally for profit; ergo, in becoming your Champion, and taking it upon myself to dispel the vile slander, was born the desire to set the record straight, but in order to do this with certainty, I needed to know just what kind of man you were, not merely what you had done; I also needed to know and understand your motivation."

> *Of the many aspects Captain Roberts did not know, came to light with V'lé's statement of being his Champion, which intrigued him. In fact, all the Captain knew was that there was a woman who adored him, & through her, if she invited him, he would no longer be forced to dwell forever in purgatory, but aside from the rules governing his tenure, for which he had pledged to keep secret unto himself, for only the power of mutual devotion would secure his freedom & more, was the extent of his knowledge. The future was not known to him, nor did he know that his freedom, everlasting, hinged on her strength, indefatigable zest & zeal, ardent love, & courage, but that must be conceived through true love & deference. 'Twas these together that would determine the very nature of their existence.*

Continuing, "To be a pirate these days, Captain, is not as it was in yours when the world was expanding, and freebooting was not limited to pirates, but heads of state as well. Today the globe is mapped out in great detail, and only the latter, those who still reign supreme, are free to pillage and plunder in gluttonous proportions. To be frank, Captain, your daring has always enthralled me. Just the idea of entire crews jumping ship, or ships vacating the area when it was believed you were approaching is intoxicating, but just so there's no misunderstanding, I want you to know that it's your moral character coupled with your daring, and an intangible air and manner that attracts me, not merely the pirate; and be that as it may, I would give anything to have served aboard your ship."

"Hast thou sail'd?"

"Yes, Captain, I have. Aside from 4 Luxury Liners, I have been on a small Sloop, and a Brigantine. Unfortunately neither of the latter two vessels left the harbor."

Asking, with an inquisitive smile, "Thou finds pleasures in the sea, then?"

Smiling as I replied to him, "I can think of few things that bring as much joy or excitement as coursing through the water aboard a sailing vessel, and one day, maybe I too will be able to live aboard a tall ship."

Finding much elation in my words brought a smile to his face, as most women he knew of, found traveling, by land or sea, a hardship to be avoided.

"Although I know that you did not indulge in alcoholic beverages, Captain, I'm sure one reason was that, like myself, you're one who prefers to keep his wits about him. Of course in your case, being in a perilous position much of the time, with your very survival at stake, and much of your success being dependent on your ability to think clearly, an attribute which is greatly impaired by liquor, you chose to be a teetotal; however, Captain, you're not at sea now, but here in my home, and as such, quite free of those responsibilities, and although I know not if you are able, I shall be pleased to offer you some refreshments."

Arising from my chair, as did he, being a well-bred gentleman, I continued. "I can offer you sandwiches and sweets, spiced tea or coffee, and perhaps a snifter of brandy. As for myself, not caring for the taste of beer, wine or strong spirits, I too am a teetotal. Nonetheless, I do occasionally indulge in a modicum of Sambucka, which, if I had to choose one, I would name as being my favorite alcoholic beverage."

Replying with a pleasant smile. "Altho' I possess no neede, madam, I am able, and such, I would not onely relish a dish of tea, I shall be most pleas'd to sup with thee, and if I may be permitted both, I would also delight in sampling thy favourite."

Eager to be the dutiful hostess to my unexpected, yet most welcomed guest, I flash a cheery smile, "I shan't be gone for more than a few minutes. Please, make yourself at home."

While leaving the room with a huge toothy grin, it was all I could do to restrain myself, I mean just having the opportunity to serve the great Captain Roberts caused me to practically fall all over myself as I raced down the hall like a kid on her way to the tree on Christmas morning.

All along the way, I became increasingly giddy, and when entering the kitchen I closed the swinging door. Engulfed with tremendous excitement from the sheer delight of his presence, no longer being able to stand independently in my weakened state, I leaned against the wall across from the stove where I waited for my heart to calm down.

Whilst waiting, I thought of the Captain's voice being a beautifully articulated Pembrokeshire accent, 'twas among the most captivating I had ever heard, and I could only hope he did not notice that I positively melted every time he uttered a sound. After a few moments I regained enough of my composer to fill the electric kettle and get it heating.

BLOOD and SWASH, The Unvarnished Life (& afterlife) Story of Pirate Captain, Bartholomew Roberts.........pt.1 "BOLT OF FRUITION"

Getting down my Moss Rose, China Tea & Coffee Service, I arranged 2 teacups and saucers, with teaspoons, alongside 2 sandwich plates, atop which I placed 2 linen napkins beside the sugar bowl, and filled the creamer with milk.

Returning the milk to the refrigerator, never was I so glad than at this moment that Katie always keeps a plentiful array of finger foods on hand, and taking out an assortment, I arranged them neatly on my three-tiered, folding hors d'oeuvre salver.

> *After his hostess excused herself, knowing she would be gone for several minutes, Captain Roberts, curious about the four doors in the room, took the opportunity to investigate. The French doors open to a charming balcony overlooking the sea; second was the route his hostess took when wishing to exit her bedchamber. The third, he discovered, led to her private bath, & behind the fourth was found a spiral staircase, & finding such to be a particularly hopeful avenue, he ventured upward to have a look see.*

Lighting one of the candles on the mantle, I venture to see where it leads, and climbing the steps to the top, I find another door. Upon entering the well kept, V-shaped room, I am pleas'd to find it fashioned in an array of red fabrics contrasted with both black and white accents. From what I canne discern in the dim light, the room is tastefully decorated with a variety of maritime appointments consisting of books on tall ships, and sev'rall more about pirates (myself in particular,) a small model of a Fregate, some bric-a-brac, a chandelier, 2 tapestries, ostrich plumes, mine owne flags, the Welsh Dragon, and another flag which is unfamiliar to me. All and all, the room as a whole maintains a nice nautical air. Also within, rests an ornate chess set upon a glass table supported by a dragon, twixt two chairs. On the corner table sits an oil burning lamp and a picture of myself. The black box situated between the two tall, yet slender bookcases at the opposite side of the room is foreign to me. Against the far wall sits a mirrored wardrobe across from a large four-poster bed shrouded by layers of sheer draperies, and not to far from the fireplace sits a large, deeply carved, ornate desk. Altho' not knowing why such be my feelings, my thoughts be that this room is for the most part, unused, and hoping my supposition to be fact, I quietly utter, "This room would suit me well." After looking about a mite longer, I return to what I assume is my hostess' bedchamber below.

Being curious, I walk out through the same door as did my hostess and find myself within a passageway bordered by an opulent balustrade. Looking over the side, I see a large room divided in to two sections, both suitable for entertaining a goodly gathering comfortably. To the left is a wall with a large archway leading to another area of the house. As I look about, glancing behind me into her bedchamber, and then again over the railing, and into the large room below, I express my thoughts quietly, saying, "She lives well," during which time I see my hostess enter the room below, hurriedly.

Not noticing my guest was in the upper hall looking downwards as I dashed into the music room, I went behind the bar and took two brandy snifters from the wall cabinet. Removing the stopper from the Wexford decanter containing Sambucka sitting on the tray atop the bar, I poured about one shot of the warming liqueur into each, and returned the decanter to its proper place. Suddenly; as I picked up the glasses, I remembered the very nice tobacco that a recent guest had left behind, and setting the glasses back on the bar, I scurried into the conversation area.

Some time ago I found a handsome humidor and pipe in the attic. After giving them a thorough cleaning, I placed the lovely antiques on the cocktail table located behind the large sofa just left of the hearth. Hoping that they would, at last, find their way into the hands of one who would truly appreciate them, totally unaware that Captain Roberts was watching my actions with great interest, my fingers, as they caressed the craftsmanship, slowly slid along the edge. Taking hold of the leather handle, I returned to the bar, and taking the tobacco from the cabinet and placing it within, I secured the lid. Sliding the leather handle over my arm, I picked up the two brandy snifters and left the room.

By the time I returned to the kitchen, the water, having come to a boil, the kettle had shut itself off. Making both tea and coffee, I filled the respective pots, and gathering the remaining items that I wanted to take upstairs, I took a deep breath, grabbed the salver in my left hand, and picking up the heavy tray with both, I headed for the stairs. Reaching the top, I saw my visitor awaiting my return at the end of the hall, just outside my room.

No less than gallant, Captain Roberts, seeing the heavy tray, walked up to me and relieved me of the burden.

"Thank you, Captain."

Espying a large sized plant stand against the far wall, Captain Roberts sat the tray momentarily upon my vanity table in order to relocate the heavy flower pot onto the floor before carrying the plant stand out onto the balcony to serve as a table, which he placed between the two chairs. After seating me, the Captain picked up the heavy tray, and placing it upon the makeshift table, he created for us a lovely dining area on my, then, rarely used balcony.

Still holding the salver and humidor, I placed one on the floor next to me as I sat down, and the other on the table.

By now, being rather calm, I place a finger bowl containing a slice of lemon, and filling it with warm water, I placed it before the Captain whilst handing him a napkin. As he washes his fingers, I take from the tray, a sandwich plate, to which I affix a dip cup, and as place an array of munchables upon it, I continued with what I had been saying earlier. "I know a great deal about the many pirate captains and their way of life, and although I probably ought't say so, Captain," smiling amid a chuckle whilst handing him the plate, "you were in a class by yourself."

Taking the plate from my outstretched hand, Captain Roberts graciously uttered, "Diolch 'chi."

Liking the way he periodically injects Welsh whilst speaking, I smiled at him, saying, "You're welcome."

"Doth thou speaks Welsh?"

"Only a few words and phrases, Captain." Picking up the remaining plate, I continued speaking while I took for myself a similar assortment. "I have always been envious of your democratic society, but aside from you, none of the other pirates interested me. To that, I attribute what I believe is the most important element of your personality."

While he took a bite of a small sandwich, I could see he was filled with much curiosity, and after patting his mouth with the linen, he asked, "And what, pray tell, dost thou believe that element to be?"

"Well, to put it simply, it's your nature; such being that even when push came to shove, you remained true to yourself, and such, never once did you abandon your moral principles, whereby each individual, whether for good or ill, was always treated as they deserved."

"Indeed. Never meeting me before his night, I am delightfully surpriz'd thou surmised such a conclusion."

Pouring him a cup of my mom's spiced tea, "The formation of my opinion, Captain, is supported by a combination of considerable facts and perhaps a modicum of perceptive intuition; then again, regardless of how I drew my conclusion, do you not consider yourself a valiant man who cherishes his honor and morality above all else?"

Taking the cup and saucer from my hand, he replied, "Emphatically. My honour was my life, and my valour above reproach." Within his voice was a slight chuckle as he added, "Nevertheless, regardless of how much it may please thee to perceive otherwise, and disregarding how justified my actions may have bin, I did become, and die, a pyrate."

Pouring myself a cup of coffee, "Should one who is forced into a life by circumstance, not then make the best of it?"

Taking a sip of his tea. "Methinks thee understands my mind well."

Smiling at him, I change the subject. "I'm sure my mother's spiced tea is to your liking, if not, just say the word and I'll look into ordering some Black Bohea."

Speaking with a modest smile, "Thou art familiar with my favourite tea?"

"Of course, Captain, but regarding the understanding I have for your way of thinking, and your statement regarding how justified your actions may have been, and that you did become, and die a pirate, you no longer consider yourself one do you?"

With a slight smile, "And if I did?"

Giving myself a few moments as I attempt to surmise his thoughts, I take another sip, and looking into his eyes whilst trying to maintain a proper sense of both modesty and rectitude, "One can not steal that which is freely given, Captain."

Lingering over his tea whilst giving my rather revealing crop top and hip hugger jeans more than a passing glance as he muses over my statement, he replies, "An intriguing assertion to be sure. Wouldst thou be referring to thyself, or thy possessions?"

Noticing that he had given me the once over, I could not help but project a smile as I replied. "Even a well-bred lady of chastity will yield her treasures to the right man, Captain, especially if she's in love with him."

> *Observing she blushed easily, Captain Roberts was pleased to learn she was shy, yet being ever tactful, made no comment, nevertheless, his modest smile, which served to enhance his twinkling eyes; spoke vividly.*

Observing that Captain Roberts' had, had enough supper, as well as the breeze freshening, I reached for the humidor. Placing my arm once again through its leather handle, "Finding it a bit chilly, Captain, would you mind terribly if we went inside?"

"Not at all." Rising from his seat and walking behind mine, he graciously holds my chair as I stand.

Appreciating his manners, "Diolch 'chi, Capten," and picking up the two crystal snifters, I go indoors, whilst adding, "The rest I shall take downstairs later."

Upon entering, whilst closing the French doors behind him, he skillfully threw the latch.

"Would you like to see my retreat?"

Not familiar with the expression in relation to my usage, he asks, "Thy retreat?"

"It's a place where one can go to escape the turbulence associated with everyday living." Walking to the door leading to the upper section of the turret, I open the door, and striking a match, I light sconce just inside before climbing the stairs.

Knowing it would be chilly, and fancying the idea of spending a couple hours just talking, perhaps even playing a game of chess, and seeing my shawl draping the back of the office chair, he picked it up as he walked by.

When entering the room upstairs, as he graciously placed the shawl about my shoulders, "Permit me, madam."

"Thank you, Captain." Setting the snifters on the mantle, I slid the leather strap off my arm, and clutching the humidor close to my chest, I turned to face him saying, "Although I haven't any Snuff, I do have some very nice pipe tobacco that was left behind by a patron, and," holding it out, offering it to him, "although I do not know if you indulged, but knowing that many of your crew, especially in deliberations, were fond of their pipes and punch, I thought you might fancy it."

"Aye, madam," and taking the humidor from my hands, "I would indeed. Diolch 'chi."

Walking to the table the lies before the mantle, he placed the humidor down. Taking the pipe from its secure holder, he lifted the lid to expose the tobacco. Filling the pipe's bowl and packing it firmly, he opened the small compartment on top of the humidor wherein was a stowed flint, Sterno®, which had long since replaced the original tallow, a steel striker, and a small piece of smooth wood, called a spunk. Being quite familiar with its usage, the seaman, as I watched carefully, lit his pipe with ease.

Wearing a slight grimace, "You did that so quickly, I missed it."

The Captain, most pleased by my interest, offered me a slight smile as he asked, "Would thou care to have me demonstrate?"

Taking another sip of my Sambucka, "Yes, I would, very much."

Noting that I seemed to be enjoying my drink, the Captain, lifting his snifter to his lips was a little caught off guard by the smell of anise, and as I gave him a smile, the master mariner, however dubious, took a small sip, and afterwards, he gave me a rather odd look.

A typical reaction, I thought to myself as I assured him, "After a few more sips your mouth will be numb, and only then will you enjoy it." Of course when I spoke, it never occurred to me that perhaps his mouth wasn't capable of getting numb.

Sounding doubtful, he replies, "Time will tell."

"Like you, Captain, I would not say it if I did not believe it to be true." Taking another sip, "Ne'er will I lie to you."

"Nor I to thee." Setting his pipe down, "Come, stand beside me."

Rising, I stand beside him, and watching carefully as Captain Roberts, who, after taking another sip of the Sambucka, picked up both the flint and the steel striker. With a measure of force, the healthy spark created when Captain Roberts swiftly drew the flint against striker, ignited the Sterno,® and as it burned gently, Captain Roberts continued, saying, "This spunk," as he picked it up, "is placed within the flame. Once burning, 'tis used to light that which needes to be lit."

"May I try?"

"Certainly," and closing the cover to extinguish the flame, he reopens it.

Picking up the steel striker, I drew the flint across it, but when nothing happened, I looked at him with rather sorrowful eyes.

"Thou must draw the flint across the striker with sufficient force to create a healthy spark, thereby igniting the tallow."

Trying again, the Sterno® was burning. Do my best to contain my adoring emotions, "I would've loved living in your time, Captain."

"Coming forward in time and learning new things, will always be simpler than going backwards.

Seeing him take another sip of the Sambucka, it was evident he had taken a liking to the liquorish liqueur. "Not to sound previous, Captain, but there is much I could learn from you."

Appreciating the fact that I was eager to learn, and having pride in the fact that his knowledge was sought by others, "What exactly wouldst thou like to learn?"

Well, I have always wanted to learn how to navigate. I learned quite a bit from my parents, but not nearly as much as I would like to know."

" 'Twould be an honour to teach you." Offering a slight bow, "To have such a willing, and dare I say, attractive pupil, will be a great pleasure."

Replying to both his willingness to teach me, and his remark about my appearance, I again smiled up at him as I said, "Thank you, Captain."

Turning towards the crimson chairs, "Shall we sit down. madam?"

Having been seated only a few moments, "Please excuse me for a minute, it's getting a bit chilly."

Before I could rise out of my chair, the courtly seaman arose from his seat. "Permit me, madam." Taking with him his drink, he walked to the mantle and after placing his glass upon it, he knelt before the fireplace. Reaching to his right, he picked up several logs from the rack, and after arranging them within the hearth he arose. Upon standing, his feet some sixteen inches apart, he elegantly waved his hands before the fireplace, and just like a magician, a blazing fire magically erupted.

"Seeing how we have promised to be forever honest with each other, am I correct in my thinking that we may both be candid with one another, including feeling free to state how we feel without repercussions?"

"Of course, madam." Returning to his chair, "Is there something in particular on thy mind?"

"No. I just wanted to lay the ground rules regarding this and future conversations."

"Masterfully accomplished, madam. 'Tis a blessing to know that ne'er shall we be crippled by our owne emotions." And in taking his seat once more, looking at the chess set on the table betwixt us, he asked, as he made his opening move, "Dost thou play?"

Replying whilst moving my king's pawn two squares forward, "Yes, Captain, I do."

As we continued our game, "Tell me, Captain, how long will I have the pleasure of your company?"

"That depends upon thee."

"Me? Are you saying it is I who will decide how long you will stay?"

"Aye, madam, it is."

"Well," smiling amid a chuckle, "providing that you're agreeable to the idea, and it would please you to stay, then it's my wish that you remain forever."

As a satisfied, closed-mouthed smile appeared on his face, "Then dwell here I shall, madam, and most happily. May I consider this my room?"

Chuckling a mite as I reply amid a giddy smile, "Having decorated it with you in mind, Captain, you certainly may."

Chapter Five

The Surreptitious Henchman

The ringing apparatus of *Inn Finistère's* internal communication system, one of our few semi-modern gadgets dating to the early 20th Century, brings me back to the present, and seeing it's from the kitchen, and using the intercom, "Good morning, Katie. What's up?"

Katie's room, being equipped with a night buzzer, "We have guests, Miss; a young honeymoon couple from Spain, I believe. They arrived very late last night." Standing in front of the stove, Katie, removing the scrambled eggs from the skillet, adds them to the Bubbles & Squeak and Splatter Dabs already on the platter. "I am preparing breakfast for them now."

"Thank you, Katie. I'll be down directly." 'So much for reminiscing,' I say to myself as I turn my thoughts to the present.

Having guests, I must dress before exiting my bedchamber. Opening my wardrobe, I don my crimson, off the shoulder, close fitting peasant blouse with billowing sleeves and my new, side-laced, black breeches over my body tied my floor length, open front gored skirt consisting of various shades of pink, and my black, laser cut Granny boots. After arranging a quantity of my all-over curls in to an up sweep, using the ivory comb carved by my Captain to secure it, I blissfully enter the hall, gamboling along as I make my way down the stairs and into the kitchen for my morning coffee.

"Good Morning, Miss," states Katie as I walk in. "I'll get ya a cup of hot coffee right quick."

"Thank you, Katie." Yawing, "I over slept this morning."

"I thought you might be up late," states Katie, handing me a cup of coffee.

"Thank you, Katie. You're a treasure." Taking a sip, "Are our guests having their breakfast?"

"Yes, Miss."

Setting my half-empty cup on the small table, I push through the saloon type swinging doors and enter the dining room.

"Bueno Días, Señora," says the young man of no more than 25, adding, "We arrived about 2 this morning. Katie, taking pity on us, was kind enough to take us in."

"I am Miss V'lé, Châtelaine of *Inn Finistère*, and your hostess."

"Bueno Días. Sorry we arrived so late, Señorita. We were to arrive last night about eight, but got caught in the storm," explains the young woman. "Your place is on our list of Gothic Places of Interest. We intended to ring, but the wind carried off our brochure. By the time we found our way here, it was very late."

Listening with interest, "No bother. I hope your room and breakfast are to your liking."

"Sí, Señorita," replies the young man whilst taking a bite of his Bubbles & Squeak.

"Sí," echoes the woman.

Smiling as I start to turn, "If you need anything, feel free to call on either Katie or myself." Leaving the room, I re-enter the kitchen to enjoy my morning coffee. Sitting at the breakfast nook, I take a sip of the warm liquid. "Needing your help with my stays, let me know when you can spare a few moments."

BLOOD and SWASH, The Unvarnished Life (& afterlife) Story of Pirate Captain, Bartholomew Roberts.........pt.1 "BOLT OF FRUITION"

"How 'bout right now?"

"Great!" Arising from my chair, the two of us trod up the stairs. Entering my room, I take my new stays from the bureau. Handing it to Katie, I remove my skirt and bustier while she loosens the laces. Unbuttoning my pants and lifting my blouse, I arrange my steel boned stays over my camisole, and giving her the go ahead, Katie snugs up the strings. Taking hold of the bedpost, and a deepest breath I can, "Pull the strings tight, Katie, but not too tight around my ribs."

As she tightens the strings, "You and the Captain looked wonderful dancing together last night."

"It was a wonderful evening," says I with a smile.

Continuing as she ties the strings in to a bow, "Not to speak out of turn, Miss, but in light of things, it seems to me that Captain Roberts could 'ave helped you."

My cheeks turning pink as I turn to face her, I smile as I reply, "His place would not be to help me dress, but to undress me, would it not?"

Katie, replying whilst laughing blusterously, "uh, yeah."

While getting back into my skirted bustier, "I'm in love with him Katie."

"I know ya are, Miss. I've known it ever since I came to work for ya."

"But you arrived only a week after Captain Roberts did."

"I know Miss, but it was pretty obvious."

"But I've never even skirted the subject."

As we leave the room and start back towards the kitchen, Katie explains. "The sparkle in your eyes when he's present is a dead giveaway; even when he's angry you're glowing."

"You're right, Katie, I have been in love with Captain Roberts since the night he arrived, but I wasn't aware it was so obvious."

"A lot longer than that, Miss."

"What do you mean?"

"I've seen your website on him, and to be frank, it's not just a website, it's a shrine! Anyone who goes there can see that it's much more than admiration you feel. Even a visiting stranger, as I was when I met you, could easily tell that you're in love with him."

Sitting back down at the kitchen table to finish my coffee, "I feel a little unsettled with that."

Picking up her teacup, "Don't be Miss, there's nothing wrong with you being in love with him," states Katie as she refills her cup before sitting across from me at the table. "Nor he with you."

Having no idea that she knew his feelings also, "What's that?" I ask quietly.

"The Captain loves you too, Miss. Very deeply." Pausing a moment to take a sip of her tea. "The sad aspect of your relationship is that he is, in fact, a ghost, but even so, I doubt anyone has ever come so close to a perfect, or happier relationship, nor ever will." Rising from her seat, and while walking over to the stove, where she begins to make my breakfast.

"You're right Katie. I know it may seem a trifle bizarre to most, but even though he's a ghost, I want no other man in my life, and never will."

"And that being said, all that really counts is the happiness the two of you share."

"Thank you for understanding, Katie." Smiling at her as I finish my coffee, "You're a true friend."

"Eggs Benedict, Miss?"

"Yes, thank you," adding, "I know my mom considers it a bother, but she loves it, so make it for her as well."

"Very good, Miss." Refilling my cup, "Being how it's damp and gloomy, may I ask Captain Roberts to start a fire of the reception room?"

"I think that's a lovely idea. I'll tell my mom that she and I shall have breakfast in the conversation area."

Arising from my seat, "I'll check on our guests and see if they need anything." Picking up my cup, and leaving the kitchen by way of the dining room, I stop and turn. "Have we the makings for Quiche Florentine and a Caesar Salad?"

"I believe so."

"Terrific!" Says I smiling. "I'll let my mom we're having it for dinner tonight."

"Very good, Miss."

"Well, having several books that I picked up from the library yesterday, as well as a couple of videos that I want to look at, I'd best get started. Being they're in the music room, I'll ask the Captain to start a fire in both sections."

Moseying through the dining room along the way, "May I get you anything?"

Shaking her head slightly, the young woman replies, "No thank you."

Gesturing to the lead crystal bell on the table before them, "Well, If you need anything, just ring."

"Gracias."

With my coffee cup in hand, I enter the rather dark reception room. Before making my way to the sofa, I pause a moment to open the drapes. After seating myself, I moderately call out, "Captain, I'm about to start researching my new wardrobe, if you'd like to join me, you'll find me in the music room?"

Dressed in the same sexy outfit he wore yesterday, Captain Roberts materializes behind me.

Showing obvious lustfulness, I quietly add, "Very sexy indeed."

"Did you say something fy melys?"

"Nope, just muttering to myself."

Shortly thereafter, the young couple, having finished their breakfast, enter the music room. Turning towards them, Captain Roberts quietly says, "Present them."

"With pleasure." Speaking happily, "Captain Roberts, I would like to present, Señor and Señora Tomás González. They're honeymooning."

Making a slight bow, "Congratulations. May the two of you wallow for many years in wedded bliss."

The young couple simultaneously replying their thank yous, Señora Gonzalez adds, "We would like to visit The Bishop's Palace and Saint David's Cathedral. Can you instruct us in which road to follow."

"Yes, of course." Looking at her map for a moment, I point to Saint David's. "Just follow this coastal road. From Little Haven, follow the signs leading up the steep road to Broad Haven. Continuing on to Newgale, will be a sign for St. David's, and after which, for parking and the Cathedral. There will be one tricky, almost hairpin turn to the right." That'll take you right to it. The drive takes 30-40 minutes. Newgale has a very nice beach; lots of activity, clean restrooms and sometimes a food vender. If you like picnics, Bishop's Palace, is an excellent place, especially up high, on the battlement."

"Gracias," states the man as he folds the map. "Adios, Señorita. Señora."

"You're welcome."

Our guests having departed, Captain Roberts, turning towards me, speaks soothingly. "Thou art looking well this morning, fy melys. I trust thou had a pleasant night's rest."

Unconscientiously emanating an air of shyness in my demeanor as I spoke, "Yesterday, afternoon, and all that followed, was glorious."

"Thou amazes me; last night, a wildcat, this morning, a reserved creature, and your attire, all together they be an aggregation of personality traits. 'Tis utterly charming. In regard to thy timidity, there be no reason for it, for that which wee shared was the realization of our most sought after dreams, and altho' to others, that which wee possess may appear trivial, wee shall pardon them, for they know not what they miss, nor do they understand that our bond, and with no less vigour since our meeting, will continue to grow. 'Tis destiny, our being together, has been since the dawn of mankind, and as long as wee remain ever vigilant, no power that exists canne keep us apart."

Before the echo of his sentiment dies, the skies darken, and except for the firelight, the room is dark as pitch. Suddenly, a storm breaks loose with a brilliant bolt of lightning which is so brilliant, the Captain's image disappears intermittently as the brightness flickers, for even though the Captain possesses substance, he is still, in fact, an apparition. Knowing that loud thunder will follow, I want to cover my ears, but instead, I am compelled to hold onto my little tea table as it shakes violently, and as the cannon like shots of thunder continue to reverberate through the walls unlike any I have ever heard before, my sketch of Captain Roberts falls to the floor.

> *Although unbeknownst to those within the walls of Inn Finistère, there were evil forces just outside, who, in using the intensity of the storm compiled with the Captain's profound thoughts, rendered him incapable of detecting the presence of the interlopers.*

My mom, who has been working on her novel, quickly pulling the electrical cord from the wall, shifts her computer to battery. Getting up from her seat, she quickly comes out to the foyer and looking into the reception room. "Wow! That was a nasty one."

Lighting the sconces above the mantle, I holler back, "Everything okay in there, Katie?"

Joining my mom in the foyer, Katie replies, "Yes! Your mum and I are fine."

Returning the heavy frame containing his image to its place above the mantle, "Art thou all right?"

"I'm fine, fy Nghapten, but thee looks different somehow."

"Thou art a trifle tense is all."

"My residence in Arizona was destroyed by a storm if you recall."

Laying his hands upon my shoulders, caressing them gently, "Worry not, fy melys, for this gale will pass soon enough."

His gentle, yet firm touch helps to calm me as my eyes close for a few moments whilst leaning back upon him slightly. "Lightning will always terrify me, I suppose."

Entering the reception room, carrying a tray, Katie calls to me. "Breakfast is served, Miss."

"Thank you, Katie."

Later ⇁

Come afternoon, the storm raging still, Captain Roberts joins me in the reception room where I have been uploading the pictures of the outfits inside the books my Captain and I am are considering to the big screen monitor. "Good afternoon, fy melys."

"What is that you've been calling me? Vinmeleze? Is that French?"

" 'Tis Welsh for my sweet."

"Oh, that's nice." says I smiling.

"Are these the picture thou took earlier?"

Although trying to ignore the lightning strikes right outside, I flinch once again. "Yes, they are. I thought we could look 'em over."

Captain Roberts, determined to take my mind off the storm, picks up the small brown frame that rests upon the mantle. Holding it in his hand, he wanders about the room a mite. Stopping directly behind me, he asks, "This dress," as he looks at the picture of my daughter, "I remember thee saying 'twas thy dress she be wearing." Holding it over my shoulder so I can see to what he is referring, "Wouldst be amongst thy wardrobe still?"

Looking at the picture, and with just a hint of a giggle, "At one time it was my favorite disco dress."

"Disco? Is that like the Kizomba?"

"Nope, not at all." Walking to the fireplace, "Disco was similar to Swing, but the latter was more lively."

Following me, he repeats his question amid a roguish grin. "Is this dress still within thy wardrobe?"

"No, but I have dark red one like it that I've yet to wear."

Placing his gloved hands on my arms, sliding them slowly upwards, "Then it will be for me alone, will it not?"

As I turn my neck to look into his eyes in response to what I took as an authoritative statement, I unavoidably speak amid lustful breaths, whilst softly replying, "Yes, it will."

> *As it was quite apparent that Captain Roberts took much delight in the knowledge that the object of his lust was aroused by his slightest touch, he ventured to see how much motivational influence he wielded.*

"Waste no more time then." And slapping my behind, "Go change thy frock."

His statement, being an obvious command, sends tingling shivers up my spine, and as the look of demanding desire on his face possesses me more with each passing moment, I give him a wispy smile amid a curtsey whilst responding, "As thou commands, fy Arglwydd," and dash out of the room.

Removing my outer clothing as I scurry down the hall, I toss it on my bed, kicking off my shoes as I enter my room. Quickly pulling my blouse over my head, I throw open the doors of my wardrobe. Still wearing my steel boned stays, and knowing that I won't be able to Kizomba wearing such a restrictive garment, I unfasten the busk closure, drape the restrictive garment over the dressing screen and remove my camisole. Leaving only my body stocking, I quickly thumb through the hangers to find my dark red wrap-around skirt. Removing the garment from the hanger, the flowing, acetate satin material is just as luxurious to the touch as I remember. Slipping on the matching teensy-weensy tie on bikini bottoms, I grab the skirt, and placing it behind me, arranging it high under my arms and bringing the ties in front, I twist them together thrice before tying them in a bow behind my neck. Overlapping by a scant two inches, the front of the dress drapes sensuously over my breasts. To secure the front, I fasten a narrow silver belt around my waist. Standing before my 3-way mirror, "My hair needs fixing." Removing the elegant comb, I pick at my hair briefly with my fingers. Grabbing two pairs of surgical gloves from within my bureau, I put on a fresh layer of my new, *'stay-all-day®'* lipstick, a hint of rouge, and within 5 minutes I'm out the door. Along the way I glance into the reception room, and seeing my beloved thumbing through the recordings, each being marked as to the type of dances it is suited for, I am reminded of the mini CD containing mp3s I had made years ago containing a variety of sensual music perfectly suited for the evenings mood, and seeing how my Captain is in the mood for some sensuous dancing, which I hope will lead to a glorious evening of uninhibited lovemaking, I quickly return to my wardrobe and begin rummaging through the bottom drawer. Finding the mini CD, I grab it, and slipping it beneath my belt, I make for the stairs and start down.

Noticing my return, he starts a CD containing a medley of sultry melodies. Meeting me at the bottom of the stairs, eyeing me up and down as I make my descent, "Thou, as I knows thee would, does great justice to a minute quantity of material."

Upon reaching the foyer, my gallant Captain escorts me to the music section of the reception room, and unbuckling the belt holding his sword and scabbard, he tosses it onto the sofa.

Myself having curtsied, he bows.

Noting that he looks into my eyes with a piercing gaze as I take his outstretched hand, he, in quiet deliberation, asks, "Ready?"

Responding softly, "Yes."

Instructing me, he says, "Place thy legs two feet apart." Placing his right hand in just beneath my left shoulder blade, he takes my right hand in his left, and standing as he requested, my dress, exposing a small amount of the matching bikini bottoms, parts in the center from my pelvis down, an aspect which does not go unnoticed by him. "When thou danc'd in the green dress, 'twas in publick, was it not?"

"Yes," speaking with a slight giggle, "but I was wearing more than most."

"Aye, so I notic'd," he says smiling, referring to my dance video. As he stands with his feet about two feet apart, placing his right leg between mine, he pulls me forward until my pelvis rests upon his mid-thigh. "Dost thou mind?"

"Not as long as you're my dance partner." And as we start to dance the Kizomba, I think to myself, 'If he only knew how much his movements arouse me.'

And well of course he knows, and throughout our impassioned dance, as our pelvises and torsos constantly brush each other, I am entranced by his mesmerizing gaze. Captain Roberts' perceptive intuitiveness was a large part of his success as a pirate, and such, he is keenly aware of the changes in my emotional state.

Having danced our way to the stereo system, I pop in the mini CD. When the music starts again, I am pleasantly surprised to learn that he is not only one with the music, but is seductively inviting, and as he sensually caresses my body as we dance, it's plain to see this is to be a 'no holds barred' evening.

Meanwhile →

Outside in the rain, although we are unaware of them, there are two figures looking in through the window watching us.

"We shall wait until they are through dancing," utters the ghastly figure. "Then, as they become entwined within the rapture of passion, I shall liven up the storm. Amid the fourth lightning bolt's thunderous boom, rap loudly upon the door."

Making no reply, the second man makes his way to the front door, and as he awaits for the prescribed number of lightning bolts, he prepares himself in mind and body to play his role.

Within the Music Room →

"My stamina, fy Nghapten, is not that of thine. May we listen for a few minutes whilst I catch my breath?"

Wearing a slight smile as my lover's seductive eyes undress me, "What then?"

Except for a twinkle in my eyes, enhancing his intense gaze as I place the surgical gloves on the mantle, I make no reply beyond a seductive grin.

Standing before the warm fire, both Captain Roberts and I remove our respective dress gloves, but before putting on the smaller sized surgical pair, I allow my hands to breathe a spell first. Captain Roberts; on the other hand, amid the repeated excerpt from Beethoven's 7th, takes from the mantle, his pair, but before he has the chance to put them on, lightning lights up the sky with dramatic fury. Searching for comfort, he holds me tightly within his strong arms as the sound of thunder shakes the house.

Neither of us noticing, the Captain's astrolabe teeters dangerously on the edge, and as I slide my hand across the mantle, I unintentionally bump the delicate instrument, causing it to fall. Instinctively, both the Captain and I reacting simultaneously, we catch it together, and as our bare hands entwine, I am too stunned to speak.

Clearing his throat whilst gently taking his astrolabe from within my grasp, the Captain carefully returns that which is one of his prize possessions to its rightful place on the mantle as we look at one another in awe.

> *Both knowing there was some rational reason for what is happening, V'lé searched the face of the only man she trusted for an explanation, but as he gently coupled her hands within his own, his eyes didn't contain bewilderment, but rather liberation, for the deliverance of regeneration was what he felt, & with the closing of his eyes, inhaling slowly, he took into his lungs a considerable amount of air, & upon the opening of his eyes, looking very much alive, he slowly exhaled the breath of life.*

Suddenly, lightning courses through the house a second time, but on this occasion, as I continue to look at my Captain, he does not disappear amid the flash as always before. "What's happening!" I exclaim, trembling.

"I have—" but before my Captain can continue, the lightning, it being the final phase prior to that which is next to come, again rocks the house with booming thunder.

Seeking safety in the arms of my beloved, who holds me securely, " 'Tisn't anny neede to be so fearful, fy annwyl. Thou art safe."

As I cling to him, I need— well, to be kissed, but I am afraid. What if I discover I am going insane, but then, as I look into his eyes, Captain Roberts, as his bare hands continues to hold one of mine, seems to know that this day would come, and such, his manner suggests one of resurgence.

Without giving anymore thoughts to the matter, Captain Roberts states, "There are no barriers between us now, fy Nghariad anwylaf." Again taking me in to his arms, and kissing my lips with great passion, the long curly locks of his mane and abundant moustache, brushing against my face and neck, creates within me a surge of passion unlike any I have known before.

With our minds racing with tremendous thoughts, neither of us care why or how, as my Captain kisses me again, and how superlative it is. As we begin to sway with the music, the powerfully erotic waltz engulfs us, and in the course of our dance he unfastens several of the buckles along the seams of his knee-length trousers, exposing his well-muscled thighs. With the change of music, as our emotions become increasingly fervid, he blows out the candles, and as we move about the room, Captain Roberts shuts and bolts the door between the two halves of the reception room.

Seductively, as the room becomes increasingly dark, I fondle his imposing physique whilst pushing his Boléro jacket back off his shoulders as we glissade by the fireplace.

Allowing his jacket to fall to the floor, leaving himself bare from the waist up. Again the music changes, this time playing the sensuous midi version of the theme from, *Dangerous Minds,*' that I had vamped for his website, as well as the same music he had heard over the computer's speakers the night we met, I am only now learning that my Captain finds the piece equally piquant. Throughout the duration of the chantey, my intrepid lover, whose lustful desires overwhelm him, again brings my pelvis against his thigh, only this time, the knowledge that he is able to literally feel the sodden undergarment of his lover, serves to further increase his sinuous movements as he takes delight in being able to feel my flesh against his.

Unhooking the narrow silver belt about my waist and tossing it onto the sofa, thereby permitting his hands free and easy movement beneath the silky material, he unhurriedly slides the body stocking off my arms and down to my waist exposing my breasts, and gazing upon the bare flesh of my torso for the first time he speaks in a most entrancing manner.

"Dost thou desire to be ravish'd beyond the realm of ecstasy?"

Answering his question by seductively pressing myself up against him, he maneuvers me before the fireplace. Gently encouraging me to lower myself onto the bearskin rug, he places a pillow upon the rug to cushion my head, are he lays me backwards. Bending forward from his kneeling position, my gallant begins to undo the front buttons on his trousers when a powerful bolt of lightning alights the room. Following the tremendous clap of thunder comes a loud banging noise. At first, I am thinking that the banging comes from within my head, but as it continues, we both realize it comes from outside.

The shock of the realization that someone is banging on the front door causes my valiant Captain to grab for his scabbard, and as he leaps to his feet, he spins 180 degrees. Unbolting the door between the 2 sections of the reception room as he hastens to the foyer whilst quickly buttoning up, I, being shocked out of my delirious passion, follow him.

Katie, also hearing the banging, tentatively steps in to the foyer with Sue close behind her. "Miss V'lé. Captain," shrills Katie, "Someone's at the door!"

Replying in an anxiety riddled voice, "We know!"

"No one in their right mind would be out in this weather!" exclaims Sue.

As my hand reaches for the doorknob, Captain Roberts intervenes. "Avast!"

Taking the opportunity to protect his woman, Captain Roberts takes my arm as he gently, ever firmly, shoves me behind him, and shielding me with his body, "Stay behind me, V'lé. Ladies, to the galley, for 'tis evident it be a madman which descends upon us!"

Backing into the kitchen, Sue and Katie peer out, but as they look around the corner, it is not the Captain's actions that evoke their curiosity, but both of ours. Looking at us and then at each other, their attention is drawn to our semi-undressed state.

Redirecting their attention to the matter at hand, the courageous seaman, drawing his cutlass with great flourish, flings open the door. When the heavy door bangs against the wall, lightning again strikes. Amid the illumination, an ambiguous form shrouded by a thick cloud of fog invading the foyer can be seen. When the mist clears, the figure of a man, soaked to the skin, stands before us.

Squinting my eyes, not believing what I see, my mouth drops open as I try to speak, I am unable to do so. As the stranger walks inside, closing the door behind him, my puzzled Captain looks from me to the man. Slowly, as I creep out from behind my fearless protector, the Captain feels I must know the person of whom I have not taken my eyes off since the door opened. Remaining motionless for several moments, finally mustering the courage to reach out, I touch the stranger's cheek with the tips of my fingers.

While closing his hand over mine, the stranger says, "Hello, V'lé."

"Keith?" Suddenly as my knees weaken, I fall unconscious into the arms of the stranger.

With this event, I shoot a terrifying glance at the man who hath instilled such distress, as to cause my woman to swoon, and without forethought, I move towards the stranger to take my woman from his grasp. Picking her up and carrying her in to the parlour, where I gently lie her upon the chaise settee, I immediately overlap the front of her dress that had fallen open when she fainted, exposing all but her breasts. "Katie, my jacket and Miss V'lé's silver belt, please retrieve them from the music room."

"Without delay, Captain," replies Katie as she makes haste. Having located both items requested, Katie returns to the parlour. Handing them to me, "Can I help, Captain?"

"Many thanks, Katie, but I can manage." and having fitted my woman with the narrow silver belt, I slip on my Boléro jacket.

A few moments later, as I come to, I can feel someone, both holding my hand and caressing my brow, and the feeling, being so wonderfully soothing, I don't want to wake up.

"V'lé," says my lover as he gently moves the hair off my face, "Deffro fy melys."

> *Kneeling beside his lady fair, Captain Roberts, speaking in his native Welsh whilst trying to wake his woman, was thankful that amid the ensuing chaos, no one had mentioned his tactile helpfulness by being able to touch his woman with his bare hands, but even if they had, he would've cared not; he knew only that he was able to touch her, & touch her he would, for all that mattered was that his woman needed him, & regardless of the possible consequences, he was not about to abandon her.*

When my eyes flutter open, I look up at my Captain, and although still half dazed, but feeling safe and secure in his presence, I smile at him lovingly, and speaking to him in a semi-conscience state, "I'm all right, my darling."

Though not truly aware of my wordage, calling Captain Roberts, 'my darling,' for all to hear pleased him immensely.

Carrying a damp washcloth, my mother enters the parlor, and in hands it to me.

"Thank you, mom."

As both my mom and Katie continue to look at both the Captain, me, and each other repeatedly, still surprised by our outspoken show of affection, my mom asks, "Are you all right, V'lé?"

Not wishing to look away from my Captain, I continue to smile at him lovingly as I reply, "I could not be in better hands."

Trying to sit up, with help from my Captain, who is still holding my hand, I express my feelings of quiet distress concerning my actions, saying, "Please forgive me, fy Nghapten, but overwhelmed with all that's happened of late, I seem to be imagining things."

"You're not imagining things, V'lé," states the stranger.

Unsettled upon hearing a familiar voice from behind me, causes me to hold my breath, and as the stranger moves in to my view, I can only stare in disbelief as I see who appears to be my late ex fiancé, Keith McClure.

For Captain Roberts, this deception takes on a totally different aspect, and although I do not generally dwell on the past, my Captain does know who Keith was, and also that I was told he had died, and now, years later, to discover that his death was a lie, my Captain becomes instilled with an immediate aversion towards Keith, and his vile behavior.

Closing my eyes for a moment to compose myself while also getting hold of my manners. Opening them once more, "Katie, please get something dry for Mister McClure to change in to before he, again, catches his death."

"Right away, Miss," replies Katie as she heads towards the laundry room to fetch one of the freshly laundered, terry cloth dressing gowns *Inn Finistère* provides her guests.

"Forgive me for fainting, Captain, but as I am sure you can imagine, I thought I was looking at a malevolent poltergeist."

After a few moments, Katie returns. "Here you are, Mister McClure. You can wear this whilst waiting for your clothes to dry." Pointing him in the direction of the bathroom, "Within the foyer, past the front door, take the first door on the left."

"Perhaps not a poltergeist," begins my mom, "but malevolent just the same."

With Keith now out of earshot, my dutiful Captain suggests, "Dost thou not agree, fy melys, that a faster recovery might be achiev'd 'fore the warmth of the fire?"

Smiling, "Yes, fy Nghapten," and trying to rise off the chaise settee, "I do," but, finding myself weak, I sink back in to the cushions.

Bending down, my Captain says, "Try not to stand." And as he cradles me in his strong arms, I happily wrap mine about his neck, and feeling secure, I snuggle my head against the soft black thicket of hair upon his muscular chest.

Setting me upon the sofa, Captain Roberts, seeing my mom had been following close behind him, turns to her and says, "Mrs Montgomery, please bring the Blackberry Brandy."

"Right away, Captain," and turning, she heads for the bar.

Returning with the crystal decanter, and a snifter; taking advantage of Keith's absence, my mom asks, "How is it you can touch V'lé without gloves on?"

"I knows not. But onely moments ago, not that I would have departed for more than a instant, I tried to dematerialize, but alas, found myself unable to do so."

"That's curious," states my mom. "Could you have been resurged?"

"Possibly, but whatever the miracle is that has blessed us, I intend to make the most of it."

With a quizzical look on her face, Katie asks, "Resurged, you mean mortal once again?"

Seeing my gallant pouring a measure of Blackberry Brandy into the glass, I push myself up in to a seated position while indicating that I wish for him to sit beside me.

Handing me the snifter while replying to Katie as he seats himself, "Aye, Katie, I believe it to be so."

After a moment's pause, my Captain focuses his attentions on my earlier reaction, enquiring, "Since when dost thou faint at the sight of ghosts?"

Jokingly, but with a serious overtone, I ask, "Wouldst thou prefer running and screaming?"

"Thou speaks as from memory."

" 'Tis indeed, fy Nghapten, from my youth, but now…" Giving his question a few moments thought, "I suppose it's because I knew Keith personally, and believed him to be dead, but when thee first appeared, well to be frank, I was more stunned than scared."

"I'll bring tea," states Katie.

"Can it be, fy Nghapten, thou dost not realize, that, that night was the beginning of a dream come true."

Smiling just enough to be noticed, whilst gently squeezing my hand, "Aye fy melys, I do indeed."

As Katie returns with both coffee, tea, a salver containing assorted finger foods, and a supply of napkins, Captain Roberts, arising from the sofa, takes from Katie, the heavy tray and places it on the coffee table.

"Thank you, Captain."

"You are most welcome, Katie," and returning, he sits back down beside me.

While everyone helps themselves to the tidbits, Katie fills the cups and glasses with the desired liquid refreshments.

Chapter Six

The Proposal

Our situation is unusual to be sure, and as we bandy about an array of speculative ideas in the midst of the incessant storm, Keith, having donned the robe provided by Katie, appears at the entrance to the reception room clutching his wet clothes.

"What should I do with these?" asks, Keith.

As the lot of us look towards him uneasily, Katie, with respect to her duties, bounds from her chair. "I'll be back in two ticks."

Speaking to Keith as she walks past him en route to the ground floor guest bath off the hall, "This way please."

While lugging his sopping bundle, Keith contumaciously follows her in to the bathroom.

Fetching a few hangers, en route, "Just set those down there, Mister McClure, over the drain."

As Keith plunks the wet articles down, Katie says, "Normally, after rinsing, those could be popped in the electric dryer, but," as she slides the shower curtain to one side, "being without electricity at the moment, you'll have to hang them up to dry."

Moments later, seeing Katie returning alone, my mom asks, "Where's Keith?"

"He'll be along directly," replies Katie, adding, "Is his manner always less than agreeable?"

"Why do you ask, Katie?" inquires my mom.

"Well, when I suggested he rinse out his clothes in the basin before hanging them up, he looked a bit put out."

Chuckling a bit, I explain. "Infuriated would be a better description. Keith comes from Texas where male arrogance still reigns supreme, and things such as laundry is considered 'woman's work.'" Only moments later, before I have the chance to speak to the Captain about his role at *Inn Finistère*, I see Keith making his way to the hearth; ergo, I must count on Captain Roberts' perceptive qualities, and requiring a co-operative effort, I enlist my mother and Katie to help. "Please go along with whatever transpires between Captain Roberts and myself."

Both Katie, who is just settling herself on the chair next to the sofa where I am still resting, and my mom, indicate they'll play along by quietly nodding their heads.

Katie, leaning forward to fill her teacup, asks, "Are you feeling better now, Miss?"

"Yes, Katie. much," replying amid a brief smile. "I was just a little spooked is all. It's not every day that we have a storm of such intensity and a dead man comes as a guest."

"Well, around here," utters my mom, somewhat comically, "such an occurrence is not that uncommon." Seeing the offended look on our faces as she glances about, she quickly adds, "In your case, Captain, your presence has been a blessing, while his," motioning in Keith's direction, "will be vexatious. Besides, Keith's only true talent would be more in keeping with that of a sycophantical prevaricator. Don't believe a word he says."

Finally feeling strong enough I stand, and remaining a gracious hostess, despite my feelings, I address Keith cordially. "Welcome to *Inn Finistère*, Keith."

"Nice old place," Keith says in reply, "but there seems to be a lack of modern conveniences."

"Really, Keith? Just what off hand would you say is missing?"

"Well, to start with V'lé, I didn't see a television in the guest bedroom."

"You won't find a light switch in there either," states Katie.

"With a few exceptions," my mom adds, "*Inn Finistère* is just as it was in the late 17th and early 18th centuries, and the majority of the exceptions are as old as V'lé could make them."

"Yes, I noticed the brass tub and antique commode in the bathroom. As for the wall sconce near the door, I thought it was just for show."

"My guests come to *Inn Finistère* because they want to experience life as it was during the days of yore, as so stated in our brochures and advertising. As for our impromptu guests, most find their stay to be a delightful experience, and during the seasonal holidays we have variety of entertainment, including Theater, Minstrel Shows, Fireworks, a Masked Ball, and we generally host at least one Cotillion."

Changing the subject, Keith states with his usual impudence, "I heard that the news of my untimely death came as quite a shock to you, V'lé."

Having no patience for impertinence, I feel no reason not to be blunt. "Quite to the contrary, Keith. When I was told of your death via telephone my comment was simply, 'One down and four to go,' after which I hung up."

Choosing to ignore my comment, Keith turns to my mom. "Good to see you again, Sue."

Feeling decidedly less than friendly, my mom kept her reply short. "Hello, Keith."

Gesturing towards my domestic, "Katie is my housekeeper, cook and good friend."

"Mister McClure," states Katie, with a nod.

Replying, "Howdy," Keith answers in his typical 'wanna-be' cowboy fashion.

In keeping with her duties, Katie asks, "Can I get you a drink, Mister McClure?"

"Thank you, Katie. I'll have a brandy."

As Katie steps to the bar, I continue with the introductions. "And," as I nestle as close as possible to my Captain, "this is Captain Roberts, he and I are keeping company." Just incase Keith might recognize the name, and knowing the Captain won't lie, I purposely left out his first name.

> *Understandably, Captain Roberts loathes Keith; nevertheless, suspecting Keith's presence would lead only to more depravity, perhaps even dangerous in nature, he intended to keep a watchful eye on him for the duration.*

Whilst Captain Roberts reluctantly summons all the charm he can muster, he stands. "My pleasure, sir," and following through with the customs of his time, he makes a modest bow.

Before Keith can offer his hand in a gesture of friendship, Katie, returning from the bar, carries a small salver, and although not intentionally to thwart his coming gesture, she walks between Captain Roberts and Keith.

Taking the snifter from the salver as it is offered, Keith says, "Thank you, Katie."

Eager to hear the goings on, Katie sets the salver down on the table before her as she returns to her seat and picks up her cup of tea.

Immediately thereafter, Keith, shifting the glass from his right hand to his left, offers his hand in friendship. 'Tho this custom had been known since the days of the Roman

Empire, the bow, a long-established method as a greeting, and the only one known to Captain Roberts, I whisper, "Firmly grip his hand, fy Nghapten, and follow his actions."

As they shake hands, Captain Roberts says, "Any welcomed guest of my treasur'd V'lé shall be treated as decorum dictates." Then, displaying his intentions, Captain Roberts encircles my waist with his arms as he moves behind me, whilst whispering, "Steady, fy annwyl. All is well, I promise."

Keith, noting my Captain's blatant intimacy, "Regarding your question earlier, Captain. It is yourself who is being openly familiar," and pretending to show a measure of responsibility, "may I ask your intentions regarding my former fiancée?"

"Ne'er did such a relationship exist 'twixt you and Miss V'lé, for such would require honest intentions, and of those, you had none."

"Your insulting remark may be true, Captain, but it does not answer the question."

Captain Roberts, speaking as if it were just a plain and simple fact, states, "Miss V'lé and I are to be wed."

Katie's and Sue's eyes widen in surprise.

"Seems I heard right. May I offer my congratulations?"

Thunderstruck as I turn my head, my weakened knees are effortlessly supported by my Captain's strong arms, and amid his sincere, although near unreadable expression, his slight, comforting smile creates a sparkling glow within me.

Fearful that Keith may read my reaction correctly, Captain Roberts redirects any such thoughts masterfully. "Miss V'lé is still a trifle shocked at seeing you and," as he looks directly at Keith, "I am sure you be acquaint'd with her fear of thunderstorms."

Holding me firmly against him, knowing I will feel his inner emotions, my Captain, nuzzles my shoulder in a prelude of forthcoming activities. "Rest assured, fy annwyl, for the disagreeable friction lurking herein, shall soon be replaced with exhaustive pleasuring."

His wedding announcement brings me more happiness than I thought possible, and the firmness of his personage, coupled with his nuzzling, creates a tingling sensation, as does his luxuriant moustache as it brushes against the back of my neck. Knowing he awaits an answer to his invitation, I do my best to be equally cryptic in my reply. "Sharing thy desire la jouissance de la vie exubérante, I await thy proposed curriculum with impatient expectancy."

Giving us both a baffled look, "I see you haven't lost the knack to skillfully speak above others, V'lé."

"Yes, a good vocabulary is rather useful at times, is it not," states Sue.

Deciding to just ignore our secretive comments, Keith returns to a previous topic. "When is the happy day?"

Not knowing the true circumstances of the situation, Katie, trying to help, speaks out of place. "They haven't set a date yet, Mister McClure. Captain Roberts is at sea a great deal of the time. Isn't that right, Captain?"

Being somewhat dismayed by Katie's boldness, speaking above her station, and blatantly lying in the bargain, Captain Roberts, without revealing Katie's lie, rectifies the situation. "Recent events have made it possible for me to stay on indefinitely, so unless Miss V'lé wishes it otherwise, she and I shall be wed as soon as the law allows." Pausing for a moment, noting the shocked faces of all present, he takes the awkward situation in hand whilst guiding me to the sofa. Bending down and gently kissing my hand, and noting that I am trembling still; my grip on his hand being solid, he whispers, "Let go of my hand, fy annwyl."

As I sit quietly, assessing all that's transpired during the past three days, I quizzically mumble, "Certainly," and releasing my grasp, he stands.

Whilst Captain Roberts gathers his thoughts, Katie freshens everyone's drink, during which time, Keith takes a seat opposite me.

"Now that we all be settl'd, 'tis my wish to address other matters." Captain Roberts, walking to the hearth to empty his pipe, turns, and accusing Keith directly, "Whyfor were you skulking about *Inn Finistère* during a torrent?"

Katie, injecting her thoughts, "You could 'ave been struck by lightning and vaporized!"

"No such luck," mumbles Sue.

For an instant, everyone glances at my mom, after which, returning their attentions back to the Captain, he continues his tirade. "I presume the head lamps on yon road 2 nights past belonged to your motor car, and the muddy footprints found upon the verandah the following morrow, they belonged to you also?"

"Do you always speak to the guests in such a rude fashion, Captain?"

" 'Tisn't rude to be assertive whilst making enquiries pertaining to another's rather nefarious activities."

"Well, I suppose I can't blame you too much for being upset."

"Just why are you here, Keith?" asks Sue brashly.

Hearing no reply, the Captain, chiding Keith firmly, "Come, sir, enlighten us!" Becoming increasingly irritated by Keith's further reluctance to reply, "I warn you, Mister McClure, my patience is wearing thin."

Assuming the Captain's hostility is merely his nature, as indicated by the unworried glance he tosses in my direction, the wayward Keith, wishing not to create too much friction, replies. "It's yes to all of your questions. I apologize if I scared anyone the other night; it was not my intention." Taking a sip of his brandy, "How do I explain?" As he half laughingly begins, "This being my first trip abroad, and hearing that V'lé owned a bed and breakfast in Wales, I decided to come here on my vacation, but until tonight, I didn't have enough nerve to knock on the door." Shrugging, Keith takes both my hands in his before I can react, "I'm only here now, V'lé, because my car is stuck in the mud about three-quarters of a mile down the road."

> *Keith shrugged a bit too nonchalantly for the Captain's taste, & as he moved behind the sofa, pacing to & fro, he began to stew. The very idea of someone of the masculine persuasion trying to comfort his woman made his blood boil. In the Captain's book of rules, gentlemen did not touch a woman's person unless she invited him to do so, & even though Captain Roberts knows this custom to be rather lax in present times, he knew his future bride preferred the rules of propriety from his era.*

Pulling my hands from Keith's before my gallant Captain comes drawn for bear, "Even though you know I love to have guests, you ought to have warned me of your impending arrival."

Captain Roberts, knowing I am not merely upset, but truly uncomfortable with Keith's presence, peers over my shoulder, and speaking to Keith rather sarcastically, "There is a remarkable invention known as the telephone. Having been in use for well over a century, perhaps you have heard of it."

Noting Captain Roberts persistently less than friendly attitude towards him, and being too egotistical to shoulder the blame, replies saying, "Yes, I have, Captain, but not knowing if I'd be welcome, I took a chance, and well, here I am." Grinning at me sideways, "I'm sorry that you're a little put off by my presence, V'lé."

Sue, letting off a memory riddled sigh, "What do you think, Keith? First we hear of your death, then out of the blue you show up without warning, and lastly, your manners are atrocious, but then they always were."

Keith, stating with a measure of resentment, "My manners? What about his temper!" pointing at Captain Roberts. "You might ask him to exercise some control."

Sporting a modest smile, "But he is, Keith." Seeing the look on my Captain's face after my statement, I maintain a more serious expression as I continue. "Considering the circumstances, how else would you expect a well-bred gentleman to behave?"

Rising, "I'll keep that in mind," replies Keith.

"How did you even know I was here?"

Replying while walking to the bookcase, showing a mild interest in its contents, "Having kept in touch with mutual friends at the 'Whatever Shop,' I asked a few questions, and well, here I am. Most of your old friends ask about you, V'lé, and now, having been here, I can tell them you're fine and engaged to be married."

"They know most of that news from my letters."

"From what I hear, you haven't written any of them for months."

"I suppose I have been rather lax lately. After I return from my honeymoon, having something to tell everyone, I'll put pen to paper."

> *Positive that Keith's, 'realitas objectiva,' was nefarious in nature, the Captain, although listening with awareness, was unable to get a firm hold of the suspicious thread that lurked in the back of his mind; therefore, knowing it's a good thing to keep your friends close, 'tis better still to keep your enemies closer, & thus, Captain Roberts extended an invitation.*

Speaking smoothly, Captain Roberts makes his position quite clear. "We shall see to your motor in the early morning light. Thitherto, you may remain as a guest, but come morn, having seen that my intended is quite well, you are to seek lodgings elsewhere."

Eyeing my Captain in utter surprise, "He's going to spend the night?"

"Fy annwyl, where be thine humanity? For onely the cruelest of creatures would deny even a knave shelter and a hot meal on a night such as this."

Looking somewhat bewildered by the Captain's questionable manner, "Thank you, Captain, I think, but regardless, I am grateful for your hospitality."

This entire evening, baffling to be sure, has Katie somewhat unsure of her duties, and as she arises, asks, "Can you help me upstairs for a few minutes, Miss?"

"Certainly, Katie." Before exiting the room, I turn to my Captain smiling; and whilst giving him a peck on the cheek I whisper, "Be nice." Trodding along after her, "I'm a coming, Katie."

Catching her on the stairs, Katie asks, "Are you and the Captain really going to be married?"

Reaching the end of the hall I open the linen closet. "That's what he said, Katie."

"But how can you marry him, Miss? He's— umm, I mean— there are laws."

Whilst gathering up an assortment of linens, "I know it's hard to take in Katie, but by some miracle he has been given a second life." Reading Katie's bewildered expression, "I do not profess to understand it myself, nor do I care. I only know that we have every intention of making the most of it for as long as it lasts."

"Good for you, Miss."

Handing her a mixture of crimson, and black towels, and a set of black sheets and crimson pillow cases. "The sheets are for my bed Katie."

"I don't recall seeing these before," states Katie, running her hand over them. "Oooo..." she coos. "My gracious, these are real silk aren't they."

"Yes they are. I bought them in Cardiff a few days ago."

Taking out more towels, and set a set of crimson sheets and black pillow cases, "And these will go on the bed in the Captain's room," handing her the sheets.

"You want me to put these in the Captain's room?"

Closing the linen closet door, "Yes, Katie."

Entering my room, carrying sheets in one arm and a load of towels in the other, I toss the sheets onto the bed. "After I hang these up I'll be right up to help you."

Walking towards the door leading to the upper section of the turret, Katie replies, "Thank you, Miss."

After quickly changing the towels in my bathroom, I dash in to my room, and stripping off the bedding I toss the linens onto the floor in a heap. From within the chest at the foot of my bed, I take out a reversible, black and crimson satin comforter. When finished, I go upstairs to help Katie. When I enter the room, she hasn't even started. "What's wrong, Katie?"

Startled by my arrival, "This room, never having been up here before, I feel as though I'm intruding."

Pulling off the crimson colored bedspread, "Don't be silly, Katie," and together we strip off the sheets and pillow cases. "Now that Captain Roberts is mortal, I'll let you take over the cleaning chores up here."

"Oh no, Miss," utters Katie, almost fearfully as we begin to put on the silk sheets. "I couldn't invade the Captain's personal space."

"Continuing my assurances as I return the crimson satin bedspread to the bed, "Captain Roberts always leaves the room when I come in to dust and run the cleaner." After a moment, I add, "Woman's work you know," chuckling a mite.

Momentarily adding the Captain's linens to the growing heap in the middle of my bedroom floor, Katie fetches the wicker basket from the hall closet, and after filling it with the linens to be laundered, "With two men joining us at the dining table, shall I add the standing rib roast to tonight's menu?"

"Yes, and now that you mention it, there will be another dish as well." Walking over to my computer and turning it on, I print out the recipe located on my website for Solomon Gundie[1] and handing it to her, "You'll have to use the more common ingredients, Katie.

Quizzically, "Solomon Gundie?"[1]

---

[1] Solomon Gundie is a hodgepodge of cooked meat or fowl fried in a bit of water, sautéed onions or peppers, salt & pepper, hard cooked eggs (sliced,) steamed vegetables, meaty fruits (e.g. melon or papaya,) cubed, grapes &/or raisins, & soft nuts. Mixed together, he lot is moistened using the au jus. Best when served at room temperature.

It's the Captain's favorite. It'll take a bit of time to prepare so you'll need to get started immediately. As well as delighting him enormously, it should make a good side dish.

Looking over the recipe. "Yes, Miss, I think I can make this with the ingredients we have in the larder," and picking up the wicker basket, she heads for the door.

> *Having spent hours over the last few months trying to envision V'lé's former husbands & ex fiancé, seeing that she had long since destroyed any photographic memories, the Captain realized he had created a rather unsavoury image of them, but after seeing that Keith looked like one of those unkempt ruffians he'd seen on T.V., wearing what is referred to as, 'trail clothes,' & possessing the manners of a buffoon, his preconceived notions were justified, & yet, even though he fully understands V'lé's loneliness at the time, he found it difficult to fathom how it was possible that any woman would allow herself to be seen with such a blackguard, much less keep company with one. At first the Captain thought her apprehension at seeing Keith was a reminder of happier days, when love's promise was all one needed to live on, but after his beloved had spoke to him, the Captain knew that all she felt for him was contempt, and for his beloved, Keith was nothing more than a grim reminder of an endless array of broken promises, & the Captain hated to see V'lé's heart ache; even so, he knew he had no choice but to tolerate Keith's presence long enough to discover his true purpose.*

MEANWHILE IN THE RECEPTION ROOM—

"This is marvelous wine, Captain," announces Keith, taking another gulp.

"This Madeira was part of the cargo aboard the, *Sagrada Família*, a Portuguese treasure ship during the reign of John V, and is considered some of the finest ever bottled. There be many hogsheads of fine wines, spirits, and brandies in the cellar, as well as a number of other rarities that are a continual interest to connoisseurs, collectors and museums, but V'lé, insisting they are for our enjoyment, refuses to part with any of them."

Having a moderate pleasantry in his voice. "If it's not too much trouble, Captain, I would enjoy seeing the wine cellar, as well as the rest of this old place."

Although loathing the idea, his woman did ask him to be nice, and such, the Captain replies, "My pleasure, of course." Excepting the wine cellar, you have already seen the areas accessible to *Inn Finistère's* guests. Leading the way, "This way, Mister McClure."

Following, Keith says, "I'd prefer it, Captain, if you'd stop calling me Mister McClure. My friends call me Keith." After several seconds with no response from Captain Roberts, either verbally, nor through his manner, Keith sighs.

Coming down the stairs and seeing the two men walking in to the dining room, I ask, "Where are you two headed?"

"Mister McClure requested to see the wine cellar."

"We dress for dinner here, Keith." Addressing my Captain, "When you come back up, fy Nghapten, wilt thou be kind enough to bring a couple selections to serve with dinner?"

His voice trailing off as the two men disappear from view, "My pleasure."

SOMETIME LATER—

Both Captain Roberts and I having dressed for dinner, and whilst adding a few finishing touches to the dining room table; a particular pleasure of mine, I take pride in my 'Royal

Albert' patterned, "*Moss Rose*" English Bone China,' dinner service; my gold engraved Waterford crystal stemware, and elegant silver service.

Picking up the crystal bell, and jingling it, Katie bellows, "Dinner is served."

Captain Roberts and Keith, returning from their stroll of the grounds and stable, comment on the beautiful table as they enter the dining room.

In the center of the table, beneath a dome cover, sits a magnificent standing rib roast surrounded by Solomon Gundie. About the table is found an array of foods for the most discerning palate, and the three bottles Captain Roberts brought up from the cellar, include a bottle of Chateau d'Yquem 1855, and an 1893 Massandra Red Port, the latter to be served with dessert.

Upon entering, "Is that the famous necklace?" asks Sue.

"It's breathtaking," injects Katie.

"Aye, it is that," replies Captain Roberts whilst picking up the 1818 Cognac Grande Champagne, and as we all sit down to dinner he pours in to his fluted glass, a small amount and takes a sip. "Exquisite." Setting his glass back on the table, he picks up the others in rotation. Filling first, the glasses belonging to the ladies, then Mister McClure's, and lastly his own. After which, raising his glass, "I offer a toast."

Everyone, in observance of this time honored tradition, happily lift their glass as Captain Roberts states, "May the splendor of true love transcend all obstacles."

"A beautiful sentiment," raves Katie.

"It is indeed," echoes Sue. "I know the two of you will be blissfully happy."

"For all eternity, fy Nghapten," and as I pick his left hand off the table, he gazes in to my eyes as I kiss the back of his fingers saying, "Fi cariad dy," and while smiling lovingly at him, I return his hand to the table.

The Captain, appreciating that I have learned more Welsh, returns my loving smile with his magically expressive eyes. "And I thee."

As everyone waits, Katie removes the dome cover from the serving platter.

"Solomon Gundie!" Exclaims Captain Roberts.

"Yes, Captain," states Katie. "Miss V'lé gave me the recipe when we were upstairs."

" 'Tis my favourite dish," he proclaims smiling, and slapping his hands together, rubbing them briskly, resplendence is evident in his voice as he says, "Thank you." Rising again, he adds, "Both of you." Reaching for the serving spoon, "You must all try it." Picking up my plate first, he gives me only a dab as he jokingly says, "She hates everything." Continuing around the table, serving everyone a good size dollop, he heaps his own plate high. Obviously in a festive mood, he continues serving everyone from all the dishes until only the roast remains. Lastly, picking up the carving set as he rises, Captain Roberts, with speed and precision, carving the roast in to equal sections, doles them out as everyone in turn as they hold out their plate. After which, being eager to sit down to supper, he takes his seat.

As each of us take a bite of the Solomon Gundie, the reactions about the table are very different. Hacking, as expected, I quickly take a big drink of water in an effort to wash down the overwhelming spices.

Remembering the first glass of Sambucka we had together, Captain Roberts, amid a sly grin, slaps me on the back as he humorously spouts, "After thy mouth becomes numb thou wilt enjoy it."

Seeing the enjoyment brim on his face as he got his own back for that first swig of Sambucka he took, I snidely reply, "How sweet of you to remember, darling!"

Laughing heartily, Keith spouts, "She gave you some of that fire water she drinks? That stuff would choke Godzilla."

Sue, who loves spicy foods, takes a bite saying, "It's delicious. The blend of flavors is wonderful Captain," and takes another mouthful. "As for Sambucka, it too is delicious, but only a fool trying to commit suicide the hard way would gulp it."

Katie, who had nibbled in the kitchen, agrees with Sue, and taking a big bite, "I like it."

Keith, who likes his food practically tasteless, takes a small bite and whilst scowling, utters, "I think I'll just let the spicy food go by."

Sue, remembering how difficult he was to please, "Both with little or no seasoning, Keith would prefer Navy beans and turnip greens."

Lastly, Captain Roberts takes a bite, and obviously relishing the flavors, "Simply mouth watering, Katie. Wee must have this sev'rall times a weeke."

Quizzically, Keith asks, "If this is the Captain's favorite dish, why is it you haven't served it before now, Katie?"

Seeing that Katie was not quite sure how to reply, I inject, "Because I just gave her the recipe today, Keith."

"Yes, so I heard it said earlier. What I meant is, why did you wait till now to give it to her?"

"I just happened to come across the recipe online, and knowing Captain Roberts fondness for the dish, I printed it out as a special treat." Looking at him, seeing how much he enjoys it, I continue saying, "I'm sure Katie will be pleased to serve it often."

"It'll be my pleasure," states Katie, happily.

Changing the subject. "Tell me, V'lé, what kind of name is Finistère?"

Answering his question I reply," 'Tis French."

"French?" asks Keith, curiously. "Why not a Welsh name?"

Captain Roberts replies for me saying, "Canne it be you knows not of her fondness for all things French?"

Before Keith can reply, I reveal my reason. "True, fy Nghapten, but that not be the reason."

Finding himself curious, Captain Roberts asks, " 'Tisn't?"

"Nope." Continuing with a modest smile, "I did toil with naming it Ffortiwn Brenhinol in homage to a master mariner, but after considerable thought I decided instead to name it in honor of Dona St. Columb and Jean-Benoit Aubéry."

"Who are they?" asks Katie.

Jumping in, Sue states, "They're characters from V'lé's favorite movie."

"Ffortiwn Brenhinol? What's that?" asks Keith, "Another French name?"

"Nay," says Captain Roberts, with a reminiscent smile on his face, " 'Tis Welsh for *Royal Fortune*, the name of my beloved ship."

Everyone at the table is baffled except my mom, who states, "Jean-Benoit Aubéry is the captain of the French pirate ship in Daphne du Maurier's novel, 'Frenchman's Creek.' Finistère was his home."

"And Dona St. Columb?" enquires Katie.

Answering her question, I reply, "She was not only an English noble woman, but the only woman Aubéry would ever love, and with no right."

"You named this place after a bloodthirsty pirate!" spouts Keith, adding, "And what do you mean, with no right."

Again dismayed by Keith's lack of knowledge regarding protocol, Captain Roberts says, "A man has no right to love a woman who is married to another."

Jumping in, "As for him being a pirate, you Keith, like most people, having been filled to the brim with fairytales and movie lore, you have no conception as to what it meant to be a pirate, or a seaman during the Golden Age, nor of the devastation that drove honest men to such an extreme. Even so, taking those hardships in to account, I would love to have lived then, and perhaps if I had been fortunate enough to 'ave married a man of independent means on his last fling, I could've helped somehow."

"How, fy annwyl?"

"I don't know, fy Nghapten," as a slight sadness becomes apparent, "but I would've found a way to ease their suffering without compromising their dignity."

"And would of become a pirate given the opportunity, I suppose," spouts Keith.

"What I would've done," as I flash a look of desire towards my lover, "was to find a way to sail with one particular pirate."

"The one from your website no doubt." Musing a moment, Keith adds, "A distant relative I suppose."

"Not so distant," states Sue quietly.

As dinner continues, everyone enjoys a leisurely meal, and the conversation, no longer comprised of depth and insight, is delightfully peaceful, yet as I consider the company, I know it's only a matter of time before the tides change.

Looking at me, "Why," begins Keith, "do you call Captain Roberts, Venhapten? Is that his first name?"

Answering his question, I reply, "Fy Nghapten is more personal. It means, my Captain, in Welsh."

"Why not call him by his first name? I know this isn't America, and even considering the formality here, it seems to me that a fiancée would have that right."

"Because it's his due, Keith," I tell him.

Reaching for the dinner rolls, Keith asks, "Where are you from, Captain?"

"Castell-Newydd Bach. 'Tis a small village about fifteen miles from where we be, and here tell," speaking with a modest smile, "as I have not been there since I was a young man, the village boasts proudly as being my birthplace. And you?"

Answering with a big grin, "Texas, the Lone Star state. Turning to face Captain Roberts, he asks, "Have you been to America?"

"Aye, that I have."

"You have!" Katie states in surprise.

" 'Twas a long time ago, Katie."

"Real long," states Sue with a chortle.

"Where did you go?" asks Katie with a smile.

"Virginia's coast mostly." Continuing as he helps himself to another slice of the roast, "For a time it was a good place to sell trade goods, and once, following the course as set down by the legendary mariner, Sir Francis Drake, me crew journeyed around the horn to your America's west coast where we visited sev'rall of the small islands that lay westward, as well as a beach on the continent with numerous tidal pools, a couple caves, and a natural rock arch."

Knowing that the trade goods Captain Roberts referred to was pirate plunder, I do my best to hide my smile with my napkin.

"You found Captain Roberts' statement amusing?" asks, Keith. "Why?"

"It's an inside joke."

Sue, realizing my last statement was an attempt to dissuade Keith from further questions, endeavors to close the topic. "Well, it's been a wonderful meal, and the conversation's been charming, but I want to get back to my writing."

"Idle dinner talk generally is," chuckles Keith, but being he's got a job to do, he ventures to, stir things up, "but in this instance, I must confess I am pleasantly surprised."

"Why do you say that?" asks Katie.

"I wasn't sure Captain Roberts could carry on a conversation without being insulting."

"Excuse, me?" says I, obviously irritated.

Speaking as he turns to face me, Keith voices his complaint. "When I arrived your intended was quite, well… shall we say merciless where I'm concerned. I'm just glad to know that he's not a rude Son-of-a-Bitch all the time."

While the look on Katie's face is one of shock, the Captain's is instant fury. It was sheer audacity to speak thus about the Captain in the first place, and his reaction, being insulted to the nth degree, is more than justified.

"Keith! We do not speak thusly in our home." Knowing Captain Roberts has killed men for less, I add, "Apologize immediately, and in the future refrain from using expletives within these walls."

"Expletives?" asks Keith.

"Profanity," chides Sue.

Directing his comment to the Captain, "Sorry. Cuss words are commonplace in the states. I only meant to say that I'm sure you're more polite to your other guests, and hopefully the members of this household, than you are to me."

Keith's manners, still decisively deplorable, pushing Captain Roberts to the limits of his forbearance, begins to rise from his chair. "You risk much, Mister McClure, I warn you!"

Knowing the small amount of provocation needed to incite a duel in the time of Captain Roberts, and painfully aware that Keith is deliberately trying to provoke him, I quickly intercede before the gauntlet is thrown. "Please, fy Nghapten, what Keith said regarding the use of foul language in the United States is correct; ergo, being fairly certain 'twas nothing personal, thou hast no need to be upset."

Looking at Keith, "As for you, Keith," motioning to the various weapons that grace *Inn Finistère's* walls, "having no skill with a blade, and as I recall, a rather poor marksman as well, and certainly no match for Captain Roberts hand to hand, I'd say, considering these things, that dueling is definitely out." Turning back to my Captain, "Keith's so called lurking the other night, that can be chalked up to faint-heartedness, and as for his unannounced arrival, I'm sure you've noticed his constant posturing. Finally, in regard to his annoying impudence, that comes from ill-breeding and lack of schooling, so please, fy Nghapten, try to keep thy celebrated temper in check."

The Captain, in an effort to acculturate himself, listens intently to what I tell him, and keeping these thoughts clearly in his mind, "I shall, fy melys; however, I must confess I be at a loss to understand what attracted thee to this unkempt lout in the first place?"

"There he goes again," complains Keith.

"What?" I ask him.

Perturbed, "Calling me an unkempt lout! Didn't you hear him?"

"Well of course I heard him Keith, but Captain Roberts wasn't calling you names, he was simply describing you."

"And quite accurately," states Katie.

"You can hardly hold Captain Roberts accountable for your unfamiliarity with the English language," adds Sue.

Smiling at my Captain, "Keith is pretty much the average guy these days, not to say there are not nice guys out there, I just hadn't met one until thee came in to my life, and that being the case, perhaps now, thou understands why I swore off all men for so long."

Captain Roberts, nodding his head slightly, replies, "Aye."

Still trying to instigate a brawl, "Tell me V'lé," begins, Keith derisively, "You always did enjoy the lavish costumes from period movies, wearing them where and when you pleased, but must you incorporate olde world English in to your game?"

"Meaning what?"

Gathering his thoughts in an effort to display innocence as he continues in his pretended role while taking a drink of his wine. "I assumed that your olde world clothing and speech, especially Captain Roberts', is just a put on for the tourists."

Luckily for Keith, this is not the Golden Age of Piracy, for if it was, Captain Roberts would've killed him on the spot for such an insult; even so, as my Captain nears his boiling point, it's obvious Keith is about to be dealt a fierce blow; therefore, I once again intervene.

Putting my hand gently atop his forearm, "Fy Nghapten, please grant me leave to handle this, for being of a different epoch than thyself, he knows not the gravity of what he speaks."

Doing his utmost, the Captain gives me an approving nod.

"I see you still have the ability to soothe the savage beast, V'lé."

Turning to Keith, warning him sternly, "If you knew the possible consequences of your remarks, Keith, you wouldn't speak so. As it is, I advise you to put a lid on it."

"Captain Roberts dresses this way because he wants to, Keith, and for no other reason, which is his privilege, same as you; he's just not much for idle chitchat," states Sue.

Adding to my moms statement, "As for his speech and manner, he is a cultured gentleman, well-bred and educated who speaks English for our benefit, for Welsh be his native tongue. If you're having trouble understanding him, the blame falls upon you, not he.

"Is that all?" asks, Keith.

With a laugh, "No," begins, Katie, "He's also fluent in Latin, and he speaks French."

Making yet another attempt, "I see those olde world tendencies I spoke of in you, V'lé," and taking a bite of his roast, "With a little effort on your part, you'll sound just like him."

Smiling, "Really, Oooo. I'm most pleased to hear that. Nevertheless, altho' I shan't make a conscience effort to increase the alterations regarding my linguistic articulation, neither shall I thwart them, or apologize to those who lack understanding, for I should think that any reasonably intelligent English speaking person would readily understand my words. When it comes to others, I shall exercise a little tolerance."

"Well spoken, fy melys."

Sporting a toothy grim as I turn to look at him, "Diolch 'chi, fy Nghapten."

While Katie pours him another cup of tea; Captain Roberts thanking her with a slight nod, Keith continues to rattle on with less than friendly chatter.

"As always, V'lé, your flare for the dramatic has not diminished."

As I take a bite of my roast. "Did you expect me to change?"

"But you have."

"Really? In what way?"

"You've allowed yourself to become subordinate."

"Wherein by your definition that all women should be slavishly obedient, that I shall never be. As for Captain Roberts, he does not try to own me, nor does he consider himself better."

"Very profound, V'lé," states Keith, almost complimentary, "but regardless of what you say, you have allowed your independent self to become dominated?"

"What I have done is merely given myself, without reservations or conditions, to the man I love and trust, and such, although he does not often make demands, I shall, more often than not, bow to his vast experience and wisdom, as I hope he will, should said be reversed."

> *Although she was not speaking to him, nor giving prior thought to her words, Captain Roberts, knowing the words flowed from her heart, listened intently to what his intended was saying with great interest, & in the doing, he discovered, not only why she so often thought of him, but also why she proclaimed herself his champion years before they had met. Her words also explained why she so readily invited him into her home, & later, into her bed. Full of pride he was, for her statement not only put any remaining doubts he might've had to eternal rest, he knew his search for her was not in vane.*

"Just out of curiosity," asks, Katie, "when did all this deference begin?"

"I've been hopelessly enthralled from the day I first knew of him."

"Doesn't it embarrass you to discuss your feelings openly knowing that Captain Roberts is right here?" asks, Katie.

"Why should it, but then I can not speak for him."

Answering the question, the Captain says, "Let us just say I am an interested spectator."

Smiling, "That being the case, I'll continue. In regard to when my deference for him began, I suppose one could say I've always compared all men to Captain Roberts, or more specifically, his moral fiber; the type of man he is, his personality if you will. But that's not the problem here, Keith, and you know it. You're just upset because, as was every other man of romantic interest in my life, because I did not place you, or them, on a pedestal as I do Captain Roberts. You see Keith, not only does he possess an ample supply of both knowledge and common sense, it's not his nature to behave recklessly, and on those occasions when he has or will require obeisance, I know his reasoning will stem from either his vast experience or incredible acumen, whereby, unless I am absolutely certain he's in error, I shall bow to his wisdom."

"Back up a bit, and explain," barks Keith harshly.

Stabbing a potato and putting it on my plate, "Specify."

With the look of a hungry animal having just trapped his prey, Keith spouts, "That bit about knowing of him, it implies a relationship prior to actually meeting him."

Amid his persistent badgering, I hack up my potato with a vengeance.

Enjoying the fencing, my mom utters, "This is better than daytime television."

Looking at my mom as I continue to pulverize my potato, then at Keith, "To begin with, I didn't imply anything, I said it straight out. As for knowing about Captain Roberts, it was decades ago that I first read about his seafaring adventures."

Altho' his jealousy is obvious, Keith tries to speak calmly in order to have his questions answered. "When exactly?"

"What difference does it make, Keith?" asks Katie.

"I am understandably curious."

Knowing Keith's true reasons, a childish act manifests itself in my mind as I reply, "Right!" And not being able to resist the temptation, I scoop up a spoon full of potato, and whilst glaring at him, using my spoon as a catapult, I feel thoroughly satisfied as my mashed potatoes hits its mark.

While both Sue and Katie bust up laughing, the Captain, stunned by my actions, stands.

Grumbling as he wipes the potato off his face, Keith asks, "Why did you do that?"

Trying not to laugh, "It slipped, and now that we're in better humor, but only because I believe Captain Roberts would also be interested in my answer, I see no reason in not answering your question." After a moment to consider, "Well, I could go as far back as a book report I wrote during my formative years, and reading it again, that was on March 1, 1996, when, with Captain Roberts as the centerpiece, I built a pirate website.

"Such a precise date?" asks Katie.

"That's the day I got on the internet for the first time, and during the course of turning my book report in to a website, I embarked on an exhaustive research campaign which, as it led me in a dozen directions, I learned a great deal about Captain Roberts, and during the course thereof, my love for him was rekindled."

"When we were still a couple!" spouts Keith.

"Wow, what a novelty that must 'ave been," states Katie sarcastically. "Who would ever suspect such illicit happenings could occur in real life."

"Living under the same roof does not make two people a couple, Keith, in any case, most of my research took place after I had left the United States."

"The point is, V'lé, is that you were dreaming about this guy when we were living together."

Speaking as I sprinkle salt and pepper onto what remains of my potato, "You had no claim on me."

Pouring himself another glass of wine, Keith spouts, "You admit it!"

"Admit what?"

"That you fell in love with a sea captain while living with me."

"No, Keith. I fell in love with a man who just happened to be a sea captain, and that occurred years before I ever met you."

"Same thing," spouts Keith.

Speaking now in an obvious angry tone as I throw my napkin down on the table. "Hardly. The Captain's profession has nothing to do with my feelings for him. As for you and I, we had no relationship."

Still combative, despite my reasoning, Keith jeers, "How can you fall in love with someone you never met?"

Shaking my head in disbelief, "You really are narrow minded, Keith. Love and Lust are not the same thing. As for lust, it is not sufficient to maintain a lifelong relationship, where Love, and I mean real love, has nothing to do with the person's looks, what they do for a living, or their bank balance, but who they are, not what they are; it's the personality belonging to that person, that's what they're in love with. All the rest is fleeting or precarious in nature and therefore immaterial, and even though it's generally a physical attraction that draws people together, that was not the reason in this instance."

"You'll never know that for sure."

"But I do, Keith. You see, until recently there were only a couple of woodcuts and drawings of Captain Roberts in books and online; the one at Whydah where his hair was loosely tied back with a ribbon is my favorite; however, I must admit that when I first saw the oil portrait of him, in Cardiff, I believe, I was pleased, but in reality, his looks have nothing to do with the love I feel for him."

"Yet because of him, you moved from America to Wales." Taking a swig of his wine, "But why Little Haven and not the town where he lived?"

"First of all, I did not move to Wales from the U.S., but from Ireland. You are partially right tho'; Captain Roberts was only one of the reasons my mom and I moved to Wales, but it was not the only reason. Secondly, this is the closest I could get to Little Newcastle and still own a Gothic B & B. Thirdly, I wanted to live on the coast, but mostly, Little Haven just happens to be where I felt, and consequently feel at home, an attribute I credit with having lived here, for a spell, in my previous life."

Curious, Captain Roberts states questioningly, "I wasn't aware thou lived here before; in a previous life you say."

"Yes, Captain, for about 18 months. Arriving during early Spring of 1701, and nearing my 16th birthday, I moved to Little Haven with my Godfather, Captain Rees, who resided in the big house on the far side of the square; the one with all the ivy."

"Do you remember the name you had then?"

"Yes and No. I do not personally remember it, but with the help of a Quija® board, and both a psychic and an astrologer, whom I trust, I did find the person I was then within my family tree, her name was Aspasia, but she went by her middle name, Rebekah. Her last name, though false, was recorded as Rees, before her mother died, but in reality, Captain Rees was her Godfather. Her biological father was Philippe, duc de Charters (a nephew of Louis XIV) who himself is better known as Philippe II, Régent of France. These knife rests, a family heirloom, once belonged to Marie Antoinette, of whom I hold in high esteem."

Taken aback, "Thou art sure of this?"

Noting my Captain's strange look, I pause a moment before continuing, "Yes, fy Nghapten, quite sure, but aside from knowing this village, S. Wales' past industry, and my way around Pembrokeshire, I remember nothing about my life then, it was my research regarding your life that led me here; however when my mom and were en route to Ireland, and I first stepped off the Hakin train the night before catching the ferry to Ireland in the morning, I knew this was where I belonged, and thus, I did not want to leave, but we were committed to Ireland. We didn't move to Pembrokeshire until 2 years later. Ne'er in my wildest dreams did I ever expect to actually meet you in person, at least not in this lifetime."

"Yes," injects Keith, "I suppose meeting under such circumstances would be difficult."

"Stranger things have happened," injects Katie.

Realizing he misspoke, Keith tries to sound innocent. "Tell me Captain, wouldn't it have bothered you to know the woman you thought was yours loved another man?"

"A great number of people often long for something they are never likely to have, Mister McClure: wealth, power, as well as people. In regard to the latter, jealousy in such circumstances would be fruitless; better to do ones best to improve their owne relationship, or simply move on."

"An interesting outlook," remarks Keith. "How did you happen to meet V'lé?"

Sounding like an upfront question, the Captain replies as truthfully as he can. "Being informed that she wished to meet with me, I paid her a call, and soon after, miss V'lé offer'd me permanent lodgings, but 'twas not the first time wee had met."

"We've meet before? When?"

"We will discuss it later, in private."

"As you wish, fy Nghapten."

"Returning to what we were discussing," Keith asks, "why not an apartment or other place where single men commonly stay as opposed to a lodging operated by an attractive, and dare I say, available woman?"

Captain Roberts, stating somewhat angrily, "I care not for yer implication."

"I'm only thinking of V'lé."

"Oh rot! The fact that Captain Roberts and I are—"

"Avast! Thou shan't finish such a sentence."

'Tis obvious to Captain Roberts that I am quite upset by Keith's unremitting persistence, but even if I were not, ne'er would he permit a conversation to continue that subjects his woman to undignified questions.

"My god man," begins Captain Roberts. "By delving in to areas of a highly personal nature, your impudence goes beyond the realm of decency, but in either case, a gentleman does not discuss personal relations concerning the fair sex."

Not giving any credence to the Captain's warning regarding his offensive behavior, believing himself to be invincible, Keith persists. "Lots of people who are not married, sleep together, Captain."

That was the Final Insult! As his eyes narrow, the Captain, in one smooth motion whilst rising from his seat, swiftly and decisively picks up the carving knife, and with precision, embeds its point into the table just inches before Keith.

"Well done!" proclaims my mom, cheeringly.

Mocking Keith, the Captain states, "Your knife lacks balance, Katie."

"I need a drink," states Katie as she gets up from the table.

His anger now subdued, Captain Roberts asks, "May I pour you a glass of wine?"

"No, thank you, Captain," and heading for the bar in the reception room, "I believe I'll have a shot of Green Spot."

It's difficult, but as I cover my mouth with my napkin, I do my best to contain the snickering brought on by the sheer pleasure of seeing my Captain's gallantry first hand, not only in the protection of my honor, but his own, and being fully aware that my Captain could easily clean Keith's clock, and secretly wishing he would, a mite of snickering sneaks out whilst stating, "Boy did you get off cheap."

"It's been a very long and tiring day," states Sue, and rising from the table, "I suggest we all go our separate ways for the remainder of the evening."

On my Captain's arm, seeing Katie at the bar as we enter the foyer, I bid her good night.

"Good night, you two," and tossing the drink back, Katie returning to her duties, and laughing as she passed us, "That was great, Captain. I'll turn in after I do the washing up."

Both my Captain and I state, "Goodnight, Katie."

Speaking to Keith as the Captain and I head for the stairs, "Katie informed me earlier that she already showed you to your room."

"Don't you want me to sign the guest register, V'lé?"

"Why?" asks the Captain, "One 'X' looks much like another."

"Tell me, Captain, what is it about me that you dislike so intensely?"

" 'Tis your supercilious nature, inquisitive posture, and prevalent impudence that riles me, Mister McClure."

"My what?" asks Keith.

"He said you're a rude, arrogant snoop," states Katie from the Dining Room.

"Me! As I see it, you're the one putting me down, Captain, and in a most conceited manner."

"For your information Keith," says I, Captain Roberts doesn't have an arrogant bone in his body."

Making yet another obnoxious statement, Keith snidely remarks, "No, of course not, but for a guest he sure wields a lot of power."

"Captain Roberts is not a mere guest, but rather a member of this household, and such, not that it's any of your blasted business, he has an equal say in the running of this Inn."

"Pardon me for my choice of words, fy Nghapten, but I seem to be having a hard time controlling my temper when speaking to that…that impertinent loon."

"You've done admirably. In any event, fy melys, I am most certain that ne'er would thee wilfully do me dishonour."

"I hope I never do, but we all have our breaking points and extreme moments, and in the realm of ones choice of words, I am reminded of an incident that took place in Sierra Leone back in 1721 between thyself and one Governor Plunkett.[B8]"

Amid a chuckle, "As thou said, wee all have our breaking points, and should I ever witness thine, I shall endeavour to understand."

Despite my being angry at Keith, Captain Roberts can see that I am deep in thought, but what he does not know, is that my pondering is caused as a result of his actions, and not Keith's. Pausing at the bottom of the stairs, and turning to gaze at my brave Captain with thankful eyes, I raise the pedestal upon which I placed him, higher still.

As the Captain looks in to my eyes, Governor Plunkett aside, it is clear he's trying to surmise the other thoughts preoccupying my mind, but before he can, I turn back towards the stairs. Gently stopping me, he takes my hand. Knowing that he is as eager, as am I, to familiarize ourselves with the pleasures of intimacy now that he is mortal, I not only follow him as he takes several steps backwards into the parlour, I close the door as we enter.

"I doubt anyone will search for either of us in here." And drawing me into his embrace, my Captain, lightly brushing his lips against the velvety softness of my cheek, maneuvers me over to the antique fainting couch where he sits upon it. Lifting the skirt of my elegant gown, I to straddle the couch, and as I rest my bareness upon his thighs, he discovers that altho' not as prudent as he, I am better prepared for the current situation.

Her actions are thus that the question I was about to ask her is gone from my mind, and how could such be otherwise with my woman caressing my lips with hers.

Shoving my coat down off my shoulders 'fore gently pushing me backwards onto the pillows, the look of impending rapture upon her face changes to fright when the great house suddenly explodes with dreadful noise.

Failing to shut off certain appliances in the kitchen that were running at the time of the power outage earlier, sends my mom rushing into the foyer, and Katie charging down the stairs, hollering, "Oh my lord, the garbage disposal!"

Captain Roberts, undeterred by the disturbance, quietly utters, "Leave it to Katie."

Amid a hint of a smile and a chuckle, I shake my head slightly as I ask, "Is there nothing that alarms thee, fy Nghapten?"

Speaking seductively, "Only the thought of thee leaving the room," and continuing to bring forth our mutual gratification by means of his less than gentle persuasion, I grip his powerful biceps tightly, relishing every moment when suddenly the parlour door flings open.

To my embarrassment, Keith, Katie and my mom, taking note of our romantic escapade from the doorway, display toothy grins as they hypocritically crave forgiveness.

Whispering, "Caught in the act," and burying my face within his lusciously thick mane, I let out a sigh of discomfiture.

"Aye, fy melys," chuckling a bit as he strokes my hair, "that wee be," and altho' careful to keep me tightly against him, his fruitful emissions are released as he sits up.

Purposely attracting attention to myself while the three of them stare at us from within the doorway, I take a deep breath, and with a look containing daggers as I exhale loudly, I harshly state, "Would you PLEASE excuse us!"

Both my mom and Katie, ne'er uttering a word, depart.

Continuing to hold me firmly, feeling fortunate at this moment that his back is to the door, my Captain, whilst fighting to regain control over his body, manages wondrously to conceal his emotions.

Keith, on the other hand, still lurking in the doorway, smirking, sarcastically spouts, "You might try locking the door next time."

Captain Roberts' face, darkening with contempt, commandingly says, "Up woman."

Complying forthwith, I lift my right leg out of the way, and swinging his leg over the couch, he begins buttoning his trousers, amid which, whilst giving Keith a belittling sneer. "Yes, do button up, Captain, we wouldn't want our guest to get an inferiority complex."

"If you can refrain from patronizing me, V'lé, I'd like to speak with you privately, if'in your sailor will leave us alone for a moment."

My gallant, struggling for control as he takes a deep breath, manages a neutral tone. "My intended, worn to a frazzle, needes a bit of restful time to herself."

Keith, speaking sarcastically, "Yes, I can see how much she's in need of rest."

"You will honour those who reside within these walls or my gracious offer to allow you to remain whilst your motor car is stuck in the mud shall be withdrawn."

Keith, almost sneering, "I see your Lord and Master has spoken, V'lé."

Affixing Keith with a cold, beady eye, Captain Roberts irately states, "Methinks a healthy flogging would benefit you immensely!"

"Would you two stop this fencing already," I spout coldly. "You're driving me crazy! If you don't like one another, why converse at all?" Heading towards the door, "And now, if you will excuse me, Keith, as my Lord and Master has already informed you, I've had enough excitement for one day." Stopping for a moment to address my Captain, "May I expect thee within the quarter hour?"

"Unquestionably."

Curtseying to my Captain, followed by his nod, I turn, and exiting the room, I make my way upstairs.

"We will visit more in the morning, V'lé," announces Keith as I head down the hall and out of sight.

"If you again cause my intended distress, you shall find yourself in a place you wont like so well," and turning, the Captain heads upstairs.

Opening the bedroom door and finding the room empty, he looks in the bath, but I am not to be found. Thus, even though I rarely encroach upon his private room unless specifically invited, Captain Roberts goes aloft. Upon entering, finding me staring moodily at the wildly racing clouds blowing across the storm filled sky, he takes care to close the door noiselessly as he compassionately asks, "Art thou well, fy melys?"

Sighing heavily as I snivel, "I'm fine, fy Nghapten. I didn't mean to intrude, but I needed a moment in a place where I feel absolutely safe," and when he opens his arms, I demonstrate to him my unwavering trust by running in to them.

Tightening them about me, his jacket smells of the salt air, and his muscular arms are most reassuring, but as I turn to look up at him, my eyes are shining with tears, and not wanting him to see me this way, I turn away and try to muffle my weeping.

Ever compassionate, my lover gently pulls me close against him, and kissing the top of my head, he holds me securely. I don't even know why I am crying. The only thing I am sure of is that it means everything to me to finally feel the physical touch of my ageless lover.

Guiding me down the steps, "Thou art exhausted."

Murmuring apologetically as my tears ease a bit, "I must look a fright."

"Not so, fy Nghariad. Thou art lovely, as always."

But even though he smiles a mite, I can see the pain of uncertainty within his sable eyes as he gazes at me.

Cutting the lacings of my restrictive waist cincher when reaching the bed and helping me to lie down, he covers me with the soft quilt, "Shhh, fy annwyl, thee must rest now. If thou should neede me, I will be right in the next room taking a most welcomed shower."

Stammering whilst asking the depressive question that's been hanging between us for several hours, "Will we be able to touch come morn?"

Looking away for a moment and then back again, the Captain's troubled eyes speak in volumes of confusion. "Even tho', 'twas what I had been promised if all went as prescribed, I canne state onely that 'tis a great gift to be able to do so now."

My tears being replaced by curiosity, "You knew of your potential rebirth?"

"Aye, but I knew not when, how, or why, as 'twas not a certainty." Removing his coat, "Now lay thine head down and rest whilst I shower."

"And afterwards, wilt thou come back here to me?"

"Is it not also my bed in which thee sleeps?"

"You know it is."

"Then I shall return presently."

Still worried, I hold him tight as he tries to stand. Assuring me tenderly, "Thou needes not be affrightened," but knowing how upset I am, he gently picks me up and carrying me across the room to the big crunchy chair by the fireplace, he seats himself. Cradled in his arms; my head against his bare chest in contentment, I drift off to sleep.

After a quarter hour, satisfied she is sleeping soundly, I stand, and returning her to the bed, and gently laying her down, I cover her as I bid her goodnight.

> *Looking forward to a hot shower, the Captain proceeded to the bath, but still concerned, he opened the door noiselessly to gaze upon his woman for a moment. Later, after showering, when Captain Roberts returned to lie next to his woman, she awoke.*

Speaking quietly, she asks, "Would thou be opposed to us getting away from *Inn Finistère*, just for a night and a day?"

With concern for my need for a peaceful sleep and our other desires as well, "Ah, methinks I understand, thee desires complete privacy?"

Replying affectionately, "Yes." And with an understanding smile, "Hurry along then and pack for us a bag, and inform Katie of our plans whilst I dress; after which, wee shall meet in the mudroom."

Taking both a skirted bustier, and the overnight case out of the wardrobe, I toss a couple items inside. Having laced my frock, I quietly make my way to Katie's room. Knocking quietly, I whisper, "Katie." Hearing no reply, I crack her door and call out a little louder.

"Hmm?" Stirring a mite before sitting upright, Katie asks, "What is it? Has something happened?"

Hurrying to her bedside to quietly explain, "The Captain and I are going elsewhere for the night."

Sympathizing with my dilemma, "You and the Captain want to be alone, is that it?"
"Yes."

"Never you fear, Miss. I'd do the same if I had your chance, and don't worry 'bout a thing. I'll take care of everything until you return."

"Thanks, Katie. You're a true friend." Leaving her room, I close the door noiselessly.

Slipping back into the master bedroom, I grab the overnight case.

Meeting my Captain in the mudroom, he asks, "Art thou sure thee wants to do this?"

"Yes, fy Nghapten. Quite sure. I don't know what it is, but I feel that Keith is, well, I can't explain it."

Replying with a harsh attitude, "I wish that blast'd bilge rat had never come."

My eyes, sad for a moment, shadowed with bad memories, "Well he did; ergo we need a place of refuge where we can think things out without his constant presence."

Altho' quietly, Captain Roberts spouts, "Altho' ne'er before have I fled from mine enemies, thou art right; wee neede to not onely ascertain why McClure is here, but why at this particular moment in time, and as wee have not beene free of his bombardment for a moment since his arrival, and being 'tis unlikely wee will find the answers here, wee must search elsewhere."

"Perhaps Mister Cullen, or the Vicar canne help."

Unbeknownst to the Captain and myself, two figures from within the reception room, hidden by the natural cover of darkness, watch us furtively as we make our way down the path to the car. Struggling to maintain his composer, "You're right," says Keith to his confederate amid an angry voice driven by obvious jealousy.

Settling into the driver's seat, I am beset with a chill, and seeing me shiver, knowing I keep a couple of crocheted throws on the backseat, Captain Roberts, taking hold of one of them, drapes it across our laps.

"Thank you, fy Nghapten." Starting the engine, I cautiously maneuver my 1938 Jaguar SS around Keith's rental as the clinging mud oozes beneath the tires. Leaving the thick gunk behind us, I head for Broad Haven, but less than half way there, my car, hydroplaning, slides off the road and in to a mud hole.

Clenching my fists tightly around the leather that encases the steering wheel as my head droops a mite, I utter, "Story of my life."

My Captain, jumping out of the car, bellowing forth thunderously, "If neede be, I shall push this infernal contraption the remainder of the way!" Storming around to the back of the car he puts his shoulder against the left rear quarter panel, saying, "Go when I give the word."

Turning my head and looking towards him, "I don't think that's such a good idea, fy Nghapten."

In ill temper, "Humour me."

Doubtful of the outcome, I take a deep breath, and letting it out with a sigh, "If thou insists."

Captain Roberts, leaning hard against the car, hollers, "Now!"

Reluctantly putting my foot gently against the gas pedal, the rear tires spin, and as I feared, the Captain gets coated with mud. Half laughing whilst hollering, "I was afraid that would happen."

Scrambling to get out of the car, whilst trying to get control of my laughter without much success, I begin to slip, and even though my gallant manages to catch me, the weight of my body in motion causes him to fall over backwards with me landing beside him in the mud.

"Damn!" says he, cursing loudly.

Together with the sound of crashing thunder, large droplets of rain begin spattering us. Grumbling, "I am sorry I have not the power to transport us there, nor to get this blast'd motor car out of the mud."

Laughing louder than I have in years, "I'm not. I'm delighted thou has not the power."

The Captain, after giving it a moments thought, begins to laugh also. "Thou art right as rain, for I too am delighted." Rising to his feet, helping me up also, he asks, "Any suggestions?"

"Well, seeing that we'd be hard pressed to get much muddier, we could wait in the car until the storm passes, and then try again."

"Good idea." Quickly spreading the throw atop the leather seats to protect it from our muddy clothes, he covers us with the other one once we're settled in.

Raining fairly hard for about 10 minutes, the storm subsides. Captain Roberts, using his ingenuity, gets out of the car, and trudging thro' the muck, he locates a suitable limb from a felled tree and a good size stump, and employing them together they serve as lever and fulcrum, he moves the car out of the mud hole, and once the cars in motion, he jumps in.

Blowing him a kiss, "Thou art a genius."

Again on the road, and seeing a vacancy sign reading, 'Rooms Available,' I pull into their drive, and park.

Touching my cheek lovingly, "This should be a beautiful, moonlit night, perfect for cavorting in and around *Inn Finistère*, and instead 'tis wet and we are away from home."

Shivering again, the Captain, blocking me from the harsh wind as he rings the door chime, holds me close, and whilst patiently waiting for someone to answer, his index finger trails along my arm in a seductive manner.

After a couple of minutes, "If they're sleeping, they may not 'ave heard the bell."

As his lips trail over my cheek to my ear, "Ring again, fy melys?" Continuing his nibbling, "At least the rain hath washed the mud off thy face."

When the door opens, Captain Roberts moves to a respectable distance.

" 'Tis a blistery night to be out," says the woman as she backs up, opening the door so we may enter. "Come in out of the weather."

Removing our mud caked shoes and setting them in the box containing others just inside the door, we enter. "Sorry to disturb you at this late hour, madam," explains the Captain, "but our motor car got stuck in the mud."

"Looks like you did also," quips the innkeeper.

"Aye, madam. That wee did." Chuckling amid a charming smile, "But there's no harm done that won't rinse off."

The innkeeper, returning his smile, "I have a lovely double, en suite, on the first floor."[1]

"Thank you."

As we walk to the reception desk, "You look familiar, miss. Don't I know you?"

"I am Châtelaine of *Inn Finistère*. With the road there being impassable, my fiancé, John Roberts and I, were hoping we could stay here tonight."

All of a sudden, everyone in the place is staring at us, and as she curtsies, "Your presence, sir, honours my humble establishment."

Looking about at their staring faces, I feel that something's amiss, and although I am at a loss to understand the reason for their universal reaction, Captain Roberts' returns her greeting with a slight nod of his head, as he replies, "Our thanks be to you, mistress, for having us."

Graciously taking me gently by the arm, the Captain, escorting me to our room, unlocks the door and holds it open for me.

---

[1] In the U.K. the First floor is what the U.S. calls the Second floor.

Chapter Seven

Alone, At Last

Entering the room, the Captain, locking the door behind us, sets the overnight case on the table. Setting my purse alongside, "Did you get the odd feeling that the people in the lobby know exactly who you are?"

Shaking his head a mite, "I care not, fy annwyl. 'Tis onely bathing that concerns me, at this moment."

Being of the same mind, and his attire being more complex, I offer my assistance. "Let me help you out of those wet clothes." Unbuttoning the sleeves of his damask jacket, and vest, I exclaim, "You're soaked to the skin!" Dashing in to the bathroom, I turn on the taps. Rushing back, I kneel on the floor, and after undoing the buttons and ribbons about his knees, and he steps out of his breeches, I strip off his over the knee socks. "Go get warm under the running water; I'll be along in a moment."

Not questioning my commanding statement, the Captain walks in the bathroom and stepping in to the shower, he enjoys the warm water as it lashes over his body.

Seeing a plastic bag on the dresser, and as eager as he to wash, I remove my clothes quickly, and placing them in the plastic bag along with his, I drop it on the floor as I enter the bathroom.

Pulling back the curtain, my imposing Captain encircles my waist, and as he lifts me in to the freestanding tub with his strong hands, mine rest atop his muscular shoulders.

Each helping the other remove the mud, our minds, at least for awhile, are free from that lout, Keith. As time passes, both of us dry and in bed, our thoughts are only about our lives together, and as my Captain envelopes me within his arms, the two of us sleep peacefully throughout the night.

When the early morning light begins to stream through the curtains and I begin to stir, pleased to find myself safe and secure within my Captain's arms, my pillow, the warmth of his bare chest, it being the most wonderful feeling in the world, I want only to wallow in it, but to my dismay, it is time to get up; however, as I attempt to move away from him, my Captain sleepily whispers, "Art thou well, fy Nghariad?"

My eyes widening as he speaks, "Very well, fy Nghapten."

Continuing to hold me securely, "Then continue thy kip, for thou needes thy rest."

"But what about Keith and home?"

"Katie will do nicely for *Inn Finistère*, fy annwyl. As for Keith, he canne go hang."

Noting my Captain's voice change from one mood to another as he uttered Keith's name in vain, "And what would you do if he were to show up here?"

Gesturing his head towards the window, "I would hesitate not to heave him thitherward. Now return to sleep, for I wish to hold thee for some time longer."

Burying my cheek in the warmth of his chest, I do as he bids, and as I allow myself to fall back asleep, my dreams are very lovely.

LATER⇁

A couple hours have passed by the time my generous lover begins to awaken me, and as he delivers kisses about my body, I incur the sweetest of my recurring dreams that begin in

1718 where I had purposely set out to be abducted by the Great Pirate Roberts, and every time the dream returns, I travel further along the path as I journey in to a wondrous life filled with exciting adventure and romance on the high seas.

Slowly as I wake up, and as not to take unfair advantage of me whilst I slept, my Captain slowly moves upward along my torso until at last, when I open my eyes, he softly speaks. "Bore da, fy Nghariad," but unbeknownst to him, I have been very aware of his movements, and thus, being in need of him, hoping my tone is beguiling, I beckon his attentions by speaking in a breathy voice. "Ewch â fi, for I want to feel the awing power of y môr-leidr mawr, Bartholomew Roberts.'"

The words no sooner leave my lips when an almost wicked expression befalls him as he grasps my wrists, and to my delight, his lovemaking is as aggressively robust as was the pirate captain in battle.

Late Morning ¬

Hungry, as I always am in the morning when away from home, I walk in to the bathroom, and wrapping myself in one of the guest robes hanging on the door, I ring the reception desk and order breakfast. About thirty minutes later, just as I finish my make-up and hair, a knock comes on the door. "Just a minute," and tossing my Captain the remaining robe, altho' physically drained, he robes himself as he heads for the balcony.

Passing before the mirror as he crosses the room, Captain Roberts discovers that for the first time in nigh on 300 years, personal grooming will again be part of his daily routine. Stopping for a closer look, stroking his face with his hand, he says, "I neede barbering."

Opening the balcony doors, enjoying the morning air as he takes a deep breath, he pauses momentarily before seating himself before the small table.

Answering the door and seeing a young man of no more than 16 carrying our morning meal, I says, "Be a love and set the tray outside on the balcony."

"Yes, madam." Heading outside, the young man sets the tray on the folding stand he brought with him and lays the table.

Purposely lagging behind, I take a small handful of £2 coins from my purse before walking out onto the balcony.

Addressing the young man, Captain Roberts asks, "Would there be a barber in the house?"

Wearing an almost gaping expression, "I'm afraid not, sir."

Taking my seat while the young man holds my chair, he asks, "Is there anything more I can get for you?"

Handing him the coins, "This will be fine, thank you."

"Thank you!" But just as the young man turns to leave, finding himself unable to repress the urge, "Are you really Captain Roberts, the famous pirate from Little Newcastle?"

"Aye, laddie. That I am."

Upon hearing the Captain's reply, the young man quietly utters, "Wow!" and after backing up a few steps, he darts out.

Gobsmacked, "Art thou aware thee just confirmed for that boy, thy true identity?"

Replying questionably, "What of it?"

"By the end of the day everyone will know."

"But, that being who I am, whyfor art thou disturb?"

"I'm not sure. Last night I introduced thee as John Roberts, but that boy asked specifically if thou art Captain Roberts."

"Aye, that he did."

Returning inside, I pick up the phone.

Taking another bite, "Come eat, fy melys, for thy meal grows cold."

Turning to address him as I dial, "I'll be there presently, but first I need to ring Katie to tell her to bring us some clean clothes."

When the phone rings at home, my mom answers, "*Inn Finistère.*"

"Mom, please put Katie on, and don't let on that it's me calling."

"She's fixing breakfast, hang on a minute while I get her." Putting the phone down, my mom walks in to the kitchen announcing, "The telephone's for you, Katie."

"Thank you, Mrs Montgomery," and setting the spatula down on the spoon rest, Katie walks in to the foyer to take the call. "Hello?"

Speaking in a serious tone, "Katie, I do not want Keith to know it's me, so please, just pretend it's one of your friends in town."

"All right."

"Our clothes, having been saturated by mud, we need you to bring us clean ones. We're stopping at the same place you did when you first came over from Ireland."

Being both cautious and sure of my meaning, "In Broad Haven?"

"Yes."

"I'm in the middle of fixing breakfast, so it will be a good half an hour before I can leave."

"That's fine, Katie." Impatient to have my breakfast, but needing to know, "Has Keith asked for me this morning?"

Replying with noticeable resentment as she recalls his rudeness, "Yes, several times."

"Well, Katie, if he asks again just tell him I went to town early this morning."

"I have," Katie informs me, "and should the need arise, I shall again."

"Thanks, Katie. I'll see you in a bit." Hanging up the phone, I return to the balcony. "Katie should be here in about an hour."

Meanwhile, at Inn Finistère →

While Sue is just placing the syrup onto the enormous platter containing an array of breakfast foods, Katie, who is returning to the kitchen to fetch it, says, "After I put this on the table and gather up the items going to the cleaners, I'll do the marketing." Picking up the platter, "Will you please be good enough to inform Mister McClure that breakfast is ready."

"Sure thing." Finding him in the reception room, Sue announces, " Your breakfast awaits you in the dining room."

Rising from the sofa as he sets the magazine back on the table, Keith replies, "Thank you, Sue."

Katie, who had eaten earlier, is washing up, and Sue, already having helped herself to a plate of Splatter Dabs, two of the sausage patties, and a half grapefruit, moseys back to her room, leaving Keith to eat alone.

MEANWHILE, BACK AT THE BED & BREAKFAST IN BROAD HAVEN →

"The point I was trying to make, fy Nghapten, is that it appears that a great deal of people seem to know of your rebirth."

Showing enthusiasm, "Such being the case, our task of finding the answers should be fairly simple."

As my Captain finishes the last of an enormous breakfast, I return to the balcony carrying my razor. "I can give you a shave this morning, and on the way home we'll get you a shaving kit. In the meantime, sit back and relax."

Although a little apprehensive, Captain Roberts takes a deep breath and tries to relax.

"The beauty of being shaved by one's woman, fy Nghapten, is it be she who hath the last word on how he wears his facial hair, not that I would make any changes in thy case."

Captain Roberts, returning my compliment, flashes me a slight smile, which in most cases, tends to be the extent of his outward display of emotion, yet however limited, his eyes and body language speak quite clearly to me.

Carrying the items needed on a tray to the table, I begin, and as I pick up my razor, seeing his nervousness, a condition rarely known to him, "Don't fret so, fy Nghapten, thou art not the first man I've shaved." After several passes, my Captain, leaning his head back against the cushion, settles in.

AT INN FINISTÈRE →

Katie is not having an easy time of it.

Backing out of my bedroom carrying a poke containing our change of clothes, Katie is just closing the door when Keith accosts her in the upper hallway. Turning around quickly, she glares at him. "You oughtn't be up here, Mister McClure?"

"I was just about to knock on V'lé's door."

Regaining her composer, "I told you earlier, Miss V'lé and Captain Roberts went to town early this morning."

Seeing how Keith already knows we left late last night, but being unable to trick Katie in to revealing where, he asks, "When will they return?"

"I don't know." Squeezing past him, "But rarely are they away from home for more than a few hours."

Hurrying after her, "Whatcha got in the bag?"

Thinking fast, "The laundry. I pick it up every morning."

Hurrying down the stairs, "Aside from my daily routine, I have a host of errands to take care of, so if you will allow me."

Stepping out of her path, "Certainly, Katie."

Dashing in to the laundry/mud room, knowing Keith will continue to try and pry information out of her, Katie grabs the canvas shopping stroller and assorted bags off the shelf. Having transferred our clothes into the stroller, she dumps the cloth shopping bags on top, fills and starts the washing machine, and heads for her car via the mudroom door, but to her dismay, there, lying in wait, is that boorish Keith.

"Hello again, Katie. Do you always take such a load with you to the store?"

"Yes," slamming the boot shut, "Not only does Miss V'lé not wish to pay a tariff tax per bag, she insists we make an effort to be green."

In a pretence to appear satisfied with her answer, Keith moseys back towards the house.

> *Soon thereafter, whilst speeding towards town, Katie discovers that Keith was following her.*

Back at the Bed & Breakfast in Broad Haven →

Cleaning up after shaving my Captain, the telephone rings, and putting the damp cloth on the tray, worried as to who may be calling, my voice carries within it, a slight quiver. "Hello."

"I don't know what to do, Miss."

"About what; can't you manage to slip away?"

"I'm en route to you now, but it's Mister McClure." Looking back over her shoulder, "I told him I had errands to do, but he's following me."

Speaking in a furious tone, I cry out, "Damn!"

Shocked by my words, "What is it that makes thou speak so foul this time, fy annwyl?"

Katie is trying to bring us our clothes, but Keith is following her."

Boiling with rage, the Captain snatches the phone from me. "I have endur'd enough from that bilge rat. Should he durst present himself here, I shan't hesitate to carve him up for fish bait!"

Taking the phone back from him, "Katie."

"Yes, Miss?"

"Make a couple of stops and pick up a few things like, postage stamps and cough syrup. Then go to Londis and do a little shopping. Whilst there, go to the manager's office and ask him, as a special favor to me, to stow our clothes until I'll can get someone from here to go collect them."

"Right O, Miss."

Hanging up the receiver, "I thought thou was for throwing him out yon window."

"Aye, and so I shall!"

It is clear to see my Captain's fit to be tied. Leading him over to the bed, "Lay down on thy stomach, my gallant, and I'll massage thy back. Just let me call the front desk first to ask if there's anyone here who can go collect our clothes."

"Tell them also wee shall be staying one more night," states Captain Roberts.

Smiling, "I would like nothing more, fy Nghapten, but I'm afraid Keith is not going to go away no matter how long we try to avoid him."

Lying down on his stomach, "McClure's presence is as welcome as an outbreak of scurvy."

Picking up the phone, I ring the front desk. "I realize this is a tremendous imposition, but I have a few items of clothing at Londis. Is there anyone who can collect them for us?"

"Yes, Miss," replies the proprietor. "I'll send my son."

"Thank you." Hanging up the phone, I climb onto the bed, and straddling my Captain's back, I begin rubbing his shoulders. "Thee really must relax, fy Arglwydd."

"I have been thinking about something McClure said that troubles me."

"What would that be, fy Nghapten?"

"Well... Altho' thou hast addressed me as both Bart and Bartholomew, much of the time, as McClure pointed out, thou tends addresses me rather formerly.

"By addressing thee, fy Nghapten, I thought I was being familiar."

"Aye, but why not by my name?"

"You heard me explain my reason last night."

Rolling part way over and propping himself up, "What thou said to Mister McClure was not the whole truth."

After considering his statement, "The first thing that comes to mind is the fact that I have always believed you had been in love once before and believing she was untrue is the main reason you returned to the sea, thereby protecting thyself against further heartache, but I also feel that you may have misunderstood something, I state the last because, in knowing of your incredible ability to read people, I find it difficult to imagine you falling in love with a woman who would do such a thing." Pausing in order to gather my thoughts, and hoping to have found the best words to describe my feelings, I look directly into his eyes. "Let me say that I am very proud to be the woman of the legendary Bartholomew Roberts, I honor thee as, fy Nghapten out of respect to thine accomplishments. However, that is not where it ends, but rather where it begins. What I feel for thee goes much deeper, but I doubt those feelings can be expressed verbally, except that addressing thee as, fy Arglwydd, has to do with how I feel about thee, personally. I feel safe and protected when thou art near thee, and altho' I admit thy piratical adventures leave me breathless, it's important thee understands that those aspects is not what attracts me, if otherwise, I would be in love with all great men and not with thee alone.

> *Having heard about V'lé & Rebekah, who are essentially the same person, the latter being she who had jilted him when he was but 18, Captain Roberts, feeling uneasy, has questions.*

"About what thee said living regarding living in Little Haven in 1701. Tell me more."

"Well, shortly after having an astrological chart made, I had a reading done by a friend who is a renowned psychic. 'Twas she who told me what my name was back then. The oddest part was that this same name appears in my family tree. When I returned to the astrologer to pick up the astrological chart, and have it explained, she told me that I was living in the wrong time and place, and that in order to become both happy and content, I needed to return home. Unfortunately she did not know were that was. Putting this together with what Greta, my physic told me, it's as if Rebekah and I are one, which also explains why, as an adult, I never felt at home in the United States. It is also why I moved. I thought Ireland was where I belonged. It was not until my arrival here, in Pembrokeshire, that I discovered my mistake.

"And if I told thee thine feelings has not deceived thee, and that there was a woman, and she did, in affect, end our relationship; and that Aspasia Rebekah Smith-Rees, daughter of Captain Rees of Little Haven, was my intended, and that you are she, reborn as was I, only with thee 'twas thro' reincarnation, how would you feel?

"I would say, 'twas destiny, us being together. In addition to that, I want you to know, my love for thee is such, whether it be now or then, and regardless of our stations in life, that I would follow thee in rags to the ends of the earth, if necessary, to be with thee. And just for the record, I do not believe she could have jilted thee anymore than I."

Suddenly, the door bursts open. Within the doorway stands Keith with glaring eyes, smirking at us, and chucking our sack of clothes onto the floor, he spouts, "Did you spend a pleasant evening?"

With a dramatic flare as Captain Roberts leaps from the bed, an action that inadvertently sends me rolling to the opposite side of the bed and off onto the floor in the process, hollers, "You contemptuous swine!" And in a fury, catching Keith off guard, my Captain, grabbing him by his belt and pulling him towards him whilst turning, proceeds to shove him backwards through the picture window and out onto the lawn below.

Drawing by Laura Smith & Sue Montgomery

    Moving swiftly to the window, looking at Keith laying upon the grass, not realizing he's unconscious, Captain Roberts delivers an ultimatum. "Be gone to whence you came, for should I see you at *Inn Finistère* again, by God's grace, I shall kill you."
    Ever heroic, my Captain, seeing me lying on the floor, rushes to my side. Gently helping

me to my feet, " 'Tis sorry I be, fy annwyl, for knocking thee off the bed. I hope thou art not injur'd."

Wrapping my robe about myself, "I am wounded in dignity only, my valiant Captain."

Within moments, the owners of the Bed & Breakfast are at our door. Looking around in disbelief, breathing hard from the excitement, the mistress of the lodgings, putting her hand on her chest as she gasps, walks to the broken window. " 'Tis the gentleman who called for you only minutes ago."

Her husband, looking fairly upset over the incident, "What the hell happened? Did he slip and fall?"

In a desperate attempt to keep from laughing, I reply, "No, not exactly."

Motioning to the broken window, Captain Roberts says, "Thro' our door burst yon madman. I showed him out thus."

Looking at the broken window and beyond, "So I see." Continuing, "When our son returned with your clothes from Londis, that man," pointing towards Keith, "arrived moments later saying that he was a friend and was expected, and having no cause to doubt his words, we saw no reason not to allow him to take up your clothes."

"As you could not have known he would be unwelcome, I offer ye both reimbursement, and my humble apologies for the hooligan's intrusion, for if not for our presence here, this incident would not have happened."

The innkeeper, impressed by the Captain's olde world manners, and feeling equally at fault, "Being we should have, at the very least, rang your room and enquired first, I insist that we share in the cost of the damages."

"I thank you, sir, for your generosity," replies Captain Roberts amid a slight nod.

Picking the bag of clothes up off the floor, and laying them out on the bed, I gather up my attire. Excusing myself, I head for the bathroom to dress. Coming back out several minutes later; the innkeepers having left, I find my beloved fully clothed and ready to depart.

Offering me his arm, "Shall we go?"

Whilst en route to the car, I suggest we drive to Aberdaugleddau and promenade along the wharf before beginning our search for answers.

Chapter Eight

Returning Home

Our stroll has been lovely. Just now, looking at all the boats rocking serenely upon the rippling motions of the moonlit water, we are seated at a charming little restaurant enjoying a leisurely meal alfresco.

Captain Roberts, having consumed a generously filled plate from the bountiful seafood menu while I indulged in more than my share of deep fried jumbo shrimp and Caesar salad, is ready to head home. Altho' we found no answers as yet, we have so thoroughly enjoyed our day, his first day, that we had not noticed until now that it is long since dark.

"It must be after 9 o'clock, says I."

"Aye, and what a grand daye it has bin, fy melys, both briskful and thought consuming; a new beginning."

For a moment I wasn't sure what he meant by, 'thought consuming.' We talked all through the day. It wasn't until thinking about his comment that I realized that much of his day was consumed by current events: His new lease on life; Keith, and his true purpose, and what, if anything, the two have in common.

Upon arriving home and seeing Keith's car, I become so upset that while stepping out of the car I, lose my footing, but even as I am falling into large puddle, I begin to laugh hysterically, and as par for the course, my Captain, in his efforts to help me, finds himself in the same puddle.

"Blast! 'Tis the fault of that interloper. Getting both of us back to our feet, my Captain, ranting still, "His end be at hand for inviting my wrath."

Knowing him to be quite serious, "Thou can not!"

Paying me no heed, Captain Roberts marches with purpose towards the house.

Following in his hurried strides, "There must be a reasonable excuse for him to still be here."

As we reach the door, "Wait, thy muddy boots."

Looking at me momentarily with a queer look, helps by pulling his feet out of his boots as I further my plea.

"Please, fy Arglwydd, wait." Rising to my feet. "I've heard it said that tired minds do not think well."

Vexed, the Captain, still grumbling as he begins to open the door, has me terribly worried, and such, speaking with earnest, I grab his arm gently, "Let's just get a good nights sleep. We can settle things in the morning."

Questioning my concerned attitude, Captain Roberts looks at my hand, and then at me strangely, but does not reply.

Sliding my hand down to his as he turns the doorknob, "Please, fy Arglwydd, I beg thee."

Realizing that killing Keith would no doubt lead to his incarceration, and 'tis this be what prompts my actions, his eyes, indicating that he understands my fears, brighten a mite whilst giving me verbal assurance. "I promise to cause the lout no permanent damage this daye."

Relieved, I am kicking off my shoes when the mudroom door suddenly opens, and to my dismay, Keith stands before us. "Why are you still here?" asks I.

Ignoring my question, Keith, whilst staring at the clinging wet material outlining my figure, states, "You look delectable, V'lé."

Tired of his lecherous remarks, I speak in utter contempt as I push past him. "Excuse me!"

In the doing, he rudely adds, "A little more voluptuous than I remember. Your current concubine must agree with you?"

Slowly I turn, and as a defiant stare of unmitigated indignation appears upon my face, I abruptly slap his face.

Chuckling as his hand smoothes the red mark on his cheek, "You still pack quite a wallop."

"I have had more than enough of your loathsome presence. Come morn, I want you out of my house. If your rental is still stuck, you can take a hack to the Hakin train."

Captain Roberts, glaring at Keith, places himself directly between us. His voice, triggered by my violent act, is low and dangerous. "'Tis onely by my promise to my intended that you are still among the living." Turning, "Come, fy nghariad," and taking me by the arm, we retire to our room.

Downstairs ¬

Although none of within my household are aware of it, two figures are conversing in Keith's room.

Speaking with uneasiness, Keith says, "I'm doing the best I can."

"Then I suggest thee takes more drastic action, for my patience is wearing thin," instructs the second man, who we again see lighting his cigar from a self-produced flame emerging from the tip of his thumb.

"The pirate does indeed have a quick temper, but V'lé has some kind of calming effect on him."

"Thou art a fool! Canst thou not see that she uses reason to appeal to his need to modernize himself in the workings of today's society." Taking a puff of his cigar, "Tonight, however, he did come very close to ripping thee to shreds."

Keith, putting on a confident look, boasts, "I'm not bothered by that, no harm can come to me."

Possessing a healthy measure of wickedness, the ghoulish creature warns, "If'in I were in thy shoes, Keith, I wouldn't get cocky." Adding, after taking an unhurried puff on his cigar, "Thou art not altogether impervious to pain, injury and death, Keith."

Having had cause to believe otherwise, and now unsure, Keith begins to speak, but before having the chance to find out exactly what the repugnant figure meant, he vanishes, leaving only cigar smoke and ash where he had stood only moments before.

Upstairs ¬

Feeling clean once more, Captain Roberts pulls back the covers, and as my lover takes his rightful place, an act that brings me extreme happiness, he lays down beside me.

Snuggling my naked flesh against his as he bids me good night, "Wee shall settle things come morn. Trust me."

Whispering in response, "I do, Bartholomew, with my life."

Chapter Nine
The Captain's Out & About

Morning came quickly. Donning my peignoir as I gently slide out of bed, I tread softly in to the bathroom to brush my teeth and hair. Returning minutes later, I find my Captain awake.

Greeting me as I walk in to the room, "Bore da."

"Bore da, Bartholomew," giving him a peck. "Within the bathroom, thou shall find a new toothbrush, a straight razor, and related equipage. Keith may still be asleep, so let us be quiet."

Donning his robe, and apparently irritated by my comment, "Thou canst seriously be concerned about being unduly quiet in case that loon sleeps still?"

"I'm afraid I am, Bart."

"Why should I shew anny consideration to—"

Interrupting him, "Because I can not bear the idea of seeing that lout before I've had my morning coffee."

Laughing a mite, he speaks softly whilst moving towards me. "Altho' such will be difficult at times, I shall endeavor, fy melys, to refuse thee not which lyes within my power to give." Lifting my chin with the tips of his fingers, he gently kisses my lips. "I shall go see Katie regarding breakfast. By the time thou art dressed, I should be returning with a pot of coffee."

Opening the wardrobe whilst smiling, "Diolch 'chi."

Watching me as I choose a pair of shoes, "What's, fy melys, going to wear?"

Pointing to the dress hanging on the dressing screen, "That."

Smiling, my Captain replies, "Very nice."

Downstairs →

Still wearing his elegant dressing gown, the Captain enters the kitchen. "Bore da, Katie."

Welcoming him, this is the first time Katie has ever seen him dressed in such a relaxed fashion. "Good morning, Captain. I trust you slept well."

" 'Twas one of the best nights sleep I have had in centuries."

Chuckling, "Very funny, Captain. What is it that brings you to my kitchen?"

"Your mistress craves her morning coffee, would you be so kind as to prepare a breakfast tray?"

"Right away, Captain. I already have the coffee ready, and the water for your tea is heating. In the meantime, I'll fix your breakfast. Any requests?"

"Have you cockles and laverbread?"

"No, but I will get some for you when I do the marketing."

"Thank you, Katie. Until then, whatever you have on hand will be fine. I shall collect the tray after I am dressed."

"No need, Captain. It'll be my pleasure to bring it up."

After thanking her, he departs.

Upstairs: About a half hour later ⇁

Hearing someone knocking on the door, and asking, "Who is it?" my anxiety is evident.

"Katie."

Happy to hear it's not that rabble-rousing Keith, I cheerfully say, "Come in."

"Good morning, Miss." Making her way across the room and out onto the balcony through the already open French doors, "You look content this morning."

"Katie!" says I with a smile, "The things that go through your mind," and giggling, "I'm shocked at you."

Setting the tray on the table, "Having merely said you looked content, 'tis your mind you need to worry about, Miss."

With an astute look and modest chuckle, "Okay, so it's my mind that's in the gutter."

"No Miss," smiling at me, "just on Captain Roberts. Well, I best be going, or your mum's egg muffin sandwich will burn. Enjoy your breakfast."

"Thank you, Katie."

When I see Keith, I'll let him know you're having breakfast in your room this morning and shan't be down until later. That should satisfy him, but bolt the door just in case."

"Good thinking, Katie," I reply smiling, adding, "you're a gem."

Standing outside the door, Katie waits several moments, and having heard the bolt move in to place, and following a nodding smile, she proceeds down the hall towards the stairs.

Entering our room from the door leading to the uppermost section of the turret, which is now our retreat, the Captain hath donned another one of the outfits I bought for him some months back. The colorful waist sash looks sharp against the billowing, cream-colored shirt, and loose fitting high-waisted, dark chocolate pants that are neatly tucked inside his over-the-calf boots as intended.

Flashing a smile, "Thou cuts quite a dashing figure in those duds."

"Please, madam, my modesty."

"Not that I'll ever tire of crimson, but it is nice to see thee in a different color."

Still wearing only my peignoir, stockings and shift, my Captain says, "I thought thee would be dressed by now."

"I decided to wait and see what thou would be wearing. Returning my original choice to my wardrobe, I take out my off white, Egyptian cotton peasant blouse with gold rickrack trim; the brown, multi-ruffled, just below the knee skirt; and my dark brown, lace-up waist cincher; and hanging hung the ensemble on my dressing screen, I take out my brown granny boots and place them beside my vanity. "Being a lovely day, perhaps we can lunch in town."

"Je serai ravi de vous accompagner à la ville lorsque vous êtes prêt."

"Fy Nghapten, thou amazes me. Thy French is beautiful."

"When one travels to foreign lands, it helps to know the language."

"Yes, it does." Fiddling with the clasp on the purse, "Umm, fy Nghapten?"

"Aye?"

"Wouldst thou do me a tiny favor?"

Amused somewhat by the modern clasp that is giving me so much trouble, he replies, "Of course."

"My limited French being a mite rusty, wouldst thou be kind enough to translate."

"Certainly. "Byddaf yn falch iawn i hebrwng chi i'r dref pan fyddwch yn barod."

Altho' my head is lowered as I continue to struggle with the clasp, and despite the problem I am having, I look up at him. "That was beautiful, fy Nghapten, but I meant in to English."

Finding joy in the knowledge that I find his language pleasing to the ear. "Aye, fy melys. I said I shall be delighted to escort thee to town when thou art ready."

Fed up with the purse, giggling in spite of my difficulties, I toss it onto the bed. "Should be a fun day."

Picking up the purse and unlatching it with ease, he hands it to me.

Smiling, I reach out, "Merci Beau Coup," and taking him by the hand, I lead him out onto the balcony. "Let us have our breakfast before it grows cold."

As always, my charming lover pulls out my chair, and upon sitting, I commence our breakfast by pouring for him a cup tea, then coffee for myself. Removing the napkin from its ring and placing it gently in my lap, "I can't believe Keith had the gall to be here last night when we arrived."

The Captain's voice, grim as he takes his seat, picks up his cup of tea. "I knows not, however," as his voice takes on a determined tone, "it is my intention to find out his true reason for being here 'fore this day is over." As he begins to eat his meal, his voice softens. "Tell me about Mister McClure and why he believes he hath hopes regarding thee?"

When I sigh, and turn away, my Captain slides his chair towards mine, and speaking with concern, "Canst thou not tell me what bothers thee?"

Remaining quiet for several moments, and while thinking over his question, his hand smoothes away the wisps of hair from my cheek. "Our relationship was very poor, and although I wanted to throw him out, I couldn't."

"Why, what stopped thee?"

"My mom was living at his house and I couldn't get anyone to help me move her stuff over to mine. When I finally did, I figured I could just avoid him by not going to the places I knew he frequented. The last I heard, he was dead, and until he showed up here, I had no reason to believe otherwise, and as cold-blooded as it may sound, perhaps as a result of all the lies he told me, his death seemed like some form of poetic justice."

Even though I did not explain in detail, Captain Roberts realizes from my sad tone, that, that part of my life was distressing, and speaking tenderly, "It must 'ave bin a horrible time in thy life." Holding me for a spell, pleased by my desire to snuggle up to him as I tilt my head towards his shoulder, he is touched by my willingness to share something so traumatic with him. "I quite understand why thee had little use for those of the male persuasion for so long a time."

"One of the oddities, is that up until a couple days ago, even though I had never consciously revealed my feelings for thee to anyone, except my mom, that is, everyone seems to know about them."

"Everyone?"

"If you recall, just a few nights ago, you said that you knew of my feelings for you long before I told you, and according to Katie, and quite a few others, my website is more like a shrine than a biography. And Keith said he heard that we were in love. By tomorrow, the whole country, and probably the world, will know thou hast been reborn. The toughest part will be dealing with both the curiosity seekers and the inquisitors."

"Aye, but what pleases me is that Keith will know."

"But he knows now," I remind him.

"Be that as it may, he believes thou wilt return to him."

"I'd rather die!"

"Thou hast no neede to fret, un annwyl. I shan't allow that regurgitated worm to upset our lives much longer. Now sit up and eat thy breakfast, after which, thou must hurry and get dressed. After our morning's search for answers, wee shall lunch in town."

Finishing his breakfast, my beloved rises from the table, and looking at the outfit I intend to wear, notably the stays hanging over the dressing screen, "As thou requires assistance with thy wardrobe, I shall summon Katie to attend thee."

Replying softly as he leaves the room, "Diolch 'chi."

Approaching the stairway; seeing Katie in the foyer, the normally soft-spoken man hearkens, "Katie," and as she looks up towards him, he continues by stating, "Your mistress requires your assistance getting dressed this morn."

"I'll be right up. Making her way up the stairs, "You look wonderful, Captain."

"Thank you, Katie," offering a slight bow. "I hear voices coming from the reception room. Have we guests?"

"Yes, Captain. They arrived an hour ago. I have already served them a hearty breakfast. And Mister Cullen is in the reception room. I told him you would be down directly."

> *Mister Cullen was the only person outside of the household who knew about the Captain, & even though Katie had informed him there had been some changes, the Captain's presence never failed to make him nervous.*

As the good Captain enters the reception room, Mister Cullen stands up. "Umm—" obviously shocked, not aware that Captain Roberts often mingles with the guests, he speaks with a quiver. "Bore Da, Captain." Continuing whilst motioning to the small rack he had set up in the reception room, "I have brought the clothes Miss V'lé ordered."

Extending his hand in observance to his newly acquired custom, "Bore Da, Mister Cullen. Thank you for coming."

Unsure about reciprocating the Captain's gesture, the jittery Mister Cullen backs up.

Waiting as Mister Cullen gives the matter consideration, Captain Roberts' mounding impatience becomes evident as his voice becomes a trifle gruff. "You simpering barnacle! Canst be you thinks not of returning my goodwill gesture." Pausing for a moment to regain his composure, Captain Roberts softens his voice, and whilst flashing a modest smile, still holding out his hand, "Look Mister Cullen, I am only trying to be friendly. 'Tisn't my fault you be the nervous sort?"

Not understanding the situation, Mister Cullen, knowing only that in the past they couldn't touch, reluctantly extends his hand, and as Captain Roberts grasps it firmly, Mister Cullen faints dead away.

Sue, witnessing the incident when entering the room, noting also the expression on the faces of our understandably bewildered guests, tries to explain away the tailor's reaction. "He does that a lot," states Sue, chuckling. "Iron poor blood or something."

"Mrs Montgomery, would you be good enough to fetch a bowl of water."

"Of course," she replies, and departs for the kitchen.

"Good morning ladies, sir," as he bows to them. "I be Captain Roberts. I trust you enjoyed your breakfast."

"Yes, Captain, we did," replies the elder of the two ladies present as she glances again at Mister Cullen still lying on the floor.

"It was delicious," remarks the younger woman while snickering. "I never saw anyone faint before."

"May I enquire in what capacity you hold the rank of Captain," asks the rather prim and proper Englishman?

"I be a man of the sea. My last command was the Fregate, *Royal Fortune*."

Enquiring further, "Was that a naval vessel, Captain?"

"Not whilst I command'd her, sir. Altho' some years earlier whilst serving in the British Royal Navy, I atchieved the rating of Sailing Master[SBA3], and later, before I was elevated to the rank of Captain, I had bin 3rd Mate[B2 pg 80] on a merchant, and 1st Mate of a Privateer." To avoid more questions, Captain Roberts turns his attentions towards Mister Cullen.

Sue, just returning, hands the bowl of water to Captain Roberts, who, without hesitation, throws the water in Mister Cullen's face.

As Mister Cullen comes to, shaking like a Christmas goose, Sue and Captain Roberts help him to the sofa. "Could it be your sleep is not what it ought be these days?"

"I suppose that could be one reason, Captain," replies Mister Cullen.

"Miss V'lé told me she rang you. 'Tis glad I am you were able to come on such short notice."

"My pleasure, Captain. As you know, my seamstresses enjoy creating your impressive attire, and it's an honour to have a notable person such as yourself as a customer. I just wish I was free to advertise it."

"Be my guest, Mister Cullen."

"Why thank you, Captain. As my way of saying thanks, it will be my pleasure to create your next garment gratis."

"Thank you, Mister Cullen. There is one special ensemble I require. I shall discuss it with you later this day."

After talking with Captain Roberts for a few minutes, Mister Cullen says, "Excuse me for saying so, Captain, but you look different somehow."

Ignoring his comment, Captain Roberts says, "Whilst we wait for Miss V'lé, both Châtelaine of *Inn Finistère*, and my intended, please make yourselves at home."

"Your intended?" asks Mister Cullen with questioning reservations.

"Aye, Mister Cullen, and now that you know, I might as well tell you of the garment I wish you to make for me.

Meanwhile Upstairs ¬

Half dressed, wearing only my black silk stockings, a white silk, mid-thigh length, Edwardian romper with a spilt crotch and spaghetti straps, and my white steel boned stays, lightly drawn, I await, Katie.

Upon entering, Katie finds me seated on my vanity chair wrestling with the buttonhook needed to fasten my new boots, "Could you use some help, Miss?"

With a sigh of relief, "Yes, Katie." Showing her the buttonhook, "Do you know how to work this thing?"

"I can't say that I do, but I'll give it a go." After fiddling with it for a moment, "I know," says she, and does the buttons easily. "What's next?"

Walking over to the bedpost, "Will you tighten me up, please."

Shaking her head in disbelief, Katie says, "Hang on Miss, and suck in." Pulling as hard as she can, "Any particular reason for this torturing attire?"

"Of course there is Katie. It's like I told you before, I want to please him, and the Captain loves the older, more feminine fashions." Gasping, "Only snug on the top strings."

Whilst tying the drawstrings in to a bow, "He loves you the way you are, Miss."

"I know, but he is, after all, from a different era. Why should he have to give up all he loves just because he's in ours. So since I can not go to his, as much as I would like to, I'll do my best for him in this one. Besides, I love the dresses of old, and," speaking with a slight grimace on my face, "I love my stays. Besides, they do wonders for—"

"For ones sex life?"

Clearing my throat a mite, "Umm," Displaying modesty in my voice, "That too, but I was going to say is that I have always did like form fitting garments. Besides, what's the purpose of working at keeping ones figure if the woman isn't gonna show it off."

Laughing as her head gestures in the general direction of the drawer where it is laying, "Well at least this outfit doesn't call for that bustle."

Slipping the peasant blouse over my head, I step in to my skirt, "I love my bustle, and the black & white gown is my favorite dress."

Whilst helping me on with my waist cincher, "Seeing that you're wearing this, why also wear the stays?"

"This waist cincher, being just garnish, doesn't hold you in like stays do, Katie." Stepping back a few steps, "Well—" giving myself the once over, "excepting the hair comb Captain Roberts carved for me, that's everything."

"Yep. You're thoroughly laced, buttoned and hooked."

"I feel a little like a trust up chicken, Katie, but more than that," continuing with a gleaming smile, "I feel like a lady who's fit to grace the arm of the Great Pirate Roberts."

"You look beautiful, Miss. I want to be downstairs to see the Captain's face when you come down. He's in the conversion room with our guests, and Mister Cullen."

"Thank you, Katie. I'll be down in two shakes."

Glancing upward, Captain Roberts, seeing Katie in the upper hall, knows his lady will be down directly.

On her way downstairs, and seeing that the front of Mister Cullen's shirt is wet once again, she spouts in her usual boisterous tone as she enters the room, "Fainted again I'll wager."

Sue, attempting to hold back a chuckle, "I'm afraid so, Katie."

"Will, Miss V'lé be down soon?"

"Yes, Mister Cullen," replies Katie, "any minute." Adding with a smile, "and just wait 'til you see her new ensemble, it's lovely, and it will complement your outfit perfectly, Captain." Turning to the newly arrived guests, "Let me show you to your rooms." As Katie leads the way, our newest guests follow her upstairs.

Just after my guests turn the corner leading to their rooms, I exit mine, and closing the self-locking door behind me, I head down the hall.

Keith, having spent the better part of an hour lurking just inside the slightly open door of his room, heard Katie inform the others of my impending arrival, and upon hearing my high-button boots upon the stone steps, waits for me at the bottom of the stairs. "Good morning, V'lé."

Speaking in a rather irritated manner as I walk past him, "Are you still here?"

Within the arch betwixt the foyer and the reception room, all eyes are upon me as I await my Captain's approach, and having met me at the threshold, offering me his arm, he whispers, "Thou looks good enough to eat," and escorting me to the music section of the reception room, he adds, "Thou art perfectly dressed for a stroll along the boardwalk."

Turning to face him, placing both my hands in his as he looks me over, I cheerfully reply, "Especially when accompanied by such a dashing escort."

Flabbergasted, Mister Cullen ekes out, "You mean— that is to say, the two of you are going to town, together," pointing his finger, shaking it back and forth between the two of us. "But you can't, you're dead!"

Katie, who is rushing back down the stairs, is carrying her camera.

"I have bin reborn, Mister Cullen."

"What! But how?"

"You left out when, why and where," proclaims Katie, giggling whilst taking a snapshot.

"We don't have any definite answers yet, but we believe it began with a bolt of lightning," says I.

Interrupting, the Captain injects, "Excepting our heavenly father who hath blessed us, the reasons be unimportant, for his divine intervention, that wee believe this is kin to, wee be most grateful indeed."

"Perfectly stated, fy Nghapten, and I, as does Captain Roberts, intend to make the most of every moment. So, if you will excuse us, 'tis a lovely day for a stroll by the seaside, just the two of us."

Trying to hide his dysphoric feelings as he wanders in, "Good morning everyone. Looks like it'll be a nice day, doesn't it," says Keith, looking like his usual, unkempt self.

" 'Tis fortunate for you," states Captain Roberts amid a sneering expression aimed at Mister McClure, "that I not be of an umbrageous ilk."

"Since when," I ask him? "'Twas forbearance in regard to ignorance, and thine audacity when in the presence of cowardice thou art famous for. Ne'er did thee give way to impertinence."

"Whom, fy annwyl, if I may enquire, hath bin more forgiving than I these last few days?"

"No one, but—"

"One will not uncover particulars, fy melys, by throwing dirt upon that which hath inadvertently surfaced."

Taking what he said to heart, I reply, "Good point."

About to prepare his breakfast, Katie, entering the room, asks, "Anything special for breakfast, Mister McClure?

"What ever you have on the stove will be fine, Katie."

"Would you like some coffee before your meal?"

"Yes, Katie. But," turning to me, "it'll take a stiff drink to get me through this mush of yours, V'lé."

Feeling somehow insulted, "To what mush are you referring, Keith?"

"This archaic speech of yours, the 50¢ words, and having to hear it all day again today."

"I think the way they talk to each other sounds pretty, and as for the words they use, none have been unknown to me," states Katie, and as she turns to leave the room, "I'll call you, Mister McClure, when your breakfast is ready."

Replying to Keith, "Since the Captain and I will be out most of the day, your ears will be spared."

As the Châtelaine of *Inn Finistère*, I always do my best to be gracious, and such, I introduce my guests to one another. "Mister Cullen, this is Keith McClure, from Desertville, U.S.A.," and as the two shake hands, "Keith, this is Peter Cullen. He made Captain Roberts' garb."

"You're a tailor then?" confirms Keith.

"I wear several hats, Mister McClure, including that of the superintendent registrar."

"What's that?"

Answering Keith's question, I reply, "it's similar to a small town clerk, and a Justice of the Peace, meaning he is also licensed to officiate at civil marriages."

"Yours, I suppose," states Keith sarcastically.

"We haven't made our plans yet," says I.

When Katie returns, she is carrying a large handled tray brimming with breakfast tidbits: welsh cakes, sausage crescent rolls, donut holes, mandarin orange slices, tea, and coffee.

Seeing Katie enter the room, Captain Roberts, relieving her of the weighty equipage, sets the large tray on the coffee table.

"Thank you, gallant sir," says Katie amid a smile, but instead of taking a seat before Miss V'lé's prized, George I, silver service, she asks, can you serve, Miss, I must get back to the kitchen."

"Of course, Katie."

"Are you going someplace special, or just making a fashion statement?" inquires, Keith.

As I begin to fill the cups, my eyes narrowing in response to Keith's impertinence, "Unlike some people I know, the majority of those in Wales prefer not to dress like an unkempt buffoon. But in any case, as dictated by etiquette, when a lady accepts the company of a gentleman, it's her duty to conform to his sense of gentility."

"Very profound, V'lé, but—"

Before Keith can utter another word, I quickly continue, adding, "I must, however, add that in this case, it's not so much a duty, as it is both an honor and a privilege."

"Well spoken," says Mister Cullen in a complimentary fashion.

Outflanked, Keith, changes the subject. "I was thinking, since I'm checking in to the Lord Nelson Hotel today, perhaps ya'll will be my guests at supper tonight, say 7 o'clock." And whilst looking directly at Mister Cullen, "And since we are all friends here, you're invited also, Mister Cullen, as are Sue and Katie."

Thinking it might not be a good idea to allow Mister Cullen, as gullible as he is, to be alone with Keith, nor wishing to deny Katie and his future mother-in-law the privilege of dining out at such a fine restaurant whilst also affording him the opportunity to discern Keith's motives in a more relaxed atmosphere, Captain Roberts states, "It will be our pleasure to accept your invitation, and perhaps afterwards, go dancing. I hear there is a discothèque within the hotel."

"Oooo, we can dance the Kizomba," I said smiling.

"I look forward to seeing you all later," states Mister Cullen. Setting his empty cup and napkin on the coffee table, "And now, it being a working day, I must get back to the office." Turning to address Captain Roberts, "I saw Miss V'lé's car stuck in the mud, and one other car also just a little ways down the drive. Shall I send a recovery vehicle?"

"What?" Irritated, I dash to the window. "It figures."

"Thank you, Mister Cullen," Keith begins, "I have already called for one. That's why I'm still here, V'lé," explains Keith. "Yesterday afternoon, when I came to pack, my car sunk into the mud, and being after 5 p.m., no one was open.

"May I offer you and Miss V'lé a ride, Captain?

"Aye, Mister Cullen," expressing his thanks, "that you may."

"I must fetch my shawl from the cloakroom," says I.

"I too shall return momentarily," echoes Captain Roberts.

Upstairs within the Captain, & V'lé's retreat ⇁

After a minute of rummaging through his sea chest in search of an Emerald ring, he exclaims, "Ah!" and placing the ring in his pocket, "This should bring a handsome sum." Closing the chest, he rejoins the others.

Carrying my shawl as I return to the reception room, I am closely followed by my newly arrived guests. Once at my Captain's side, he introduces me. "I would like to present Miss V'lé, Châtelaine of this great house."

Amid a slight curtsy, "Welcome to *Inn Finistère*." Turning to Mister Cullen whilst gesturing towards my beloved, "As Master of *Inn Finistère*, I am sure my fiancé has already told you of our impending wedding."

"Yes, Miss V'lé, he has," replies one of the new guests.

"We can leave whenever you're ready," states Mister Cullen, and foiling Keith's plans, the three of us depart.

Driving along Barn Street towards the Car Park off High Street, Captain Roberts commandingly states, "Stop here."

Honouring the Captain's request, Mister Cullen pulls over, and as the car comes to a stop, Captain Roberts gets out. I begin to follow, but before I have a chance he shuts the door saying, "Nay, fy melys. Thou needs to accompany Mister Cullen to his office."

Once again beginning to sweat in his boots, "But why?" asks Mister Cullen nervously.

"My business necessitates I get out here. In the meantime," states Captain Roberts instructionally, "I neede the two of ye to create for me the identification documents used in today's society."

"But they won't be legal."

Questioning his reasoning, "Why not Mister Cullen, have I not been reborn, and am I not, therefore, one of her majesties subjects?"

Snivelling, he replies, "Well— yes, of course."

"You be the superintendent registrar, are you not?"

"Yes."

"And your office, does it not contain the proper forms?"

Feeling trapped, "Yes, but—"

Giving my Captain assurance, "No problem, fy Nghapten, thou go along and take care of thy business. I shall see that everything is done properly."

"Diolch yn fawr iawn, fy melys, I shall join thee there later."

As we depart, I can see my Captain's duster swaying elegantly in keeping with his proud, rolling gait as he heads towards High Street.

HIGH STREET, HWLFFORDD ¬

Following the bend in the road, remembering well, the steepness of the grade, I take comfort in the knowledge that many of the buildings are as I remember them. Reaching the bottom, I stop 'fore one of Pembrokeshire's oldest jewellers.

Entering the shoppe, I am greeted by a dignified looking gentleman, who greets me warmly. "Bore da, sir. May I be of assistance?"

Returning his verbal greeting with a slight nod, I walk up to the glass display case, and reaching into my pocket, I bring out the superlative 17th Century Emerald ring I had placed there earlier and set it atop the velvet cloth already lying upon the glass counter.

Taking a jeweller's loupe from his pocket, "May I," asks the jeweller as he reaches, tentatively, for the ring.

"Certainly," says I.

Holding the folding magnifying glass against his eye, the jeweller begins by examining the setting. "The gold, Aztec, if I'm not mistaken, is splendid." Continuing, as he moves his eye about the 29 karat, transparent gem, he smiles, and as he continues, slowly turning the ring as he inspects the 18 blue white baguette diamonds framing the flawless dark green stone, anny onlooker canne easily see the sheer delight in his eyes.

"It's exquisite. This Emerald is, unquestionably, the finest I've seen. All the stones, in fact, are flawless. May I ask why you have brought it here today?"

"Your shoppe, sir, comes highly recommended, and if it is agreeable to you, I would be interested in trading for an equally impressive Garnet suitable for a wedding ring, and both the garnet riddled, horse-drawn brooch timepiece, and the well equipped, jewel encrusted, sterling silver Châtelaine which lyes in yon window."

"Not that I would dream of turning away a customer," begins the jeweller, "but this ring would dazzle any bride worth her salt."

"To be sure, but my intended, altho' possessing a lifelong passion for Garnets, has ne'er been so privileged to owne one of quality."

"I see. Well, I am afraid I haven't anything in my shoppe nearly as valuable as this; however, if I may, permit me offer you your choice from the rings I do have, the Châtelaine, as well as the timepiece, and shall we say, £100,000.00 cash."

Offering my hand to seal the deal, "Thank you, 'tis a splendid offer."

"How would you like the payment to be made?"

Answering his question, I reply, "Will £25,000.00 be sufficient to take my intended on a memorable holiday in celebration of our wedding?"

"A honeymoon? Yes, very much so."

That being your opinion, I shall have £30,000.00 in notes, and for the balance, I shall accept a bank draft made payable to V'léOnica Roberts."

"Cash... Of course, sir," replies the jeweller as he brings forth a company cheque to be signed. "Would you prefer the cash to be large or small denomination bills?"

"A mixture. Mostly large, but with plenty of pocket cash as needed by a bon vivant on the town frequently with his lady."

"Very good, sir." Moments later, having put his pen to the cheque, the jeweller flags his trusted assistant, Neville, who hurries on over. Whilst waiting, the jeweller jots a note regarding my wishes on his personal stationery.

Having arrived, Neville says, "Yes, sir?"

Slipping both the note and the cheque in to a matching envelope, and sealing it, the jeweller hands it to Neville. "I need you to dash over to HSBC. See the manager, and return with the pouch he gives you as soon as possible."

"Yes, sir," and scurries off.

"Our branch, being just down the street, it shan't take more than a few minutes." Continuing, the jeweller asks, "In the meantime, may I offer you some liquid refreshment?"

Assuming such to be alcoholic, I reply, "No thank you," and with my hands folded behind my back, I look about the shoppe.

"Over here, sir," calls the jeweller as he unlocks the wall safe.

As I approach, the jeweller places several trays glistening with beautiful cocktail rings and wedding sets, as well as a few other items atop the counter. "We keep the more valuable items in our safe."

As I look on, one ring in particular catches my eye, and reaching down, I pick up an exquisite ring having a delicate filigree depiction of a magnificent dragon's head encrusted with a multitude of blood red garnets in various sizes.

Holding it up to the light, "The Garnets reflects the dark auburn highlights in her hair."

Congratulating me. "My compliments, sir, you possess a keen eye. This unique piece contains 85 Garnets, but do you think a dragon is appropriate for a wedding ring?"

"My intended adores dragons."

"That being the case," begins the jeweller, "she's sure to love this one."

"May I have the ring engraved forthwith?"

"You mean right now, whilst you wait," asks the jeweller?

"Aye, unless it presents a problem?"

"Not at all. What would you like engraved?"

Putting pen to paper, I jot down the Latin phrase, "Virtus Junxit Mors Non Separabit."

"Very Poetic." Gesturing to one of his clerks, the man hurries forth. Handing the clerk both the ring and the slip of paper, "Take these to Claire. She is to drop whatever she is doing and take care of this immediately."

"Yes, sir," replies the clerk, and taking both from his employer's hand, he hurries away.

"It shouldn't take more than half an hour." Again offering refreshments, "May I offer you a cup of Glengettie Tea, or perhaps something stronger?"

As I turn to face him, I reply, "Thank you, sir. A cup of tea will suit me well."

Milk & sugar?

"Aye."

Walking across the room to the tea cart in the corner, the jeweller pours a wee bit of milk into the cup, adds a sugar lump, and after pouring the tea, he places 2 macaroons on the saucer, and upon returning, whilst handing it to me, asks, "Have you set the date?"

"In a manner of speaking. Last night when I announc'd my intentions 'fore witnesses, stating wee were to be married forthwith, she smiled."

Speaking warmly, "Well, in that case, I would say that she's happy about it."

The clerk and, Neville are returning. Arriving first, Neville hands his employer a locked leather pouch, and departs. Moments later, the clerk hands me the ring for my inspection.

Taking a look at the engraving, paying no attention to the price tag which dangles on a piece of thread, I compliment him. "Well done."

Handing the ring to the jeweller, who removes the tag before placing it inside a velvet hinged ring box, he then returns both to me whilst stating, "If the ring does not fit, she needs only to bring it in and I will happily resize it for her, gratis."

"Thank you, sir."

Alone once more, the jeweller hands me both the pouch & a key, and a handsome jewellery box. Having unlocked the pouch, I reach inside my duster and bringing out my leather money purse, I insert the cash, and returning it to my inside coat pocket, I set both pouch and key upon the table.

More than a little surprised by my actions, "Excuse me for saying so, sir, but wouldn't you feel better if you counted the money?"

With a quizzical, familiar manner, "Dost thou intend to cheat me?"

"No sir, of course not, but not only is it expected, it's highly recommended that all customers count their change."

"I don't feel the neede, sir." Holding the bank draft in my hand, I fold it in half, and then half again.

"Miss Roberts, that would be the name of your intended?"

"No, 'tis V'lé Onica, but her wedded name will be Roberts."

Looking inside the 2nd jewellery box to inspect both the pendant and the châtelaine, I am pleas'd to find they are secure in their respective places on opposite sides of the velvet-lined box, and to my surprise, I find an additional item, and picking up the jewelled encrusted fibulae, "And this?"

Smiling, the jeweller, hoping his gift is not considered too familiar, replies, "When the weather turns cool, instead of the norm, I picture your intended wearing a delicate shawl. Thus, being a woman with an appreciation of antiquities, I have taken the liberty of presenting you with this jewelled Germantic fibulae dating to the 5th century as my gift to your bride."

"A most generous gift, sir." Returning the fibulae to the box, "I am sure my intended will be most pleas'd to wear it. Thank you." Placing the draft inside, "The timepiece, châtelaine, and bank draft are the gifts I am giving her."

"You're very generous, sir."

"Not nearly as munificent when compared to what she as already given me."

Curious, "Tell me, sir, being that you look familiar, and if you do not mind my asking, may I inquire where it is you hail from?"

"I was born in Castell-newydd bach. My intended, an American of Welsh/Irish, French, and English descent, makes her home in Little Haven."

"Castell-newydd bach." Musing a moment, he speaks with a measure of excitement, "Little Newcastle?"

"Aye."

As the jeweller links the town with the name of Roberts, his interest is suddenly peaked. "Will you be settling nearby?"

"Aye, at *Inn Finistère*."

"Sounds familiar. Would that be the Gothic Bed and Breakfast on Settland's Hill?"

"Aye. My intended is Châtelaine of *Inn Finistère*."

Although trying to remain calm, "Oh my lord, you're Captain Roberts aren't you."

"Aye, sir. I am indeed."

Grabbing my right hand with both of his, the jeweller shakes it briskly. "I'm so very happy to meet you."

Altho' a bit puzzled, "Thank you," says I with a measure of relief. "I imagin'd there would be quite a different reaction from people when they learned my identity."

"Well, I can only speak for myself, Captain," obviously brimming, "but I for one am delighted."

"May I ask how you heard of my rebirth?"

"Whilst attending church Sunday last, those of us present were told of a miracle happening, and that the late great Captain Roberts had been given a new lease on life. Naturally, especially since the man was dressed like a cowboy, many of those present didn't believe him, but I assure you that those of us who took what he said on faith, were delighted to hear the news."

"I appreciate the knowing of it, sir." As the jeweller and I shake hands once more, "My intended is waiting for me, so I must be on my way."

"Take care, Captain, for very few such gifts are awarded."

ARRIVING AT MISTER CULLEN'S OFFICE ¬

Seeing the bemused look on the Captain's face, Mister Cullen rises from his chair and hurries to the refreshment counter. Pouring for his guest a cup of tea, "What is it, Captain?"

With trepidation as he leans against the counter, the Captain asks, "Where is Miss V'lé?"

Handing him the cup and saucer, "She's in the back room printing the documents you requested. She'll be out directly I expect."

Taking the tea from Mister Cullen's hands, Captain Roberts politely replies, "Thank you."

"I have only just finished making the entries needed in today's society into the computer.

"Thank you, Mister Cullen."

When I enter the room, I see my Captain, and noting his faraway expression, I do not take my eyes off him whilst handing the documents to Mister Cullen, saying, "You need only to add the finishing touches, stamps and such." Walking slowly towards my beloved, who looks stricken, I ask, "What is it, fy Arglwydd?"

Not receiving a reply, I turn to Mister Cullen, and asking with a quiver of worriment, "What's wrong with Captain Roberts? Did he say anything to you when he came in?"

"Nothing unusual."

Beginning to worry, suddenly my Captain looks at me, "Sorry, fy melys, I was deep in thought."

Displaying a measure of fear, I ask, "Is something wrong?"

"Nothing per se," taking a seat, "it's just taking a few minutes to come to grips with the reality."

Suddenly feeling an emptiness engulf me, I become teary-eyed as I slowly ask, "What… um, what reality?" Closing mine eyes for a moment, terrified I will find my beloved has returned to a ghostly state, I take a deep breath whilst mustering the nerve to slowly reach out to touch his skin, until, though skittishly, touching his cheek with the back of my fingers, I am happy to discover my fear was unjustified. Letting out a quiet sigh of relief, "For an instant I thought that— well, no matter." Learning that such worriment was for no purpose, I am wondering what else can be upsetting him so. "Thou looks bewildered."

Turning to Mister Cullen, my Captain speaks in a solemn tone. "Did you not attend church services Sunday last?"

Being evident to Mister Cullen that Captain Roberts is very disturbed, he is careful not to say any more than absolutely necessary.

"No, I did not. My alarm clock, failing to wake me, I overslept."

"Miss V'lé was with me, and Katie, as you know, is Catholic. Tell me Mister Cullen, this alarm clock of yours, has it ever failed you 'fore?"

"No, as a matter of fact it hasn't."

Very concerned about where this conversation might be leading, never seeing my Captain in this mood before, I am beginning to get frightened.

"V'lé, dost thou remember pointing out his clothes on the morrow following McClure's arrival?"

"Yes, of course." As it finally occurs to me what the Captain is thinking, "Oh my word."

"At last the light begins to shine." Arising from his seat, Captain Roberts offers me his arm, "Come fy melys, I shall ponder the events of the past few days whilst wee dine, for I be famish'd."

Together, as we walk to the café that lies just across the car park, several of the local residents appear to be gawking at us. Ignoring them, we enter the restaurant. As my Captain maneuvers me to a corner table, "I can not remember when I have felt so happy."

Reaching in to his pocket, "I ought not have taken liberties the evening of McClure's arrival, for I had no right without first presenting thee with a suitable offering." And taking my hand, he places white velvet ring box in my palm. " 'Twould afford me endless pleasure, fy annwyl, if thou wilt accept this as a token of my love, and honour me by becoming my wife."

Smiling broadly as mine eyes become tear filled, "Yes, Bartholomew, I will!"

Releasing my hand, allowing me to open the box, "It's breathtaking." Then with a sly smile, thinking it was among the treasure he procured whilst a *'Gentleman of Fortune,'* "And to whom did this treasure belong?"

"I know not, fy Nghariad, for I only procur'd it this day."

Flabbergasted by his statement, "Thy business earlier?"

"Aye."

Knowing he was wearing his magnificent necklace, and being relieved to know does still, "It's too beautiful. I don't deserve such a wonderful—"

"Shhh…" Slipping the ring on my finger, "fy annwyl, all I possess, belongs equally to thee. Until wee art wed, let this be the symbol of our betrothal; thereafter, thy wedding ring."

Seeing how we are in public, I pick up the menu to shield us from the rest of the patrons, and leaning forward, I give him a small kiss. Lowering the menu as I lean back against the seat, I am happier than ever did I dream was possible.

Coming to our table to take our order, the waitress asks, "What will you have, Miss?"

Being overwhelmed and unable to think clearly, whilst holding the ring close to my cheek a moment, "Wilt thou order for me please, fy Arglwydd."

Pleased by my obvious adoration of his gift, he says, "Bydd gan y ddynes wyau Benedict, tatws wedi'u ffrio, sudd oren, a choffi gyda llaeth. O ran fy hun, rwy'n credu y bydd dau wy wedi'i botsio, cocos wedi'u ffrio a chic moch, crempogau, bara laver wedi'i ffrio, sudd grawnffrwyth, a phot o de sbeislyd poeth pibellau yn addas i mi."

"I'm sorry, sir," begins the waitress, "but I have no idea what it is you said."

Seeing my Captain's slight dismayed expression, "I'm afraid that these days, a great number of the natives, altho' Welsh, do not speak the language."

Sighing a mite, my Captain states our order again, this time in English. "The lady will have egges benedict, fried potatoes, orange juice, and coffee with milk. As for myself, methinks 2 poached eggs, a heap of cockles fried with rashers, a stack of Welsh cakes, fried laverbread, grapefruit juice, and a pot of piping hot, spiced tea, if available, will suit me well, and it pleases us to have our hot beverages served forthwith."

Still writing, "Very good, Mister—"

"Captain," he corrects her.

Staring at him intently, "Captain Roberts?"

"Aye."

"Oh my lord." Struggling to get her order pad back in her pocket, "Please forgive me for being flustered, Captain. I heard about you during church services; rebirth was the term the man used, but naturally, as did most of us present, I thought he was tetched."

" 'Twas onely natural," he responds.

Though puzzled, I listen intently, but just can't believe what I'm hearing, and asking with great concern, "What man?"

"I don't know his name, Miss."

Captain Roberts, speaking in a commanding tone, "Deskribe him."

"Well, let me see. He was tall, wiry, had jet black hair and a heavy moustache. Oh, and he was dressed like a cowboy."

"My thanks."

"You're welcome, Captain." Turning the waitress resumes to her duties.

"She described Keith perfectly," I begin, "but how could he have known, and what would he be doing in a church here in Wales; in all the time I knew him in Arizona, he never attended church, and perhaps even more important, how could he have known who you are?" Stopping a moment, I then add, "Perhaps that lightning bolt wasn't the cause."

"Nay, fy annwyl," the Captain says to me quietly. "Not the reason, nor the cause. 'Twas simply the mode of delivery."

Taking a drink of my water, "I don't understand."

"I, on the other hand, am just beginning to," states Captain Roberts with a degree of disquiet.

The waitress, whilst rudely ogling my Captain, is returning with our breakfast. Setting my plate down in such a manner that one would think I wasn't here, and in the doing, brushing up against him as she sets his plates of food before him. "You have a hearty appetite, Captain."

"That will be all, miss."

The Captain's statement, being delivered in a manner that suggests she return to work, the waitress departs.

"She's impertinent."

Captain Roberts shrugging a wee bit, "Dost thou understand the reference, the one regarding women letting men know."

"If thou art referring to what is meant by subtly letting the other person know they're interested, I'd like to know your definition of throwing oneself."

"Unlike you, fy melys," speaking with a chuckle, "The wench lacks finesse is all."

"Wench? She's a regular Madame du Barry." As I continue to cut up my breakfast, "Imagine, trying to pick up a man when he's with another woman."

Speaking with the hint of a smile, "A lady would not have." Picking up his cup of tea, "After breakfast I shall have Mister Cullen marry us forthwith."

"You mean this morning?"

"Aye," he states firmly.

"I'm afraid there are required timeframes involved, Captain. The bands must be read in our local parish, as well as the parish where we wish to be married for 3 weeks running, or 28 days notice must be given to the Register office before the marriage can take place. Either way provides time for me to shop for a wedding gown."

Telling me in no uncertain terms. "Then we shall buy for thou a goune this daye, Mister Cullen can wave the time, and immediately following dinner wee will be wed." Adding, "That scallywag, Keith, can give thee away."

I can't help but laugh as I reply sarcastically amid a chuckle, "He'll like that!" Having finished my breakfast, I've just been enjoying my coffee, but now, seeing my Captain is all but finished, I call for the waitress. "May we have the check, please?"

Still trying to entice my man as she hands him the cheque, she says, "Yes miss, of course."

"That's my fiancé you're flirting with, deary."

Ne'er looking at the cheque, my Captain takes out forty quid, and hands it to her. "Thank you."

"Thank you, Captain." And putting on her most seductive look, the waitress, blatantly ignoring my objections, adds, "If there's anything else I can do for you, I get off at five."

Being fit to be tied, picking up my glass of water as I stand, I dump it over her head, saying, "I don't think you'll be dry by then, missy!"

Chuckling as we leave the table, the Captain says, "That, fy annwyl, was not lady like."

Replying to him with a slight smile, "A lady knows there's a time and a place for everything, and that, fy Arglwydd, was the proper time for that."

Chuckling a mite, "Shall we return to Mister Cullen's office?" asks the Captain as he offers his arm. "He needs to prepare our Marriage License. Afterwards we shall saunter down the walk to that boutique thou art fond of where, hopefully, thou wilt find a wedding goune to thy liking."

Smiling as I take his arm, "Sounds wonderful. I know it isn't proper, seeing how we're outside on the street, but may I kiss thee anyway?"

Pulling me close to him, my Captain envelopes me within his strong arms, and as he meets my lips with the same eagerness as mine, I melt in his embrace.

Releasing me slowly, "Come, fy Nghariad," and offering his arm once more, we jovially walk back to Mister Cullen's office.

Opening the door, "Mister Cullen," I call out, "Are you here?"

Coming from out of the back room, "Hello, Miss V'lé," and when the Captain comes in, Mister Cullen, jittery as ever, takes a step back.

Glowering at him, Captain Roberts spouts, "Command yourself!"

Trying to do just that, "What can I do for you, Captain?"

"I have a small, yet most important task for you to perform this evening."

"M…m…me?" stammers Mister Cullen.

"Listen up!" says Captain Roberts demandingly, smacking the counter with his hand.

Retreating a mite, "I'm listening, Captain."

"Wee neede you to perform a wedding this evening."

"A wedding. Whose?"

"Ours!"

Quaking in his shoes, whilst looking at us, "I can't."

Jumping when the Captain puts a hand on his shoulder, "Mister Cullen, we know it's an unusual situation, but we want to be married immediately, and we want the ceremony held at *Inn Finistère*."

"But—"

"Please, Mister Cullen, try to understand that Captain Roberts and I love each other, and we may not have much time. You, being a Superintendent Registrar, can create all the official documents necessary."

"Umm," starts Mister Cullen, "what's in it for me?"

Again, restraining my beloved by way of gentle mannerisms, "Calm thyself, Bart."

"Rest assured, Mister Cullen. You will be adequately compensated," states my Captain.

"No Dubloons coins this time, Captain," complains Mister Cullen, "only modern currency, I beseech each you."

"This time, Mister Cullen," Captain Roberts assures him, "I shall pay you in the paper money that is held so dear in this age."

Smiling, "Thou hast some gold coins, fy Arglwydd, like doubloons?"

Glaring at Mister Cullen, still, "Not just some, fy annwyl; the bottom half of my sea chest is layered with Doubloons, Reales, Escudos, and gold Moidores."

It's obvious that Captain Roberts hasn't done any investigating, and therefore, is not aware just how valuable his coinage is, and neither is Mister Cullen, who out of ignorance, must've taken a huge loss when he sold the last ones he was given. It also explains how my Captain purchased the gifts he gave me.

Speaking quietly, "fy Arglwydd?"

"Aye, fy melys."

Asking meekly, hoping his reply will be favorable, "May I have some of them?"

"Take what you like, fy melys, for all that is mine, belongs also to thee."

Being sure the idea that just sprung to mind will please him, "Whilst thou finishes up here I shall shop for thy wedding gift." Walking towards the door. Shall I meet thee at the boutique down the street in, say 3 hours time?"

As the door closes, my Captain replies, "Aye."

Rushing home in a cab to look at the coins, I make an accounting, and having taken one of each to a local coin dealer, I have the cabbie drop me off at Milford Harbour. Locating Mister Baines, a boat merchant, he shows me several pictures of both boats and ships in the harbor, and elsewhere, that are for sale.

My first thought is for something big enough to live on comfortably, but able to be handled by a master mariner and a willing novice.

"There's a newly refitted forty-eight foot sloop available."

"Sounding doubtful, "I think my fiancé has had his fill of Sloops. He prefers square riggers." And as my vision grows, "Besides, a forty-eight footer may be fine for a local pleasure cruise, but it's hardly adequate for adventuring hither, thither, and yon." While thumbing through the pictures in his album, the majority of the boats he has contracted for sale are pretty small, only a few are even yacht size. "Don't you know of a two-masted Schooner for sale, or a Brigantine perhaps."

"A two-masted Schooner requires a crew consisting of one person for each mast, one at the helm, and a fourth to do the other chores, like cooking, which doesn't permit any togetherness time for you and your fiancé, and a Brigantine, would require a sizeable crew; twelve at least. More if you carry a full complement of officers and a physician."

Suddenly I see it. "Wow! Is this beauty in the harbor?" pointing to a three-masted, square-rigger. "She's a Clipper Ship, is she not?"

"Aye, that she is, but such a ship requires a sizeable crew of perhaps 40."

Knowing the Clipper Ship did not come in to being until long after my Captain had died, I know he'll love 'er once he experiences how she'll relish a force 8 gale, as well as her ability to reach speeds of 18 knots. Drooling as I eye the photograph, "Yes, I know, but oh how Captain Roberts would love 'er."

"Bartholomew Roberts?"

"The one and only," says I smiling.

Ecstatic, "If you like, we can pop over and see 'er right now."

"Great!"

En route, Mister Baines explains that she is more or less a reproduction composite of both the Flying Cloud and the Comet; sail plan and luxurious appointments, respectively.

MEANWHILE AT MISTER CULLEN'S OFFICE →

Demandingly, the Captain asks, "Why have you suddenly decided to be so reasonable?"

"Since it's obvious I cannot dissuade either of you, let's just get down to brass tacks."

Unknown to Mister Cullen and Captain Roberts, there's a figure crouched behind the door outside who is rubbing his hands together in glee. "So he's here making wedding arrangements is he, we'll just see about that."

BACK AT THE HARBOR →

Enjoying the tour, "She's beautiful," says I in delight as I walk about on the open deck. Yes, this is the one I want." Turning to the sailboat merchant, "You're sure the owners will accept my payment."

Thinking of the huge commission he will make on the sale, and smiling. "Positive."

"Terrific!" Forgetting we are to dine out this evening, I invite him to *Inn Finistère*. "If you can come for dinner this evening as my guest, I will ask the Captain to choose a bottle of wine from the cellar, during which time I can give you the payment. That way, Captain Roberts will be totally surprised.

"And please, not a word of this to anyone beyond the ship's officers, or Captain Roberts might find out and spoil the surprise."

"Yes, miss, I'll be discreet, and I'll get you a good crew. I am sure there will be no end to men who are eager to sign on."

"Great! Dinner is at 7 p.m. and bring a guest if you wish. In the meantime, can I rely on you to take care of those other matters?"

"Aye, Miss, I'll take care of everything."

Walking down the gangplank and smiling, "I must run now, I have an appointment in Hwlffordd."

Waving, "See you at 7."

Hurrying to the cab, I'm clutching the tote wherein can be found a nicely framed picture of the Clipper ship.

As the cab turns the corner, knowing the boutique is just a little ways down on a charming cobble brick road, I ask the cabbie to let me off just around the corner. As I close the door of the cab, I see my beloved rounding the corner. Waving my hand, I holler, "Here I am, Bart."

Seeing me, he acknowledges with a wave of his hand, and within minutes we meet up just outside the door to the boutique where my forever gracious Captain opens the door. As I walk in, he follows, closing the door behind him.

Within a minute or so, the shop manager greets us at the service counter. "Good morning, Miss, nice to see you again. Good morning, Mister uh—"

"Captain, will suffice."

"Oh yes, of course. I should've guessed. Nice to meet you, Captain Roberts."

Replying with a slight bow, "The pleasure is mine."

Turning her attentions towards me. "What can I do for you today, Miss V'lé?"

Flashing a smile, "I would like to see some wedding gowns."

"You and Captain Roberts, of course." Speaking cheerfully, "Familiar with your tastes, may I show you a few of our period styles?"

"That would be lovely," I says smiling.

"Great! I'll ready the models." Handing us a flier from the counter, "In the meantime, take a look at these."

Sitting on the two wing chairs, the Captain and I speak quietly. "This is too odd. Everyone but us and Mister Cullen seem to know more about your situation than we do."

"Aye, fy melys, 'tis most disquieting, but let us not think of it now. I am sure we will be inform'd when they want us to know."

"They? Who are they?"

Speaking seriously, "McClure for one. I have onely suspicions about the other."

"Wouldst thou care to share thy suspicions with me?"

Wanting to keep his feeling of dread to himself, he replies, "Nay, fy melys, not yet."

"Alright, but only because I trust thee implicitly."

"Diolch 'chi, V'lé. Thy faith and trust mean a great deal to me."

With the manager of the boutique returning, we give her our full attention.

Little Haven, sometime later ⌐

Katie and Sue, having just arrived in the small car park adjacent to the walk, see us. "There they are, madam," states Katie.

With an anxious quiver, Sue asks, "Where?"

Pointing, Katie replies, "There, near the water's edge."

Relieved to find us, Katie helps my mom traverse the uneven walkway.

"V'lé, Captain, is everything all right?"

"We're fine, mom. We've just been pondering all that's happened of late."

Both my mother and Katie can see the anguish displayed in my Captain's face, and in an effort to try and change the moods of both the Captain and myself, Katie declares, "You must have faith! I believe it is the love you two have for one another that has created this miracle, and," smiling at both of us, "I know the two of you will be forever happy."

> *From behind the cliffs, the foursome was being observed by a man whose face, darkened at the sight of their merriment, rejoices in the knowing that the next 2 phases of his comedy are about to be skillfully set in motion by his unscrupulous henchman.*

Getting in the car, Katie drives us home, but seeing Keith parked none too far from *Inn Finistère*, mine eyes narrow. "Stop, Katie," says I, commandingly. "I want a few words with Mister McClure, alone."

When the car comes to a stop, I get out. "Take Miss V'lé and Mrs Montgomery up to the house and get them inside."

Understanding his meaning, Katie replies, "Yes, Captain."

Noting the concerned look on my intended's face, I kiss her lightly on the forehead. "I shan't be long."

Cautioning me, V'lé states, "Please be careful, for I believe Keith to be dangerous."

"All shall be well, I promise," and standing back from the car, "Go along now, Katie." and closing the door, Katie drives off.

Stepping out of the car and onto the walk, Katie, noticing I am angst-ridden, puts her arm around my shoulders, and as she adamantly nudges me towards the house, she reminds me, amid my effort to twist my head around, "Captain Roberts' charged me with getting all of us into the house."

As the distance between them continues to close, my mom, sensing my fear, and as they usher me indoors, says, "Come on, V'lé, Captain Roberts can take care of himself."

When Keith and I come face to face, his insolence is obvious. "You want a word with me, I take it," states Keith brusquely as he meets my cold gaze.

"More than just a word, McClure," placing my left foot atop the rather large rock; resting my left hand on my knee. "You are no gentleman, nor are you welcome in our home. Your rather bizarre call on the church, and the chicanery entangled throughout your past is despicable; what's more, the recollections awakened within my betrothed since your arrivall hath afforded her much suffering. A person of your ilk is not fit to be in the company of a lady, and altho' I knows not the full purpose for your presence, I suggest you depart Wales forthwith."

To my surprise, Keith simply laughs. "Despite the fact that I do not know what you're saying half the time, I understand your meaning perfectly, and although I'm not a gentleman, I am alive, while you haven't been until a couple days ago, but don't let that fool you. I'll tell you this much, your time among the living is short." Seeing fierce anger come over my face, Keith adds, "Before you spout again, pirate, let me inform you of this. I intend to win this battle, and as for my 'bizarre calls and chicanery,' you're right again. And after you're back among the dead, despite her loathing, it will be me, as she pines for you, who'll fulfill the sexual emptiness that will overpower the woman you love."

Without forethought, I backhand Keith whilst shouting, "You miserable wretch!"

Feeling the corner of his mouth, Keith wipes away the blood. "Careful Captain," taunts Keith, "If you kill me in your present state, it won't speak well for your soul when you return to your watery grave."

"You be a poor excuse for a man, not fit to wipe the mud from her shoes; furthermore, be I dead or alive, Miss V'lé and I shall marry, and even if I were to cease living this daye, and am forced to whence I came a yeere ago, she will not onely don widow weeds, she will wait for me, as I for her, and when that daye comes, wee shall at last be together."

"I wouldn't count on it, Captain."

As I turn to leave, Mister McClure states, "See you at the Lord Nelson hotel at 7 o'clock."

Trudging back to *Inn Finistère*, McClure, not onely admitting he was the man at the church, but also that he knew in advance of my becoming mortal, has provided me with a few answers, but even so, there is much I neede to find out.

Walking across the street to the stone patio that lyes above the steps leading down to the beach, needing to bethink, I am reminded by the freshening breeze of my dayes at sea. Such, however, 'twas a fleeting moment, for as much as I'd rather recall happier times, and those still to come, my mind is packed to the gunwales with who and why anyone would wish me harm after all these yeeres, and considering the possibility of my woman being used as a cat's-paw, gives me cause to fear for her safety.

As the Captain stared out to sea, the need for his woman so dominated his subconscious mind that, as if hearing him call to her, V'lé darted out the front door. Seeing her approach, he could only wonder if it was a vestige of his ghostly renderings that brought her running, or if their love had, in some ways, joined them together as one.

BLOOD and SWASH, The Unvarnished Life (& afterlife) Story of Pirate Captain, Bartholomew Roberts.........pt.1 "BOLT OF FRUITION"

AT MISTER CULLEN'S SHOPPE ⇁

After entering Mister Cullen's small haberdashery tucked in amongst the businesses not far from *Inn Finistère,* Keith casually strolls around examining the collection of books within his office, while idly jingling coins in his pocket, when suddenly, he flips a wad of £50 notes onto the desk.

Eyeing the crisp new bills, Mister Cullen's greedy eyes grow wide. "If you're attempting to get my attention, Mister McClure, you've succeeded."

Noticing V'lé and Captain Roberts walking along the ridge, Keith, pretending to act casual, "I suppose you perform lots of weddings, being a sort of Justice of the Peace."

His greedy eyes trained on the pile of dosh, Mister Cullen replies, "Most couples have a church wedding."

Speaking quite frankly to Mister Cullen as he casually walks in front of his desk, "A great many wealthy and influential people would be interested in the wedding of, shall we say a well-known innkeeper and a certain other famous person residing in this burg, or should I have said infamous!" Keith's eyes, grow dark as he places his hands on the desk, and bending down low enough to come eye to eye with Mister Cullen, "That is of course if an announcement of such a wedding was released to the papers and television."

Stuttering, "I...I, I'm sure I don't know what you mean."

Standing erect and placing his hands behind his back, being careful not to look at Mister Cullen, Keith resumes his pacing to and fro. Stopping short, Keith spins around, and again looking into Mister Cullen's beady little eyes, "I wonder just how much people would pay to find out the specifics."

Leaning firmly against the back of his chair, his voice quivering. "They're in love; what more is there to know? The whole village has known for months, but seeing that Captain Roberts was, that is to say, he being only a—" Suddenly, realizing what he was about to say, Mister Cullen, held his tongue.

"A ghost, Mister Cullen, you can say it. Such would be the wedding of the ages. Why there's millions just waiting to roll in."

MEANWHILE AT INN FINISTÈRE ⇁

As depicted by his body language as we stroll, the woe engulfing my Captain is evident. "What is it?"

My strong protector, exhaling deeply. "My mind is cluttered with the events of the past few days: myself becoming mortal, McClure's sudden appearance, the townspeople knowing before we knew ourselves. 'Tis chilling," says he. Stopping, he embraces me, and whilst rubbing his cheek against my hair while feeling the need in his body grow both warm and taut, "Thy love is my salvation, yet still my mind is preoccupied, for I am at a loss to discern Keith's true motivation."

"I don't know what is, fy Arglwydd, but surely jealousy can't be Keith's motive."

"I believe it is. McClure's motive, anyways. He believes my present state is short-lived, he said as much, and in that belief, he's convinced thou wilt prefer him to a mere spirit."

"He's just trying to Gaslight thee. Pay him no mind." Stopping to rethink, "What do you mean, McClure's motive?"

" That thought is mere speculation." Grabbing me gently, he looks deep in to my sapphire blue eyes, "I told him thee would marry me even should I return to a ghostly state, does that hold true?"

"You know it does. "I love only you, and I want only you. I always will. To be apart from you is death of my heart; of my soul. We were meant to be together, fy Arglwydd, Nghapten, and thus, we must have faith to that end, but if by chance thou dost return to a ghostly state, our lives shall simply return to the way they were, for in that too, we found completeness, but if that too is taken from us, I shall don a black veil until the day comes that I too am laid to rest, and on the day we will at last be together; just on a different plain of existence, is all."

"For a few minutes I was unsure, but I knows now that we shall be together always, whether in this lifetime or the next, for all eternity."

Kissing him, I echo his last statement. "You and I, together for all eternity."

Reminiscing, my Captain quietly says, "I wish we could sail off into the sunset, ne'er to return."

Noting a bit of sadness within his eyes, I reply softly, "Perhaps one day we shall."

"The world is full of splendour, fy Melys, and the sea, for the most part, is a wonderful place."

"I would love to sail with thee, but once I am aboard a tall ship, thee might have to drag me, kicking and screaming, to get me off again."

"Then, should we become so fortunate as to owne a ship, I shan't ever force thee from her, but for now," holding me tightly, " 'tis that scallywag, McClure we must concentrate on."

"What dost thou suggest we do next, fy Arglwydd, Nghapten?"

"I suggest we head upstairs to change or wee shall be late."

As he places his arm around my shoulders, snuggling me close for a moment, just relishing the contact, I says, "I don't want to go to his dinner tonight; must we go?"

Gently moving the wispy hairs from my face, "Both thy mother and Katie are looking forward to the evening out. 'Twould be unfair of you to disappoint them. Now upstairs with you and change thy frock, for I wish not to be late."

When the Captain goes topside to change, I make a quick call to the harbormaster asking him to meet me at the Lord Nelson, covertly, for dinner, to which he agrees.

Chapter Ten

One Too Many

Approaching the front doors of the Lord Nelson, "Ah, Mister McClure, so nice to see you, here that is," states Captain Roberts, reservedly.

Smiling, Sue quips, "And wasn't it a lovely day."

Replying to Sue, "Yes, but…" looking at me, "I had hoped to spend most of it with V'lé." After which, focusing on Captain Roberts, Keith adds, through gritted teeth, "but you spirited her away, again."

" 'Twas hardly that dramatic, Mister McClure."

"Shall we go in now," asks Sue, "it's a bit chilly out here for me."

"Shouldn't we wait for Mister Cullen to arrive," asks Katie?

"He's already inside," states Keith. "When I saw him last, he was enjoying a before dinner cocktail."

Distressed by his appearance, "I have no objection to Westerner clothes, Keith, but must it appear as if you just came off a roundup?"

"Just because Captain Roberts is dressed in fancy duds doesn't mean I have to be."

"Captain Roberts' attentiveness in regard to personal grooming suits me perfectly, but that being set aside, I would like to point out that this is not a fast food joint, but a fine restaurant, and everyone here is dressed appropriately except you."

"You call that late nineteen century gown appropriate?"

"Yes I do, because it's not the era we are discussing, but the locale and time of day, and in this instance, etiquette maintains that formal attire is obligatory after 5.

In the mist of criticism, Keith, ignoring my comment, catches me off guard, and taking me by the arm, escorts me into the restaurant. "Come, Vamp, Mister Cullen is waiting, and since the appetizers have already been ordered, we wouldn't want him to get too much of a head start, now would we."

Not wanting to create a scene, I refrain from making a fuss. Even so, as I twist my neck, it's evident my Captain is annoyed, but in keeping with propriety, he banks his irritation, and whilst being careful to keep Keith within his view, he offers an arm to both my mom and Katie, escorting both of them to our table.

Approaching our table and seeing that Peter Cullen looks like he's been in a fight, I am taken aback, and giving Keith an accusing look, I dash to where he is seated. "What happened, Mister Cullen?"

"I fell," he says, grumbling, taking another gulp of his drink.

"Off what," ask Sues, "the back of a moving truck?"

"The poor man, he told me he has a terrible headache," begins Keith whilst trying to look innocent, "but knowing we were all looking forward to this little get together, he forced himself to come."

Glancing at his adversary, Keith's cold, narrowing eyes return to a seemingly concerned expression as he looks at Mister Cullen again. "Would you care for another cocktail, Peter? In fact, let's all have one."

"By all means," states Mister Cullen, swaying somewhat in his seat, "fill 'er up."

Seeing that Mister Cullen has already had at least one too many, Katie, rather disapprovingly, states, "Must be a particularly good year for scotch."

"Your behavioral attributes, Mister McClure, are deplorable to say the least," remarks Captain Roberts.

"What are you talking about?"

"First your actions concerning, Miss V'lé outside, and now wee find Mister Cullen inebriated."

"Just being a good host, Captain." Moving on, "Sue," pulling out her chair, "you're here, across from Mister Cullen." Walking to the opposite side of the table and pulling out my chair, "You're here, Vamp, diagonally from your mom, and Katie, you're next to Sue.

Taking her seat whilst Captain Roberts holds it for her, Katie utters, Thank you, Captain."

Irritated as I take my seat, I spout, "Don't call me Vamp."

Ignoring me, Keith, whilst taking the seat next to mine, "Being the only seat left, it must be yours, Captain, but never fret, you and your fiancée can ogle each other and play footsies all through dinner."

I can't think of anything nicer than ogling my Captain whilst playing footies," and as I say it, I stretch my leg up to my Captain's, and as I stroke it with my foot, my Captain gives me a look, after which I say, "Yee Haw, " and bust up laughing.

Having flagged the waiter to bring the appetizers, Keith argues, "On the subject of manners, you're hardly in a position to criticize, Captain, considering your, shall we say, rather colorful history."

Despite his efforts not to glare at Keith, "What part of my history would you be referring?"

"Oh, I think you know, Captain."

While the waiter sets the large tray containing a variety of tempting morsels in the center of the table.

The cocktail waitress, seeing we have all taken our seats, comes over. Speaking to me first, "May I bring you something from the bar this evening, miss?"

Before I have a chance to reply, Keith jumps in. "The lady will have Sambucka, straight up in a snifter." Gesturing towards Peter Cullen, "Another Scotch for my friend, as for myself, I'll have another Brandy."

"Very good, sir," states the waitress as she turns towards my mom.

"I'll have a Mudslide," replies Sue without hesitation.

"A Perfect Rob Roy for me," Katie says with a smile.

"I know you're basically a teetotal like Vamp, Captain, but seeing she's having a drop, will you not join me in a Brandy?"

"Aye, Mister McClure," speaking with a modest smile, "I think I will."

"An excellent choice, Captain," states the waitress, giving him the once over.

The waiter, still at the table, begins with Katie.

Having a large appetite, "I'll have the roast duck, mixed greens, and a cup of tea."

My mom being next, "Madam?"

"Your Mixed Grill sounds good, both a Caesar salad and a bowl of clam chowder, a jacket potato with sour cream and chives, and coffee. I'd like my coffee before my meal."

"Yes, madam."

Speaking to me, the waiters asks, "And you, miss?"

"I'll have the surf and turf, and hold the mushrooms. I'll also have a jacket potato with sour cream, a Caesar salad, half a lemon, and coffee, but with my meal."

Speaking to Keith, "And you, sir?"

"What's a jacket potato?"

"Crike!" Speaking a mite condescendingly, I answer his question. "It's a baked potato."

Speaking to the waiter, Keith says, "Bring me the T-Bone, a large plate of steak fries, onion rings, and a chef's salad with sliced cucumbers."

"Anything to drink?"

"Yes," replies Keith. "If ya'll have Guinness on tap, I'll have that."

"Very good, sir."

Turning to Captain Roberts, "And you, sir?"

"I would be pleased to have your fisherman's feast, 2 lamb chops with crushed mint leaves, the mixed bean salad, fried laverbread, and a dish of assorted fresh fruits."

"And to drink?"

"A pot of Black Bohea tea."

And lastly, the waiter asks Mister Cullen, "And what will you have, sir?"

"I'll—" hiccup. "I'll have the rainbow trout. You choose the sides."

"Yes, sir."

As the waiter departs, the cocktail waitress, returning, again makes eyes at my intended. Paying the waitress, Mister Cullen raises his glass, and with a rather silly grin, spurts out, "To the living and the dead, may we all get what we deserve!" and hiccups.

"Good grief," states Katie, "He's sloshed!"

Katie, being perceptive, notices that despite Keith's constant disruptions, the Captain and I keep almost constant eye contact, an aspect that infuriates Keith. Knowing that someone needs to cut through some of the tension, Katie smiles, saying, "Well, I think I'll go wash up before dinner."

Being quick minded, Katie, having just given Captain Roberts the opportunity he had hoped for, stands, as a well-bred man does, which prompts Keith to do the same; furthermore, my Captain swiftly walks behind Katie's chair and pulls it out as she rises.

"Thank you, Captain," says Katie, smiling. "Will you care to accompany me, Miss?"

Seeing the harbormaster, "Yes, Katie, I will."

"Mom?"

"Having a wet nap, and this group needing a referee, I think it would be better if I stay."

As I rise from the table, Keith pulls out my chair. "Thank you." Addressing my Captain, "If'in the waiter returns, wilt thou have him refill my coffee cup?"

"With pleasure, fy Melys."

MEANWHILE ⇁

En route to the lady's room, as I make a detour to the table where the harbormaster, and whom I assume is his wife, are seated. "I'll join you presently, Katie."

"Very good, miss," and continues on her way.

Doing his best to make our meeting appear fortuitous, "Good evening, Miss V'lé. Nice to see you again."

"And you, Mister Baines."

"This is my wife, Brianna."

Offering her hand, "Nice to meet you."

Shaking her hand gently, "And you, Mrs Baines."

Setting my shoulder bag on the table, I reveal a heavy wood chest containing some €300,000 in gold coin, and 5 leather pokes.

From within his inside coat pocket, he takes out the envelope containing the bill of sale and the Ship's Papers, and showing them to me, I smile whilst saying, "Awesome!"

Opening the chest, his face is alit by the 100 antique coins: Reales, Escudos, and Moidores, all in like new condition.

"What's in the leather pouches?"

"5 pounds gold dust each; and for the other matter, here's 60 quid, and my thanks."

Knowing that I am referring to him having to meet me here for dinner, "'Tisn't necessary, Miss."

"I insist." Dashing off, "I must hurry or Katie will begin to wonder what's keeping me."

As I join Katie, she asks, "Everything alright, Miss."

"Just fine. I just stopped for a minute to say hello to some friends."

Returning to our table, Captain Roberts rises from his chair, an action followed by Keith, who, not wanting to look like a bumpkin, stands as well.

Captain Roberts, standing behind his chair, "Methinks, thou wouldst be more comfortable here, fy annwyl, being left handed."

Amid a smile, I reply, "Much." As I sit down, "Anything interesting happen while I was gone?"

"Same old, same old," jibes Sue.

Observing that Keith looks a bit peeved as he holds what was my chair for Katie, Captain Roberts says, "Surely, this being our wedding night, you wouldst not deny me the pleasure of sitting beside my intended."

> *Time flew by as the hors d'oeuvres were consumed, & despite Captain Roberts, with his gilt edged vocabulary, trading his well-cultured insults with Keith's vacuous remarks, the meal, thus far, was a welcomed one.*

Katie, who can't believe the whole conversation, spouts, "If the two of you don't like one another, why talk to each other at all?"

Smiling at my good friend, "That's what I said a couple nights ago."

"To be frank," spouts Sue, "I think that Captain Roberts would've preferred to dine with V'lé's ex husband."

"Which one," asks Katie.

"Her first," replies Sue. "Being in close proximity to Mark, well… let's just say, that for V'lé, the temptation to dispatch him would be too great."

Mister Cullen; on the other hand, delighted to see the Captain sparring with someone else for a change, listens happily as he shovels in the free meal while Keith, seeing to it that he drinks his way to oblivion, plays the role of a debonair host by way of keeping his glass full.

"At last, dinner is served," states Keith.

"Considering the wonderful conversation, I'm surprised I have an appetite," states Sue, sarcastically.

"You know Keith," deciding to put him in his place. "Since it's apparent that you know exactly who Captain Roberts is, I'm surprised you're here at all. As for his colorful past, as you termed it earlier, Captain Roberts is a master mariner, whose remarkable accomplishments and navigational feats are well documented."

"Accomplishments!" rebukes Keith, slugging back his drink, "Is that how you sum up almost four years of terror on the high seas?" Slamming his glass back onto the table, "Really woman, this man, so revered by you, was a bloodthirsty Pirate, and nothing more!"

Amid a rather tumultuous reaction, "If that's all you see, Keith, then you know nothing about his life, nor the reasoning that was his motivation."

" 'Tis be true, what he said, fy annwyl. I was a pyrate."

Spouting with a deliberate tone, "That's only a half truth, fy Nghapten," and as I leap to my Captain's defense, as I have often done, "I think it's about time Keith knew more about you."

> *Captain Roberts wasn't sure what his lady was planning to say, but her tone was serious, & knowing the only way to prevent her would be to drag her out bodily, he instead, listened with bated interest.*

As I begin with one of my well-known history lessons, not realizing that those sitting at nearby tables are also listening, "You're quite right, Keith, this is the famous pirate captain, Bartholomew Roberts, some say the most lethal, but that aside, he was definitely the most successful." After a moments pause, "Following, Queen Anne's War, after his brief association with Edward England, another pirate captain, that took place whilst Bart was first mate on board the merchant, *Terrible*, the crews having gone their separate ways, and none too pleased with the prospect of returning to his ancestral home, he, instead, despite his aversion to slavery, signed on board the Guineamen, *Princess*, shortly before she sailed out of London. As 3rd mate, his chief duty was that of ship's navigator, and such, 4th in command. When the *Princess* fell victim to the well-known, Welsh pirate, Hywel Davies in February 1719, Bart, being an intelligent man, was more than a little tired of the poverty and strife that plagued the time in which he lived, and thus, being 'twas not the first time a ship he was serving on had fallen prey to pirates, this officer and gentleman, whose intelligence, cunning, bravery, as well as brilliant navigational skills and uncanny understanding of the sea, being decidedly appreciated by Davies and his crew, eventually joined their ranks, but such was not until after Captain Davies was ambushed and killed, which occurred a mere 6 weeks after being aboard the *Rover*; furthermore, this change took place whilst Bart was acting Captain, an appointment that was made by Davies before he went ashore. With the death of Captain Davies, coupled with both the onslaught by both the shore battery and temperamental weather, the very existence of the ship and her crew was at risk, but fear not, for the illustrious newcomers intuitive perception, and fast action, saving both ship and crew from capture and death on the gallows, found himself duly elected the new Captain of the heavily armed, 3-masted Sloop-Of-War, and thus was born a great chapter in the annals of maritime history." Taking a bite of my dinner, I continue to regale both those in my company, and the captivated patrons within earshot. "Already creating considerable havoc, 'twas but a few weeks later that his well-known hatred for those of Barbados was born, and about 2 months more is when, Captain Roberts and his crew happened upon a fleet of 42 Portuguese treasure ships supposedly under the protection of two 70-gun, Ships-of-the-Line, but did the relatively new Pirate Captain sneak off in the dark as suggested by his crew? No, he did not. This magnificent seaman, assuring his crew that sheer nerve, along with the element of surprise and ingenuity would see them through, sailed right into Baía de Todos os Santos, bold as brass, and in the first of a string of daring exploits against insurmountable odds, Captain Roberts, after acquiring the intelligence needed, sailed alongside the heaviest laden ship, *Sagrada Família*, fired a full broadside, and before the smoke had cleared, the treasure ship was boarded, captured, and heading for the open sea. The booty, valued at more than 2 1/2 million pounds sterling by today's standards, included 40,000 gold Moidores, and the famous diamond studded gold cross, intended for John V, king of Portugal, which, as you can see, is still in Captain Roberts' possession.

"That's quite a story, Vamp," Keith says, "but it only confirms the fact that you're in love with a pirate."

"That be very true, Mister McClure," Captain Roberts had to agree, "but pyracy was onely a part of a much larger picture."

Returning to our table, the waiter enquires, "Would anyone care for dessert?"

"This brandy Captain," begins Keith, "is quite interesting poured over French vanilla ice cream."

"My intended will be pleased to have an orange sorbet frappe with a soupçon of triple sec drizzled atop a dollop of thick cream. For myself, I shall have French vanilla ice cream served as Mister McClure has suggested, and see to it he gets the same."

"Why not add some cherries, Captain, and set it on fire," suggests Katie.

"That would be Cherries Jubilee, madam," injects the waiter.

"Sounds enticing," states Captain Roberts. "Have you cherries?"

"Yes, sir."

"Then Cherries Jubilee it shall be, for both myself and Mister McClure."

Turning as he speaks to Sue, "And you, madam?"

Looking at the menu, "I'll have a banana split with oodles of nuts and extra cherries."

Looking at Katie. "And you, madam?"

Mulling over the many choices, "I'll have an apple tart à la mode topped with melted caramels."

And lastly, looking at Mister Cullen, who is resting his head on his hand, "I think I'll have a dish of ice cream filled profiteroles drizzled with caramel sauce."

When the waiter departs, I continue my rhetoric with a smile. "What you do not know, Keith, is that Captain Roberts also freed hundreds of slaves, as well as a dispenser of justice, especially in regard to seeing to it that the officers aboard the captured ships who treated underlings cruelly were repaid in kind."

"I see, like my childhood hero Robin Hood and his Band of Merry Men."

"Although it looks the same at a distance, the force that drove them was very different."

"What do you mean?"

"Whilst your hero's motivation was a fight against tyranny, Captain Roberts went much deeper. To state it as plainly as possible, Bart was tired of being passed over simply because he was not highborn, and despite the fact that Bart's father was a landowner (which was no small thing in his day,) and that his family had always held positions of prominence in the church, as well as their vast tract of land having several rent bearing dwellings, they were more in keeping with a Country Squire, than that of the then Landed Gentry class."

"Meaning they were middle class," states Keith.

"His family was near the top end of middle class society, but such hardly qualified him in the realm of advancement, and knowing that he would never achieve a captaincy, despite his own personal achievements, Bart wanted to show their High and Mightinesses just how wrong they were in their thinking, and he did so brilliantly!"

"Somehow I doubt the government saw his side of it," states Keith.

"They never do," replies Sue.

Continuing, "Bart's feelings went deeper still. Rising from the rank of Ship's Boy, he knew the sufferings the common seaman endured, such as rotten food, harsh treatment, and unspeakable punishment, and such, he was known to ask the crews of the ship's he captured how they were treated, and if they were treated poorly, he enquired as to which of the officers were the offenders, and those deserving of his wrath, were punished accordingly, and for the purpose of providing both a measure of satisfaction and recompense, such was dealt out in front of those who had been abused. From the officer's point of view, this made Bart a holy terror." Looking at my Captain, "Would you agree that I stated thy feelings, and the events correctly?"

"Aye."

"And to make a point regarding men being forced," states Captain Roberts, " 'Twas the Navy who was for pressing men into service. Captain Kidd himself had complained bitterly when a Naval Captain literally shanghaied 30 of his officers and crew, and did so out of spite. Left willfully under-manned, Kidd, was forced to take on a number of hardened criminals to make up for the loss."[W2 & B2 pg 11]

"I have to admit," states Keith, "that the times and events justified the means. By the way, Captain, how did you like the brandy?"

" 'Twas excellent," pronounces Captain Roberts as he gazes upon his woman, whose defensive posture regarding his days as a pirate serves well to further stimulate his needs as a man.

When the waiter brings our desserts, Keith requests, "Be good enough to send the cocktail waitress back over."

"Yes, sir."

"Care for another, Captain?" asks Keith.

Knowing he's not use to spirits, Sue spouts, "I do believe you're trying to get our good Captain drunk."

"Not so," states Keith, taking a sip of his brandy. "My only intention is to be a good host."

"It matters not, Mrs Montgomery," states the Captain, "for 'tis tea I prefer."

"Among Captain Roberts' piratical escapades, Miss, which is your favourite," asks Katie? Taking a sip of my frappe, "I'd have to say Trepassey."

Smiling, Katie urges me on. "Tell us about it."

"Well, after Captain Roberts picked up the 13 English seamen who had been marooned on the isle of Dominico by the French Guard de la Coste, Bart and his crew sailed more than 1,000 nautical leagues to Newfoundland to procure justice. When he was near, this daring seaman, in a brilliant use of psychological warfare, sent a message announcing not only that he was coming, but wished to be greeted, and when the *Fortune* sailed in to

Trepassey Bay in a tattered sloop with only 10 guns and a scant 60 men, with drums beating and trumpets sounding, every able-bodied man, despite the fort being fortified with 40 pieces of cannon, deserted their posts, as did the 1,200 sailors aboard some 22 armed vessels, that jumped ship, including Admiral Babidge, who, by the way, was first to abandon his ship, ne'er firing a shot."

"The Captain loves music," injects Katie, smiling.

Continuing, "Captain Roberts, so infuriated by their cowardice, stayed for a fortnight, and when the *Fortune's* crew was not on duty, they enjoyed the town's hospitalities."

"I'll just bet they did," scoffed Keith, adding, "raping, pillaging, and committing acts of mayhem no doubt, with your illustrious Captain leading the festivities."

"He did no such thing," I said crossly. "He never even went ashore there, but upon his departure, as further punishment, this time impudence and cowardice being their crimes, he laid waste to all within the range of his guns: the harbor, the town, the fishing boats, and vessels, with the exception of a particular French brigantine, which he kept for himself; what's more, when they came upon 9 or 10 more French ships when leaving, they sank or otherwise destroyed all but a 26 gun, 3-masted oar ship,[1] which, reminding him of his first command, he kept, and being generous, the newly acquired brigantine was left behind."

"And these acts of destruction," suggests Keith," they are the attractant that stimulates you?"

"Not the deeds, Keith, for they would mean nothing if I were not attracted to the man behind them." Retaking my seat and taking a sip of my Sambucka, I whisper to my Captain, "What a pity I wasn't there to make thy nights as exciting as were the days."

Smiling slightly, "Never fear, fy annwyl," replies Captain Roberts quietly, "that victory we shall celebrate tonight."

After acknowledging his bedroom eyes with my own inviting smile, I turn to Keith, and in a snappish tone, "And you have the unmitigated gall to come in to his home and accost his woman. The only reason Captain Roberts has not cut out your gizzard and fried it for his lunch is because I pleaded with him not to; not because the idea doesn't appeal to me, but rather to keep him from going to jail for murder."

"You really do need to learn to control your enthusiasm, Vamp, or Captain Roberts will use it to his advantage."

"Meaning what!"

"Just what I said."

"Captain Roberts is a gentleman. Ne'er would he use or abuse the affections of a woman. It may interest you to know that his sixth article," turning to my Captain, "thou wilt excuse me for paraphrasing."

Captain Roberts nods yes, while smiling slightly.

Turning back to Keith. "Within the sixth article was a clause proclaiming death to any man who took a woman against her will."

"Rah, Rah for the good Captain," states Mister Cullen.

"You give him too much credit, Vamp," continues Keith.

---

[1] Renamed *Royal Rover*.

"If anything, I don't give him his due, " says I, seriously.

"You'll see, Vamp, in time he'll become so conceited you won't be able to stand him."

"Captain Roberts did not achieve his success from thinking he was great, but by way of cunning, valor and intelligence. And stop calling me Vamp."

In an effort to change the subject, Katie, in a lively tone, "You sure have had some exciting adventures, Captain."

But Keith effectively thwarts her attempt. "I find it hard to understand how a religious moralist can also be a pirate."

"That's because you don't understand the times, Keith," states Sue, "and until you do, you can't begin to understand the answer, much less the man, but I will say this much, Captain Roberts was not merely a great pirate, and to compare him thus is to call Robin Hood a thief, because his plundering was not for the sake of piracy, but rather a means to fund the honorable state of vigilantism, pay his men, and of course repay those who denied him his due, and in that regard, when it came to not getting mad, but even, I'd have to say Captain Roberts was, and is, without peers."

Speaking to Captain Roberts, Katie says, "I seem to recall someone online calling you Captain Nice."

"Oooo—" I cooed, smiling broadly, "What a lovely thing to say, but it's true, and except for those who earned his contempt, Captain Roberts was well known for being polite and mannerly to everyone."

Paying no heed to my request, "Somehow I knew you'd react that way, Vamp. Your desire to live with Captain Roberts, and wishing you were in his time is quite obvious," states Keith in a jealous tone, "and I'm sure those little niceties, adds to fuel your desires."

"You know, Keith," states Sue as she slowly stirs her mudslide with a straw, "seeing how you're the one who's always bringing up the topic, it's you who are preoccupied with sex, not V'lé."

"How true," says I while displaying a lustful smile in the direction of my Captain.

"Do you deny wanting to sleep with him?"

"It's not sleep that I crave when—"

Protesting, Captain Roberts, slapping the table hard, shouts, "Enough! You, McClure, have the mind of a pig."

As for myself, "I beg forgiveness, fy Arglwydd Nghapten."

"That's some relationship you two have, Captain. If I had done that, V'lé would of told me where to get off, yet from you, she begs forgiveness. Isn't love wonderful."

"How would you know!" states Sue sarcastically.

"I respect his wishes, Keith." Changing the subject, I look at Mister Cullen, and noting his condition, I scoff at him. "You're suppose to marry us tonight."

Gulping his drink, he hiccups, saying, "Dearly belov—"

Slouching more and more, we're all watching as his head slowly comes to rest on the table.

"Peter!" Getting to my feet, I begin shaking him, but he's dead drunk. "Oh, that's all!"

Keith, getting up, walks over to Mister Cullen's chair, "It looks as if he can't hold his liquor." Lifting his head up off the table by the back of his hair to look at his face, Keith, dropping his head back down on the table, states, "Yup, he's out." Wearing a wicked smile, "What a shame. It looks as if you two lovebirds will have to wait to get married."

"You're insufferable, Keith!"

"I was just being a good host by keeping his glass full," replies Keith with a smirk. "He's the one chugging, not me."

"Not I," states Sue, correcting him.

"Ok, so I'm not as gifted with good English as you, but that's not what generally impresses a woman."

"If you're referring to wealth, refinement, and sexual prowess, you sorely missed the boat there also!"

Katie, together with Sue, laugh a mite.

"Looks like you finally found the prize package you've always wanted, Vamp; a wealthy man who is no doubt good in the sack, but one hell of a scoundrel to boot."

" 'Tis you who are the scoundrel, Keith, not he. As for Captain Roberts being a renown pirate, 'altho I can not deny his daring exploits enhance my desires, they are hardly the cause of them. As for being wealthy, Captain Roberts is rich in all the qualities that make a good man, in his case a great man; just the same, it was the good man I fell in love with. The rest is all just gravy." After a brief pause, "I feel sorry for you Keith, you see only the pirate, not the man." As he dislikes public displays of affection, I lean towards my Captain, and taking some of his necklace in my hand, I kiss it, and whispering in his ear, "If'in thou thinks my mom and Katie have had enough socializing, may we go home now?"

Returning my affection by kissing my hand, my Captain stands. "On behalf of all of us, Mister McClure, we thank you for the sumptuous meal, but it's time we were getting back to *Inn Finistère*." Grabbing my cloak, shrugging off Keith's hands when he tries to assist, I throw it about my shoulders while my Captain helps my mother out of her chair.

Katie, having helped my mom with her wrap, both of whom want a cigarette before leaving, make their way to the door.

Placing an gold Sovereign into the hand of our Waiter, and another onto the Waitress' tray, as I depart, Keith, sneering at Captain Roberts, states, "A private word with you, Roberts."

"Go along, fy annwyl, I shall take a hack back to the Gwesty."

Complying with his wishes, I get into the car, whilst saying, "If you want to knock his block off, be my guest."

On the way home, not a word is uttered, and after pulling up in front of *Inn Finistère*, I shut off the motor, where for several moments, we all sit in silence.

Opening the car door, my mom speaks first. "I'm sorry that your wedding has been postponed, but I'm sure all will go well tomorrow."

"So am I," adds Katie, shutting the door after stepping out. "Frankly, I don't see why you ever allowed that popinjay on your property."

While the three of us walk up the path leading to the verandah, I explain briefly. "The Captain believes Keith is somehow involved in his resurgence, and since that's all I know, ya'll go inside and get warm."

Taking a seat on the porch swing, "I'll be along in a few minutes." Not that I need to worry, because if anyone can take care of himself, Captain Roberts can, however, as his past has proved already, he cannot deflect a bullet, and thus I wait patiently until sleep overtakes me.

A short time later, I am awakened by the sound of an approaching car. As I sit up, I see what appears to be a cab turning off the main road.

Katie, also hearing a car coming, rushes out onto the verandah and sits down beside me. "Your mum, being tired, has retired for the evening."

"Thank you, Katie." Seeing my Captain step out of the cab, I run to greet him. "Did you find out what Keith hoped to gain by delaying our wedding?"

"By demonstrating that he can prevent our marriage, he believes he hath atchieved some sort of victory. In his mind, being unwed equates still available."

"I may be unmarried, but I'm hardly available. In either case, Keith may act as if he loves me, but I feel that it's more likely that he needs me for something. During those weeks that did qualify, vaguely, as a relationship, he stood me up twice, spent most of his free time with friends, expected me to wait on him hand and foot, strewn his clothes around like a slob, ate me out of house and home, and contributed nothing.

"Katie, you don't believe Keith really wants me, do you?"

"Well, he has done everything he can dream up to make the Captain look bad in your eyes, Miss."

"Thank you, Katie, for your honest reply."

"Well, you two, I'll be turning in now," and going indoors, she leaves us alone.

Suddenly occurring to him, "That's it!"

"What's it?" asks I.

"What thou said about Keith wanting thee for some reason other than love. It's not thee, per se, that he wants."

"I don't understand?"

"Something that crossed my mind earlier today. With no offence intended, I believe he's using thee as a cat's-paw."

After strolling along, neither one of us speaking for several minutes, I skillfully change the subject and the mood. "It's a beautiful night tonight, much too nice to be spent indoors."

"Aye, it is that."

"I wish I could've been with thee aboard thy ship, inhaling the clean air by day, and having the motion of the ship rocking me to sleep every night."

"The sea, altho' a place of grandeur, is not as romantic as thee imagines, fy melys. At times the sea canne be violent and unforgiving."

"But thee loves the sea, fy Nghapten. Dost thou not long to sail?"

"Aye... Altho' at times the sea canne be merciless, she tugs at my heart still. Do not, however, take that wrongly, for I would rather be here with thee, than out there without thee."

"Didst thou ever sleep on the deck of thy ship?"

"Uh-huh, often." With a sudden impulse, "Wouldst thou be averse to spending the night with me on the beach under the stars?"

Smiling; hoping he would suggest it, "What a romantically spontaneous idea."

Delightfully pleased with my reply, "Wait here, fy melys, whilst I get for us a blanket to lie upon." As Captain Roberts heads for the house he doubles over.

Terribly worried, "Bartholomew! What is it?" asks I, peering at him in the dim porch light. "Thou looks as pale as a—"

"Nay, fy melys, sayeth not." Groaning in pain, "What in thunder be wrong with me, I feel as if someone is twisting a knife in my ribs."

In a matter of moments, Captain Roberts collapses onto the verandah.

Opening the door and shouting as loud as I can, "Katie! Come quick!"

Rushing down the stairs and outside, and seeing the Captain crumpled on the verandah, "What happened?"

"I don't know. Suddenly he was in pain, stammered a mite, and fell over."

Fortunately, Katie and I manage to get Captain Roberts upstairs, and while Katie begins to remove his jacket and boots, "Quick, Miss, fetch a cold compress."

Dashing in to the bath, I grab a washcloth, and after soaking it in cold water, I ring it out thoroughly.

In removing the Captain's silk damask jacket, Katie finds it very pleasing to the touch, and having draped it over the chair, she quickly begins to remove his boots.

As I return, Katie says, "He's out cold!"

"He must weigh 14 stone," says I, and grabbing a duvet, Katie and I cover him.

"I wonder if it could be that he ate too much," suggests Katie. "After all, until just a couple days ago he hasn't had a real stomach for nigh on 300 years."

Opening the drawer beside the bed, I remove a thermometer, the kind that goes in the ear, and after taking his temperature, "Well, it's 98.6°F, but never having taken his temperature before now, I don't know if he's feverish or not."

"For his sake, Miss, I hope he's average."

As the Captain comes around, "I think you overdid it, fy Nghapten."

"I agree," states Katie. "Too much, too soon."

Exerting himself whilst trying to answer for his actions, "Ne'er have I overeaten in my life, nor since for that matter!"

Both Katie and I giggling at his joke, stop suddenly when Captain Roberts moans in agony.

"Oooo! I feel as though I have been poisoned, Oooo!"

"No one is saying that you over ate, Captain," states Katie. "We're only suggesting that your stomach is not use to food yet, and with all the exercise as well, you overdid it."

Smiling at my beloved tenderly whilst placing a second pillow beneath his head, "A sick tummy can be one of the most painful of ailments, fy Nghapten." Walking over to my vanity table to get the chair, "Katie, would you prepare the Captain a bicarb, and bring a glass of 7-up, a straw, and a dish of soda crackers."

"Right away, Miss." Hurrying, Katie departs.

Complaining, "Ne'er have I been sick a day in my life." Groaning again, "Oooo."

As beads of sweat soak his forehead, feeling helpless as he grows flush, I pat them away.

"Ohhh! If this be what it feels like to be sick, 'tis dead I'd rather be!"

Chiding him, "I don't want to hear that kind of talk again, fy Arglwydd, not ever!"

Katie is back in two shakes. Adding the straw so he can sip it, she hands me the glass containing the bicarb, whilst stating, "I'll stay if you want, Miss."

"No need, Katie. The Captain will fall asleep soon enough. Please make an appointment for him to see a doctor as soon as possible. Just to be safe, he should be inoculated against diseases."

"Yes, Miss, I'll ring Doctor Macalister's office first thing in the morning," adding, "the Captain should have a tetanus shot too."

"Good thinking Katie."

"Good night, Miss. Good Night, Captain. I hope you are well by morning."

"Have a good nights rest, Katie." As for the Captain, a moan is the best he can manage.

Holding the glass near the side of the bed so my beloved can reach the straw, "I want thee to drink as much of this as you can."

"Nay," moaning once again, "I canne not."

"Now don't be a difficult patient," I tells him, pleading softly. "I promise that in drinking this, thou wilt feel much better soon, but thee must make an effort."

Looking at me with that boyish kind of helplessness that just melts your heart, I again hold the cup for him, and like the strong man he is, he drinks it down.

Smiling at him, "Thou did just great!" Putting another cold cloth on his forehead, "I want thee to nibble on these crackers and sip thy soda; they'll help to settle thy tummy, and no talking."

Opening his eyes slightly, he mumbles, " 'Tis sorry I be for—"

Bending down and again kissing him on the forehead. "Shhh. Nibble, sip, rest."

Reaching to the far side of the bed, I pick up Bunny, one of my 2 stuffed animals. Handing it to him, "Rolling onto thy side, I want thee to keep Bunny tight against thy tummy. It will help, I promise."

Tho' moaning quite a bit, he manages to roll onto his side. Knowing how terribly painful it is when you feel like your guts are being torn out, I feel bad for him, and thankfully, after several minutes pass, he seems to be resting a little more comfortably. "Feeling better, fy Arglwydd Nghapten."

"A mite." wincing amid his mumbling, " 'Twas to be our wedding night."

"Do not think about that now, for we shall be married just as soon as thou art well."

Quite angry at Mister Cullen, he spats, "When next I see him, I shall give that blast'd pip-squeak a sound thrashing to durst incapacitate himself with drink!"

Projecting a positive smile as my hand moves smoothly over his cheek, "Believe me, fy Nghapten, come morning he'll be feeling worse than does thou now."

Turning his head, he kisses the palm of my hand, "I be thinking of a better idea," smiling with satisfaction.

"Thou needs to forget all this for now and just rest."

Altho' too ill to display his fury, "All right, but come morn I shall confine my thoughts to McClure. He's the Devil incarnate, he is."

Having forgotten how malicious Keith can be, I again try to get my lover to rest quietly. "Please, fy Nghapten, thou must direct thine energies towards getting well."

As Captain Roberts sits up just a little, "I think I be fighting this at last." but, finding himself in error, he slumps back down to the pillow.

"Let that be a lesson to thee." Being sterner still, "Be still now and rest." Seeing a slight spasm of pain dart across his face, "If 'in thou needs me, I will be right here in this chair."

"Nay, fy Nghariad, I shall be fine." Barely audible as his eyes begin to close, "I want thee to go aloft and get for thyself a good nights rest."

Stroking his forehead rhythmically for awhile longer, just being grateful to be able to touch him, I try my best not to think about Keith or Mister Cullen, and instead, whilst daydreaming about the life we will share, I fall asleep with my head lying upon my folded arms that rest atop the bed upon which my lover sleeps.

Chapter Eleven
The Morning After

> *Awakening early & seeing his woman with her head lying upon her arms on the edge of the bed, Captain Roberts, whilst being careful not to wake her, got up, & picking her up, he gently laid her atop the covers, after which, being well again, he garnished her person with tender kisses.*

As I begin to stir, fy Nghapten, aware that I am enjoying his advances, repositions himself to better suit his purpose, as I softly utter, "I love thee, fy Arglwydd, Nghapten."

Relishing the soft words of affection and devotion that are spoken as I sleep, it pleases my Captain to know he is the subject of my dreams.

Suddenly, I begin screaming, and my arms flail as if I were trying to force someone away. Grabbing my hands, my Captain, speaking somewhat loudly, "V'lé, wake up, thou art having a nightmare!" but holding my arms only makes me fight more aggressively. Thinking better of it, my Captain releases me, and calling my name tenderly whilst gently nudging my shoulder, he says, " 'tis I, Bart."

Upon opening mine eyes and seeing my lover's handsome face looking down at me, "Oh Bartholomew," and throwing my arms around him, I add, "hold me tight."

Asking urgently, "What was in thy dream that affected thee so?"

Hesitating, as I had never told anyone that for years I have dreamt about him, "I was dreaming of us making love aboard thy ship, then all of a sudden," sobbing in his arms, "thou be gone and Keith was—" Unable to hold back my tears, "he was—"

Speaking angrily as his eyes grow narrow, "He was assaulting thee."

"Yes."

Stroking my hair, " 'Twas onely a nightmare, fy melys, and holding me close as my breathing slowly returns to normal, he's delighted, for the dream reaffirmed my desire to be with him in the 18th century.

Composing myself, looking up at my Captain as I gently touch his forehead with my fingertips, "I am glad to see that thou art looking much better this morning."

The phone begins to ring, but after only two rings, it stops.

"Katie will inform thee if the call be important." Staring into mine eyes, his are beaming once again, "Being wee miss'd that which ought to have bin our wedding night, dost thou think wee might enjoy the morning after?"

My own eyes sparkling as my face displays a hint of blush, "Only if the date on the beach is still open."

"Of course, fy melys, come dark, but until then, may wee not indulge?"

"A lovely idea, fy Nghapten."

Just then, a knock is heard upon the door. Upset that we are again interrupted, my Captain takes a lounging position as I roll onto my side before stating, "Come in."

Katie, poking her head in, "Sorry to disturb you, but— Pausing for a moment, "you look much better than you did last night, Captain."

"I am well now Katie, thank you."

"It was Mister McClure who rang. He wanted to speak with you, Captain, but I told him you were under the weather and would probably be spending the day in bed. Then he wanted to speak with you, Miss. I told him you were busy and couldn't come to the phone; after which, he said he'd be right over and hung up."

"Thank you, Katie. Please be good enough to bring up a breakfast tray."

"It's already cooking, Miss."

"You are a treasure."

Smiling broadly, Katie replies, "I'll be back in a couple of shakes with Blueberry pancakes for you, Miss, and for you Captain, Cockles, fried Laverbread, and a dish of fresh berries."

"Thank you, Katie," states Captain Roberts.

"Well my darling," speaking in a tone reflecting disappointment, "it looks like our morning's activities will have to wait."

Looking somewhat grim, "Aye, it looks to be so." Perking up as he slaps my rump as I get up, "Wee best hurry and get changed 'fore that repugnant lout arrives."

Making my way to my cherished antique dressing screen, "It's a shame were not in the early 1800s where Keith could meet the same end as did the governor of Martinique."[1]

"That would be amusing, but have thee forgotten my article forbidding women aboard ship."

"I do not recall it verbatim, but I do remember it said that taking a woman against her will, or bringing one aboard in disguise, warranted death, but what about those women who wished to come aboard?"

"Thou forgets 'twas stated also that, 'No Boy or Woman be allow'd amongst us.' "

"What about, Jean François, ship's boy aboard thy flagship?"[B2 & B12]

With a chuckle, "He was not a ship's boy, but a vigilante & pyrate; and at 15, he was a man, by all accounts. Nonetheless, I commend thy research. 'Twas decidedly thorough."

Katie, having returned upstairs with our breakfast, raps upon our bedroom door whilst asking, "May I come in?"

"Aye, Katie," replies Captain Roberts.

As the Captain opens the door, Katie nervously says, "Despite the fact that I told him to wait in the foyer, Mister McClure is coming up the stairs."

"Thank you, Katie," says I while stepping out from behind the screen. "Just set the tray on the balcony table. I'll serve."

"Very good, Miss. Shall I bring another cup for Mister McClure?"

"No, Katie. He won't be staying."

> *Noticing the bleakness within V'lé's eyes, an aspect that had worsened considerably since her nightmare, Captain Roberts knew she dreaded the very idea of seeing Keith.*

Keith, now standing outside the door of my bedroom, asks, "May I come in?"

Speaking scornfully as Captain Roberts turns from his spyglass, "I have sail'd the world over, and having met all manner of men, I canne state without fear of contradiction that your impudence is without peers."

As Katie exits the room, "How you can show your face here after your performance last night escapes me."

---

[1] In 1721, Cap'n Roberts hung the Governor of Martinique from the yardarm of his own ship

BLOOD and SWASH, The Unvarnished Life (& afterlife) Story of Pirate Captain, Bartholomew Roberts.........pt.1 "BOLT OF FRUITION"

Ignoring her, Keith addresses his adversary. "Look Captain, I only want to talk to V'lé for a few minutes, what possible harm could that do?" Seeing that Captain Roberts is unyielding, Keith reminds him, "Last night you said I could speak with her."

Noting my shrug, the Captain says, "She's right there, Mister McClure, talk."

"What I need to say must be spoken tête-à-tête." With my Captain still blocking his path, Keith adds, "You know, Captain, if you had allowed me to speak with her alone the night I arrived, I might well be back in the U.S.A. by now."

"Providing thee approves, fy Arglwydd, Nghapten, I might as well hear what the bloke has to say, but afterwards he is to leave, by force if necessary, ne'er to return."

"As thee wishes," replies Captain Roberts reluctantly, and stepping aside, he allows Keith to proceed onto the balcony.

Returning my Captain's tea and breakfast dishes to the tray, I stand, and taking it to him, passing by Keith on the way, "Katie went to a lot of trouble to fix thee thy favorites. It would hurt her feelings if thou were to allow it to grow cold."

Taking the tray, "I shall be on the verandah. If thou needeth me, holler."

Sneering at Keith, "I shall, my Lord, Captain." Giving my Captain a peck on the cheek, "I expect to join thee within the quarter hour." Turning, I return to the balcony.

> *Less than 10 minutes later, Captain Roberts heard Keith's car drive off, & after waiting several minutes more, V'lé had not joined him. Becoming worried, he arose from his seat, & taking the stairs 2 & 3 at a time, he rushed up to their room. As he entered, he glanced around, but V'lé was not within their rooms. Knowing her desire to visit what she now called his man cave when she's feeling sad, he climbed the steps quickly, but alas, she was not to be found. Dashing downstairs, the Captain went to the kitchen to question Katie.*

"Have you seene, Miss V'lé?"

"Not since I took up the tray, Captain." Taking note of his anxious demeanour, Katie asks, "Why, what's wrong?"

Displaying concern, "Where will I find Mrs Montgomery?"

"She's in her room working on her book, "Terror In Hidden Springs," replies Katie as fear begins to engulf her expression.

Resuming my search, and with Katie following closely upon my heels, I walk briskly down the hall to Sue's room.

Seeing my approach, Sue looks up. Ne'er 'fore, even when angry, has she seen me less than composed. "What is it, Captain?"

"Have you seen V'lé this morn, madam?"

"No, Captain, I haven't."

Being conscious of her agitated state as Katie enters the doorway, Sue asks, "What's wrong, Katie?"

"It's Miss V'lé, madam, she's missing. The Captain and I are on the hunt for her."

"Will you be good enough to check the rooms downstairs?"

"Of course, Captain," replies Sue.

"Katie," I begin, "you check the upstairs and the wine cellar. I will check the grounds, the stables, and outbuildings."

"You're thinking that Keith abducted her, aren't ya?" states Katie as her eyes widen.

"Surely Keith would not have stooped to kidnapping her," says Sue. "He'd go to prison."

Belieeving McClure to be capable of anything, I state, "I doubt McClure's character would concern itself with possible repercussions."

Close to 30 minutes later, the three of us meet up in the foyer.

"I have searched every inch of the upstairs," states Katie.

"She's not on the ground floor either," states Sue. After a brief pause, "V'lé would not have gone anywhere with Keith," declares Sue, who is now in tears. "Of that I'm certain."

"I agree, at least not of her own volition," says I.

"Being a scrapper," asserts Katie, "V'lé would 'ave fought like a wildcat."

Agreeing with Katie, Sue says, "He must've drugged her somehow."

Fit to be tied, I tell Katie, "Ring up that inebriated clod, Mister Cullen. Perhaps he canne locate them in the village."

"Yes, Captain, instantly," replies Katie as she hurries to the telephone. Looking up the number, she dials as quickly as she canne. Ringing sev'rall times, Mister Cullen, more than a little hung over, picks up the receiver. "Yes."

"This is Katie at *Inn Finistère*. Have you seen Miss V'lé this morning?"

"No, Katie, I haven't."

"Forgive me, Katie," taking the receiver, "Captain Roberts here."

Hearing the sound of the Captain's voice, Mister Cullen becomes terribly nervous.

Paying no attention to his fearful attitude, I says, "Miss V'lé is missing. Wee suspect she's in the company of that oaf, McClure."

"I don't see how this concerns me, Captain."

"Locate the blackguard's motor, blast you. I suggest you begin your search at his lodgings."

"What's the big deal, Captain? Is there some reason why she shouldn't—"

"Just do it!" Slamming down the phone, "Whilst we wait for Mister Cullen to ring back, I shall search the area around the cliffs. Katie, please search the beach, afterwards, we'll meet back here in the foyer. Sue, I would be pleas'd if you could wait by the telephone."

"Will do, Captain."

Looking like it might rain, Katie grabs her Mackintosh and Wellies in the mudroom, and dashing out the door, she makes for the steps that lead down to the beach.

> *Knowing Katie would use the steps, the Captain took the footpath down to the cliffs & searched the few places where it was possible to climb down, but alas his woman was no place to be found, & with no more places left to search, he returned to the house.*

"She's not on the beach," reports Katie.

"And no one has telephoned either," adds Sue.

Suddenly, as it starts to rain heavily, "I shall be in the uppermost section of the westerly turret. Let me know if either of you hear anny news."

> *Climbing the stairs to what he considered their retreat, Captain Roberts was in despair; thus, he seated himself in her favorite chair in hopes that he could feel where his woman was, but to his dismay, the intuitive bond they had shared while he was a spirit was gone.*

The next couple of hours dragged by, when at last, hearing the sound of a motor car on our drive below, I hurriedly make my way to the foyer.

Sue, peering out of the dining room window, says, "It's Mister Cullen. He appears to be alone."

The minute Mister Cullen is on the verandah, I thrust open the door and quite literally yank him in to the house. "Well, what news have you learned of Miss V'lé?"

Startled, Mister Cullen, making an effort to twist away, "It's not necessary to manhandle me, Captain. I found Keith, not that I wanted to, but he owed me some money. He was in his hotel room packing his suitcase. When I asked him if he knew where Miss V'lé was, he said he hadn't seen her since leaving here."

"You simpering codfish!"

Although shrinking away from me, Mister Cullen speaks defiantly. "I'll have you know, Captain, that I searched his room, including the wardrobe, bath, and under the bed, and she was not there. Knowing you'd ask, I also searched his car, and no one on the hotel staff, nor any of the guests have seen her either. Keith said he'd call when he had his stuff packed. When he arrives, you can talk to him yourself."

Satisfied with Mister Cullen's report, I release him.

Nervously patting his pocket, Mister Cullen turns to face Katie. "Being terribly wet out, do you think I could have a cup of tea, Katie?"

Being agreeable, "Of course, Mister Cullen."

Furious, I says, "How canne you think of your stomach with Miss V'lé still missing?"

Still fumbling with whatever lyes within his pocket, "Because of you, I dashed out without any breakfast, and starving myself isn't going to help her, wherever she is."

Eyeing his fidgety actions, Sue follows them in to the kitchen. "What's in your pocket, Mister Cullen, a ransom note?"

"Of course not!" gripes Mister Cullen, following Katie, who, after putting on the kettle, begins to slice the freshly baked mince pie.

"Is that a note from Mister McClure," asks Katie?

"No, it's not! snaps Mister Cullen.

"But it is from Mister McClure," states Sue.

"If you must know, it's money. I left the house in such a hurry I forgot my wallet."

Katie, knowing him well, sarcastically states. "I'm surprised it's not locked in your safe?"

Becoming upset by the persistent questions, "I already told you that Mister McClure owed me some money."

As I enter the kitchen, "Are you positive McClure said he's coming here?"

Dropping his fork, "Yes, Captain." Reaching down to the floor to pick it up, "Why wouldn't he?"

Mine eyes narrowing in contemplation, "Why indeed?"

Cutting another piece of pie, Katie suddenly drops the knife on the counter. "I hear another car coming up the drive."

Mister Cullen, quickly shovelling in the fruit laden delicacy, and gulping the tea, winces a mite as the hot liquid burns his throat.

Both Sue and Katie rush to look out the window, "It's Keith!" exclaims Sue. "He's alone."

When Mister McClure comes to the door, again I yank it open, and snatching him up by his shirt, I haul him inside. Slamming the door with my foot, I shove him backwards against the hard surface, and with my forearm firmly against his throat, I demandingly ask, "Where is she?"

Gasping for breath, Keith, looking innocent, asks, "Who?"

"Miss V'lé, of course, you dastardly swine!" As I grab Keith by the throat, my ever powerful hand pushes him harder in to the door. "You be the last person amongst us to see her."

"You're crazy! Let go of me!" demands Keith.

> *Despite Mister McClure's efforts, Captain Roberts is much the stronger, & his already immense strength is being increased by the flow of adrenalin pumping through his body; even so, Keith tries again, but despite his efforts, he is unable to dislodge the Captain's firm hold.*

"Captain," Katie suggests quietly, "I think you'll get more sense out of him if you let him go."

Chapter Twelve

Lucifer's Playground

Moaning faintly as I slowly awaken, I open mine eyes to find myself in a dank, poorly lit room. As my head spins with what feels like the aftereffects of some sort of drug, I ask myself aloud, "What place is this?" After a few moments, as mine eyes adjust to the light as I look about, I suddenly perceive a faint figure through the gloom. The eerie looking silhouette standing motionless about ten feet in front of me appears to be on the opposite side of the room, but being shrouded in some sort of fog like glint, it's hard to tell.

"Bartholomew," asking as I slowly manage to get myself in to a sitting position on the concrete floor, "art thou he?"

"No," answers a gravelly voice, "I be thy guardian angel."

The voice, definitely not the Captain's, is almost as eerie as the room. Understandably frightened, I scrunch backwards against the wall, whispering, "My Guardian Angel? You don't expect me to believe that, do you?"

"I speak true," says the voice, "and for the sake of thyself and those loved by thee, thou must take heed."

Seeing how I've been in the middle of a Twilight Zone episode of late, I reply, "Well, why not." Looking sharp, trying to see the figure more clearly, "Having done nothing, and having little to offer, why am I here?"

"Sometimes, it takes half a lifetime, or more, before one's worth is realized, if ever. As it is, there's a man who loves thee deeply; what's more, 'tis thee alone who can save him from Lucifer's service or should he refuse, ever-lasting perdition."

Confused by the aftermath of the drug, and the ramshackle surroundings, "I can't see you very well, can you come in to the light?"

"The room is not dark, it only appears thus amid my presence, and in that, I have appeared to thee because I have knowledge of Lucifer's plans."

"Lucifer!" sinking back down to the floor, despite my efforts to stand, "You mean the devil?"

"Yes," replies the voice calmly. Moving closer, the strange figure continues. "Before departing this place, thou must first understand. To begin, the one thou knows as Keith McClure, having earned himself a bitter sentence, is no longer a man, but a Ghoul in Lucifer's service, and in that realization, only thee can preserve the life of whom thou loves."

My mind, flooding with thoughts, "So Keith really did die, just as I was told."

"Yes, but," uttering with sadness, "as he was not open to rehabilitation, he was sent to hell. 'Twas not too long ago that his decadent ways came to the attention of Lucifer."

Asking with an obvious measure of fear, "What does Lucifer want with me?"

" 'Tis not thyself Lucifer wants," the voice informs me. "However, Keith, as thou knew him, seeking redemption, made a pact with Lucifer, but unbeknownst to him, Lucifer, as he is using thee, is only using Keith to achieve his true goal."

Gropingly, "But if he doesn't want me, then who?" Suddenly, as the correct answer occurs to me, I blurt out, "Captain Roberts?"

"Yes. McClure's assignment to keep the two of ye apart and unwed until he can devise a plan to seize him."

Being struck with terror as the gloomy figure before me speaks of the life of the man I revere falling into ruin. "Can't you help me?"

The only help I can give is knowledge, and to that which I have already told thee, I can add only that for all to end well, the Ghoul must be vanquished, and that wilt happen only if thou hast both the emotional and physical strength to best him. As for thy presence in this dreary place, 'twas Keith who brought thee here, and should he win this contest, thou wilt be his prize."

Shivering, I wrap my arms around myself, "I am not a prize to be awarded!"

"Thou art mistaken, for 'tis thy destiny to be the property of the victor."

"Captain Roberts would never regard me as such."

"Thou lacks knowledge of his times, but in any case, if the two of ye are to overpower both Lucifer and his henchman, thou must give thyself to him completely, and he to thee."

With assurance in my voice, and evident love in my eyes, "I have already given myself to him."

"True love in thine heart is a powerful tool, but to win, brute force coupled with decisive intelligence is also needed if evil is to be defeated."

"Then I have nothing to fear, for Captain Roberts loves me truly. As for brute strength," boasting with a confident smile, "my Captain is not only much the stronger, he possesses vast, problem-solving intelligence as well."

"And Keith?"

"Keith couldn't command a toy ship in a bathtub." Demandingly, "Why does Lucifer want Captain Roberts?"

"Thou does not know Lucifer, but Captain Roberts does, and should either thy strength of heart or mind fail," the voice states sadly, "it is Captain Roberts who shall be the prize."

As tears fill my eyes, "For what purpose?"

"Lucifer's plans for Captain Roberts are his own. I do know, however, that once 'fore he beckoned for his soul, but even in meeting death, thy Captain's strong, honorable convictions were as he lived, and Lucifer lost. Thou being the tool Lucifer is using to distract the pirate's attentions is a fact thee best be remembering it, for such knowledge may save not only thy life, but also that of thy pirate Captain."

As my Guardian Angel begins to back up, "Now dry thine eyes, for this be no time for tears. For now, and for all time, remember, it is strength and fortitude that secures everlasting happiness."

Sniveling in to my blouse whilst drying my eyes, I utter, "But I'm afraid."

"Fear can be a valuable asset for sharpening the senses, but for whom art thou afraid? Thyself, or Captain Roberts?"

"Captain Roberts," I spout, "and losing what we share. If I lose him, nothing else will matter."

"The one true sad realization of life is that for those who survive, although pelted with pain and anguish, life goes on."

The coldness of my Guardian Angel's words bracing me up, "There's a difference betwixt mere existence and living. I intend to live, and with Captain Roberts."

"Then return thou must to thine home forthwith, but it shan't be easy, for if thou does not return to *Inn Finistère* in time, the game shall end and Captain Roberts' soul will become the property of Lucifer; furthermore, thy life will again be as it was 7 years ago, when thou be at thy lowest, only there will be no escape."

"Like Hell it will! I shall traverse the most fearsome places, and battle any creature set before me to save him."

"Even if that means to die in his stead."

"Yes!"

"But— "

"There are no buts, and only one course for me to follow. I cannot believe that God would allow us to find our true happiness only to rip us apart." With both fear and anger evident upon my face, I add, "I couldn't bear it."

"There would be nothing for thee to bear," says the voice, "for everything that hath taken place since before you moved to Wales would not even be a memory, and your memory of Captain Roberts since you met would be erased."

"You're wrong! Having been in love with him for years before actually meeting him, you'd have to turn the clock back a good 40 years!"

"In that event, Lucifer shall have both of ye as you are now."

"Then we shall be together in hell, and," announcing with a boisterous laugh, "Lucifer had better prepare to be conquered, because my Captain is subservient to no one, and that being the case, only a short time would pass before he'd take over. In any case, being it was my love for him that brought him to my home in the first place, I will not allow that love to be his downfall."

Again as I try to stand, my love for Captain Roberts giving me strength beyond imagination, I rise to my feet. "I must go to him. He needs me!"

"Yes, he does, but ne'er forget that the Ghoul will use every means possible to win, and in thine attempt to save thy Captain you fail, or if he fails in his attempt to save thee, ye both shall be lost. Only in the Ghoul's destruction can thee and thine beloved win."

"If that was meant to scare me, I thank you, for I now know to be very careful in my actions, and I shall inform my Captain of such as well."

As the shadowy figure dissipates, "Wait! One more question, please." As the figure comes slightly back in to focus, "How did I get here; the last thing I remember was eating my breakfast this morning."

"The Ghoul, having drugged thy coffee, carried thee down the trellis and to his car. He's there now, at *Inn Finistère*, trying to convince them that he knows nothing about thy disappearance. If he succeeds in convincing Captain Roberts he speaks true, and therefore permitted to leave, the man of thine heart's desire will be lost in Perdition forever," and as the eerie vision vanishes, by his word, darkness becomes light.

Knowing what I have to do, I'm thinking, as I make my way downstairs, that I must be in one of the dilapidated buildings in the area. When I get to the door and look outside, the rain is coming down in sheets, but the night sky is alive with nature's fury as lightning and thunder wreak havoc upon the landscape, nevertheless, seeing I am in the old derelict, #5, that I have mentioned several times in the past, I know I am on the far side of Little Haven, and such, quite some distance from both my home, and my beloved. Knowing it's the only way to save the man I love, I reach behind me, and grabbing one of the blankets that drapes the furniture, I wrap it around myself and venture out in to the fearsome storm.

Buffeted by the wind whilst being lashed by the rain, I struggle along, and somehow knowing I am drawing upon strength which is not my own as I become stronger with each step, I make it back to *Inn Finistère*. To my astonishment, as I near the house, I see 3 figures near the cliff side of the road. As I draw closer, while one of the men, Peter Cullen, nervously wringing his hands, is moving about them, I can see it is my Captain and Keith who are fighting, and as they grapple, both being violently attacked by the mixer of wind and rain as it lashes them with a vengeance, I try to hurry my pace.

Exhausted and panting as I draw nearer to the fierce battle that is getting dangerously close to the edge of the cliff, I shout repeated warnings to no avail. Frantic, I begin running towards them whilst calling out, "Bart!" but unfortunately I succeed only in sliding this way and that in the mud, and to my dismay, my voice can not be heard over the onslaught of rain, thunder and the howling wind. Although I feel as if the Devil himself is thwarting my efforts, I gather all the strength I can muster, and press on.

Finally near enough to hear, Captain Roberts, whilst backhanding him as he holds Keith by the front of his shirt, bellows, "Where is she?" When Keith offers no reply, my Captain roars once again as he doubles up both fists, and with the delivery of a series of severe blows, first to his stomach and then his jaw, Keith goes down.

Lying in a heap upon the drenched earth, caked with mud, Keith spouts, "I'll see her dead before I give her up!"

"You insidious blackguard!" hollers Captain Roberts as he reaches down, grabbing the front of his shirt, and once again hauling him up from the ground, his fist comes up from the basement to make firm contact with Keith's jaw yet again.

Close enough at last to interfere, I shout, "Bart!" as loudly as I can, and as I come between them, 'tis only by my Captain's sheer power that stops his fist from doing me grievous bodily harm.

"V'lé," says my Captain, and as he releases his hold on Keith, allowing him to drop backwards to the ground, adds, "thou art safe."

> *Sweeping the woman he loves up in to his embrace, Captain Roberts, though exhausted, carried her in to the house & up the stairs to their bedchamber.*

"Put me down, fy Arglwydd, for thou art hurt, and I can walk these few steps."

Ignoring my words, Captain Roberts does not rest until he reaches the big crunchy chair near the French doors where he at last sits down, cradling me in his arms still. Wiping the wet hair from my face, he gently kisses my face and lips.

> *To Keith's dismay, fuming over V'lé's escape, despite his injuries, was able to muster the strength needed to be right behind them all the way.*

When Katie makes it to the foyer, Mister Cullen informs her, "The Captain just carried Miss V'lé upstairs, and being they are both as soaked as I am, please get them something hot to drink."

"I shall," Katie says as she hurries to the kitchen.

Having climbed the stairs, Sue, with Keith only a step behind her, make their way down the hall, and upon entering V'lé's room, both see a wet blouse flop over the dressing screen.

Captain Roberts, just having come down from his man cave after getting into some dry clothes, is standing by his spyglass, when I step out from behind the dressing screen. "I have learned why you're here, Keith, and there's just no reason for you to carry on with this ridiculous quest of yours because the Captain and I, having had a civil registrar ceremony in St Brides Inn at dawn this morning, are married."

As my words echo through the minds of those present, there is a moment of stunned silence, but the quiet does not last more than a few moments before a great, almost deafening howling, reverberating within the renewed fury of the storm, is heard all about us.

The Captain, with his stern expression, knowing there must be a good reason for my statement, remains silent.

"You're not the least bit ashamed to be married to a pirate, are you?" jibes Keith.

"Proud is how I feel, and although I wish I could be more expressive, I shall state only, that no collection of words could possibly describe my feelings for Captain Roberts, nor how honored I feel to be loved by him. If knowing he truly loves me is all I ever get in this world, it'll be enough."

Although his outward expression is well controlled, it's evident Captain Roberts is touched.

My mom, unaware of most of the day's events, gives me a hug upon entering my room, whilst asking, "Where were you all day, V'lé?"

Walking over to the table by the door to get a cup of coffee from the pot Katie has just brought in, "I was just coming to that, but before I go in to detail, I must first have thy word of honor, fy Arglwydd Nghapten," and looking at him with an expression that is not only loving, but also quite serious, "that regardless of what it is I am about to tell thee, thou wilt do nothing but listen."

Speaking quietly, Captain Roberts promises as he gives me a slight nod, "You have my word."

Knowing that my Captain's word is his honor, and that ne'er would he break it, though what I am about to tell him will be the ultimate test in that regard, "Keith drugged me," and noting that it is taking all of my Captain's strength to uphold his promise, I continue. "and in my unconscious state he carried me off to the derelict house, #5, on the hill and tied me up." Waiting while Katie pours two cups of coffee, "Whilst there, I was visited by my guardian angel who told me the truth concerning both recent and forthcoming events."

Glaring at Keith, as his anger intensifies, Captain Roberts asks, "What truth?"

Taking both cups from Katie, I proceed to walk back to the Captain, telling them, "My Guardian Angel said that Keith, who did in fact die and who was sentenced to hell as a ghoul, made a pact with the devil, whereby thee," looking at my Captain, "would not only become Lucifer's prize should Keith win, but I would become Keith's chattel."

> *The tempestuous Captain, doing his best not to go back on his word, edges towards Keith. At the same time, as V'lé walked between them with the coffee, Keith grabbed her, & before the Captain could act, Keith, using her as a shield, put a blade against V'lé's throat.*

"One more step, Roberts, and I'll kill 'er; leaving you alive and alone for all eternity."

"You Son-of-a-Bitch. Killing you will be a pleasure."

Seeing that Katie, as well as Sue, is terrified, Captain Roberts gives Katie an order. "Katie, take Sue to her room forthwith, and stay with her."

"Yes, Captain!" replies Katie as she starts to escort Sue out of the room.

Fearful of losing her daughter, my mom, protesting angrily, makes it difficult for Katie to do as Captain Roberts ordered.

"Try not to worry, madam, everything will be all right." Trying to reassure her as she forcibly moves my mom in to the hall, "You must have faith in Captain Roberts!"

"I do," states Sue, as her eyes fill with tears, "but—"

"Worried she won't be able to get Sue down the stairs safely, Katie elects to take her to her own bedchamber just down the hall, where the two of them can only wait and pray.

The evil persona engulfing Keith's aura is intense. "The game's not over, Captain! One of us MUST die!"

Twisting my neck to look at Keith, "You're insane!"

"That's right, V'lé," tightening his grip, "I'm insane with jealousy, and the righteous seaman you hold in such high esteem will have to kill me to get you back. After which, Roberts, it will be then, after I am dead, that you will learn how she truly feels."

"What do you mean?" asks Captain Roberts.

Exclaiming with a calculating look in his eye, "She'll see you for what you really are, a vicious pirate who thinks nothing of murdering anyone in his way to get what he wants, and she'll be repulsed!"

"He's wrong, fy Arglwydd Nghapten. 'Tis he who knows not—"

Choking me off, "What is there to know, V'lé," states Keith, enjoying his opponent's rage as he continues to spout. "Your precious Captain was nothing more than a thieving, rabble-rousing thug; a ne'er-do-well who took the easy way out by stealing instead of working for a living."

Such were his remarks, that as my fury mounds beyond his expectations, I bite him on the forearm with all my might.

"Ah!" Screaming in agony as blood spews from the wound, Keith, pulling my hair back harder, hollers, "You bitch!" And to my chagrin, despite the immense pain, he does not release his hold.

"You're the ne'er-do-well, Keith. Never in your entire life did you ever put in a full day's work, never striving to make one penny more than what was needed to just barely pay your bills. I remember when I got online and began my pirate site, you couldn't stand the fact that it didn't revolve around you. That was the last straw. I loathed you. Reading about Captain Roberts again after so many years gave me hope that life could improve, and during the course of my research, it did. I became intrigued again, tenfold, and whilst spending 6 years researching every detail of his life, and that only covers the time spent before I left the states, I not only fell in love with him again; I love him deeply, and there's no deed that has been done, or might been done that can ever change that fact."

"Shut your mouth!" spouts Keith. "I'm tired of hearing about your White Knight! You're mine, and I shall have all of you."

"None of her!" retorts Captain Roberts.

"You'll have to kill me, Roberts, and being fearful of her reaction, I don't believe you can do that while your lady love stands by, watching. That's your Achilles heel! Your belief that she'll think less of you, and that's why I'll win."

"Don't listen to him, Bartholomew. Ne'er could I think less of thee, especially for destroying evil; what's more, such an act, by demonstrating thy willingness to protect that which we share would only serve to increase my love for thee."

"Worry not, fy nghariad, for I am fully aware of thy views."

As Keith's glare deepens, "So you have convinced, V'lé to condone the taking of a life. Well, Roberts, we shall see."

"You're wrong Keith, I have always approved of duels, providing they be truly justified, just as I believe in defending life and honor, not that either of those pertain to you."

"I was dead, but just as your Captain now lives, I do also." Glaring at Captain Roberts, "I still say you won't kill me in your lover's presence, and when your precious pirate is dead, and this time it means Perdition, I shall become the ghostly heir to *Inn Finistère*. Not only that," as he pulls my head back and kisses me, "as for this little trinket, after she becomes my property, it'll be my extreme pleasure to take her, violently if need be, whenever I choose."

The look of fury on Captain Roberts' face is alarming. Yet as intensely as he desires to free me and kill Keith, he does not dare, for any attempt could easily mean my death.

"That must've been what the angel meant by me becoming the prize of the victor," and turning towards Keith, I laugh in his face, "In hand to hand combat against the Great Pirate Roberts, you don't stand a chance." Looking again at my Captain, "No matter what happens, Bartholomew, I shall, for all of eternity, love only thee."

Calmed by the power of true love, Captain Roberts regains control of his rationality, and after a few moments, "Ah... I understand now. You will be granted a reprieve should you succeed in delivering my soul in your stead."

All of a sudden, the windows blow open and the fury of the storm, wreaking its havoc, blows small items and papers off the tables and desk as the room fills with an immense amount of smoke, fire and brimstone.

"You're exactly right, Captain," speaks a voice from within the glowing smolder. As the smoke dissipates, a ghastly creature with an unkempt goatee and jagged horns protruding from his temples stands in the center of the room. Turning to behold the eyes of whom he addresses, thereby knowing if they speak true, "How dost thou feel towards this woman, Captain?"

"She is all that I am, or will become, and as she understands me, she is the very essence of my soul."

Lucifer turns to face me, and with a penetrating look, stares deep in to my eyes. "And how dost thou feel towards this man who stands 'fore thee?"

"I feel as does he. He is both my life, and my destiny. I wish only to be with him and there's no power in the universe capable of changing that fact."

"And wouldst thou die to save this man, so that he, whom thyself hath called a saint, may live?"

"Yes!"

"Then here be my decision. Should Captain Roberts emerge the victor, I shall grant him and his woman all of eternity to enjoy all of the passion of their unbridled love."

"And McClure?" enquires Captain Roberts.

"He's very angry, Captain. In his eyes, 'twas thee who took his woman 7 years ago. Should he win the contest, his main reward will lie in the satisfaction of knowing that he hath beaten thee."

"And V'lé?"

Knowing all present to be at his mercy, such being clearly defined by the sadistic smirk upon his gruesome face, Lucifer speaks grandiloquently. "Being merely a motivational pawn, she will become the property of the victor, and as a consequence, Captain, should thee lose, thou wilt be forever aware of thy lady's eternal self-reproach, and because ne'er will she submit to thy rival's concupiscence, her existence will beggar description."

"And when Captain Roberts wins," asks I, "will it then be Keith who is made to suffer forever in perdition?"

"Yes."

"What! Now just a damn minute! You never said anything about that," shouts Keith in horrific consternation. "She's not worth that risk," and flinging me to the floor, "he can have her!"

Captain Roberts, keeping a close eye on Keith whilst bending down to help me to my feet, positions me safely behind him, and addressing Keith, "Next time don't dance with the devil unless you're prepared to spend an eternity within the fiery depths of Hell."

"Yeah, next time!"

"In the future," Lucifer warns, "make sure thou knows the consequences of thine ambitious lust for folly."

Stating in reserved anger, "But you never mentioned a penalty should I lose."

"Wanting only to know what thou would reap in the winning, ne'er did thee ask." Calmly lighting his cigar with his flame tipped appendage, "The terms are decided. Now for the rules of the game. I shall keep them simple. Thou, Captain, must rescue V'lé from Keith's clutches." After pausing for a moment, Lucifer continues. "The game shall be one of perceptive intelligence, brute strength and the desire for conquest, meaning close quarter weapons only are permitted. In thy favor Captain, thou hast wisdom, brute strength, and, no doubt, the strongest motivating force being the true love thou hast for this woman. Keith, on the other hand, as this woman so astutely put it, has only his insane jealousy, and thus, being no match for Captain Roberts, I, for the sake of a good contest, have instilled within him ruthless cunning."

"V'lé," declares Lucifer whilst looking at me, "thou holds the key. Draw upon the strength and perception of loved ones and combine them with thine owne. The game shall end in 12 hours. If all of ye live still, Keith shall win by default. The game takes place in a nearby area that is known to all of you."

Still partially shielded by my Captain, I reach up to my compass pendant, and fondling it, I take a measure of comfort knowing that at the least, I will know in which direction I am being sent.

Noticing my movements. "Oh no, missy," declares Keith furiously, and snatching the jewelled compass from around my neck, he hurls it with all his might into the far corner of the room, "You won't have anymore help like that, I assure you."

As my outraged protector responds by backhanding Keith whilst hollering, "You contemptuous swine!" a look of smug confidence is evident on my face.

As Keith feels his aching jaw with his right hand, Lucifer, interested only in the forthcoming contest, pays no heed to that which he considers a slight confrontation.

"There's one more stipulation," announces Lucifer. "Just so there won't be any misunderstandings, the contest will end sooner should either of you two," motioning to Captain Roberts and Keith, "be killed, by any means permitted, the survivor shall reign forever victorious, but should V'lé perish, ye shall both be forever in Perdition." And thrusting out his hands, waving them about as he briefly gambols about the room as a fulgurous display emanates from his fingertips, Lucifer proclaims, "With no quarter given, let the game begin!" and as his spectacular exhibition concludes, V'lé and Keith vanish.

KEITH'S HIDING PLACE ¬

To my dismay, I find myself alone with Keith in a stone cottage. Making a run for the door, he snatches my wrist, and despite my efforts to fight him, he drags me over to a chair by the fireplace.

Laughing like a crazed lunatic whilst binding my hands and feet as he forces me in to the chair, and removing my shoes, Keith throws them in the fireplace. Speaking with confidence "With all the broken glass on the floor, and the equally harsh terrain outside, being barefoot will thwart any escape attempt on your part. All we need do now is wait for the time limit to end."

"This is where I was this morning. You must be crazy if you think that Captain Roberts won't find us here."

"I have no doubt that he'll make it here eventually, in fact, I'm rather looking forward to his arrival."

Snapping at him, "Keith, you're a fool." Continuing with a rebellious smirk, "Captain Roberts will tear you limb from limb with his bare hands, and you know it." Hoping that Keith will let me go, I jeeringly tell him, "Not that it would be much of a fight, in fact, not only will Captain Roberts take great pleasure in beating the life out of you, I shall rejoice in the watching of it."

Slapping my face. "Neither will happen, Vamp. You see, I placed a variety of booby traps in this shack since you were here earlier, and when your White Knight charges in, he'll be killed instantly."

Looking about the room, I see that Keith speaks true. Suddenly realizing that this is part of what both my Guardian Angel and Lucifer meant, I study the ropes and other apparatus the best I can, and in doing so, learn that his traps can only be disarmed from within, so when I get free, I will have to not only get outside, but also find my beloved, thereby removing the necessity of my gallant coming in for me.

Looking at Keith, not wanting him to think I may be studying his traps, I condescendingly scrutinize his ineptitude. "Haven't you managed to get that fire started yet?"

Shouting angrily as the fire finally lights. "You really can be a bitch, can't you, Vamp."

"Then let me go and be rid of me."

"Not a chance," he replies whilst approaching me with a sadistic look in his eyes. "Relieving you of some of that sass will be just the beginning of the evenings events."

"If you touch me Captain Roberts will—

Snatching the blanket off my lap and spreading it on the floor before the fireplace, he pompously declares, "Should by some chance he does get in, you won't say anything, that is unless you want to destroy his ability to think clearly."

"You don't know him. Captain Roberts is at his best under pressure."

"In battle perhaps, but that's quite a different thing from knowing your woman has just been violated, especially, when the act is perpetrated by the man's most loathsome adversary."

As he abruptly rips open the front of my shirt, I shriek, "Bastard!"

As I struggle violently within the chair, "Oh my, an honest to goodness corset. You do believe in punishing yourself for him, don't you."

As he unties the ropes binding my feet, I kick him, causing him to fall backwards, but quickly getting back to his feet, he hollers, "You bitch!," and again slaps me across the face.

Moving behind the chair to untie the rope that holds me to the chair, leaving my wrists bound together, he yanks me to my feet and forces a kiss on me, and unfortunately, my futile attempts to avoid him only seem to fuel his desires. Aroused by my fury, he appreciatively says, as he shoves me onto the floor, "How thoughtful of you to wear a skirt."

Fighting him as hard as I can, screaming and biting, it occurs to me that my struggling only makes him want me more. "I shall not add to your lust, Keith," and hoping to put a permanent damper on his libido, I go limp. At first, my inactivity seems to douse his desire, but then, after a couple moments when he continues his attack, I try insulting him. "I don't know how you can obtain any satisfaction from that puny worm you call your manhood," but my insults being fruitless, I suddenly realize that all he wants is the satisfaction of knowing that Captain Roberts will know that his woman was assaulted by his adversary.

Lifting up my skirt, "What sexy little garments you wear for him; my word, and stockings too. How convenient." Savagely ripping my ninies off me, throwing then in to the fire, "these will only be in my way."

Even with the blanket, the cement floor is quite hard, and as Keith crouches over me and pulls his dinky dingus out of his pants, I close my eyes and try to just lie still, but I can't, and again amid his grunting and slobbering, I fight him the best I can. While repeatedly yelling, "Get off me," I inadvertently begin to scream for my Captain, but remembering the booby traps, and realizing that my hollering is exactly what Keith wants, my cries for help cease, and in doing so, even though the situation is not my fault, I feel sullied.

With his act of rape now completed, he rises, and sneering at my tears, he bends over, grabs me by the front of my tattered blouse, and hauling me to my feet, he slams me back in to the chair. Quickly reattaching the small ropes; securing my wrists to the back of the chair, and this time being careful not to get kicked again, he again binds my feet to the chair's legs. Once satisfied I cannot get loose, Keith returns to the blanket, and feeling rather good about himself, he chugs a beer before drifting off to sleep.

After quietly struggling most of the night, my wrists are raw and bleeding from the abrasive nylon ropes, but despite the pain I manage to loosen them enough to slip my hands free. I know that Captain Roberts is searching for me, but how can he possibly know where to look. All I am sure of is that my Captain is mortal now, and in order for him to remain such, I must escape, and as I contemplate our lives, knowing both are dependent on the Captain winning, not just for today, or in this lifetime, but for all eternity, I am beginning to understand more of what Lucifer's cryptic message meant; it's up to me to get to a safe place where Captain Roberts can find me. Even so, I know that winning the game will require full use of my gallant's rugged physical strength, which, fortunately, is accustomed to fatigue and hardships. Fortunately, that is if you can draw a line between them, his need to succeed is his strongest attribute.

BLOOD and SWASH, The Unvarnished Life (& afterlife) Story of Pirate Captain, Bartholomew Roberts.........pt.1 "BOLT OF FRUITION"

> *Captain Roberts searched all through the night for his woman, but she was not to be found, nor had anyone seen her since earlier the previous morning. The only place he had not searched was #5, the derelict on the hill in Little Haven, & as he began his trek on foot, it proved to be a long & perilous journey.*

Succeeding in untying the ropes around my feet, I loop them about my arm and slipped the coiled rope over my head. Remembering that the door opens out, I quietly pick up the chair, and carrying it with me as I exit the room, I wedge the chair beneath the doorknob. Moving towards the window, I can see a bear trap lying beneath it, and not knowing what else to expect, I carefully look outside. "Oh great," I murmur, "we're on the upper floor," and believing it's too dangerous to prowl around the ground floor in the dark, especially amid the broken glass, I try desperately to open the window. Coming to the conclusion that it's jammed from the outside, and being what I believe to be my last recourse, I go back to the door, where as noiselessly as possible, I remove the chair. With the only light source being created by the fire burning in the hearth, I re-enter the outer room where I am grateful to find Keith still asleep on the blanket. After looking at the different ropes for a couple of minutes, I trace the rope leading to the bear trap on the landing, but as I turn to leave, Keith stirs quite a bit. Having no time to waste, I quickly return to the chair and just as I sit down he turns around and looks at me.

"I'd invite you to come lay next to me before the fire, but," as the jerk chuckles a bit at his tired old joke, "I can see you're tied up at the moment." Getting up, "I'll fetch breakfast."

Watching Keith head off down the stairs, I hurriedly dash back onto the landing. Unhooking the beastly bear trap from the outer rope, I carefully shove it in to the corner, and having decided earlier that my only way out is through the window, I pick up the chair, and swinging it just as hard as I can, I fling it forward, shattering the glass.

Quick as I can, I climb out the window, and after hanging onto the ledge for just an instant, I let go only to land hard. Despite my injuries, I pick myself up and proceed through the wooded area, but even though I am making every effort, the uncertain ground, covered with debris, causes injuries to the bottom of my bare feet with every stride.

> *Upon hearing the crash of the window breaking, Keith, in an explosion of anger, threw the breakfast on the floor & dashed up the stairs. Entering the room, he saw his foiled booby trap & the broken glass. Running to the window, & although he could not see any indication of which way his captive had gone, he was sure she would head for home. Storming out of the room, he picked up a bit of rope off the floor & headed downstairs, where, in a furious rage, was forced to remove a series of booby traps he'd set until finally the mechanism was dismantled enough for him to exit the building through the front door, & slamming the door shut as he left, he went in search of her.*

Despite the fact that Keith is looking for me, I have to stop for a couple of minutes. Resting on my hands and knees, I try to block out the pain emanating from the cuts on the soles of my bleeding feet. But again, I know this is but another aspect of what Lucifer said was my part. I need to draw strength from someone I love, someone else who had continued on despite his injuries. In this, I pray for help from my son who had overcome great obstacles associated with life threatening wounds, and as I pray, I find the strength needed to keep going.

Getting myself turned around, I look about frantically, but to my dismay, I have no idea where I am. If I can find either the ocean or a clearing, I can get my bearings. Until then, all I can hope for is that Keith won't find me before I find my Captain.

Faintly, hearing a bloodcurdling cry calling my name, I find myself terror struck, and as he stomps along through the leaves, it becomes quite apparent that Keith has gone completely mad. In my fright, I start to go to pieces. "Get a hold of yourself," says I quietly, whilst slapping my own face. Regaining my composure, I listen intently, and hearing faint sounds of what I believe to be someone moving quickly, I turn to face in the direction of the sound. But the woods are full of small critters, and as I peer in to the darkness, I find myself unsure of my senses, and hearing Keith's voice, again chillingly calling my name, I know he is all too close.

After a couple of minutes, altho' not from which direction, I can hear the water lapping against the shore, and if I can find it, I will at least know which way is North, and from there I can make my way to *Inn Finistère*. Both Captain Roberts and my parents taught me that I must learn to use all my senses, and in thinking about all the talks I have had with them in the past, my mind fills with those memories. Following my training, knowing that the ocean is close by, helps to ease the stress, and even if I can't find the shore I will at least be in an area where I can see the sky. Knowing that the moon always shines over the ocean this time of year, I remember that my Father, who had taken my brother and I out to both the woods and the desert many times when we were kids, repeatedly told us, 'Always know where you are,' and at that moment I realize that I am drawing strength, insight and knowledge from three people, just as Lucifer said. Nevertheless, despite my efforts to move quickly, Keith, beset by his madness, is gaining on me.

> *Unknown to Keith & V'lé, Captain Roberts; nearing an area where it is possible to climb the precipice, was on the beach just below where Keith & V'lé were located. It was an arduous climb, but fortunately, although the Captain did not know it, the cliffs are all that remained between himself & the woman he loves.*

Coming out of the woods, at last, I immediately look up, but to my dismay, as I pan the sky, there is no moon. I do however see the Big Dipper, and as taught me by both my parents, and my beloved Captain, I locate Polaris, and noting that Cassiopeia is on its left, I know not only that I am facing North, but that it's early morning, and knowing that *Inn Finistère* lies before me, I dash off. Once home, I will then be able to sound the fog horn, and using a signal known only to the Captain and myself, he will know that I am home safe.

Captain Roberts has also made it to the clearing, but the area is quite large, and being some distance away, we are unable to see one another in the early morning light. Starting down the path along the Cliffs edge, the Captain heads towards the old derelict, #5.

Emerging from the woods, Keith also enters the clearing, and altho' just barely, he sees me limping along in the distance. Knowing from my movement that the bottoms of my feet are hurting me a great deal, Keith not only quickens his pace, he begins yelling my name with maniacal frenzy.

Turning towards the sound, and seeing him running towards me, I dart in terror, but regrettably, even tho' I run as fast as I am able, it is not fast enough, for within less than a hundred feet he tackles me. Quickly getting to his feet he hauls me up. His grip tight about my wrist, I holler, "Let go of me!" but despite my efforts to thwart him, Keith, grabbing me about my waist and lifting me off my feet, flings me over his shoulder like a sack of grain, and carting me off, he heads back to where he held me captive.

Hearing my screams, Captain Roberts, boiling with rage, quickens his pace. Seeing us within moments he shouts, "McClure!" stopping Keith in his tracks!

Still hanging over Keith's shoulder, I look up, and seeing my lover, I call out to him tenderly. "fy Arglwydd."

Infuriated, Keith slowly turns around.

Keith, now facing Captain Roberts, and seeing the ruthless glint harboring within my Captain's eyes, Keith, undeterred, gives the Captain an immediate smug look as he holds his prize tightly.

In a demanding, almost bloodthirsty tone, the Captain roars, "Unhand her, you coward!"

Doing his best to infuriate Captain Roberts even more, Keith hollers, "Come and get your wanton, that is if you think you have enough grit, that's if the knowledge that I have just had my way with her doesn't tarnish her in your eyes."

As I continue to struggle against Keith's strong grasp, my efforts remain fruitless until another idea comes to mind, whereby I manage to bite Keith severely on his back, who in a rage, chucks me off his shoulder and onto the rocky terrain, an act that provides the very opening my Captain needed, but as he lunges forward, Keith manages to pop his adversary squarely in the jaw, but no blow from Keith, however severe, could slow down the stalwart mariner, who in doubling up both fists and bringing them up from the basement, belts Keith several times, knocking him flat on his back. Far from through, yanking Keith to his feet, Captain Roberts takes great pleasure in belting him several more times as they draw nearer to the edge of the cliff. Holding Keith up by the front of his shirt, "So you take pleasure in throwing women to the ground, do you?" and looking back at me, seeing me not only crumpled on the ground, but also my tattered clothing, and knowing that I have been assaulted, "If I were aboard my ship, I could relish the pleasure of feeding your carcass to the sharks after hanging you from my yardarm, but since we are not, I shall end the game thus," and using his other hand, Captain Roberts grabs Keith by the seat of his pants, and taking three steps forward, hurls him over the edge. Walking forward, the Captain looks down onto the beach below, and seeing Keith lying upon a boulder; his back no doubt broken, my Captain's ever quiet expression tells a tale of immense satisfaction.

Turning his attentions towards me once again, "My feet are pretty cut up, fy Arglwydd Nghapten."

Kneeling beside me as my gallant takes me in to his arms, giving me a kiss, I know my Captain is exhausted from the long trek and his brawl with Keith, but his fortitude being ten fold that of average men, I place my arms about his neck as he picks me up and carries me to *Inn Finistère* by way of the road. Resting, I lay my head against his muscular chest, but almost immediately, as the wind begins to howl, my Captain stops forthwith.

Suddenly, in a brilliant flash of fire and brimstone, shrouded in a cloud of red gray smoke which fills the air, Lucifer appears before us. "Thou hast won, Captain, and by my word, ye shall have thy prize."

Lifting my head off of my Captain's chest, "And just what would that be exactly?"

"Ye will forever be entwined together, throughout all eternity," promises Lucifer. "Thy woman hath saved thy life, for it was through her efforts thou fought in the clearing, rather than being killed instantly upon entering Keith's death laced trap. Be proud of her."

As my beloved Captain kisses me on the top of my head, "I am, Lucifer. Very proud indeed."

Anxiously, "Does this mean Captain Roberts shall remain mortal?"

"It does, and thine adventures will be as numerous as they are exciting. In parting Roberts, I shall state only that few men are born twice. Make the most of it."

"I shall."

Not the least bit dismayed by Roberts' victory, having Keith in his stead, Lucifer waves a salute as departs amid a colorful puff of smoke. Moments later, when the smoke clears, we find ourselves on the walk in front of *Inn Finistère*.

Upon entering, the Captain hollers, "We're home…"

Chapter Thirteen
A Dream Come True

"You're safe," exclaims my mother, as she and Katie rush in to the foyer.

"We're not only home, but the terror is over. There's just one thing. The Captain and I are not married. I lied about that."

"But wee will be," injects the Captain. "Is Mister Cullen still here?"

"Yes, he is, Captain," replies Katie, mournfully, whilst pointing towards the reception room, "but I'm afraid he's passed out on the sofa."

"Mrs Montgomery, please be kind enough to awaken him; he's performing our marriage ceremony, this night."

"It'll be a pleasure, Captain," responds Sue happily as she hurries into the kitchen to fetch a pitcher of water.

"Katie, Miss V'lé's feet are in neede of doctoring. She will also be needing help getting into her wedding goune."

Following us up the stairs, Katie pauses in front of the linen closet. Hurrying to catch up, she says, "I stopped to get the first aid kit."

Entering our room, Captain Roberts sets me down on the seat before my vanity, and giving me a peck of the forehead, "I shall leave thee alone whilst thou changes in to thy goune, but first, I am in neede of a quick shower."

MEANWHILE, DOWNSTAIRS IN THE RECEPTION ROOM →

Mister Cullen, now awake, follows Sue upstairs. Upon reaching the half-open bedroom door, he knocks.

Answering, Katie says, "Come in," and stepping out from behind the screen, "Have a seat, you two."

Exiting the bath, and passing thro', Captain Roberts goes aloft to what shall forever be his man cave.

My Captain, having gone upstairs to his retreat, I, with Katie's help, also take a quick shower. A few minutes later, returning to my vanity table, Katie applies Bactine® and bandages to the bottom of my feet, after which, Katie, closes the first aid kit, and helping me over to the dressing screen, she helps me in to my gown. A few minutes later, we both step out.

Seated near the dressing screen, Sue fondles the rich silk. "Your gown is lovely, V'lé."

"Most beautiful," agrees Mister Cullen, who is sitting just inside the door.

Beaming as I thank them, "The Captain bought it for me."

Speaking in a mildly shocked tone, Katie says, "You mean he's already seen it?"

"Well, sort of. It was amongst a dozen others in the boutique, but the Captain doesn't know which one I picked out, and I had a few minor alterations and some extras added."

Just then, a knock is heard on the opposite side of the door leading to the upper section of the turret. Seeing me dart back behind the dressing screen, Katie invites him in."

As the Captain enters, "You look magnificent, Captain," states Katie.

"Truly a fine figure of a man," adds Sue.

"Mister Cullen fashioned this striking ensemble for me," and noting the smile on the face of its creator, he adds, "it is just how I imagined and intended. I thank you for having it ready for me to wear on this special occasion."

"My pleasure, Captain."

Removing the jewelled Germantic fibulae from the box, "This fibulae," handing it to Katie, "a wedding gift from the jeweller, is to be worn upon, Miss V'lé's gown. Please find a suitable place for it."

"With pleasure, Captain."

As she steps back behind the screen, Captain Roberts places the box in his coat pocket.

> *The Captain's magnificent crimson coat, glistening with gold thread demarcating the Brocade fabric, matches both his boot tops & tricorne. His luxuriant, milk white shirt; made upon a broad yolk & fashioned from the finest silk, is neatly tucked in his trousers. Atop is worn a crimson & white fringed waist sash. The cuff's generously ruffled flounces; extending 3 inches beyond the coat's sleeves, & the matching jabot, were crafted from a rare piece of antique Point de Neige Venetian Lace. Upon the jabot, & consisting of 12 festoons of heavy 22 karat gold paper chain, & the sizeable jewel encrusted cross intended for the King of Portugal, was his magnificent necklace. The billowy black trousers, fashioned from heavy Egyptian cotton, are neatly tucked in the top of his over-the-calf, black boots; & upon his delicious curly, sable colored hair; loosely tied with a narrow black ribbon, was worn a fashionable, black tricorne hat adorned with 2 curled ostrich plumes; 1 red, & 1 black.*
>
> *Being in charming company, Captain Roberts, as a general rule, would've forgone his medieval sword & the matching bandoleer that holds his treasured, pearl gripped, flintlock pistols, but knowing his intended would desire him to wear the lot, he dressed loaded for bear.*
>
> *As a whole, the Captain's ensemble harmonized perfectly; what's more, his stately appearance, denoting one of command presence whilst demonstrating, not only his good taste & refinement, it obliterated any skepticism regarding his unassailable position as the most successful pirate of all time.*

MEANWHILE, DOWNSTAIRS IN THE FOYER ⇁

Another unexpected guest from afar has entered the house. Despite her natural wariness, curiosity gets the better of her, and she looks around downstairs. Hearing faint voices from above, she decides to venture upstairs, and following the sounds, she proceeds down the hall with caution until coming to the open door. Peeping in and seeing her grandmother just coming out of the loo, she enters saying, "Hello everyone. Umm, would anyone like to explain to me what's going on here?"

"Katrina?" says Sue, questioningly. "I had no idea you were coming to Wales. Why didn't you let us know?"

"I didn't know myself until a moment ago," she replies while looking the room over. "I was just leaving to go to work, and when I stepped out through my front door, I found myself standing in the foyer downstairs. Hearing voices, I searched until I found all of you in here, but just how I got here is a mystery."

Replying, Sue says, "Together, we'll see if we can come up with a reasonable explanation. First, however, we have a wedding to attend."

"Whose?" asks Katrina.

"Your mother's. The man standing by the French doors in the Crimson garb is the groom. What do you think of him?"

"He looks familiar," states Katrina, "and what a magnificent outfit, weapons and everything." Smiling, she adds, "It figures my mom would have a pirate themed wedding," laughing a mite.

Unaware of my daughter's presence, having just finished dressing my hair, I step out from behind my dressing screen and in to my Captain's view.

Gazing upon me, "Thou art lovely."

"Diolch 'chi, fy Arglwydd Nghapten." Suddenly seeing my daughter, I exclaim, "Kat!" Walking over to her, I give her a hug. Turning to face my Captain, "Allow me to introduce you to my fiancé, and walking up to him, "fy Nghapten, allow me to present, my daughter, Katrina."

"Miss Katrina," says the Captain whilst presenting a gracious bow, "thine aura and beauty, being that of thy mother, I recognized thee instantly."

"Thank you," replies Katrina amid a smile.

"Katrina, allow me to present, Captain Bartholomew Roberts."

Looking somewhat baffled, as she reaches out, the Captain gently lifts and kisses her hand. After musing a few moments, "Isn't that the name of the pirate on your website?"

"He is the pirate from my Website."

Taken aback, she moderately exclaims, "What?" And wearing an skeptical expression, Katrina, slowly turning her head to look at Captain Roberts for a moment, looks back at me. "Well, I knew he looked familiar."

"It's a long story, Trina, and between the lot of us you'll hear it all, but right now, allow me to introduce you to the others present.

Turning around, "This is Katie, my housekeeper, cook, and good friend."

"I'm happy to meet you, Katie."

Flashing her typical big smile, Katie replies, "I am very happy to meet you, Katrina."

Walking over to him, "Mister Cullen, this is my daughter, Katrina."

Rising, Mister Cullen says, "Delighted, I'm sure."

"Mister Cullen is not only the superintendent registrar, and a fine tailor, but also the owner of the haberdashery that made the magnificent ensemble Captain Roberts is wearing."

"I am very happy to meet you, Mister Cullen, states Katrina. "You do beautiful work."

"Thank you," replies Mister Cullen, smiling.

As the Captain approaches, "Thy mother, hath no Maid of Honour. I would be most pleas'd, if thou wilt grace the ceremony by standing up with her."

"I'll be happy to, Captain," replies Katrina, with a modest smile. Waiting for the ceremony to begin, she whispers, "Your gown is stunning, mom."

The cream-colored, Edwardian reproduction, is comprised of duchess satin, & a chiffon veil, both fashioned from mulberry silk.

Atop the bodice, covering the capped sleeves, was loosely pleated chiffon. Crisscrossing the bosom, the chiffon tapers to the side seams. Embellishing V'lé's back, was a congruous array of magnificent festoons consisting of strung pearls, seed beads, teardrops, & garnet danglers. The fabric covering the bosom & sleeves was bejeweled with a delicate spray of tiny garnets, & beginning where the right sleeve connects to the front of the bodice &

> ending just beneath her heart (where the 5th Century Fibula has been placed,) are 2 more like festoons.
>
> The underskirt was trimmed with a six-inch, gathered flounce, & the apron overlay, being drawn up at the sides, & attached at the small of the back, created both gentle folds in front, & a moderately sized bustle that flowed in to a chapel length train.
>
> Lastly, V'lé's hair, worn in the fashion the Captain preferred, was an array of all-over curls elegantly swept to the left side & decorated with a sprig of baby's breath held in place by the hand carved ivory hair comb fashioned by the Captain.

Walking out onto the balcony, Mister Cullen, taking notice of the town's folk gathering below on the veranda, turns, and standing with his back against the railing, "Everyone please take your places. Captain, V'lé, please stand here. You're here Katrina, next to your mother, Mrs Montgomery, you're just behind V'lé."

Removing from my finger, my Dragon engagement ring, I hand it to Captain Roberts, who asks my mom, "Will you serve as ring bearer?"

"Of course, Captain."

"Katie," begins Mister Cullen, "Have you the small Welsh bible?"

"Yup." Walking to my bureau, Katie picks up the bible, and handing it to Mister Cullen, she stands on my mom's right.

"We are gathered here today to unite this man and this woman in the time-honoured celebration of love as they become lawfully joined in holy matrimony. Theirs is a love that has endured separation and mortal danger, and in their struggle, as more obstacles were placed before them, their love grew stronger. There's is an union of true love."

Beginning with Captain Roberts, Peter Cullen states, "Whilst placing this ring on her finger, state your vow."

"Fy melys V'lé, as I place this ring upon thy finger as a symbol of my love and our bond of holy matrimony, I shall, whilst I live, shield thee with my body; honour thee with my words; share with thee all that I possess; and pledge thee my troth."

Turning to me, "Have you a ring you wish to give to John Bartholomew, V'lé?"

"Yes, I have." Taking the custom made, 22 karat gold ring from within my châtelaine purse, all can see the 3-masted tall ship, where atop the masts are placed the Captain's flags as represented by 2 black diamond chips, as well as the diamond dust sails that glistens even in the moonlight. Lastly, altho' not readily seen, Captain Roberts smiles faintly as he reads the words, *Royal Fortune,* engraved on the ship's stern.

Continuing, Peter Cullen says, "As you place this ring on the Captain's finger, state your vow."

"My dearest John Bartholomew, as I place this ring upon thy finger as a symbol of my love and our bond of holy matrimony, I shall, whilst I live, shield thee with my body; honour thee with my words; share with thee all that I possess; and pledge thee my troth."

Finishing up, Peter Cullen states, "In the presence of God, and before this company, John Bartholomew & V'lé, having given their consent, and exchanged vows and symbols of their love, I, according to God's Holy Law, proclaim them to forever be husband and wife." Joining our hands together, "Those whom God hath joined together let no one put asunder. Virtus Junxit Mors Non Separabit. Captain, you may kiss your bride."

Gently, my Captain places my veil behind my head, but before taking me in to his loving arms, he gazes in to my tear-filled eyes for a moment, and lifting my chin with the tips of his fingers he gives me the sweetest of all tender kisses.

As the Captain and I turn, Mister Cullen announces, "I present to all those present, Mister and Mrs John Bartholomew Roberts."

Amid the applause, I state, "Captain and Mrs Bartholomew Roberts, if you please."

"I stand corrected."

After hugs all around, my husband, in taking Mister Cullen's offered hand, takes him aside, pulls out a wad of dosh, and whilst handing it to him, "Please arrange for us a reception tomorrow at the Castle Inn in the late afternoon, and invite the entire village."

"I'll be glad to, Captain, and I'll do it up right well, but seeing that the village is below on the veranda," stepping out of the Captain's way, "I think they would relish being invited by you personally."

Stepping into view, "Ye and all of you, it will please both my bride and myself if you will join us tomorrow at dusk for refreshments and dancing at the Castle Inn."

Everyone below hollers, "Huzzah!"

"Not to hurry ye," my Captain begins, "but this union has been a long time coming, so if you don't mind."

Turning to my mom, Katie and Katrina, Peter asks, "Shall we go downstairs and start on the arrangements?"

Smiling jovially, the lot of 'em, indicating they love parties, shout happily as they depart.

As soon as the door closes, my incomparable Captain of the sea, seizes me somewhat roughly as he backs me up against the hardwood door. To both our liking, I reach to my left, towards the bureau, and pressing play on the boom box, the air fills with the bombastic music we both love.

There's a violent hunger in him, I can sense it. He is eager this night, eager to take that which now belongs to him. I too am eager, eager to feel the power that rages through his veins, and showing not only my approval, but also my desire to be ravished, I slam the dead bolt in to the closed position, and in raising his level of desire into a frenzy, he lunges towards me, kissing me passionately.

Knowing my lust is equal to his own, he slowly turns me around. Removing first the festoons; setting them on the table, he looks at the tedious lacings on the back of my dress, and reaching down to his boot, and pulling out his dirk, he slashes them open.

Turning me around, he is pleased to see, as he slowly pushes the sleeves down off my shoulders, that I am bare underneath, and backing up a couple steps, after removing his bandoleer and waist sash, he tosses his coat and vest onto the chair.

Holding out his hand, encouraging me to step over my gown, I reach out to begin undoing his trousers, but as I do, my Captain seizes me about my waist, and as he pulls me close, the scent of the rain and the ocean breeze upon my dark auburn tresses sends an added surge of passion throughout his body.

> *Quickly pulling his shirt over his head & dropping it on the floor, it was easy to see that Captain Roberts was eager to take that which now belonged to him, & although he dynamically backed his woman against the bedpost, the pirate, being no ones fool, knowing that her pleasure would serve to increase his own, staved off her efforts to rush ahead. Holding her wrists with his left hand whilst kissing all the areas of her body he could reach,*

whilst concurrently assiduously creating a combination of sensations about her erogenous zones, he effectively gave her cause to squeal & quiver. Knowing, as she rose to her tiptoes, that she was ready for his offering, he released her hands & clutched her firmly about the waist with his left arm, & pinning her against the bedpost to support her weight, he lifted her left thigh with his right hand & gave to her that which she begged for.

Desperate to match the power of his actions with her own, she reached above her head & grabbing the bedpost, her enthusiastic performance brought forth their concurrent fulfillment, & leaving neither of them the strength to remain standing, they crawled atop the bed and fell asleep.

MEANWHILE in MILFORD HAVEN —

As the air outside shrouds the landscape in a light fog, the harbor is bustling with activity, and as the Magnificent Clipper Ship awaits her new master, her crew studiously readies her, for on the ebbtide she sails to Little Haven. After that, who knows.

It is noon the following day when Katie knocks upon the bolted door. "I have brought breakfast, as requested."

"One moment, Katie," states Captain Roberts as he rolls out of bed. Covering himself with his robe, and nudging, me, his bride, "Wake up, fy annwyl, 'tis time for breakfast." Walking to the door and unbolting it, inviting her in with a slight smile, "Come in, Katie."

"Looks to be a lovely day, Captain," states Katie with a bright smile as she enters their room. Waiting just inside the door, "Shall I serve breakfast on the balcony?"

"Aye, Katie," and whilst passing by the bed en route to the French doors to open them for her, my Captain slaps me on the rump as he says, "Move thyself, fy annwyl, or thy breakfast will get cold."

Resting the tray on one of the chairs, Katie lays out our breakfast.

Wrapping myself in the comforter, "I'm a coming." Making my way to the wardrobe, I take out my plush chenille dressing gown, and having shrugged off the coverlet, and slipping into the red and black robe, I drag a brush quickly through my hair before wandering out onto the balcony. "Good morning, Katie. Isn't this a glorious morning?"

"'Tis a lovely day, to be sure, Mrs Roberts," replying with a toothy grin. "I trust you slept well."

"I had a wonderful night. In fact," smiling as I stretch a bit, "I can't remember a more relaxing night's sleep. As for today, it is the happiest day of my life."

Grinning, Katie says, "I would 'ave thought that yesterday would be the winner of that award."

"Oh no, Katie, that was the happiest night of my life. Actually, although today will be extra special, I think each day from now on shall be the happiest of my life."

"Why so, fy annwyl?" asks Captain Roberts.

Speaking with a smile, "Thou wilt learn the reason later, fy Arglwydd, when I present to thee, thine wedding gift.

Knowing that asking questions would be a waste of time, the Captain, as he begins to eat his hearty breakfast, puts his mind's curiosity to rest.

I, of course, am eager for the day to pass and late afternoon to arrive. It is going to be a full moon, and clear skies are predicted.

"Can I get ya anything else?" asks Katie before she turns to leave.

"In about half an hour, I will need your help getting dressed."

"Make that a full hour," states the Captain.

"Yes, sir." replies Katie with a broad smile as she quietly closes the door.

Returning downstairs, Katie sets the tray on the kitchen table and joins Katrina and Sue, who are just sitting down to breakfast on the verandah.

"So this is Little Haven," Katrina begins as she sits down in the chair facing towards the harbor. "What a beautiful view," she says, looking around. "All those boats, just resting on the sand like that, reminds me of Lake Mead."

"At high tide," beings, Katie, "all the coves will be filled with water."

"Sounds refreshing. Taking a couple bites of her breakfast, "The air is so clean and fresh, it's easy to understand why mom doesn't want to return to the United States."

Swallowing a mouthful of molasses drenched pancakes, Sue informs us, "Although V'lé loves it here, she is leaving."

"She isn't!" exclaims Katie as she pours herself a cup of tea.

Taking a sip of her tea, Katrina asks, "Where is she going, Grandma?"

Glancing at Katrina between mouthfuls whilst dipping a fork full of pancakes in to the small bowl of molasses, "I promised her I wouldn't say anything until after they left on their honeymoon."

Cutting the tomatoes on her plate, "A honeymoon trip. How exciting," states Katie just before taking a bite.

"V'lé made plans several days ago. Captain Roberts doesn't even know about them yet," explain Sues, taking a sip of her coffee. "V'lé plans to tell him after the reception."

"My lips are sealed," Katie says assuredly whilst popping in to her mouth the last bite of her toast.

"Going on a honeymoon isn't leaving, Grandma," states Katrina, while taking another bite of her breakfast.

"Well," as Sue continues, "V'lé didn't actually say, but I think they'll be gone for quite a long time, but don't say anything to anyone or it will ruin the surprise."

Rising from the table, taking her cup of tea with her, Katrina walks around a bit. "Did my mom say when she would be downstairs, Katie?"

"I am to go up in about three-quarters of an hour to help Mrs Roberts dress."

"Why," asks Katrina. "Can't she get dressed by herself?"

"Not with the outfit she plans to wear," Katie replies, smiling.

"V'lé's taken to wearing the clothes from past eras on a regular basis," states Sue.

"That's my mom, flamboyant as ever," replies Katrina, smiling.

"Perhaps so, Miss," states, Katie, "but the main reason is because Captain Roberts loves them, and she wants to please him, and loving period attire herself, makes the doing pleasurable."

Smiling, "Let me know when you're going upstairs Katie and I'll join you. In the meantime, I want to know how I got here, how my mom met a ghost, and, perhaps the most important question, why he's no longer a ghost, or is he?"

"Well," begins Sue. "It started a little less than a year ago, just a short time after we moved here. One night, about midnight, the Captain appeared to your mom upstairs in her room and he's been here ever since, but it wasn't until last week, with the help of V'lé's ex boyfriend, Keith, that Captain Roberts was reborn."

"I thought Keith died years ago," states Katrina, remembering.

"He did," replies Sue.

"Anyway," as Katie takes over the telling of it, "Keith kidnapped your mum, but she escaped, and Lucifer—"

"You mean the devil?" gasps Katrina.

"Yup. Anyways," as Katie continues, "with your mum being the prize, there was a fight to the death between the Captain and Keith, just last night." Smiling broadly, "Fortunately, as you can see, the Great Pirate Roberts won the contest, and now, as their reward, they are both immortal, and with any luck, they'll truly live happily ever after."

"Wow!" exclaims Katrina. "But how do I fit in?"

Pouring herself a cup of coffee, Sue replies, "We don't have any idea why or how you got here."

Offering as one explanation as she places the breakfast dishes on the tray, Katie suggests, "Perhaps it was because your mum missed you." Picking up the heavy tray, Katrina hurries to the door to open it for her.

"I guess I should ring Mister Cullen," begins Katie, "and find out what time he wants to go to Woolies to pick up the decorations."

Twilight Time Approaches ¬

> *As the townspeople entered the reception hall, Katie, Sue & Mister Cullen were busy welcoming them. Katrina; meanwhile, whilst the guests are happily enjoying themselves dancing & socializing, kept an eye out for the Bride & Groom.*

Looking out the door, and seeing my car, Katrina ducks back inside. "Here they come."

Whilst parking across the street, I see my daughter standing out front waving to us. "Well, fy Nghapten, art thou ready to be the center of attention?"

"Such has never beene my intention," says he with a wisp of a smile, "but be that as it may, family and friends await us."

Again dressed in his crimson brocade damask coat and black trousers, the Captain opens the door and steps out of the car, whilst I, being the driver, open my door and step out. To complement him, I am wearing a copy of Scarlett O'hara's famous red dress that I, myself, fashioned nigh on a year ago, and that he chose as one of his favorites.

Walking towards the Castle Inn on my Captain's arm, we pause on the top step where we are met by my daughter, Katrina.

"Mom, Captain." Turning, she leads the way.

Entering on the arm of my beloved, as one of our favourite tunes ('The Lady In Red') begins, we are greeted by Mister Cullen's voice as it booms over the microphone, "Ladies and Gentlemen, I present to you, the bride and groom, Captain and Mrs John Bartholomew Roberts." As my Captain and I approach the podium, everyone applauds as Mister Cullen says, "Please, Captain, will you honour us with a speech."

Hearing the roar of an enthusiastic crowd, I smile graciously, saying, "He gotcha."

Knowing he can not refuse, Captain Roberts takes a deep breath and, as instructed by Mister Cullen's deportment, walks up to the microphone.

" 'Tis grateful wee be for yer welcoming, and wee art pleasured to have ye all here. On behalf of myself, I offer my thanks. 'Tis an honour to know I am welcome."

Amid the claps, cheers and whistles, Captain Roberts backs away from the microphone.

Stepping back to the mic, Mister Cullen instructs the musicians to begin playing once more. Covering the microphone with his hand and moving slightly out of its hearing range, Mister Cullen informs Captain Roberts, "When you and your bride reach the dance floor, the musicians will play your favorite waltz, but first it's customary to step to the banquet table and cut the cake."

Amid a modest smile, Captain Roberts verbalizes his appreciation, "Thank you, Mister Cullen, for arranging this elegant reception."

Replying with a smile, "On behalf of Sue, Katie, Katrina, and myself, you are both, most welcome."

"Thank you very much, all of you," says I, smiling.

"Shall we cut the cake, fy melys?" asks my Captain, offering his forearm.

Accepting his gracious invitation, "Happily, fy Arglwydd," and placing my hand atop his wrist, crosswise, he escorts me from the podium to the banquet table. As we step up to the cake, both of us, smiling broadly, are very pleased by the beautiful a tall ship anchored in a lagoon with a castle, flying dragons, and images of ourselves sitting on the beach of a tropical island.

Picking up the knife together, we make the first cuts and place the piece on a small paper plate. Smiling, I pick up a small piece with my fingers, prompting my lover to take a bite. In turn, he offers the second bite to me.

Announcing with a gracious smile, "It's delicious."

"Would thee care to waltz, fy Arglwyddes," asks my gallant with a gleam in his eye.

"Delighted, fy Arglwydd," says I, after arising from a deep curtsey.

Again, as I lay my hand upon my gallant's wrist, the musicians start to play the haunting little waltz from 'Edward Scissorhands,' as he escorts me to the center of the dance floor, and taking my hand in his, whilst placing his left forearm just beneath my shoulder blade, my Captain and I begin to waltz. As we travel throughout the room, as the magic created by our happiness fills the air, my face, all abloom with a radiant smile, is graciously returned by my Captain in the highest fashion, and for the next 2 hours, as we continue to dance to a variety of lovely little pieces, our favorites are the Waltz & the Kizomba.

Chapter Fourteen

The Ultimate Surprise

Nearly 9 o'clock, it is, by the time we finally manage to escape our guests by way of the back exit, and once outside, he takes me into his arms and kisses me. Releasing me, "Come, ngwraig, quickly, before our guests discover wee have gone missing."

Taking me once more by the hand, we proceed to trot along the outside of the building, when suddenly, as we round the corner, my Captain stops short.

Knowing he sees the carriage, "Our transport, fy Arglwydd Nghapten."

Smiling at me, " 'Tis beautiful."

Returning his smile, mine eyes beam brightly. "I wanted us to depart in grandiose style, and an adventure filled honeymoon seemed the perfect prelude to a wonderful life."

Lifting the front of my gown with my left hand that already clutches my train as my Captain takes a hold of my right hand, we hurry down the steps to the Barouche. Opening the door, my Captain, lending a hand as I step up, follows closely behind me.

Upon closing the door, Captain Roberts, assuming the carriage was hired simply to drive us home, slaps the side of the carriage, signaling the driver to proceed.

Thoroughly enjoying the ride, "This is a wonderful way to travel, Bartholomew. I've driven jog carts and 4-wheeled buggies, and once I even drove a stagecoach, but aside from my pony cart, which I drove for years, and always driving the car, being a passenger is nice."

"Thou art one for surprises, fy annwyl, and the carriage is a most pleasant one." Looking out beyond the cove, Captain Roberts, espying a beautiful, 3-masted ship lying at anchor, hollers, "Stop!"

As the driver reins in, the Captain, opening the door, steps out. While simultaneously reaching for my hand, he speaks with much excitement as he points towards the ship. "Come quickly, V'lé, wee must have a closer look!"

Picking up my gown's train, I take my beloved's hand as I step down from the carriage. As we proceed towards the beach, I am thrilled to see my Captain is so taken by the ship.

"She's a beauty," he states with a beaming look about him as we hurry to the water's edge. "I have not seene such a ship since me *Royal Fortune*."

Ne'er have I seen him so lit up, but then this is the most magnificent sailing ship to come in to view since the 4-masted Barque, *Sedov*, visited Milford Haven, aboard which, as she welcomed visitors, we both delighted ourselves in trodding her deck several times during her brief stay.

This ship, with her distinctively long hull, narrow prow; and lightly aft raked masts, which came in to being in the 1800s, is a replica of the clipper ship's, Flying Cloud for it's design, and the Comet's luxurious appointments.

"Thou hast done a bit of research, fy melys, what dost thou make of her?"

"She's a Clipper. 225 feet long, 41 ½ foot breadth of beam, a 21 ½ foot draught, 1,752 tons burthen, a bowsprit measuring 20 feet outboard, and a mainmast reaching 97 feet into the sky." Seeing his look, I add, "I saw her for the first time last Monday, just before meeting thee at the boutique, and being curious, I made inquiries. The man at the Milford boatyard told me she's just out of dry dock after a full refit, and her new owners take on both passengers, and trainees to help offset her maintenance costs."

"It would be grand to sail on her," states Captain Roberts in a nostalgic tone.

"Yes, it would." Speaking in glimmering anticipation, "Since we're here, let's ask if there's an empty cabin this trip. Surely the Captain's around someplace."

"On board to be sure," states Captain Roberts, "for the crew appears to be making her ready to sail on the ebb tide, but how to get out there proposes a problem."

"Look," says I pointing, "there's a man in a rowboat over there. Let's ask if he'll take us out to the ship."

Elated with enthusiasm, he picks me up and swings me around, and being excited, he hurries me along.

Upon reaching the young man, and offering him a tenner, my Captain asks, "Can you take us out to that Ship?"

"Sure, hop in," replies the young man.

As we take our seats in the dinghy, Captain Roberts asks, "Is the Captain aboard?"

"No, not at the moment, but I know that the crew, who are enthusiastically awaiting his arrival, are making last minute preparations."

"Raring to head out to sea, are they?"

"Aye, madam, just as soon as the Captain's on board."

"I thought as much," Captain Roberts remarks as the sailor rows the boat. "What be the name of the ship?"

"I don't know, sir. She is under new ownership, and her new name does not yet grace her hull."

Captain Roberts wasn't aware that I had been making arrangements for our sail every free moment I was alone. After speaking with Peggy at the costume shop after meeting with Mister Baines in the restaurant, she sent over complete period wardrobes for the entire crew, including ourselves that arrived earlier this afternoon, and with the boatyard managers help, having the ship, crewed and provisioned, the ship is ready for a 30 day cruise. While the officers, cook, pastry chef, medical personnel, and my personal trainer are hired, the about half of the remaining crew, those wishing to be trained in the art of sailing, have paid to sail. In regard to *Inn Finistère*, my mother and Katie will take care of business during my absence.

Being a large ship, and quite a ways to her, it takes about ten minutes before the sailor rows alongside, Coming to the ship's affixed ladder, my Captain states, "Thou wilt have a bit of trouble climbing in that dress, fy Annwyl."

"Fret not, fy Arglwydd. When this was the only mode of travel across the sea, many ladies in fine gowns managed to board these ships."

"Passenger ships generally docked in port when the patrons came and went, fy annwyl."

"Was Elizabeth Trengrove[HCA 6, B6] not wearing a floor length dress, fy Arglwydd?"

Replying with a chuckle, "Aye, that she was."

Exposing my calves a mite, I just smile as I drape the lower part of my long gown over my right arm, and whilst climbing the ship's ladder, my gallant, to insure my safety, follows close behind me.

Reaching the top, two men dressed in historical pirate attire help me on board.

"Welcome aboard, madam," says one of them.

"Thank you."

As my Captain finishes his assent, "Permission to come aboard."

Speaking with an Irish brogue, "Permission granted, sir. I am the Bos'n, Sean Taylor."

Offering his hand, "A pleasure to meet you, Mister Taylor. I am Bartholomew Roberts."

"An honour to have you aboard, Captain."

"Pray, sir, would it be asking too much to grant me and my bride leave to look about the ship?"

"Be my guest."

Brimming with delight, my Captain, clasping his hands together and rubbing them, "She's a beauty. What be the name of the ship?"

His persistence in wishing to know the ship's name, forces me to reveal my surprise a little sooner than I would've liked, and opening my reticule, I take out a rolled document written on heavy paper and hand it to him.

Taking the scroll, "What be this, fy Melys?"

Smiling, I reply, "Read it."

Upon brief examination, he looks up in astonishment. "They be the ship's papers."

"Your gold coins, fy Arglwydd," whispering in his ear, " I traded about half of 'em." Smiling broadly as I speak, "I took the liberty of re-christening her *Royal Fortune*."

Jovially, my Captain, grabbing me up, kisses me in public. "Ne'er has their been such a loving gift. Diolch 'chi." And with great enthusiasm, taking me in tow, my Captain swiftly makes his way aft along the starboard side towards the Quarter-Deck, and upon our arrival, I see the Quarter-Master approaching.

Introducing himself, "Captain Roberts, I am Michael Llewelyn." Offering his hand, "I have the honour of being your Quarter-Master."

As they engage in a firm handshake, "'Tis pleased I am to make your acquaintance, Mister Llewelyn."

Eager to get underway, Captain Roberts wastes no time in becoming master of his ship, and from the moment he takes command, standing aplomb upon his quarter-deck, his voice and manner shows him to be a confident commander, who, ne'er forgetting a nigh fatal experience, and before giving the order to weigh anchor, asks, "What water, provisions and necessities be on board, Mister Llewelyn?"

As is part of his duties, the Quarter-Master replies, "Except for fresh water, we have sufficient supplies for a three month sail. Of water, in the realm of hygiene & necessaries, our cistern contains enough water to last 30 days. For drinking and cooking, we have laid in a supply of bottled water sufficient to last 60 days."

"And the crew complement?"

"71, which not only includes 5 officers and 10 junior officers, but a full kitchen staff, a physician and nurse, a Reverend, 3 musicians, plus 45 crewing the deck and sails, 25 of whom are trainees who have paid to learn the art of sailing."

"Excellent. Weigh anchor; make for the Atlantic."

"Aye, aye, Captain." With his megaphone in hand, the Quarter-Master relays the order to the men standing by the capstan, "Weigh anchor."

"With your permission, fy Nghapten, I shall change in to suitable attire."

"Granted."

Knowing my desire to witness everything, Captain Roberts, looking at his Quarter-Master, as I make my way to the main deck, asks, "What do you think, Mister Llewelyn?"

Knowing exactly what his Captain is thinking, he replies, "It will be interesting to see how fast she can get out of that gown and into her shipboard attire."

Speaking with just a hint of a chuckle, "Quite." Taking from his pocket the watch I gave him, my Captain looks back at me, and just as I reach the main deck, he calls to me in a loving tone. "Mrs Roberts."

Turning to look at him, "Yes, fy Nghapten?"

His expression stern and commanding, "Thou hast ten minutes."

Smiling broadly, "Thank thee, fy Nghapten." With my train still over my right arm, I lift the front of my gown and scurry towards the bow until amidship.

Noting I look lost, one of the crew, whilst pointing at the doorway in what looks like a little room on the deck, says, "Through there, Mrs Roberts."

"Thank you," says I. And again lifting the front of my gown, I descend the spiral steps to the crew deck.

Also on board is my trainer, an experienced female deckhand named Joanna, whose main job is to train me to be a useful member of the crew, is also to act as my lady's maid when I need help getting into or out of one of my period ensembles whilst in port. Reaching the passageway, I see her waiting for me at the far end.

Calling to me, "Here, Mrs Roberts."

As I hurry aft, I am glad to see my trainer is waiting to help me change. As for what my beloved Captain will say when he sees a female, and an Irishwoman to boot, as part of his crew, is anyone's guess, and be that as it may, I love Ireland, so my Captain will just have to get use to the idea.

"Quickly now, Mrs Roberts, we must get to our station."

Just as I finish pulling up my thigh-high boots, "First, permit me to introduce you to Captain Roberts." Dashing up the steps I am again on the main deck, and only 6 minutes have passed by the time Joanna and I are topside and heading aft.

Standing at the bottom of the steps leading to the Quarter-Deck waiting to be acknowledged, Captain Roberts, upon seeing me, states with a glimmer of a smile, "A pirate if ever I saw one, and in excellent time."

Smiling just a mite, "Thank thee, fy Nghapten." My voice becoming more serious as I motion to Joanna, "Miss O'Malley, my trainer, and I, are members of thy deck crew."

Raising an eyebrow for an instant, my Captain asks, "And your duty station?"

We are part of the fores'l sheet crew, Captain," states Miss O'Malley with a hint of a smile."

"Train her well, Miss O'Malley."

"I shall, Captain."

Speaking in a commanding tone, Captain Roberts states, "Man your stations."

Both replying, "Aye, aye, Captain," we turn to.

Upon arriving, our station being just behind the Foremast, my trainer begins to instruct me in my duties.

Turning towards Mister Llewelyn, Captain Roberts speaks quietly. "Ne'er before has a woman crewed upon me ship, and now there be two of 'em."

"A sign of the times, Captain," replies Mister Llewelyn, with just the hint of a smile.

"Hmm…"

The Bos'n having reported to Mister Llewelyn that the anchor is secured, the Captain of the new *Royal Fortune* orders, "Make saile."

Lifting his megaphone, the Quarter-Master repeats the order.

"Just remember what I've told you and all will be well," states Joanna as she relays to me what is happening, and exactly what we, working as a team, need to do.

Suddenly I am frightened, "Joanna?" I utter timidly.

"There's nothing to worry about," Joanna assures me. "Just keep your eyes open and follow orders. Captain Roberts will be proud of you, trust me."

As I glance his way, seeing my beloved on the Quarter-Deck giving clear and decisive orders, I see him in his element for the first time. Strong of mind and heart, his face is tense and alert. All around me, I see men scurry up the ratlines, crossing to their places along the yard arms upon the ropes that serve as stirrups, and when all are in place, and the sails begin to unfurl, my trainer says, "Following my lead, pull on this sheet with all the strength you possess." Forthwith, Joanna and I, who are amongst those manning the fores'l sheet, and the rest of those on the sheet crews, adjust the Course sails by pulling our respective sheets taut, lashing them in to place upon the belaying pins, we adjust them frequently until our heading is achieved, after which, standing in awe as I watch the Mizzen and Cross-tree sails fill with the wind, the motion of the ship is smooth and graceful as the ocean water laps against the hull, and as the next chapter in our lives begins, the great ship glides swiftly through the estuary towards Saint George's Channel.

> *Captain Roberts, overseeing from the Quarter-Deck whilst scrutinizing the performance of his crew, was decidedly pleased, especially in regard to his bride, who, as a member of the sheet crew, was no slouch as the great ship made for the open sea.*

"Course direction, Captain?" asks his Quarter-Master, who stands beside him.

Remembering the day I said that if my woman had beene born in my time I would 'ave taken her upon my ship and shown her all the wonderful places in the world, and that's exactly what I intend to do. "Upon reaching the Atlantic, after making our distance such that wee be a law unto ourselves, steer in a southerly direction, and the Mediterranean. Once there, I shall plot a course in and around the Greek Isles."

"Aye, aye, Captain!" replies his Quarter-Master with a smile, knowing they are in for a great trip, and knowing the crew will be delighted as well, he lifts his megaphone and announces their immediate destination for all to hear. "Crew of the *Royal Fortune*, we are bound for the Greek Isles."

By the sound of the crew cheering, it is evident that his announcement is well received. After the enthusiastic crew simmers down a bit, Mister Llewelyn continues. "Our course will be west by south until we make twelve miles distant, after which, we shall steer in a southerly direction towards the Med."

For some little time the crew works diligently and once our course direction is South, Joanna informs me, "You can relax now, Mrs Roberts."

"Please feel free to call me V'lé."

"Thank you, V'lé. Now that we're on course, we can take a break till we are called on, or need to perform our other duties."

"When will the Captain be free to relax?"

"He's free now, but it may be awhile before he comes down from his command post," says Joanna, smiling, adding, "If I were he, I would want to relish the moment."

"Yeah, he might at that, but being it's been long day, it's more likely he's very tired."

Asking, whilst I sees the first shift of the new day begin their eight-hour shift as the ship's pilot strikes the bell, whilst simultaneously singing out " 'Four-Bells & All's Well,' " I asks the Quarter-Master, "Aside from the Welsh Flag atop the main, is there a ship's flag?"

"As a matter of fact," replies the Quarter-Master with a slight smile on his face, "your Missus sent out a supply of flags yesterday morning."

Chuckling a little, "Considering the crew's attire, I canne almost guess." Taking a deep breath, "Waste no more time Mister, let's see it."

Speaking in to his megaphone once more, "Raise the ship's colors."

Almost instantly, mine own famous Jolly Roger, bearing the image of myself and a skeleton clutching an hourglass, is hoisted to the top of the mizzen. The other, where I stand upon two skulls, is hoisted to the top of the spirit mast.

Chuckling a bit whilst shaking my head, "Seemes my bride is just full of surprises."

"Aye, Captain," replies Mister Llewelyn, "she is indeed." Adding, "And as one of the course sheets crew, especially it being her first time out, I thought she performed well."

"Aye, that she did." After pausing a moment, I add, "Steady as she goes." As I head for the steps, "If you neede me, I shall be in my cabin."

Awaiting the command duty officer to relieve him, the Quarter-Master repeats my command, "Aye, aye, sir. Steady as she goes."

As the Captain walks down the steps leading from the Quarter-Deck to the Main Deck, Joanna says, "He's coming, V'lé. I caution you to remember that he is in command and you are part of his crew. It's very important that he maintains the crew's respect, so don't be put off if he appears either stern or somewhat distant whilst in their view, after all, he is the Captain."

"I understand Joanna. Rest assured that I shall conduct myself accordingly."

As the Captain approaches, "You did well, Mrs Roberts."

" I thank thee, fy Nghapten." Turning slightly, " May I again present, Miss Joanna O'Malley. Not only is she my trainer, she's distantly related to, Grace O'Malley, the famous pirate Queen of Ireland."

"A pleasure, Miss O'Malley. As a lad, I heard many stories about your ancestor. When time permits, if you and the crew would enjoy the telling, I shall be pleas'd to share them."

"Thank you, Captain, I'd like that. May I say that I am very pleased to be a member of your crew, and I shall do my best to instruct Mrs Roberts in her duties."

"Thank you, Miss O'Malley, and now, please excuse us."

"Certainly, Captain." Turning, she retires for the evening.

"Come with me," orders my Captain as he proceeds to walk towards the bow.

Keeping in mind what my trainer, Joanna, had told me, I walk quietly beside my Captain without question.

Seemingly to know exactly where he is going, the Captain stops by a door leading to the lower decks. Having traversed the steps, we proceed along the passageway until coming to a T-junction, "Which is the way to our cabin?"

Gesturing straight ahead with my hand, "This way."

Maintaining his commanding tone, "Proceed."

Proceeding forward, we pass numerous doors on both sides of the 80 foot passageway. "The door to our cabin lies at the end of this corridor. Measuring 12 feet deep, and spanning the breadth of the ship, methinks thou wilt find it most comfortable."

"Whyfor dost thou wish to be a member of the crew?"

"To be anything less, fy Arglwydd, would make me an outsider."

Upon reaching the door, it's a little after midnight, and as I turn the knob, my Captain scoops me up, and carrying me across the threshold, he shuts the door behind him with his foot. Looking around, "I've never seen a ship so lavishly appointed."

"I heard it's décor is similar to another Clipper, called the Comet." As my Captain puts me down, I ask, "When dost thou have to be back on deck?"

Removing his ostrich plumbed, tricorne, "I have no plans to return untill mid morning."

Always very careful of his appearance, my Captain, espying the man's valet in the far corner, walks across the room whilst unwrapping his waist sash. Having hung up his elegant damask coat and sash, he dons the smoking jacket that hangs on the lower arms of the nicely equipped valet, and crossing the room again, he takes a seat and lights his pipe.

"I was quite aroused by thy lusty manner in which thee handled the sheet at thy station."

Smiling up at him as I seat myself and begin unlacing the lower inside of my boots, "I am glad of that. For a fleeting moment I thought thee were disappointed in me."

"Thou hast no neede to fear such, fy annwyl."

"I shan't, fy Nghapten," stating with confidence as I again smile at him, "not ever again."

Looking about the cabin a bit, and then at me, "Thou looks fetching in that getup, fy melys," says he, sporting a lustful grin.

With my face lit up, "Diolch 'chi, fy Nghapten. I rather hoped thee liked it."

Setting down his pipe, "There is but one problem," he replies in a rather serious tone as he rises and walks towards me.

With a quizzical look, "What?"

"Thou art still wearing it!" And pulling me to him sharply, he kisses me with a fierce intensity. "Thee stirs my passion, fy melys, and I shall have thee now."

Quickly unhooking my bustier, my Captain tosses it on the settee, and with an almost savage demeanor, he pulls my shirt out from the confines of my black leather jeans and up over my head. All the while, as he relieves me of my attire, my entire body quivers from his touch, but even though I am under the spell of the captivating, Bartholomew Roberts, the most successful pirate in history, I am not to be tamed, nor would he wish me to be.

Breathing quite intensely in response to his passion whilst undoing the buttons of his breeches, my lust for him is a match for his own, and when his body, glistening from the tiny water droplets upon his skin, touches mine, the indescribable feeling inside me escalates, and grabbing his arm, turning him around quickly, I push him backwards against the bulkhead.

Pleasantly surprised at my forcefulness, and speaking in a low, seductive voice, "My but thou art a brazen wench."

Having tossed him a shameless grin whilst running my fingers through his delicious thick mane, I maul him, wildly kissing his chest.

Responding in kind, forcibly taking control, he pins my wrists with a single hand, and scooping me up, and lying me on our bunk, delighting in his forcefulness, I succumb to his aggressive take over as he mounts me. Matching the driving force of his movements with my own, further demonstrating to him the intensity of my desire as my nails dig in to his back as our mutual need for pleasuring is satisfied, I pull the satin comforter over us.

SEVERAL HOURS LATER →

Awakened by the sudden increase of the ship's movement, I look beside me to find my seasoned Captain sleeping peacefully. For him, the movement of the ship as she heels atop the wind's gusty swells is as relaxing as being nestled within a cradle. I, however, not yet so accustomed, would surely have rolled out of the bunk and onto the deck if my lover's strong arms had not been securely wrapped around me.

When the earliest of morning's light streams in, I peer out the window to find dawn is just breaking, and as the bright orange sunlight shimmers upon the water, the helmsman, sounding the bells twice, makes it 5 a.m. Wanting to be topside so I can enjoy my first sunrise aboard a Tall Ship, I inadvertently wake my lover as I try to wiggle out of his firm hold.

Asking in a whisper, "Where art thou going, fy Ngariad?"

"I want to go topside to see the sunrise."

"The sunrise?" After giving the matter a few moments thought, "Art thou brave enough to climb the mainmast to the crow's nest during the twilight; wherefrom, the view is like no other."

With a hopeful expression, I ask, "Is there a Lubber's hole?"

"Aye, fy annwyl."

Speaking with aspiration, "I'll climb up there if thou wilt come with me."

Slapping me on the rump as he gets out of bed, "Then let us hurry in to some clothes."

With an alluring look, "If thou continues in such a manner, fy Arglwydd, "we will not see the sunrise this morning."

"This here cabin is not the onely place where copulation is likely, fy melys."

"Considering thy rather capricious mood this morning, wouldst thou be referring to the crow's nest?"

With a rakish grin, "Such occurrences are best decided by circumstance."

In lieu of possible lustful activities, I slip in to an appropriate outfit, and when we are both dressed, we make our way topside.

Standing before the shrouds and ratlines belonging to the mainmast, I stop, and looking up, speaking somewhat timidly, "Sure is a long way up, isn't it."

Remembering my fear of heights, Captain Roberts removes my need to climb to the crow's nest in such a manner as not to make me feel as though I'd be letting him down as a result of my fears. "If thou prefers, fy annwyl, the view from the Quarter-Deck is excellent."

Looking at him, studying his face for a moment, I know that ne'er would my Captain require I do anything that frightened me that wasn't absolutely necessary; however, it being very important for me to be able to climb the shrouds and ratlines, my determination to do so is not so much to please the man I love, as it is to conquer my own fears, and as I gaze deep into his eyes, I find the courage. Taking a deep breath as I turn, I grab hold of the ropes and step onto the chain plates. Taking a moment to accustom myself to the swaying of the ship, I begin to climb.

Shouting aloft, my Captain cries out, "Ahoy the watch!"

The crewman above, looking down and seeing his Captain, replies, "Aye, Captain. Top o' the morning to ya."

"Wee be coming up. Prepare to assist Mrs Roberts."

Opening the lubber's hole, the Irishman replies, "Aye, aye, sir."

Staying alongside as I carefully make my ascent, my Captain is ready to assist me should I need him. Nearing the top, the area becoming too narrow for us both to continue abreast, "Thou must proceed alone, but fear not, for I shall be right behind thee."

Climbing the next fifteen feet alone, I reach the lubber's hole, and poking my head inside, the crewman offers his hand. As each of us grasps the other's wrist, he helps me inside.

"Thank you." Once inside, giving Captain Roberts plenty of room to join us, I quickly step aside and out of the way.

Relieving the watch, "Mrs Roberts and myself, wishing to see the sunrise, will finish your watch."

"Aye, sir," and closing the hatch as he departs, "Thank you, sir!"

> *Captain Roberts was pleased that the woman of his choice enjoyed both sailing, & those pleasures which can only be found on the high seas. Only last week he was but a spirit, not even able to touch or feel the warmth of her skin, & the sea that he loved was forever lost to him, when by way of a passel of great gifts, he was mortal once more, married to the woman he loves, & once again Captain of a magnificent ship; this time with his woman at his side, & knowing she relishes the sea as much as he, it shall always be a match made in heaven.*

Looking all around, I says, "What a magnificent view. It just takes your breath away."

"Thou takes my breath away, fy melys," utters my Captain softly as he takes me in his arms, "but dost thou feel safe?"

Replying in a like tone, "I always feel safe when thou art near me."

"As seen from below, 'tis difficult to see the goings on within the crow's nest."

As a brazen look engulfs my previous expression, "I do believe thou art propositioning me, sir."

Untying the knot securing my button down blouse, "Thou art quite right."

Following his lead, I unbutton all but the top button on his breeches.

DOWN BELOW ON THE OPEN DECK ⌐

The crewman on watch steps on the deck of the ship.

Seeing him, the Bos'n makes inquiries. "Do you not have the watch?"

"I did, but I was relieved."

"Who by?"

"The Captain and his Missus. The Captain said she wanted to see the sunrise."

"I see. Carry on."

"Aye, sir." After which the crewman departs.

> *MEANWHILE, touching her breasts in silent caresses with his eyes, the Captain encourages her to press her breasts against his exposed chest, & as she begins to move towards him, his piercing eyes never leaving hers, he seizes her, & pulling her tightly to him, whilst nibbling on her ear, he quietly commands her to straddle his left leg. In her ever burning desire to please him, she obeys without question, whereby, in order to achieve the*

> *desired positioning, he places his left foot atop one of the horizontal slats of the crow's nest's basket. Sliding his hands up her inner thighs, his skilled fingers enjoy the pleasure of toying with the edge of her tiny ninies, & after untying the bows that hold them in place, he tucks the tiny garment beneath his belt with one hand. In response to her demonstrative desires, he pleasures himself to the hilt, & bringing forth their fulfillment in an aggressive manner, the Captain is forced to muffle her vocalizations with a kiss before the entire ship is awakened & their activities become known, but knowing the full potential of her ecstasy had not yet been reached, & himself being blessed with remarkable recuperative qualities, helps himself to more pleasuring whilst concurrently satisfying hers as he cleverly conceals their sounds of ecstasy until his effusion is consumed by her inner recesses.*

For sometime thereafter, the Captain and I happily take in the beautiful scenery of the mighty Atlantic and the remarkable creatures that live within her depths, during which time we take delight in watching a school of frolicking dolphins playing near the starboard bow, when suddenly, our moments of tranquility are interrupted when the Captain who in leaning over the railing and lets loose a loud cry. "Hearken on deck!"

The Bos'n hollers up, "Ahoy the watch!"

"Two points off the larboard bow," shouts the Captain.

"Aye!" acknowledges the Bos'n, "What ye see?"

"A forest of giant kelp."

"Aye, Captain," and without delay, the Bos'n, hollers to the ship's pilot, "Mister Thomas, Bring her four points to starboard. Smartly."

"Aye, sir." Swiftly turning the highly polished oak and teakwood creation, already a point of pride with Captain Roberts, the Bos'n, joined by Mister Llewelyn, both men watch the compass as the great ship maneuvers complaisantly.

"Four points to starboard achieved, sir," states Mister Thomas.

"Well done." Turning his attention again to the crow's nest, the Bos'n hearkens, "How goes the ship now, Captain?"

Replying, Captain Roberts hollers back, "She will clear."

Relaying the message to the wheel, the Bos'n hollers, "Hold your course, Mister Thomas."

"Aye, aye, sir."

Continuing on his way, the Quarter-Master states, "She is a fine ship, Mister Taylor."

"That she is Mister Llewelyn."

"Why so much concern over a little seaweed?" Asks I.

"'Twas a forest, fy melys, one that could easily fowl the rudder; ergo, such needes to be avoided. 'Tis among of the many things the watch lookouts for."

As the helmsman rings the bell, he sings out, "'Eight-Bells & All's Well,'" signifying to all not only the time, but it is also a call to duty.

Lifting the hatch, "Be careful as you climb down the shrouds."

As my gallant speaks, I find myself beaming with the excitement of the day.

"Hearken on deck!" shouts Captain Roberts.

"Aye, watch," responds the Bos'n as he hollers up to the crow's nest.

The relief watch who stands beside them asks, "Who's up there?"

"The Captain and his Missus," states the Bos'n.

"Wee be coming down," continues the Captain. "Prepare to receive Mrs Roberts."

"Aye, Captain," hollers the Bos'n in reply. Looking at the helmsman, who had just rang out Eight-Bells, "Who has the upcoming watch?"

"I have, sir," states the crewman next to him

"Aloft, man! Do you not see the ship's mistress on the ratlines!"

"Aye, sir," states the crewman as he grabs the ropes and scurries aloft.

Having descended about 15 feet, where there is room for 2 people, alongside each other, my Captain, both skilled and agile, descends rapidly to his woman's side, reaching me about the same time as the crewman below.

"Thank you, gentleman," I tells them as I slowly make my way down, "but I'm doing quite well, as you can see." When I resume my descent, my foot slips forward through the ropes and I start to fall over backwards. Fortunately, both men being quick to act, each grabbing one of my arms, quickly haul me back up.

As I place my hands firmly on the ropes, I am trembling.

"Are you all right, madam?" asks the crewman from America.

"Yes, just a little shaken," comes my reply with an evident quiver in my voice. "Thank you for rescuing me. Both of you."

"Art thou free of injury, V'lé?"

"Yes." And refusing to let the great Bartholomew Roberts see me so fearful, I take a deep breath and resume my descent.

As I reach the chain plates, the Bos'n, taking me by the waist, helps me to the deck. "Thank you, Mister Taylor."

"My pleasure, Mrs Roberts."

As my Captain steps onto the chain plates, "I'll see to breakfast, fy Nghapten," and head for the galley.

As I hold on to the rope with my right hand, jumping the remaining distance to the deck, the Bos'n notices a tiny garment held within my waistband.

Hoping to sound discreet, as opposed to presumptuous, the Bos'n, whilst glancing unpretentiously at my waistband, states, "Impetuous folly, Captain?" A couple seconds later, he adds, "Methinks those would fair better in your pocket."

Looking towards my waist, I pull the tiny garment from beneath my belt, and with a slight smile amongst a serious tone, whilst shoving it in my pocket, "Indeed it would, Mister Taylor."

"Consider the matter forgotten, Captain."

"Ne'er did I think otherwise," and walking off, wee attend to our various duties.

Chapter Fifteen

The Storm

> *His bride, having spent several hours with him, finally fell asleep, & after carrying her below, Captain Roberts returned to the Quarter-Deck to finish his itinerary. As the horizon slowly became visible, Misters Llewelyn & Taylor, together with Doctor Byrne, joined their Captain on the Quarter-Deck for breakfast. For them, & a handful of others, 'tis a private sanctuary reserved for officers, accessible by others only should duty permit, or when special permission be granted. It is here, where each morning, the routine of the day is discussed, & this past night, Captain Roberts, whose intention was to show to his bride the world's most prestigious ports & cities, instead, such being her burning desire to see all the places he had been whilst a 'Gentleman Of Fortune,' mapped out his entire piratical journey beginning with where he seized the Sagrada Família. Although most of the islands would be quite different than he remembers them, he thought little of it, for it was not the new she wanted to see, but the places where he had been. But first, they would see the Greek Isles, take on provisions (enough for a 6 month cruise excepting fresh water which would be laid in at every opportunity,) & afterwards, set sail to Salvador, Brazil, and the Bay of All Saints, as it is now called.*

'Tis a morning following a full moon, and as I had done so often in yeeres past, I enjoy'd wiling away the night on deck. This morning, having bin at sea a little more than 2 dayes, our heading being just east of the Aegean sea, me crew, although barely a sea dog among them, have functioned well.

As my inkwell closes, my Quarter-Master asks, "Finished with your plans, Captain?"

Blotting the parchment, I close the ship's log. "Aye, Mister Llewelyn." Showing him, and Mister Taylor, the map I had drawn, together with a list of ports, "to-morrow, when the sun is straight up, wee should be rounding Sagres, Portugal, and by dayes end, the Straight of Gibraltar, and the Med. With plans to sail at the average speed of 8 knots once therein, wee will be about a weeke of dayes from the easternmost side of the Greek Isles, and Milos Island, where wee shall anchor for the better part of a fortnight. Upon our return to the Atlantic, wee shall sail south along the West African coast until reaching a good vantage point, approximately here," pointing to the lower region of Angola, "some 875 miles distant from São Tomé and El Príncipe, where the trade winds will take us to Baía de Todos os Santos." Folding the map carefully, I place it within my inner coat pocket. Turning to my Bos'n, "After I confer with my bride, I shall be pleas'd if you will make a copy and post it for the crew."

"My pleasure, Captain," replies Mister Taylor happily.

"Also, inform them, should there be anny port they wish to visit, they neede onely add it to the list, and there we shall go."

"Officer on Deck!" bellows the watch high in the Mizzen's crow's nest.

Several officers and crewmen, myself included, look up.

"Aye," hollers back the Bos'n to the crewman aloft.

Continuing, the watch hollers, "A storm aft, on the starboard side."

Rising from our seats, wee swiftly move to the ship's stern where a trained eye canne readily see the tell-tale signs of an ominous sky in the distance as the storm approaches.

Knowing his Captain's intuitiveness regarding to the weather, my Bos'n asks, "What do you make of it, Captain?"

BLOOD and SWASH, The Unvarnished Life (& afterlife) Story of Pirate Captain, Bartholomew Roberts.........pt.1 "BOLT OF FRUITION"

Un-strapping the spyglass from my belt, and looking in the direction of Newfoundland, I observe a dense mass of billowing storm clouds swiftly moving, which are not onely on an unusual course, but towards us. Relying on both my intuitiveness and instinct, I reply, " 'Tis a tantrum building to a woman scorned. Should the wench continue her present course, on the morrow, come midday, her outermost winds will be upon us; making landfall upon the southern tip of Europe's west shore thereafter."

My Bos'n, already in possession of a concerned tone, "Most of the crew have never sailed in rough seas, Captain."

"As it was for each of us, Mister Taylor."

Although already assured my assessment to be accurate, the ship's pilot, by way of the radio phone's headset, calls for a weather report. In this age, it seemes, the sailors rely heavily on new fangled equipment, but from my standpoint, me crew's assurance of my abilities with regard to reading nature's strategy is essential; ergo, the radar report confirming what I have said already, shall serve to demonstrate, first hand, my abilities, and thus, instil within them, unshakable trust.

Lowering my spyglass upon seeing the ship's pilot hang up the headset, I enquire, "And what say this radar I hear tell of, Mister Thomas?"

"Your assessment is dead on, Captain. Currently listed a Gale, she packs wind speeds of 35 knots, 18 foot waves, and a forward speed of 45 knots. It is estimated that the storm will reach Spain in approximately 30 hours, which is just about when your calculations place us near Sagres, Portugal."

Offering his suggestion, my Bos'n says, "We could make port in the upper region of the Bay of Biscay until the storm runs her course."

"Aye, wee could." Says I.

After a brief pause, my Quarter-Master injects, "With your permission, Captain, this ship's design possesses unique capabilities; in such, you will find she's unlike any you have previously commanded."

"Continue, Mister Llewelyn."

"I merely want to inform you that whilst most other tall ships, as you're aware, would be in jeopardy, the *Royal Fortune*, being a Clipper, will relish gale force winds."

"Thank you, Mister Llewelyn, but as the storm intensifies, it will not be a gale bearing down on us. Having weathered the ferocity of many a storm, and wee being in the path of its right quadrant, it is prudent wee will be; ergo, we will make the best effort possible to get out of the storm's path. Having no time to waste, muster all hands, wearing their Wellies and Slickers, amidship forthwith."

"Aye, Captain." Lifting the microphone, which sounds throughout the ship, the Quarter-Master says, "All hands, don your Wellies and Slickers and muster amidship!"

"I am always open to information you feel is, or could be pertinent, Mister Llewelyn."

"Thank you, Captain."

Altho' awakened by the ruckus on deck, 'twas not soon enough to hear the order, and whilst musing on whether or not to go topside, Joanna bangs on the door.

"Get up, V'lé!" Entering the cabin, "We have to report amidship, tout de suite."

Jumping up quickly, "What's going on?"

Replying in a calm, yet apprehensive tone, "A storm is approaching from astern!"

"Oh, my word!" Quickly moving to the edge of the bunk, I quickly get dressed. "What time is it?"

"Roughly Three-Bells," replies Joanna.

Noting the sunrise, as I tuck in my shirt, "That would be about 0530?"

"Yep. Come on, we must hurry! I only hope I know enough to work my station under duress," states Joanna restlessly.

"You!" Speaking with a measure of fear in my voice, "Being I just started, that wasn't very inspiring."

"Those of us manning the sheets are responsible for tacking the ship. With luck we can get out of the storm's path." Although maintaining her composure, Joanna adds, "Unfortunately, the majority of the crew have never weathered a storm."

Obviously agitated as I dash to the wardrobe, "Does Captain Roberts look worried?"

"Not in the least," says Joanna with a smile.

"Captain Roberts is not only a master mariner, but a brilliant navigator," I tells her. "Having him aboard ship during battle is the same as having Napoleon on the battlefield."

After it appears to my trainer that her pupil is dressed, she asks, "Ready?"

"Ready?" I reply questioningly whilst letting out a half laugh whilst donning my slicker. "I'm dressed if that's what you mean."

Heading for the door, with me right behind her, my trainer hollers, "Then let's go!"

Making our way to the main deck, it's plain to see, as we join the others, that the crew has abundant confidence in their Captain.

> *Pulling sheets & working aloft in good weather is difficult enough, but doing so during a storm is no place for the fair sex, & therefore, having 2 women crewing on the open deck was the last thing Captain Roberts needed to worry about. This being his reasoning, he hoped that Joanna had kept his bride below along with herself; but upon seeing V'lé & Joanna as they mixed in with the men, knowing he could not play favorites among the crew members, not even with regard to the women, for the doing would lose them the respect of their fellow crewmen. Thus, having no other choice before him, he forced his expression to remain indifferent, & taking a deep breath, exhaling slowly, he turned his thoughts toward the storm.*

"The crew is assembled, Captain."

"Very good, Mister Llewelyn."

Lowering his voice to speak quietly, "As you have no doubt noticed, Captain, Mrs Roberts, and Miss Joanna are amongst them. Shall I quietly have them retire below deck?"

"Nay, Mister Llewelyn, methinks not. The women are members of the crew by their owne choosing, and as such, they must be treated accordingly. Anny other course would cause them to lose face."

Turning to the crew, and speaking loudly so all hands canne hear, I begin my address. "An encroaching tempest besets herself upon us from astern to test our mettle. Our radar, as report'd by Mister Thomas, indicates a gale, but my experience suggests she'll grow to hurricane force, thus, 'tis quite a blow which threatens us. With the storm's forward speed being 45 knots, wee have perhaps 30 hours. If wee canne be within, or near, the Strait of Gibraltar when the outermost winds begin to assail us, wee, with luck, will double our speed whilst skirting the wenches hemline thro' the Med to arrive at our destination much the sooner. In order to do this, it is imperative that every hand be well rested, and fit; ergo, in order to maintain the ship's best possible speed, each crewman, sleeping and taking on nourishment in between, will work in shifts of 4 hour on and 4 hours off for the duration."

As I look about, 'tis easy to see the worry in the faces of me crew. Hoping to allay their anxiety as well as instil within them confidence of their owne abilities, I leap down from my elevated platform, and now amongst them, I speak in a calmer tone as I continue. "I am to understand that ne'er have most of ye weathered the ire of the sea, but having observed ye, I find you, one and all, to be fine seamen. The best test of anny amount of training is that which comes under stress. And now, with that having been said, and ye knowing what I will expect and demand of all of you, I want to state that it has beene suggested that wee make port in the Bay of Biscay and wait for the storm to pass by."

Immediately, before the echo of the suggestion fades, me crew boisterously shout various crys to the contrary.

"Then onward wee shall saile, and as I knows ye, and all of you shall, do me proud." Stepping back onto the platform, I add, "As you trust me, trust the ship. To yon stations!"

Having finished his address, I, together with the crew, cheer loudly as we disperse."

Being some distance away, I am awe-struck as I stand motionless, just staring at my beloved whilst expressing my devotion for him verbally. "Isn't he magnificent!"

"He is that," replies Joanna, quietly. After a moment, Joanna sharply states, "Come on, V'lé!" and grabbing my arm, "You can drool later!"

> *Over the next 30 hours, as the intensifying storm raced towards Europe's southernmost shore with a vengeance, the shipboard activities were feverish as the Royal Fortune, with the aid of the storm's outer winds, coursed thru the Straight of Gibraltar under full sail as hoped, & having achieved their goal, and seemingly out of the storms path, the ship & crew entered the Alboran Sea; altho' drenched to the skin, and decidedly exhausted, were none the worse for wear.*
>
> *Bearing down on Lisbon, where the hurricane made landfall, it hovered; meanwhile, relaxing for the first time in more than 30 hours, the crew sat down to a leisurely meal.*
>
> *Later, when resuming forward momentum, the downscaled Tropical Storm, continuing South East, made for Tangier. As for the newly refitted, Royal Fortune, altho' equipped with a modern galley, scullery, infirmary, & lavatory facilities, the ship, itself, however, not having an auxiliary engine to help during inclement weather, relied solely on the skill of her captain & crew.*

Mustering my courage, I run alongside my trainer to our station while my Captain, having just returned to the Quarter-Deck with Mister Llewelyn, gauges the outer winds to be a strong gale, and to my Captain's delight, the responsive Clipper ship is going along under full sail, as elegantly as was promised.

> *While the crew works laboriously, their heading, being due East as the storms fury trounces them from afar with wind speeds nearing 50 knots & moderate to heavy rain, the crew were pleased the storm was traveling South East as Captain Roberts, delighted by how well his new, Royal Fortune, responds, thanks God warmly. In spite of this, the Captain's uncanny sense of perception for wind & ocean currents, telling him his joy will not last long, an attribute for which he is legendary, orders the furling of several sails.*

"She's a fine sailor, this Clipper, Mister Llewelyn."

"Aye, Captain. That she is."

"Nevertheless, double the size of the crews manning the sailes."

"Aye, Captain."

Again looking thro' the spyglass, and as I watch the clouds billow up higher with unsurpassed speed, "Mister Taylor, bring down the watch."

"Aye, Captain." Flipping a switch and lifting the ship's microphone, as to speak directly to those on watch aloft, "All crew members within the crow's nests, report to the open deck and man the sails where needed, forthwith."

Suddenly, the violent change I expected occurs as the storm takes an abrupt course change, and now heading due east, the storm's intensity, lashing her fury upon us, bombards me ship with severe wind and rain. Time being crucial, I shout the orders to my crew myself. "Aloft me hardies! Shorten sail! You men there," pointing to a small group, "Batten down those loose hatches!"

As the storm overtakes us, I knows that all hope for survival relies on turning me ship directly into the oncoming waves. My voice, tho' booming, is barely heard over the roar of the wind as I bellow, "Come about! Keep 'er bow heading directly into the waves, Mister Thomas. Mister Taylor, get more positive steerage from the course sails, lest ye let 'er heel too far and wee capsize." Watching me ship come about smartly, I brim with pride.

Amid the horse tails, as me ship heels and pitches atop the rapid succession of 30 foot waves, and the troughs threaten to swallow us whole as the pilot struggles to keep the rugged ship heading directly into the onslaught of the cross current swells, the deck crew works feverishly to maintain our heading in the rough sea, whilst aloft on the yards, brave men slave laboriously to furl the majority of the sails untill only the forward course sails are left to drive the ship ahead as enormous sprays of water awash the deck.

Growing stronger still, while the *Royal Fortune* is tossed atop the sea's crests like a toy, one of the men crys out, "This one looks like it was forged by Thor himself." Another crewman, whose station is such that he is being particularly battered by the horizontal rain as the storm continues to mercilessly assail me ship and crew with all the ferocity of hell, adds, "Aye, and Lucifer too!"

Minutes later, pleased the men aloft have safely descended to the open deck, a huge swell slams nearly full broadside against the ship's freeboard, whilst another enormous wave breaks concurrently across the bow, and me crew, lest be washed overboard, hang on for dear life, I knows wee be in the worst of it now, and 'fore long, if all goes well, wee will see calm seas once again.

Standing next to the ship's pilot, I adjust the wheel a mite to correct the ship's rudder. "Keep her headed straight and true, Mister Thomas," adding, "Our onely chance is to go straight through the belly of the turbulent wench." After the course is corrected, I glance to me brides station, and altho' worried for her safety, I espy her near the mainmast, and as I once again see her, and me whole crew performing well, pride wells up within me. At that moment, whilst the ship pitches up and over a particularly choppy wave, and a huge swell backwashes over the stern, most of me crew are knocked off their feet, including Mister Thomas who slides across the Quarter-Deck's rain soaked surface and down to the main deck. Grabbing the wheel, it takes all my strength to regain control of the resilient Clipper Ship as she wallows dangerously. Amid the doing, I espy a crewman in the rigging struggling to untangle a sheet from the shroud of the mainmast when a sudden gust jars him loose from his precarious perch as the mighty Atlantic, roaring her fury, hurls him to the deck below. Moments later, after the ship's physician examines him briefly, sev'rall crewman carry the man below to the infirmary; meanwhile, as the rest of me crew be pelted by the relentless rain pummeling down in sheets, the lot of 'em, in spite of the slippery decks, accomplish their assigned duties in superb fashion.

V'lé, Joanna, and the rest of the crew, despite their transparent slickers, having bin blown in every direction, are soaked to the skin. Looking forward towards the bowsprit, and catching sight of the foremast course saile as it breaks loose, I holler, whilst pointing toward the bow, "Belay that rigging!" Working together, several crew members manage to catch and haul in the sail, tie on a new rope, and within a couple of minutes, when it is secure, one of the crewmen runs to the Quarter-Deck to report, "Shipshape and secure, Captain."

BLOOD and SWASH, The Unvarnished Life (& afterlife) Story of Pirate Captain, Bartholomew Roberts.........pt.1 "BOLT OF FRUITION"

> *Nearly five hours had passed since being overtaken by the storm when again it changed course, & at last, the crew knows the worst is over. Within a half hour more, the sea quieted to the high side of a force 8, as described as white foam atop the lashing swells amid a wind speed nigh 40 knots, whereby the Clipper ship, again in her element, rolled jauntily along under half canvas, relishing the weather other Tall Ships would balk at.*

As me *Royal Fortune* cruises briskly in these now relatively moderate winds, and comparatively light rain, my exhausted crew knows there is much work to be done before they canne rest.

"Damage report, Mister Llewelyn."

Speaking with a grin, "I'm happy to report only minor damage, Captain. The ship and crew functioned well, and given calmer seas, with one exception, we will be able to make all necessary repairs at sea."

"And the exception?"

"The circuit board in the radio room. Both the Radio and the Satellite phone are out, but when we reach port, one of the ship's radiomen will purchase the parts needed, and afterwards, make the necessary repairs."

"And the man that fell?"

Replying confidently, "He had the wind knocked out of him, Captain, but good. Doctor Byrne says he'll be back at his station in a couple of days."

"Very good, Mister Llewelyn. Resume our original course."

"Captain?"

"Wee shall follow the storm, Mister. After each saile has been checked for damage, decrease to the main course saile onely untill all repairs be made. After which, drag on all the canvas the yards will hold untill wee again near Gibraltar. Once thro' the straight, maintain 8 knots until our destination is reached."

"Aye, Captain."

"Mister Taylor."

"Aye?"

"Have the crew don dry attire in rotation, and assign duties. I also want the kitchen staff to deliver hot chowder to each crewman. Afterwards, get some rest. As for myself, after I tour the ship and survey the damage, I shall speak with the physician; thereafter, I will be in my cabin. When I return, later in the day, I want the *Royal Fortune* to be shipshape, in Bristol fashion."

"Aye, Aye, Captain."

As I begin to make my way down the steps to the main deck, I heave to. Turning, "Mister Llewelyn, do you know the whereabouts of Mrs Roberts?"

"No, Captain, I have not seen her since the man fell. Perhaps she is with the Doctor."

"Upon locating her, have her report to the Captain's cabin."

"Aye, Captain."

Before going below to change, I saunter around the deck inspecting both the rigging and general condition of me ship. Observing a busy crew either cleaning or making repairs, the musicians, that I am delight'd to have on board, be playing a jaunty sea shanty, and am pleas'd most of the crew, as they sing along, be in high spirits. Continuing on my way, I open the door leading to the corridor and the lower decks. En route, I hear the ship's pilot strike the time bell as he simultaneously sings out, "Five-Bells, and we thank both our Captain, and the Good Lord that all is well."

Wearing a modest smile as I slowly make my way to the berth deck, I stop by the infirmary to check on the crewman who fell during the storm. "How is he, doctor?"

As he approaches, Doctor Byrne speaks softly as not to disturb his patient, "Finding no serious injuries, I am happy to report that Mister McBride, will be fine. He just needs a few days bed rest."

" 'Tis pleas'd I am to hear such news," glancing at the injured man and noting he appears to be sleeping soundly, I add, "My compliments, Doctor."

"Thank you, Captain," says Doctor Byrne, contentedly. "By the way, Mrs Roberts was here until called away some minutes ago."

"Thank you," says I, as I turn about.

Noting my condition, the doctor advises, "You look exhausted, Captain. I suggest you get a couple hours rest."

"Sound medical advice. Please so inform Mister Llewelyn."

"Aye, Captain."

> *Continuing down the passageway, the exhausted mariner finally reached his cabin, & upon opening the door he found his bride, already changed into dry clothes, waiting for him.*

As I turn from the stern's window, "I was ordered to report here."

"Aye, fy Ngariad," answers my Captain whilst walking to the wardrobe, and taking out his robe, he enters our private bath and removes his wet clothes.

With a slight laugh of relief, I say, "That was some storm."

"Aye… for a blow, 'twas quite a blood pumper."

"More like a curdler," I reply with a shake as I walk over to him.

"I found it exhilarating," says he with a slight chuckle.

"Exhilarating?" retorts I whilst kneeling down to help my Captain remove his boots, "I was terrified!"

"Thou had good cause, for wee could 'ave lost the ship."

"Until now, the thought of a storm as being a part of the voyage never occurred to me."

Removing his sodden garments, "Dost thou desire to return to land?"

"Not a chance, fy Arglwydd," I reply with a big smile. "Ne'er have I been happier. I love the sea. I love this ship, and I love thee. I just don't like storms."

Rinsing off in the shower first before drying myself with one of the Welsh Dragon patterned towels, I chuckle a mite. "Thou must take the good with the bad, fy annwyl." Musing a mite as my mind ponders the perilous storm, I am delightfully surpriz'd to see how well me bride handled herself. "Wee be suited to each other perfectly, fy melys."

Sufficiently dry, I toss the towel onto the rack and don my robe. Being quite tired, not having slept the night before, I seat myself on the settee. "Come sit beside me and let me hold thee for a few minutes."

As I sit beside him, "You're exhausted, fy Arglwydd, and hungry too. Which first, food or sleep?"

"A light meal will do me well," I reply as my mind contemplates the wonders yet to come. "As a result of our love for one another, our most ardent dreams have become a reality, and my intention is to not waste a single moment."

As he spoke, mine eyes shining with all the devotion one can have for another, it makes me happy to know such pleases him, especially when he knows it is the man and not merely the intrepid hero that I adore.

Picking up the phone, I buzz the galley. "This is the Captain's cabin. Please bring Captain Roberts a bowl of Chowder, a variety of cocktail sandwiches, prepared fruit, and a large cup of Bohia tea."

"Right away, Mrs Roberts."

As I hang up the phone, "Thou amazes me, fy annwyl."

"I do?"

"I ne'er thought of thee thus."

"Thus? I don't understand. Thus how?"

"Athletic," says he as he kisses my forehead. "'Tis delightfully surpriz'd, I am."

"I was pretty active most of my life. My dad taught me how to fence and shoot, and all through school I was on the track & field, and archery teams. I also studied gymnastics, ballet and tap. In my early twenties, for employment, I was in Burlesque, and I belly danced; the ladder being an art which I continued throughout a goodly part of my adulthood. In my spare time, I spent many a weekend camping, hiking and fishing, often with my brother. On top of all that, being a full time Horsewoman, training and showing horses, since I was 9 years old; I also gave riding lessons, occasionally boarded horses, and during the early 1990s I ran a sizeable, as well as very successful horse show."

Nodding his head in recollection, "Aye, I remember seeing all manner of activities in thy picture album, but for the past year, aside from riding or driving thy Morgan horse, thou hast spend much of thy time indoors."

"When my life changed, so did my lifestyle; I am pleased to be active again, and am thrilled to be here on this ship with thee. There's no place or time I would rather be, except perhaps, with thee in thy time. I would love to have been with thee then, knowing what I know now, of course."

"Indeed? And why the last stipulation?"

"Well, knowing thee as I do, I would not have known how to persuade the confirmed bachelor to want me aboard his ship."

"Thou art quite a woman to wish for such excitement, and durst I say that altho' I disapproved of the presence of you and Miss O'Malley top side when the storm was upon us, I was compelled to allow thee to remain."

"I'm glad thou felt such; if thou had not, we would've felt like outsiders."

"Ne'er neede thee worry in that regard, fy annwyl, for thou hast proven thy worth as a crew member, as has Miss O'Malley."

Hearing a knock on the cabin door, I says, "Come in."

Pushing a tea cart is a young man about 12. Entering the room, he walks over to the table where his Captain and I are seated. "With your permission, Captain."

Giving him a slight nod, the lad sets the table.

Although surprised to see a youngster on board, "You be in good time, Master…"

"Jackson, sir."

"In what capacity are you aboard, Master Jackson?"

Replying cheerfully as he removes the last item from the tray, "Ship's Boy, sir."

Smoothing his moustache whilst musing a moment, he adds, "Carry on."

Myself, having tossed the young man a wink tells him the Captain approves, he replies to me with a slight grin, and then to his Captain.

"Thank you, Sir," and departing, he shuts the door behind him.

With a raised eyebrow, "Methinks thou hast no use for my sixth article regarding women and boys."

"No, not entirely, but I can understand it. A pirate vessel is no place for a youngster, nor most women. I do, however, approve of the last part about protecting women; as for boys, you began as a Ship's Boy, did thee not?"

Chuckling, "Aye, that I did, and I was younger than he. With regard to women, ne'er have I voiced them to be unworthy; it's just that they tend to be an unwitting distraction."

"How old were you when you signed on as a Ship's Boy?"

"Well, let me see. 'Twas during the year of the Massacre of Glencoe. The ship having sailed from Solva before that brutal conflict, it having taken place in the Winter of 1692,[①] I would 'ave beene 10 yeeres of age."[B3]

"Where's Solva?"

"It lyes on the North end of Saint Brides Bay, 'twixt Newgale and Saint Davids." Changing the subject, he reaches into the pocket of his robe and withdraws his proposed itinerary. Unfolding the parchment, "Look, fy annwyl."

While picking up one of the sandwiches, "What is it, fy Arglwydd?"

Laying the heavy paper across the sandwiches, "Before the storm, I had worked on this in hopes 'twould please thee."

After studying the map for a couple of minutes, "'Tis all the places thou visited whilst a pirate, is it not?"

"Aye, fy annwyl, it is. All these places, I shall take thee," he says smiling, "as I wish it could 'ave beene, the first time."

"All except for Parrot Island," says I. "I couldn't bear it."

And using the pencil that rests on the table, he scratches the foreboding location off the list. "There, 'tis deleted. Art there anny places thee wishes to add?"

"I have but three requests. 1st, on those occasions when we do stay on shore for a few days, and thy plans permit, for I shall miss the horses, I would like to stop where riding is offered. 2nd, I have always wanted to see the White Cliffs Of Dover in person, from the sea, and 3rd, being particularly fond of Marie Antoinette, I would like to visit Versailles."

Smiling, "Then adding them to the list I shall." Taking the last morsel from the plate, "I should like to rest for a spell. Please awaken me at Eight-Bells."

"I shall, fy Arglwydd." As Captain Roberts lays back on the bed, I gently kiss the hair atop his head as I cover him with the duvet. Creeping away silently, he makes a request before drifting off to sleep.

"Having much to be thankful for, this day, I should like the Reverend to hold a non-denominational service just prior to twilight, for which, the crew is to dress appropriately; thereafter, methinks a celebration is in order, please see to both. I would be further pleas'd if thou wilt again wear thy crimson bejewelled gown with the feathers."

Seeing my Captain hath drifted off to sleep, I depart noiselessly.

---

① The Massacre of Glencoe took place in Glen Coe in the Highlands of Scotland on 13 February 1692.

Chapter Sixteen

Jubilation

Arriving on the open deck, I see the crew full of activity. Everyone is quite busy cleaning and repairing various parts of the ship. Climbing the steps to the Quarter-Deck, I see Mister Llewelyn at the wheel, and seeking information, I ask, "Where will I find Mister Taylor?"

"He's changing into dry clothes."

"Thank you." Pausing for a moment. "May I have a word with you?"

"Of course, Mrs Roberts."

"As you know, the Captain, having been up since before the storm, is resting. I have orders to wake him at Eight-Bells. For the duration, short of disaster, please see to it he's not disturbed."

"Aye, madam. I shall give orders to that effect."

"Thank you, Mister Llewelyn," smiling. "I am also under orders to arrange for a religious service tonight, prior to twilight, but I have not been able to locate Pastor Pyle. Do you know where I can find him?"

"No, madam, but I will be happy to give him the message when I see him."

"Thank you." As I turn to leave, I see Mister Taylor returning.

Departing, Mister Llewelyn gives me a nod.

Addressing Mister Taylor, "Just the person I was looking for."

"Aye, madam?"

"Captain Roberts requested that I wear a gown this evening, and asked me to arrange both a celebration and a church service, the latter to be held at twilight followed by a party; ergo, please have the entire crew dressed in their finest, and regardless of their religious affiliation, they are to be on time for a non-denominational Church Service to be held on the open deck."

"I shall, madam."

Still learning Military, Bell, and Solar Time, "How long until Eight-Bells?"

"Four hours, one each half hour. There are only 8 bells, and they go around 6 times."

"Oh… I get it, there's one bell for each half hour."

"Aye."

Looking about the ship, "There seems to be a lot of work being done, Mister Taylor."

"Aye, there is at that."

"Is there anything I can do to help?"

"Well… with Cook and the galley staff having their hands full getting the dining room back in order in time to prepare dinner, Miss Joanna and young Master Jackson are attempting to prepare the afternoon meal. I am sure they would appreciate any help you can give them."

"Thank you, Mister Taylor. I shall report to the galley forthwith." Turning, I make my way back to the corridor leading to the lower decks. As I enter the galley, I am shocked. "Oh my word, what a shambles."

Greeting me as I enter, "Good day to you, Mrs Roberts," states Master Jackson. "What can I get for you?"

"Not a thing," says I, smiling. Reaching for the apron hanging on the wall, "I am here to help you prepare the afternoon meal for our deserving crew."

"That's fantastic!" says Joanna smiling as she comes out of the pantry. "We can use the help."

"But— I mean— you're…"

Chuckling, "What I am, Master Jackson, is a member of this crew," and looking around at the pots and frying pans already in use, "What can I do to help?"

"Well," looking at the timer on the oven, "the chickens will be done baking in half an hour. In the meantime," asks Master Jackson with a hopeful look, "Can you prepare those potatoes for deep frying?"

"Sure can." Pointing to the one lying on the drain board, "Can you hand me that potato peeler?" As Joanna places it in my hand, I ask, "How do you intend to serve them?"

"We're making steak fries," replies Joanna.

"And deep fried chicken nuggets and onion rings," adds Master Jackson joyfully.

"You've got to be an American."

"Aye, from Oregon. I was visiting my Great Uncle for the summer. Working at the docks in Milford Haven, is how I learned about this job."

"And what's cooking in these stock pots?"

In reply, Katie says smiling, "Having seen your website, I'm making Solomon Gundie."

Smiling, "That'll please our Captain." Looking around, "Speaking in confidence, of Captain Roberts, thus far, is happy with your work. Yours also, Master Jackson."

Being such was the best news they could've received, both Joanna & Master Jackson smile broadly.

Back to menu ideas, "How about some cream of chicken noodle soup?"

"What a great use of the chicken drippings, V'lé," states Joanna whilst reaching for two stock pots hanging from the rack overhead.

"I'll fetch some spaghetti noodles," states young Jackson, darting towards the pantry.

Having assembled the ingredients, "Just as soon as I finish with these potatoes, I'll prepare the soup, and I'll also see to getting some veggies heating too."

"I signed on to escape the drudgery of the, so-called, women's work, but if we're not careful, the men will stick us in the kitchen permanently," remarks Joanna bitterly.

Adding to her cynicism, "Where most of them think we belong, but right after lunch," I tell her, "the galley and scullery crews can have their jobs back."

"That's for sure," Joanna declares, laughing.

Sometime later: Time flying by as it generally does when you're busy, I hear the ship's pilot sound Two-Bells over the ship's speakers.

Because the mess hall is still a shambles, the crew's gathering around the tables we've placed about on the open deck.

As the crew sit down to eat, Joanna, Master Jackson and I, plus a couple of the crewmen, carry the afternoon meal topside to be served buffet style.

Later, after the afternoon meal dishes are being washed and put away, I hear the ship's pilot merrily sing out, " 'Seven-Bells & All's Well,' aboard the Clipper ship, *Royal Fortune*."

Jumping up, I remove my apron, and grabbing the tray containing the meal I prepared for my Captain, "Sorry to run Joanna, but I'm under orders to wake the Captain at Eight-

Bells."

Entering our cabin quietly, and finding my lover sleeping peacefully, I hate to wake him, but his orders stipulate otherwise, and having sat the tray on the table, I sit on the edge of the bed. Shaking his shoulder gently, "Time to wake up, fy Arglwydd."

Opening his eyes and looking at me, "What time would it be?"

"I came in shortly before Eight-Bells, as thee requested."

> *Giving his bride a slight smile as he arose off the bunk, now suspended from the overhead on chains, it pleased Captain Roberts to know she was making the effort to learn the bell system of telling time.*

"I best get dressed and survey the progress, lest we shan't have time for tea before twilight."

"I have brought thine afternoon meal down to thee."

Looking at the table before the large window aft, "How thoughtful, fy melys. The crew, have they eaten?"

"Yes, fy Nghapten. With the regular cook and galley crew being busy cleaning up after the storm, Miss Joanna, Master Jackson and I made and served the crew the afternoon meal about 2 hours ago. We only just finished washing up a half hour ago. Under the circumstances, tea will not be served until late, and it'll be buffet style again."

"A trying day for all, I'm sure." Giving her a warm smile and a light kiss, "I thank you for this lovely meal, but first, and 'fore I dine, I must tend to duty. Wilt thou be good enough to have my meal taken up to the Quarter-Deck?"

Proud he puts duty before personal pleasure, "Of course," I reply, smiling.

As Captain Roberts dons one of the several outfits I had specially made for him, "After church services, wouldst thou care to wile away a couple of hours dancing? And afterwards, as I find myself exceedingly hungry for thee this day, I shall seeke thy favours."

Having flashed him a smile, I move to the table, and picking up the phone, I ring the Quarter-Deck.

"Quarter-Deck, Mister Taylor speaking."

Smiling at my Captain in response to his statement, "Just a moment," as I place the phone against my thigh, "Art thou in need of Master Jackson's assistance?"

"Nay, but methinks I should get accustomed to his presence, and thus, I shall welcome his service with joviality."

Giving my Captain a smile as I lift the phone again, "Good afternoon, Mister Taylor."

"Good afternoon, Mrs Roberts. What can I do for you?"

"Please send Master Jackson and Miss Joanna to the Captain's cabin."

"Aye, madam. Right away."

Until now, I have only worn female pirate outfits whilst on board, and although I love them, it will be a pleasure to wear a beautiful gown.

Picking up his hat, he slaps me on the rump. "I shall see thee on the Quarter-Deck within the hour, fy nghariad."

Replying to him with a smile, "I'll be there, fy Nghapten."

Placing the plumbed Tricorne upon his head, he opens the door and finds Joanna just arriving.

"Good afternoon, Captain."

"Good afternoon. You're in good time, Miss O'Malley. Mrs Roberts is in neede of your assistance in getting dressed this evening," and without further comment, he departs.

Closing the door behind her as she enters, Joanna finds me at my wardrobe looking at the different dresses. "Hello Joanna. Captain Roberts wants me to wear my crimson gown with the marabou feathers."

Moments later, having passed Captain Roberts in the corridor, Master Jackson knocks.

"Come in," says I.

"You sent for me, ma'am?"

"Yes, I did. Please take this tray to the Quarter-Deck. On the way, stop by the galley and have the tea and soup warmed. Upon arriving, lay out the Captain's meal, and do not forget the tablecloth, finger bowl and napkin. After which, you are to quietly stand by on the Quarter-Deck until either dismissed, or until your Captain indicates he's finished, after which times you will clear the table and depart."

Standing by on the Quarter-Deck to wait on the Captain, being considered a special privilege, Master Jackson replied with great enthusiasm. "Aye, aye, ma'am," and picking up the tray, he departs.

Joanna, looking at the beautiful gowns from many eras, "These are simply breathtaking, V'lé. I've seen some of these before."

Smiling, I inform her, "Most of my gowns are copies of what I consider the most beautiful in movie history." Thinking for a moment, "Did you think to bring an evening gown with you?"

"No. It never occurred to me that one would be needed."

"We look about the same size."

Speaking in a meek tone as Joanna's eyes light up, "Oh no… I couldn't, could I?"

"Go ahead. Except for this one, pick whatever dress you like. I'll get us some under garments."

SOMETIME LATER ⇁

All eyes are upon us as we appear on the open deck.

Joanna's gown is a copy of the pastel yellow dinner gown worn by Janet Leigh in the movie Houdini. My gown, and the one I wore at our wedding reception, is a copy of Scarlett O'Hara's famous red velvet gown.

As Joanna and I climb the steps to the Quarter-Deck, Captain Roberts and his officers rise from their seats.

"How enchanting you look, states Captain Roberts whilst pulling out my chair.

Joanna, being offered a seat next to him, Mister Llewelyn holds the chair for her.

As the gentlemen take their seats, Captain Roberts, picking up his glass, states, "Men of the crew, a toast. To the ladies," and raising his glass, "Two of the loveliest creatures, ever to grace a ship."

Shouts of agreement are heard from the crewmen.

Setting his glass on the table, Captain Roberts arises from his chair, and walking over to the railing, looks over the crew. "Men, and Ladies," turning slightly towards us and then facing the crewmen again, "in triumph over the tempest, I belieeve ye, and all of you, would enjoy a party to celebrate, and altho' wee have but three ladies on board, 'tis sure I am that they will honour ye who so desire, a dance."

"All the men on the deck cheer, "Huzzah!"

"But first, 'tis fitting Reverend Pyle offer a few words in prayer." Looking around, I ask, "Where is the Doctor and his missus?"

Mister Taylor replies, "Both are in the infirmary with the man who fell."

"Master Jackson, taking along the 4 men sitting nearest to you, dash below and inquire if the patient is well enough to be in attendance. If he is, bring back the lot of them."

"Aye, Sir," replied the young man.

As they scurry below, Reverend Pyle stands. "Let us bow our heads." As the entire crew complies, he begins. "We thank thee, oh Lord, for watching over us, and also for the bounty that enrich our lives, and we especially thank thee for restoring to him, the life of our Gallant sea Captain. Amen."

The entire crew respond by saying, "Amen."

The good Pastor, taking his seat at the Captain's table, is replaced at the railing by Mister Llewelyn. "I think it's time we reveal to our Captain just how proud we are to be members of his crew.

The cheers and jubilation give Captain Roberts cause to stand once more, and altho' he makes an effort to maintain his composure, such is thwarted by the overwhelming emotions as he learns just how revered he is, and such, walks to the railing once more.

"I thank ye, all of you." Signaling me to accompany him, my Captain states with sincerity, "You all know this amazing creature to be my bride. 'Tis she you have to thank."

Once again, all the men on the deck cheer, "Huzzah!"

As Master Jackson returns, he is accompanied by the Doctor, his missus, and the man who fell, who being seated in a wheelchair, is carried by the 4 men to the Quarter-Deck. Following them, Master Jackson places a box on the Captain's table. Opening it, he lifts out a large, Custom-Made, music box in the shape of a Frigate.

"We would be pleased if you will both accept this small offering as a token of both our appreciation and admiration."

"'Tis beautiful," and offering me his arm, my Captain escorts me to the main deck, whereby the crew cheers once again.

Standing aft, the Bos'n says, "We all know how much the two of you love to dance," and as he opens the lid on the music box, a beautiful rendition of one of our favorite waltzes, altho' untitled, is from an episode of the TV show Outlaws entitled, 'Madrid.' As it begins to play, my gallant bows, and extending his hand, "Wilt thou do me the honour, Mrs Roberts?"

Amid a curtsy, "I would be honored, fy Arglwydd," and taking me in his arms, we begin to waltz.

As the music box begins to come to the end, the ship's musicians pick up the tune.

Rising from his seat, Mister Llewelyn walks over to Miss Joanna, and following the example set by their Captain, he bows as he asks, "May I have the honour, Miss Joanna?"

Upon rising, she curtsies. "A pleasure, sir."

The Doctor and his missus also grace the dance floor.

Between dances, the six of us change partners, and after a brief spell, other crew members take turns by tapping the gentlemen on the shoulder. All throughout the evening as the musicians play a variety of music we have great fun engaging in all types of modern dance, including of course, an occasional tune to which my Captain and I can dance the

Kizomba, which Johanna and several of the crewmen also learn.

Come ten o'clock, I walk to the rail to catch my breath. "Look! Another ship," says I, pointing towards the bow.

"Where?" asks Captain Roberts.

"There!" pointing again, "it's white, like the horizon, but denser."

Looking sharp, he espies the ship. "Thou hath the eyes of a hawk."

"So I've been told the whole of my life, fy Arglwydd."

Mister Llewelyn, handing his captain his binoculars, "What do you make of her?"

"She appears to be a Schooner, and sailing due East, same as we."

Asking with anticipation, "Could we not give chase? Just for fun."

"She is perhaps four leagues distant, fy melys, perhaps more."

"Art thou not the same Captain Roberts who, after plundering the *Samuel* in July of 1720, gave chase to another ship spotted on the horizon, catching it by midnight that same evening?"

"Aye," he states with a chuckle. "that I am."

"It's a shame our radio has a blown fuse," grumbles Joanna. "We could've invited them to dine with us tomorrow."

Mildly rebuking her, I state, "Where's the fun in that?" 'Twould be much more fun to catch them and invite ourselves to their ship for breakfast."

Smiling, "thou would have made a splendid pyrate, fy Melys." Hollering to me crew, "Men, a 3-Masted Schooner lyes some four leagues off our bow. 'Tis the request of me bride that wee spread more saile and pay her a call, and altho' wee shan't plunder her, perhaps ye would enjoy the sport of giving chase."

All feeling the excitement already, the crew cheers wildly.

"Then me hardies, drag on canvas sufficient to reach 12 knots, and post a watch atop each mast, and thus, with God's grace, by dawn wee shall bid her a good morning."

Breaking away from the festivities for a

brief spell, half of the crew climb aloft while much of the remaining crewmen see to the tacks and braces.

> *As everyone aboard enjoyed a fantastic time as they made chase for the ship in the distance, the party continued most of the evening with much revelry, & as they closed in on the Schooner, most of the crew felt the same emotion their Captain's pirate crew must've felt each time they took a prize. To insure all had a good time, the crew members took short shifts so that no man would be separated from the carousing for more than an hour.*

As midnight approaches, both me bride and I be quite weary. "Let us go to bed, fy nghariad, for it will be some hours 'fore wee catch yon vessell."

THE END

To Follow this Saga to its exciting conclusion in the 'WILLING CAPTIVE'

YOU NEED ONLY TO TURN THE PAGE

BOOK 2

The Willing Captive

This latter book contains, in it's entirety,

Captain Bartholomew Roberts, A Pyrate's Journal

Unchanged

Written With Purpose by V'teOnica Roberts

To Set The Record Straight
& Dedicated To
Pirate Captain, John 'Bartholomew' Roberts

TABLE OF CONTENTS

Chapter		Where	Page
01	Devil May-Care	'Bermuda'	184
02	First Glimpse	'Bound for the Palace of Versailles'	194
03	Plan "B"	'Britannia'	217
04	Borne is a Legend	'Isle of Princes & Annamaboa'	231
		'Cameroon Bay & the Isle of Princes'	236
05	Captain Roberts	'S.W. Coast of Africa & E. Coast of Brazil'	242
06	Luck of the Ages	'Bound for Brazil'	247
	Sheer Audacity	'La Baía de Todos os Santos'	248
07	Return to Plan B	'Britannia'	264
08	The Articles	'Coast of Caiana [now-Guiana], S. America'	271
09	Hatred Displayed	'St. Christophers, Barbados & Martinico'	274
10	A Lady's Well Laid Plans	Small Islet nigh Bermuda's Coast -1720'	281
11	Victory		300
12	An Offer Of Clemency	'Newfoundland Region'	310
13	Royal Fortune, Ranger, & Saint Christophers	'Newfoundland Region to the West Indies'	316
		'Saint Barthélemy to Surinam via Brava'	340
		'Martinico & Saint Lucia'	349
14	Wolves in Sheep's Clothing	'Bennet's Key'	352
15	Captain Anstis	'Bermuda, West Indies & Africa'	363
16	Fetch and Carry	'Sierra Leona River'	374
17	Plundering a Plenty	'Calabar'	387
18	Whydah Road	'The West Coast of Africa'	392
19	The Muster Sheet	'Isle of Annamoboa' & list of Captain Roberts' Crew	395
20	The Final Hour	'Parrot Island / Nigeria's Estuary'	403

BLOOD and SWASH, The Unvarnished Life (& afterlife) Story of Pirate Captain, Bartholomew Roberts......pt.2 "THE WILLING CAPTIVE"

---Notation---

With reverence to Captain Roberts, the author presents such as it would have been written &/or spoken during his lifetime.

CONSEQUENTIAL INFORMATION
BOTH PROTAGONISTS, HAS HER/HIS OWN FONT.

Fonts Uses: V'léOnica in Book One / Aspasia in Book Two.

Unchanged throughout: Captain Roberts, NARRATOR, & *Associations with Captain Roberts piratical career, inc. Mates, Governors, Captain & Crews from other ships, locations, &c.*

☠×☠×☠×☠×☠×☠

In the realm of spelling, each holds true to their own; each person's speech will be written in keeping with their raising. This shall also hold true in regard to that which is not spoken; fluctuating if you will, depending on which of the 2 protagonists is telling the story. e.g. American & Welsh, etc, and also to the particular time frame; Modern 21st Century wherein e.g.: harbor, jeweler, check are spelt harbour, jeweller, cheque, and early 18th Century British English wherein the spelling differs again: e.g. cried, loudly, & show equals cry'd, lowdly, shew, especially by those who were living at that era. In either case, with regard to Book 2, it was the cusp of change of the late phase of Early modern English (c1500-c1700 - notably the King James Bible & Shakespeare) to Present; the spelling, altho' more so than before, 'twas by no means standardized; what's more, those who received a formal education tended to speak and write in the most modern fashion, whilst those without, did/do not, & even then (as still today) most tend/tended to combine both the old & the new. This was also the case in reference to region, inlands in particular, being less influenced by travellers. I am also pleased to relate that several areas still speak in the melodious fashion of olde: e.g. Yorkshire, England, whose speech is particularly mellifluous; furthermore, apostrophes frequently replaced the e in ed ending and elsewhere. y instead of i & an e ended many words (the e being silent) & and others, e.g. Davies, which is pronounced Davis.

Exception to this lies with V'lé, who, in her efforts to conform with her chosen country's spelling & other differences, as well as the spelling & differences in the time of Captain Roberts, & altho' far from perfect, she does make an effort.

☠×☠×☠×☠×☠×☠

The LONG s: 'Twas the Firſt & middle, lower caſe, letters of a word, and generally the firſt when abreaſt (ſſ ff or ſſ, and on the occaſion when Sufficient type not be available, 'twaſ, fs or ſs was uſed). Ne'er was the long ſ/ſ uſed when it was the laſt letter.

THE REASON SOME OF THE YEARS ARE PRINTED, e.g. 172½ or 1720/1 is in direct relation to the Julian & Gregorian calendars which were in flux.

TO ELABORATE, the Gregorian calendar was not yet in use, exclusively, in most countries, e.g. Great Britain & the Eastern seaboard, until 1752 (Spain & France adopted it in 1582,) Most of the Dates, Henceforth, reflect the Julian Calendar.

Chapter One
Devil May-Care

Location: 'Bermuda'

Upon waking, I feel a little out of sorts, and finding my surroundings totally unfamiliar as I sit up, I discover that I am no longer aboard ship as I was when I drifted off to sleep last night, but within a spacious bedroom upon land. Dumb-founded, I sit on the edge of the bed rubbing my forehead with the tips of my fingers in a manner one would when trying to think while suffering from a severe headache, when suddenly the date **1 September** plainly written on a silver framed calendar sitting on the bedside table, with the year **1717** just below, scorching my mind's eye, I find myself mesmerized and unable to look away until the realization that I had been thrust back in time sets in.

Being the cautious sort, I slip into the dressing gown lying on the foot of the bed and quickly creep barefooted over to the door beside an enormous mirrored dressing table on the far side of the room. Opening the heavily built door as noiselessly as possible, I peep into a spacious hall bordered by a magnificently carved balustrade. Seeing me, 2 female servants in livery, who curtsy in unison whilst saying, "Good Morning, Madame," scamper down the hall.

Closing the door as I duck back in, I muse a moment, and deciding that the best thing to do is to get dressed and go investigate, I wander over to the ornate wardrobe against the far wall, open the doors and begin to rummage through the raiment. "Wow!"

Despite my bewilderment, I try to get a grip on my worrisome thoughts when my eyes catch a mirrored reflection of what my instincts tell me are hints of fire and smoke. Knowing that most big houses in past eras were equipped with numerous fireplaces, I begin to turn, when suddenly, from within the red-grey cloud, a ghastly creature billows forth.

Finding myself once again confronted by Lucifer, who, wearing the same grimace expression as the last time we met, leaves little doubt in my mind that he's conjured up a new game by which to amuse himself.

Like the sadist he is, the ghastly creature speaks cheerfully. "Good day, Madame." Amid his salutation, his bow is gesticulated to the extreme, and despite his rather polite greeting, 'tis easy to see he basks within the turmoil of those who are besieged, especially when they're fighting for their very survival.

However my expression may be while letting out sigh, I reply, "Ah, Lucifer," shaking my head a bit, "I should've known. I suppose this is what you meant when you said life would never be dull."

"Just a little adventure. Thou may recall I mentioned such occurrences at our previous meeting."

"And what's it to be this time? Last night when I went to sleep it was 2014, and now—"

As I walk to the bedside table to pick up the calendar, Lucifer murmurs," 'Twas 1869."

Not hearing him, I continue, saying, "Judging from what's written here, it's 7..." Suddenly realizing what he had just said, "What was that? Say that again."

"The year was 1869, had been since the storm; thee simply were not yet aware of it." As a hint of a sadistic smirk appears, "And as you observe, things have changed a bit."

"A bit!" Not seeing any evidence of my husband's presence as I look around, and becoming angry. "Where is Captain *Roberts*?"

Looking rather smug, "Currently anchored off the west coast of Africa, Mister Robert is first mate on board, the privateer, 𝒯𝑒𝑟𝑟𝑖𝑏𝑙𝑒.[B15]"

"Mister *Robert*?" I'm really not sure which emotion is most prevalent, the fear of being in a strange time and place, alone, or the knowledge that Captain *Roberts* is not here with me. Trying to maintain my composure so I can gather information, "And where am I, exactly?"

"Thou art within thine husband's magnificent villa in Bermuda, in thine own bedchamber."

Uttering in a rather glum tone, "Bermuda? A long time back I dreamt of visiting Bermuda, but," as my voice perks up again, "that was before I learned all the pink sand was gone."

"Well, there's plenty outside now," pointing towards the window. "Have a ball!"

As I stand before the ornate design carved deeply into the windowsill's framework whilst looking out to sea, thinking only of my situation, things like pink sand are very unimportant. Again growing angry, I turn to face him. "The storm, that was your doing wasn't it," scoffing at him. "If not for Captain *Roberts*' superb seamanship, and the confidence he instils in the hearts of his crew, the ship could've been lost with all hands."

Wearing an almost, 'hoping it would have,' look on his face, "Knowing Captain *Roberts*' efficaciousness, I was confident of the outcome."

Snarling whilst becoming disillusioned about the promise he made us after winning the last contest. "Are you saying that we all could've perished?"

"Thou best be remembering, Madame, that 'tis only Captain *Roberts* and thyself, who have reaped immortality, so be prudent, for there be other souls awaiting their day of judgment, and now," as he mellows, " 'tis here and now where thou must concern thyself." As he lights a cigar with the flaming tip of his thumb, he calmly changes the subject. "On the morrow, thee journeys to France. A duty call."

Displaying my anxiety. "A duty call?"

Ignoring my animosity, Lucifer continues. "On the way back, thou wilt stop to call on friends. Mrs Robles, who will accompanying thee, is most efficient, and being a native of Pembrokeshire, she hath invaluable knowledge of the Welsh countryside and its populace."

"And who is Mrs Robles?"

"As the widow of an English Baron's youngest son, and a kinsman on thy mother's side, she is the Honourable Mrs Neville Robles. Having been placed in her charge, chiefly due to Louis' Queen, Françoise d'Aubigné,[H4] originally as thy Governess since thy birth, she hath the honour, by Royal appointment, of being thine official Lady-in-Waiting and Companion."

Chuckling a mite, "Uh, yeah," and thinking this is just a game, " and what about me, just who am I supposed to be, and how am I introduced and addressed?"

"Holding a French title, thou art introduced as Madame Aspasia Rebekah Jourdain, la Marquise d'Éperon-noire; thereafter, depending on who's talking and to whom, those present will address thee as either Madame, my Lady, my Lady Aspasia, or Madame la Marquise. And now, being that Court convenes late next month, thou must ready thyself for an important appointment at Versailles. A matter of state."

"Court! You expect me to attend court. I, I can't! I don't—"

"Calm thyself. Mrs Robles, as will the attendants at Versailles, as is their duty, shall guide thee."

Speaking with great anxiety, "But why do I have to go there?"

"Because here and now, thou art a Marquise, and le Régent, himself, hath commanded thine attendance."

"Charming, but what has all this to do with my relationship with Captain *Roberts*."

"Directly, nothing, but indirectly, it shall be because of thy personage that the road to thy beloved can be traversed."

"After the last contest you said Captain *Roberts* and I would be together for all eternity."

"What I said was that, ye will forever be entwined together, throughout all eternity. I further said ye would know adventure, and eternity, Madame, is a very long time. Ne'er did I say ye be joined at the hip."

As I do my best to hold back the tears as the evil that besieged my life is here still, Lucifer continues. "Whyfor the tears, did thee not spout several times thou would sell thy soul to be with him in reality?"

Looking downward a moment, I let out a sigh. Looking up, I quietly reply, "Yes, I did."

"Then thou should be able to surmise his resurgence; even so, ye, both of you, had to play and ultimately win a deadly contest requiring skill, cunning, and courage to achieve thy dream."

"But we did win!"

"So ye did, however, if thou recalls, the first part of thy dream was realized after thee penned and sent a heated message in the defence of thy beloved. That was the night he appeared before thee as a ghost. Yet as time marched on, thine unfulfilled desires becoming desperate needs, they too were granted."

"But those were gifts from the Almighty."

"Thou art mistaken, Madame, for 'tis I who be thy benefactor."

Shrouded by a measure of fear, I withdraw a mite to take a moment to consider before asking a rather daunting question. "A moment ago you said 'for all time,' by this are you saying that these adventures, as you tend, are to continue forever?"

Shrugging, "Possibly." Taking a puff of his cigar, "Now then Madame, was it not thy fondest wish to go back in time and sail with thy beloved upon his ship and share in his piratical adventures?"

Realizing that these adventures are born out of my own dreams, I courageously reply, "Yes it was, and ever shall be."

"Then whyfor art thou complaining?" Taking another puff, "If thou desires to continue thy relationship, thee must win his love again, here, in his time; ergo, thee must devise a plan to meet him. Should thee fail, thou shall remain here, in this time, ne'er to be reborn, and—"

Grabbing him by the arm, forcing him to turn around whilst hollering, "Just a damn minute! Because of you, Bart might not sign on board the *Princess*, and thus, shan't fulfill his destiny as, *'The Great Pirate Roberts,'* so dubbed by the High and Mighties in his own time."

"Oh, I see. Thou art keen on his piratical activities."

"It's his greatness, damn you, and you've changed history!"

"How so?"

"You said this villa belongs to *Bartholomew Roberts*."

"Nay, Madame, I did not. I said this villa belongs to thine husband."

"*Bartholomew Roberts is* my husband!"

"In the 21st Century yes, but not now, not in the 18th Century. As for, *John Robert*, he is, at present, living the life which thou art so familiar, and unless thou art successful in thine intervention, history shall remain unchanged."

"But—"

"Heed my words, Madame, and listen well. Here, thou art Aspasia Rebekah Jourdain, la Marquise d'Éperon-noire.[H1] Thy late husband, Sir Guillaume Jourdain,[H3] 1st Marquis d'Éperon-noire, and 32 years thy senior, was descended from the Australian Huguenots who migrated to Bermuda in the beginning of the 17th century. As a paternal grandson of François de la Béraudière, marquis de l'Ile-Jourdain, seigneur de Rouhet, chevalier de l'Ordre du Roi, and a courtier of Louis XIV of France. With regard to thee, 'twas Françoise d'Aubigné, Marquise de Maintenon[H4], Louis XIV's 2nd wife, whose keen interest in thee as a child, is how thy marriage in 1702 came about."

"I see, a marriage of state."

"Quite. Thy late husband, a nobleman of vast wealth, and the last to bear his families name, and desperate need to sire a legitimate male heir, was obliged to take a young wife, however, being from a family who had enjoyed, *'Pride of Place'* for centuries, 'twas necessary that his bride be a well-bred, accomplished *'Lady of Quality,'* educated in scholastics, heraldry, and schooled in the arts, dance, song, and able to play a musical instrument, as well as being fluent in the modern languages. Considerable polish, a refined carriage, and manners were also required, as was beauty of face and figure; and lastly, it was imperative that the Marquis' prospective bride's skills in estate management be finely honed."

Giggling, "Wasn't asking for much was he." Returning to serious reality, "Well, you've explained the late marquis' need for a young, well-educated wife, but—"

"Because thy mother had dallied with the King's young nephew's affections—"

"Meaning they were lovers."

"Yes, and as a result of that liaison, thou art not only a natural daughter, but the first issue sired by Philippe Charles d'Orléans.[H7] Some years later, in 1693, after Philippe was married, the King declared thee a légitimée of France. Afterwards, in the care of thy Nursery Governess, Mrs Robles,[H2] thou journeyed to France, and within the Palace of Versailles, thou was brought up in court society. Soon after, thee was called la petite dame du palais by Madame de Maintenon."

"Petite dame what?"

"la petite dame du palais, which in English means, 'the Little Lady of the Palace.'"

Doing my best to absorb the telling of what is presently my life history, I seat myself upon one of the elegant chairs. "Let me be sure I understand. Aspasia's mother was an American colonist of Welsh/Germanic and French decent whose dalliance with the King's teenage nephew, Philippe Charles d'Orléans, who has since become Régent of France, begat the female child who, now, a mature woman, is the Marquise who lives here."

"Most correct. What will become important later is the fact that because of thy loyal services to the crown, thou hast been granted unparalleled privileges, which includes the fact that thy title, estates, and wealth can never be stripped from thee; what is more, due to supplications made by the church, thou possesses the right to choose thine owne husband."

"Excuse me for pointing this out, but la Marquise's life, no doubt a complicated one, how can you expect me to just take her place, and now that, that thought has cropped up, where is she?"

"She stands before me."

"What! Are you saying that I am she, like reincarnation, and I'm here to re-live a past life?"

"Dost thou remember when thou told Keith how a physic, an astrologer, and the Quija® board said that in a previous life, thou had lived with thy godfather in Little Haven back in 1701, and that her name was Aspasia Rees, but used her middle name, Rebekah."

"Yes."

"And dost thou recall the look on Captain *Roberts'* face?"

"Yes, his expression was rather queer."

"That was because at that moment he knew thee to be the reincarnation of she whom he loved. Thou hast the rare opportunity to rectify the wrong doing that kept two people who were truly in love, forever apart."

Chiding myself, "That means Captain *Roberts* was serious when he said that I was she, reincarnated?"

"Yes, but in this time he knows his Rebekah, only as Rebekah Rees, the daughter of a retired merchant ship's captain, not as the celebrated Marquise, Aspasia Rebekah Jourdain."

Trying to grasp the situation, "Are you saying that this," pointing to myself, "Aspasia Rebekah Jourdain and his Rebekah Rees, are the same person. If so," as my eyes become tear filled, "that means I am the woman who broke his heart?"

"Yes and no. They are one in the same, yes, but 'twas a misconstrued occurrence, reinforced by wagging tongues spouting vile slander, that collectively drove a dagger into his heart, not thee; and that being the case, the situation can be righted.

"How?"

"To achieve this, thou wilt have to be both clever and decisively courageous; in addition, despite thou art a French Noblewoman of prominence, thy beloved may know nothing of thee, especially with regard to recognizing you as being his Rebekah after all these years." Changing the subject. "As well thee knows, Madame, the man of thine hearts desire, thrives on flattery, admires bravery, and appreciates a well-bred, virtuous lady, especially when she's beautiful, and with all thy memories from whence thou came in tack, and as stated thee would have it, all thou needs now is a plan capable of fulfilling his most searching dreams."

Dishearten, a tear drops onto my cheek. "Even if I do find a way to get where I may have an opportunity to meet him, just how am I supposed to win the heart of the reigning paragon of masculine virtue when only on rare occasions does he leave his ship?"

Brushing my cheek with his long, bony index finger, wiping away the tear, "As thou hast seduced and won him once, thee can again, for thee hast qualities he admires, and as thou knows already, even strict religious moralists have been known to fall in love."

"Thank you, but even so, I know of no instance of Captain *Roberts* visiting Bermuda."

"Ah…" says he, "but he will pass by."

"When?"

"En route to Trepassey."

"Trepassey! But that won't be until June 1720."

Speaking with a chuckle, "Quite, but don't fret, Madame, 'tis not so long. Besides, by my calculations, the time allotted shall leave you none to spare. Following thine appointment in Versailles, thee shall journey to Britannia. From that moment forward, thou wilt need not only all of thy creative talents, but all the moxie thee can muster, and as such will prove invaluable later on, study the trade winds. If thou art to achieve thy dream, everything thou doest must serve thine objective; if one tactic fails, thee must try anew."

Walking to the corner table, Lucifer pours a small measure of the flagon's contents into one of the ornate silver goblets, and wetting his throat before continuing, he samples the wine. "Already thou possesses maturity of thought, youthful beauty, intelligence, and a nodding acquaintance with the Augustan way of speaking. Those, together with thy flare for conniving and scheming, and thy personal history of sexual abstention outside of marriage, as well as being more or less a teetotal, I see no reason why thee would not succeed." After a moment of pause, "But perhaps thou art correct, and thine attributes alone are not enough; ergo, for the sake of a good contest, I shall aid thee in thine endeavour by providing thee unlimited means available at any bank thou enters, fluency in all needed languages, wielding power, and a copy of thine owne writings."

Magically, as a book appears on the table, he picks it up and hands it to me, "Thy reference material, Madame."

"Can you at least fill me in on the goings on here, in this villa, so I'll know who's who, what's what, and my place in it?"

"As an extremely wealthy widow and Châtalaine of d'Éperon-noire plantation, thou dost as thee pleases."

Feeling rather lost and uneasy, "Surely I have some sort of schedule, and manner."

"Just continue to be the wilful nonconformist thou hast always been. The servants will do the rest."

Walking over to the bureau, Lucifer opens the top drawer and removes a gilt-edged book and carries it with him as crosses the room.

Knocking back what remains in the goblet, "Mrs Robles is busily preparing thy breakfast." Stretching out his hand, "The answers to all thy questions are located within these pages."

Taking from him, the DIARY, "One last question."

Setting the goblet on the table, "And that is?"

"What will it take to restore our lives together, the Captain's and mine, as a loving couple, and for this game to end?"

Waving his arms about as he vanishes, a voice is heard amid a cloud of red-grey coloured smoke. "When his love for thee equals thine owne for him, thy lives shall be as ye desires."

Coughing a bit whilst waving away the smoke I spout, "Show off!"

Altho' I have no idea why a diary of my past here would be of help, I carry, both it, and my book of the Captain's memoirs, which contains future events with me as I go on the hunt for the kitchen. Wandering thro' the enormous gothic manor house, and after passing thro' the dining room, I find the kitchen, where I see an older woman cooking over an impressive wood burning stove, whereupon, I make my presence known. "Good morning."

Noticing me, the woman looks in my direction, and whilst continuing to stir the pot, "Bore da, my Lady, I shall serve breakfast presently."

"Thank you, Mrs Robles." Relaxing some, I return to the dining room, where after taking a seat, I open the diary.

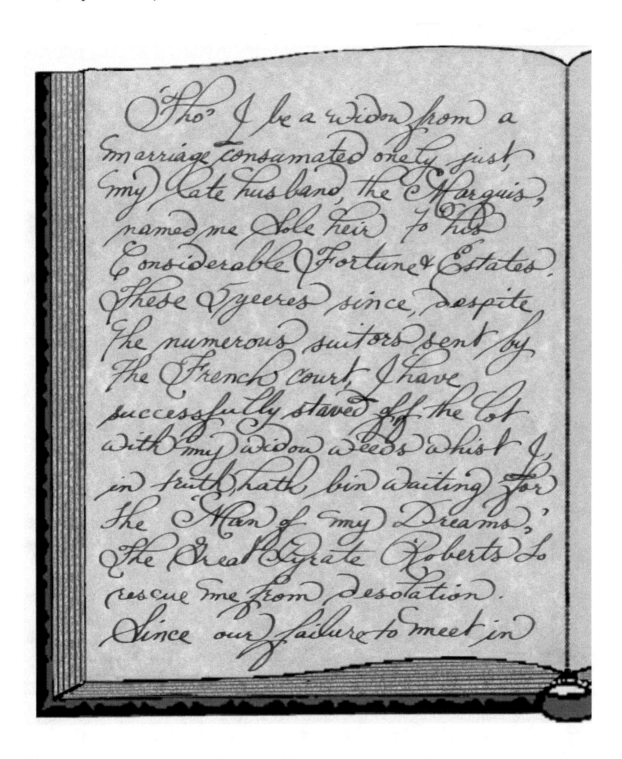

"Tho' I be a widow from a marriage consamated onely just, my late husband, the Marquis, named me Sole heir to his Considerable Fortune & Estates. These 5 yeeres since, despite the numerous suitors sent by the French court, I have successfully staved off the lot with my widow weeds whist I, in truth, hath bin waiting for the 'Man of my Dreams,' The Great Pyrate Roberts to rescue me from desolation. Since our failure to meet in

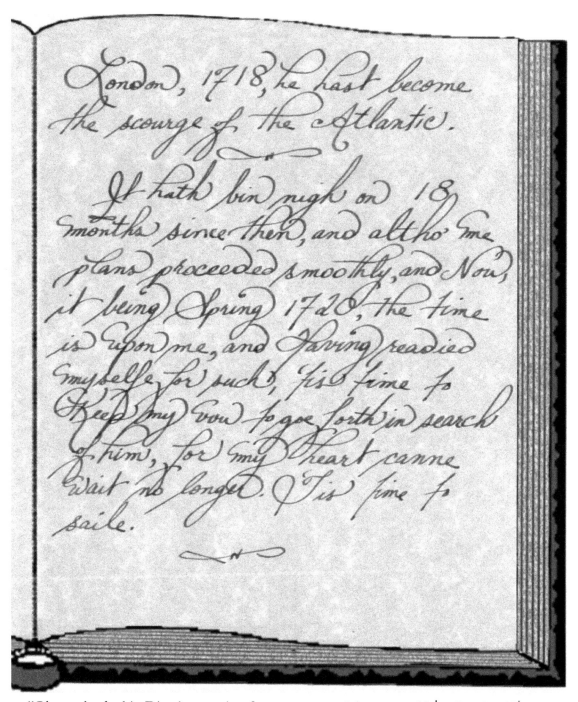

London, 1718, he hast become the scourge of the Atlantic.

It hath bin nigh on 18 months since then, and altho' me plans proceeded smoothly, and Now, it being Spring 1720, the time is upon me, and having readied myselfe for such, 'tis time to keep my vow to goe forth in search of him, for my heart canne wait no longer. 'Tis time to saile.

"Oh my lord, this Diary's contains future events. I have a guide! On the 2nd page, as opposed to being in chronological order, it speaks of events well into the future." Looking one page further, I see it returns to less far off days. Obviously the 2nd page was to instil hope. Closing the diary, I find myself thinking of the various ways people met up with pirates.

Lucifer, knowing me well, is an aspect which in itself is unsettling, but however my life may be in regard to these circumstances, being totally different if not for my love for Captain *Roberts*, it will never be my wish for it to be otherwise, for I chose to be his Champion, and he in turn, tho' later, accepted me as such, and as a result, I have placed myself in the perilous position of being the one who must now and forever fight to keep him from perdition. This, as strange as it may seem to some, is a great honour that ne'er shall I forgo, for the road upon that which I have travelled since our meeting, despite the looming dangers, has afforded me a wealth of happiness beyond compare. As things are now, that is unless I get lucky enough to be captured by him during my journey to and from France, or elsewhere, I will have to go in search of him. As for just what Lucifer expects, is anyone's guess.

Hearing footsteps, I look upward and see Mrs Robles and a kitchen maid bringing breakfast upon a large silver tray, and as my Lady-in-Waiting takes a seat on the opposite side of the table, it becomes evident that she takes her meals with me, and as my role begins, I get into character, otherwise I may be here until the end of days.

Opening the morning's conversation, Mrs Robles says, "Although being named as your godfather's executrix was an unwelcomed duty, I trust you managed a bit of diversion during your visit to the Collonies."

Playing my role as best I can, hoping not to say the wrong thing, "The task afforded little time for pleasantries, Mrs Robles."

"And now, barely home a day, another duty call. The urgency of your attendance in France leaves little time to prepare, my Lady, for the crossing takes 5 to 6 weekes; nevertheless, David awaits you at the mews."

"All this travelling, and yet, where I find myself longing to visit is Wales. Shall we make plans for an extended visit?"

Eager to visit the land of her raising, "And Pembrockshire, my Lady, will the trip take us there as well?"

Smiling broadly, "Shall we begin our holiday in The Havens, and go on to from there."

Decidedly happy, "Sounds splendid." Taking a happy bite of her breakfast, she pauses a moment. "On the receipt of the crown's notification informing me of your need to sail forthwith, I ordered several items from the shoppes in town. The Merchant and Couture both sent word this morning that the items I ordered for you are ready."

Having just taken the last bite of my breakfast, I cover my mouth as I speak. "Surly you need some new fixins too; shall we go to town as soon as I return from my ride."

"Perfect." Arising from her seat, Mrs Robles informs me, "By now, Noémie will have your riding habit laid out."

"Thank you for a lovely breakfast." In the realm of other tasks, knowing it will take a bit of time to absorb all that has happened this morning, I pick up my two books and slowly make my way back to my bedchamber. Going back in time is difficult indeed, but fortunately I am not entering cold. Perhaps, as Lucifer stated, having lived here in the past is no doubt the reason I've always had a fondness for what most contend as being antiquated speech, period attire, and decorum. Such may also be the reason why I never felt at home in my own time."

Entering my bed chamber, the young woman waiting for me can only be Noémie, my Lady's Maid.

"Good morning, my Lady," says she amid a nippy curtsey before scurrying over to help me to remove my bed gown and wrapper.

As she strips me naked, thinking to myself as the young woman flits about; doing as Lucifer suggested, to just go with the flow, my thoughts at the moment, being I haven't ridden in a fortnight, are that I will enjoy going out for a ride.

Within about 30 minutes, I am ready to go out and survey the grounds. Years ago, before Captain *Roberts* entered my life, I dreamed of places like this, but now, in truth, with my mind consumed with thoughts of how I am going to get back to him, I find that the only thing that truly matters is the happiness we share with those we love.

Whilst looking into the full-length mirror and seeing myself in a beautiful green velvet, riding habit, my thoughts turn to the present. Not knowing where the stables are located, I walk out onto the balcony hoping to see them, but all that can be seen is a dense tropical forest. Thinking quickly, I call to my lady's maid. "Noémie," who, whilst hurrying to stand just behind me, "I thought I ordered the flora cut back before I left."

Smiling some, " 'twas, my Lady. Yer turned 'round again." Walking to the proper balcony, she opens the drapes. "The mews can onely be seen from the Southern exposure."

"Thank you, Noémie," says I whilst walking to the opposite balcony. After a minute, having a general idea on which way to go, I leave to take care of what I understand is my usual business. As I exit the house, I flip my crop upside down, and using the handle, I snatch up the train of my riding habit. Carrying it behind me as I go in search of the stables, I utter, "This is a big place." Then, hearing a horse whinny, I head in the direction of the sound, and within a couple minutes, I find the stables. "Wow," says I, as I look in the different stalls, "Nice horse flesh." Coming out of the paddock area, I see who I assume is David, and looking at the two horses he has saddled, again my heart sinks. Though adept in most of the equestrian disciplines, the one I need is the only one I never learned, and speaking quietly under my breath, 'Lucifer probably planned it that way.' 'Well,' thinking to myself, 'I always wanted to learn to ride side-saddle.'

Seeing me approach, "Good morrow, my Lady. Cocobahn missed you."

"Good morrow, David." and stepping up to the 17hh Friesian stallion, David helps me mount. After arranging my riding habit, I balance my weight in the saddle, and in giving the high sign, I am happy to state that although we unexpectedly depart at the canter, my fears were unjustified.

By the time I return to the house, change my dress, accompany Mrs. Robles to town and back, and have my dinner, more than 9 hours have gone by before I can retire to my bedchamber and begin making plans. Unfortunately, all I know is that Captain *Roberts*' piratical adventures won't bring him anywhere near *Bermuda* until he's en route to *Trepassey*, nigh on 3 years from now. Perhaps I can dream up a way to go out and meet him, and until then I shall make every effort to become not only knowledgeable, but proficient in the era Lucifer has placed me. A marksman with 20th Century handguns, I know very little about the pistols in the 18th century, and not knowing what type of situation may present itself, and not having fenced, nor handled a bow and arrow for several years, as well as needing to re-learn how to load and fire black powder pistols as well, I am sure that all of these skills, which I hope shall come back to me swiftly with the aid of a tutor, will be useful in my life here, especially considering my plans for the future, and whilst becoming proficient, I can fashion for my Captain a garment fit for a King. The hardest, whilst being also the most exciting, will be learning all there is to know about sailing the tall ship I have decided to purchase in Britannia. As for the lingo, although the spelling will remain a constant battle, at least the speaking of it has been made easy by Lucifer. The one thing I know for sure is that every aspect of my present life must be as real to me as it is to everyone else or I shan't succeed.

Chapter Two
First Glimpse
Location: *'Bound for Versailles'*

Ne'er before have I enjoyed travelling so much as I have aboard Monsieur Pomier's French Brig. The air is fresh and clean, and for a fortnight, since leaving Castle Harbour, the motion of the ship upon the water each night has been like a cradle. The sea, ever so peaceful whilst concurrently invigorating, is beyond description, and altho' there have been a few days when the sea has been heavy, I have loved every moment.

Altho' I learned much from my Captain, and more still during the short time I was aboard the 21th century Royal Fortune, most every day, whilst also becoming familiar with the terminology used on board, I have, in some capacity, performed as a member of the crew, during which time I have gained invaluable knowledge pertaining to the various stations about the ship, most of my free time is spent formulating my plans whilst perched high up in the crow's nest; it is there where the purest of all freedoms can be found, especially in the sense of escaping my entourage. I had no idea so many were required to perform the tasks associated with one person of rank and privilege. There's Mrs Robles, of course; Noémie Bizet, my lady's maid, hairdresser, and modiste; Julie, a fine cobbler, who also runs my errands, as well as for Mrs. Robles, including being her relief chaperone when she is under the weather. Whilst most of these persons duties require only a partial day, Mrs Robles is ceaseless; she even sleeps in my bedchamber, and except when we're home in Bermuda, the only time Mrs. Robles is apart from me is when she's cooking, and during that time, Julie is in attendance. Also in my entourage, is Katrine, my laundress; Catherine, the scullery-maid; Philippe, my footman, who, together with Noémie, will be very useful in learning the ways of the French; and lastly, Betsy, a kitchen-maid/cook. Must be a sign of wealth, all these servants clattering about, why their very presence can be unnerving, and they never leave me alone for a minute. Fortunately, working 'bout the ship is one way to escape my chaperones, which, in itself, gives me cause to scurry up the mizzen at every opportunity, and when I am not mapping out my proposed itinerary, I quietly read the Captain's biography to refresh my memory; thus, there is hardly a moment when my thoughts, in some way, are not devoted to my Captain, and the events that pertain to his life. All in all, I'd have to say that, thus far, the hardest part about being thrust back in time is dealing with simple ignorance, mostly due to the fact that since I'm supposed to already know the answers, it's difficult to ask or phrase questions without revealing the fact that I am, in essence, an impostor, and the constant skulduggery, which is, in itself, exhausting.

Woodcut: Captain Edward England

Whilst en route to West Africa, the *Terrible*, captained by the Welsh privateer, *John Williams*, our ship was taken by the pyrate, *Edward England*, Captain of the *Pearl*. Seemingly, not onely did most of the crew of the captured ship remain on board, wee, with myself as first mate, remarkably, kept our places. Sailing on, sev'rall prizes were taken. The next ship seized and kept was renamed *Victory*, and *John Taylor*, a member of Captain *England's* crew, was voted as her new Captain.[B15]

Despite the new prize, the pirate's recent engagements, being nigh on profitless, created unease, and as a result, much animosity began to ensue 'twixt the senior officers, Captains included. Irrespective of their opinions, they abided these laxities in accordance with the lawes that faithfully governed their democratic society. *Edward England*, whose languorous crewmen, favoring his easie going nature, remain'd Captain of the *Pearl*. Consequently the impertinent opinions, which would 'ave beene considered wilful insubordination, remained at bay untill one man, myself, so motivated by *Edward England's* determination to not onely saile for the Indian Ocean, but to be elevated to the rank of Commodore, led to an outright debate; however, the proposed voyage and concept whereto, was one I disagreed with, wholeheartedly,[E] and with so many being content with an easie life, I affeared the Captain's wishes would come to fruition; ergo, utterly refusing to abide by what I considered ineffectual and power craving leadership, I could hold my tongue no more, and thus, in keeping with my owne beliefs, spoke openly and with conviction when the opportunity arose amid conflicting suggestions made by the senior officers with regard to which heading to take. Subsequently, being unable to resolve their differences, the pyrates broke rank. Of the combined crews, the malingers, dividing themselves 'twixt the *Pearl* and the *Victory*, sailed with Commodore *Edward England* to the Indian Ocean. Some of the others, them who craved action and riches, sailed elsewhere aboard, the *Terrible*. The remaining men, those who believed and trusted my judgment, returned to their lives as honest seaman.

Turning to the last section of my pocket-sized book, I begin making a 'Things to Do,' list which will commence as soon as my appointed court appearance in France is concluded.

1st item: Excepting Mrs Robles, send my entourage back to Bermuda.

2nd item: Secure passage on a ship sailing from Le Havre to Dover.

Knowing *John Robert* will sign on as Third Mate[B9 pg 80] aboard the Guiney-man, *Princess*, it's my intention to arrive in London before she sails, that way I can personally hire him to

Captain my ship. But 'tis more than just a Captaincy that I wish for him. Somehow, I want him to understand the feeling of trust and faith he instils in people, myself included. Still thinking, "Admiral of the Leeward Islands," says I quietly, "that's what he call'd himself," as a smile slowly emerges, I'll give him complete autonomy, and that being the case, I shall allow him to purchase a ship of his own choosing, or, if he wishes, even design it himself; what's more, having Carte Blanche, he will have the opportunity to make the most of his incredible talents. My one and only stipulation being that Mrs Robles and I will be on board, as passengers, myself hopefully taking care of the business aspects with regard to the exporting of raw silk, and both manufacturing and marketing of the fabric therefrom, as well as the mulberry wine also produced on my plantation, will be agreeable to him.

Not knowing exactly when the *Princess* will make sail, and being fearful of missing her, I decide it best to write my beloved a letter, and upon reaching port in Plymouth, I shall hire a courier to take it to him, and such, I add another item to my list.

3rd item: Hire a courier in Plymouth to deliver my letter to John Robert in London.

After climbing down, I go directly to my cabin, and having carefully placed my little writing desk and quill into a leather haversack, I quickly return to my place of sanctuary to write my letter.

After about an hour, my letter now completed, I place my calling card beneath my signature; a ribbon attached with red sealing wax to which I firmly imprint the Coat-Of-Arms seal afforded me by the French court. Folding the parchment thrice, being careful not to crease the ribbon, I place it within the leather pouch with a front flap I made specially for this purpose. Securing the leather pouch closed by way of a leather thong tied in a falconer's knot, I slip my ribbon beneath the flap, and pouring on a generous helping of sealing wax, I dampened my seal and depress it firmly into the wax.

Momentarily, as I stare out over the ocean whilst waiting for the wax to harden, I find myself dreaming of the man I love and what is to come for several minutes before packing up my writing slope. Climbing down the rigging; my haversack flung over my shoulder, I am completely happy with my proposal.

Proceeding on deck with the letter, I approach the officer on watch. "I know that within the week we are due to dock in Plymouth where the ship will take on fresh water and provisions before sailing on to Calais. Whilst there, I have need of a special courier who can deliver a letter to London."

Replying, the officer says, "Once docked, should you permit me, it shall be my singular privilege to escort your Ladyship to the finest messenger service in Plymouth, and when your business is concluded, safely back to the ship."

"Thank you, Lieutenant."

The week passes quickly, and as promised, Lieutenant Main has hired a carriage, and together with Mrs Robles, we head for town.

Arriving in jig time, the charming officer helps us ladies from the carriage, and dutifully escorts us into the shoppe.

"Excuse me, sir," says Lieutenant Main whilst dinging the heavily built bell that rests on the counter, "la Marquise d'Éperon-noire wishes a word with you."

Fawning over the delight and prestige of doing business with nobility in person, the owner of the shoppe hurries giddily to our side of the counter.

Bowing, "A great pleasure, my Lady."

Lifting my hand, the shoppe owner immediately takes the opportunity to kiss it.

Speaking in a jovial tone, "Welcome to my humble shoppe, my Lady; how may I be of service to you?"

"Her ladyship, la Marquise," begins Lt Main, "wishes to hire your most competent courier."

Removing the leather pouch from my haversack. Showing it to him, "I need this letter, delivered with all speed to *Mister John Robert*, in London. He will be signing aboard the Guiney~man, *Princess*. Not only must it be placed in *Mister Robert's* own hands, he must be made to understand the urgency of its contents, before his ship sails."

"It shall be done, my Lady."

"I dislike sounding doubtful, but I prefer to speak to your courier personally."

"But of course, my Lady."

Looking over his shoulder, he calls to his young apprentice assistant, "Master Barnes, has William Crandall returned from his Hakin holiday?"

"Yes, sir. He returned last night. Shall I fetch him?"

"He lives but a few minutes from here; will your Ladyship wait?"

Replying jovially, "Of course."

"Run, Master Barnes. Bring back William at all speed."

"Thank you," says I, smiling, happy in the knowledge that my plan, thus far, is going well.

Grabbing his hat and coat, Master Barnes runs past me, bowing briefly as he quickly says, "Yer Ladyship," and bolts out the door.

"May I offer your Ladyships some refreshment?"

"Thank you. If'in it's available, I shall have café au lait."

"Very good, my lady." Turning, "Mrs Robles?"

"I take tea."

Snapping his fingers, the shoppekeeper gets the attention of his clerk, who dashes over. "Run to the Plymouth Inn and inform the Maître d'Hôtel that I need café au lait, tea, hors d'oeuvres, and sweets suitable for a Lady of Quality and party of 4."

Without uttering a word, the clerk dashes off.

"Will you join me in a glass of port, Lieutenant?"

"Thank you, sir, I believe I will."

Moving to the cabinet concealing a hidden bar, the shoppekeeper, lifting the lid, raises a decanter of port & several glasses. Filling two, he hands one of the glasses to the Lieutenant.

"Thank you, sir."

The returning clerk holds the door for Plymouth Inn's, Maître d', who is followed by a busser pushing a tea cart lavished with refreshments upon a heavy silver tray.

" Nice to see you Mister Croswell, and Welcome." Turning to Mrs Robles and myself, "Allow me to present Mister Coswell, Plymouth Inn's Maître d'."

Mrs Robles, as do I, respond graciously.

Being dutiful, the Shoppe Keeper continues with the introductions. "Mister Coswell, 'tis my pleasure to present la Marquise d'Éperon-noire, and the Honourable Mrs Robles."

Bowing courteously, as both ladies nod respectively, "A great pleasure, ladies." Turning to the Busser, "You may go."

Bowing to Mrs Robles and myself, the busser departs without a word.

Proceeding with his purpose, the Maître d' pours a cup of tea and handing it to Mrs Robles, she utters, "Thank you."

Continuing his duties, the Maître d', having poured a cup of coffee, adds a mite of cream, before handing it to me.

Taking the cup, "Thank you," says I whilst adding a scraping of raw sugar.

Picking up the tray, the Maître d' offers it to each of us, who in turn, take a dessert fork, a napkin, and a few tidbits from the tray. Turning, "Would you care for a bite, Lieutenant?"

Picking up a napkin, the Lieutenant helps himself to a sweet, whilst saying, "Thank you."

Taking a sip of my café au lait, "This man William, how reliable is he?"

"Very, my Lady. He'll deliver the letter for you, rest assured." Showing pride in his employee, he jovially adds, "He's the best courier in the whole of *Britannia*."

Taking another sip of my coffee, "You mentioned Hakin. Is Mister Crandall a Welshman?"

"Yes, my Lady. Born and bred."

Happy to hear this, for I too am Welsh, tho' not having seen my home for many years, I think only to sweeten the pot, as my plans for this hard working, young Welsh courier, be much more involved then simply delivering a letter. Just then, scurrying back into the shoppe, comes young Barnes.

Huffing from running, he announces, "He's coming, my Lady."

Replying with a smile, whilst handing him a Guinea, "Thank you, Master Barnes."

"Thank you, my Lady," he says with a broad grin, before returning to his work.

Just finishing my coffee, William enters, brashly.

"Master Barnes tells me you have for me a mission of great importance."

"Yes, William, that I do."

His coat and hair being as brazen as his manners, William is not at all what I expected, altho' just what I did expect, I'm sure I don't know.

Turning to introduce me, "I have the pleasure of introducing la Marquise d'Éperon-noire, and her companion, the Honourable Mrs Robles."

William bows graciously to Mrs Robles and myself.

Setting the cup upon the silver tray, "I understand you to be the best courier in Britannia."

"So they tell me, my Lady."

Courtesy of TheFairyGodfather.com

Rising from my seat, I show him the leather pouch, "It is of grave importance that this letter be delivered to John Robert, placed in his hand, before he boards the Guiney~man, *Princess*, which is scheduled to sail sometime in November. I know not what day John Robert will arrive in London, or at the ship, so you must arrive prior to the end of October and wait at the ship until he arrives."

"Just as you say, my Lady."

"Being aware that more than one man named John Robert could be in London, even aboard the *Princess*, makes it vital that you be sure he's from *Nghastell Newydd Bach, Pembrockshire, Cymru*. I have," showing him, "written it here, on the back of the pouch."

Taking the pouch from me, "I shall, my Lady."

"Is it possible for you to depart forthwith?"

"I canne leave within the hour."

"Excellent!" Reaching into my haversack, I take

from within the first of two velvet pouches. "Please hold out your hands." Placing the heavy bag within his hands, I open it. "Herein, in all manner of denominations, rests £100. in both sterling and gold coyne. Once in London, you will need to take lodgings near the docks. This money will provide for your meals and lodgings en route, as well as a comfortable room and meals whilst you wait." Whilst taking a smaller velvet pouch from my haversack. "To be sure no misfortune can delay you," taking out a fist full of £20 banknotes. "Here, is an additional £500." Handing it to him, "These additional funds should be more than sufficient to cover any unforeseen emergency. Please ride with all speed. Use whatever funds you deem necessary to purchase indomitable mounts as need'd en route. The balance, as will be the horses you purchase on your journey, are yours to do with as you will."

"Your generosity is too great to accept, my Lady."

"Superior service, William, deserves payment expressing appreciation. If not for such, wherefore would the incentive to improve stem."

Although holding within his hand more cash than e'er has his eyes before seen, being nigh on half a lifetimes wages, his mind is only on the success of his mission. "I shall not fail thee, my Lady."

"You must wait each day at the docks from dawn until midnight. Eventually, John Robert will arrive to sign on. So you will recognize him, I brought a miniature of him, a drawing." Removing it from my haversack, I hand it to him. "Will it suffice?"

" 'Tis more than adequate, my Lady."

"When you find him, make him aware of the urgency contained within; it's imperative that he reads the letter before he signs on."

Whilst slipping both pouches and portrait within the deep recesses of his inside pockets, he speaks confidently. "Consider it done, my Lady."

"Thank you, William."

Turning to the shoppekeeper. "Mister Coswell, I realize I am taking from you your finest courier for some time to come, please allow me to compensate you for your loss," and stretching out my hand, I hold five, £20 banknotes, " 'Tis my hope this will be satisfactory payment."

Speaking with much delight as he takes the money, "Oh yes, my Lady, most assuredly."

"And now, gentlemen, we must return to the Merchant Ship, *Mary and Martha*."

As we turn to leave, Mrs Robles, who's getting on in years, is appreciative when Lieutenant Main offers her the support of his arm.

"Thank you, Lieutenant," says she kindly as she arises.

Dashing over, the door is graciously opened by young Master Barnes.

Upon exiting, and after tossing the lad a coin, I turn to again speak to William. "If all goes well, I, myself, shall be in London before the *Princess* sails."

"I look forward to seeing thee there," replies William with a confident smile.

The passage to France was uneventful, and since being in Versailles, time is moving along quickly. My first appearance at court was not quite as noisy as it was tedious, not to say that I would not have enjoy the visit if'n my mind was not so preoccupied elsewhere, but as it is, my heart and mind have but one ambition, and thus, having a great fondness for France, I shall holiday there often. As to matters regarding my late husband's Château in Havre de Grâce, Normandy; having let it be known that I wish to sell the property, 'tis where I shall be stopping until time necessitates my departure for Britannia.

Altho' 'tis been but a few days following my arrival to this lovely place, a wealthy merchant has paid the handsome sum of 250000 Pistoles[①].

My aim now is to hire a ship to cross the Channel and land me at Dover, where my journey will continue via coach to London. Being that I shall be carrying with me, a large sum of emergency money, I have fashioned for myself a red satin lining for my bustier, specially designed to securely hold and conceal, 100 Gold Sovereigns, and 20 notes valued at £1000*l*. sterling, and altho' my attire as a result, will be somewhat cumbersome, 'tis a necessary precaution should we be beset upon by highwaymen. As for the balance of the purchase price, it travels with me; well hidden within a secret compartment located beneath the seats that must be dismantled in order for the contents to be observed, much less removed. Upon reaching London, the entire sum will be deposited at the Bank of England on Princes Street, in Grocers' Hall. I am also carrying a quantity of travelling money, and altho' an assortment of gold and silver coynage from all over Europe and Britannia, pursed within a small pouch located in the upper region of my stomacher, it is accepted any place I choose to spend it.

The channel crossing, from Le Havre to Dover, taking from dawn to dusk, goes smoothly. Whilst on board the 142 foot, three-masted Ship, I became very fond of her. She is what Captain *Roberts* would term yare, meaning she is quick to respond, and easy on the helm. Her lower decks are nicely arranged with generous cabins. The galley and scullery, a cook's dream. Yes indeed, she's a very fine ship.

---

① 250,000 Pistoles in 1718 is equal to about 7,860,000 U.S. Dollars in 2016.

As the watch hollers, "Land Ho!" all passengers on board dash to the railing. The approach to Dover, with its towering white cliffs, is a magnificent sight to behold, and until  one actually sees the tiny homes dotting the landscape, they cannot fully realize their grandeur. Upon disembarking, a dockwalloper escorts myself & Mrs Robles to the dock supervisor's office where I am given a note. Opening it, "It's from William. He's in London. There's an Inn, The Pelican, situated on Pelican Wharf, on the south side of the River Thames."

"Perhaps there will be time to see the Tower of London," states Mrs Robles.

"We'll make time," I reply. Continuing to read the letter, happily jiggling my companion's arm, "He says the Inn has a fantastic view of the *Princess*, whish can be seen from both our rooms and the Inn's upper dining balcony." Having made arrangements for our accommodations already, William also enclosed a map which I am to give the coachman when we reach the outskirts of London, pinpointing our lodgings in Wrapping; marked by an X.

Curious, Mrs Robles asks, "What about lodgings en route?"

Continuing to read, "In order to maintain a fast pace, William has reserved rooms and fresh horses for us at each of the Coaching Inns along our route."

As time passes swiftly, we still have 3 full days and nights, a 70 mile journey, via coach before we reach London; ergo, I have engaged a rider to go before us at each stop, who shall inform each Inn we are en route.

As we hurry along, the Coaching Inns, treating us with the utmost respect, are most accommodating. 'Tis always advantageous for business concerns to give their all to the nobility; the advertisement of such patronage promotes custom. But I, unlike so many of my fellow nobles, not one to take advantage, pay them well for the comforts provided me, and happily so. Best to be well thought of, methinks, by all the people. As do all of the towns and villages we stop in, the local gentry tries to hold me with promises of parties and other entertainment, but as always, I must beg off, saying to them I have urgent business in London, but when next I pass, I shall be most pleased to stop and visit for several days.

When at last the coach reaches London, Mrs Robles be nearing exhaustion; being, nigh on 70, it has been a long and tiring journey for her; ergo, in a sympathetic gesture, I have the driver, who was so informed as to The Pelican's location by my hired rider when last we changed horses, takes us directly to our lodgings, that is, after I deposit the funds within the carriage's hidden compartment at the bank. Immediately thereafter, he is to drive straight on to our lodgings where my ever faithful companion can rest for a few hours before accompanying me to the docks. Altho' I would like to go forthwith, wait for her I must, for to go alone in today's society, well… it just isn't done; a *'Lady of Quality,'* on the docks, especially when she is not going on a sea voyage, would be quite out of the ordinary.

All the while, as Mrs Robles sleeps, eager to meet with *John Robert*, and not knowing just when the *Princess* is to make sail, I am a nervous wreck.

Finally, Mrs Robles wakes, and observing my agitated state, makes haste, and throwing about her neck, a clean fichu, we venture out to locate both the *Princess*, and William.

Seeing William in the distance, I call out to him.

Hearing his name, he glances around, and seeing me, comes straight away. "My Lady," says he, amid a bow. " 'Tis good to see thee, and you also Mrs Robles."

Whilst fanning myself fretfully, "Have you delivered the letter yet?"

"No, my Lady, Mister Robert has not yet arrived."

Asking anxiously, "Have you been able to learn anything in his regard?"

"Very little, my Lady. I've been here for a solid week, waiting as you instructed on the docks, and each day I have made enquiries, but altho' many know of him, no one has seene him in quite a spell. For the past 3 days, most of the crew have beene making preparations to sail, and judging from the amount of stores being taken aboard, this har ship is making for a long sail."

" Damn ? " I curse, closing my fan abruptly. "Forgive me William. I do not understand," speaking whilst rising from my seat. " I know he sails on this here ship."

"How do you know, my Lady?"

"I just know, William. Please accept that answer." Calming back down, I resume my seat. Once again opening my fan, "Where are you stopping?"

"At the Pelican, same as you. I am, by dawn each morn, waiting over there," pointing to an old wooden chair, "just before the gangplank until long past dark each night, leaving onely when nature calls, even my meals be brought to me, and each time I return, I made inquiries."

Most appreciatively, "Thank you, William." Glancing at my well thought of attendant, "These last few days have been most draining for Mrs Robles; ergo, I shall take to her room now, and perhaps get a bit of rest myself." Rising from our seats, "Please wait here the whole of the day, and if you should hear of him, or see him arrive, please send me word at once."

"I shall, my Lady."

Showing Mrs Robles and myself to the carriage. "Come 9 o'clock, this eve, will you be my guest for supper on the Pelican's upper terrace?"

"Thank you, my Lady. It shall be my extreme pleasure to accept your kind invitation."

For several days, while we wait, much of the day is spent either on the upper terrace, or at the Pelican's quaint dockside café that sits just across the wharf from the *Princess*. On this particular day, after seeing Mrs Robles to her room, I spend my afternoon at the dockside café reading, *'Daphnis and Chloe.'*

Waking about half past four, Mrs Robles wanders onto the balcony. Observing that I am not on the upper dining terrace where I have spent much of my time since arriving, but rather below at the dockside café, she leaves her room forthwith and joins me for tea.

Upon arriving, noting my frustration, Mrs Robles motions for the waiter to deliver the earlier ordered medicinal libation.

Frustrated that no word has come, and unable to wait any longer, altho' quite out of the realm of etiquette, I, whilst my companion is distracted by the waiter, venture alone on foot to personally address the crewman on muster watch at the gangplank.

"Young man."

Altho' the crewman finding the presence of a *'Lady of Quality'* on the docks, unattended and odd, he bows. "How may I be of service, my Lady?"

"Would you be good enough to tell me the name of your 3rd Mate?" B2 pg 80

"Our Third Mate?"

"Yes. Would it not be *John Robert*?"

Mrs Robles, having turned back around to face me after speaking to the waiter, realizing that I have wandered off, looks about. Seeing me off in the distance, she makes her way hurriedly thro' the bustling activity.

Looking at the muster sheet, the young man says, "The position of 3rd Mate has not as yet been filled, my Lady, but it does indicate that someone is expected."

Reaching my side at the foot of the gangplank of the *Princess*, Mrs Robles is in a snit. "A woman of your position mustn't be out and about by her lonesome."

"But I am not alone, Mrs Robles."

Reproaching me, "You know perfectly well what I mean."

Irritated by the fact that a female aristocrat is not allowed to venture out in public without a chaperone in attendance, "Yes, Mrs Robles, I'm afraid I do." Speaking to the Crewman on Muster Duty, "Allow me to present my companion, Mrs Robles."

"Good day, madam."

Mrs Robles having nodded her head in reply, I continue. "Mister John Robert will be signing on. Having a letter of great importance for him, I need to be notified of his arrival."

"Are you family, my Lady?"

"No, I am not."

"I am permitted to relay onely fam—"

Noting I am close to being in tears, Mrs Robles interrupts. "Young man, This is la Marquise d'Eperon-noire."

Giddy in the presence of a celebrated *'Lady of Quality,'* "Forgive me, my lady, I shall be pleased to relay thy message."

"Thank you. Simply tell him that I wish to offer him a Captaincy—"

Mrs Robles, again interrupting her charge, "Surely that will be sufficient to gain an audience with the decidedly tardy Mister *Robert*."

Stunned upon hearing the offer of employment, "Aye, to be sure."

Handing him my card and a gold Doubloon, "For convenience, I have taken rooms at the Pelican Inn. Please give him my card along with my verbal message the moment he arrives, and tell him I will be available to meet with him, regardless of the hour."

Ecstatic from such generosity, "Aye, my Lady, I will."

Turning, Mrs Robles and I return to the Inn.

All day I wait anxiously, but ne'er does word come. Finally, from the sheer exhaustion brought on by worry, I fall asleep on the sofa.

Come morn, I am up decidedly early, and being certayne I will meet with *John Robert*, I dress in a copy of the Crimson velvet goune he loved only a week ago when we danced the night away in 2014, and I shall continue to wear this dress each day until he arrives and has received my letter. As we leave the room, it being rather chilly, I take with me my delicately fashioned, white cashmere fichu.

As with each previous day, hoping to hear some news during breakfast, 'tis most obvious that I am as jittery as a fly caught in a web, but still no word pertaining to John Robert comes.

Obviously frustrated as we wait to be seated, I glance at the Bill of Fare posted on the wall. Moments later, when the Maître d' returns, he escorts us to our usual table window.

Talking aloud to myself, "Where can he be?"

"Your usual, my Lady?" asks the Maître d'.

"No! Yes!" Rising, I toss a few coins on the table. "But serve it to us downstairs at the dockside café. Come on, Mrs Robles, let's dine alfresco."

"What's wrong, my Lady?"

Bordering on a snappish tone, "The sun's glare inhibits my view."

Making our way downstairs, "Ne'er have I seen you like this."

Wishing we could dine at a more fashionable establishment, Mrs Robles, whilst taking her seat murmurs, "Again, my Lady, I do not understand all this fuss. Who is this man you are so determined to find?"

"I told you. He is the man I want to Captain my ship."

"But you have no ship, my Lady, and in any case, why him?"

Pushing a tea cart, a Busser comes to lay the table.

"I intend to buy one. As for *Mister Robert*, he's a great seaman, and well respected."

"But, my Lady, having never met him; he may be an ogre and a tyrant."

Amid a soft chuckle, "He's most handsome, Mrs Robles, but more importantly, his navigation expertise and excellent personal success with regard to his handling of men makes him the perfect choice."

"And his family?"

"I hire people for their expertise, Mrs Robles, not their family."

Looking ever forward, my journey takes me to London, in search of work, where, shortly before the ship is to saile, I have secured for myself the position of 3rd Mate[1] B2 pg 80 aboard the Guiney-man, *Princess*, within the Merchant Navy under the command of Captain Abraham Plumb. Altho' my duties are the same, being but 3rd Mate, 'tis not onely a tremendous reduction in rank with regard to my most recent ship board situation, I regard this type of work to be a deplorable trade; nevertheless, these feelings notwithstanding, being it is employment that will sustain me, I sign on.

Suddenly, jumping to my feet, "Look! There he is," says I, pointing towards the ship.
Seeing several men boarding, "Where?"
"The last man trodding the gangplank."
"How can you be sure at such a distance?"
"I just know." Ne'er before have I been so flustered; my heart's pounding in my ears. Obviously enamoured whilst I tells her, "He is strong of character, and gentle of heart, Mrs Robles. Look at how majestically he carries himself; fiercely proud, yet not at all arrogant."
Seeing the onset of tears, she says, "By your description, my Lady, one would think you were deskrybing the essence of a God."
Smiling whilst muttering to myself, 'He is that, to be sure.' Suddenly, as I see the men gather about the capstan, and knowing the ship is about to depart, I stand abruptly. "No!" And lifting the front of my dress I dash across the crowded dock towards the ship.
Following me, Mrs Robles, hollers out, "My Lady!" Catching up to me about half way to the ship, she grabs my arm. "Such blatant disregard to your reputation!"
"Ridiculous!"
As men stand by for the unfurling of the ship's jibs, tears well within mine eyes. "I'll never see him again." Yanking my arm from her, I hurry my pace, and forgetting myself in my despair, I call out, "Captain *Roberts!*"
"Have you lost your mind?" screeches Mrs Robles.
Turning from her, seeing William walking towards the *Pelican Inn*, I call out to him.
Looking about and seeing me, William hurries on over.
Again calling out to my beloved, this time being sure correct myself, *"Mister Robert!"*
Mrs Robles, whilst trying to catch her breath, scolds me. "Carrying on like a wanton, is it your intention to make an exhibition of yourself?"
"I don't care!"
Happy to see him as William joins us, he gives me good news.
"There's no need to fear, my Lady. I delivered the letter just moments ago."
Why then is he aboard the ship."
Reassuring me, "Look amidship, my Lady," says he, pointing to *John Robert*. "I delivered the letter to that man there, the tall, swarthy one by the railing."
"But—"

---

[1] Navigator aka Ship's Master SBA3

"Perhaps he merely boarded to retrieve his belongings," my Lady.

Beside me stands our 2nd Mate, *John Stephenson*, who, sounding somewhat shocked, "Would you look at that!" pausing a moment, " 'Tis not often one sees a beautiful woman.

Looking down from the Open-Deck, I add, "Much less a, 'Lady of Quality,' who be beautiful, especially nigh the docks."

I do not wish to appear presumptuous, states *Stephenson*, "but I belieeve 'tis to one of us she points.

After getting the attention of the crewman standing just below me on the lower deck, I ask, "Would you be knowing that woman standing nigh the gangplank, the one dressed in red?"

Looking up at me, the crewman on the lower deck replies, "I cannae say that I do, matey, but 'tis of herself that she has beene making a spectacle of."

"Aye," replies *Stephenson*, "she has that."

Amid a modest chuckle, John Robert states, "I would venture she attracts attention wherever she goes."

"What is that you carry, matey? Looks to be of some importance."

"This?" Holding up the pouch, "It came by special courier."

"Speaking vibrantly, as tho' the letter was his, "And you have not yet opened it?"

Not having taken notice of the seal, "'Twas delivered by courier onely minutes ago, but being that no one except my family knows I am in London, and judging by what's written on the back, leaves little doubt, and neither farming, ranching, nor the clergy is for me."

"Must be mighty important to be sent by courier."

"Onely to themselves. As for myselfe, my life is the sea."

Walking up to the midshipman at the foot of the gangplank holding the manifest. "Young man, her ladyship, la Marquise d'Éperon-noire, wishes to have a word with you."

Bowing as is proper, "How may I be of service, my Lady."

"Where is the young man who was here yesterday afternoon?"

"Young Charles took ill last night, my Lady. I am taking his shift."

"Damn! Then he did not get my message."

"Who, my Lady?"

"*John Robert*. This ship's 3rd Mate."

"Not if your message was given yesterday."

"Can you take a message to him?"

"I cannae leave my post."

An officer, seeing the mild disturbance, intervenes. "Canne I be of service, my Lady?"

"How can I get aboard?"

Dubious of why a gentle woman would make such a request, "No one except those on this here muster sheet may board."

"Then how do I get that man there," pointing, "the one looking down at us, to disembark?"

"He can not."

Knowing that the gentleman who attracts me looked right at us when I pointed at him, Mrs Robles slaps my hand, "You know it's not polite to point."

Rather irritated by propriety's constraints, I spout, "Who made that preposterous rule?"

Scanning the muster sheet, "I'm sorry, my Lady, but if he's aboard, it's because he signed on." And showing me the muster sheet, "He signed on not more than 20 minutes ago."

"But I have a matter of great importance to discuss with him."

Looking up at my beloved, I can see him holding in his hand the leather pouch, and seeing my seal unbroken, I know he has not read the letter inside. Beginning to wield my considerable power, I speak in a commanding tone. "Do you know who I am?"

"Aye, my Lady," replies the officer.

"Good! I am ordering you to stop that ship from leaving."

"Me?" he asks, astonished by my demands. Knowing what might happen to him if he fails to obey a direct order from a high-ranking Aristocrat, he replies, "I'll have to send for the Dock Master."

Spouting demandingly, "Then do it!"

"Aye, my Lady." Speaking to the crewman on muster duty, "Run and fetch the Dock Master!"

Nervously replying, "Aye, sir," the crewman dashes off.

Again, Mrs Robles reproaches me. "Has your Ladyship taken leave of her senses?"

Although the lady is quite upset, I cannae hear what is being said; nevertheless, I am sure, being she is in the company of the man who delivered the leatther pouch, and should this letter be from her, such would explain her rash behaviour. If it were possible, I would disembark and have the courier, whom she obviously knows, present me to her, but alas I have not the time, for the *Princess*, currently hoisting her anchor, is getting under way.

"All hands, to yer stations," comes a voice from the 2nd Mate.

Whilst looking up at him I can see him pondering the idea of opening the leather pouch. Hearing another man call to him, and seeing the anchor is being hoisted, I know there be duties requiring his immediate attention.

Ignoring the first call to duty, I begin to open the pouch, and whilst doing so, I canne see the woman grow happy.

"Look Mrs Robles!" says I, hopping with delight, "He's opening it!"

Once more *John Stephenson* calls out, lowdly and with conviction this time. *"Mister Robert, to yer station."*

Whilst looking right at her, I have no choice but to return the delicate flax linnen writing paper to the pouch, replying, "Aye, aye, sir."

Kissing the pouch, I salute the Lady In Red, and securing the leatther pouch beneath my waistband, I hurry to my station. In the doing, being on familiar terms with procedure, I knows that honest saile canne not be spread until the ship has beene towed out of the harbour, thus, 'twill be the better part of an hour before anny time canne be call'd mine owne, onely then will I have the opportunity to read the letter.

With all that I could hope for being but a few feet away, yet unbearably out of my reach, tears begin to stream down my cheek. Suddenly, as the gangplank is being removed, and seeing the smile upon *John Robert's* face as he is called away from the railing, it is too much to bear. Unknowingly beset with hysteria, I knock the midshipman who blocks my path into the water below as I hastily scurry over the ropes.

"My Lady!" hollers Mrs Robles. Grabbing my arm, "What be ya doing?"

In my state of anxiety, trying to break her hold, I inadvertently knock her to the ground.

"Have you gone mad?" she cries out.

As William helps her to her feet, Mrs Robles hollers, "Stop her!"

Free of the ropes, I begin to run towards the ship. Glancing back over my shoulder, and seeing William, quick and agile as a cat, leap over the ropes, he catches me about the waist just as I reach the ship.

Kicking and screaming like a wildcat, I am, but his hold is too strong. Seeing 2 long boats with tow lines, and several men along the railing equipped with long staffs pushing against the seabed, and 2 jibs unfurl, the ship is underway, and as I see other sails begin to unfurl, realizing my efforts are futile, I begin to sob uncontrollably before swooning in William's arms.

Picking me up, William carries me back to the dockside café where I sit silently, head bowed for several minutes; after which, looking up, I just sit and stare into nothingness as the *Princess* leaves port.

In her effort to console me, "Do not lose heart, my Lady, you will see him again; ergo, I must insist we have a nutritious, full-bodied meal at a fashionable restaurant."

"William," begins Mrs Robles, "Please be kind enough to have the front desk ready her Ladyship's carriage."

"Certainly." Rising to his feet, William enters the Inn.

A couple minutes later when he returns, Mrs Robles, rising from the table, states, "I am afraid you'll have to assist her ladyship, William," and supporting me as I half heartedly walk, the 3 of us step into the carriage.

In the wake of the *Princess*' departure, our companion ship, the *Bird*, commanded by Captain William Snelgrave, setts saile in consort.

Time passes quickly, and as I sitt upon my bunk located within the officers quarters, I take from my waistband, the leatther pouch.

BLOOD and SWASH, The Unvarnished Life (& afterlife) Story of Pirate Captain, Bartholomew Roberts......pt.2 "THE WILLING CAPTIVE"

Looking at the coat-of-arms. Not recognizing the seal, I open the pouch carefully, and taking out the neatly folded sheet of fine linnen with great curiosity, I begin reading.

> My Dear Mister John Robert, 17 September 1718
> of Nghastell Newydd Bach, Pembrokeshire, Wales
>
> I am writing thee in regards to a Captaincy. At present I am bound for France, but come November, I will be in London Towne, where I hope to learn thou hast accepted the position offered herein.
>
> If I may, having heard of thine outstanding seamanship throughout Queen Anne's Warr, & on board the Terrible, wish thee to chose a a ship worthy of thy seamanship, and as such, knowing all will be well within thy capable hands, I afford thee a Carte Blanche.
>
> I confess a fondness for square riggers; Brigs & Fregates, but please, sir, understand that her design is to be that which thee prefers. Please see to the hiring of her crew, & her outfitting; personally picking her sea artists, offering whatever thou deemes fitting. For thyself, 70% of the profits. As for the ship's destiny, that, sir, is to bee of thy choosing, for from this moment, thee has absolute autonomy.
>
> For myself, I have but one desire, to be aboard her, but, mince no words here, I shall be but a subordinate passenger, or, should thee find me worthy of thine esteem, a most privileged crewman, whose identity, should thee so desire, be kept secret.
>
> Should you be in acceptance, take this letter to anny Bank of England, & honoured it shall be.
>
> I look forward to meeting thee in November.
>
> Aspasia Jourdain
> la Marquise d'Emperor noire

Jumping to my feet, I shout, "My owne command!" The woman on the dock, I begin thinking to myself, she must be this here Marquise. That must be why she was making such a fuss. "Damn! And this here merchant, she wont return for months."

Feeling dismayed, knowing that if I had opened the letter when the courier placed it in my hand only moments before I signed on this voyage, that which I have dreamt for the whole of my life would 'ave beene mine, and now the command shall be afforded someone else. As I begin to fold the letter, I instead, read it again. Suddenly replete with happiness, "She wants *me* for her captain, and judging from her phrasing, and her actions on the docks, she will have no other. Oh, what a woman she is, so full of zeal." Concerning her presence on board, methinks her ladyship loves both the sea and adventuring, and one cannae argue that her charming company would make way for pleasant diversions, and with this in mind, my neede for work, forcing me again into a repulsive occupation, shall be less intolerable now.

Drawing up in front of, *The George Inn*, situated on Borough High Street, London, one of the 2 Footmen who rides at the rear of the carriage jumps down from his perch to open the door and lower the steps.

First to depart the carriage is William, who, after helping Mrs Robles and myself out, escorts us to the upper dining room.

All thro' the meal, as my solemn air eats away at my heart, hardly a word is spoken. I am sure *John Robert* has read my letter by this time, and the tear which falls upon my cheek is not merely for myself, but for him as well, for I know that the initial loss of the position I offered must've been a tremendous disappointment, and even tho' I am sure he will discern that the exuberance displayed by both my actions, and my letter, will convey to him the knowledge that 'twill still be his upon his return, and yet, I know that it shall not come to pass, for come February he will be pressed into service upon the pirate Sloop, *Rover*,[①, B8 & 9] and some 6 weeks thereafter, it's Captain.

"My Lady, you must calm yourself; in a few months, when the ship returns, he will come to you."

"No, Mrs Robles, he won't."

"Thou art beside yourself, my Lady," states William.

"He won't be coming back, William, not ever."

Looking at me in a sad sort of wonder, neither of my companions have any effectual words to offer.

After brief moment of solemn stillness, a fresh idea springs to mind. "Have you any family, William?"

"My mother, and two brothers are all that remain of my family, my Lady."

Pleased to learn he has no wife or children to care for, I start to lay the groundwork for my new plan. "Would it interest you to work in my employ, full time? The pay will be better, and being full of adventure, the work may be more to your liking."

"Just what, my Lady, is going on in that conniving mind of yours?"

"Conniving, Mrs Robles, Me?" Lowering my head slightly whilst lifting and opening my fan in the pretence of cooling myself, "Surely you jest."

---

①Author's Note: Shortly before sailing into Anamaboa Bay, after a fierce battle lasting 20 hours, Hywel Davies captured a 30 gun Dutch Galley which he renamed The Rover.[sic] Haverfordwest Castle PRO in 2004, B12

"Nay, my Lady, I do not, and you know very well I do not."

Having thought it over, "Sounds intriguing, my Lady," says William, "I accept."

"Splendid!" says I, smiling, "And it's your opportunity, Mrs Robles, to enjoy an extended holiday in Pembrockshire. As for myself, I have much to do here in Britannia."

"But, my Lady, who shall tend to your needes."

"I'll tend myself."

Fearful for my safety and reputation, "But without a chaperone—"

Interrupting her, "It will be my privilege to guard my Ladies virtue," proclaims William.

Sparkling, "See," says I whilst flashing a wispy smile.

"Be mindful of what I am about to tell you, William. la Marquise, altho' quite intelligent, is tenacious, and this plan that races through her mind, is no doubt in connection with that sayler, and will lead to trouble."

"Well, of course it is," I reply amid a smile. "But no ill will come of it."

Frowning, "You heard 'er, William, and wilful want makes woeful waste."

"Fret not, Mrs Robles, I shall keep her ladyship's wilful demeanour in check."

"Does that please you, Mrs Robles?"

"I suppose it will have to, my Lady."

Speaking to Mrs Robles, "To ease your fears, I shall see to it la Marquise writes you each fortnight."

"Thank you, William."

"I shall afford you a Letter of Credit. When my plans are complete, William and I will come collect you."

Taking on a serious attitude whilst turning to William, "Once Mrs Robles is safely en route to Milford, we shall discuss my plan."

Having finished our meal, being filled once again with enthusiasm, I say, "Shall we go?"

Rising, the three of us make our way downstairs and onto the front walk. Upon returning to our lodgings at the Pelican Inn, William escorts us inside.

"If I am to leave on the morrow, I must pack."

"Goodnight, Mrs Robles."

"Goodnight, my Lady."

"Henceforth, William, your room will always adjoin mine; as my steward, such is perfectly respectable. Once we leave London, wishing not to appear as a high tone, *'Lady of Quality,'* methinks simpler apparel will best suit my cause over the next few months; ergo, I shall ship the majority of my apparel and trappings on to d'Éperon-noire house. Please see to it."

"I shall, my Lady."

Reading over the shipping news posted on the wall of the Inn, I give my first orders to William as my steward as he follows me upstairs. "The *Mary and Martha* departs for the Americas on the morrow. Please go to the harbour and book passage for Mrs Robles." In my sitting room, I jot a note for him to deliver, "Speak to the Captain personally." Affixing my ribbon and seal, I fold the parchment and hand it to him. Starting back downstairs, "If'n his route does not take him to Milford Harbour, this note will inform him that he needs to divert there long enough to drop off Mrs Robles before sailing on to *Bermudas* where, among the cargo, they are to deliver a message to my household together with my trunks. Should he balk, agree to whatever amount he requires to fulfil my needs. When you get back, arrange for the trunks to be taken to the Merchant at dawn. I shall visit the shipbuilder in the morning with Mrs Robles, after which my carriage will take you and her to the ship before she sails. Please be sure she is settled on board before returning here to me."

"I'll take care of everything, my Lady."

Seeing the Innkeeper scurry over to greet me, "Nice to see you Mister Rivers."

"And you, my Lady. Mrs Robles tells me you're leaving us to-morrow. "It will be sad to see you leave, for your presence here has brightened our staff considerably."

Replying with a smile, "Thank you, but only Mrs Robles will be leaving. Once gone, William, my steward," indicating in William's direction, "will occupy her room. Please treat him with the respect that is his due."

Speaking with a nod, "Your servant."

"My Steward requires a clothier. When he inquires, will you be good enough to direct him? For myself, I shall be pleas'd if you will send for London's most prestigious couture."

"My Pleasure, my Lady." Raising his arm, and snapping his fingers, the he shouts, "Page!"

Seeing his employer, the pageboy dashes on over. Stopping before us, he bows. "Good afternoon, my Lady. Turning to Mister Rivers, "Yes, sir?"

"I want you to run to the fashion house on High Street. Tell the proprietor that a Lady of Fashion who is stopping with us desires his services."

"Yes, sir." Bowing, the page dashes off.

When a different page hands a note to William, he, in turn, hands it to me.

"Thank you, William." Whispering, "Give the young man a shilling." Reading the note, not aware they had not yet been invented, I open the reticule I fashioned during the crossing from Bermuda, and taking out 10 gold Sovereigns, I hand them, and the note to the innkeeper.

"Thank you, my Lady."

Speaking to William, "Before visiting the clothiers, I need you go to the docks. Afterwards, see about a wardrobe consistent with you new title, Mister Rivers will direct you." Again opening my reticule, I take a small quantity of coinage and one of my cards and hand the lot to William. "Give the Shoppe Keeper my card and tell him to send the bill to me here."

Placing the items in his pouch, "I shall, my Lady, and thank you." Bowing, he departs.

Finding myself in an inspired mood, I retire to the writing desk located within my rooms. Taking from my lap desk a piece of fine parchment, I make a list of what needs doing whilst awaiting London's finest couture to arrive. As I start to write, a knock comes upon my door. Rising, I place the list beneath the blotter.

Upon opening the door, a well-made young woman in her twenties toting a book containing fashion plates, and wearing a measuring tape about her neck, enters. Accompanying her is a much older, well dress gent carrying a receipt book. Lastly, a Negro slave carrying a large bundle of Fabric swatches and trims enters.

"Thank you for coming so quickly."

The gent nods graciously, "I be most honoured, my Lady. I am Richard Meyers from the small, yet notable shoppe on High Street, and this young lass is Lizabeth."

"And," demonstrating my lack of bigotry, "the name of your manservant?"

"Nathaniel, my Lady."

Taking the measuring tape from about her neck, "May I take your measurements?"

"Yes, of course."

Whilst Lizabeth takes my measurements, Mister Meyers opens the first book of pattern templates.

"Before you begin, Mister Meyers, let me inform you that what I require is a wardrobe befitting that of the upper Gentry class."

Flummoxed, Mister Meyers asks, "Why would a high-ranking noble wish to don cloathes so beneath her station?"

"As part of my charity efforts, I am going to appear in a number of divertissements."

"Sounds exciting, my Lady," states Lizabeth.

Speaking to Nathaniel, I ask, "Do you not agree?"

Rather timorous, the manservant replies, "Yes, my Lady."

"I also need a rich looking coat, vest, and britches, but as I intend to embellish the coat myself, I do not want the lining stitched down at the cuffs or hem." Handing him a list, "Here's a list of the details and materials; the embellishments I'll take with me, and lastly, I also want 4 holes drilled in each of these 50, gold doubloons. They are to be the buttons."

"As you wish, my Lady."

"I also need 5 gross pairs of men's cotton socks, 1 dozen silk; 2 dozen of your finest curled ostrich plumes in wine red, black, each with good stems for quality writing instruments, and 5 gross, average quality in assorted colours. Lastly 5 gross men's shifts and breeches, assorted."

"Most assuredly, my Lady."

After spending about half an hour thumbing thro' the book of fashion plates, I pick 3 styles, and the materials in which they are to be fashioned. "Nothing too fancy, you understand, but nevertheless aesthetically pleasing, and well made."

The first pattern is a riding habit of which I choose to have 2 made. "I want one fashioned from a moderately weighted flax linen in crimson, with black trim suitable for day wear. The second, which shall be worn in the late evening, is to be fashioned from black cashmere. I want it to have an extra long, silvery gray fox muffler that can be worn as a coverlet about my head and neck." Pointing at the picture, "I also want 3 fancy shifts fashioned out of Mulberry silk, with these sleeves: One from black twill, another damask in crimson, and the last is to be made out of 2 layers, cross-grained, of white chiffon atop red satin. Next, 2 reversible vests and matching full skirts attached that open in front, 1 black and white, the other red and black, both with complimentary trim. While waiting for these to be made ready, I shall require a couple long shifts; just send me any 2 you currently have on hand." On the next plate, "I would like this dress in Crimson silk taffeta. It's to be open in the front in a V-shape from the waist down," indicating on the picture with my finger, "Lower the neckline to here. Next, I want a moderately full, ruffled petticoat fashioned from matching fabric, only black. Excepting the riding habits, he hems on all are to be 1 inch from the floor. Lastly, my steward, William, is in need of a couple items as well: 2 new outfits suitable for riding, 2 cashmere jumpers, and a woolen overcoat. I shall send him to your shoppe in the morning to have his measurements taken." Lastly, handing him my red velvet gown, "I want this copied."

"Very good, my Lady. I'll have my entire staff get to work on your order forthwith."

Having taken my measurements, Lizabeth, whilst packing up her supplies, "I shall send over the 2 shifts you requested late this evening. In 2 days time I will have one suitable riding habit ready, my Lady. Your personal garments will be ready by the weeks' end."

"The rest of your order," says Mister Meyers, "excepting those for William, which will also be ready within the week, will take nigh on six weeks to complete. To-morrow evening, I shall have an array of materials and trims brought over to you for your approval, as requested."

"Thank you Mister Meyers, Lizabeth, and you also Nathaniel."

After they leave, it being time for supper, and I promised Mrs Robles that I would take her to the finest dining establishment in London her last night in town, I hurry myself into my silver trimmed, purple and green gown, the only other evening dress of quality I am keeping with me. William is also to accompany us. Seeing the Innkeeper as I pass thro' the lobby, I and call him over, "I have worked out my agenda and altho' my steward and I will be away, sometimes for weeks at a times, I would like to reserve our rooms for 8 weeks more, that is, if you can accommodate us."

"Your presence will be our extreame pleasure, my Lady."

"Thank you." And handing him 8 weeks rent, "I must dash now, I have a carriage waiting."

Stepping out onto the verandah, the footman opens the carriage door, "Where to, my Lady?"

"First to the Tower of London, after which, The George Inn."

Whilst helping myself and Mrs Robles into the carriage, taking the coin from my hand at the same time, "Very good, my Lady." Closing the door after William steps into the carriage, I hear the footman repeat our evening's agenda to the coachman.

"Right O," says the gruff sounding coachman, and off prance the high stepping horses.

Arriving at our 1st destination, and later, all thro' dinner, I repeatedly found myself daydreaming of the exciting adventure William and I will have collecting all of the goods I intend to present to Captain *Roberts* and his crew to show to him my good faith, my main concern is how I shall go about persuading him to take me as his woman. Keeping to his codex: *'All female prisoners are to be protected by sentinel, one who will protect her from the others,'* and even tho' I am knowing that whoever he is who holds this honour reaps as his reward, the Lady's favors, should she chose to offer any as payment for his protection, I am not worried in the least, for I am sure that when, *'the Great Pirate Roberts,'* learns that I am the woman who offered him the Captaincy, he will assign the task to himself.

Come morning, Mrs Robles and I make our way to the shipbuilders.

Strolling into the office, I see a portly man sitting at his desk. He is so engaged with the paperwork that clutters his desk, he does not even notice us. Seeing the heavily built silver bell on the counter, Mrs Robles taps it several times before getting his attention.

Looking up and seeing us, he arises. "Good Morning, Ladies. I am Mister Johnson."

Introducing me, as is part of her duties, my Lady's Companion says, "I am the Mrs Neville Robles, and this," gesturing towards me, "is la Marquise d'Éperon-noire."

"Good Morning, Ladies. How may I be of service to you?"

"I wish to commission your company to build me a ship."

Opening the side panel that separates the inner from the outer offices. "Come in, ladies. May I offer you any refreshments?"

Both of us reply, "No thank you."

Gesturing with his right hand, Mister Johnson says, "Please be seated."

As Mister Johnson moves behind his desk, I take a seat in the chair opposite side while Mrs Robles sits down in the big comfy chair against the wall.

"Being of mine owne design, you are to retain the services of John Jenner."

"Britannia's finest Naval Architect? But he resides in Portsmouth."

"Yes I know. Offer him anything he wants, but get him here."

"By your command, my Lady, I shall write to him forthwith."

"May I use your pencil and a sheet of parchment?"

Placing both before me, "Of course, my Lady."

Quickly sketching the hull design, "The ship must be both functional and luxurious. Her length is to be 198 feet from bow to stern with a 40 foot beam, a 22 foot draught, and outfitted to carry 56 gun ports sized for 36 pound shot on the 2 gun decks, all hidden from view, plus 32 gun ports sized for 8, long nines on her bow and stern, and 10, 24 pounders on both sides of the open deck. She is to have 3 masts. Her mainmast is to be 200 feet, her foremast 180, and her Mizzen 155 feet. Her rigging is to be similar to that of a Full-rigged ship, adding fitments to support square, fore & aft rigging, spanker, and gaff capability on her mizzen. Her sails, Crimson in colour, 10 full sets, are to be fashioned out of the finest canvas, and I want her rigged for a Spinnaker sail fashioned out of your best silk."

"A Spinnaker, my Lady?"

Whilst sketching it for him, "A Spinnaker is a special new type of sail that is designed specifically for sailing off the wind from a reaching course to a downwind, with the wind 90°–180° off the bow, resembling a very large hemispherical shaped kite that balloons out in front of the ship when deployed. The head of this kite type sail is connected to the top of the foremast, and the tack corner is attached to a specially designed retracting bowsprit. The clew corner is connected to a sheet; this last, is used to control the shape and position of the sail. Are you with me on this?"

"Uh, yes. It sounds similar to a gybe."

"Yes, I suppose you can look at it as a gigantic gybe sail, but larger than the mainsail. Now for her Masts. They are to be raked 10° aft; in addition, she is to have a very thin prow, some 22 feet, before gently widening to her 40 foot breadth. She will need a deep draught to accommodate her hull, which is to be nigh on V shaped from the waterline to keel, but not so much that she cannot be maneuvered with the same ease as a Sloop. Completely encompassing the cistern, is to be a hold similar in fashion that a Smuggler might have, or wish they had, and it needs to measure 4 feet wide and 7 feet tall inside, and it will have but two entrances, a trap door located on the Quarter-Deck, and the other in the great cabin."

Shaking his head, "I don't follow you, my Lady."

Drawing a top view of my proposed layout, using a dotted line, "The only open deck access shall be here," indicating the Quarter-Deck, just before the great cabin, which also sits atop the Quarter-Deck. It must be designed in such a fashion that heavy cargo seemingly rests upon it, yet in reality, such can be moved with ease by one who knows how. You see, I wish to be able to transport rare cargo. As I'm sure you know, I own a silk and mulberry wine plantation, and just in case my ship is attacked by pyrates, I want her cargo unfound."

" 'Tis brilliant, my Lady."

There will be 4 decks in all. Divided in to 2 sections, the Great Cabin is to be behind the Quarter-Deck, 1 small, 1 large, the latter is the Bed Chamber. Below the Weather Deck is the Gun Deck and the Crew's Quarters. Directly below the Great Cabin, in the overhead, lies a concealed hatch with a dropdown, folding staircase. On Deck 2, surrounding the galley and Crew's Quarters/Dining Area is a 2nd Gun Deck. The Stores and Officers Quarters/Dining Area is on Deck 3, as is a 3rd Gun Deck. In the Lower Hold, there's to be a Massive Cistern that runs the length and breadth of the ship that feeds 2 specially designed rooms equipped with both a bathing tub and an enclosed area for the men to relieve themselves. A similar room will be adjacent to the Great Cabin. The waste is to flow out the rear of the ship through a special tube made from brass connected to a specially designed waste tank." Marking them with an X, "They're astern here." Setting down the pencil, I says, "I think this about covers it."

As my prescribed terms are looked over, "This is a tall order, my Lady. A commission such as this will require 12 months."

"6," I counter.

Shaking his head, "So little time for such an enormous undertaking."

"I care not how many men you need to hire, Mister Johnson. Just get it done."

"Your servant, my Lady."

"Having glanced at my specifications, can you give me a guesstimate?"

Jotting down some rough figures, he says, "Doubling the workforce, the luxurious appointments and other specifics, roughly £16,500 sterling."

"I shall make arrangements at the Bank of London to allocate funds as needed to cover costs. Your commission, and Mister Jenner's fee will be placed in a special account, payable the day of the christening. Send me word as soon as you hear from Mister Jenner."

"Very good, my Lad, I'll do what needs doing. Mister Jenner will receive the commission papers within 2 days time, and pending prior obligations, he could be here by week's end."

Satisfied that I've done all I can here this day, I jot down The Pelican Inn, 57 Wrapping Wall, London. Arising from my chair, "I'll be in and out, but here's where I'm stopping." Handing him the address where I am stopping, Mrs Robles and I depart.

Chapter Three
Plan B

Location: 'Britannia'

It hath bin 3 dayes since the departure of Mrs Robles, and even tho' I hate to dwell on it, the ending of the warr left thousands of men without jobs, and tho' I cannae employ all of them, I canne pay those I do hire sufficient means to sustain them for sev'ral yeeres to come.

This morning, William and I have purchased for ourselves 2 fine mounts, and at dawn, to-morrow, wee ride forth to our destination; a cannon maker. William hast learnt of a man who lives some 10 miles South who hast bin unemployed since the warr with

BLOOD and SWASH, The Unvarnished Life (& afterlife) Story of Pirate Captain, Bartholomew Roberts......pt.2 "THE WILLING CAPTIVE"

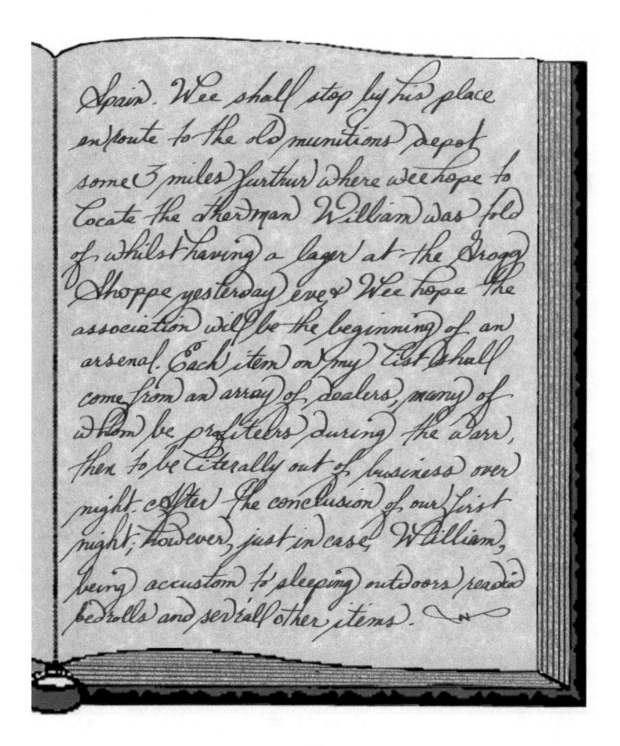

Spain. Wee shall stop by his place enroute to the old munitions depot some 3 miles furthur where wee hope to locate the other man William was told of whilst having a lager at the Grogg Shoppe yesterday eve. Wee hope the association will be the beginning of an arsenal. Each item on my list shall come from an array of dealers, many of whom be profiteers during the warr, then to be literally out of business over night. After the conclusion of our first night, however, just in case, William, being accustom to sleeping outdoors readied bedrolls and several other items.

Time, of late, has flown by. Mrs Robles is enjoying Pembrokeshire, and already the crews who will build my ship are being hired; my adventure upon both land and at sea, which will be soon be upon my own ship, is about to begin.

'Tis early when William quietly knocks upon my door. "'Tis time, my Lady. I'm off to ready the horses."

"Thank you, William. I shall be ready within the quarter hour." Getting out of bed, I swing the coffeepot over the hot coals which are kept burning throughout the night by the chambermaid assigned to our rooms. As I dress, I also make ready a loaf of bread, and several rations of fruit and oven-dried meats that I place into my haversack. Being I wish for my true identity to be kept secret, I have decided to wear my specially fashioned stays so I can carry with me, sufficient gold coins and banknotes to secure the dealings whilst on this first of many ventures in the procurement of the items on my list, many of which I expect shall be made special to order, and occasionally, when possible, purchase used. In either case, the majority shall be in a clandestine fashion, and once purchased or made ready, they are to be taken to a place where the goods can be loaded into my ship's smugglers' hold.

As I fling my cloak over my shoulders, William again knocks quietly upon my door whilst uttering, "my Lady."

Opening the door, "Good morrow, William. Do come in. I have prepared for us coffee, and," holding up a poke, "our breakfast, which, as you suggested, we can eat en route."

"Excellent, my Lady," says he with a smile whilst taking from my hands the hot cup. Taking a sip of his coffee, "Being this journey is a surreptitious operation, I mean, lest those with whom we conduct your business will learn of your true identity, ought we not travel incognito."

"Very good, William. I hadn't thought of that. Humm, let me think." Smiling, "I know, I'll call you Billy and you will call me Aspasia." Pausing a moment I add, "As I'm sure you know, Billy, this undertaking is a hanging offence for any of us who get caught; nevertheless, it must be done; ergo, before we start, I want to give you one last opportunity to decline."

"I admire your goal in wanting to help those who have been displaced since the war, my lady, I mean Aspasia, and I am with you to your mission's conclusion."

Drinking our coffee, I asks, "In which way do we ride, William?"

"East by South, towards Dover. The majority of our journey shall be conducted within a few miles of the coast."

Setting down the empty cup, William grabs the poke contayning our meal, and leaving by way of the side door, we quietly make our way to where our mounts are ty'd and waiting.

"Thank you, Billy," says I, as my dutiful aide helps me aboard my robust mount, a Darley Arabian mare.

Standing beside his grey thoroughbred, Pan, William secures the poke to his saddle, and untying the reins from the fence, he mounts. "Let's away, Miss Aspasia," and at the gallop, we leave town.

Not wishing to be seen by them who may be up in the wee hours of the morning, we keep at our pace until well clear of the last house. William rides at the trot quite a ways before deciding it is time to walk the horses. At first, I was wishing I was astride and able to post the trot, but fortunately, my mount took to a wonderful ambling gait, and such, the ride was quite comfortable. As we ride east, the sunrise is glorious and the air peaceful.

Some little time has passed when William, pointing to a fallen tree, "Yon log will be a good place to rest our mounts whilst we eat our morning meal." Spurring on his mount, he reaches the log within a few strides.

Dismounting, he unties the water bota and poke from his saddle, and carrying them, "Altho' I do not understand your desire to win the heart of this *John Robert*, any man to have the love of one such as you, one who risks all for him, is indeed most fortunate." Handing me both the poke and bota, after helping me to dismount, William tyes a soft cotton rope to the front legs of the horses, creating with ease, two pairs of hobbles whilst I, spreading a bed sheet atop the log, prepare a suitable place to lay our meal.

Taking a seat, William continues speaking. "An unhappy prospect to be sure I, also understand fully what is at risk should either of us be caught."

"I do not wish to sound ungrateful, Billy, but I need to ask a question."

Seeing that my words be sticking within my throat, William, being an understanding bloke, places my mind at ease. "Feel free, Miss Aspasia."

Smiling at him, altho' still apprehensive, "Considering we'll be hung if caught, whyfor are you risking your life to help me?"

His face takes on a look of quiet surprise, and as he takes a drink from the bota, I can see that he is considering his reply. "This man who so attracts you, he does not know you does he, nor was he a pyrate when I met him."

Lowering my head as mine eyes close slowly, reopening amid a slight sigh as I look up at him briefly, it becomes apparent to him that he spoke true.

"There's much going on here, Miss Aspasia, much more than you have chosen to reveal to anyone, not even to Mrs Robles. This quest of yours is a good deal more than just chacing a would be lover, no woman would risk so much for that alone." Noting that I am too upset to even manage a swallow, he, whilst taking a bite of banana bread, cleverly gives me a moment before continuing with his reasons.

"Altho' my life as a courier was humdrum, and the pay provided only a marginal living, it did bring me notoriety, and you. You, my Lady, are the reward for all my efforts."

"How do you mean, William?"

"I hastened to your offer, not merely for adventure or monetary reward, but because of the passion of yer quest regarding the man to whom I delivered your letter. The contraband you wish to acquire, 'tis for him, is it not?" Taking another bite of the bread, "It must be, why else would we be gathering cannon and munitions thus, when Nobility has the right to outfit their ships anny way they choose. Am I wrong?"

Looking at him, seeing the sincerity in his face, I know I'm at liberty to answer his question truthfully. "No, Billy, you are not wrong. *John Robert*, altho' not yet a pyrate, will become one, and not only a pyrate, but the most successful in recorded history."

My words cause him to stop chewing, and as he looks at me with bewildering curiosity, "But how could you know this, my Lady? Are you a witch?"

His words support quite a question, one that requires answering; ergo, in order to continue in my effort, which I cannot do alone, I must take William into my complete confidence, otherwise I have no right to expect him to continue helping me, and in the doing, knowing our adventure will be full of great excitement, Lucifer will enjoy it immensely.

"No, Billy, I am not a witch, I'm from the future, the 21st century to be precise."

His eyes grow large, and his face, unlike what one might think, is not speculative, but intrigued.

"Captain *Roberts* came to my home in Wales as a ghost about 16 months ago."

Being that he is taking a drink of water whilst I am speaking to him, he begins to cough, spatting it back out.

Patting him on the back, "Are you okay, Billy?"

"Fine, my Lady," says he whilst trying to gain control of himself. "Continue, please."

"Well, 'twas nigh on a year later when Lucifer…"

"You mean the Devil," asks he with a look of nigh dread upon his face?

"Yes, Billy. Lucifer beset us in a deadly game, and in the winning, Captain *Roberts*, who had been given a new lease on life, and myself, were given immortality, but the price, so it seems, are further games, which, like this one, are both deadly and sporting in nature."

Whilst taking from the bota another drink, wishing it were spirits to ease his restless thoughts, "Are you saying this is but a game?"

"In the eyes of Lucifer it is; however, for us, and all those involved, it's as real as it gets. Both of us, and all those who help us are at risk, and can be hung. I believe this aspect excites Lucifer, but on the other hand, should we succeed, the lives of those who help us will improve greatly; and that is also their reality."

"And this pyrate of yours, how do you know he will take kindly to yer actions?"

"I don't, but like Robin Hood, Captain *Roberts* is a vigilante, as well as a freer of slaves, who, aside from paying his crew, and outfitting his ships, he will use piracy to finance his good deeds; ergo, his upstanding morals and beliefs that govern his being will appreciate my efforts."

"To hear you preach his good will, I canne onely say that it will be my esteem honour," picking up my hand, "to help you in yer endeavour, my Lady," and bending his head, he gently lifts my hand to his lips and kisses it.

Lowering my hand, William says, "I have, but one more question, my Lady."

Speaking with a confident smile, whilst taking a bite of bread, "Ask your question."

"Being that history already boasts of his remarkable career, what be the reason for our undertaking?"

"I take your point, Billy." Lifting the bota, I take a drink of water, and holding it in my lap whilst replacing the lid, "Lucifer has made the terms of the game simple. I must be able to win, not only *John Robert's* affections, but his true heart. Only after I have achieved this, will the game end, but in order to accomplish this feat, I must not only get to him, but concurrently be seen in a favourable light, by all accounts. My thought is, that if I am to convince him of my loyalty, I must bring the fairest of gifts, and not just clothes, food, medicines and the like, but items that will show to him that I have risked my very existence to obtain and deliver them to him, these, however, are the simple aspects. You see, Billy, Captain *Roberts* is not easily wooed. His first love, to whom he was betrothed; a young woman he believed to be untarnished, suddenly, in his eyes, appeared to be your archetypical wanton."

"How so?"

"Well, although the circumstance was quite innocent, it appeared coquettish to the young *John Robert* when he made an unannounced call on her father to discuss a business matter. 'Twas through the parlour window, which was situated along the path to their front door, that he saw what he took to be his intended spooning with a common sailor." Fidgeting with my kerchief, I continue sadly, saying with considerable doubt, "And for that reason, and my greatest task, I'm afraid, will be in convincing him that I am for he alone, and such, a woman worthy of his love and affection to whom he can entrust his heart. Only in this way can I win his true heart and subsequently end the game."

"There's more to it isn't there, my Lady."

"Yes, Billy, there is. I have learned that what he thought he saw is not how it happened; the young lady's bracelet got caught within the lace doily on the back of the settee, and the sailor, who was the son of her supposed father's guest, was simply trying to free it for her."

"How do you know this to be true?"

"Because I am she, and because of me, the man I have been in love with since I was a girl, in both centuries, suffers not only from a mortal wound to the heart, but of the soul, for if not for me, his greatness would've been alongside *Alexander, Caesar, Nelson*, and the like."

Standing, "Then I should say we have little time to waste."

Pulling the drawstrings to close the poke, I hold out my hand.

Drawing me upward, William asks, "And what of history, his brilliant career, will you change that?"

"No, Billy," I tells him whilst walking to my horse. "I shall do my very best not to interfere with that which brought him greatness."

As he helps me to mount, "But is that not what you attempted with yer letter, my Lady?"

Mounting his own steed, I reply, "Well taken, Billy. That I did, but himself having told me when we were betrothed in my time, I know that a Captaincy is what he dreamt of; therefore, what better way could there have been of introducing myself. He shan't forget the woman who offered him a Carte Blanche Captaincy aboard a ship of his own choosing."

As we ride off, "And altho' I know that I could get to the Isle of Princes before he, I no longer wish to stop him from becoming a pyrate; there is, however, one aspect I shall make every effort to change."

"And what might that be, my Lady, besides yerself re-entering his life."

"To prevent his untimely death."

"Indeed, and how will you accomplish that feat?"

"I don't know yet."

"And if you can not, I mean that with such a worrisome probability, how can you allow the game to go forth when by getting to the *Isle of Princes* before he, you could prevent his capture and thereby prevent him from becoming a pyrate."

"First is that even tho' he would be my Captain, he may not fall in love with me, and second is because even though his greatness will be as a pyrate, I shan't begrudge him the everlasting fame that will be his, first as a legend in his own time, hailed as, '*That Great Pyrate*', but for all time." Pausing a moment, "Besides, Lucifer promised me that after the game ends we shall be able to live as we choose, and that, of course, can only take place if he lives."

"But as you also said, my Lady, will such only atchieve the placement whereby you will be but pawns within yet another game."

"You would think of that." And with a grim reality blessed only by fleeting moments of everlasting love, the two of us gallop off.

Choosing not to talk for a spell, knowing William is most likely right, I instead spend time contemplating what he had said, and thus, I shall try only to think of the tenderness of his touch, and the strength of his resolve, altho' I do not think tender is the right word; robust, I think, better serves my meaning.

Riding on for a spell, occasionally cantering, nigh on two hours pass before William says we must rest the horses again; this time leading them for about 15 minutes, whilst we, in turn, stretch our legs. Coming to a stream, William fills our water botas whilst the horses consume their fill. Taking a handkerchief from my satchel, I submerge it into the cool water, and using the dampened cloth; I wipe my face, neck, and hands.

Having returned our botas to our respective saddles, William returns to the stream and splashes his face with water. Shaking his head a mite to throw off the excess, he lets all I've said sink in, and after a couple moments, "We must be moving along, Miss Aspasia."

"I'm ready, Billy," and once again helps me onto my sorrel mare, we are off.

After an hour or more, we arrive at our first destination. The place seems sadly deserted, but after a few minutes, amid our looking around, an older man, nigh on 65 years, comes from around the corner of one of the old, dilapidated buildings. It saddens me to see what was once a flourishing foundry, faithfully serving her country in her effort to bring peace for all, is now neglected. But more so, even than that, is the reality of knowing them who worked here be forgotten also, and by those they faithfully served, and the sights that come alive in this reality makes it plain to understand the deprivation which Captain *Roberts* had spoke. I only hope that this man will look kindly upon us, and together with many of those who worked here in the past, will accept my offer of employment and manufacture the cannon as specified on my list, and after completing the contract, deliver them to the specified location where they will be hid before being stowed aboard my ship.

Seeing William dismount, the old man, gruff and suspicious, addresses us in a somewhat hostile manner. "What be yer business here?"

Helping me down from my sorrel mare, William takes charge. "We have come here to offer you, and them in the village, profitable employment."

"Of what sort?"

"The making of 10 score bronze cannon." Moving towards the gruff man, William takes from me my list, saying, "I have here a list. Read it fer yerself, if you be able."

Having some learning, the crotchety old coot looks the list over, "What fer would ye be needing such a quantity of so expensive a cannon? Have ye not heard, the war be over."

"This contract the lady offers be fer a private venture."

"At what rate of pay? Fer we have much work to do tending our fields in this har poor soil and being tenant farmers, our tedious chore of tending the crops will neede to continue atop any employment if 'n we are to remain here?"

"To ease that burden," I say, "the contractor, glancing at William, shall provide an ample supply of livestock and chickens, which will, in turn, provide the nutrients that will aid your crops as well as provide meat and milk, as well as wool, bacon, poultry and eggs."

Jumping in, William adds, "How many men live in yon town that would wish to benefit, fer this place is badly neglected and is in neede of much repair, also which, on a separate account, will also be paid for by the contractor."

"Well…" ponders the old man, scratching his head, "there be about 50 men who live in and about the village. Among them art those who not onely be skill'd in the making of cannon, but also in carpentry, as well as other relat'd jobs, including a Millwright."

William, being not only intelligent, but intuitive, knows that once the crusty old farmer hears my offer, he will change to a sweeter tone. "The contract, being held by the widow Jourdain, offers the sum of £5000*l*. plus the cost of materials, and anny repairs that neede be undertaken to work efficiently, in addition to the farm animals mentioned."

"Five Thousand!" Screeches the old man.

The man's reaction being as William believed would be so, did happen; the old man's attitude did, in fact, alter to that of a pleasing quality.

Making sure, the old man asks, "This sum, it be what you offer to us personally, and not to our landlord?"

I ask, "Who owns the foundry, your landlord?"

Replying, the old man replies, "It was abandoned by it's owner years ago."

Knowing he speaks true, "On the morrow the contractor shall buy it." Proceeding directly with business, I add, "The money is to be divided betwixt the workers, and paid weekly from a special account via the foreman, the contractor shall hire."

Thinking that the old man may try to gouge me, William quickly adds, "We hope this amount will be sufficient. If not, speak thusly and we shall be on our way, for there be many other foundrys such as this, who, like yerselves, be in dire neede of employment, and we have no wish to haggle."

I am impressed greatly by William's business acumen. The old man, knowing William speaks true, quickly takes it upon himself to speak for the entire village. "Wee of this village shall be 'appy to fulfil yer contract, Madam, and wee shan't be breathin' a word beyond the confines of our village except as neede be to procure the required materials."

Putting the man at ease. "The contractor will hire a bronze merchant who will deliver the materials to you here. Upon acceptance of this here contract, signed by you and those in the village who wish work, we shall hold a modest celebration, wherein, I hope canne be found accommodations for the night. On the morrow we must be away at first light, as there is much more that needs doing, and we haven't time to dally."

The old man, obviously overjoyed, "Yes, Guv. If ya follow me to the pub, I shall inform those present of yer generous offer." Heading for his horse and cart, the old man's manner lyes within the realm of thinking an angel has sent work to his village, and once again, having enough funds to support all the people in the village for many years to come, they will prosper, "and by nightfall everyone shall know."

Hiding my inner smile, I says quietly to Billy, "My plan, going more perfectly than e'er did I dare to hope thus far, I am most pleas'd." Turning to the old man, "Thank you, Mister…"

"Just call me Jacob, Madam."

"Thank you, Jacob. I know we shall enjoy a splendid working relationship." As the three of us approach the village, I ask, "How long will it take to manufacture the cannon?"

"After the foundry's repaired, I should think the better part of 3 months, and a fortnight more to deliver them to Erith on the River Thames, between Erith Reach and the Rands."

"That's splendid," says I, smiling. Mounting our steeds as Jacob climbs into his cart, William and I follow him the short distance to the village.

Upon arrival, William, having tied up his horse, helps me dismount. Jacob also ties up to the hitching rail.

Espying the Inn across the street, "I should like to repair to my room to freshen up, so if you will excuse me, gentlemen."

William and Jacob happily walk into the Publick House as I cross the road. Entering the Inn, I am pleas'd to see that altho' old, the large room is neatly kept. Continuing on, I see who looks to be the Innkeeper, and whilst approaching the reception desk, "I would like two rooms adjacent, please. One for myself, and another for a friend who rides with me. We shall also require and two hot baths."

"Very good, Madam."

"My friend is across the way at the Publick House with Jacob arranging a community gala to be held there to-night. I hope all of you here will attend."

Curious, as I expected, several people want to know why.

Smiling at them, "My friend and I have come with a contract for the production of 10 score of bronze cannon,[1] and 2 score of swivel guns. Jacob has accepted on behalf of anyone who wishes employment."

"But the foundry, it be in ruins."

"It is to be repaired."

Cheering wildly, several of those present run out. As I watch them, I see a couple of them enter the tavern, joining, even if only briefly, those few beset with only sorrow in their hearts that are inclin'd to tipple away their lives. Terribly pleas'd that William and I be here, the Inn-keeper shews me upstairs to my room.

After she leaves, I wash up a bit. Feeling somewhat done in after the long ride, I decide to take a short nap on the settee; meanwhile, a hell raising party is well underway across the road.

Arising from my nap, I look at the clock in the corner of the room to find that I have slept for a little more than an hour. 'Tho' feeling refreshed after the long ride, I am rather rumpled, and thus, after smoothing down my dress, I preen myself in front of the mirrored wardrobe before leaving the room.

Coming down the stairs and entering the lobby, I find it to be empty. Nearing the door, I hear the sound of much gaiety. "They must be having a joyous time indeed, judging from the noise," says I, speaking aloud. Being in good spirits, I step out onto the wood decking that runs before the building, and wishing to establish good relations with those who will be working for me, I hurry myself along to join in the festivities.

Seeing me as I enter the room, "Ah, Madame Jourdain," says William. "Everyone, this be yer benefactor. It be fer this fine woman that ye, and all of you, will again have employment."

Altho' quite shocked by William's announcement, having wanted to appear as an envoy, I force a smile as I find myself duly gathered about by the villagers, all of whom be holding pints in their fists. As they cheer me, I had no idea that bringing work to the village, especially under unscrupulous circumstances, would be met with such warmth, and again find myself remembering Captain *Roberts*, altho' ne'er is he far from my thoughts, I recall him telling me of the poor conditions, yet not until it actually comes into view, very few are able to truly understand. These peoples cloathes be in tatters, and even tho' I am hardly dressed in cloathes in a league equal to my station, my attire is posh by comparison. Being I can not offer to buy them new cloathes and wares, for such would be detrimental to their dignity, I decide to see what is in the town that I can buy, thereby I can bring prosperity whilst I shop. Surely there must be a merchant locally, and perhaps I can hire a private seamstress, and a couple other workers who would not otherwise benefit from the manufacturing of the cannon. I shall have to give the matter a little thought. Whatever my random thoughts may be, there is one thing I be most sure; that being; however small a pittance it will be in comparison to my means, shall seeme like riches to these people. Naturally, being it is my wish for them to believe my generosity is genuine and not charity, I join in the fun, but first the contract must be signed. Getting William's attention, I holler. "Billy, 'tis time to gather the men around."

"Everyone," says William, shouting to be heard over the noise of jovial conversation,

---

[1] *Author's Note: Cannon to be manufactured will fire 24 & 36 pound shot.*

waving his hands in the air, "please gather 'bout, for 'tis time to sign the contract."

One of the village folk, one whom others look up to, speaks his mind. "But what of Sir Walter? He owns the land upon which we live, and since the closing of the foundry, we have become but poor tenement farmers who have had to pay both rent and tribute to farm the land that now belongs to him, and for the privilege of remaining in our homes."

Being that the knowing may make a huge difference, I ask, "What rank is this, Sir Walter?"

"He's a Baronet."

As an older, well-dressed man walks in, purposefully attracting everyone's attention, he starts to boisterously harangue the village folk. "What be the cause for this gathering, have you no work to do?"

Disliking people of his ilk, I speak sharply, "Excuse me, but just who might you be, and what gives you the right to speak thus to these people?"

Uppish, "I am Sir Walter Shotts, Baronet of Sidcup, and not that it's any of your business, but most of these people work on my farm, and if they wish to keep their places, they best get back to work."

Leaning his head towards mine, "The Landlord," states William with quiet disdain.

Despising his kind, I spout, "William, inform this man who I am!"

"Good people of Sidcup, allow me to introduce yer benefactor, Madame Aspasia Rebekah Jourdain, la Marquise d'Éperon-Noire."

Gasps and the like are heard amid curtsies and bows.

Addressing those in the pub, "I am here to procure 10 score Bronze Cannon for 9, 24 and 36 pound shot, and 2 score of Swivel Guns for my new ship, just as William informed ye."

Doubting my identity, Sir Walter spouts, "Your attire is hardly fitting that of a marquise."

"Her ladyship hoped to do her good deed incognito," states William.

"I believe it not," states the Baronet, and addressing the village folk, "Why, are there no cannon factories in France? And why would one of her declared rank, and a foreigner, care for Britannia's peasant class?"

"Not only am I half Welsh, but those who know me, know not only that I do not live in France, but also that one of my proclivities is to help those displaced by Queen Anne's war."

"As a Champion of 'Noblesse Oblige, her Ladyship," begins William, "was so described simply because she chooses to not only provide work for those who need it; she buys slaves only to set them free, many of whom she employees at a fair and honest wage on her mulberry plantation and silk textile mill; but most of all, she despises the treatment most persons of rank inflict upon the common folk."

Again addressing the village folk, "Just words, I tell you, even her speech, for one of rank, and therefore educated, is rather antiquated." Turning to face me, "Either prove your claim, or move along."

"To he who doubts my sincerity, I propose a bargain."

Shaking his head in disbelief, "Name it."

"First, have you a wife, children?"

"No."

With a chuckle, "No doubt this be the reason for your ill temper." Pausing a moment, "Well, I can fix that. How much value do you put on your estate, the house and land?"

"My estate, being comprised of an eighteen room house, tenements and servants' quarters resting upon eighteen hundred acres of farmland, would be well beyond your means."

Making a chuckle, "Hearing no mention of its value, I can not imagine a fine house. It must be frightfully run down."

"I'll have you know, Madame, that my estate is valued at £20000l."

Laughing, "So small a sum," Suddenly pompous, "but then you being but a mere Baronet."

The Baronet, having gone from uppity to irritated, "Put up or shut up!"

Whilst jotting down a simple contract of sale, "And if I do?"

Confident that I am just jesting, "I shall renounce my Baronetcy and depart forthwith, ne'er to return."

Amid an impudent chuckle. "Done! Sign this please, or are you afraid to put up or shut up?"

The agreement having been signed, I walk to the table, and removing my bustier, and laying it down, I undo the fancy lacing across the top that closes the pocket, and as I pick it up, a grand display of banknotes and coins, totaling £35000 tumbles out.[1]

As the coins topple down, everyone's eyes, amid various sounds reflecting their feelings of wonderment, grow large.

Counting out twenty, £1000 banknotes, I walk up to the humiliated, yet humbled Baronet, and roughly shoving the money in the vest pocket of his coat, "You've been paid, Mister Shotts. Now go!"

Altho' feeling dejected, the former Baronet bows as is proper, "By your command, my Lady," and with his head held low, the former landlord, hat in hand, leaves the publick house.

Happier than they dreamed possible, everyone present rejoice, as he departs.

"Looks like you have a new home, my Lady."

"No William, I have no neede of it."

"Then why did you buy it, my Lady?" asks the Inn Innkeeper.

"To rid your village of that impudent swine." Musing a moment, "Methinks the estate will serve well to house the orphans and the infirmed. As such, perhaps the current taxes on the property can be abolished. William, make a note for me to look into it."

Cheers abound!

Quieting the cheers, I convey my plans. "On the morrow, I shall delay my business long enough to return to London to record the land transfer, engage a surgeon, a nurse, a tutor, and hopefully a member of the clergy. William and I shall ride out to the Big House momentarily. Will you be good enough to show us the way, Jacob?"

"A pleasure, my Lady," bowing.

"But first, let us get to the signing of the work contract."

As each man in turn steps forth, he signs or makes his mark.

Now, for the next order of business. Getting everyone's attention I ask, "Would there be a seamstress, a lace maker and milliner in the village, William and I shall be gone for about a week, would it be possible to have a new change of cloathing for each of us made in that short of time?"

---

[1] *Author's Note: In 1719, banknotes, not having been issued in denominations of less than £50ſ for many years, & average salaries being less than £20ſ per annum, most persons had never seen them.*

"Oh, yes, Miss," says the woman nearest to me, and from still another who curtseys, "I canne create for you a new bonnet, as the one you be wearing this afternoon shall be quite done in by the time you return."

Not wanting to be outdone, the other three women clamber for work as well.

"Ladies, as the menfolk will need work clothes, hats, footwear, and hearty meals, there's plenty of work for all. Your salary, regardless of your trade, shall be 8 & 6 per week. I shall establish accounts between the local mercantile with the suppliers, courier and freight service in London. That way you can place your order for materials when need'd, and a subsequent courier will inform you when the order is ready to be picked up."

Being most grateful for both the work and conveniences, the lot of 'em curtsy whilst awarding me with their thank yous.

"Shall we go investigate the Big House now, my Lady?"

"Yes, William, lets." Heading towards the door, "Ready Jacob?"

"Yes, my Lady.'

Looking forward to seeing that which I just bought sight unseen, we depart the pub.

Come morning, I feel fresh as a daisy, and within the hour, I am on my way to the quaint dining room for breakfast where I am joined by William.

"Good morrow, William. I trust you slept well."

"Quite well, my Lady," says he whilst gallantly pulling out my chair. "And yerself too, I hope."

Taking my seat, "Very well, thank you."

Entering the room, the serving wench sets the two plates of food and a pot of coffee on the table before us. As she pours the coffee, "The breads shall be served presently, my Lady."

"Thank you," says I, offering a slight smile.

"The villagers, were most eager to thank you during last night's festivities."

"So I noticed, but being what we be doing is not exactly, 'above-board,' I want those we hire henceforth to be under the impression that we are acting for others."

"I understand."

As he replied, the Innkeeper brings forth a nice assortment of breads to complement our eggs and back rashers. Filling our cups with more coffee, "Thank you," says I, as does William.

During breakfast, we make plans to leave promptly at noon, returning to London so I can meet with the shipbuilders to discuss the configuration of the ship I want built. I also need to pick up the newly fashioned clothes I ordered for William and myself before heading out on our journey. I hope the inhabitants at our next destination will be less likely to inspire such jubilation, being instead, complacent with regard to getting the work done, but somehow I know that each town and village will be as was the first, and I have an entire crew of some seventy pyrates, all of whom need cloathing, plus sails of all sorts, and rigging, so from now on a simple to-do and we'll have to ride off, spending the night outside in the woods in order to save time, for Britannia be bulging with folks who need work, and even tho' I wish to do the best I can for them, mingling wastes time, and I have none to waste.

Weekes having passed by, I take time to record the recent events in my diary.

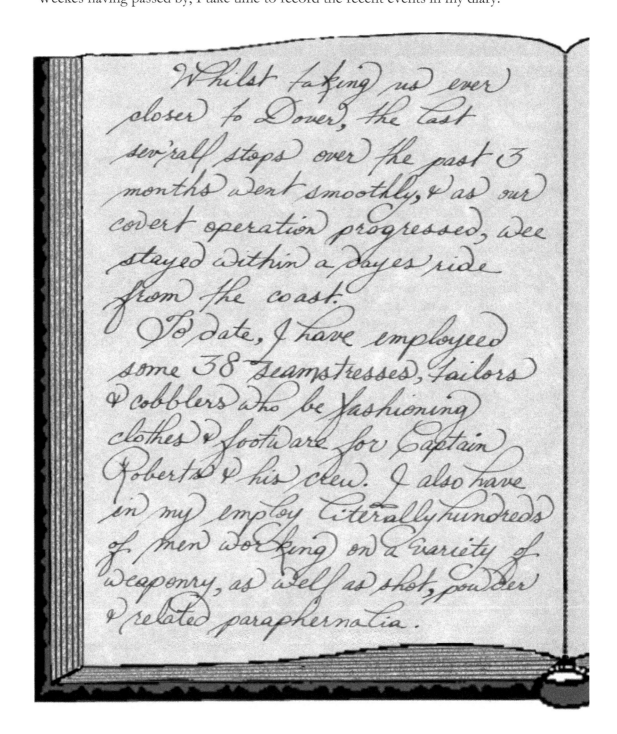

Whilst taking us ever closer to Dover, the last sev'ral stops over the past 3 months went smoothly, & as our covert operation progressed, wee stayed within a dayes ride from the coast.

To date, I have employeed some 38 seamstresses, tailors & cobblers who be fashioning clothes & footware for Captain Roberts & his crew. I also have in my employ literally hundreds of men working on a variety of weaponry, as well as shot, powder & related paraphernalia.

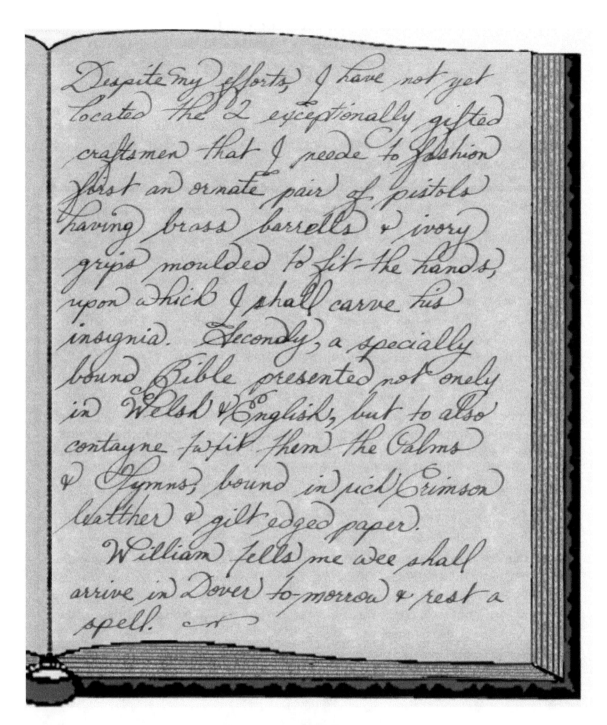

> Despite my efforts, I have not yet located the 2 exceptionally gifted craftsmen that I neede to fashion first an ornate pair of pistols having brass barrells & ivory grips moulded to fit the hands, upon which I shall carve his insignia. Secondly, a specially bound Bible presented not onely in Welsh & English, but to also contayne fwfit them the Palms & Hymns, bound in pick Crimson leatther & gilt edged paper.
>
> William tells me wee shall arrive in Dover to-morrow & rest a spell.

Packing up my diary, I continue on towards my quest.

Chapter Four
Born is a Legend
Location: 'Isle of Princes & Annamboa'

Below is contained the True Life story of Pirate Captain, Bartholomew Roberts. ALL actual, 'true-life', quotes are italicized: Black & White version shall be present thus, **Bold**. *The COLOR version, thus shall be presented in* Red.

A Brief 'Historical Narrative' of Importance, containing future events.

Unbeknownſt to thoſe upon the merchant ſhips, the crew of the *Prince*'s were about to be beſieg'd by none other than the well~known Welſh pyrate, *Hywel Davies*,[1] who whilſt commanding the *Royal James*, had no more than a month earlier, captured the 30 gun *Dutch* Interloper, *Marquis del Campo*, off Cape *Three Points Bay*. The fervent engagement laſted from one o'Clock in the afternoon until nine the following Morning, each crewman giving their all until the *Dutch* Captain, being regrettably unable to continue the fight, ſtruck his colours.

The *Marquis del Campo*, an impreſſive ſquare rigged *Dutch* crewed *East~Indiaman*, carry'd a crew of 90. Proud of their Captain, their ſhip, and of her 30 cannon; all of which gave them a ſenſe of ſecurity, and rightly ſo. Among her many attributes was a magnificent great cabin located juſt below a high poop deck; ſuch ſo, that it alone was enough to breathe aſpirations into any Captain worth his ſalt, and that be not all, for her three maſts be tall and ſtout, her conſtruction throughout, ſolidly built. Laſtly, and in mine eyes moſt important, they tell me ſhe is yare.

As is cuſtomary aboard pyrate veſſels, all unneed'd bulkheads within the mighty Sloop be promptly removed as ſhe was outfitted for their purpoſe; furthermore, even tho' ſhe be armed to the teeth, Captain *Davies* ordered ſtill more cannon be mounted until ſhe boaſted not only 32, 8 pound cannon upon carriages, but 27 ſwivels upon her railing, making her as formidable as any Naval Fregate. Newly fitt and ready to ſerve, 'twas time, it was, that a new name be given their prize, and what was decided by them was, *Rover*." B8 & 9

---

[1] Captain Hywel Davies (aka Captain Howell Davis) the spelling listed first being correct, as documented by the author in 2005; the source: the PRO in Haverfordwest, Pembrokeshire. Said is also cited in the book *'Open Secrets'* which is located in Bibliography.

BLOOD and SWASH, The Unvarnished Life (& afterlife) Story of Pirate Captain, Bartholomew Roberts......pt.2 "THE WILLING CAPTIVE"

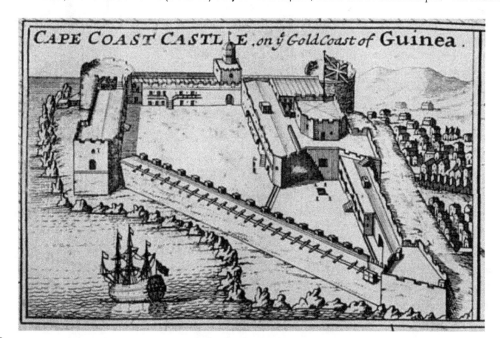

It has beene quite some time since wee left Britannia, and to our good fortune, the journey, sailing in consort with the *Bird*, has beene pleasantly uneventful. Business flourishes, and finally, with the *Bird's* holds full, wee sett about on different paths.[N1] In keeping with her orders, the *Princess* makes course for her last trading stop along the west coast of *Africa* before returning home to *London* with a shipment of Negroes, gold and teeth.[B8 & 9]

Having arriv'd, at the steaming hell hole of *Annobón*, wherein lyes a derelict outpost functioning primary as a storehouse, with a mere 9 cannon, is where the nearby *Royal African Company* keeps supplies for passing ships, the *Princess* came upon two other merchant ships, the *Morrice*[sic] Sloop, and the *Royal Hynde* already anchored in the harbor.[B8 & 9] This was our last preskrybed destination, and 'twas not long before Captain *Plumb* and our First Mate be ashore conducting business. For myself, 'tis forward with relish that I look, for it shan't be long before I shall be bound for Bermuda and the Captaincy offered me by her ladyship, la Marquise d'Éperon-noire, will at last be mine. It will be my singular ambition to justify her faith in me, and thus, I shall make for her a splendid Captain, and what a crew I shall have.

Just then, me thoughts are interrupted by a cry from the man on watch in the crow's nest who has espy'd approaching ships in the distance, but unbeknownst to us, the ships bearing down on *Annobón*, be a band of rovers led by *Hywel Davies* on board the *Rover*, with the *Royal James* in consort.

> ### A Brief 'Historical Narrative' of Importance.
> 'Twas betwixt the hours of twelve and one on a fine February, in the Year of Our Lord 1719, when the pyrates efpyd three fhips, one being a Guiney~man entitled, *Princefs*, aboard which *John Robert*, was Third Mate. 'Twas lying peaceably at anchor under the fuppozid protection of the Royal African Company, which was protected by 9 guns pofitioned at *Fort Cape Corfo Caftle*. This, however, not be the cafe, for 'twould be a rude awakening that the lot of 'em be in for.
>
> Alongfide the *Morrice*, where alone can be found 140 Negroes, dry goods, and a confiderable amount of Gold Duft and feveral canoes, fome of the crewmen from the aforementioned fhip manage to row afhore to feeks help. Thofe who witnefs their courageous act, could feel only defpair, as it was to No avail, for when the fort fired at the pyrate, fhe be out of range. Be that as it may, Captain *Davies*, in a defence pofture, raifed his black flag and returned fire.
>
> Immediately, and without hefitation, thofe having the temporary power of command of their fellow merchants, alfo riding at anchor; their Captains being afhore conducting bufinefs, knowing they could expect not onely a heated engagement, but undoubtedly lofs of life among them, promptly furrender'd and afk for quarter. Captain *Davies'* helmfmen, well fuited to their duties, kept both the *Royal James* and the *Rover* out of range of the harbour's gun emplacements. After capturing both the Sloop, *Morrice*, and the French Pinque, *Royal Hynde*, the pyrates proceed to fail alongfide the *Princefs*.
>
> The date: February 6, 1719

This is a fine ship, the *Princess*, her Second Mate; however, whose name be John Stephenson, brims with less desirable qualities. Being as nervous as anny man that ever I have seen, informs the pyrate as she draws alongside, that both the Captain and the First Mate be ashore, and that he, being Second Mate, is acting Captain; ergo, having hardly a skeleton crew on board, he wishes not to engage. Thus, in hopes to safeguard those of us on board, as did the others, he asks for quarter forthwith, whereby the pyrates were treated to an easie victory.

The orders given him, be simply, *"Come on board with all hands."*

Experience and faith told *Stephenson* that discretion being the better part of valour, does as he is ordered, and followed by his seven shipmates: *John Eshwell,* ship's carpenter; *William Gittus,* gunner; *James Bradshaw; John Jessup; John Owen; Thomas Rogers*; and lastly, yours truly, *John Robert,* 3rd mate/navigator, the lot of us board, the *Rover.* [HCA1 & B2 pg 80]

If'n I were to deskrybe myself whereupon them whom be reading these writings in yeeres to come, canne better identify with me, I shall state that it be a sable eyed man that I am, standing more than two yards tall, and older than most. I am said to be broad-shouldered, and I confess to that of a decidedly serious expression that is worn beneath a heavy mane of sable coloured, wavy hair atop a swarthy complexion, browned from yeeres at sea, stern with regard to duty, and I have heard it said that I possess a goodly amount of personal bravery.[B8 & 9, F]

That same day, after placing upon them a prize crew, Captain *Davies* sails with 2 more prizes. Still having on board the crew taken from the former, *Marquis del Campo*, and in lieu of Captain *Finn's* less than co-operative attitude, Captain *Davies* gave to the Dutch

Captain, the *Morrice*, rewarding him, as it were, for the impressive effort made by him and his gallant crew, whereby they, the lot of 'em, went on their way, whilst us, meaning the crews of the *Morrice*, *Royal Hynde* and *Princess*, having no choice, accompanied Captain Davies upon the *Rover* and *Royal James* as he made his way down the coast towards the Portuguese colony residing upon the Isle of Princes, which lyes within the *Gulf of Guinea*.[B8 & 9, CSP-CSY2]

Woodcut: Captain Hywel Davies

Come early morn, the man on watch espy'd a sail. Wasting no time, Captain *Davies* gave chace. The Captain of the potential prize, packing all the canvas the yards could hold, made an attempt to run his ship aground in an effort to escape to the safety of land. Captain *Davies*; on the other hand, being both shrewd and intelligent, surmising the Hollander's intention, ordered all sailes to be trimmed forthwith, and foregoing the pretence of discussion, sail'd alongside and fired a broadside. Affrightened, the Hollander immediately struck his colours and call'd for quarter, which, as it is among the majority of pyrate vessels, was granted. With regard to the same, such granting is outlined within the Articles belonging to Captain *Davies*, which specifically states: *"Under pain of death, Quarters, whenever call'd, Must be granted,"*[B8 & 9] The Hollander, presently delayed in her return to her homeland, carried not onely a wealth of valuable merchandize, but the Governour of *Acra*,[sic] who himself possessed 15000l, all of which is jovially plunder'd.[B8 & 9]

Captain *Davies* and his duly call'd, 'House of Lords,' being delighted with their New success, voted in privy council, whereupon Captain *Hall's* ship, the *Royal Hynde*, is returned to him.[B8 & 9] As for me, Captain *Abraham Plumb*, the *Princess*, and her crew, less 35 men collectively, which included sev'rall taken from the *Morrice* Sloop, who, with the exception of one, joined readily; the One being yours truly who was pressed into service at point of pistol, marking the Onely exception of his Captaincy in such an act,[①] once again places me in the company of pyrates. After which, feeling especially charitable, *Davis'* crew also voted to allow the plundered Hollander, and her passengers, to depart without further molestation.

At first, aside from the obvious reasons, I, being a well-bred man, possessing a good education, am none too pleas'd with my situation.

Over the course of sev'rall days of my capture, however brooding, I find myself talking with *Hywel Davies*, Captain of these here pyrates, at great length, during which time he and I have become great friends; and it pleases me to say that as opened mine eyes to the Mundane way of life that had besieged me, and the Despotic relationship existing 'twixt the Common man and his Oppressors, otherwise known as the Degenerate Aristocracy, who in possessing wealth and social position, use their high and mighty status to increase their own selves whilst trampling upon those, who without recourse, are relentlessly forced to perform laborious tasks to maintain the so stated oppressors in their exalted rank, ne'er has he attempted to force nor sway me. Also throughout these profound conversations, I have learned much about their democratic society; 'tis

---

① Author's Note: Captain Davies undoubtedly saw a special quality within the man, John Robert, as did the crew of, the Rover, & the Terrible as well.

altogether different than the totalitarianism regime that runs rampant throughout Naval and Merchant vessels, and the rather haughty Masters who command them. I also, as enlightenment befalls me, find myself softening to that which I have beene, for the whole of me life, repulsed by, one aspect being that all forms of thievery, including privateering, as well as pyracy, to be a moral sin, which is why I am not an active member of this crew; nonetheless, whenever I see that which I feel needes correction, or when I canne be giving assistance to those needing my helpe, I do, and ever shall, be of assistance, for it be my way.

Tho' strange it may seeme, I find myself pleas'd, for in the few short weekes that have passed, Captain *Davies* and his crew, Lords and Commoners, as they consider themselves, have complemented me on my adeptness as a seafaring mariner. Some, especially them of high regard, have commended my natural leadership abilities. In regard to these thoughts, 'tis my pleasure to write herein, that I was offered, this day, the position of Quarter-Master aboard the *Royal James*; however, not yet keen to the idea of officially joining their ranks, whilst at the same time wishing not to insult those who think so well of me, I graciously refus'd.

As time goes on, I need to convey that their placement, in what is their owne private commonwealth aboard ship, is one of commanding interest, especially being this here vessel be a pyrate ship; their officers, being known as their *'House of Lords,'* is conducted with the utmost respect; furthermore, I find the crew, All in All, to be for the most part, men of honour (mostly displaced after Queen Anne's War,) whose word, once given, is a bond that canne be trusted; the lot function as a brotherhood for the betterment of all, and their ship is their country. Again being in contrary to that of a Naval vessel or Merchant which serves onely for the gain, both in wealth and social position of its commander, and even more so, to them he serves in loyalty, being especially the land lubbers whose highborn status reap the benefits from them who toil; the latter, being the common man who, and it grieves me to admit thus, atchieve no benefits beyond a meager subsistence for their labours, which is far less than one thinks when you consider disease, injury, sickness,[①] and punishment, the average lifespan for a common sailor is a mere 2-3 yeeres.

These thoughts have plagued me, and after much deliberation and soul searching, I have come to the conclusion, despite the loathing I have for their incessant drinking, reprehensible language, and deplorable lack of propriety, that I shall thenceforth be a willing member of the company; and to those who enquire as to my reasons, I shall state, *" 'Twas to get rid of the disagreeable Superiority of some Masters I have been acquainted with, and the Love of Novelty and Change, Maritime peregrinations has accustom'd me to."* [B8 & 9]

This decision is not made without the consideration of the promised Captaincy offered me by la Marquise d'Éperon-noire, for should things not go as I expect, belieeving that here I canne make a name for myself, which be my aim, I canne return, for I knows she will have me still.

---

① As reported by the *Victualing Board*, a sailor's official rations were listed as: 1 lb of bread (hard tack) & 1 gallon of beer per day, plus 1 lb of pork twice a week, 2 lbs of beef also twice a week, or butter and cheese the other 3 days. For the common sailor, these meats were salted. Only officers were allotted fresh meat.

NOTING the absence of fruit and vegetables, not to mention fresh water, it is easy to understand why so many fell victims to illness, e.g. Scurvy & Rickets, as well as dehydration.

Also as a added note, especially to you readers relishing the idea of a gallon of beer everyday. Beer (provided due to the lack of fresh water available) is not a substitute for the water a body needs.

An Interesting Statistic regarding British Royal Navy casualties - *Source: deseretnews.com - A Sailor's Life*

In ALL major fleet actions: 5,000 killed in action - 70,000 killed from disease

Location: 'Cameroon Bay & the Isle of Princes'

Whilst en route to the Isle of Princes, the *Royal James* springs a leak. Once again, Captain *Davies*, knowing my familiarity with these waters, and having already accustomed himself in the seekement of my advice, asks where a suitable place to make repairs canne be found.

In reply, I suggest *Cameroon Bay*, letting it be known also that whilst repairs be made, both timber and fresh water canne be taken on board. Unfortunately, come low tide, 'tis discovered the damage to her hull, having beene ravished by the savage Teredo Worm, far exceeding our previous knowledge, the ship, deem'd damaged beyond repair, Captain *Davies*, orders her armament, and all other items of value, to be transferred to the *Rover*. Afterwards, with the *Royal James* being left to sway at anchor, wee depart.

Continuing forth to our destination, wee soon come in sight of land. Both the ship's Quarter-Master's, Lords *Walter Kennedy*, and *Richard Jones*, respectively, as is our Bos'n, be for direct action, but once again, I, *John Robert*, the intrepid newcomer who knows the *Isle of Princes* well, voices the particulars. "We ought not rush in, Captain. This here port, she is well protected. As ye sees," pointing to the fortification of both yon cliffs and *Fort James*, "There be a battery of no less than 12 cannon that guards the mouth of the harbour and the town. Even should wee sail in unmolested, 'twould be nigh on impossible to leave once the warning bells be sounded."

Heeding my words, Captain *Davies*, devising an alternate plan, orders the hoisting of English colours, specifically those belonging to that of a Man-of-War. 'Tis by this time, them ashore, seeing a large, heavily armed, three-masted ship approaching, send forth a small, single-masted vessel to learn our intentions. After hailing, our Captain, himself properly donned in finery, and having seene to it that his crew on deck also be properly attired, tells 'em wee be an English Man-of-War in search of pyrates, and having receiv'd intelligence

A Prospect from Sea of ye Harbour of Princefs belonging to ye Portugueze.

of such being upon this coast, wee have sail'd forth to investigate.

As for myself, I am amazed by the gullibility of these here islanders, who, without question, belieeve the Captain's twaddle, and such, wee be well receiv'd.

As is customary, Captain *Davies*, salutes the fort with cannon fire. After being answered, our ship anchors just under the harbour gunns, and immediately thereafter, Captain *Davies*, orders his boat hoisted out, and together with eight hands and a cox'n, he goes ashore.

Over the next few days, whilst our *Rover* is careened and stowed with fresh water, bottled beer (a necessary commodity when no drinking water canne be found,) provisions and other much need'd necessities, all appears to be going as plann'd.

Various members of the crew, other than those gathering supplies, venture ashore sev'rall times learning, not onely the lay of the land, but the routine of the inhabitants, and where valuables be kept.

BLOOD and SWASH, The Unvarnished Life (& afterlife) Story of Pirate Captain, Bartholomew Roberts......pt.2 "THE WILLING CAPTIVE"

Our ship, for practical reasons, has been strategically anchored where wee appear to be inadvertently blocking the harbour entrance, and as a result, a French ship has beene brought in to our lap. Wishing to enter port, the Frenchie requests wee make way, but instead, to their dismay, our Bos'n informs them that with that most of our crew be ashore, wee be unable to oblige them, and having no choice, the Frenchie drops anchor. Within minutes, three of our longboats carrying a goodly number of our company row on over, capturing her easily. Tho' small, replacing the *Royal James*, she will be of use. Wanting not to alarm the inhabitants, the Governour herein is told that these Frenchies be of such an ilk as to partake in unlawful dealings with pyrates, and, as is our Captain's sworn duty, their vessell has beene seiz'd in the name of the King.

Nigh on a fortnight having passed, makes it a trifle less than 6 weekes since being forced, at point of pistol onto this pyrate vessel, and much has happened. I, of course, 'tho a member of the crew, have not as yet participated in anny plundering, or, excepting the newly acquired French ship, the taking of prizes. Since my willingness to join his ranks, Captain *Davies* and myself, being born and reared less than 20 miles apart, have at liberty, openly enjoyed one another's company, being fellow Pembrockshires. Assuming 'twould be of interest to me, Captain *Davies* discusses with me his plans which included his intentions of invading the women's quarters, and invites me to join the shore party, but not approving of his plans beyond the pilfering of this port, and having said as much, Captain *Davies*, leaving me in command, ventures ashore with his lords as originally plann'd. Below be the telling of it.

> ### But First, A Brief 'Historical Narrative' of Importance.
> 'Twas that fame eve that, Captain *Davies*, again, ventur'd afhore, this time with 14 of his mates, but alas, for reafons unbeknownft to them, their plans went awry. Upon return to the fhip, 'twas voiced that they be quite fure they had not been recogniz'd.
>
> Confidering the events, *John Robert* fuggeft'd 'twas beft to fally, but the crew being, *Gentlemen of Fortune*, chofe firft to fack and loot the ifland; ergo, with the fhip careen'd and provifion'd, Captain *Davies*' plan commenc'd. To the Governour, in appreciation for the fine hofpitalities afforded them, Captain *Davies* was to prefent to him a dozen Negroes with his compliments, and afterwards invite the Governour and his entourage on board for fome fhip board entertainment, whereby the lot of em, fave one (the meffenger) fhall be flapped in irons and held for 40000*l*. ranfom.[B9]
>
> According to *Charles Ellms,'The Pirates Own Book*,' "A Negro, who was privy to the horrible plans of *Davies*, fwam on fhore during the night and gave information of the danger to the Governour.[sic]"

Hardly have they beene gone when those of us aboard the *Rover* see *Walter Kennedy* returning in haste. As wee hoist up our boat we grow disheartened, for instead of treasure wee find Lord *Kennedy* wounded. Terribly shaken, he relays the details.

"The shore party was ambushed," says he. "I alone managed to escape. To this feat, being but three and twenty, aided me as I fled in the awaiting boat, whereby my brawn, I successfully sculled the heavy longboat, and returned to the ship."

Abreast of the situation, it may be unwise to remain here whilst awaiting the return of our mates who be fishing. In a few minutes, as our anchor be hoisted, 'tis blessed wee be, thinks I, as I espy them come alongside, and with 'em, another man from the shore party.

Still in shock, speaking amid stammer and his gulping, *Kennedy* adds, *"Davies was shot through the Bowels, yet he rose again, and made weak Effort to get away, but his Strength soon forsook him, and he dropp'd down dead; just as he fell, he perceived he was followed, and drawing out both his Pistols, fired them at his Pursuers; thus, like a game Cock, giving a dying Blow, that he might not fall unrevenged."* [B8 & 9]

Taking a few moments to catch his breath, the man who was picked up by the shore party states, "Whilst Lord *Kennedy* dashed towards the shore with the others, I took to the high road. Finding myself cliff side with sev'rall of them yobbos close upon my heels, I had no choice but to dive into the shark infested waters and swim fer it."

'We were ambushed!' he said. 'When the slaughter began, most of our officers fell prey to hideous deaths. *"Captain Davies fought brilliantly, firing both his pistols as he fell mortally wounded, demonstrating to the last, the strength of his resolve."* Still in shock, speaking amid a gulping stammer, he added, *"They slit his throat."*

The Ambush & Murder of Captain Hywel Davies & several of his crew.

With half the crew wanting to flee and the other half bent on avenging our Captain and mates, the hullabaloo on board is deafening.

Despite the devastation brought to my soul regarding this news, being that *Hywel Davies* was not onely our Captain, but to me personally, an inspirational friend whom I held as a brother. I; therefore, altho' it greatly pains me, knows 'tis a necessity that wee, who be anchored beneath the harbour's 12 gunns, depart in due haste, as I says to 'em, "We be in grave danger. First wee must escape this harbour, for 'tis death she holds for us all. Once out of harm's way, then canne our plans be made."

Rallying the men, my advice is heeded, but alas more ills surge upon us, for out of the blue, a fast moving squall breaks loose and the winds do not favour us. To ensure our survival, I exercise the command entrusted to me by our late Captain, and altho' not spoken with conceit, 'tis by virtue of my adroitness, the necessary speed is made getting our great ship under saile, and despite the heavy gale, the crew, under my direction, works feverishly to tack us out of the harbour.

'Tis not too long before our *Rover*, and a fine sayler she by all accounts, is positioned off the coast of *Cabo de Lopo Gonsalves*, and now, limping to our Leeward side, our French acquisition joins us. Free from danger, saving both ship and crew, I step down. Plans now are able to commence. First, however, as the perplexity of ensuing chaos arises, one member of the company points out a necessity, saying: *"The good of the whole, and the maintenance of order, demands a head, but the proper authority be deposited in the community at large; so that if one should be elected who did not act and govern for the general good, he could be deposed, and another be substituted in his place."* B8&9

And thus, altho' I be not amongst them, this second week in July 1719, Lords *Walter Kennedy*, *Henry Dennis*, *Thomas Anstis*, *Valentine Ashplant*, *Christopher Moody*, *Dennis Topping*, *James Phillips*, *David Sympson* and *Thomas Sutton* stand for Captain.

Having had his fill of their debate, our master gunner, Lord *Henry Dennis*, rises and makes a memorable speech:

> *That it was not of any great Signification who was dignify'd with Title; for really and in Truth, all good Governments had (like theirs) the supream Power lodged with the Community, who might doubtless depute and revoke as suited Interest or Humour. We are the Original of this Claim (says he) and should a Captain be so sawcy as to exceed Prescription at any time, why down with Him! it will be a Caution after he is dead to his Successors, of what fatal Consequence any sort of assuming may be. However, it is my Advice, that, while we are sober, we pitch upon a Man of Courage, and skill'd in Navigation, one, who by his Council and Bravery seems best able to defend this Commonwealth, and ward us from the Dangers and Tempests of an instable Element, and the fatal Consequences of Anarchy; and such a one I take Roberts to be. A Fellow! I think, in all Respects, worthy your Esteem and Favour.*

His speech, so eloquently presented, is afforded a great deal of jubilation by all, except Lord *Sympson*, who after growing sullen, his reason, I have been told, being that his owne father had been a sufferer in *Monmouth's* rebellion, left us saying; *"I care not who ye choose as Captain, so it is not a papist, for against them I have conceiv'd an irreconcilable Hatred."* B8&9

Despite being but a mere six weeks amongst them, I find myself elected accordingly to a position I have dreamt of since going to sea as a ship's boy, and thus, amid the joyous feelings so prevalent within my heart, I stand and accept the honour afforded me, saying, *"Since I have dipp'd my Hands in muddy Water, and must be a Pyrate, it is better being a Commander than a common Man."* B8&9

A couple of crewmen, not belieeving what they had heard, made comments. After a moment's pause, I state my disposition thus: *"A merry Life and a short one, shall be my Motto."* B8&9

Our first order of business is to replace those Lords killed in the ambush. The voting on matters of such importance gathered together the makers of punch, and them who smoaked brought out their pipes whereby much talk commenced.

After a spell, the vote is taken, and our new government is settled. Captain *Davies'* good nature and affability gained him much respect, creating a unanimous concord, and after a brief discussion, a plan for avenging his murder is decided upon. Nigh on a weeke has passed since that fateful daye, and wee now be en route back to the *Isle of Princes*, determin'd to avenge not onely Captain *Davies*, but our other shipmates as well.

Lord *Kennedy*, tho' wicked, and a profligate,[B8] is known also for his boldness and daring. His placement as Quarter-Master, and his familiarity with the terrain, having beene ashore here sev'rall times, suggests the best course of action is to venture overland and attack the fort's rear flank. My better judgment goes against his proposed expedition, and instead, I offer up my strategy for a frontal assault. After deskrybing me plans of having Lord *Kennedy* lead the ground assault as he suggested; going ashore with 30 men, I shall command the seaside attack with cannon from aboard ship. The crew, tho' ready for action, have reservations. I tells 'em that such a shew of daring will implant such awe within their minds, that the soldiers and towns people will flee.[B8 & 9]

Tho' unsure at first, I am, after careful explanation, able to impress upon me company the logic of my proposal, me plans for our line of attack be readily accept'd.

Once making land fall, displaying tremendous fortitude and courage, off they march'd up the steep embankment directly towards the harbour gunn emplacements, they fearlessly trudge beneath the bombardment of our gunns.

Looking thro' the spyglass and discovering our shore party, the Portuguese fire into their ranks, and just as I had predicted, and seeing their gunns have no effect, the Portuguese quit their posts and flee towards the town, whereupon, Lord *Kennedy* and his men march onward without opposition. Even at such a distance, and knowing the men's disposition, I canne see, as well as feel, both their fury and sense of satisfaction as they heave the heavy cannon over the ridge and into the sea below. After the completion of their task, they sett the fort ablaze whilst displaying some merriment before quietly and quickly making their way back to the ship without casualty.[B8 & 9]

However successful be the delivery of our revenge, 'twas not look'd upon as sufficient satisfaction for the loss of Captain *Davies*. The majority of the company be for burning the town, which I am agreeable to, providing a means be proposed that shan't bring forth our owne destruction. When no such ideas are suggested, I point out that the town, having a thick wood coming almost upon it, provides cover to the occupants, and under such an advantage, it having a securer situation than the fort, is a thing to be affrighted, and state, *"Would fire stand better than cannon? Besides, the burning of bare houses would be but a slender reward for our trouble and loss."*[B8 & 9] With that implanted in their minds, I once again suggest to me crew a very different plan of action.

Altho' my prudent advice prevails, I think against using the *Rover*, for the water here, being shoal, is not fitting for our purpose. "However," I explain, "Within our possession still, wee have the French Pinque, and having a shallow draught, will better suit our purpose."

The Lords and Commoners concurring, light'n the vessell that will do our bidding, and fitting her with cannon until she numbers twelve, and towing even more which be lashed upon rafts, wee position them to float nigh as possible to the beach.

Once ready, those of us who will be aboard 'er, myself commanding the assault, run the French vessel along the shore, therewith, wee thoroughly and well, shell the town, and in doing so, batter down many of the outlying houses. After which, returning to our *Rover*, and having no further use for it, wee abandon the French Pinque. With our revenge, now satisfied, wee saile out of the harbour by the light of two Portuguese ships, which I am pleas'd to say 'twas ourselves who sett them ablaze.[B8 & 9]

Chapter Five
Captain Roberts
Location: 'S. W. Africa to the East Coast of Brazil'

Nigh on August 1719, it is, and wee be sailing Southward. After having sail'd for a short time onely, wee meet a Dutch Guiney-man.[B9]

After having plundered 'er, wishing to sett an example that will speak Lowdly to all, I tells them, "To them who freely co-operate with me, whilst maintaining the proper respect, shall be permitted to depart unharmed, less anny swag, or other need'd items found on board. All seamen thereof wishing to join with me shall be welcome, providing he agrees to the signing of me Bible, whilst pledging to me his loyalty; however, being I owe it to all who saile with me, I shall have onely the best crewmen and sea artists available, those worthy of our endeavours; ergo, should anny man prove not so, he will choose for himself a place along our route, and together with a paper, should he so desire such, I shall state, written in mine owne hand, that he was forced, thereby allowing him to escape the halter and return home should he so choose; furthermore, all non-compliant vessels will not onely pay a price for their Arrogance, but such shall be in a manner which pleases me at the given moment." After which, the Dutch Captain, being respectful enough, and having no neede of his vessell, 'twas voted that both her Captain and crew be allowed to depart.

Two dayes later wee take an English ship call'd the *Experiment* off the coast of *Cabo de Lopo Gonsalves*. 'Twas one of the oddest of happenings, for it seemes that none, barring her commander, Captain *Cornet*, and Sailing Master, one *Thomas Grant*, of the Brigantine's crew like that which earns 'em their bread, and therefore, the lot of 'em eagerly joined me crew; what is more, although the cause being unknown to both myself and the rest of me company, our quick-tempered Quarter-Master becoming enraged, hauled *Mister Grant* into the Great Cabin whilst cursing at him.

"Damn you!" Says he, in obvious anger. *"I knows you, and will sacrifice you!"* whereby his deliverance, hitting him in the mouth with a severe blow, sent the Sailing Master to the deck, bleeding profusely from the wound.[B13]

As Lord *Kennedy* begins to beat him mercilessly, 'twas evident *Mister Grant* be fearful for his life. 'Tis lucky he was, indeed that sev'rall of me crew saw fitt to intervene, for I myself not being of a mind to offer anny assistance to that self-aggrandizing sea rat, instead be writing a note to Captain *Cornet* inviting him for Tay and Conversation whilst me crew conducts business. As for those who be restraining Lord *Kennedy*, whilst shouting for the Sailing Master to get out, he pays heed. The note, delivered forthwith, was hence, a standing invitation extended to all my guests, Captains and Governours alike.[N1]

Captain *Cornet*, a pompous man, to his owne regret, declines my invitation, for which, I, in response to his arrogance, and to further shew those who will later be within my grasp, maketh known forthwith that his be not a wise decision, whereby; carrying on with business, Lord *Kennedy*, in accordance with his duties, sees to it, the *Experiment* is thoroughly stripped of her valuables before setting the torches to 'er.[HCA2], after which, *"This daye, the Experiment, Captain Cornet, master, I was obliged to send to the bottom since the good Captain refus'd my offer of Tay, so we put him ashore in a smale boat and less dignity."*[B9]

Sometime later wee enjoy reading, as came to be a pastime of infinite pleasure, a newspaper saying:

> "See what the rafcal does," faid the Colonial Governor who chofe to pen his wrath concerning the punifhment he was delt in refponfe to his arrogance, fpouting boifteroufly onto fine parchment,"within the majefty of Government! He writes me letters inviting me to take Tay with him— A Governor of His Majefty, fipping Bohea and fwopping fmalltalk with a pyrate[B9]!"

Meaning me of course, for I be the rascal of whom he spoke, the blow hard.

Come morn, wee capture a Portuguese trade ship bearing little cargo. Two dayes more, whilst sailing westward, wee fall upon the *Temperance*, command'd by one Captain *Sharman*. Well supply'd in pot, pans and metalware, she is; a cargo intend'd, tho' unsuccessfully, to trade for slaves, will serve us well; furthermore, being she is a fine ship, I shall keep 'er. Not wanting to deprive her former Captain, being he was most co-operative, wee afford him the Portuguese craft still within our possession.[C01]

Steering for *São Tomë*, we meet with no ships and thus continue on until reaching the Isle of *Annobón* where wee anchor. 'Tis here wee water and provision the ship, and upon gathering for council, 'tis put to a vote to make saile for either *Brazil* or the *East Indies*. The company, by majority vote, setts saile for to *Brazil*. The journey, a distance of some 2,700 nautical miles, takes us onely a span of 28 dayes, whereby wee arrive, by design, to the tiny uninhabited island of *Fernando de Noronha*, some 125 miles off the Easternmost tip of *Brazil*.[B8 & 9] The speed and accuracy of this sailing, altho' not out of my ordinary endeavours, forever imprints my much talked 'bout navigation skills; instilling not onely a goodly amount of confidence into the hearts and minds of me crew, but also within the annuls of history, for such skills be of a sort that gives birth to legendary proficiency.

Enlargement↗

BLOOD and SWASH, The Unvarnished Life (& afterlife) Story of Pirate Captain, Bartholomew Roberts......pt.2 "THE WILLING CAPTIVE"

Upon arrivall, our *Rover* be in neede of the tedious chore of careening, which in order to atchieve the best possible performance from a ship, ought be done every three to four weekes, and 'tis here that wee have dropped anchor to carry out this task.

Once beached, me ship is light'ned. Her cannon, stores, water casks, and other heavy cargo is plac'd on shore, and her topmasts removed. After which, using ropes

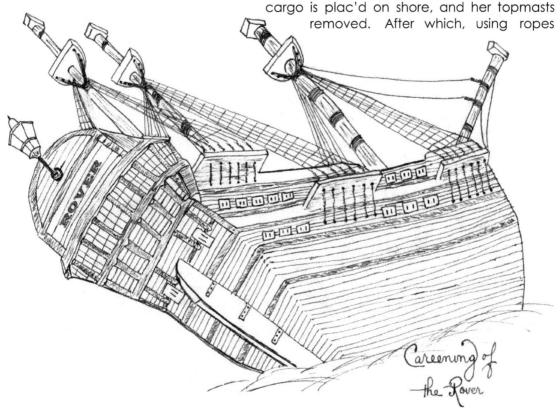

Careening of the Rover

and pulleys attached to her lower masts, and the usage of stout timber in the woodland, the *Rover*, is heeled over, onto her side, to lie upon the beach whilst the work is done. By night fall, being wee shall reside upon land during the cleaning, tents are sett up along the shore, and come morn, Lord *Main*, our Bos'n, as is among his responsibilities, issues work assignments.

One crew scrapes her hull thoroughly of the infectious marine life and weeds, whilst the ship's carpenters follow closely behind making anny need'd repairs. Lastly, me ship is caulked with a mixture consisting of Red Lead, Sulphur and Tallow, me owne recipe, is generously apply'd to her hull.[B3] Such a mixture not onely deters encrustations, but helpes her to better slip thro' the water; adding speed whilst also giving her an Impressive, as well as Fearsome appearance. Once complete, the entire process is repeated, after which, the opposite side of her hull receives the same start to finish treatment.

Amid this work, there are many crewmen who be assigned the tasks of filling the water casks and barrels, whilst others gather provisions. After working laboriously for one weeke and a half more, all tasks being complete, wee be ready for our *South American* cruise.

Sailing on the ebbtide, wee cruise on the cusp of the horizon, just beyond land's sight, but for a period of nigh on nine weekes, to our dismay, wee sight not a single saile. Me crew, as am I, disillusioned by these empty waters, belieeve 'tis best to depart, and upon the vote of me company, wee sett saile for the *West Indies*.

I have only just this moment arriv'd in *Dover*, yet from across the street I hear a familiar voice calling out. Turning, I see Mrs Robles. Knowing she would not have come unless it be a matter of great concern, I hurry over to her.

"What is it, Mrs Robles?"

"This letter, my Lady, it's from Dragonwood Plantation. Your sister, the Lady Trilby, is gravely ill and is calling for you. It is requested that you come at once."

'My sister,' says I to myself, raising an eyebrow, not knowing until this moment that I even have a sister, and knowing I mustn't falter, I gather my composer. "Where is she?"

"At her late husband's sugarcane plantation in *São Salvador, Brazil*."

"Is that near *La Baía de Todos os Santos*."

"Yes."

Knowing it's nearing the time that Captain *Roberts* will be there, I'm ecstatic. "Then to *Brazil* we shall go." Motioning for us to go inside, I says to her in a concerned voice, "How long have you been waiting for me?"

"A few days only, my Lady. I have both the shipping news, and your wardrobe trunks in our rooms. The next ship departing for *South America* is a merchant, and is scheduled to depart by week's end. If'n I hurry, I can make arrangements before night fall."

"Waste no more time then, Mrs Robles. Go now and book our passage, but not on any lumbering merchant. Procure the fastest ship in the harbour; speak directly to her Captain. Tell him la Marquise d'Éperon-noire, on urgent business, needs to be taken with all speed directly to the dock that serves the Dragoonwood Sugar Plantation."

"Yes, my Lady."

"Tell him also that we shan't require him to remain."

"How then will wee return?"

"The Portuguese Treasure fleet sets sail soon, we shall return thus."

"Just as you say, my Lady." Turning, Mrs Robles departs.

Altho' the circumstances are not the best, the outcome is more than I could've hoped for. My chance, I'm thinking, knowing that should I be lucky enough to get myself on the proper ship, I'll be able to see the fun. I may even get face to face with Captain *Roberts*.

Whilst at the front desk, William enters the lobby. Espying me, he comes directly to the reception desk.

Seeing him, I move towards him, out of earshot of others present.

"The horses have bin well groomed, fed, and bedded down, Miss."

"Thank you, William." Changing the subject, "Mrs Robles is here. She has brought me grave news concerning my sister Trilby, the Lady Dragoon, widow of the 6th Viscount of Dragoonwood, and she is not only gravely ill, she's asking for me; ergo, I must depart for *Brazil* forthwith. Being that Mrs Robles already has rooms for us, I shall resume my true identity, which will, conveniently, procure the passage I need."

"Position does have rewards."

"Indeed it does, William, but such privileges, altho' often abus'd, never should be."

"What about —"

"I shan't be gone long, William. By the time I return, the ammo and pistols should be ready, and stowed nigh the dock. I am counting on you to handle these matters during my absence."

"Good as done, my Lady."

"I never thought otherwise, and now, I think a bath and a hot meal will suit us both."

"Aye, my Lady, they will indeed."

Stepping back up to the front desk, I begin speaking to the manager of the hotel. "I, as does my steward, should both like to bathe before dinner. Please arrange for two hot tubs without delay."

"Most assuredly, Miss…"

Introducing me, William says, "This is her ladyship, la Marquise d'Éperon-noire."

"My apologies, my Lady," says the hotel manager whilst making a couple of quick bows. "Mrs Robles said you were expected. We have your rooms all ready." Taking the keys from the pigeon hole slot, the reservations clerk, who is also the manager of the hotel, steps from behind the counter. "Allow me to personally shew you to your rooms."

"Thank you," I reply with a slight smile.

"The finest rooms we have," speaks the Hotel manager with obvious pride.

"But of course," utters William snootily under his breath.

"And they cost plenty too, William," I respond in similar quiet.

As we begin to walk towards the stairs, the manager of the hotel, whilst lifting his arm high, snaps his fingers. Responding is one of the maids, who comes running. Speaking to us first as is proper, she demi-curtsies, "Good day, Miss. Sir," turning her attentions to her employer, "Yes, Mister Simmons?"

"I want you to prepare 2 hot baths immediately. One for her ladyship, la Marquise, and the other for her steward."

Flustered, as nobility generally let Fashionable Houses or Villas, are rare in Inns, the youngish maid, smiling, curtsies again, "With your permission, my Lady, I shall draw yer bath first, and yours, sir," speaking to William, "I shall draw next."

Simply replying, "Thank you." to the girl, letting her know I approve, responds only with a curtsey before scampering off.

Chapter Six
Luck of the Ages
'*Bound for Brazil*'

Morning comes quickly, and within the hour we board the Pinque, *Seagull*. It took some convincing, but after speaking directly with the French ambassador, special arrangements were made for me to pre-empt the fastest ship in port, and without further ado, Mrs Robles and I are bound for *Brazil*.

We are just departing the estuary, and with a bit of weather on the horizon, already the swells in the mighty Atlantic, being a goodly size, Mrs Robles innards do not take kindly to the motion of the ship upon the water, nevertheless, the urgency of my sister's needs makes for no allowances.

Becoming sickly already, I says to her, "Lett us get you to your berth," supporting her by the arm as the ship, rolling with the current, begins to heel, I, on the other hand, oblivious to the motion, am preoccupied with thoughts of my beloved, and knowing he will be in *Brazil* soon, I am eager for that day to come.

Mrs Robles, who never ceases to amaze me, even tho' she acts as if she were on her deathbed, still manages to remind me that being a French Aristocrat in a territory where scores of French are migrating, I am again obliged to wear a powdered wig for the duration of my visit.

The voyage passes quickly, as did my visit with my sister, who passed away this morning, I, having but three days with her, was all too short. Being barren, and her late husband having no kin, she hath left me sole heir to her vast estates here, and in Europe, and tho' I must concern myself with the settling of her estate, my mind is preoccupied with getting aboard the Merchant before it departs on its voyage to *Lisbon* this night. Should for any reason I be delayed, I shall miss the excitement of my Captain's derring-doo; ergo, I must hurry.

Stepping into my late sister's rose adorned carriage, pulled by her prized Connemara Pony, en route to the barrister's office, I tell the driver to hurry along.

Sheer Audacity
Location: 'La Baía de Todos os Santos'

Meanwhile, Captain Roberts is making plans of his owne

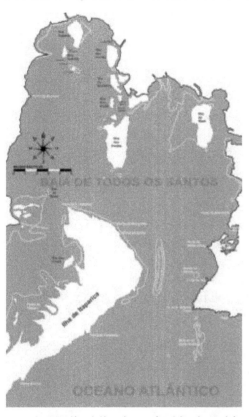

'Tis September 1719, and with the intention of watering and provisioning our ship for the long saile, I make course for *La Bahía de Todos los Santos*. By dusk, wee be steering into the harbour, where, to my delight, I espy a fleet of heavily laden Merchant ships, as does me crew, altho' their reaction be of a considerable difference to that of mine. This be a rare occurrence, and in an effort to study the situation, I give orders for the *Rover* to hove, during which time, a series of intense discussions are taking place all about the ship, the consensus is the same, me crew thinks to slip away unnoticed. My thoughts, however, be of a different sort.

The affluent presence of saile here explains to me the lack of such, elsewhere, these past two months and more. Here, anchored before me, almost within my grasp, is gathered the treasure fleet of the Portuguese, and I be a-knowing that anny one of these here ships will afford us our fortune, for each is sure to contayne, not onely a yeeres quantity of riches, but a hearty amount of much need'd supplies and necessities, all of which I surmise to be in good assortment, and it be most sure I am, that the heaviest laden ship ought be the richest in the fleet.

Nine weekes is a long stint for a pyrate vessel to saile without reward; however, I find myself to be greatly pleas'd, for in a remarkably short time I have impressed upon my capable, yet rowdy company, a great deal, whereby they have rapidly become a well-greased attack force, and altho' their manners and moral conduct have not changed, their courage is beyond compare, and in time, I knows their seamanship abilities will be without peers. Of late, however, despite the rigorous training, 'tis increasingly restless I see them becoming, and thus, even tho' much of which be consider'd by them to lay in superstition and omens, I knows I neede to restore within them uncompromising thoughts of my abilities, and yet, however superstitious the average seaman may be, a Captain, when blessed with a measure of good luck within his repertoire as I be, is revered. My luck, of course, not subscribing to superstition, is not onely to be proficiently skill'd in navigation and seamanship, but also in possession of a healthy supply of audaciousness. Altho' here and now, the flotilla within my view is just the good fortune I've beene needin', I know, 'tis not by luck that wee shall prevail, but vigilance, skill and cunning.

Back in Brazil. Offices of Franklin and Amberly, Barristers

"Then it's clearly understood, Mister Franklin, that Dragonwood Plantation; lock, stock and bank account, is to go to Jane; my late sister's devoted companion."

"As you wish, my Lady."

"And now onto the other matter I mention'd."

Shuffling the papers about on his desk, he picks up a rather large file. "Yes, I have the papers for the transference of ownership of the ship, *Willing Captive*, all ready for you. Lastly, your *'Last Will and Testament.'* It, too, is ready for your signature. I am impressed by the generosity regarding your staff, especially the Honourable Mrs Neville Robles, and the dispersal of your estate in case of either your death or disappearance for more then 5 years without a letter. Yours is a generous and kind spirit; however, there is one aspect, well, to put it bluntly, it's damn irregular."

"What bothers you, Mister Franklin?"

"Your bequests to Miss V'lé Onica, whom you state as having been born in Santa Monica, California. You've written here that she is heir to your collection of Gold Coynes, Banknotes, Jewellery, Estates or other Property, and your account at the Banque of England in Grocers' Hall. It further states here that you want the first three items sent by special courier to Harvard College, in the Collonies for safekeeping."

"I assure you, Mister Franklin, I know what I am doing. As you can see, I've made provisions for a sizeable endowment to the college," pointing at my notes, "in return for which, they are to provide for me a secure place within the college for my sea chest until my heir, or if need be, her heir, or theirs, calls for it. I'm counting on you to take care of the details for me. By the way, I have the only key to this chest, and I am sending it by way of a different courier to my kinfolk in the Collonies. My note to the College states that the heir will have the key and that only the person with the key will have the right to claim the chest."

"Of course, my Lady, to be sure, but the size of this bequest, being that it's for my files, I need to know the location of Santa Monica, California, and lastly, who might this V'lé Onica be who is to receive the bulk of your estate? Some sort of identity reference must be made that would dismiss any questions that may arise when/if she is to inherit."

"Santa Monica is a town in the Collonies. As for Miss Onica, she's by way of being a relative of mine."

"Yes, of course," he replies whilst smiling. "Still, however, some other article of identity is needed."

"Your point is well taken." Giving it some thought as I fondle the pendant about my neck, I am inspired by the unique piece of jewellery given to me by another ship's Captain. "I shall send to her this pendant." Removing it from my neck, "This 2-reale coin, set within an Aztec Gold bezel, is comprised of a skull & crossbones above crossed cutlasses. The claimant must possess both proof of identity and either the key, the pendant, or have proof of her identity or genealogy."

As I describe it, Mister Franklin writes down the detailed description. "I am sure that the pendant, and/or the key, together with your relatives' papers, shall be quite adequate. In regard to this last matter, I shall send a copy of these papers, as per your request, along with your note, to John Leverett, President of Harvard College, Cambridge, Massachusetts, a copy of which will be forwarded to your residence in Bermuda."

"I prefer to pick up my copy. Sailing at noon, I shall return at half past 11."

"I shall draw these up personally."

"Thank you, Mister Franklin."

Finally, as I am getting pressed for time, all the papers being duly signed, I return to my late sister's estate to change my dress and don my specially designed bustier before proceeding to the ship. En route, I realize the extreme importance that I have just placed upon both the key and the 2-reale pendant about my neck. Suddenly they have become the single most important items that I own, and as such, I must forever guard them carefully.

Whilst lacing me up, Jane, Trilby's lady's maid, informs me of the events of the day. "As ordered, my Lady, your trunks were packed and have bin stowed in yer cabin. Your late sister's open carriage is being loaded, along with her prized Connemara Pony. Lastly, the carriage you ordered awaits you on the south side of the veranda. It will take you with all speed to the longboat."

"And Mrs Robles?"

"She left for the ship an hour ago."

"Thank you, Jane." From my sister's barrister, I have learned that Jane, who is in her sixties, was my sister's nursery governess, who rose to the honour of being her personal companion. Such should not be rewarded by reducing her to a life of hardship simply because my sister has passed on. Of course, as her sister, I would no doubt know this already, and thus, I can not let on that such is news to me.

"You've been with my sister ever since I can remember, Jane, and I know from her letters that she thought a lot of you."

"To be in the Lady Trilby's service was my singular pleasure. I would like to think she was both satisfied, as well as happy with my services as both her lady's maid, and companion."

"She must've, Jane, to keep you on these 30-odd years. Such deserves a reward."

"Oh no, my Lady. I have a small pension and—"

"Be that as it may, I have already taken the liberty of procuring for you, a suitable reward." Taking from within the vanity drawer, drawn up on a sheet of heavy linen and rolled in scroll fashion, I hand her the deed to my late sister's sugar plantation. "You are mistress of Dragoonwood now, Jane."

Unrolling it, she gasps. "Oh no, my lady, this is much too generous."

Ignoring her objections, "I have furthermore designated a few articles to some of the remaining staff, but the bulk of her estate, and bank balance goes to you. You've more than earned this, Jane. I have but three requests of you whilst you reign as the Lady of the Manor."

"Anything, my Lady."

"Free the slaves and pay them an honest wage. Treat those who do you a service with kindness, and as your last act, be sure Dragoonwood is left in good hands."

"I shall, my Lady."

"Regarding the latter, I shouldn't delay too long in deciding on an heir. Choose well, but above all, keep your choice confidential. I must go now, but as a last word of advice, a secret Will in the hands of a trusted friend, as well as a sealed copy with an honourable barrister," my voice trailing, "and an additional copy in your locked jewelry box is best." Speaking loudly as I exit, "I engaged a seamstress who will make my sister's clothes over for you."

Meanwhile, Captain Roberts' plans proceed ⇁

In all, wee be counting more than two score of ships, two of which be 70-gunn Man-of Wars. The Lords, as does me crew, wishes to depart, silently and in haste, but I think otherwise saying, *"Nay — Wee shall attack!"* [B8 & 9]

The Portuguese Treasure Fleet, including the *Sagrada Família*

Continuing with enthusiasm, "Plundering brings not onely wealth in the form of Gold, Jewells and Plate, but also Provisions and other much need'd Necessities, and that which lyes before us, is in all respects, the wealth of a lifetime. To take such a prize would afford each of us a luxurious retirement."

During the course of council, my company be understandably dubious.

" 'Tis a large number of ships to combat, Captain," begins *William Main*, "and wee be one lone band of Rovers."

"With one ship," adds *Walter Kennedy*.

But as the plan formulated itself within my mind, knowing it to be sound, I propose it to them thus. "It is blessed wee be, for this night there will be no moon. Under the cover of darkness, wee will mix in with the fleet, and until the proper moment, the crew shall keep themselves hidden from view. Upon me word, ye and all of you, armed for bear, shall spring upon them. This me hearties, I assure you, will breed fear within their hearts."

With this plan, convincing the lot that the element of surprise, coupled with sheer audacity will see us thro', as did our attack on the *Isle of Princes*, I perswade 'em. Judging their reactions, I call for Bohea to be served all around, and upon the open deck I raise my china cup to toast that which will be our greatest victory, as I proclaim, *"Damn to him who ever lived to wear a Halter."* [B8 & 9] And in the doing is born the ritual that shall precede all future engagements, whilst also is born my jack. Standing full figure I am, 'Toasting Death' as it be called, and standing beside my image is a skeleton holding within its grasp, a flaming arrow.

Meanwhile, la Marquise & Mrs Robles board the Treasure ship ⌐

Having traversed the steep, narrow steps, Mrs Robles and I are helped aboard by two of the Portuguese officers.

"Thank you," I says to them. Of the two men, one of whom I met yesterday, is Tenente Duarte Gonçalves, the ship's first mate. 'Tis he whom provides the proper introduction.

"Capitão Cane, permit me to present her ladyship, a Marquesa de Espora Negra, and Senhora Robles."

"minha Dama, may I present Capitão Cane.

With a curtsey, "Boa tarde, Capitão."

Welcoming me aboard, the Captain offers a gracious bow, "Boa tarde, minha Dama. Bemvindo a bordo."

Extending my hand whilst bidding the Captain my thanks, "Obrigado, o Capitão Cane."

Graciously, the prepossessing Captain takes my hand, and speaking English with a heavy, yet well enunciated accent, gently brushes the top of my hand with his lips; after which asking, "minha Dama speaks Portuguese?"

Wanting to hurry to my cabin in order to change into the gown Captain Roberts saw me wearing in London, I pray my reply will dissuade the Captain from a prolonged conversation. "O suficiente para sobreviver, o Capitão."

"My officers and part of me crew speak some of English. The rest, I'm afraid, very little."

Smiling, "I'm sure Mrs Robles and I shall get along fine, Capitão."

"To help in that regard," turning to his 2nd mate while gesturing with his hand, "Allow me to present, Tenente Gamas," who presents a sharp bow whilst clicking his heels together. "Being the Tenente speaks English quite well, he not only has the honour of being your escort while you're aboard, he is also responsible for securing any requests you may have."

"And now, minha Dama," again taking my hand, gently brushing it with his lips, "I must be tending my ship, for we sail at dawn." Bowing to Mrs Robles, "Senhora," he departs.

Amid a slight nod of my head, "Obrigado, Capitão."

His Captain having taken his leave, Tenente Gamas, following his orders, proceeds to escort us to our cabin. Gesturing with his hand, "This way minha Dama. Senhora."

Making my way thro' the corridor en route to my cabin, which is situated just below the Quarter-Deck, I am grateful that, just as Lucifer promised, I was again fluent in the language needed at the moment, if not, Mrs Robles and I would have a difficult crossing to be sure. Reaching the door of the cabin, graciously opened by Tenente Gamas, I thank him, saying, "Obrigado, Tenente. I shall call on you later if I need you. Right now we wish to rest a spell."

"Very good, minha Dama. Senhora."

Closing the door, and seeing that Mrs Robles has seen to the unpacking, knowing that Captain Roberts will be along soon, and hoping he'll recognize me as the lady on the docks the day the *Princess* sailed from London, I change in to the Crimson velvet gown and underpinnings I was wearing where last he saw me. Nigh on an hour has passed when from my window I see what I believe to be, the *Rover* coming alongside. Tossing the items I am holding onto the bunk; I grab the front of my gown, and bursting out the door of my cabin, I rush out onto the open deck. Remembering that the *Rover* is trying to creep upon us, I quickly gather my composure, and positioning myself accordingly, I stand motionless in the shadow of the mainmast. As the ship comes alongside, my heart beats furiously as I search the *Rover* for Captain Roberts.

The Rover Approaches →

Me ship, as she sailes thitherward slow and quiet, creates No noise upon the water that is distinguishable from anny other a-swaying at anchor. As wee come abreast one of the smallest ships, a Portuguese crewman, who be standing along the larboard railing, noticing how close wee be, becomes concerned and calls out to his officer who joins him at the railing forthwith.

The officer, understandably curious as to my intentions, being all he canne see on board, is myself and my Quarter-Master, sends the crewman, to first notify the Captain, and second to escort anny passengers that may be aboard, to their quarters.

Seeing me within moments of his arrival, the Captain bids the officer to relay his query, and in such, lifting his voice trumpet to his mouth, and speaking with a heavy accent, nonchalantly asks, "Senhor, state your business."

'Tis laughable to be sure, thinks I, this treasure ship being so undisturbed by our presence. "An easie catch," says I quietly to my Bos'n who has joined me. "Wee shall have our pick of the fleet."

Seeing him standing there proudly upon his Quarter-Deck, my heart races with unmitigated excitement as every fiber of my being becomes flustered, but hardly a minute passes when I am accosted by one of the non English-speaking crewmen.

"minha Dama, Aspasia."

Somewhat annoyed by the fact that he's encroached upon my excitement, I, nevertheless, turn to face him, and replying in his native tongue, "Sim, tripulante, o que i la?"

Speaking with a solemn voice, he replies, "Todos os passengers deve retornar para seus quartos."

"Mas estou feliz aqua," I reply calmly.

Returning in kind, yet still speaking in a commanding tone, "Lamento, minha Dama. Ordens do Capitão."

Being robbed of the opportunity to observe my beloved by this crewman's insistence, I reply, "Essas ordens não me incluem!"

Noting my continued resistance as he repeats his plea, "Por favor, minha Dama, você deve chegar até você cabina, agora!" the crewman as he grabs me by the arm and roughly pulls me thro' the corridor towards my cabin.

Desperately trying to escape his hold as he hustles me below, shouting in disgust as he literally shoves me thro' the door, locking me in the cabin with Mrs Robles, I blurt out, "Damn!"

"My Lady!" says Mrs Robles scoffing me, "Your language."

Ignoring her, I frantically pull on the door handle, but alas, I am unable to open it. Turning around sharply, stamping my foot, I espy the portholes on the larboard side. Dashing to it, I fling the window open and proceed to climb out.

"My Lady! What pray tell be ya doing?"

"I shan't miss this opportunity to see him, Mrs Robles, nor shall I be denied the witnessing of his valour and fortitude."

"Whose?"

"Captain *Roberts*, of course."

Shrieking in horror, "The pyrate of infamy?" Rushing to me, grasping frantically at my skirt, "Nay, I shan't allow it. You may be killed or captured."

Uttering, "I should be so lucky to be captured by him." As I continue my efforts to climb thro' the window, speaking vociferously, "Lett loose of my skirt!" whilst trying to pull free of her grasp, "It's *John Robert!*"

Asking with much anxiety prevalent in her voice as she clings to my skirt tightly, trying to pull me back inside, "The man in London? How be ya knowing?"

Pleading as tears begin streaming onto my cheeks, "Just trust me to know what I speak be the true and lett me go, or I'll miss him, and ne'er shall I forgive you."

Seeing my tears, she knows that by some miracle I do know, and letts loose of my skirt.

Proceeding, I climb the mast. Once finding a good vantage point, I listen intently whilst clutching onto my precarious perch; I drink in my Captain's every movement.

My reply to the rather baffled looking Portuguese Captain be a simple one. Despite being within hailing distance, I make no verbal reply to him, giving to my gunner, instead, the word.

Without delay, I call out, "Open all Starboard ports!"

Forthwith, as the port doors fly open, sixteen cannon be hauled swiftly into place. Neede I say, that upon threat of a broadside, my opponent's face beholds an expression which can be deskrybed onely as sheer pannick. Most unbecoming for that of a commanding officer. Better to have been awestruck, 'twould 'ave beene more complimentary methinks; nevertheless, putting my hand to my mouth to better direct my voice, I holler, *"Hoist out yer boat."* B8 & 9

Before the echo dies, he, who is obviously the Captain's First Mate, points to his ear, saying, "Wee cannae hear ye."

Drawing my cutlash, I take within my grasp the cargo line affixed betwixt the underside of the mainmast's crow's nest and the quarter-deck, and whilst stepping up on some crates, I concurrently reach out to my Bos'n, "Give me that thing." With the voice trumpet's strap about me left wrist, and me sword in my right hand, I boldly swing amidship with great flourish, landing firmly atop the starboard rail. Placing the voice trumpet to my mouth, I demandingly state, *"Hoist out yer boat, Senhor Capitão, and come aboard me ship."* B8 & 9

To be in the midst of one of history's most daring piratical acts, I am enthralled; all the same, trying to keep my beloved in sight as he moves about is easier said than done; ergo, in my attempt to climb across some barrels whilst vying for a better position, I am sent plummeting into the crates below as they give way. Luckily for me, hard as they are, they do brake my fall.

Feeling rather indignant as I scramble to my feet, and finding that my A-line dress is torn at the waist in such a manner that my undergarments are more than a mite exposed, but not having time to change, I'm hoping that being dark in colour, my movements will go unnoticed as I venture aloft into the mizzen's rigging.

'Tis clear he be hesitant, and hearing a crash, suppozing the noise be the impendence to alert the fleet, I say once again, tho' now, being so close, I find myself speaking in relatively sombre quiet, dispelling anny doubts of my intent; his fear being that which prompts my attitude, as I say to him, "Non-compliance, Captain, is most unwise. Should resistance of anny kind be offered, to the hoisting of your pennant, will find you amid such an onslaught which I shall afford ye, and all of you, no quarter." At this moment, knowing now is the time to shew the strength of my resolve, I enthusiastically add, "See here me crew duly drawn up before yer eyes."

Upon my word, me crew, a bullish looking lot, jump to their feet brandishing their cutlashs and pistols, and upon such a shew of force, being that of a well-armed gang of cutthroats, the gulping Captain gives the order to hoist out his boat.

From aloft, I have a fantastic view. The Portuguese Master, ne'er before witnessing such audacious behaviour as that of Captain *Roberts*, is obviously in shock upon seeing the multitude of formidable pyrates before him, and such, he complies forthwith. Whilst waiting, Mine eyes take in his manner of dress; his rich Crimson damask waistcoat and matching breeches, being just as I knew they would be, are complimented by his white silk stockings, the full-bodied ostrich plume upon his tricorne, his medieval sword, and the 2 pairs of handsome pistols upon a silk bandoleer slung over his right shoulder. So stylish is his ensemble, such would be worn with much pride by even the most flamboyant of French Admirals.

'Tis a few minutes only before Captain Cane reaches the *Rover*, the place I long to be.

When the Portuguese Captain steps upon the *Rover's* deck, my beloved Captain, John Robert, gives his distinguished visitor a most gracious salute.

Within minutes, the grapnels are swung by the *Rover's* crew, who tie the two ships together with the deck railings being perhaps a dozen feet apart, but being not near enough, I can hear only parts of the conversation as Captain Roberts informs him they be, *'Gentlemen of Fortune;'* further stating that their business with him is merely the seekement of information. Determined to hear better, I begin to move to the other side of the rigging when suddenly I hear Walter Kennedy, whom I knows to be the *Rover's* Quarter-Master.

Drawing his pistol, "Look, Captain! There," points *Walter Kennedy*, "Aloft in the rigging. A man attempting to send a signal."

Affrightened by the sight of the pistol aimed at me, I freeze.

Looking thro' my spyglass, "Hold! 'Tis a woman." Moving about her form, and recognizing her goune, I have upon my face a glimmer of a smile. "Go fetch that wench."

Upon the order, *Walter Kennedy's* face lights up as he dashes off; swinging on a rope to the Portuguese ship."

Having seene the lecherous look in my Quarter-Master's eye as he departed, I holler, "Treat her gently, *Mister Kennedy*."

Looking sharp, the Portuguese Captain searches thro' the rigging using his owne spyglass, and altho' fitt to be ty'd, he sharply crys out, "No! Leave 'er be. I beseech you!"

Upon hearing the order, knowing that within minutes I am to be in the presence of, *'The Great Pyrate Roberts,'* my face becomes alit with joy, and as such, I happily start climbing down.

"Fear not, Captain." states Captain Roberts, "She shan't be harmed."

As I look down to the deck, that rat, *Walter Kennedy*, waits directly below, so in an attempt to avoid his grasp, I rotate my decent to the opposite side of the mast, but as my foot touches the deck, he seizes me nonetheless.

"Unhand, me you brute," I says demandingly; putting up a fierce struggle.

Laughing, "Oh, a fiery wench!"

Altho' my legs be kicking and my arms flailing, my grand struggle, holding me as he does, with my back to him, is futile.

Seeing me twist my neck and glare into his blue eyes, he looks back at me with a lecherous smile. " 'Tis fortunate for you that I be under orders to deal gently with you."

"I can walk, *Mister Kennedy*."

Setting me upon my feet, he says, "Go along then."

Seeing that my dress, being ripped away from the front of my bodice, is causing me quite a problem, *Mister Kennedy*, pulling out his dirk, and leaving only my frilly black pantalets to guard my virtue, slashes the front of my dress to the hem.

With a chuckle, he says, "That should make things easier."

"Will you not permit me to robe myself?"

"You will be presented as you are."

'Tis obvious, knowing this man's manner as I do, that I have no choice in the matter, and thus, taking the lead as instructed, I find myself walking before him with what's left of my gown trailing just in front of his feet as he follows.

Upon reaching the larboard railing, and being there is no gangplank in place twixt the ships, the strapping young Quarter-Master, after offering me the skirt of my gown as if it were an elegant train, takes a firm hold of the sheet. "Well Missy, canne it be the wench needes instructions."

Understanding his meaning, I snatch my train from him, and as I firmly wrap my arms about his neck, he takes a running leap, launching us towards the deck of the *Rover*, and altho' I shouldn't admit it, the ride, surpassing all the E-Ticket rides I've been on, I am unable to refrain from openly displaying the thrill of it all.

Landing backwards, I am unaware that my beloved stands but a few feet behind me, and in backing away from *Mister Kennedy*, I step right into Captain *Roberts*. Being startled momentarily, I whisk myself around, and finding myself close enough to be kissed, I am inundated with the intense breaths of desire as my body brims uncontrollably with lustful emotions.

After all these months, when I am, at last, standing before *the Great Pirate Roberts*, in his element, he is exactly how I imagined he would be: Formidable, Authoritative, Effectual, and Decisive. Coupling these with his Swarthy appearance and Majestic Carriage, all of which do great justice to that which he considers his uniform, well… the motif leaves me breathless.

Looking deep into my eyes, he asks, "Canne it be, seeing you possess the nerve to climb the rigging, and the obvious enjoyment regarding how you boarded this vessell, that my presence frightens you, ou y a-t-il une autre raison, peut-être physique, pour vous de respirer et de vous acquitter ainsi?

Knowing I could not openly divulge my reasons, I am grateful my Captain spoke French; nevertheless, displaying shyness before truth at first, I bite the lower corner of my lip. Then, looking at him with telltale eyes; and replying in Welsh, I demurely utter, "Yr olaf, Nghapten."

The Portuguese Captain, concerned for my well-being, as it would be his head should any harm befall me, asks, "Are you injured, minha Dama?"

"No, Capitão *Cane*, and to be honest," I says laughingly, "I found the ride exhilarating!"

Fearing what may happen should he lie, Capitão *Cane*, taking to heart the reports he had heard, and believing honesty would please the pyrate, speaks out. "Allow me to present la Marquise d'Éperon-noire, wife of a prominent nobleman, and kin to *Philippe II, Régent of France*."

"Widow," I correct him. Projecting a modest smile, "Mae'n bleser cwrdd â chi, Nghapten *Roberts*." Following with a well-cultured curtsey, low to the deck to demonstrate deference, I extend my hand to shoulder height to let him know I await his physical permission to rise.

Following thro', Captain *Roberts* places his hand beneath mine, and as he draws me upright, I say, "Diolch 'chi, Nghapten." Upon rising, hoping he recognizes my name from the letter I wrote him some months back, "Fy enw i yw Aspasia, Nghapten, and, as thou art thyself, I am fiercely proud of my Welsh heritage."

Addressing me in Welsh, 'tis obvious she wants to be sure that, I, alone, knew what she said, and knowing exactly who she is, and understanding the great care she has taken, I am cautious not to offer anny reaction beyond the glint of a nod and smile; ergo, to keep the others from assuming an acquaintance, I says, whilst looking her up and down, "Praise be, for wee are blessed not merely by beauty, and a member of *Philippe's* owne court, but a most intrepid lady to be sure, would you not agree, my Lord, *Kennedy*."

Further demonstrating his lecherous thoughts, "Aye. As an alluring woman of fire, as well as a high-ranking aristocrat, she ought bring a handsome price, eh Captain."

"Aye, my Lord, she would indeed, however..."

Having easily read his sideways glance, I am happy to learn that Captain *Roberts* approves of moxie in women in this era too, and thus, I pay no mind to Mister *Kennedy's* remark; still, however, I can not help but think I look a fright when so much I wanted to look my best for him, yet instead, I stand before he of whom I both admire and adore with muffed hair and tattered attire, nonetheless, as a new plan emerges in my mind, I, being forthright in nature, speak right out.

"Captain *Roberts*, a moment, please." Altho' I had wished it otherwise, the lot of them have their eyes trained on me, and thus, "I propose to bargain with thee. May we speak in private?"

"Beware of her, Captain, for the wench knows my name," quips *Kennedy*.

"Indeed; is this true?" asks he, his eyes narrowing a bit.

Realizing the gravity of my mistake, "Yes, Captain, it is. Having a particular weakness for thine adventures, and knowing the Quarter-master is almost always the first to board a prize, I deduced that this man," motioning to my left, "must be *Walter Kennedy*."

Smiling, Captain *Roberts* says, "It seemes, my Lord, *Kennedy*, that wee be better known than I realized."

Demonstrating that he enjoys the aspect of meeting a woman who finds him fascinating enough to read and learn all she can about him, I tells him, "Thine adventures, being in the papers more often than not, thou art talked about constantly."

I am taken by this woman who knows much about me, and me crew, but I dare not lett the crew know that I know anny more of 'er, and such, I suggest instead that she states her proposal openly so all may hear. "Feel free to speak your mind, my Lady."

Taking a deep breath, "Herein may lie tremendous wealth, but I, my dear Captain, have riches beyond the dreams of avarice." As I begin to speak what lies in my heart, the weighty spur being my own fears in the realm of things not going as planned, has finally given way to some relief. "The rub lies in the fact that I have no kith or kin who could authorize payment, but to that, I have a remedy, and it, Captain, be my proposal." After taking a moment, hoping that he, whom I know to be most insightful, utilizes his ever calm, relaxing demeanour.

Intrigued, "Pray continue, my Lady. What be your proposal?"

"Take me with thee upon the *Rover*—"

As I speak, fear is easily read upon the faces of the Portuguese seaman present, and such whilst one of them blurts out, "Não, minha Dama!" another crewman from the ship abreast us, shouts, "Não sacrificar-se para a gente como nós."

This sentiment is echoed by both his First Mate, and lastly, Capitão Cane, who attempts to reiterate his crewman's plea in English. "Sacrifice not—"

Giving my would be protectors assurance, "Por favor, Capitão Cane, não interferem!"

Switching to English so both Captain *Roberts* and *Walter Kennedy* can also understand me, "No harm shall come to me, for Captain *Roberts* is a courtly gentleman whom I trust implicitly."

Perplexed by such a statement, Captain *Roberts* asks, "Is her ladyship one to presume?"

"No, I am not. A man's life may change, Captain, but he himself generally does not."

Capitão *Cane*, speaking with grave concern, "Mas, minha Dama!"

Ignoring the Portuguese Captain, I continue speaking whilst looking into the eyes of my beloved. "I shall go with thee freely, and when convenient, providing no force that is not absolutely necessary is used with regard to these Portuguese seaman, I shall afford thee a king's ransom."

Before replying, Captain *Roberts*, looking deep into my eyes, seems to be studying me.

It is impressed I am. She knows not onely sev'rall languages, but the name of me ship, and some of me crew as well; and the way she speaks to me, unlike them of rank and privilege, is rather subservient in manner. I must confess I am deeply touched, and now, having met the woman who made such a spectacle of herself on London's dock, and altho' she seemes determined it be otherwise, I shan't reward her generous nature by subjecting her to the dangers and hardships of a pyrate ship; however, such must be done with tack, not onely as not to raise suspicion within me crew, or within the minds of the Portuguese, but to be sure that she, herself, does not feel snubbed.

Turning away from the others, hoping they belieeve I am considering her proposal, she walks a mite with me. "Wee have but a few moments, my Lady." When she begins to reply, I stop her with a slight raise of my

Bartholomew Roberts doodgebleeven.

hand. "Lett me say onely that I knows you be the woman who honoured me with the offer of a Captaincy; 'twas my dream fulfilled, but this is not then. Life on a pyrate ship is difficult at best. Supplies, more often than not, are woefully inadequate, privacy is scarce, and danger forever looms upon nature's most volatile element. With these being my reasons, my Lady, I must refuse yer offer."

Her face displaying despair, "Lett me add that ne'er would I subject a such decidedly feminine woman, especially one that I hold in high esteem, to the perils and hardships of a pyrate's life." Pausing a moment whilst turning around, "And now lett me tell the others of my decision, and reason, in such a manner that will not onely be most truthful, but will also prevent them from suspecting anny acquaintance." Thus, whilst again facing the others, I say alowd, "Not that having you aboard wouldst not prove a pleasantry, the hazards accompanied by your presence would be unceasing."

"What hazard could she possibly create, Captain?" asks Lord *Kennedy*.

"The French Navy for starters." Turning to speak to her Ladyship, "As for these Portuguese seaman, lett their fate rest within Capitão *Cane's* hands, not yours."

"Meaning?"

"Meaning, that providing Capitão *Cane* speaks true, No harm will befall them." Turning to his Quarter-Master, "My Lord, Kennedy, return her ladyship to whence she came."

"But Captain," bellows Lord *Kennedy*, "she be worth a fortune."

"Wee be Pyrates, my Lord, not kidnappers. All the riches anny man could hope for is here upon the water, and in our quest, wee shall not tarnish purity in the bargain."

Altho' reluctantly, the greedy *Walter Kennedy*, doing as he is ordered, replies, "Aye, aye, Captain," and goes to fetch the sheet.

As I am once again to be parted from the man I love, there are no words that can do justice in describing my sorrow.

Wishing not to be heard, Captain *Roberts* takes me gently by the elbow, and moving several feet to the starboard, he speaks to me quietly.

"My Lady, lett me say to you again that yer offer of a Captaincy, and the terms therein, was utter bliss, but things be different now. No longer am I an officer and a gentleman, but a pyrate, and aside from being hung and sun dry'd, I have no place within yer world."

"To me, thou wilt forever be a gracious and gallant gentleman, and as sure as I stand before thee now, I know the annals of history will paint thee bright."

As she speaks courageously from her heart, 'tis clear to see she be melancholic, and even tho' this be the first time wee have met, her ladyship's phraseology and mannerisms suggests she cares for me deeply, and of course the fact that I would enjoy her presence aboard my ship, the decision I have made is the onely realistic course to follow.

Seeing that *Mister Kennedy* is returning, "And now, my Lady, 'tis prudent we Must be, so off with you." Hoping she understands my reasons; wishing not to place her in anny danger, I shift my attentions to the business at hand.

Whilst awaiting *Mister Kennedy*, I listen to what is being said, and upon the asking which ship to be the richest in the fleet, I hear Captain *Roberts* assure the Portuguese Captain that his proper reply will achieve his forbearance, and afterwards he and his crewmen will be released without incident, whereas, misdirection shall yield not only an unpleasant end to his ship, and crew, but most especially himself.

As a tear rolls down my cheek, "Captain," continuing when he focuses on me, "may I be granted one small request before I go?"

"And what might that be, my Lady?"

"Wilt thou kiss me goodbye?"

Finding her request a pleasant one, I move towards her, and in the doing, despite the disapproving looks from those who heard her request, she presents me with a loving, nonetheless respectful, kiss upon my lips.

As *Mister Kennedy* waits impatiently, knowing I have no recourse, I turn towards him, and as I take a firm hold, as before, I hear Captain *Roberts* say, "As for her Ladyship, she and hers will be safe, regardless. On that, Capitão *Cane*, you have my word of honour."

Within less than a minute, I find myself back aboard the Portuguese vessel and *Mister Kennedy* is gone. Overcome by immense sadness, I slowly descend to the deck and begin to sob.

Belieeving my words, and rightly so, the Portuguese Master, without hesitation, whilst pointing towards the mouth of the harbour, names, the *Sagrada Família*. In the attainment of further information, 'tis learnt she mounts 36 cannon and carries a crew compliment of 150 men, a discovery that instills more than a slight amount of affrightment within me crew; however, these facts in no way dismay me. As for me crew, in observing my demeanour; regaining their nerve, they remain steadfast. Knowing all orders be mine alone, and anything less than courage will be deem'd by me as cowardice, wee saile towards our objective.

Onely now, whilst glancing discreetly in the direction of Captain *Cane's* vessel as wee depart, and seeing her Ladyship sink to the deck in despair, I realize without doubt, that her ladyship's feelings go deeper than I presumed. "She's in Love with me." says I; nevertheless, despite that I wish it were otherwise, for there is something about her that is familiar, I am, as wee saile upon the Treasure Galleon, *Sagrada Família*, obliged to turn my full attention to the task at hand.

'Tis difficult to see in the dark night, but still I canne see that which I be told to be true; as she is indeed a much larger ship, and observing the activity aboard 'er amid the lanterns, she boasts, without question, a vastly larger force.

Taking with us as our captives, for a brief time, that is, them being the Portuguese Captain and those of his crew who rowed him to my ship, wee saile forth. Coming alongside the heavily armed ship, I order my high-ranking prisoner to hail her Commander, ordering him to ask, *"How Seignior Capitain did?"* [B8 & 9], and to invite him onboard for confidential communication of some importance.

Doing as he is told, he replies, *"He shall wait upon you presently."* [B8 & 9]

Whilst awaiting his arrivall, as his boat must be hoisted out, I be paying heed to details, whereby a collection of actions made by the *Sagrada Família's* crew, I perceive that yon Captain is manoeuvring his ship into a posture fitt for defence; ergo, without further consideration, knowing that wee have either beene discovered, or at the very least, be under suspicion, I commence with me plans for refusal. Hollering, I says, "Raise our Jack!"

Immediately, whilst our black flag finds its place atop my mainmast, I holler, "Open all larboard ports!"

Forthwith, the gunn ports upon the *Rover* be manned and ready for action, and without delay, whilst the cannon be hauled into position, I cry out, "Grapnels at the ready."

Within a few moments, seeing the cannon be in place, my voice booms as I holler, "Fire!"

Upon hearing cannon fire, I rise to my feet and run to the railing. Noting that the ship I'm on begins to ready for action, I shriek, "No!" And lying to beat all, I shout, "I gave my word that upon my release, and the promise for the safe return of your Captain and mates, this ship would do nothing."

One of the few crewmen on board who speaks English replies, "That, my Lady, was a bargain made under duress. No one would hold you to it."

"I shall," speaking commandingly to whom I know to be the ranking officer, and consequently, Seignior acting Captain, "so will he."

"Who?"

"*John Robert*, of course, the scourge of the Atlantic, and the Captain of them pyrates." Speaking high handedly, "And I warn you that, should you, or anyone aboard this ship do anything to give a signal, or otherwise hamper their flight, I shall speak of it to my kinsman, *Philippe II, Régent of France*, and I assure you, it will lead to your downfall."

Upon my words no action is taken, and as I stand beside the larboard railing, 'altho' I durest not chear, nor shew even a modicum of enthusiasm, I watch *'The Great Pyrate, the Admiral of the Leeward Islands,'* make the most impressive capture in maritime history.

After pouring in a broadside, I immediately shout, "Grapnels away."

Without delay, me crew quickly draws upon the ropes, bringing the grand Galleon within boarding distance, and before the smoak clears, she be boarded.

Cutlashs drawn, and pistols ready, my men, boldly led by our brash *Walter Kennedy*, attacking her company without mercy, race across the deck of the treasure ship in a short, yet bloody clash of steel, whereupon, with a loss of but two from me owne company, many of the Portuguese fall. Leaving the *Rover* in the command of my Bos'n, I, together with Captain *Cane*, board the *Sagrada Família* just as she makes saile for the open sea.

By this time, much of the fleet is alarmed as flags bearing signals rise, and guns are fired in a desperate attempt to raise the attentions of them who be commanding the two Man-of-Wars that be lying at anchor still, and who else but yon commanders of them Warships could be blamable, in the highest degree, for 'tis their negligence that allowed such freedoms within the very fleet they were assigned to protect. They be unworthy of the positions afforded them, and yet in the world of so-called, *'Honest Labour,'* men of their ilk be the holders of such positions throughout the world, whilst men like I, who be undeniably more qualified, and had keenly sought well deserved positions of honour, they were deny'd me.

The *Sagrada Família*, is heavy to saile, but resolving not to lose so faire a prize, I order the ship's pilot to lay by the headmost of yon, inept Portageese Captains, as I shall call 'em henceforth, who finally, be spreading canvas with intentions, I be most sure, to give chace as they prepare for battle.[83] The lead Man-of-War, tho' of superior force, having in command, a spineless buffoon, is obviously affrighted, and therefore dursts not to confront me and my company alone, has chosen to heave to and await his consort, who be dawdling. Even so, their hesitation making our task of departure nigh on effortless, all speed is made in our flight.

Soon after, I call for the men to assemble before the Quarter-Deck, whereby, as battle will not again ensue this daye, I give to them much congratulations regarding their performance and courage.

Upon examination, the exceedingly rich booty consists of furs, jewells, a multitude of hogsheads and chests contayning sev'rall tunns of sugar, rolls of tobacco, hides, chains, trinkets, and 40000 Moidores;① also among the booty is found a magnificent gold cross

---

① Moidore: An old Portuguese gold coin equal to about 27 shillings (£1. 7-) 40,000 of them = £54,000 (1721).

embellished with diamonds of considerable size. This, methinks, admiring the craftsmanship, I be keeping for myself, whilst muttering, 'tis fitt for a King.' Soon after, I am to learn this be the case, as told me by Captain *Cane*, who says the cross was designed and intended for *John V, King of Portugal*. Superlative in all respects, 'tis truly well-suited as intended, and shall; therefore, be forever worn, for I resolve to be the Greatest of all Pyrates, and whilst hunting for myself a suitable gold necklace, equally rich in elegance, me thoughts be thus, for I have, this night, become equal in daring to that of *Sir Francis Drake*, Captain of a Privateer who was Knighted on the deck of his ship by Her Gracious Majesty, *Elizabeth I*, and *Sir Henry Morgan*, a Buccaneer and sea Captain, who in exchange for ratting on his brethren, was made Lt. Governour of *Jamaica*. All them pyrates, buccaneers and privateers who came before me, I shall surpass, and in the doing, make for myself, such a reputation and degree of atchievement in the taking of ships, that ne'er shall it be equaled, and with these thoughts heavy in me mind, I continue searching thro' the treasure until at last, I find for myself an immensely heavy, multi-strand chain of gold.

Having hung the cross upon it, I place the chain about my neck, and in the doing, I am knowing I shall wear it for all time.

Now that the threat of all danger has passed, 'tis time to release the Portuguese Captain and those members of his crew as was promised, and upon reaching landfall, it shall be done.

Carrying on, my company elated with more riches than ever did they durst to dream, have no more to think about beyond our destination; the tiny islet, *Île du Diable* (aka Devil's Island,)[N2] which lyes a distance of some 650 leagues North, off *French Guiana's* coast, within *Îles du Salut*. Here, off the coast of *Cayon*[1], canne be found a place of divine pleasure and much luxury, where the needs of me crew for wantonness canne be satisfy'd.

In due time wee pass the Amazon estuary off *Surinam*, anchoring as plann'd. Captain *Cane*, wishing a word with me, is brought to the Quarter-Deck.

"You wish to speak with me, Captain?"

"Aye, Capitão *Robert*. I wish not onely to thank you for yer kind treatment of myself and that of me crew, but especially for your generosity in not holding the Marquesa for ransom."

'Twas no neede to subject her thus, Captain." Speaking under my breath as I walk away, "She wanted to be captured, and by me specifically, that's why she proposed to me such a bargain." Continuing to quietly muse, "And now; our prize being astronomical, having provided sufficient means for the lot of us to retire in luxury for the remainder of our dayes, I feel I am now worthy of her admiration, and canne now, make plans to saile for Bermuda." Smiling a faint, yet forward looking smile, murmuring still, "But should such not come to pass, she and I shall still meet again, and soon; she'll see to it. 'Tis written in the heavens."

---

[1] aka Cayenne.

As me crew and I disembark, wee be greeted warmly. Almost immediately, considerable trade commences betwixt the Governour, factory workers, their wives, and me crew as they extensively exchange wares, but this is because those supplies which wee had sought, their owne nearing exhaustion, be the very items the settlers avidly bargain for. Fortunately, there is treasure to be found here, for in this river wee seize a Sloop from the Americas. Upon the questioning of 'er crew, wee gain knowledge of a Brigantine who sail'd with her in consort. This long awaited vessel that hails from *Rhode Island*, is said to bring forth the urgently need'd cargo of sundries, medicines and foodstuffs;

ABOVE: *Îles du Salut* (the top island being the famed, Devil's Island).

ergo, as there be very little to be had at the settlement beyond that which wee brought, wee await the inbound prize.

Hailing from the masthead, whilst rifling thro' the treasure laden, *Sagrada Família*, I hear the watch announce the afore descry'd Brigantine is tacking in.

Even tho' wee are to disband, a goodly portion of me crew, as a last hurrah, want to take 'er.

As Captain, feeling the responsibility lyes with me, I take a complement of 40 men consisting of those most eager to go, among whom be many of our Lords, including *Henry Dennis*, *Christopher Moody*, *Valentine Ashplant* and *Thomas Anstis*. Leaving behind, and in charge, as is customary, be our Quarter-Master, Lord *Kennedy*. He alone is to have charge of the prisoners, and not onely the *Rover*, but that of our newly acquired Portuguese prize as well. Her booty, together with the swag which lies in the deepest part of the *Rover*'s hold from the time of Captain *Davies*, and also the recently captured Rhode Island Sloop, which wee, in honour of our plunder in *Bahia*, have christened the *Fortune*.[SCHA1, HCA4]

Chapter Seven
Return to Plan B
Location: 'Britannia'

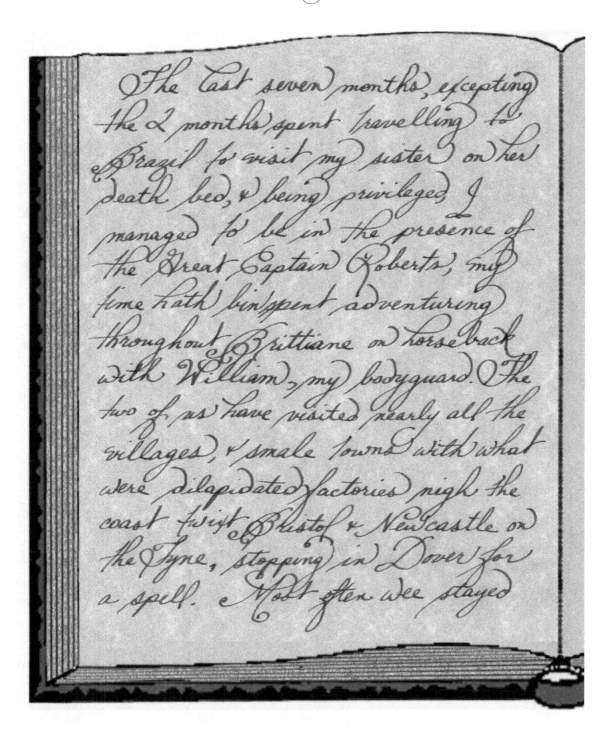

The last seven months, excepting the 2 months spent travelling to Brazil to visit my sister on her death bed, & being privileged, I managed to be in the presence of the Great Captain Roberts, my time hath bin spent adventuring throughout Brittiane on horseback with William, my bodyguard. The two of us have visited nearly all the villages, & smale towns with what were dilapidated factories nigh the coast twixt Bristol & Newcastle on the Tyne, stopping in Dover for a spell. Most often wee stayed

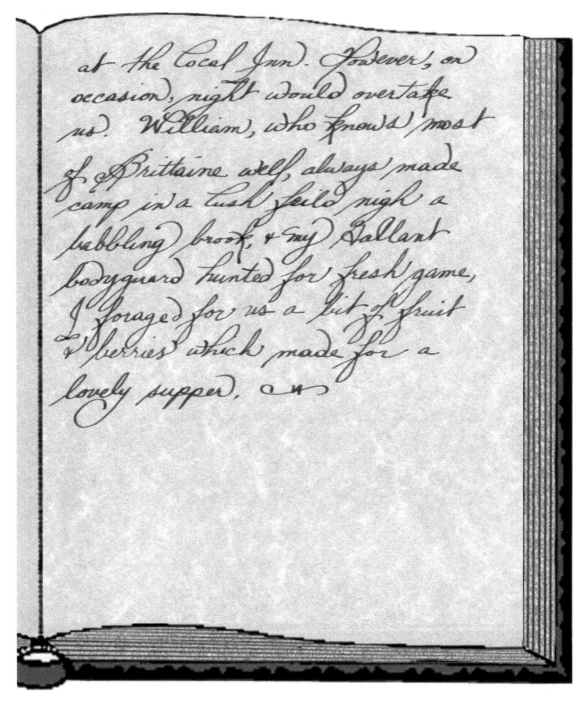

at the local Inn. However, on occasion, night would overtake us. William, who knows most of Brittaine well, always made camp in a lush feild nigh a babbling brook, & my gallant bodyguard hunted for fresh game, I foraged for us a bit of fruit & berries which made for a lovely supper.

'Tis just outside Newcastle on the Tyne we be this day. Here, we will rest briefly before heading back. Travelling in a barouche on the return trip, we will be making only 15 miles a day. Whilst William drives, I travel in both comfort and style. As myself, the chances of being stopped are nil, and with the large trunks William secured to the rear of the carriage, there's plenty of room to gather up all the cloathes that have been fashioned for the seaman within my beloved's crew that we'll then stow aboard my ship at Dover before we put out to sea; Dover being one of the Harbours where my ship is taking on lawful cargo. Soon after, we shall set sail for the tiny islet off the *Bermudas*.

The Inn here, altho' meagre, is quaint. Being fond of both scones and bara maen, I take several of each with me to my bedchamber. Setting my haversack upon the bureau, I take a handkerchief from the top drawer, and after folding the cloth about the breads, I place it in my haversack atop the hunks of cheese and fresh fruit. Going to take my bath, I stop by William's room.

Knocking upon his door I call out, " 'Tis I, Billy."

"Come in."

As I enter, "Well, my Lady, according to my calculations, wee shall reach Bristol come mid-May. 'Tis beene a long and tiring journey; art thou looking forward to the return trip?"

"Needing only to pick up the clothing in the various towns and villages where I hired dressmakers, I think it will be rather boring."

"I doubt it will be that simple, my Lady."

"But of course it will, William," I says smiling. "Your splendid record keeping, and superb management of this little enterprise, compiled with your vast knowledge of Britannia, has made this trip a pleasure to be sure."

"Thank thee, my Lady. Yer words are as generous to me as the helpe thou hast given to Britannia's starving populace."

"It's very kind of you to say so, but it is my love for a pyrate that has provided them with work and an income, William, not I."

"No, my Lady, 'tis thee. Most would not concern themselves so with the small towns and villages. All the cloaths, sails, rigging and cannon thou hast gathered could 'ave beene bought easily in the bigg towns and deliver'd with little fuss, but thou took it upon thyselfe to not onely provide jobs to the forgotten needy, but paid them top wages within their specialized fields as well. Thou afford'd them a sense of purpose and dignity, and even tho' for a short period onely, thou repair'd the factories in the bargain, and now they hast the means to be self sufficient for yeeres to come."

As per my request, a knock comes upon the door.

William says, "Come in."

Upon his word, both a chambermaid, and a serving wench carrying trays containing our supper enter the room. As the trays are set upon the table nigh the window, I see a newspaper with the word Pyrates written in bold lettering within the pocket of the chambermaid's apron.

"Would that newspaper," pointing to her pocket, "be for this room," I ask her?

"Yes, Madame," she replies, handing it to me.

As the table is laid, my complete attention is drawn to the article on the front of the single sheet newspaper entitled:

'!La Bahia de Todos los Santos. Attacked by Pyrates!'

"Very exciting reading, my Lady."

"Yes, I'm sure it is."

As I look further, I see clippings from several newspapers already atop the table.

Weekly Journal or Britiſh Gazetteer   13 February 1720
The pirates off Brazil, of the number of 2000 or ſo; purpoſe to make a baſe in Madagaſcar.

Weekly Journal   2 January 1720

By our letters from the Weſt Indies, we have an account that the pyrates continue to be very numerous there, and do incredible damage to trade by taking, plundering and deſtroying the Ships of all nations without diſtinction that come in their way.

Weekly Journal   2 January 1720

'Letters... tell us that a pirate ſhip of *14* guns in company of a ſloop of 8 guns had done a great deal of miſchief upon the coaſt of Brazil: and that in the height of the undertakings a Portugueſe man-of-war which was an excellent ſailor came a very unwelcome gueſt among them and gave the chaſe. The ſhip got off but the ſloop being cloſely followed and giving herſelf over for the reſt aſhore. There were *70* men on board, *12* of which were killed and all the reſt taken priſonerſs of whom the Portugueſe hanged *38* Engliſhmen, *3* Dutchmen, *2* Frenchmen and one their own nation.'

                        The following be the inventory carried by
                              the Brazilian Treaſure Fleet:

Daily Courant   6 February 1720

Liſbon. TwentyFirſt January. On the inſt. The Brazilian Fleet arrived, conſiſting of thirtytwo ſail.

    Man-Of-War that conveyed them: ſhips from the Weſt Indies, *3* ſhips from Fernambuco and *25* from Bahia de Todos os Santos.

Their cargo conſiſted of *7794* cheſts of ſugar, *128* baſkets of ſugar in cake, *21751* hides, *92* barrels of honey, *957* quarter-cheſts of ſugar, *11238* rolls of tobacco, *205* raw hides, *104* ſlaves, Large quantities of planks and Eaſt Indies goods. Gold in ſpecie and duſt not yet declared. For private people, *759128* octaves of gold duſt, and *164161* moedas of gold. For the King, *10270* of the ſame.

Weekly Journal or Britiſh Gazetteer   6 February 1720

The Liſbon Fleet from the Bay of All Saints, Brazil, has arrived. But one veſſel of thirtyſix gunns was taken by a pirate Ship (formerly an Engliſh hog boat) and two others plundered.

With their duties performed, the two young women leave the room, and it's about time too, for it's just about all I can do to contain my excitement as I tell my news. "I was there, William," showing him the article. "I was right there; I stood face to face with Captain Roberts. First, I was manhandled by that rat, *Walter Kennedy*, the *Rover's* Quarter-Master, and then, after swinging on a rope, we landed right on the deck of the *Rover*. It was exhilarating! Even now, just remembering what it was like, my heart beat faster."

Knowing that to be thy one ambition, William asks, "Why then did you not stay there?"

"I tried to get Captain *Roberts* to take me with him, but he wouldn't hear of it. Methinks he was concerned for my safety; he said as much, and nothing I said could sway his persuasions."

"And this dost not dismay thee?"

"Not in the least. My next attempt shall be far bolder, for it shan't be a mere woman of rank with untold riches in the offering, but, with the gifts we've been gathering, it shall be a woman who has risked all for him; besides, I think he likes me."

Belieeving the *Fortune* had beene made ready as ordered, wee sett out after the Rhode Island Brigantine, which apparently, in suspecting danger, fled. Amid the chace, an unsavoury current seizes our new sloop, and wee lose sight of the Brigantine, further misfortune abounds as wee are ensnared within a doldrums pocket and wee be condemned to drift upon a merciless sea.

For sev'rall dayes following; suffering such hardships as thirst and hunger that most cannae not realize, wee must now battle unfavourable winds and currents. Finally, when the sea pacifies, wee find ourselves 30 leagues to the leeward of whence wee came, and with the current still much in opposition to our desires, our fresh water nigh on gone, and having drifted all thro' the night, most of the men have lost all hope; however, as dawn breaks, finding ourselfes within sight of land, and able to anchor, 'tis praise I give to *Our Lord*, for I knows the *Almighty* is on our side.

Desperate to inform our mates of our extreame neede, I send forth Lord *Moody* together with five men in our boat to *Îles du Salut* to bring back aid. Still, however, wee who be left, must muster all our strength to tear up the flooring below deck, and still more if wee are to fashion a raft whereby myself and sev'rall others possessing a mite more endurance canne paddle to shore where, God willing, wee will find fresh water.

Shortly after landing, a babbling brook, and meagre, yet much welcomed nourishment is found. Quickly as we canne, we refresh ourselves, and upon having regained a measure of strength, wee return hastily to our newly acquired, *Fortune*, taking to those who be wither'd and dying, the much need'd water and nourishment.

'Tis three days later when our long awaited boat returns, bringing with her, grave news. Our owne suppozid trustworthy, 25 yeere old Quarter-Master, Water *Walter Kennedy*, who'd beene chosen and held, not onely in high esteem by much of the crew, but as one who be within our owne, 'House of Lords,' has abandoned us. 'Tis a tremendous blow it be to learn this man, together with them whom were to wait for our return, has absconded with both, the *Sagrada Família*, and, the *Rover* bursting with swag and necessities taken from Bahia, as well as, tho' durest I say, the lot be nowhere nigh as rich, all booty acquired in our preceding adventures. This, of course, which is echoed with much sentiments from us who be mortify'd, instilling within me, and the lot of us, an aversion to them hailing from Ireland, being how that wretched land robber, *Kennedy*, altho' Spanish, be of Irish decent.[B9,N3]

With regard to my first command, I shall be forever reminiscent, for ne'er does she reach Nevis, but as such events onely distress me, I shall return to the happenings of the moment.

A Brief 'Historical Narrative' of importance

With vague reports trickling their way, they came to learn that their once truſted Quarter~Maſter, after waiting nine days for them to return, believing they had periſhed, is the reaſon they left. This; however, does not abſolve them, for they ought not to have preſumed.

'Twas alſo learnt that after tranſferring the ſwag, which was the combined haul from ſix or ſeven ſhips, *Kennedy* releaſed *Captain Cane* and his crew; however, the greateſt betrayal was when *Kennedy* gave the *Sagrada Família* to *Captain Cane*, and if that was not injury enough, it was further learnt that the Portugueſe Captain ſailed to *Antigua* where he, in turn, gave the ſhip to the Governour of the *Leeward Iſlands* who then wrote the following letter to *Miſter Popple*, the Secretary Of The Commiſſioners Of Trade and Plantations in *London*.

> *February 16, 1720*
>
> *Secretary of the Commissioners of Trade and Plantations in London,*
>
> *Wee have of late heard of several pyrates that rove in these considerable seas, particularly one of about 30 guns that had bin for a considerable time upon the coast of Guinea where she had done a great deal of damage, afterwards took a Portuguese ship upon the coast of Brazil, which he brought to the island of Cayon, a French islet lying off of Surinam; and there plundered her of a vast booty, mostly in moidores, not valuing the rest of the Cargo (which consisted of sugar, tobacco and Brazil plank) would have sett the ship on fire but meeting a Rhode Island sloop which they took and fitted out for their use, they gave Portuguese ship to the master of the R.I. Sloop who with the Portuguese that were left on board brought her into Antegoa where I have ordered a merchant to take care of her, and what remaining on board for use of the owner or owners.*
>
> CSP 31/14

Furthering their diſmay, was learning that *Kennedy* ſailed the *Rover* to the *West Indian iſlands*. After which, when a Snow named *Sea Nymph* was ſeen on 15 December 1719, ſailing towards *Barbados*, is when *Kennedy*, as Captain, fought his firſt capture, and after a chaſe laſting ſeven hours, he caught and plundered her, but what infuriated Captain *Roberts*, and the others moſt was when *Kennedy* abandoned their formidable, and moſt beloved *Rover* in favour of another Snow named the *Eagle* becauſe the *Rover* was too much ſhip for the incompetent buffoon of a Captain with a hamhanded crew of five and twenty, and to add to that injury, the *Rover* was ſpotted by Major *Richard Holmes*, and *Mister Thomas Ottley*, and knowing they could claim the rewards, towed her to *Saint Croix*, a diſtance of forty miles to the South, wherefrom the following meſſage was ſent to Governour *Hamilton*, who added a poſtſcript to *Mister Popple*.

> Post Script for Mister Popple,
>
> I was told that last Sunday morning on the way to St. Eustatius and St. Thomas, that a pyrate lay under the Isle of St. Thomas, most of the pyrates being on shore. Major Richard Holmes of Colonel Richard Lucalls Regiment and Mister Thomas Ottley went to the ship at anchor. She was well-armed with severall pyrate colours on board. As they were not able to bring her to anny of my Inhabited isles, they tooke her to Saint Croix Isle where they left her in charge of officers of the Regiment till the Major could tell me. So I sent Captain John Rose of the Seaford to bring her back. He sailed on February 15.
>
> Mister Hamilton,
> Governor of the Leeward Islands
>
> CSP 31/14

Chapter Eight

Location: Coast of Caiana, South America

The Articles of Captain Bartholomew Roberts

1. Every Man has a Vote in the Affairs of the Moment; has equal Title to the fresh Provisions, or strong Liquors, at any Time seized, and use them at pleasure, unless a Scarcity makes it necessary for the good of all, to vote a Retrenchment.

2. Every Man to be called fairly in turn, by List, on Board of Prizes, because, (over and above their proper Share,) they are on these Occasions allowed a Shift of Cloaths. But if they defrauded the Company to the Value of a Dollar, in Plate, Jewels, or Money, MAROONING is their Punishment. If the Robbery is only between one and another, they shall content themselves with slitting the Ears or Nose of him that is Guilty, and set him on Shore, not in an uninhabited Place, but somewhere, where he is sure to encounter Hardships.

3. No Person to Game at Cards or Dice for Money.

4. The Lights and Candles to be put out at eight o'Clock at Night: If any of the crew, after that Hour, still remain inclined for Drinking, they are to do it on the open Deck.

5. Each man shall keep his Piece, Pistols and Cutlash clean, and fit for Service.

6. No Boy or Woman to be allowed amongst us. If any Man is found seducing anny of the latter Sex, and carries her to Sea, disguised; he shall suffer Death.

7. He that shall Desert the Ship, or his Quarters in time of Battle, shall suffer Death, or Marooning.

8. No striking one another on Board, but every Man's Quarrels to be ended on Shore, at Sword and Pistol.

9. No Man to talk of breaking up our Way of Living, till each had shared a 1000. If in order to do this, any Man should lose a Limb, or become a Cripple or in our Service he will receive 800 Dollars, out of the publick Stock, and for lesser Hurts proportionably.

10. The Captain and Quarter-Master to receive two Shares of a Prize; the Master, Boatswain, and Gunner, one Share and a half, and other Officers, one and a Quarter.

11. The Musicians to have Rest on the Sabbath Day, the other six Days and Nights, none without Special Favour.

After recovering from the ordeal that cost many men their lives, I sought to draw up that which would be our Articles. After conferring with the Lords and Commoners, all who make up my company, wee sett forth, on fine heavy paper, such to be that wee feel will best govern and maintain order in an effort to better preserve our society.

"In keeping with our aversion for the Irish, as be the one named *Walter Kennedy*, each crewman, excepting Irishmen, whom wee will forever hold responsible for the cause of our aforesaid peril, shall be forever excluded, will swear an oath of allegiance upon this here Bible, in my presence."

After commencement, those in our company, as each comes forth to sign or make his mark, I says, "These, which lye herein, be our laws. The breakage of such shall be considered a heavy crime against our society. All remaining offences, those wee deeme minor, or rather not important enough to require that of a jury, shall be under the judgment of Lord Anstis or myself, and us two alone, by way of thrashing or whipping, may preskribe and carry out such punishment; and lastly, within my Government, my power shall not be unlimited merely in chace and battle, and anny decisions pertaining thereto, but also, if I so choose, the destruction of anny who durst deny, or otherwise challenge my authority until which time, by majority vote, ye no longer wish me for Captain."

Hearing none objecting, I pick up my cup of tea, and take for myself, a healthy drink before continuing.

To replace the other officers, who belieeving their mates had perished, left with the *Rover*, a general election is held. *Jones* is re-elected Bos'n. *Henry Dennis* remains our Gunner, and the long time Lord, *Christopher Moody*, altho' his skills at navigation are not what they ought be, is elected Ship's Pilot; however, being 'tis I who shall provide all the navigation details necessary, shall permit Lord *Moody* to sett saile according to my preskribed orders, all shall work out well, and now, as our plans for retirement be dashed, 'tis time wee go forth and plunder, during which time wee shall continue to mete out justice on behalf of the populace who are greatly starved in that regard.

Our *Fortune*, altho' she not be as mighty as was our *Rover*, being it is a good crew that I have, shall serve me, and all of us, well.

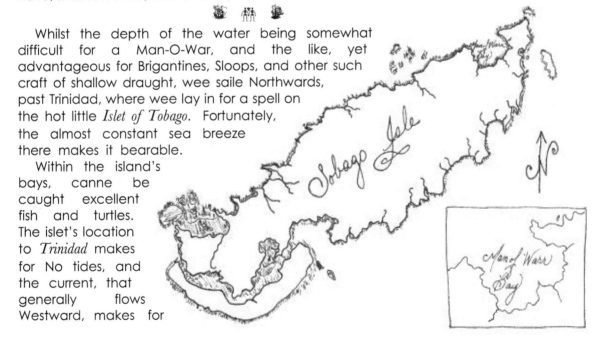

Whilst the depth of the water being somewhat difficult for a Man-O-War, and the like, yet advantageous for Brigantines, Sloops, and other such craft of shallow draught, wee saile Northwards, past Trinidad, where wee lay in for a spell on the hot little *Islet of Tobago*. Fortunately, the almost constant sea breeze there makes it bearable.

Within the island's bays, canne be caught excellent fish and turtles. The islet's location to *Trinidad* makes for No tides, and the current, that generally flows Westward, makes for easier careening than the *Carribee Islands* to the Northwest. Also here, there be Indians that dwele on the Northeast shore occasionally. 'Tis their scattered huts that are used to house the French Turtlers during their even more infrequent visits, whereas the sporadic trading habits of the London merchants who acquired possession of the Island in the yeere of my birth, suggests that onely a brief visit is in order.

Chapter Nine
Hatred Displayed
Location: *'St. Christophers, Barbadoes & Martinico'*

Within the *Laquary Roads* at Dawn, on 10 January 1720 wee find the Sloop, *Philippa*, lying at anchor, and whilst her gout suffering Captain, *Daniel Graves*,[sic] rests himself, the ship's crew takes their orders from the first mate, John Wransford, who espies our approaching canoe. Being ever cautious, he not onely warns off the encroachers, but also orders his crew to fire upon us. Seeing that the mouth of the smale harbour is blocked by our well-armed vessel, and that his cannon failed to deter Lord *Anstis*, and his band of scallywags, *Mister Wransford* sees to it that he and his mates quickly prepare for battle; however, as me prize crew draw alongside, the crew of the *Philippa* are boisterously informed that No quarter will be given should anny resistance be offered.

In swift fashion the *Philippa* is boarded, and having beene maneuvered to where she rests at anchor alongside me *Fortune*, wee anchor just off *Sandy Point*, but being a poor sayler, the *Philippa* is plundered onely, and whilst Lord *Dennis* takes her 2 cannon, Lord *Jones* carries off a cable, a hawser, and an anchor; returning once more, Lord *Jones* helps himself to some tackles. In the meantime, Lord *Anstis* orders the taking of her provisions: consisting of bread, 10 casks of oatmeale and 6 of beefe; a 60-gallon cask of rum, 300 pounds of sugar, and an abundance of cloaths, as well as all the Musquets and other firearms on board, together with 5 barrels of powder, 5 and 20 bales of goods, plus the smale amount of money found amongst her crew.

Having words with the officers and crew of the *Philippa*, I says, "Be it known, All of ye, that I alone have charge over anny prisoners, and being anny punishments lye in my hands rather than one who may not onely be much the harsher, but less forbearing than myself, ye ought be grateful." For obvious reasons, I cannot shew anny signs that common decencies be my master, lest the necessary terror that ensues in my presence would not exist, otherwise such would onely bring forth more death and destruction. "In spite of this," as I tells 'em, "it is ruthless I canne be, and have beene; ergo, 'tis best ye be remembering, *there is none of you who will hang me, I knows, whenever you canne clinch me within your power.*"[B8 & 9]

Strangely enough, so think all those present, I present to Captain *Graves*, an Indian and a Negro whom wee had taken off a French ship, and in what appears like that of an unprecedented gesture, is in actuality, part of my plan, for I knows that such an act will not onely enhance my reputation as a pyrate, but the telling of such a noteworthy deed will perpetuate widespread, whereby others will see the sense of yielding, and thus, they reap for themselves my favorable attitude, thereby atchieving victories without bloodshed.

This venture increases not onely our holds, but our ranks as well, for three of the *Philippa's* crew enthusiastically join me company, one being a most capable fellow named *Mister Sympson*, or rather, '*Little .David,*' as he is affectionately call'd by his mates.[C02]

On the 17th, nigh Trinidad, wee plunder the Sloop, *Happy Return* of St. Christophers, William Taylor, Master; where Robert Crow joined my company.[B2 page 40]

February, altho' busy, has not rewarded us. Our plundering of the Sloop, *Mayflower*, and a Bristol Trader of ten gunns nigh Barbados, brought little if anny rewards to justify our efforts. Wee further captured a ship from *Liverpool* nigh the twelfth named, *Benjamin*, who, altho' carrying a meagre cargo, wee detain her for three dayes.[C03]

As is customary, Lord *Thomas Anstis*, our Quarter-Master, is first to board prizes. The *Benjamin's* commander, being inexperienced, not onely misunderstands his name, belieeving it to be Hanse, but also, not knowing how things be done, belieeved him to be Captain.[①]

---

①Both the incorrect identification and spelling, believing, in error, that it would be the Captain who came aboard first, is found within the official records.[C03]

The 18th of the month brings us yet another prize, the *Joseph*, commanded. by *Bonaventure Jelfes*. Carrying a meagre cargo, and little provisions, wee proceed untill meeting up with the French pyrate, *Montigny le Palisse*, Captain of the *Sea King*.^{CSP-CS14} He and I, tho' for reasons that escape me, decide, in spite of my intense dislike of the man, and his ways, who, being like *Calico Jack*, is more than content to pick up the leavings like the carp and gulls, whilst I, true to my bold and decisive nature, wants ships onely worthy of me crews efforts; nevertheless, 'tis partners wee become.^{CO4}

All I canne fathom which possessed me, not that anny saile that has come within my reach has escaped me clutches thus far, be the notion that perhaps a combined force, sailing a league apart, will locate and plunder a sizeable ship carrying a cargo of riches worthy of our efforts.

Steering South by West, wee saile for *São Tomë*. Espying no sailes, wee continue on to Annamaboa, where wee anchor. 'Tis here wee careen, water and provision our ships.

A weeke having passed, wee be ready to sett saile, and by vote, wee return to the *West Indies*.

Sometime later, as time marches on, wee discover, despite our charity, having taken onely that which wee need'd from the recent ships encountered, being poor, as are wee, seeing not to deprive that which they did have, including the Sloop, *Philippa*, and not pressing into my service, their crews, nor stripping their ships clean as would most of them who call themselves Pyrates, or taking them as prizes, building for ourselves a formidable fleet, or as other, less than generous rovers who simply sett unwanted ships aflame, but does this on again-off again,^{W1} Governour *Robert Lowther* of *Barbados* pay heed and consider himself fortunate that, 'twas I, and not some others band of rovers, and lett sleeping dogs lie? No, not this pharisaical son of an English landowner.

Below be the telling of it.

But first: A Brief 'Historical Narrative' of Importance

Upon the *Philippa's* arrival, when the ſhip's log, which duly contayn'd the incident, when reported to the Governour, as preſkrib'd, many were outraged. But upon hearing the ſtory, one muſt aſſume that 'twas either Captain *Graves*, or one of his crew that relay'd Captain *Roberts* goodwill geſture, becauſe the incident was more or leſs ſhrugged off. Sometime later, numerous tellings began to circulate, each of which deſkryb'd in ſome detail, the prodding, by means of continual communiqus, obviouſly by them who did not appreciate Captain *Roberts* niceties, ſought retribution, and thus, the loon of a Governour, who no doubt did ſo in an effort to better ſecure his precarious poſition, allowed himſelf to be ſwayed. With all ſaid and done, two veſſels for the expreſs purpoſe of hunting the pyrates, one a Naval Veſſel, the other, an appropriated merchant.^{CO2}

Conſidering there be no Man~of~War, or other ſuitably armed veſſel within that port, the *Summerſett* Galley was outfitt'd with 16 guns and one 130 men. Alſo therein, lain the merchant Sloop, *Philippa*, which was outfitted under proteſt with 6 guns and 60 men. The petitioners, feeling 'twas they who paid for the refit, wanted the former Captained by a man of courage and fortitude. In port, by chance, was one Captain *Owen Rogers* of *Briſtol*, a man duly noted for his ſeamanſhip, bravery, and leaderſhip. Qualities that earned him, not only command of the Galley, but a ſpecial commiſſion from the aforemention'd Governour, who himſelf, appointed Captain *Rogers* Commodore.^{CO2}

Having no objections from the newly appointed Commodore, the *Philippa*,[CO2] remained under the command of, Captain *Daniel Greaves*, also of *Barbados*.

It be mid-daye this 26th daye of May 1720, and a fine Friday it is. As I stand beneath my jack, sipping Bohea, I of course know nothing of the aforemention'd goings on that be taking place within the port of *Barbadoes*. 'Tis beene a lazy daye when suddenly sighting the aforesaid vessels, I forthwith give the order to give chace.

Sailing easily upon them, I order our manoeuvring accordingly to flank their stern. Once in range, I order the firing of our forward cannon, givin' 'em a taste of our gunns. Expecting both to strike their colours and yield as all others have done since the *Experiment* at *Cabo de Lopo Gonsalves*, I brazenly order my pilot to saile betwixt them. As wee course on thro', seeing an inordinate number of crewmen, yet neither laden with cargo or provisions, I determine they not be ordinary vessels, but rather outfitted with specific purpose.

Onely moments pass when, upon recognizing the Sloop as, the *Philippa*,[CO2] I am suddenly knowing yon ships have beene sent out specifically to engage me, and knowing also that my charitable acts of grace are to be repaid in blood, an overwhelming resentment settles deep within my bones. In my wrath, I hearken, "It be a trap," and hollering as fury beset my veins, "Spoiling for a fight they be, my Lord *Dennis*. Let us not disappoint them."

Storming across the deck, barking orders, I shout, "Rig all sails!" and as wee pass close behind 'er, whilst concurrently gesturing my forearm, I bellow, "Rake her stern!" with obvious vengeance.

Immediately, as my Gunner pours in a broadside, our consort, the *Sea King*,[CSP-CS14] Captained *le Palisse*, as he makes for an immediate and hasty departure without firing a single shot, portrays him exactly for the scurvy dogg that he is. Despite his cowardice, I holler, "committed us I have, and fight wee shall."

Despite the odds being against us, leave wee shan't, at least not before reparation has beene dealt to Captain *Graves* for his return gesture regarding my previous benevolence. Whilst me men drag on every inch of canvas the yards canne pack, both Warships force us to receive their broadside. At full tilt, my men return both in grand style, which is the commencement of a fierce engagement that takes place in a running battle as wee get off.

As both opposing ships fire their cannon continuously, as do wee, my gunner uses every manner of shot available to us, including a belly full of hot coals from the galley.

Having a well trained crew, the *Summersett* Galley, keeping abreast us, is,

without question, being led by a most determined man whose mettle not onely impresses, but infuriates me as well.

With the attacking Galley, free from burden, and our vessell heavily laden with a full store of provisions and fresh water, extra anchors, cannon, and our holds bursting with swag, 'tis obvious wee will not escape.

Having no choice, I holler, "Heave the cargo and heavy stores over the sides, men!"

Reluctantly following the order, me deck crew, whilst other crewmen hurriedly bring up heavy stores from within the holds, the deck hands jettisons much of our burdensome cargo from the open deck, and yet, after much effort, it not be enough, for the Galley, whilst relentlessly hammering us with constant bombardment, is sailing exceptionally well, and altho' wee return her fire in kind, wee make no headway in our flight.

To my dismay, with our remaining stores weighing us down in the water, still, I am forced out of desperation to order the jettisoning of all wee have acquired since the signing of my Articles, and thus, holler to my men, *"Get clear or Die!"* B8 & 9

Understanding my meaning, me crew Frantically shedding our remaining burdens in swift fashion, heave the majority of our fresh water and provisions overboard together with anchors, newly acquired cannon, shot and powder; all items of hindrance, excepting that swag in the lower hold, is pitched over the side, and this accomplished, our *Fortune*, now light'ned, gets clear.

From this occurrence is born a hostility so fierce, that I cannae stomach the mention of those who be from, or otherwise have affable relations with *Barbadoes*, and this I be upholding to both my selfe and that of my company, that when meeting ships whose crew be men of their ilk, wee shall be particularly severe, whilst not at all to them who strike their colours without incident.

MORE NEWS ITEMS

TO THIS INCIDENT WEE LATER READ THE FOLLOWING NEWS ITEM.

Weekly Journal   *25* June *1720*

From Portfmouth in N. Hampfhire they tell us that a brig arrived there from Barbadoes in *22* days and reported that a Briftol Galley and a Sloope were out fitted to take a pirate Sloope of *12* guns that lay to the windward of the ifland; they came up and engaged her, but the pirate, having a great number of men on board, gave them fuch a warm reception that they were obliged to go back to Barbados without her. In this engagement many men were loft on both fides.

Sailing on, wee have little left but our pocket money and personal jewelry. Twenty of me crew have died thus far, and more of the injur'd shall follow them to a watery grave. Not having a surgeon, as *Archibald Murray* had beene amongst them who left with *Kennedy*, wee make our wounded mates as comfortable as possible, and whilst sailing for the isle of *Dominico*, wee bandage our mates as best wee canne. Upon arrivall, having beene careful to maintain peaceful relations with the Spanish, wee take on a fresh supply of water and provisions.

Trading our welcomed booty betwixt the inhabitants, who being in a rather neglected outpost, cares not the means by which wee afford said trade, nor our profession.

To me and my crew's surprise and outrage, wee discover thirteen English seamen who were sett ashore by a *French Guard de la Coste*, detached to *Martinico*.

As seasoned recruits, having had their fill of so-called honest labour, the lot of 'em enthusiastically join our ranks.

Their spokesman, *Robert Botson*, says that nigh on three weekes ago they had beene taken off two ships, one being from the Collonies, and the other being the Sloop, *Revenge*, belonging to *Antigua*, which had beene seized by the aforesaid Frenchies, and it was them who Marooned them in this place.^{HCA3}

Upon the hearing of such infamy, I propose to me crew the commencement of a worthy occupation as *Avenging Angels*, telling them that with piracy being the means to atchieve this end, and vengeance being the force that will drive us to victory, they will be handsomely paid. To my delight, my proposal being well received, our new careers as, '*Vigilantes,*' as well as, '*Gentleman of Fortune,*' is born.

Altho' our *Fortune* be in dire neede of careening, I be against *Dominico*, for it not, in my judgment, be none too suitable or proper for our task, whereby weighing anchor, wee saile directly for the *Grandillos*.

Hauling our vessell into a lagoon at *Corvocoo*,^{N12} great speed is made in the careening, watering and provisioning of our Sloop, during which time, being little more than a weeke, I have deduced from the accounts told by our new English recruits, that *Trepassey* being the destination of the scurvy Frenchies from *Martinico*, it is there where wee shall go, and by me word, wee shall deal the lot of them a severe blow of our idea of justice.

After leaving, wee learnt that my judgment, once more, is right on both occasions, for it came to be known to the French colony that the Governour of *Martinico*, having equipped and manned two vessells, had sent them forth to not onely seeke me out, but to destroy me, first at *Dominico*, secondly, at *Corvocoo (aka Carriacou,)* and again at *Martinico*, for those Frenchies had sail'd into the place wee had departed the night before, onely hours after wee had weighed anchor.

'Twas fortunate timing to be sure, especially considering that it was by chance alone, and not from anny fears of discovery, that my company, hungry for vengeance, made haste from the island. For myself, *Trepassey* is where wee will embark on our new career, wherewith, wee shall effectually avenge our 13 new mates in the process.

'Tis the beginning of March. During our leisurely saile to *Newfoundland*, wee be amus'd by many diversions.

These new men, and all those upon the ships encountered by me, I must allow them to presume the worst in order to atchieve an easie victory, and as a result, belieeve my words. In turn, numerous stories telling the consequence of non-compliance verses those who tamely submit, for it being necessities, provisions and valuables that wee seeke, and not lives, spread swiftly. To those, it must be said, that harsh treatment shall be apply'd, are them who seeke our destruction, especially the ship's Masters who ridicule, or otherwise

BLOOD and SWASH, The Unvarnished Life (& afterlife) Story of Pirate Captain, Bartholomew Roberts......pt.2 "THE WILLING CAPTIVE"

impugn my honour when it be them, and the merchants they serve, who be the ones that have committed crimes upon the greatest number, not I, and as such, thro' the spreading of my forbearance, and how to atchieve it. As a result, colours are struck, quarters call'd for, and as so it should be, is respectfully granted.

In April, wee plunder the Dutch Guineyman, *Jeremiah and Ann*, from whom wee take on fresh men.[B8&9] Two dayes later, off *Cabo de Lopo Gonsalves*, wee plunder another vessell, which, by chance, also bears the name *Experiment*.[B8&9]

NEWS ITEM
Daily Poft　　　　　　　　　　　　　　　　　　　　　　　　7 May 1720

By a fhip arrived this week from Barbadoes we have an account that the pyrates continue upon that coaft and few or no fhips efcape them; that fome they plunder, others they carry carry off which together if an incredible detriment to the trade.

Chapter Ten
A Lady's Well Laid Plans

Location: 'Small Isle nigh Bermuda's Coast'

Time, as it always does when one needs every moment, has flown by, but at last, after more than 18 months preparation, the great day is finally here; my ship, which cost a considerable amount to build and provision, is loaded to the hatches with good faith offerings, and ready to sail.

For the past fortnight, since arriving in Bermuda, I have been plagued with numerous objections regarding my sail, but to their chagrin, there is nothing they can say that will keep me from my goal, and outside of Mrs Robles and William, not a soul knows where I plan to venture, and early this morn, whilst jerking my chin at those who persist in trying to tell me how to run my life, I tote the perishable supplies on board as, William sees to the livestock.

Over these past months whilst procuring my cargo and supplies, William and I, having ridden like the wind, have journey'd great distances overland, and altho' our journey has been swift, resting a day here and there only when necessary, we have enjoy'd Britannia's serenity and lush countryside.

More recently, and much to the contrary, life aboard the *Willing Captive*, which be the name I have christened my elegant ship, has been most comfortable. Mrs Robles, William and myself, having spent much of the past 3 months at sea learning to sail, had, until this day, a splendid crew headed by Lieutenant Main, the officer who escorted me to the courier office where I met William, has returned to Britannia only last night, and now, having become proficient sailors during the gathering of the contraband goods located within various coves 'twixt Dover and the Northern tip of Scotland, and around to Bristol by way of Haverfordwest, we are prepared to sail across open water to Bermuda.

At last, with Mrs Robles at the wheel, while William weighs anchor, I stand ready to hoist the forward jib whilst saying a little prayer to Our Lord, hoping that our training be sufficient, regardless.

As the great ship begins to course forward smoothly, William rushes to my aide and together we hoist the remaining jibs, which alone will be sufficient until we be clear of the bends.

Once in open waters, and beyond the sight of land, we unfurl her spinnaker. Being so large a sail, William is doubtful at first as to its manageability, but it does not take long before he finds the sail rather easy to control, and 'tis most pleased I am to find that even with just us three, my ship is incredibly yare, and in addition to her impressive size and graceful lines, the *Willing Captive*, unlike most other ships which are fitted with a whipstaff, is steered solely by way of the relatively new, ship's wheel, which I am hoping, together with her generous allotment of innovations and conveniences, including an infirmary, my Captain will be decidedly pleased.

Months ago, from a smuggler who helped with our cargo, I learnt of a tiny islet nigh Bermuda where those engaged in nefarious activities go for provisions and fresh water. What makes the islet special is its perfectly camouflaged rattail shaped inlet, which do to the quality of its illusion, makes the island appear to have no place to make a landing.

The journey takes most of the day before reaching the little islet where I believe my beloved will come for fresh water and provisions. Having sailed clear around, we enter via a rock bordered narrow inlet that does in fact project a natural illusion of solidity. Carefully navigating thro', we find the hidden lagoon the smuggler told us about and drop anchor. After rowing to shore, while William gathers wood and kindling, and Mrs Robles sets up a makeshift camp on the beach, I go foraging. About half an hour later, returning with a basket of fruit, I tell my companions that the smuggler spoke true, for this small uninhabited islet is in fact brimming with edible vegetation, fruit trees, timid game, fowl, and fresh water. It's a true paradise.

It has been nigh on a fortnight, and today, as I stand on the bow, just about to cast my fishing line, I sight a sail, and as my heart races, I pray it be he whom I revere.

"Look," says I, ecstatic as I turn to Mrs Robles and point.

The weather is perfect, and as I wait breathlessly for the vessel to come closer, Mrs Robles becomes more and more concerned.

My elegant, 180 foot Ship, is larger than any of Captain *Roberts*, and as the still unidentified ship draws nearer, I pray it be, the *Fortune* stopping to take on water and provisions.

William, who had been below deck preparing the fish he had caught earlier, comes topside to see what be the cause of the ruckus, for I am hopping up and down in delight.

"What if yon ship not be the one you seek so desperately, my Lady?"

"You would think of that, Mrs Robles," I says to her smiling.

As the ship approaches, no more than a mile distant, I find myself surging with anticipation as I unknowingly place my hand upon my chest. "I must change!" Grabbing my skirt, I spin around quickly and make my way first to the main deck, "Come help me, please." Hurrying to my cabin below, Mrs Robles follows close as she can behind me.

Untying the lacings of my bodice, "my Lady, you must calm yourself."

Removing my rather plain garb hastily, "I'm trying to, Mrs Robles;" kicking the pile of clothes out of the way, I add, whilst donning my crimson evening goune, "truly I am."

Moving about so, Mrs Robles can hardly finish the lacings. "This Captain *Roberts* of whom you are so determined to be acquainted, will not be impressed by you if you continue to act like a giddy child," and thus, yanking hard upon the cords, she forces me to stand still for a moment. Tying the strings in a bow, she pats me on the back, saying, "All finished, my Lady."

"Thank you." Returning to the bow, I see the approaching vessel has furled all but her lower jib.

As I stand beside him, William says, "I have carefully looked her over, my Lady, yet I can espy no flag identifying the ship, nor any indication that suggests she be a pyrate. Do you not find this to be odd?"

"Yes, William, I do. Captain *Roberts*' flew his jack 'round the clock." Noting my fervent demeanour, William hands me the spyglass.

Suddenly shrieking, ecstatic to see the jack I know so well, knowing that the worst I can expect would be a warning shot across my bow, I dash below quickly to joyfully inform Mrs Robles. "He's here, Mrs Robles," says I, breathing hard from excitement. "He's really here!" Turning to make my way back up to the Quarter-Deck, "He'll be here soon. Please begin to heat the bath water and prepare the meal for myself and Captain *Roberts* as plann'd."

Convinced I've lost my wits, she none the less complies. "All will be just as you request'd, my Lady, even if we hang for it."

Chuckling as I begin to run out of the cabin, again, Mrs Robles stresses, "Command yourself!"

Stopping short, I look back at her, "Thank you, Mrs Robles," and taking a deep breath, I gather my composer and exit the cabin as a well-bred lady ought.

Standing on the Quarter-Deck of my Ship next to William, I search for my beloved thro' the spyglass when I suddenly feel frighten'd. "Suppoze I hold no attraction for him. Perhaps that's why he would not take me on his ship in Bahia. What if he's not onboard?"

"Methinks you have no call to distress yerself on that score, my Lady; Captain *Roberts* will take to you, of that much I am certayne. As fer him being aboard, where else would he be."

Smiling at him, I again raise the spyglass, and as I see a man on the approaching ship raise his, I immediately lower mine, hiding it behind my back.

"What is it, my Lady," asks William anxiously?

"Someone from the Sloop is looking us over." Altho' unbeknownst to me, 'twas Captain *Roberts* himself, who was having a gander, just before handing it to his Quarter-Master, Lord *Sympson*.

"'Tis important, William, that we in no way look threatening."

"Look at the size of that ship," verbalizes one of me crew, "She must be 180 feet."

"And fresh looking," Remarks another.

"Yon ship bears what appeares to be a Coat-of-Arms, a Red Dragon wind sock, and the white flag. Could be a peaceful traveller who stumbled into the cove and merely wishes to stave off trouble, or a ruse, for no smuggler or pyrate would raise such flags."

Speaking to my Lord *Sympson*, whilst handing to him the spyglass, "You boast knowledge of heraldry, what do you make of yon pennant?"

Taking the spyglass, my Lord *Sympson* looks sharp. "It appeares to be the banner belonging to the late Marquis d'Éperon-noire."

Recognizing her ladyship's name at once from the letter given me on the docks some months back who was also the same woman who kissed me in Brazil, I do my utmost to contain my delight regarding her tenaciousness, and therefore, in an effort to seeke information indirectly, I play ignorant. "Do you know anything about him?"

"He was a favourite courtier of *Louis XIV*, of some importance who enjoyed not onely immeasurable wealth, but power. No man would dare fly the pennant belonging to one so honoured if not entitled, such would mean his head should the crown get wind of it."

"His son perhaps?"

"The Marquis sired no children. It is said that both his wives were barren."

Thinking the woman who offered me a captaincy is a passenger aboard the elegantly appointed vessel, I utter, "Do tell..." as I happily remember meeting the woman in Brazil, and altho' she had beene on board the *Rover* briefly, I knew then that wee would meet again; still, things being as they are, I must guard my manner and keep these thoughts to myself. Fortunately, the onely member of me crew who both saw her up close, and also heard her name, was *Walter Kennedy*.

As our *Fortune* draws near, my Lord *Sympson*, who is generally addressed as *Little David* by me crew, noticing the absence of cannon and crew, says, "I canne see no crewman nor cannon on board. Wait!" chuckling, "Now there be a sight to behold."

"What is it? What do you see?"

Chuckling still, "Look for yourself, Captain." Passing the spyglass, "Aft, Captain, standing upon yon Quarter-Deck."

Looking through the spyglass once more, and knowing fer sure, mine eyes open wide, and for a moment I find myself paralysed with delight. Amid a noise within my throat, I thinks to myself, 'It is she; and flying a Red Dragon wind sock too.' But being cautious with respects to her identity, I create a bit of a falsehood of amazement in front of me crew by exclaiming, " 'Tis a woman!"

By now, I'm sure that they be close enough to see I am female, and except for William, quite alone on deck. I am also sure their first inclination is to believe my ship is a velvet trap with myself as bait. I, however, knows the crew will know differently once they search and discover only us 3 on board, and thus, will be delighted with that which be contained within my holds. As for Captain *Roberts*, I pray he will remember me.

As a gesture of goodwill, not only do I have the cannon, munitions and cloathing that William and I have spent months gathering, but also a rich supply of many staples and luxuries, fruit, meats, necessaries, and an apothecary chest, as well as 100 bottles of Madeira, 1000 of beer, and of course a huge supply of brimstone, potassium nitrate, and coal.

As this moment finally arrives, I am very happy that a little more than eighteen months back, when Captain *Roberts* was a ghost residing in my home, that I had sought his opinions concerning women's clothes. I am sure that in the present, knowing his specific tastes, as well as proper etiquette and deportment, will greatly enhance my efforts, and such being the case, I outfitted an entire wardrobe composed from the elegant attire throughout the ages that he himself chose. The Crimson gown I am wearing this day, replacing the one that was ruined in Bahia, was created just for this meeting. I am also wearing a necklace similar to his, only mine being fashioned out of Sterling silver, as well as the garnet and diamond dragon heads ring, also Sterling, that he placed upon my ring finger, but being that had been in another time, when he was within mine; and now, blissfully I hope, being in his, I hope to again win his true heart.

My ship's colors are White, Crimson and Black. The top of her hull is white, as is the open deck, masts and all bulkheads and overheads. Her sails, the lower part of her hull, plus all adornment are Crimson, trimmed with a fine black pinstripe, separating the Crimson from the white. To enhance my ship's opulence, the lanterns that light my ship by night, made of Bronze, are quite elegant upon the bright whiteness of my newly painted ship.

One of the 3 special gifts for my Captain is a specially bound bible that I intend to present to him as a gift shortly after he comes on board. Time being short, I can only hope that I know my beloved well enough to awaken his desires, later his affection, and eventually his love. To do this, I intend to not only cater to that which I know he enjoys, but by honoring his beliefs; and lastly, being that I know he loathes loose women; myself, being a well-bred lady of practiced abstinence, especially with regard to chastity, I pray that, despite what needs to be a rather forward presentation of myself, I will fit within his stringent criteria.

At last, as they draw alongside, they be scrutinizing my ship with great interest.

"Still not a crewman in sight," says I, speaking to my Quarter-master. "Ready yer grapnels, my Lord. Wee shall board her." Turning to look beside him, noting my Bos'n has joined us, I says to 'em, "Give 'er a hail, my Lord *Main*."

"Aye, Captain." Picking up his voice trumpet, he hollers, "Prepare to be boarded. Offer no resistance and ye shan't be harmed."

⚓ 🏴‍☠️ ⛵

"Make no reply, William," I tells him. "By remaining steadfast, the Quarter-Master will be forced to come here to me."

"Thou art not concerned for yer safety, my Lady?"

"Not in the least. Go now, William. I shall meet with *Captain Roberts'* Quarter-Master alone."

"But, my Lady…"

"I know the type of man Captain *Roberts* is. To hurt me would mean the man's death."

"As you will, my Lady, but should ye be in neede of my assistance, I shall be within earshot."

"Thank you, William."

Within a couple minutes, as the *Fortune* draws alongside, several of the crew toss their grapples, securing the two ships together. After fixing a gangplank, a stout fellow armed to the teeth, presents himself. "I am Quarter-Master of yon vessel.

"Where be the ship's captain and crew?"

"I am captain of this ship. As for her crew, 'twas my Lady's Companion, Steward, and myself who piloted the *Willing Captive* here from Castle Harbour."

As he searches my ship, it is obvious that he doubts my words, and knowing this man's history, I do nothing except follow him as he looks around whilst asking many questions.

"Who might you be?"

"I am Aspasia Jourdain, la Marquise d'Éperon-noire."

"Seems I have heard much of you."

Shocked for a moment, could it be that my Captain and that rat *Kennedy*, 'No, he wouldn't, I assure myself, Captain *Roberts* is a man of honour, *Kennedy*, however, he might've told of them. Naaa… that lecherous blackguard wouldn't have remembered a thing beyond my attire; then again, remembering what Lucifer said, I am quite well known.

Breaking my momentary gloom, the *Fortune's* Quarter-Master states cruelly, "You be the widow of that old codger, the Marquis d'Éperon-noire, who died some yeeres back. What be your purpose to anchor here, alone, and so far from yer home in Bermuda?"

"I have come to meet with Captain *Roberts*, says I with a smile."

As he continues to search, now below, within the bowels of my ship, "Indeed. I am most sure such will please him."

As my face shines brilliantly. "I have brought all that you see here, and more, for he and his company."

As the Quarter-Master eyes the overwhelming supplies: food, necessities, cloathing &c, 'tis obvious by the look upon his face, that he took note of my fervidness. "You say you have brung all this for Captain *Robert?*"

"That which you see is for the *Fortune's* crew, *Mister Sympson.*"

With a measure of distrust evident in his voice, "How be it you know both my name, and that of yon ship?"

Realizing that once again I used a name that I perhaps should not have, reply, "Did you not state yourself to be Quarter-Master under Captain *Robert?*"

Speaking somewhat quizzically, "Aye."

"Then yon ship be the *Fortune*, and you are *Little David*. I am an avid reader, *Mister*

Sympson, and reading about Captain *Roberts'* adventures is a particular hobby of mine. When you see your Captain, tell him of your concern. I am sure his reaction, knowing that he and his crew are becoming well known, will be a pleasant one." As I turn to head back to the main deck, he follows me closely. "I have other items for he alone; will you be kind enough to inform that I am eager to meet with him."

When we arrive on deck, I follow him, and in the general area of the gangplank he finally replies, "I shall relay to my Captain yer desire for a meeting. Should he choose to come, he will come to you on the Quarter-Deck."

Speaking with a modicum of outwardly expressed joy, "Thank you, *Mister Sympson*," which I follow up with a modest curtsey.

After satisfying himself that I be alone on board with only Mrs Robles and William, *Mister Sympson* returns to the pyrate vessel to report.

⚓ ☠ ⚓

Looking at my Quarter-Master intently, "Well, my Lord, *Sympson*?"

"To begin with, Captain, the woman standing upon yon Quarter-Deck, an old woman she says is her companion, and her steward, be the onely ones on board, and Captain, not onely does the Lady possess a comely face and a healthy body, she not onely appeared unafraid, she was decidedly cordial as well."

Lifting my spyglass to look at her closely, observing that altho' she stands tall, she does so without projecting anny haughtiness. As did my Quarter-Master, who is still going on about her, I canne see that this woman is different.

"What's more, Captain, she has a generous nature."

"You surmised all those qualities in such a brief encounter?"

"Aye, Captain. I did."

Smiling slightly, "I would say the pulchritudinous lady has a mind of her owne; nevertheless, why, pray tell, would a woman be out so far alone; wanderlust do you suppose?"

"I did not get that impression," replies *David Sympson*.

"Did you find out who she is and what be her business here?"

"She introduced herself as Aspasia Jourdain, la Marquise d'Éperon-noire."

"A French title."

"As to her business here, well, to be frank, I'm thinking her presence here is, well... highly personall in nature."

"What do you mean?"

"Before I tell you, I want it said that she is a genuine Lady of Quality, Captain, of one whom I have heard much."

"Really. What have you heard?"

"I suggest wee talk privately."

Thinking his to be an odd suggestion, wee; nevertheless, head for the great cabin. Upon entry, allowing *David Sympson* to speak freely, I shut the door behind us.

"Her late husband, who died some yeeres back, as I stated earlier, was an old Marquis who possessed untold riches. 'Tis said la Marquise refuses to receive suitors, including those proposed by her sovereign, *Philippe II*.

"To refuse a Marriage of State, she must wield great power, but why..."

"It is said that she awaits another."

"And could it be you know the name of the gallant who has captured the lady's heart?"

"Aye, Captain," replies my Quarter-Master, pausing before finishing his thought. " 'Tis you."

"Me?" Yet as my shocked reply leaves my lips, her display on the docks, the offer of a Captaincy, and her sawcy performance in *Brazil*; everything suddenly becomes clear.

"Aye, Captain," replying with a modest chuckle.

As a moderate smile settles upon my face, " 'Tis an interesting situation, is it not?"

"Aye, but there be more. The generous nature I spoke of," states *David Sympson*.

"And?"

Continuing, *David Sympson* says, "She comes bearing gifts. Hearing that food and other necessities are often short, yon ship is filled to the hatches with offerings, all of which she says was stowed for us. She says also to have gifts that be for you alone."

"Methinks I shall pay her Ladyship a call, but before I head on over, is there anything else you be knowin' of her."

"Onely that her marriage of state to the late Marquis, by order of the late King, commenced when she was hardly more than a child, especially in relation to her husband who was considerably older."

Having conversed with her in *Brazil*, I am bewildered. She told me in a roundabout fashion that she is half Welsh, but her accent was neither Welsh nor French, nor did she sound European, and she spoke to that Portageese Captain like she was born to the language; perhaps, being a traveller, she has mastered many languages. Thinking that perhaps my Quarter-Master may know, I ask, "She is French then?"

"You would not know such by talking to her, Captain, and myself having beene most everyplace, including the Collonies I can not guess. Perhaps hers is a combination of several regions. Long time back, *John Stephenson* told me about a woman he saw on the docks the daye you signed on board the *Princess*, and as it just so happens, this is the woman *Kennedy* told us about on board, the *Rover* in *Brazil*."

Trying not to lett on that I have already linked all those occasions, "Is she now."

"I doubt, however, that anny of the crew saw her up close that night, and I doubt that even *Stephenson* would know her by sight, her name; on the other hand, which generally precedes her, is well known, and thus, many of the crew may know of her as well."

"If you knew of this woman, and that it is I she pines after, whyfor did you wait untill now to tell me of 'er?"

"Untill this daye I knew not that it was you she sought."

With a look of unsettled bewilderment, "How is it you be knowin' now?"

"It be written all over her, Captain. She asked about you specifically, and after establishing your presence, which made her knees weak, she made no secret about the fact that she knew not onely our ship's name, but mine as well."

"Interesting. How did she account for that?"

"She said that being a particular fascination of hers, she reads everything she canne about yer adventures."

Chuckling, "She actually said that?"

"Aye, Captain."

" 'Tis rather flattering, isn't it. How do you suppose la Marquise, who is nigh on alone, came to be anchored here?"

"It be her ship, Captain. She, together with her two companions, saile it themselves."

"She intrigues me to be sure." In order to pay proper respect to this unusual woman of rank, I don my finest, and upon placing my hat upon my head, my Quarter-Master and I walk out of the great cabin and onto the open deck.

"One last item, Captain. Altho' I perhaps oughtn't say so, it is said she has known no man but her late husband, and such, together with her other attributes, she may prove to be the one who will fill the bill in regard to yer unyielding predilections where women are concerned."

Having a fascination for this woman already, I reply, "You may be right, My Lord."

Taking my leave of him, I walk towards the gangplank leading to the large white ship. Standing alone on the Quarter-Deck, her Crimson goune, of unusual design, flatters her tall, slender figure. Her abundant, dark auburn hair, displayed in long, tumbling, all-over tresses, beautifully frames her faire, yet sun kiss'd complexion. Climbing the steps to the Quarter-Deck, I observe, as told me by her rapid deep breathing, that her Ladyship awaits my arrivall most eagerly, and altho' she trys to conceal her excitement, there is an libidinous look about her, as well as a reverent love coupled by stardust in her eyes.

As my long awaited Captain trods the deck of my ship, praying my feelings are not overly conspicuous, it takes all the inner strength I can muster to contain my excitement.

When I come to within a fathoms distance, I canne see what was meant by, my Lord *Sympson's* statement regarding my necklace, for hers being similar is an aspect that pleases me. Stopping before her, I remove my hat with my left hand, and passing it to my right, I bow and speaking in Welsh, I says, "Prynhawn da, fy Arglwyddes," and with all the refinement of a cultured lady, she curtseys low to the deck.

Upon rising, she extends her hand whilst returning my greeting. "Prynhawn da, Nghapten. Croeso ar fwrdd y *Willing Captive*."

Gently, I place my hand beneath hers, and as I lower myself, kissing her soft skin ever so delicately, I canne sense the vehemence of passion that radiates all about her. After which, as etiquette dictates, she slowly removes her hand from mine, and henceforth, I find myself a captive audience.

Complementing the diamond studded cross dangling from a heavy, multi-strand, gold chain about his neck, "Your necklace is stunning, Captain."

"As is your gown. It appears, my Lady, that wee have similar tastes.

Knowing she speaks sev'rall languages, I ask, "Ai Ffrangeg, Cymraeg neu Saesneg fydd hi, fy Arglwyddes?"

"Altho' my breeding is Welsh and French, Captain, I prefer English."

"I find that somewhat uncharacteristic."

"Altho' born in Wales to a Welsh mother, where I lived until I was 7, my father, altho' said to be a Collonist, is actually a renown Frenchman, which is why the bulk of my raising was in France. After I was married off, I lived with my late husband on his silk plantation in Bermuda. Being it was there where I spent the majority of my time, and conversing mostly with those who spoke English, and the majority of my travels also seem to lie in regions where English is prevalent; it is what I have become most accustomed.

From the deck of the pyrate ship, me company watches the goings on with fascinated interest.

"Now would you look at that," says the young *Thomas Sutton* who hails from the town of *Berwick*, to his mate, *William Main*, the latter of which, signifying his position as Bos'n by wearing a silver call, says, "What a pair they be, eh."

"Aye that, *Mister Main*," adds *John Stevenson*, "It seemes the faerie maid holds our worshipful Captain spellbound."

"Wouldst thou like to see the cargo I brought for thee and thy crew, Captain?"

"My Quarter-Master has informed me of your generosity."

"The cargo of which I speak, lyes within an area that *Mister Sympson* did not discover."

"Indeed. That being the case, I would be most pleas'd to see it."

Leading me to a hogshead of water, "As thou wilt soon see, all is not as it seemes, Captain," and whilst portraying a modest smile, she says, "First this barrel would needed to be moved."

Knowing that this single barrel canne hold some 63 gallons, and weigh upwards of 35 stone, I reply, "To move this barrel, my Lady, providing it be full and such is done with minimum spillage, the effort of sev'rall of me crew would be required."

Smiling broadly, "Thou art quite right, Captain, but look." Lifting the hinged lid, she scoops out a dipper of water to show the barrel's contents.

" 'Tis full, my Lady."

"It only appears full, Captain, but in reality this barrel contains only 2 gallons of water."

Closing the lid, she rotates the top portion which contaynes the water, counterclockwise, and then with one hand, she moves the lower section of the barrel, exposing a staircase. Lifting her train, and placing it over her forearm before kneeling down to show me, she says, "It's a powerful magnet, and when the top portion of the water barrel is in place, as thou saw, the magnetic field engages."

"Ingenious."

"I Thank thee, Captain," says she amid a modest smile.

Asking with a look of captivation, "You designed this, my Lady?"

"I borrowed the idea from a tale about the sword Excalibur, but I did design the ship's plumbing, and other areas as well. The ship also contaynes a massive cistern." Gesturing, "These stairs descend into the smugglers' hold."

"And her aft raked masts and narrow prow, were they also yer design?"

"In a manner of speaking."

Upon descending into the hold, her Ladyship explains that the passageway, which engulfs the entire parameter of the ship, is completely hidden within the design, and from neither the topside view, nor from within, canne the smugglers' hold be discerned, and the pride she feels in the design as she carries the lantern is obvious.

As she leads the way, my investigation beholds wonderment as I see before me five score of newly made bronze cannon, most being 24 pounders, a dozen 36 pounders, a score of swivell gunns, and an enormous supply of shot all neatly stowed in well-marked crates. Continuing on, are more crates, and having their lids open, 'tis obviously they are awaiting my inspection. Moving along, I see a multitude of small arms consisting of a wide variety of flintlocks and muskets, and sev'rall crates of shot, and another contaying strikers. As wee round the corner, I find espontoons, bayonets, swords and knives of every description. Rounding out the arsenal is an enormous supply of gunpowder makings, unmixed, no doubt to maintain a safety factor. All in all, there be more than sufficient armament to take over and hold a small country, and if such was not enough, there also be rigging, sailes, and a host of other implements, all of which be for maintaining the ship.

"How did you amass such an enormous quantity of weaponry, my Lady?"

Smiling, "Oh, I get around Captain."

With a quick laugh, "I canne well belieeve that."

"I purchased these goods on the quiet, Captain, especially for thy ship and crew; an endeavour I began shortly after thee signed on the *Princess*. When I missed the opportunity to speak with thee then, I made to myself a vow to seek thee out, and remembering you mentioning in Bahia that supplies, more often than not, are woefully inadequate, privacy is scarce, and danger forever looms, I have brought a shipload of those items I thought thee wouldst be needing most as a shew of my good faith."

BLOOD and SWASH, The Unvarnished Life (& afterlife) Story of Pirate Captain, Bartholomew Roberts......pt.2 "THE WILLING CAPTIVE"

Chuckling a mite under my breath, I find myself needing to ask that age old question, 'Why;' ergo, I stop, and turning to face her in order to look her square in the eye, thereby allowing my perceptive prowess to tell me that which I neede to know, "Not to appeare ungrateful, my Lady, but whyfor do you wish to help, *'Gentlemen of Fortune,'* when by the doing you could be hung for treason?"

Her answer is a simple one. "I support your reasons. I knows that even tho' thou has worked hard, and simply because thy parentage, not being highborn, second mate is about the highest thee canne expect. I also know that many who make up thy company have been displaced since *Queen Anne's War*, the same war that also left thousands with no way to earn their bread. I am only a woman, Captain, but still, I feel there must be something I canne do to help the populace. It may please thee to know, that those who manufactured what I have brought ye and all of you, live in a hundred small towns and villages throughout *Britannia*, and as they did my bidding, they again had jobs, and in return for their efforts, I not onely rebuilt their factories, but I paid them well."

As she continues to explain her reasons, a smile emerges by way of a gentle laugh, as tho' she be greatly excit'd by my pyrating ways.

"I could've purchased for thee a magnificent, first-rate Ship-of-the-Line, Captain, but, um... What I mean to say is, would it not be more exhilarating to seize one instead?"

Speaking amid a hearty laugh, "Aye, my Lady, it would at that."

What becomes clear is not learned from her spoken words, but rather what she did not say, and it was them that spoke the lowdest. To put it plainly, she is enamoured, and altho' I am sure she is not aware of it, her every move, to the smallest inflection, is most demonstrative. Her unpretentious, yet forthright nature, delights me, and as she said, altho' a provocative statement to be sure, pyracy being most exciting, I laugh heartily, responding, "Then I shall seize a vessel worthy of that which you have bestow'd upon me and my company," and as her face lights up, 'tis easie to see that my comment excites her.

Continuing within the smugglers' hold, I am truly amazed by all that she has gathered, but being curious, I asks, "With all the cannon on board, whyfor are there no gunns within the ports on the weather deck?"

"Things are not always as they appear, Captain; nevertheless, wouldst the mere sight of them not make my ship a more sought-after prize?"

"I should think that most seaman would find this vessel highly desirable in either case, still, however, you are most correct; the bronze cannon you have on board would behoove a crew of cutthroats to make a fight worthy of the telling; therefore, prudent actions are always advisable, but if you had a good crew, one worthy of her, this ship would not be overcome."

Smiling, she says, "You have no idea how much it pleases me to hear you say that."

As her Ladyship leads me thro' another secret passageway, "The *Willing Captive*, for all her splendour, is a fully operational, 84 gunn Man-of-War." Stopping, she opens a concealed hatch in the overhead to expose a pull down staircase which she says leads to a hidden gunn deck, wherein, as I poke my head thro' the hatch, I see a battery of what she says are 56 bronze cannon, situated upon 2 decks, all of which are in place, and ready to fire.

Upon entering the room, she reaches for a lever attached to the overhead, "You'll appreciate this, Captain," and as she pulls effortlessly upon the lever, a row of well-concealed gunn ports become visible forthwith.

"Truly remarkable, my Lady."

Smiling a mite. "Within less than one minute, if need be, William and I can each fire a full broadside on both sides of the ship, concurrently." Returning the lever to its original position, she smiles whilst saying, "The gunns are again hidden. It may also interest thee to know that the majority of this ship, as well as her masts, were built out of Live Oak."

Looking at her and smiling, "What speed does she make?"

Stopping so she may speak whilst looking at me, she expresses a happy smile, as she replies, "18 knots, 12 with her present cargo, and a good deal faster should we deploy her spinnaker sail."

"Spinnaker, my Lady?"

"I will show it to thee."

Her reply alights my being, for that be a tremendous speed, especially for such a heavily laden ship as this one be. As for her construction, such would make it nigh on impossible to sink such a vessel.

"And now, Captain, if thou wilt do me the honour of accepting them, I have brought 3 gifts that are for thee alone. May I present them now?"

Affording her a nod of my head, "I shall be pleas'd to accept them, my Lady, and with great pleasure."

Turning, she walks a few steps to what I assume is the door leading to the main corridor. Standing to one side, she graciously waits for me to open it. Following her, she leads the way to the end of the passageway, whereby climbing seven steps, wee enter the great cabin thro' an open hatch in the flooring. Closing the hatch, she says, "Mine are the only rooms accessed from that particular route, Captain. The remaining rooms on this deck, as well as this one, are entered by way of doors along the main passageway."

Seeing two doors, and gesturing towards them, "And those, where do they lead?"

Smiling, as she points to them, "The one back here grants access to a smaller room contayning a bathing tub, washbasin and necessary, which I call a washroom. The other, altho' undetected from outside, grants access to and from the main passageway."

As I look about, noting that the Great Cabin is also her bedchamber, I find her tastes pleasingly genteel. Possessing very little in the way of unnecessary items, the cabin contaynes an oversized bed which is suspended from the overhead; a massive, 6 door, burled mahogany wardrobe and matching dressing table; a well appointed writing desk, above which hangs an oil lamp. The décor itself; Crimson, White and Black, 'altho striking, is not garish, and with the curtains drawn, as they are at present, the lighting is supply'd by an array of candles encased within sev'rall Bronze wall sconces. As a whole, the room affords an ambiance of Seduction. I must confess that ne'er before has a woman beene so bold as to take me into her bedchamber who be not a harlot, and altho' her motives do not elude me entirely, she has made no action that could be considered anything less than what is both dignified and proper for a well-bred, virtuous Lady.

Upon entering, she walks to the far corner of the cabin where she opens a wooden box that sits on her dressing table, and taking out a large Crimson leatther bound book adorned with both gilt lettering and edges, she hands it to me. "This be the first of my gifts for thee, Captain. Pray, take it with my compliments."

Taking the book from her delicate hands and looking upon it, "A handsome bible, my Lady. I thank you." Opening the bible to thumb thro', I am even more taken by her thoughtfulness. " 'Tis written in Welsh," says I with a thankful smile.

"And English. Turn it over and read from the back side."

Suddenly, upon hearing a noise from the room her Ladyship called the washroom, I inadvertently drop the bible as I draw two of my pistols. "Come out," I shout, demandingly, "or Die!"

As her Ladyship places herself before the door, she speaks with a measure of fear. "Wait, Captain! 'Tis only Mrs Robles, my Lady's companion & maid." Slowly, stepping out of the way, and speaking reassuringly, "Mrs Robles, pray come in here at once, but slowly, I beseech you."

BLOOD and SWASH, The Unvarnished Life (& afterlife) Story of Pirate Captain, Bartholomew Roberts......pt.2 "THE WILLING CAPTIVE"

Slowly emerging from the washroom, terrified and shaking, is an elderly woman of 70 odd, and seeing such, I lower my pistols. "Forgive me, madam."

As her sereneness returns, the elderly woman asks, "Have you had your afternoon tea yet, Captain?"

"No, Mrs Robles, I have not."

Speaking in a reassuring manner, her ladyship says, "Please see to tea for Captain *Roberts* and myself." Glazing at me for a moment, then back at her, "We shall dine here, Mrs Robles. Please have William see to it."

"Very good, my Lady."

After she departs, I reach to the floor to pick up the bible. "My apologies, my Lady."

"Perfectly understandable, Captain." Smiling once more, "The second gift I have brought thee is behind the far right hand door of the wardrobe." Following her to the far corner of the large room, "Open the door and thou wilt see it."

Doing as she bid, I open the door. Within I find a magnificent Crimson coloured silk suit embellished not onely in rich gold embroidered edging upon black silk; but a multitude of gold doubloon buttons. The ensemble further includes a contrasting bandoleer contayneing two richly decorated pairs of pistols with Mother of Pearl grips, and an ostrich plumb trimmed tricorne hat, and black boots. " 'Tis a most generous gift," I tells her amid a heart-felt smile."

Being fairly sure that her ladyship knows I have entertained thoughts of not onely taking both her and her ship, wee seat ourselves upon the chairs placed about a small table. "Please forgive me, my Lady, it's not my intention to sound unappreciative, but why would a woman, especially one such as you, place such temptations before a Pyrate?"

Remaining ever gracious, "Well," with a wispy smile, "at the risk of sounding unseemly, I am merely following the course that began with the letter I wrote thee. 'Twas just after thyself and John Williams parted company that I first heard about thy navigation skills, daring and intuitive intelligence, and being impressed, I decided to offer thee a Captaincy. As time went on, I found that the feelings I have for thee be, well, shall we say mesmeric, but more to the point, Captain, let me bluntly state that one can not take by force that which is freely given."

Momentarily taken aback, I find that her forthright candour, altho' cryptic, attracts me; ergo, wanting her to state from her owne lips, thereby to confirm my suspicions, "Wanting not to tread upon the innermost feelings that are deeply rooted within your heart, I would like to know what your Ladyship hopes to reap by your declaration?"

"Adventure, Captain. Adventure and... um..." As she fiddles with the doily on the arm of the chair, suddenly appearing withdrawn, she is barely able to look at me.

"Adventure and what, my Lady?"

Taking a deep breath, her ladyship asks, "Is it not law upon thy vessel to place a female captive within the protective custody of a formidable sentinel, thus protecting her from harm?"

"Aye, my Lady, that be so."

"Well," speaking amid a delicate chuckle, "um... since I know thou wilt allow no woman to join thy crew, I wish to be thy captive, under thy personal protection, mind thee, and as such, I would relish hearing thee alone addressing me by my given name."

I canne scarcely belieeve what I be hearing; 'tis the most extraordinary request I have heard tell of. This woman, a refined lady of quality, is actually asking to become my chattel, and as such, I canne lye with her whenever it pleases me to do so, but then why else would she be here if these things be not what she longs for, and yet, how canne I not be enthralled by her boldness, as thus, I ask, "Whyfor does a well-bred lady of meanes wish to be treated so?"

"With thou as my sentinel, Captain, I can not imagine being treated poorly; what is more, being la Marquise d'Éperon-noire, I am able to further thy cause in many ways."

"How so?"

"Well, to begin with, the *Willing Captive*, whilst serving concurrently as a storeship, would make for thou a splendid private retreat, thus relieving the *Fortune* of the burdens associated with heavy cargo and stores; and if neede be, the *Willing Captive's* smugglers hold, which I might add was not found by thy owne Quarter-Master, would be equally useful in hiding thy plunder. Lastly, as la Marquise d'Éperon-noire, I can sail thy ship into any port and be both well received and generously provisioned."

"My Ship?"

"Yes, Captain, 'tis my third gift to thee," says she whilst placing within my hands a small bejewelled box. "Having her built especially for thee, the *Willing Captive* has always been in thy name."

As she continues speaking, I open the elegant box, and taking out the papers I see written upon them, *John Robert*, village of *Nghastell-Newydd Bach*, *Cymru*, Owner and Captain.

Looking up at her, she adds, "Not that it is a condition, mind you, I am just hoping that thou wouldst not be averse to the idea of allowing me to share in at least one adventure with thee."

Stunned, "You mean a pirate venture?"

"If it's too much, or if being my sentinel does not appeal to thee, thou needs only to set my party and I ashore in *Bermuda* or other French or English port and sail away."

Speaking with a modest smile, " 'Tis impressed I am, my Lady, and before you refuse my address, I belieeve it fitts you. And the name of this ship, 'twas named for your most searching dreams, was it not?"

With the barest hint of a shy smile, "Thou art very perceptive, Captain."

Ordinarily, I would avoid such advances by a woman, especially one so eager to lye down with me, but this woman, by affording herself to no one but myself, howe'er bold she may be, is a genuine lady who, for reasons that elude me, not onely loves me truly, she is not afraid to make her feelings known.

> *As she awaits his reply, it's easy to see, as he mulls over her proposition, that he is in deep thought.*

Having made my decision, her breaths increase as I begin to lean towards her, and lifting her chin with the tips of my fingers and giving her a light kiss on her lips, "Already I find that I am fond of thee, Aspasia, and such, I will treat thee gently as thee deserves."

"Does this mean—"

"Aye, Aspasia, it does, for I accept thy proposal, and such, thou art henceforth, under my personal protection, and in due time I shall take thee pyrating; what is more, as my 'Willing Captive,' thee and thine shall enjoy all the privileges ye be accustomed." Standing, "but first, I neede to speak briefly to me crew. When I return, I shall be pleas'd to not onely dine with thee, but I shall stay the night."

In a relaxed tone, amid a happy expression, she says, "During the intervening time, fy Arglwydd, William will set the table."

Taking notice of her new entitlement for me, I excuse myself for a few minutes to go topside. Returning to my *Fortune*, I am quickly surrounded by me crew who be eager to hear the news. As I begin the telling, they gather about. "la Marquise, and a fine Lady indeed, has brought the lot of us, as Lord *Sympson* has no doubt informed ye, many fine gifts and provisions; however, unknown to our Quarter-Master, there be a smugglers hold encompassing the perimeter of yon ship simply brimming with munitions; furthermore, because our gracious benefactor has stowed yon Ship to the hatches with a bounty of clothing, and provisions fitt for a king, the lot of us will address her as, my Lady, and refer to her as her Ladyship. For myself, and a most generous gift it is, her ladyship has afforded me her fine Ship; the ship's papers having already beene conveyed into my name; moreover, her Ladyship has boasted that the ship, not onely be yare, but will make 18 knots, 12 with her present cargo. To this wee shall see for ourselves before night sets in, and in that, I will leave it to ye to choose 16 to crew the *Willing Captive*, plus master *Jean François*, after which, wee shall see just how fine a sayler she is. As for myself, I be privileg'd to dine with her Ladyship in private, but shall return to the open deck thereafter, for I wish to clock the ship's speed myself. On the morrow, as supervised by Lord *Sympson* and *William Main*, ye shall take orderly possession of both the gifts and provisions her ladyship has bought us in a quiet, well ordered fashion. Thereafter, following the careening of our *Fortune*, wee shall sett saile for *Trepassey* as plann'd.

After my address, I return to her Ladyship's cabin where I find William placing our dinner upon the table whilst her Lady-in-Waiting stands by to serve. The tray William had beene carrying is empty, but nevertheless, he awaits both my introduction and permission to take his leave.

"fy Arglwydd, Nghapten, I would like to present my Steward, and treasured friend, William Crandall. William, this is *The Great Pyrate Roberts*."

William, not the least bit shocked or surprised by the way she introduced me replies, "Captain," amid a nod.

"You may leave us now, Mister Crandall," she tells him.

"Thank you, Captain. My Lady?"

"Thank you, William."

"One of us shall ring should wee neede you," says I politely amid a nod.

As William departs, "You as well, Mrs Robles," her ladyship tells her.

"But who will serve?"

"I shall," states her Ladyship, "and as Captain Robert stated, one of us shall ring should we need you. Lastly, this ship, henceforth, and all those aboard her, are under the command of Captain Roberts. Is that perfectly clear?"

Amid a curtsy, "Yes, my Lady. By your leave, Captain," and turns to leave.

"Wait, Mrs Robles," says I.

Turning to face me, "Yes, Captain?"

"Her Ladyship spoke in error. Whilst this ship and its crew be under her Ladyship's and my joint command, you and William shall remain in her service. As fer myself, I want onely the respect I am due; nothing more."

"My gratitude, Captain," says she whilst curtsying.

"Please so inform, William."

"I shall, Captain, and thank you." As she curtseys again, she adds, "Good night, sir." Curtseying once again as Mrs Robles takes her leave from her ladyship, "Good night, my Lady," and upon exit, she closes the door behind her.

"As thee canne see, fy Arglwydd, I live rather simply, but such as it may be, I am sure thou wilt find my humble faire most palatable."

"Aye, I am sure I shall, my Lady." As I look about the table, I observe a nice arrangement of roast squab, a tureen containing fisherman's stew, new potatoes cooked in their skins, an array of vegetables and cheese, bread, assorted fresh fruits either or sectioned or cut in to bite-sized peeces, and a couple sweets.

"Thy faire, my Lady, is not as humble as thee thinks, in fact, by a seaman's vantage point, 'tis a veritable feast."

As wee dine, limiting herself mainly to answering the questions I put to her, her Ladyship does not talk much, and in doing, I venture to suppoze she wishes not to appear loquacious. During our conversation, due to her obvious fondness for the ship, I tells her that I consider the *Willing Captive* to be our joint property; hers as well as mine. As for the ship's papers, they shall serve mainly to disavow anny belief that the sailing in me company be of her owne desire, and thus, she will be considered irreproachable should ever wee be taken.

As the ship gets underway, "I see thou hast placed a crew on board."

"Just a short cruise, my Lady. In a few minutes wee shall be upon the open sea." Rising, I hold her chair. "Wilt thou join me whilst I go topside? I wish to clock her speed."

Removing from her lap the heavy linnen cloth covering her goune, she stands. "I shall be Delighted, fy Arglwydd."

Following her, wee go topside.

Within a few moments wee be on the open deck, and as I await for the sailes to be sett, I make conversation. "How does my Lady generally fill her day? I am sure thou art very skilled with a needle."

"Yes, fy Arglwydd, I am. I enjoy the making of many of mine owne garments, and took much joy embellishing the Crimson suit I had made for thee."

"And what of other interests, what might they be?"

"Well, before I began my trek with William, gallivanting all over creation gathering, the *Willing Captive's* present cargo, I was saddled with the tedious chore of managing the estates my late husband left me, which is why I recently sold the *Château in Havre de Grâce, Normandy*, for the grand sum of 250000 Pistoles, which, by the way, is what I paid for this ship and its cargo. In my free time, trained in horse management, I ride quite a bit. I also became proficient with bow and arrow, rapier and pistol. I love musick, play chess, backgammon and go, and am a faire cook. 'Twas I who prepared both the fisherman's stew and the sweets."

"Seemes, my Lady, thou hast a number of interests."

"Oh, I keep myself occupy'd, but my main pleasure is that which I find aboard ship."

"Thou art fond of the sea then?"

"Passionately, fy Arglwydd. I really enjoy'd roaming around collecting her present cargo."

As she tells me of some of her adventures, I am quite impressed by the ship's speed, and hearing that she loves the sea is refreshing, for most women do not like anny form of travel.

As wee stand by the bow, I know already this ship's speed is faster than anny other vessel I have beene aboard in the past, and being enthusiastic I says, "A few minutes, my Lady, please, whilst I count."

Before thee proceeds, I should like to introduce thee and thy crew to a new type of sail." Calling William, who be not far off, I says, "William, will you be good enough to deploy the spinnaker."

"With Pleasure, my Lady."

Following him, William opens a huge wooden box on the bow just beneath the jibs. "Will you give me a hand, Captain?"

"Certainly."

As William fastens the lower clew corner to a specific sheet, he says, "It's important the saile is attached in this prescribed fashion, and thus, onely 2 crewmen are needed to get it airborne, and furled again." Taking into his hands the head of the saile, William attaches it to a rope for hoisting it high upon the foremast, and then lastly, whilst attaching the tack corner to a specially designed retracting bowsprit, "This massive saile will balloon out in front of the ship when deployed." Handing me the sheet, "Yer job, Captain, is to swiftly take up the slack, and securer the sheet."

"I'm ready, Mister Crandall."

As William deploys the massive saile, I swiftly take up the slack in the sheet. Quickly, as wee tie off our respective lines, William says, "This saile is designed specifically for sailing off the wind from a reaching course downwind, with the wind 90°–180° off the bow."

As the ship surges forward with incredible speed, myself and me crew are amazed, and dashing aft, to the stern with a Chip Log, I toss the Chip into the water. After less than a minute, I arise from the railing, proclaiming, "14 knots!" there is surely a gleam in mine eyes.

'Tis a fine crew thou hast placed aboard thy ship, fy Arglwydd. Ne'er has the *Willing Captive* atchieved such speed whilst so heavily laden."

Speaking to me crew, "Return us to the cove, and drop anchor. Being its master, Mister Crandall, will you take in the spinnaker?"

"My pleasure, Captain."

Addressing me crew, "Those now on board shall crew the *Willing Captive*, and after gathering yer effects, ye shall spend the night within yer new quarters aboard this ship. Mister Crandall will acquaint you with them." Turning, and taking her Ladyship's elbow gently, I escort her back to the great cabin to finish dinner.

When wee take our seats, a knock is heard upon the door.

Inviting who she suspects is her Companion, her Ladyship says, "Come in."

Opening the door is Mrs Robles. Is there anny thing I canne get for you? More Tea, Captain, coffee, my Lady?"

Giving her maid, or rather, her lady's Companion an ever so slight, sly looking smile, her Ladyship replies, "No thank you, Mrs Robles. I shan't have neede of you until morning. As for the tray, I shall place it outside the door later."

"Please leave us now," adds I, "and advise William and the others that wee wish not to be disturbed."

"Yes, Captain," replies Mrs Robles as she curtsies. "Good night, my Lady," curtsying once again as she takes her leave, closing the door behind her.

After the door is closed, her Ladyship rises and walks to the door. "'Tis not that I do not trust her or the others, fy Arglwydd, but," and having bolted the door, she returns to her seat.

Doing my best to refrain from speculation whilst trying not to shew anny of my inner thoughts, I continue with the conversation as wee finish our meal. "Not to pry into your personal affairs, my Lady, but um..."

"Go ahead, fy Arglwydd, I have no secrets from thee; ask whatever it pleases thee to know."

"Was your marriage not consummated?"

Although obviously shocked by my question, she answers it just the same. "Onely just, but such was nature's choice, not the Marquis'."

"And ne'er didst thou seeke a paramour?"

"To willfully indulge libidinously with one not my husband whilst he lived, or to voluntarily lie down with a man whom I did not truly care for, of mine owne volition, would be a sin against myself, fy Arglwydd."

As I take the last bite of my supper, I sit back for a moment, and gazing upon my faire prize, I find myself eager to lye with her. To the best of my knowledge, ne'er have I met a woman such as she, and the idea of being with this unspoiled lady, methinks the delight in pleasuring one another shall reward us both.

Within a couple minutes, having finished her modest meal, she arises. "May I draw thy bath, fy Arglwydd?"

"A bath?" asks I, looking up at her whilst also arising.

"Surely thee wilt honour me by bathing before..." Again the shyness of her persona preventing her, she instead looks upon her hands as they fidget with the kerchief gracing her right wrist, "um... before retiring."

Upon the completion of her sentence, I find myself captivated more than ever. With my thoughts focus'd, belieeving the words she cannae utter alowd be of a carnal nature, a modest smile grows upon me lips as I cheerfully reply, "Methinks a bath will suit me very well indeed."

"I shall call thee in a few minutes, fy Arglwydd," and whilst walking into the next room she leaves the door 'twixt us, ajar.

Waiting within the Great Cabin as I ponder some of her remarks, her love for adventure and of the sea, and other activities, it is my opinion that even tho' she is able to take care of herself, she wants to be taken care of. She needes to love, and be loved, and she wants to be protected. To the right man, she will yield herself both freely and fully, and saying quietly, "And as I am that man, the reverse could be true as well." Arising, I remove my pipe from the elk skin smoking caddy attached to my belt and place it on the table. Opening the lid of the ornate tinderbox before me, I graze the steel striker sharply against the flint, lighting the tallow. As I return to my seat, I am just about to light my pipe when the door leading to the anti-chamber opens fully, and whilst standing gracefully in the entry, my beautiful 'Willing Captive,' who has changed her frock, announces, "Thy bath be ready, fy Arglwydd."

Arising from my chair, I extinguish the flame, and return both the spunk, and my pipe to whence they came. Preparing for my bath, I remove my weaponry, powder flask, belt, and lastly my coat, and utilizing a specially designed coat holder by the door, I deposit the aforementioned items upon it. Turning, I note that her Ladyship, who awaits me patiently, watched my actions with great interest.

The room, contayneing an enormous tub filled with steaming water, is elegant to be sure. In the corner of the room a pot belly stove heats, not onely the water, but keeps the room warm as well.

As I enter, she kneels beside me, "Allow me to remove thy shoes and socks, fy Arglwydd?"

Placing my hand upon the bulkhead to steady myself, methinks one could easily become quite fond of such attentions.

Chearfully she pulls my shoes off one by one, after which saying, whilst gesturing to the chair just inside the door, "Please seat thyself."

Having done so, she unbuttons my britches at the knees and begins to strip off my stockings, and as she does, I observe her sapphire eyes as they drinke in the sight of my legs, which are beset with a moderate thickness of curly black hair, and not able to resist, she briefly fondles the hardened muscles of my calves a moment with one hand whilst the other setts the socks atop my shoes. "I shall wash them for you, fy Arglwydd."

As she stands, she makes slight tugs on my shirt, pulling it from beneath my britches. Becoming aware of her plans, I rise to my feet asking, "Canst be, my Lady, thou plans to remain?"

Whilst beginning to untie the lacings of my shirt she asks sweetly, "How else canne I wash thy back and hair, and afterwards give thy shoulders a rubbin'."

"Well, um," Being unaccustomed to such, "It onely be that I..."

Altho' ne'er saying a word, 'tis obvious by the sadness that engulfs her face, belieeving I wish for her to go, she turns to leave, but 'tis not that I wants her to leave as much as I am surpriz'd by her intention to remain, and letting her know this, I quietly call to her. "My Lady, Aspasia."

Stopping, yet refraining from turning to face me, she replies, "Yes, fy Arglwydd?"

Being obvious that she be overcome by a feeling of being less than desirable, and I wanting her to know otherwise, "How canne my hair and back, as well as the rest of me be cleansed to thine satisfaction without thy gracious assistance?"

As she slowly turns 'round, I am pleas'd to see her jovial attitude has returned.

"The doing for thee, fy Arglwydd, will afford me great pleasure."

Whilst undoing the lacings, I notice the deepening of her breaths, and as she gazes upon my well-muscled torso; taking particular delight, methinks, in the thicket of hair, black as pitch, upon it, as she removes my shirt. As for meselfe, I canne onely smile, for already I be most pleas'd with my 'Willing Captive,' and when she looks up at me, as she melts against my chest, how could anny man resist the ravishment of her lips; she makes it most difficult to resist her charms long enough to bathe first as she request'd.

Having stripped off my britches to submerge myself into the hot tub while she gathers a cloth and the soap, the look on her face when she turns back 'round, even tho' she doth not speake of it, gives me the impression that she desired to see me in a state of total undress. To this, I surmise her to be as bold as she is shy. Once the latter is overcome, methinks she'll be like a wildcat who shall forever await my return.

Kneeling beside the tub, she begins by scrubbing my chest and legs with the rich lather. Her touch, tho' decidedly gentle, is most invigorating, and her owne emotions add to this feeling, for she appears to be thoroughly enjoying herself.

Nudging me forward, "You have a wonderfully thick mane, fy Arglwydd," says she as she runs her fingers through my hair whilst her other hand washes my back. Using the washcloth, she gets my hair quite wet before applying soap to it.

After a quarter hour, leaving no part of me unwashed, she smiles. "Thou art most decidedly clean now, fy Arglwydd," and moving to the back of the tub, she kneels on the floor behind me and massages my shoulders and neck muscles for sev'rall minutes.

Speaking in a low, soothing voice, "Thou ought have a thorough rubbin' often to relieve thy tension, especially after an engagement. I hope thou shall permit it to be my pleasure to fulfill that need."

Finding myself quite comfortable with her, I think that now is the best time to confess to her. "A few months ago I would 'ave jumped to the position offered by thee, but now I am thinking I have found my Destiny, and being that I am now, a Pyrate Captain, art thou displeased?"

"Hardly, fy Arglwydd," says she, cracking a smiling, and whilst shaking her head just a mite, "It delights me to know thou hast not onely found thy calling, but excels in thy profession."

As the tub drains, she wrings the wash cloth tightly, and whilst calling my attention to the contraption overhead. "Just pull the lever, and the showerhead shall rinse away the soap." Laying the cloth over the side of the tub, she rises. "Whilst thou dries thyself, I shall tidy up the outer room." Pointing to the back of the door as she departs, "Here is thy dressing goune."

Having rinsed, I am feeling quite relax'd as I step out of the tub, and robing myself, I find the sumptuous garment a delight to put on. Upon opening the door slightly, I espy her in the bed, and hearing the door creak, she rolls onto her tummy and flashes me a coy smile.

"Does my 'Willing Captive,' intend to deprive me the pleasure of gazing upon the beauty of her form?"

"Canst, fy Arglwydd, not wait until he be laying beside me before indulging in such pleasures?"

Her eyes, altho' lowered, are inviting, and as I undo the sash, opening the dressing goune that covers me, an act that appears to reward her eyes, I allow it to fall to the floor. In return, amid a look of sweet delirium as she lifts the Crimson coverlet, she silently invites me in to her bed.

In the doing. whilst laying myself beside her, altho' greatly pleas'd, I am surpriz'd, for I expect'd to see her wearing a bed goune, but instead, she is in the altogether, and as added bonuses, I am not onely pleas'd to find that her ample breasts are well made, but also by the creaminess of her white skin against the black silk sheets.

Impassioned, I am eager to take her favours, and as I lay beside her warm flesh, her chest heaving heavily, I asks quietly, "Is it the pleasurable expectation of sweet love, or the fear of such which causes thee to breathe so?"

Rising to a seated position, she looks into mine eyes for a moment, and speaking in a soft, breath filled manner, she completes the sentence she began earlier. "Adventure, fy Arglwydd. Adventure and the absence of chastity."

Her motives, spoken at last, are made plain. As for mine, I intend, with much delight, to make full use of the delicacies she offers, and in the doing, give to her all that she has confessed to be her desires.

"And so it shall be, Aspasia, and in such, wee shall find both fulfillment and ecstasy."

Come morn, I don the rich Crimson suit my Lady fashioned for me, which to my amazement, fitts perfectly, and as I step out onto the open deck, I am met by Mrs Robles, who hands me a cup of the finest Bohea tea.

"Being that her ladyship hoped it would please you and your crew to take breakfast aboard, the *Willing Captive*, I would appreciate it if you would lett it be known that such will be served on the open deck within the quarter hour."

Speaking with a measure of pride, William, just coming up from below, carrying the morning coffee, "On Deck 3, there is a dining room capable of seating 200 people, but being such a beautiful spring morning, Mrs Robles thought yer crew would prefer to dine on the open deck." Continuing, William, looking about and not seeing me, asks, "Will her Ladyship be topside soon do you think?"

"Methinks wee canne expect her momentarily, Mister Crandall."

Walking to the starboard railing, I holler to those of my company who be on deck, "Come aboard, men. Ye, and all of us, shall enjoy our breakfast this morn aboard the, *Willing Captive*, but first wee will thank both her Ladyship, and her companions for the rich gifts they have seene fitt to bestow upon us, one and all."

"And then, Captain," hollers one of the crewman, "what be yer plans for her ladyship?"

Hearing the door to the corridor open, knowing I must abide by mine owne articles which specifically state that no woman, under pain of death, shall be taken against her will, I turn my head just a mite, and knowing it is she, I turn towards her, and in grand *Shakespearian* style, I throw open my arms and say, "Shew to my company thy feelings for me," and as she runs into my arms, which close about her, I reply to my crew, "I shall keep her."

Chapter Eleven

Victory

This May and June [1720], the waters have yielded much to satisfy our needes and wants. Nigh on a Dozen vessells have come into our view, all of which wee have happily plundered.[B2 page 61]

In the latitude of *Deseada Island*, in June, wee garnered provisions and other necessities from two Sloops, the *Expectation* of *Topsham*,

and the *York* of *Bristol*, which wee plundered with little or no resistance.

A few dayes later wee caught and plundered with ease, the aforementioned Brig belonging to *Rhode Island*, as well as the Sloop, *Happy Return*, and the *Mary and Martha*.

Having sold our booty along the *New England* coast, wee continue towards our objective, but being quite a distance, wee first cruise North along *Newfoundland's* Eastern coastline, and with intentions of watering and provisioning our Sloop, wee saile to *Feryland*.[sic CSP-PRO1]

Initially, wee enter the port as peaceful voyagers looking to pay or barter for the provisions wee neede, but being recognized, and a fuss being made, wee are forced to take what wee came for. After a brief skirmish, our opposition quit their posts. Before departing, seeing fitt to shew the Admiral herein the error of his ways, by way of not better protecting the region put in his charge, I order his ship to be burnt.

Over the past weeke, the *Fortune* and, the *Willing Captive* saile southward in consort towards *Trepassey*, and altho' dividing my time 'twixt the two, I, as it must be, spend the majority of my waking hours with me crew aboard the *Fortune*; however, and I say this with much delight, all but one of these nights, that being the night of the full moon, when her Ladyship and I slept atop a blanket beneath the stars upon the *Fortune's* open deck, have beene spent on board the *Willing Captive*.

Needing my sloop fitt before proceeding to our objective, wee anchor as close as possible to a small islet of black rocks in order to boot-top. During this tedious task, throughout which time her Ladyship

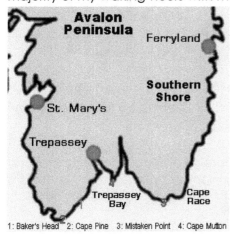

1: Baker's Head 2: Cape Pine 3: Mistaken Point 4: Cape Mutton

and Mrs Robles prepared for me and my crew wholesome meals, me crew enjoyed the hospitality and grandeur of her ship; nevertheless, now that our *Fortune* has beene cleaned, I am, as Captain, constrained by duty to order that wee continue on our way. Rounding the southeast portion of *Newfoundland's* coast on a direct course for *Trepassey*, wee anchor off *Mistaken Point*. After breakfast, whilst her Ladyship watches from the deck of the *Willing Captive* in earnest, my company gathers for privy council, and altho' her Ladyship proposed to saile the formidable *Willing Captive* into battle in with us, it is decided that while the *Fortune* sailes forth alone, she is to anchor off *Cape Mutton*.

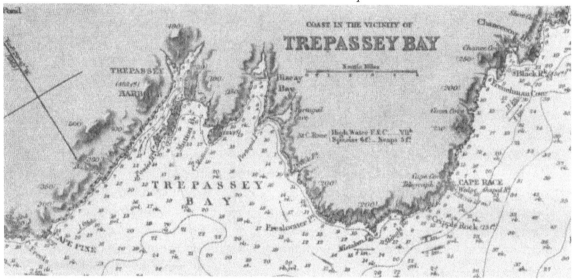

The day of revenge is here, and within a short time only, we shall part for a time whilst my brave Captain sails into battle. Even now, I am sure that his crew readies themselves, for within an hour, the *Fortune* shall bear down upon not only the *French Guard de la Coste*, with a vengeance, but anyone else who crosses his path, and as I am sure Captain *Roberts* knows, this being a most important port, not only because of its strategic location, but also its flourishing fishing industry, it is well guarded.[C05]

Just as my Captain is about to step on to the gangplank, fearful that my presence could somehow change the outcome, I holler, "fy Arglwydd, Nghapten," and run to him.

Stopping, he turns to face me, and giving me assurance, " Worry not, fy Arglwyddes, all will be well."

"I…" Trying desperately to compose myself, I pull from my hair, the gold edged, crimson silk scarf he gave me only days before. "Wilt thou carry my kerchief into battle?"

Kissing me atop my forehead, "An honour, fy Arglwyddes," and tucking the delicate fabric into the jewelled cuff of his gauntlet, he, tho' nigh whispering, speaks seriously. " 'Tis time," and stepping onto the gangway, he departs.

Just about the time the morning sun hits the water, following thro' with my Captain's plans, the *Willing Captive*, as she prepares to sail for *Cape Mutton*, the *Fortune*, herself, is getting under way.

Today, on the 21st daye of June, our objective lyes roughly 5 nautical leagues distant, and as I stand on my Quarter-Deck watching sev'rall members of me crew turn the stout handles of the capstan to haul up the anchor, I am knowing that this bright and sunny

Friday shall indeed be a morning that will be long remembered.

Whilst more than half me crew scurry aloft into the rigging, and the tacks and bracers on deck await my order, I turn to face her Ladyship briefly; and taking from my gauntlet her silk kerchief, I hold it to my lips for a moment before tying it about my neck.

Seeing a well-trained crew, each knowing that what is expected of 'em, it is Proud I am as I look about me ship, and knowing the time is right, I put all my thoughts towards our objective, as I order, "Make saile."

A typical French fishing shallop of the period.

'Tis a feeling one cannae deskrybe, watching the sailes unfurl; feeling the motion of the ship as she begins to move forward; the wind being the propellant that drives her thro' the water. But this morning, the feeling is different, for Justice shall be served this daye before the noon bells sound.

Altho' unknown to her Ladyship, and even tho' I knows full well, as does me crew, that the fortification that guards this here fort, and that the ships that serve to protect her industry have more than enough armament to blow our ship from the water, I sent forth a messenger to *Trepassey* whilst in Feryland, informing them of my intentions to pay 'em a call, and why. Me crew, of perhaps 60 men,[C05] and onely 10 cannon,[B8 & 9] be driven by a warlike hunger in their hearts, and therefore shan't be deterred, for they be a-knowing that even should the worse come to pass, our objective shall be met, and thus, wee saile brazenly towards the closest ships.

With intentions to saile betwixt 'em, I look at Lord *Sympson*, whom eagerly awaits my command, and in a calm, methodical tone, whilst also giving my musicians the nod, I order, "Hoist our colours."

Without hesitation, Lord *Sympson*, placing his voice trumpet to his mouth, repeats my order.

The crewmen who waits his command, proudly runs our Jolly Roger up to the topmost of our mainmast straight away. Within moments our guns be in range, and as I knew they would be, the crews on the opposing vessells are unprepared for our arrivall.

Speaking in a deliberate tone, cupping me hand about my mouth to better direct my voice, I shout, "Up all ports!"

Instantly, as the cannon port doors fly open, the men on the gunn crews, heaving upon the hulking ropes, haul the heavy cannon speedily into place. With the ship's musicians beating their drums and sounding their trumpets with intensity, I thrust down my sword whilst bellowing, "Fire!"

Sev'rall of our cannon be loaded with mast shattering balls, attached by twos with heavy chain. Of those that remain, half be loaded with exploding cannon balls, and the remaining cannon be loaded with a fierce anti-personnel weapon known as grapeshot. To our delight, both our broadsides burst atop the Frenchies open decks simultaneously, and knowing at once the ferocity of the ammunition they be up against, the Frenchies are sent a-whirling, but not a one thinks to return fire, or otherwise engage. Obviously affrightened for their lives, and rightly so, ne'er should a man abandon his post, and it greaves me to watch as some men dash for cover, whilst others still, jump ship, either into longboats or by jumping over the side. With the dread ridden crews of the 22 ships taken utterly by surprise, despite being forewarned, me crew quickly reloads our gunns, and as our *Fortune* courses swiftly thro' the water, using our opponent's agitated state to my full advantage, I holler, "Hard-a-starboard." Moments later, as wee clear the Frenchie's bow, I order, "Fire!" As the cannons release their load upon a second sett of ships, I shout, "Hard-a-larboard," whereupon, our blessed ship, altho' decidedly worn, yet ever yare, quickly responding to both the artful direction of her pilot, and the skilful deck crew, who being quick on the sheets, adjust the ship's sails, I holler, "Come about." Pleas'd with our ship's maneuverability whilst again coming within firing range, whilst the gunn crew, again ready the cannon, and as our vessel slips nigh boarding distance 'twixt two more French Sloops, and as I again holler, "Fire!" another volley barrels away, and most of those that remain of the twelve hundred pannick-stricken sailors, flee in terror.

Meanwhile Upon the Willing Captive ⇁

With my ship anchored off the western point of *Cape Mutton*, whilst in the crow's nest of the Willing Captive, with spyglass in hand, I watch the excitement, leaping and cheering, and as the battle ensues, my heart pounds at the very idea of this multitude of seamen fleeing to shore in fear of he whom I love, the ever present lust I have for him multiplies 10 fold.

Cannons Blazing aboard the Fortune ⇁

Sailing on thro', wee continue our barrage of cannon fire upon the ships that come into the path of our gunns. Being interested in a certayne Brigantine Galley,[B8 & 9] wee saile abreast 'er, and with the intention of seizing her, I bellow, "Grapnels away!"

Promptly and accurately, the grapnels are thrown, and the crews on the ropes swiftly secure the two ships together. Being in the mood for fighting, I lead the prize crew, but seeing the remainder of the Galley's crew jump ship the moment wee swing on over, and noting there's no one to fight, I find myself disappointed.

Looking over the ship, wee be deciding that not onely will she will be well suited to our needes when modified, she is decidedly more seaworthy than the dilapidated sloop wee arriv'd on. Upon the transference of our Jolly Roger, I am outraged as wee continue, for a multitude of seaman and 40 cannon make for strong harbour defences, and yet, when they could 'ave easily blown me ship and crew out of the water when wee enter'd the harbour, every man and jackal by quitting their posts without firing a single shot, allowed us to saile thro', unchallenged.

Me crew, having served well, are deserving of a holiday, and my ill temper, enraged by the blatant shew of cowardice within this port, is evident; ergo, allowing my emotions to dictate, it shall be here where I shall allow me crew to dally, and considering the circumstances, it shall be at the expense of the populace and shoppe keepers, for 'tis they who have bred such cowardice.[B13]

With the town under siege, me crew, when not working their shift, be free to enjoy themselves ashore to the utmost; especially when one considers that all is theirs for the taking, an aspect, mind you, that I would not normally condone; however, tho' it be a tough lesson indeed, these here people must suffer the consequences of their cowardly behaviour.[CSP-CS7]

> Applebee's Original Weekly Journal   1 October 1720
>
> Two light men-of-war are ordered for Newfoundland in queſt of Roberts and other pirates who continue to commit great depredations on our merchant ſhips that way.'

Not being inclined to gamble, being a teetotal, and having no use for loose women, there be no purpose in my going ashore; ergo, whilst concurrently overseeing the plundering of the ships that dot *Trepassey's* harbour, I canne efficiently supervise our new Brigantine's refit, which will include adding to her weaponry until she, whom wee have christened, *Good Fortune*, mounts 16-gunns.[B8 & 9]

Thus far, since arriving in *Trepassey*, my men, it seemes, are so efficient in ravaging the ships, there is little neede for the preskrybement of duty assignments. Thus, leaving me little to do, I sent sev'rall of my crew to the *Willing Captive* to fetch her ladyship. Charged with la Marquise's safety, they are, and thus, I knows she shall be within my arms by nightfall. With the rest of me crew off either pillaging the ships or conducting business ashore, all the pleasures I could possibly hope for shall be here, upon this ship, relaxing in this place of solitude. Caution, however, in regard to her Ladyship, must be maintained, for no one ashore, excepting those amongst me crew, are to know of her presence in these waters.

Knowing it shall be quite a spell before the longboat returns, I go about my business. First of course, before anny cargo is brought on board, our new prize needes to be refitted for our use. Being essential that the areas below deck where arms and powder be stowed have a clear line of sight, many of the interior bulkheads, being of main concern, are taken down first. For sleeping, open areas being much easier to move thro', serve well for hammocks, wherein, taking less space than bunks, are also easily stowed when not in use.

'Tis long since dark when the longboat returns with la Marquise, and knowing that much of me crew is ashore, wee being free to enjoy the pleasures awaiting us this night, I take care to be on the open deck when she comes on board.

"Welcome aboard our latest acquisition, my Lady," states one of my crew.

Graciously, whilst looking about, her ladyship, as she espies me nigh the door leading to the passageway that leads to the great cabin, replies, "Thank you," to the sailor.

As I watch her slowly approach like a seductress, mine eyes become aware of her body's little indicators, and as they demonstrate just how much the dayes events have excit'd her, I grow increasingly fervent.

With a demure expression, and a breath filled voice, "Thy valour, fy Arglwydd, is beyond measure, and thy crew, one and all, be a credit to their profession, but above all, it be the enchanted moments, those that create the passions which motivate us, and the fulfilling of them, they are what makes living worthwhile."

As she finishes speaking, she stops a few feet distant from me, and despite her desire to be in my bed is apparent, she remains, whilst in view of others, a gracious, well-mannered Lady of Rank.

"I thank thee for thy generous praise, my Lady."

Her hand, not being presented, I take it upon myself to gently take her left hand within mine, and in lifting it chest high, observing that her breathing grows stronger, I bend forward to tenderly kiss her soft flesh.

"Thou art the perfect embodiment of what every sea captain ought be. To you sir, I humbly kneel," and having said such, she not merely curtsies, she Genuflects.

Her praise, for flattery is not in her nature, stems from her heart. As a Captain, I am decidedly pleased that she finds me most capable, and as a man, her words, taking me outside the ability to curb my lust, compels me to take her below and make love to her beyond corporeal limits; 'tis all-consuming.

Still holding her hand as she arises wearing a look of fierce desire, I, who took care when she approached to position her so that her back be to the door, move towards her. Ushering her backwards, ever so slowly, as not to cause her to step on her modest train, wee are at last before the door leading to the corridor and the Great Cabin. Knowing that profound pleasuring lyes just beyond, I reach beside her, and turning the knob, the door opens. Aware of such, her ladyship turns somewhat, and lifting her dress slightly, she descends down three of the five steps. Stopping momentarily, she glances sideways into mine eyes teasingly before continuing.

Reaching the bottom of the stairs; allowing me just enough room, she stands just a foot beyond. Waiting, projecting a come hither look, she baits me, and resist her, I can not. Standing before her, hardly a moment passes when I snatch her by her arms, drawing her not so much to me, but rather turning her, and in the doing, I pin her against the bulkhead. Grasping the front of her dress, I all but tear her bodice as I hastily unfasten the closures, sev'rall at a time, I find her, to my delight, to be bare beneathe her goune, and thus, I indulge myself greedily without fuss.

In turn, as she sways slightly from the onslaught of my lustful attack, being overwhelmed by her owne powerful emotions, my woman takes hold of my breeches, and as she forcefully begins to undo the buttons, I slam door to the corridor shut.

For nigh on a Fortnight, whilst the 21 ships within *Trepassey* harbour be efficiently plundered, me crew spends a goodly amount of time on shore taking full advantage of the situation; yet despite their drinking bouts, which be as constant as is their wenching, ne'er do they neglect the duty of their shift: taking provisions, fresh water, plundering not onely the harbour ships as ordered, but on land as well, they bring on board need'd necessities, including medicines, rare spices and other similar items of considerable value. But these not be the onely pleasures. Each morning a cannon is fired from me ship, a signal directing all the Captains in port to come on board and take breakfast with me whilst the issuance of orders be made, including Admiral *Babidge*, who I had order lashed to the mast of his owne ship, the *Bideford Merchant*, and flogged severely for his cowardice, and despite his wounds, he is summoned as well. Why ye be thinkin' did this man peeve me more than the other Captains? The reason be a most simple one. He was the onely one amongst 'em who paid heed to my letter of introduction which formally announced my arrival, and as he ought, he made his ship ready to do battle in defence of both the harbour and the town, but at the sound of my first gunn, he, along with his crew, fled like frightened sheep, ne'er firing a shot. Leaving his gunns loaded, and jack flying, punishment aboard anny ship was in order. To some, my punishment may seeme severe, but 'tis onely that they do not know that what was dealt him was less than which he himself would have preskrybed.

'Twas not without strong argument that her Ladyship, having always felt as I, joins me at breakfast as I dine with the Captains of this port each morning, saying that she has always beene apart from their world, and such, like anny other backdoor dispenser of justice, one must use unusual methods; ours is pyracy, and each morning as wee dine, in our efforts to conceal her true identity, she is addressed falsely, for I shan't have anny harm come to her, her title, nor them within her household; furthermore, if they knew who graced their table, and belieeved her to be held against her will, I would surely find myself being sought by the entire French Fleet, and perhaps, should England and France become allies, the British would, at the least, double their present efforts in securing my demise.

With all ships now plundered, our provisioning complete, and me crew having their fill of taverns and wenching, and being no further reason to stay, wee make plans to saile.

Despite the forced appearances to dine with me, and the punishment dealt out, I find myself still greatly upset by the lack of courage found here, not onely by both the common seaman and those in powerful positions ashore, but most especially by these here highbrow Captains, and that Admiral. He who Commands a ship ought be one of daring and fortitude, but these here be the definitive examples of what is meant by the word Coward, make my blood boil with such rage, that now, even tho' our business here is concluded, me thoughts be that the punishments have not equalled the crime. Thus, my proposal is complete destruction of the sailing vessels within Trepassey before leaving, but let it be known that my motive is not for the purpose of sinking ships, but rather to instil humiliation upon those who have not the bearing and courage to be so positioned as a Commander, on land or sea, and thus, after taking a vote, it is decided that wee shall wreak havoc on all those that lay before us as wee depart; moreover, with regard to her Ladyship, who desires the taste of action, I not allow onely her to remain, but to accompany me on the Quarter-Deck whilst my plans be carry'd forth, and knowing that she deemes such to be a great privilege, I knows I neede not instruct her to keep clear.

Not a ship nor boat in the harbour, of which lay more than 200 shallops,[N13 & C05] most being in the general vicinity of the hatcheries, remains unscathed as me crew amuses themselves; blastin' the majority with cannon whilst others, those reluctant to sink, be met with fire from torches that be hurled atop them. This obliteration, not confined to the boats and ships, but eradicates also the sheds and machinery, and by the time wee depart, the shore is lain to waste, along with the livelihood of the populace with just as much vigour as wee mete out our owne version of justice.

So that she herself canne officially call herself both a vigilante and a pyrate, la Marquise, herself, helps to load and fire sev'rall cannon; not onely because she be angry as are wee, but because she longs for the crew to accept her. By dayes end, which ends also our long excursion, her Ladyship graciously accepts a share of the swag when it be unanimously offered her by me crew. 'Twas to our owne satisfaction, and that which I felt is to my credit, was when me company be joined by sev'rall of the local inhabitants.

Lastly, on the deck of our new Brigantine, is placed our booty, and tho' 'twasn't swag wee came fer, wee have quite a haul.

All on board be enjoying their triumph, especially the 13 Englishmen wee have avenged, for their jubilation is beyond description. As for my company, the majority spend most of the evening carousing atop the open deck whilst I do my celebrating with her Ladyship below in the great cabin, for come morn, being obliged to remain with me crew, I must bid her farewell for a time, but even as I depart, I knows, as does she, that I shall return to her.

Come morning, with her Ladyship safely aboard the *Willing Captive*, wee saile. Whilst cruising along the banks of *Newfoundland*, meeting with no less than nine French saile, wee, still beleaguered with hostility, destroy all except one ship, a fine ship of 26-gunns. This three-masted vessel, I be feeling, will be the equal of my first command, and thus, being overwhelmed with sentiment, I re-christen her *Royal Rover*, and thereafter, being a charitable sort, I order our worn down *Fortune* left behind for the Frenchies.[CSP.CS5a-251 iii & Pg. 465]

THE PIRATE ROBERTS. (PLACED HERE BECAUSE THIS INCLUDES REMARKS ON TREPASSEY.)

May ye 31st, 1721.

To the Board of Trade:

My Lords:

Inhabitants here, w'ch are yet unrepaired, has cost this Governm't near a thousand pounds, including the Bounty money given by the Gen'l Assembly to the men that went in ye Flagg of Truce. A Ship is lately arrived here from the Isle of May, w'ch in her passage a little to the So' ward of Burmuda, was taken by one Roberts, a Pirat Commanding a Ship of 38 Carriage and 12 Scowell Guns, and 240 men, and in his Company a Briganteen of 38 Guns, also well mann'd. He told the M'r of this Ship that he expected speedily to be joyned by a Ship of 46 Guns, and that he would make Virg'a a Visit and revenge the Death of the Pirats w'ch have been executed here, and considering the boldness of this Fellow, who last Year w'th no more than a Sloop of 10 Guns and 60 men ventured into Tenassy, in Newfoundland, where there were a great number of Merch't Ships, upwards of 1,200 men and 40 p's of Cannon, and yet, for Want of Courage in this heedless multitude, plundered and burnt divers Ships there and made such as he pleased prisoners, I thought it prudence to lay hold of this opportunity to put the Country in a better posture of Defence, and have got the Council Unanimously to Consent to ye Erecting of Batterys at the mouth of James River, York and Rappahannock, where I shall in a few days have 54 p's of Cannon mounted, and hope when these Batterys are finished according to the Plan I have laid the Country will be under no dread from any Alarm at what the pirats may be able to do, and the Ships in our River may ly in safety, but in order to prevent the danger to the Trade of these Plantations, I am humbly of opinion that Ships of greater force than those now station'd here are necessary to be sent to Guard the Coasts, for there is not one of the Guard Ships on this Coast fit to encounter such a one as Roberts has now under his Command, and it is no easy matter for two or more of the men of War to joine of a sudden, so remote as their stations are from one another, for suppressing any great force of the pirats appearing on these Coasts. Certainly a 50 or 50 Gun Ship is absolutely necessary to Convoy our Merch't Ships out to Sea and a smaller Vessel, such as a Sloop or Briganteen, to pursue little puckaroons in Shoal Water where a great Ship cannot come at them, would be very serviceable towards the Security of our Trade and driving the Pirats from this Coast, where they frequently resort to furnish themselves w'th provisions as well as to wait for good Ships when their own is grown out of Repair, And if, last Year, there had been two Men of War here, the One to have Cruised while the other Cleaned, the great loss this Colony, and the Trade of Great Britain in gen'l, suffered here from the Spanish privateers had been prevented.

My Lords, &c.^{sic}

The Letter above was copied, verbatim, from the book noted below.

The Official Letters of Alexander Spotswood (Lieutenant-Governour of the Colony of Virginia, 1710-1722, see pages 349 & 350 --- found within the Collections of the Virginia Historical Society. Vol. II Published 1885.

CSP version (it having the spelling corrected in keeping with the period) & most of the contractions written out, can be found in the Calendar State Papers, Colonial Series, America and West Indies March 1720 to December 1721. Published 1933. Within 513, found on page 328.

BLOOD and SWASH, The Unvarnished Life (& afterlife) Story of Pirate Captain, Bartholomew Roberts......pt.2 "THE WILLING CAPTIVE"

A SECRETARY OF PLACENTIA, NIGH TREPASSEY, 3 JULY 1720 WROTE:

> There are many ships drove in here by the pyrates who infest their coast and in one of our next ports they have burnt and destroyed twenty-six ships with a great number of fishing craft. Those pyrates have now plundered near 150 boats and 26 ships at Trepassey and St. Mary's which, if a communication had been cut overland, had not been above a two days march to have rescued these harbours where the pyrates have been repairing their ships for 14 days past, nor could any vessel sail from hence to reprieve 'em if wee had any ships of force [COP5].

News Clippings

One obferver of the daye remarked: "Roberts' men were, a parcel of furies."

After hearing of the occurrence, Governor Shute of New England ftated: "One cannot with-hold admiration for his (Roberts) bravery and daring."

Weekly Journal or Britifh Gazetteer   26 November 1720

"St. Lawrence. 28 June. A pyrate in a fmall floope of 12 gunns and 160 men entered Trepafsy on Tuefday the 21 ft inft, and made himfelf mafter of the faid harbour and of all the fhips there, being 22 fail and 250 fhallops. He made the mafters all prifoners and beat fome of them heartily for their cowardice for not making any refiftance. The Admiral, one Babidge, in the *Bideford Merchant*, fuffered moft becaufe he and all his hands left their fhip with jack, enfign and pendent flying, his gunns all loaded, in order to defend themfelves, but the pyrate was clofe alongfide him, ftruck his colours, hoifted their own, and fired all his guns. They cut his mafts and fevrall others clofe by the deck. He cut all the other fhip's cables in junks and their fhrouds. He feized one of Coplefton's fhip for himfelf, and fett all the fhips carpenters to work to fit her for his purpofe. He threatened to burn all the reft, and to hang one of the mafters, at leaft for their incivility in not waiting upon him to make him welcome at his entrance, he deftroyed about 30 fail, French and Englifh, on the Banks.

Two accountings regarding Lt. Gov Glenhill chastising his fellow high officials for their unreasonable attitude towards Cap'n Roberts for destroying Trepassy, when they, themselves, had been trying to figure out how to do it for sometime.

> *Facsimile*
>
> **CALENDAR OF STATE PAPERS**
> AMERICA AND WEST INDIES,
> MARCH, 1720 to DECEMBER, 1721.
>
> Pirates raid the Fishery. Lt. Governor Glenhill remarked that if the Government intended to destroy or remove the Fishery from Newfoundland, the pirates were helping to do that very effectually. In the summer of 1720 they raided the Fishery Fleet at Trepassy and St. Mary's, capturing or destroying 150 boats and 26 sloops. They remained there for a fortnight whilst they compelled the crew of the captured ships to git out one of the ships for their use—the *Royal Fortune*, under Bartholomew Roberts. Roberts was a savage and brutally cruel barbarian. But if Spotswood's account is correct, and he sailed into Trepassy in a sloop of 10 guns and with only 60 men, and there dominated in this way the confused and leaderless Fishery Fleet with 1200 men and 40 pieces of cannon, one cannot withhold admiration for his barvery and daring Mary s, capturing or destroying 150 boats and 26 sloops. (200, 251 iii, iv, 281 i, 325)

Requested Citation: *Calendar of State Papers Colonial Series, America and West Indies: Multiple Volumes, March 1720 to Decenber-1721*. Cecil Headlam (London, 1933).

> *Excerpt*
>
> 281. i. Lt Governor Gledhill to Mr. Secretary Craggs. Placentia, July 3, 1720. If what these proclamations suggests that H.M. intentions are to destroy or remove the fishery, the pyrates are doing it effectually. There are many ships drove in here by the pyrates who infest our coast *etc. Refers to his* scheme for making roads *etc. v.* 1st Oct. 1719. *Continues :*—These Pyrates have now destroyed near 150 boats and 26 ships at Trepassy and St. Maryes, wch. if a communication had been cut o're land, had not been above two days march to have rescued those harbours where the pyrates have been repairing their ships for 14 days past. Asks for particular instructions on these points *etc. Signed,* S. Gladhill. *Copy.* 3½ *pp.* [*C.O.* 194, 6. *Nos.* 83, 83.i.]

Chapter Twelve
An Offer of Clemency

Come the end of June, sailing our two ships in company on another raiding expedition, wee took sev'rall prizes; among them, the Sloop named *Success* at *Newfoundland*.

Early in July, wee plunder the *Norman Galley*, a Pinque called the *Richard* belonging to *Bideford Jonathan*, whose Master be named *Whitfeld*; the

Willing Mind of Poole; the *York*, again; and the *Blessing* which hailed from *Leamington*, from each of which, wee increased our company, but should the truth be known, many of those wishing to join me company lack the high calibre skills comparable to those of me crew. Of the lot, there be but a handful who possess anny talents as sea artists befitting our purpose.

SPEAKING RETROSPECTIVELY ⇁

'Twas the 13th of July 1720, when wee came upon the *Samuel*, commanded by Captain *Samuel Carey* of *London*. She was a distance of perhaps 35 nautical miles east of the *Newfoundland* shore when they espy'd our two ships on the horizon, so wee learned. To hear tell, Captain *Carey* watched our approach with increasing concern, and even tho' he was on the King's business, he was affrighted when wee fired our gunns; his worst fears, however, unconfirmed until he saw within his spyglass our pyrate flags, confirming such, belonged to yours truly. Knowing such, Captain *Carey* reckoned there be nigh on 100 men on board each of my vessels, out numbering his crew 20 to 1. The *Samuel*, having a mere 6 gunns, Captain *Carey* knew he was completely out-gunned as well.

Our splendid new, 220-tunn French Ship, *Royal Rover*, carried 28 gunns. From her main topmast head, wee flew our jack, which from nigh on all angles, was clearly visible. Tho' smale, our 80 tunn Brigantine, *Good Fortune*, is serving us well. From her main topmast flys the *Cross Of St. George* emblazoned with four blazing balls.[N13]

When the larger of our vessels sailes on in, and hailing the *Samuel*, I ordered her Captain to hoist out his boat and come on board my ship. Being an intelligent man, Captain *Carey* did as he was told. During our relatively brief discussion, I learn he carried intelligence concerning me and my company, specifically, with regard to our latest saile off the coast of *North America*, where is stated, *"Left in our wake, a trail of destruction."* He went on to say that *"it is the English King's hope, that a pardon will put an end to the devastation, and what he presumed to be our need for acts of vengeance."* To this, Captain *Carey* presented papers offering to myself, and me crew, a full pardon.

Be that as it may, me and my shipmates thought little about such an offer, which, strange as it may seeme, the audacity of it, serving onely to enrage us, I wrote to the King, the following note.①

> To My Sovereign
> King George,
> Wee shall accept no Act of Grace that the King and Parliament be Damned with their Acts of Grace For Us. Neither will wee go to Hope Point to be hanged up a sun drying as Kidds and Braddish's company were But if we be overpowered, we shall sett fire to the powder and all go merrily to hell together.
> Bath. Roberts

Immediately thereafter, agreeing with what I had written, my company swarmed upon the *Samuel's* decks, whereby they began taking her apart, tearing open hatches, they be, attacking the cargo like madmen as they cut open bales, trunks and boxes with boarding axes and Cutlash's, whichever be within each owns grasp.[CSP-CS2]

Some goods, as ordered by Lord *Anstis*, be plundered; making off with sailes, arms, powder, cordage and no less than £8000/ of the choicest goods, including two of the carriage gunns, all of the ship's spare rigging, and, of course, her stores.

Still outraged by such impudence, and rightly so, much of the cargo was simply hacked to pieces and cast into the sea together with her anchor and cables.

My company, finished in their looting, focusing their attentions on the crew, invited each to join, and excepting the Captain, three passengers and an Irishman, me crew still remembering *Kennedy*,[E2] the remainder of *Samuel's* crew joined readily.

Whilst the company debated whether to burn and sink the Merchant, another saile was spotted on the horizon, and with barely a word, wee scurried forthwith to our respective vessels to give chace.

---

①RE: Captain William Kidd[E6] & Joseph Bradish[E7] trusting in the 1698 *ACT OF GRACE* which offered a pardon to pirates who willingly surrendered, were nevertheless tried & hung for piracy, as were countless others.

These two men, altho' having no other association, were frequently associated due to similarities regarding ship's names, scuttling their ships, piracy, jails held, & death.

Expressed their allegiance and loyalty to each other one pirate who brandished "a lighted match in order to Set the Magazine on fire Swearing very profanely let's all go to Hell together."[B17 & HCA 1/99/152]

Wee later learnt that, Captain *Carey*, having return'd to *Boston* with the aid of them left on board, had reported onely our rage, tellin' 'em, *"Incessant cursing and swearing, they were more like fiends than men."* [B8 & 9] with ne'er a mention of that which provoked such behaviour.

Despite my dislike of expletives, I will not begrudge me crew for their use of such vulgarity on this occasion, for I too was greatly piqued by the King's offer, whereas, not pursuant to that of my usual standards, 'twas an emotional experience that was rekindled when it was further learnt that Captain *Carey* also reported that his crew had beene forced, at point of pistol, to join my company. This was a monstrous falsehood, for onely one, the *Samuel's* chief mate, *Harry Glasby*, did I strongly urge. Ne'er on anny occasion did I take recruits by force.[B2 & B12] Even the musicians, whom I employ, are free to decline. The rest of me crew, the lot of 'em, 'tis of their owne volition to saile with me. As for the few passengers who must come aboard after their vessel is made either unseaworthy or sunk, they be aboard my flagship for a brief spell onely before being either sett ashore in a safe port, or upon another vessell; moreover, being a gracious sort, I am always willing to provide new recruits with a certificate stating they had beene forced;[B15] the main reason being, considering our profession, that after a time, those who prove to be unworthy of my esteem are either put ashore in a port of their choosing along our route, or should they prefer, they be free to depart with anny ship wee later encounter.

With regard to the ship that gave leave for the *Samuel's* departure, our pursuit, which ended about midnight, proved to be a Brig from *Bristol*. En route to *Boston*, she was under the command of one Captain *Bowls*. The news that he not onely sailed a ship from *Bristol*, but also hailed from such, sent me crew into another uproar, and tho' barbarous they be when motivated, me crew resisted the temptation to make sport of the fellow in remembrance of that cod's wallop, Captain *Rogers* for his relentless attack whilst wee be off the coast of *Barbadoes*, for he too, hail'd from *Bristol*.

Calendar of State Papers Colonial, America and West Indies: Volume 32, 1720-1721, ed.

REQUESTED CITATION: Cecil Headlam (London, 1933), pp. 97-106. *British History Online* http://www.british-history.ac.uk/cal-state-papers/colonial/america-west-indies/vol32/pp97-106 / [Direct Link]. https://www.british-history.ac.uk/cal-state-papers/colonial/america-west-indies/vol32

ON DIRECT LINK ABOVE SEE: AUG. 19. BOSTON, N. ENGLAND. - #200

Capt. Carey who left London 29th May was taken by a pirate ship of 26 guns, and a sloop of 10 near the banks of Newfoundland who took and destroyed so much of his cargo as amounts to about £8000 sterling; and also reports that they had fallen upon and destroy'd the fishery of Newfoundland. *Signed*, Samll. Shute. *Endorsed*, Recd. 27th Sept. 1720, Read 7th March 1720/21.

ADDITIONAL INFORMATION

Captain Samuel Carry, with a crew of ten men to work the ship, and several passengers, was bound for Boston with a cargo of ironware, forty-five barrels of gunpowder, and an assortment of English goods in bales and trunks.[sic]

SATURDAY *October* 15. 1730.

We have the following long Story from Boston in New-England of a famous Pirate Ship, viz.

Boston, August 22. The 15th current arrived here the Ship Samuel, about 11 Weeks from London, Capt. Sam Carry, who in his Voyage hither the 13th of laft, in Lat. 44. a-about 30 or 40 Leagues to the Eaft w. of the Banks of Newfoundland, was taken by 2 Pirates, viz. a Ship of 26 Guns and a Sloop of 10, both commanded by Capt. Tho. Roberts, having on board about 100 Men, all Englifh.

The firft Thing the Pirates did, was to ftrip both Paffengers and Seamen of all their Money and Cloaths which they had on board, with a loaded Piftol held to every one's Breaft, ready to fhoot him dead, who did not immediately give an Account, of both and refign them up. The next Thing they did was with Madnefs and Rage, to tear up the Hatches, enter the Hold like a Parcel of Furies, where the Axes, Cutlaffes, &c. they cut, tore and broke open Trunks, Boxes, Cafes and Bales, and when any of the Goods came upon Deck which the did not like to carry with them on board their Ship, inftead of toffing them into the Hold again, they threw them over-board into the Sea. The Ufual Method they had to open Chefts, was by fhooting a Brace of Bullets with a Piftol into the Key-hole to force them open. The Pirates carried away from Capt. Carry's Ship on board their own, 40 Barrels of Powder, two great Guns, his Cables, &c. and to the Value of about Nine or Ten Thoufand Pounds Sterling worth of the choiceft Goods he had on board. There was nothing heard among the Pirates all the while but curfing, fwearing, damning, and blafpheming, to the greateft Degree imaginable, and often faying they would not go to Hopes-Point in the River of Thames, to be hung up in Gibbets a Sun-drying, as Kidd and Bradifhs Company did: for if it fhould change that they fhould be attacked by any fuperior Power of Force which they could not mafter, they would immediately put Fire with one of their Piftols to their Powder, and go all merrily to Hell together. They often ridiculed and made a Mock at the Acts of Grace with an Oath, that they had not got Money enough; but when they had, if then they could obtain a Pardon, after they fhould fend Work to London, they would be thankful for it. They forced and took away with them Capt. Carry's Mate, and feveral of his Men, but whilft the Pirates were difputing whether to fink or burn the Ship, they fpied a Sail the fame Evening, and fo let him go free.

At Midnight they came up with the fame, which was a fnow from Briftol, Capt. Bowls Mafter, bound for Bofton, of whom they made a Prize, and ferved him as they did Captain Carry, unladed his Veffel, and forced all his Men, defigning to carry the Snow with them to make her a Hulk to careen their Ship with.

The above faid Capt. Roberts was born at Bridgwater in Somerfetfhire, in Nov. 1718, was third Mate of a Guiney-Man, out of London, for Guiney, Capt. Plummer

Commander, who was taken by a Pirate, and by that Means Roberts himſelf became a Pirate, and being an active, briſk Man, they voted him their Captain, which he readily embraced.

The ſaid Roberts, in the above ſaid Sloop, Rhode-Iſland built, with a Brigantine Conſort Pirate, was ſome Time in Jan. laſt in the Lat. of Barbadoes, near the Iſland, where they took and endeavoured to take ſeveral Veſſels: but the Governor hearing of it, Fitted out one Capt. Rogers of Briſtol, in a fine Galley, a Ship of about 20 Guns, and a Sloop, Capt. Graves Commander. Capt. Rogers killed and wounded ſeveral of Roberts's Men, and finding Capt. Rogers too ſtrong for him, run for it, as alſo did his Conſort Brigantine, which he never ſaw, nor heard of ſince.

From Barbadoes, Roberts went to an Iſland called Granada, where he careened his Sloop, and from thence with 45 Men he came to Newfoundland, into the Harbour of Trepaſſi, towards the latter End of June laſt, with Drums beating, Trumpets ſounding, and Engliſh Colours flying, their Pirate Flag at the Top-maſt Head: and there being 22 Sail in that Harbour, upon Sight of the Pirate, the Men all fled on Shoar, and left their Veſſels, which they proffeſſed themſelves of, burnt, ſunk and deſtroyed all of them, except one Briſtol-Galley, which they deſigned to be their beſt Pirate-Ship, if a better did not preſent. After they did all the Miſchief they could in that Harbour, they came on upon the Banks, where they met 9 or 10 Sail of Frenchmen, one of whom if the Pirate-Ship of 26 Guns above ſaid, taken from a Frenchman, unto whom Roberts the Pirate gave the Briſtol-Galley, but ſunk and deſtroy'd all the other French Veſſels, taking firſt out what Guns were fit for his own Ship, and all other valuable Goods.

Roberts the Pirate deſigned from Newfoundland to range through the Weſtern and and Canary Iſlands, and ſo to the Southward, to the Iſland of New Providence, proffeſſed by Negroes, in the South Latitude 17, which they ſay if the Place of the Pirates General Rendezvous, where they have a Fortification, and a great Magazine of Powder, &c. where the intend to ſpend their Money with the Portugueſe Negroe-Women. Roberts the Pirate ſays, that there if a French Pirate on the North-Coaſt of America, who gives no Quarters to any Nation, and if he met him, he would give him none. The Pirates ſeem much in raged at the Briſtol Men, for Capt. Rogers's Sake, whom they hate as they do the Spaniards.

Sailing with a good wind and a steady current, wee make for *Baker's Point* near the low green point where wee are not onely to rendezvous with the *Willing Captive*, but also where both timber and fresh water canne be obtained with ease, and being aboard different vessels than when previously here, wee are paid little notice. Arriving in the twilight, wee anchor on the lee side of the Ship that beholds her Ladyship, la Marquise d'Éperon-noire. As the three ships rock gently, 'tis eager I be to pay her a call, but matters concerning me crew be in neede of settling.

By tea time, our business being concluded, I hoist out a smale boat, and whilst rowing myself on over, I find that I have missed not onely her Ladyship's favours, but her company as well. As I trod the deck of her ship, the door leading to her cabin opens, and it's clear to see that her ladyship, as I expected she would be, is overjoyed to see me. As I stand before her, I open my arms, and to my delight, she runs into them. Sweeping her up into my arms, I carry her thro' the door, down the corridor, and into her bedchamber, where, without hesitation, after I place her atop the bed, she, being a feisty wench, begins to unbutton my cloathes; what's more, knowing she hath drawn me a bath, it be into the tub I go.

For sev'rall minutes I relish the relaxation as she scrubs me from head to toe, but after she is thro', she sets the soap on the table behind her and starts to leave the room, " 'Tis lonely within this big tub," says I, grabbing her hand, and as she kicks and shrieks, knowing she's but playing hard to get, I pull her in atop me.

Soaked to the skin, altho' in the falsest shew of anger, she hollers, "You beast!" and as she rises to her feet, stomping her foot, she demands my assistance. "Well, art thou going to unlace my goune, or canst be thee intends me to remain thusly cloath'd until I catch my death of cold?"

Adoring her little tantrum fitts, as she be gorgeous when angry, and even more exciting, altho' ne'er did I expect to admit such, I am but a mere captive audience whenever I be with her.

As the last of the laces be undone, she quickly slips out of the goune and begins to dry off with soft linnen, but in my haste, wastin' no time, I seize 'er. "Come here, wench!"

Still keeping up the pretence as I pull her back into the enormous tub. "It hath beene nigh on a fortnight, and thee shall deny me not."

"Deny thee!" she exclaims, whilst shoving me backwards, "I be starv'd for thine attentions, fy Arglwydd," and as she coos, 'tis difficult to discern from which I obtain more pleasure, the divine feeling of copulation, or the look and sounds of her enjoyment as sweet sounds of pleasuring fill the air.

SOMETIME LATER →

Her Ladyship wakes me. After dining, wee talk for a spell whilst she gives me a deep shoulder massage. Later still, after all three ships proceed southward in consort, and just before turning in for the night, 'tis time, methinks, to present her with a gift. Dashing to me *Royal Rover*, I fetch the elegantly appointed peignoir that I have had in my possession for some 20 yeeres. Returning to her, "I purchased this garment in my youth for my then intended, and why I have saved it thro' the yeeres, I canne venture onely to guess. Perhaps I ne'er gave up hope that one daye I would find for myself the woman who would fulfil my most searching dreams."

Amid a delightful smile she utters, "It's beautiful, fy Arglwydd," and whilst leaning towards me to give me a gentle kiss on my lips, she adds, "Thank thee."

Her Ladyship's demeanour, coupled with her addressment moves me deeply. "I hunger to see thee wearing it."

After removing the dressing goune she be wearing, the feelings that possess me at this moment, as I help her to don the delicate garment, are indescribable. Such a demanding, yet rewarding wench is she, it shall please me to fulfil her every desire that lyes within my ability.

What's amazing is that this is the same peignoir he gave me whilst he was a spirit living in my home almost 300 years in the future, and now, to have the one I love gives it to me again, here, in his own time, well... all I can say, as the soft fabric caresses my face, is that the doing has brought me immeasurable joy, for he, as I am his, is mine.

Waking with the sun, I find that last night was the first peaceful sleep I have experienced since arriving in this time period; what is more, I feel, at last, that all will turn out well.

Later that day, as my Captain sails forth, taking care of business, wee aboard the *Willing Captive* sail to *Carriacou Isle*, where he shall meet up with us.

Chapter Thirteen
The Royal Fortune, The Ranger, & Saint Barthélemy
Location: 'Newfoundland Region to the West Indies'

Two dayes later, on the 18th daye of July 1720, wee take a Virginian named *Little York*, of which, *James Phillips* was Master, and the *Love* of *Lancaster*; both of which wee plundered and lett go. The next daye wee encountered the *Phoenix*. She was a snow from *Bristol*, *John Richards*, Master. Also plunder'd, wee let 'er go, but not before two of her crew joined my ranks.

A couple of hours before dawn breaks, wee come upon another saile, the Brigantine *Essex*, captained by *Robert Peat*. Loaded with passengers, and some goods, the latter of which, me crew took their fill. In this, except that whilst mine has beene satisfied, I cannae venture to guess just when the rage that brought us to *Newfoundland* will subside.

Below are the New clippings and pertinent letters and recorded information that followed.

Boston News-Letter   **22-29 August 1720**

The briganteen Essex was taken by Two Pirates, one a French Built Ship of about Two Hundred and Twenty Tons, Twenty-six guns mounted, and One hundred Men, Commanded by one Roberts, the other a Sloop of about Eighty Tons, Ten Guns mounted, and 40 men, who did him considerable Damage, and abused several Women, that was Passengers on Board The pirates declared they would have sunk Capt. Peates Briganteen if they could have known what to have done with his Servants and Passengers; the next Day being the 18th about Two a Clock they parted with him, and said they designed for Madera.[B10]

Author's Note: Regarding the word 'abused' in the Boston Newsletter above: Altho' there are some reports of Pirates raping European white women, it was very rare, but more importantly were The Articles wherein states, in part: "If any Man is found seducing anny of the latter Sex [meaning a woman] and carries her to Sea, disguised, he shall suffer Death." Knowing the delicate sensibilities of the upper class of the period, being handled with anymore force than they were accustom would have been regarded as abuse in their eyes. Cap'n Thomas Anstis, however, after absconding with the Good Fortune 18 April 1721, with 21 from his crew of thugs, which Bart was happy to see go, 'twas learned that Cap'n Anstis, & his crew, did in fact successively rape a female captive, and after which, after breaking her back, they flung her into the sea.[B8 & 9]

The Following statement was made in an *Essex County* Court Records on August 31st, 1720.[B10]

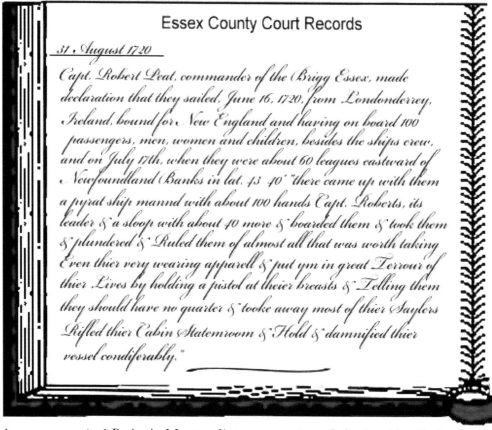

Essex County Court Records

31 August 1720

Capt. Robert Peat, commander of the Brigg Essex, made declaration that they sailed, June 16, 1720, from Londonderrey, Ireland, bound for New England and having on board 100 passengers, men, women and children, besides the ships crew, and on July 17th, when they were about 60 leagues eastward of Newfoundland Banks in lat. 43 40' there came up with them a pyrat ship mannd with about 100 hands Capt. Roberts, its leader & a sloop with about 40 more & boarded them & took them & plundered & Ruled them of almost all that was worth taking Even thier very wearing apparell & put ym in great Terrour of thier Lives by holding a pistol at theier breasts & Telling them they should have no quarter & tooke away most of thier Saylers Rifled thier Cabin Statemroom & Hold & damnified thier vessel condiferably."

Below is an account of *Benjamin Marstons Jr.'s* voyage from *Ireland* to *New England* in 1720.[B10]

Bofton News-Letter   **10-17 October 1720**
Daniel Starr of Bofton, by Trade a Joyner, but lately a Mariner on board the Briganteen Effex, whereof Robert Peat was commander, related that in his voyage from Ireland to Salem on the 17th of July laft he was taken by one Captain Thomas Roberts, Commander of a Pirate fhip and floop of 150 men, and forced the faid Starr to go along with him againft his will.[B10]

> *Author's Note: A Similar report with regard to Daniel Starr's misfortune written up in the American Weekly Mercury correctly named the Captain of the pirates as John Roberts.*[B10]

Acquiring additional information, directly below, the Boston News-Letter did a follow up their previous report concerning the *Essex*.[B10]

> **Boston News-Letter** 22-29 October *1720*
> Laſt week arrived at Salem Capt. Marſton from Ireland with ſeveral Paſſengers, both Men and Women, who taken by Captain Roberts, the Pirate, about two Days after he had parted from Captain Carey. The ſaid Pirate had alſo taken a Briſtol veſſel bound for Virginia from Briſtol, out of whom the Pirate took his goods and Forced ſome of moſt of his Men, and put on board ſeveral of Captain Marſton's Men or Paſſengers to go with her for Briſtol.[B10]

John Leverett, President of Harvard College, a friend of a man who was on the merchant, *Samuel*, wrote a letter to the family in regard to the incident.[B10]

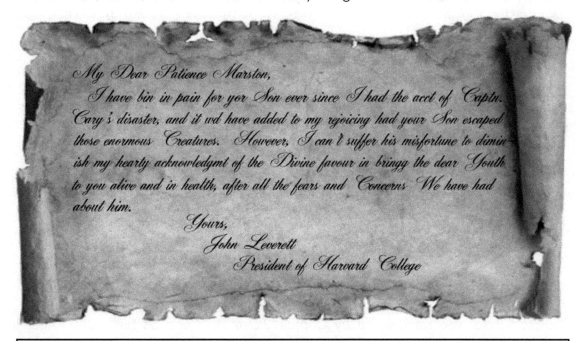

My Dear Patience Marston,
I have bin in pain for yor Son ever since I had the acct of Captn. Cary's disaster, and it wd have added to my rejoicing had your Son escaped those enormous Creatures. However, I can't suffer his misfortune to diminish my hearty acknowledgmt of the Divine favour in bringg the dear Youth to you alive and in health, after all the fears and Concerns We have had about him.
Yours,
John Leverett
President of Harvard College

Author's Note: In relation to Ocean-Born Mary, none of the reports as yet discovered, except as relayed by the infants' parents &/or others aboard the brigantine Essex, mention just when Elizabeth gave birth to the child, including the Captain's Log; however, having complete understanding of Captain Roberts persona, knowing also that he returned to sea in 1701 after the loss of his betrothed, & the documented proof of his ship's being in the area at the same time, as well as Captain Roberts well-known benevolence & generosity, lends considerable credence to Jeremy D'Entremont's well presented account.

The waters be plentiful, and me crew, being a self-indulgent lot, plunder them plenty. Next came a Sloop, followed by the Brigantine, *Sadbury*, under Captain *Thomas*, but 'twas not as easie for her. This ship bore an unusual amount of willing recruits, the entire company in fact, and after joining me crew, valuing her not, her former crew strips 'er of all that was deem'd to be of value before sending 'er to the bottom of the sea.

With none of the aformention'd ships carrying much, wee vote for the *West Indies*. Making saile forthwith, wee sail'd in the latitude of the small isle, *Deseada* which lyes in the Northern region of the *Leeward Islands*, just East of *Guardaloope*.

Being the isle farthest east of *Dominica*, wee ought find ships bearing provisions, and with the absence of advantageous offerings during the voyage, our supply of water, provisions and necessities became short in supply.

Sailing on, wee cruise past *Barbadoes*, our heading, the general latitude of *Grenada*; my intention being to boot-top me ships whilst taking on the necessary fresh water and provisions need'd before sailing forth to the Isle of *Saint Barthélemy*, that lyes in and amongst the *Leeward Islands*.

Being a rather overlooked, and under supplied Port, she openly welcomes the trade from pyrates. 'Tis here where, '*Gentleman of Fortune*,' such as ourselves, canne trade our plunder for rigging, necessities, and Gold-Dust, whilst also indulging in the hospitalities found within the Taverns.

On 4 September, wee saile into the lagoon at *Carriacou Isle*,[N12] where wee come upon a smale Sloop named, the *Relief*. 'Tis plain to see as wee approach, that her crew, as well as the crew of the *Willing Captive*, is having a Grand time harvesting the succulent turtles so prevalent within these waters.[CSP-CS5a-251 iii & CSP-CS9-Pages 465 & 466]

Once anchored, myself, and much of me crew go ashore where wee be greeted by Captain *Robert Dunn* and his First Mate. After the introductions, graciously provided by her Ladyship, wee, being myself, Captain *Anstis*, and our Bos'n, *Richard Jones*, who himself altho' onely recently amongst us, possesses fine seamanship skills, and thus, was elected Bos'n soon after signing our Articles, be invited to refresh ourselves. The latter, however swift to accept their invitation, excuses himself, no doubt for his usual hurriedness to survey the situation, issue duty assignments, and after which, states that he shall join us later.

Making enquiries with regard to their business as wee dine, I quickly learn that Captain *Dunn* and his crew; in addition to their legal activities, were not above a bit of smuggling, and for a period of 3 weekes, I am pleas'd to convey that all hands get on splendidly.

Having much booty to sell, a bargain is struck, wherein 'tis agreed to meet off the *Black Rocks* that lye on the windward side of *Saint Christophers* in a fortnight where Captain *Dunn*, whilst disposing for us a goodly amount of contraband, will supply to us fresh water and provisions before continuing in consort to *Saint Barthélemy*, whither wee shall share equally in the revenue. 'Twere a faire price, wee felt, for the hiring of Captain *Dunn* and his crew, whom wee have high hopes regarding the successful dispersion of our plunder.

Sev'rall restful dayes pass before Captain *Dunn* sailes onwards to *Saint Christophers* in consort with the *Willing Captive*, during which time me crew transferred a great deal of highly sought after merchandise from both the *Royal Rover* and *The Good Fortune* to the *Relief's* hold.

The crew of the *Willing Captive*, being at liberty to enjoy the port's hospitality until the 24th when they are to hove on the horizon untill my arrivall, be eager to get underway.

Tho' I have my doubts that her Ladyship will enjoy herself, not being particularly keen on court life, she will see to it that those who crew her vessell be properly versed, attired, and introduced in a manner that shall afford 'em grand treatment, and knowing me crew, as I do, leaves no doubt in my mind that they will enjoy hobnobbing with the blue-bloods on that quaint little Isle during their stay.

Both Captain *Dunn* and her Ladyship, on their respective vessels, sett saile on the ebb tide. Before leaving ourselfes, nigh on a weeke of dayes more be spent in the gathering of provisions and fresh water need'd for our voyage.

Having beene at sea a few dayes onely, wee find ourselves strangely becalmed. Scrutinizing the sky, me sees a lone ominous looking thunderhead forming directly overhead, and recognizing the subtles signs, I knows this part of our journey shall not be an easie one, but before the crew canne be rallied, the heart of this unusual circumstance besieges me ships with cyclonic winds as an abundantly thieving twister plummeting from this thunderclowd, dances betwixt me ships. Tho' small, the mildly insidious rogue, altho' it did not inflict anny serious injury to me crew or ships during its raid, it did carry away much need'd supplies before it departed as swiftly as it had appeared.

After an accounting be made of our remaining provisions, and me ships restored to a neat and orderly state, wee, as we ought, be duly thankful for the rest of the daye as wee continue our voyage peacefully upon a calm sea.

Later, with full dark upon us, not a star be visible. The brief, though intense brush with the seas fury earlier this daye, put us behind schedule in our forthcoming rendezvous with the *Relief*, and such being the case, I choose to keep us under full saile well into the night.

As dawn breaks, 'tis manning the whipstaff, I am, and gazing into the brightly lit sky, her beautiful red and yellow hews, as ever, be one of life's greatest joys to behold, and yet such splendour, as fleeting as is each new swell, ne'er is to last. This yeere being inundated with bizarre weather, nature's fury, again, suddenly and without warning, interrupting violently, deals us a wealth of foul weather beginning with a powerful gust of wind slamming against our starboard side. Being on familiar terms with the intense moods of the sea, I knows at once wee be within the eye of yesterdayes squall that, on the quiet, has beene forming all around us; ergo, and knowing wee are to be besieged by a violent storm, I, without hesitation, give the order to muster the crew.

"All hands on Deck!" hollers, Lord *Jones*.

In a few moments, the crew duly gathers before me on the open deck. As always, being the sort who prefers to issue mine owne commands, which I use as a means to reinforce their unswerving confidence in me, I address me crew.

"Men, wee be in for quite a blow, but courage and skill shall see us thro'."

In my ceaseless efforts to further secure the faith and trust me crew has in my abilities, I leap over the crates situated before me, and as the great thunderhead forms, blackening the sky, I point to the barrels and crates containing fruits and vegetables, and sev'rall hogsheads of water, and whilst swiftly taking the stairs leading to the Quarter-Deck, seeing them still cluttering the open deck, I bellow, "Get those provisions stowed below!"

Hardly two minutes pass when wee are beset with heavy rain.

"You men thar!" says I, hollering still, this time to the men just below me on the Main-Deck, and pointing, "Give 'em a hand."

Following their orders, the crew works quickly. More than half the men climb aloft into the rigging to take in saile, whilst the remaining hands, mostly those assigned to the tacks and braces, work feverishly to stow the provisions below as ordered.

Within a few minutes, the majority of the sailes now reefed, wee hove. The howling winds force the men to abandon their labours with regard to the stowing of provisions in lieu of maintaining the position of the sailes on the mainmast.

Incessant rains, driven by cyclonic winds, sting the faces of me crew whilst huge swells continually slam nigh broadside against me *Royal Rover*. Breaking across her deck high enough to soak me crew to the waist as me ship heels violently, the gunnels awash in the sea's wicked cross tides give me crew cause to hang on to ropes and railings, lest be swept overboard.

Shouting to *Stephenson*, our pilot, "Mind the helm, lest you lett 'er heel too far and wee capsize!" is joined by *Mister Oughterlauney*, who together struggle to hold the whipstaff as it is churned by the heavy sea. Moments later, altho' shouting still, my voice; however booming it ought to a beene, canne barely be heard over the roar of the wind whilst fiery horse tails stream in rapid succession as dramatic sprays of white water wash over the bow. As wee plunge deeply into each new swell, I canne barely make out the *Good Fortune*. As are wee, she be heeling and pitching whilst swells approaching, what I estimate to be nigh 29 feet, threaten to swallow me ships in its troughs as the storm's fury tosses 'em about like toys upon its crests.

Once again the bow dips low as the mighty Atlantic roars her fury, causing more sea water to surge over the gunnels whilst the onslaught of the raging wind threatens us. But reading the signs, I knows wee have past thro' the worst of it, and soon the storm ought pass us by.

Nigh on an hour since the onset of the storm, as her ferocity slowly begins to abate, the powerful winds begin to subside, and a thankful crew knows the worst be over. Within the next half hour as the sea calms, both ships roll jauntily along.

Looking over me *Royal Rover*, my Lord *Jones* returns from the *Good Fortune* with what I hope be good news. "Damage report, my Lord."

My Bos'n, speaking with the grin of satisfaction, " 'Tis 'appy I be to report the crew has sustained minor injuries onely, Commodore, and minor damage onely to the ships. Given calmer seas, wee ought be able to make repairs whilst en route."

"Very good, my Lord. When permissible, have the crew don dry attire in rotation. After which, assign duties to repair the damage and see that both ships are made shipshape in Bristol Fashion."

"Aye, Commodore."

Turning aft, bound for the Great Cabin, I get into some dry cloathes.

With the sea now calm, a scrutinized search for damage progresses, and as found, the ship's carpenters commence with repairs. Altho' a quantity of our stores survived, much was washed overboard.

Returning to the Quarter-Deck, as I meticulously inspect my ship, 'tis pleas'd I am to see my company, altho' quite exhausted, is working diligently repairing the damage.

MEANWHILE, THE WILLING CAPTIVE SAILS INTO SAINT CHRISTOPHERS' HARBOUR →

With all the hands duly gathered, I think it's best I give 'em one more talking to. "As I said en route, all of you will partake in the grandeur that surrounds court society whilst in this port."

As the entire crew cheers in grateful appreciation, it's plain to see, eager as they are to go ashore, that they're all chomping at the bit.

"Do you all remember your lessons regarding etiquette and deportment, and the persons you are to impersonate whilst on yon Island?"

To my satisfaction, all in my crew replying that they know their roles well, "Then let us make for the island."

Beginning my turn to the left in order to speak to *Mister Crow*, the most trusted member of my ship's crew, I sweep my skirt back with my right hand and walking back towards my Pinnace, "*Mister Crow*, please prepare the smaller boat for myself, Mrs Robles, William Crandall, and *Maître François*. It is my intention to speak with him and invite him to be in attendance with William, serving, as it were, his apprenticeship as my aide-de-camp." Turning to look at him, "That is if it's alright with you, William?"

"Aye, my Lady. I shall be privileged to train him."

Mister Crow, pleas'd with my offer, replies with obvious gratitude, "That's right kind of you, my Lady."

"Then you believe he will accept?"

"Aye."

Smiling, I set my bag down, and turning, I return briefly to my cabin to rewrite the note I had previously written that will not only introduce myself and my entourage, but young *Jean François*,[B2 pg 68] and as soon as I can brief him, his first assignment will be to deliver the note to the Governour's house.

Either William Crandall or *Jean François* will always be in attendance, and *John Philips*, who joined Captain *Roberts'* crew in Trepassey, will fair better aboard the *Willing Captive*, will be among the second of the two rotating shifts.

The first boat to reach shore is my Pinnace, whereby *Jean François*, leaping from the boat, scurrys away with the message.

In no time, my new aide-de-camp, in training, reaches the home of *Governour Mathew*, Lt General of the Leeward Isles. Climbing the steps, *Jean François* raps on the heavy door, which is opened by a tallish, older servant, who, upon hearing his somewhat winded explanation, takes the note and strides off.

Applying two rather sharp knocks upon the door leading to the study, the butler opens the door.

From within, a voice asks, "What is so important, Clinton, that you find it necessary to beat on the door in such a manner?"

"la Marquise d'Éperon-noire, sir."

After a day sorting thro' a mountain of letters, the rather tired Governour, in a grumpy tone, asks, "What about her?"

"She's here, sir, and with a Full Retinue."

Leaping out of his leather-covered chair, he screeches, "You mean now? Are you a fool, show her in!"

"She's on the beach, sir." Crossing the room, the butler presents the message he had placed atop the silver salver he carries. "This was just delivered by her Ladyship's boy."

Picking up the note rather abruptly, the well-dressed gent slips his thumb beneath the wax seal bearing the unmistakable ancestral, Joan of Arc, signet belonging to la Marquise d'Éperon-noire, and removes the sheet of lace edged parchment. The use of an envelope, and the unique seal atop a distinctly folded red ribbon, was all the Governour needed as proof of the sender's identity.

The rather flustered *Jean François*, as he waits at the front door whilst observing a distinguished looking fellow opening the envelope, he utters, " That must be *Governour Mathew*."

Having quickly read the note, *Governour Mathew*, in a state of giddy agitation, must quickly prepare for the arrival of a notable Aristocrat whose presence will present him with the rare opportunity to demonstrate his gracious hospitalities, from which he hopes will beget more visits from court society, therewith creating wealth and prestige for both himself and his family.

Still witnessing the Governour's actions, young *Jean François*, can only stand and stare in amazement by the fanfare generated by my letter as the

Governour hurries out of his private rooms and into the large foyer whilst hollering for his wife.

Speaking to his butler, "Clinton, summon all the servants, quickly." Hollering to a young man, "You, houseboy. Run to the stables and have the footmen ready the carriages for la Marquise and her party. They are to be picked up at once." Seeing my messenger, "Young man, come here."

The young pyrate, looking around for a moment before realizing the Governour is speaking to him, "Me, sir?"

"How many are there in her Ladyship's party?"

Hurrying over to the Governour, "Fifteen in all, sir, but only eight be ashore. The rest, not having made the journey well, are recovering aboard her Ladyship's vessel, but plan on coming ashore on the morrow."

"Accompany the carriages and shew the lead coachman where her Ladyship awaits."

As the remaining household servants enter the foyer, the Governour's missus does also, and without delay, orders are issued. Addressing his wife first, he tells the Lady *Catherine*, to put on her best day dress, and noting the tone and concern present in his voice, she dashes off to do as he tells her without question. Next, he orders the kitchen maids to begin preparing a court banquet for 3 dozen people.

Jean François, who waits in the doorway of the great house, is not sure which amazes him more. The fact that the Governour addresses him respectfully, or all the fuss caused by la Marquise's arrival. Furthering his surprise, seeing 4 carriages of various types that have been made ready in record time, he climbs up to sit with the lead driver.

Carrying on, the Governour sees his wife returning wearing a beautiful gown of blue taffeta and silk. "You look lovely, my dear."

Understandably curious, "Now that I am dressed, will you please explain to me what all the fuss is about?"

"la Marquise d'Éperon-noire, she's here."

"His wife, greatly flustered, "Here? You mean now?"

"Yes, dear."

"Oh Lord, she's famous the world over. Before the old Marquis passed on, she hosted the most divine parties, and I heard that she loves to dance. We must have music." Thinking quickly, she calls out lowdly for one of the houseboys. "Samuel, come here quick." Speaking to her husband, "You must write out invitations to all those of importance on the island and have them delivered at once."

"Yes, dear, I am writing the first one now. Where's Clarissa?"

"Thank the Good Lord that we thought to have her tutored in penmanship," voices the Lady *Catherine* jeeringly about her inept niece. "I'll have the doxy write out sufficient copies, and afterwards she can retire to her room for the duration."

Still writing the original, the Governour tells his wife, "I'll get her to copying as soon as I'm finished, my dear."

Running into the room comes Samuel, "Yes'um?"

Hurrying to the writing desk where the Governour is preparing the initial invitation, his wife takes a piece of parchment and quill, and quickly jots down a note whilst giving the lad verbal instructions. "I want you to have Fennington saddle you a fast mount, and riding as swiftly as you can, deliver this message to Mister Stevens at the theatre. He'll arrange for musical entertainment during la Marquises visit." After folding the note in thirds, she pours an ample supply of sealing wax onto the letter before using the Governour's signet to seal the message securely. Handing it to the young boy, "Hurry now," she tells him, displaying her obvious keyed up state.

"Yes'um," he replies whilst dashing out the front door.

Talking to her chambermaid, "Marie, I want the West wing aired out and made ready at once, and I want the best silk bed clothes in la Marquises' room."

Curtsying, she replies, "Yes, my Lady," and trots up the stairs.

Speaking to two more of her maids, "Lorna. Carla," she continues, "we're having dinner in the formal dining room, with a reception in the ballroom to follow. Be sure there are flowers in every room.

"But, my Lady," begins Carla, "we haven't enough flowers in the garden for such displays."

"Then send someone to get what is need'd in town."

"Yes, my Lady." Turning quickly, she begins to fetch Jonathon, the second of the 2 house boys, but before she's out of the room, the Lady *Catherine* calls to her.

Voicing lowdly to gain the young woman's attention, "Carla!"

Stopping short, Carla turns around abruptly and nervously answers, "Yes, my Lady?"

"I recall hearing that her Ladyship prefers Carnations and Wildflowers, and adores them best when engulfed in scads of those tiny white flowers and greenery. Be sure to order an ample supply."

Replying amid a curtsy, "Yes, my Lady." Continuing on, she races out of the room in order to fetch Jonathon.

"Lorna, using our finest silver service, best china, and crystal, I want you to set 36 formal place settings, and be sure to light every candle."

Amid a curtsy, "Yes, my Lady."

MEANWHILE, ON THE BEACH ¬

Waiting, as does my entourage, and what a lofty bunch of well-dressed pyrates they be, I see the carriages coming 'round the bend. All having practiced relentlessly for more than a fortnight, and in the realm of learning the art of being suitably pompous in their mannerisms, I knows they are most ready, and being a swell bunch, I can not help but snicker, just a mite.

"Well, men," says I, as the carriages pull before us, "here we go, but durst not forget that I did say already that adventuring is by far, more fun."

As the first carriage stops, out hops *Jean François*. "There be an enormous fuss being made as those at the big house prepare for your arrival, my Lady. One man, the one who read yer note," speaking worriedly, "he kept staring at me. Perhaps he has seene me before."

"Calm yourself, *Maître François*. My note to the Governour not only informed him of my presence, but of my entourage, to which I introduced you, the bearer of the note, as the great nephew of the late 7th Viscount of Dragonwood, who, as a junior Aristocrat serving his gentleman's apprenticeship under my wing, as my aide-de-camp, and are to be treated with respect, and as my attendant, you will be present at all the soirées and such. Are you pleas'd?"

"Aye, my Lady, and thank you. I'll do you proud."

Smiling, "I am sure you will, *Maître François*."

"Just one question, my Lady?"

"Yes, *Maître François*?"

"Who is the 7th Viscount of Dragonwood?"

"He was my late sister's husband, the 7th Vicountess, a plantation in Brazil."

"What if someone on this island knows him personally and asks questions, like how's he been keeping?"

"Well, Considering it common knowledge that his whereabouts has been long since unknown, 'tis unlikely. As for my sister, she died some months back. Just say you've been in my care since your great uncle died."

> *Her Ladyship is no fool. She knows full well that the best way to get a good performance, as well as service, is to make the doing beneficial for all concerned.*

ABOARD THE ROYAL ROVER ⌐

'Tis the 25th of September 1720. The recent storm stripped such a quantity of provisions and fresh water from us, that our necessities have beene rendered dangerously low.

From within the great cabin, as it is hearkened from the crow's nest, followed by the sound of the men of my company chearing, I hear, "Land Ho!" Going topside, taking with me my spyglass, I look yonder, saying, " 'Tis the Isle of *Saint Christophers*, men."

Their reaction is one of being doubly delighted. Not only shall wee be able to replenish our supplies, but wee have, despite our plight, arrived in time to keep our scheduled rendezvous with the Sloop, *Relief*, and her master, Captain *Dunn*.

With our fresh water all but gone, wee heave to, off the coast, nigh the *Black Rocks* as arranged. Once sure our harborage is secure, wee furl our sailes and wait.

Sev'rall hours pass and to our dismay there be no sight of the *Relief*, or the *Willing Captive*; nor anny sign of a messenger Thus, in keeping with my usual practices, I ask, *"Who will go?"*

Sending forth our boat, one of my ambitious crewmen goes ashore hoping to locate the good Captain and his band of smugglers; not merely to conclude our business, but more importantly, to inform them of our dire need. After three hours, and there be no sign of our crewman ashore, I order the unfurling of our sailes, after which wee begin to make our way 'round the island and into the *Caribbee Sea* with intentions of entering the bay on the Leeward side, whereby, it'll be myself and a few hand picked officers who will go ashore to investigate.

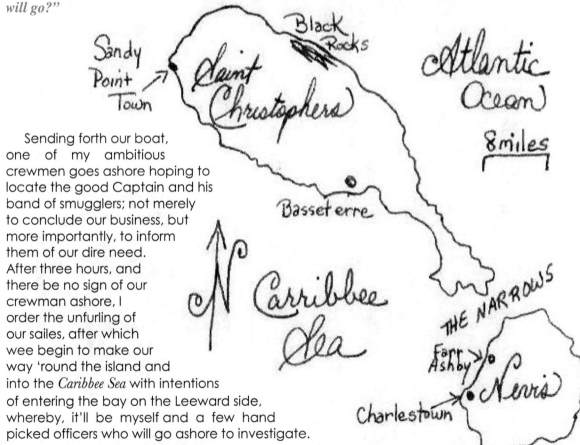

Nearing the mouth of the harbour, in consort with the *Good Fortune*, I knows at once by the vessell's unusual lines, brilliant white hull, and crimson sailes, which, tho' furled, be clearly visible, that the ship anchored off the west bank be the *Willing Captive*. Further, knowing that in order to project peaceful intentions, wee must furl all but our jibs and main course saile, wee do so before as wee enter the harbour.

About halfe way to where wee plan to anchor, wee are besieged by foul winds, yet again, and after making great effort to saile in as planned, wee find ourselves being fired upon by the island's elaborate fortification, which not onely makes clear wee were expected, but 'tis also apparent that wee are to be denied all succour from the government;[CSP-CS15] and to this end, wee be affeared that our messenger had beene

captured. This, however, does not thwart me in my attempt, as Captain, to provide for me crew. At this point in time, I find myself assuming that Captain *Robert Dunn* had beene arrested for the possession of contraband, and it pains me to think that others have considered disloyalty on his part, or that of his crew, for they ought not have. Such betrayal has led onely to their own downfall; consequently, ne'er did such a possibility enter my mind.[CSP-CS4]

In a continued effort, I order the opening of our gunn ports, whereby wee return fire, but alas, as the gale slams into me ships, knowing wee be in for another blow, I have no choice but to seeke a safe haven for the safety of all hands.

The wind, nigh on 50 knots, brings with them moderately heavy rain, and as me ships heave and pitch violently, I lowdly order, "Batten down them loose hatches!"

As the storm takes a sudden and violent directional change, heading back towards us, the ship's pilot struggles to keep the ship heading directly into the storm amid the onslaught of 18 foot waves streaming in rapid succession, and each new cross current swell threatens to swallow us whole in its troughs as the rugged ship heels and pitches violently, enormous sprays of water awash the deck of the *Royal Rover*. All the while, the deck crew works feverishly to tack whilst brave men aloft slave laboriously to reef the majority of the sails, untill onely the forward course sails are left to drive the ship ahead, the situation is grave to be sure, for being deep within the harbour, the danger of running aground, or having our hull torn out by the reefs and coral, is a significant threat to me ships and crew.

Altho' visibility is poor, I canne see the *Good Fortune* is much the better sayler in our present circumstance, and as our situation worsens, I reason our best hope for survival, should the ships come abreast one another once more, is to attempt to board 'er, either by jumping or swinging onto her deck; ergo, all our efforts are to be geared to that end.

Within minutes, whilst the storm's howling winds batter us, both ships slam into each other, and knowing the undertaking risky, the men, seeing me bravely take a running leap over the railing to safely land on the deck of the *Good Fortune*, waste no time in seizing their chance. Thro' the onslaught, I see dozens of men making running jumps, whilst others swing across on ropes. To my dismay, seeing sev'rall slip and fall, I knows not all will be so lucky as to make it, and as one man slips upon landing, and is sent sliding towards the broken railing, I run towards him. Grabbing his arm, just as he begins to go over, I too am clinging desperately to the railing; all the while, my efforts to pull up the dangling seaman is compounded as the ship heels at an alarming rate.

After pulling the young man up and onto his feet, I race to the *Good Fortune's* helm, hollering, "Keep her headed straight and true through the belly of the storm, Mister, and out to sea." As I grab hold of the whipstaff correcting the ship's rudder, "Our onely chance is to go straight through the fiery wench!"

With our course corrected, I glance towards me *Royal Rover*. Far in the distance behind us she is now, as the *Good Fortune*, altho' still deep in the squall, heads out to open sea and away from the hazards of yon harbour. At that moment, a huge swell backwashes over the stern, and as my remaining ship plunges up and then dives straight down, causing the lot of us to lose our footing, I nevertheless find myself searching the harbour for my Flagship still, as I make my way to the leeward rail. With no success, I turn aft where I espy Lord *Moody*, the *Good Fortune's* Pilot, still adeptly manning his station, when suddenly, more terror strikes. Amid the next pitch, losing his footing, he falls hard atop the rain soaked surface. Before he canne recoup, he is sent sliding across the deck. With the ship wallowing dangerously, I dash to the whipstaff as the rugged ship pitches forward on the next swell. Barely regaining control of the helm, I see a man, who despite peril to his life, steps on the chain plates, and in an effort to untangle a loose sheet caught within the shrouds of the mainmast he climbs aloft into the rigging. Fighting with the rope, he gets it free, but as he begins his descent, a sudden gust, tearing him loose from his precarious perch, sends him falling heavily to the deck. With the man lying unconscious, and not having on board a surgeon, I see *Richard Jones*, the *Good Fortune's* Bos'n, examining him. Minutes later, informing me of his condition, "I cann find no broken bones, Captain."

"Take him below and see to it he's looked after."

"Aye, sir. The galley is the best place, I'm thinking."

"The galley it is then," says I.

Relentlessly, the rain pummels down in sheets atop the slippery decks, yet still, all hands manage to follow the orders given in superb fashion, and picking up the injured man, being careful as possible in this horrid weather, they carry him below deck. As they disappear from view, the fo'most jib sheet breaks loose. Captain *Anstis*, shouting to be heard whilst pointing forward toward the bow, bellows, "Belay that rigging."

Working together, sev'rall deck hands manage to catch and haul in the saile. After tying on a new sheet, one of the crewmen reports to both myself and Captain *Anstis*.

Breathing hard from the struggle, "The rigging is secure."

Captain *Anstis* replies, "Very good."

Lowering my voice a mite as the wind dies to a gale, "And the man who fell?"

"The lad had the wind knock'd out of him, is all. Lord *Jones* says he ought be able to return to duty by weekes end, Commodore." While my crewman tells me the news, the rain becomes little more than a drizzle.

Whilst my mannerisms indicate the stoppage of rain as the sun begins to shine, I reply, "Very good."

As the young pyrate departs, the ship's Bos'n approaches from behind. Turning to speak to him, Captain *Anstis*, knowing my compassionate manner, issues the following orders. "My Lord, disperse a dry shift of cloathes to the entire company, after which, assign duties to repair the damage, and see to it the *Good Fortune* is made shipshape, in *Bristol* fashion."

Lest riling Captain *Anstis*, a rather short-tempered fellow, the man swiftly turns to as he replies, "Aye, aye, Captain."

Turning towards me, Captain *Anstis* states, "You best get out of those sodden cloathes yerself, Commodore."

Wearing a rather dubious smile, I asks him, "I trust you have a suitable coat and breeches I canne change into?"

"We'll see what wee cann do," replying with a slight chuckle. Giving me a brief pat on the back, "Surely there must be something on board fitting the tastes of the *'Admiral of the Leeward Islands.'* Afterwards, as weather permits, I suggest wee saile windward and return to the *Black Rocks* where wee canne hove in relative security whilst plans be discussed."

"Excellent advice. That's just what we'll do," I tells him as the two of us make our way to the Great Cabin.

'Twas Nature's Fury, and none other, that thwarted us, forcing us also to abandon me *Royal Rover*. As it is, I consider ourselfes fortunate that a sufficiently close passing of the *Good Fortune* was atchiev'd, and that most of me crew, myself included, managed to make the transference betwixt ships.

With the sea calm once more, and having anchored, wee again begin to wait, but after many an hour, no word comes from Captain *Dunn*, nor has there beene anny sign of our mate who went in search of him.

Fairly positive that *Dunn* has beene arrested or worse, and thereby not able to obtain the goods he was to deliver to us, leaves our food stuffs dangerously low for all wee took from the *Willing Captive* was aboard the *Royal Rover*; furthermore, wee haven't an adequate supply of water to last until wee canne reach an alternate island, excepting Nevis, which shan't help, for upon that barren little rock, food is scarce and no fresh water source exists. Methinks 'tis best, that is when twilight is upon us, I shall venture on over to the *Willing Captive* in a smale boat, for it is there where I stand the best chance of learning the goings on, and with luck, replenish those items wee have the greatest neede for.

MEANWHILE, ON SAINT CHRISTOPHERS ¬

Altho' out of breath, young *Jean François*, all done up in Livery, remains calm as he approaches me in the Grand Ballroom where another social gathering in my honour, this time a ball, takes place. I am hoping that this evening's festivities will permit me some relief, as the weather is giving me cause to worry for my beloved Captain *Roberts*, whom I was to meet yesterday afternoon. Altho' I was suppoze to hove on the horizon on the opposite side of the island, when twice I attempted to weigh anchor, the reoccurring bad weather prevented me from putting out to sea, and as a result I am ashore still.

Looking grand in his white satin brocade jacket, trousers and crimson shirt, *Maître François*, taking to his borrowed position well, bows graciously.

"You look quite stylish this evening, *Maître François*, but I was expecting William."

"I have come on a different matter, my Lady."

Holding my breath a mite, hoping he has brought news of my beloved.

Handing me a note, my aide-de-camp says, "The *Castell-Newydd Bach* môr-leidr sends his humble apologies for being late and asks if it would be possible to speak to your Ladyship privately."

Employing a gentle nod as not to draw attention, *Maître François*, ensuring proper manners as he circles behind me and to my left, extends his right forearm.

Placing my hand atop his, he leads me from the ballroom, but en route, several people intervene.

As the bouncy wife of the Governour approaches, I'm hoping she is the last of 'em. "My Lady Aspasia, surely you are not leaving."

Speaking with an intermittent smile whilst removing my hand from *maître François'* forearm, I try not to give rise for concern. "Fret not, Lady *Catherine*. *Maître François* has brought a note from my ship, is all." And showing it to her in only the briefest sense, "*Maître François* is escorting me to a place of quiet where I may read it."

"Shall I send Clinton to you?" she asks as she looks around for him, "You may have neede of him, should a reply be necessary."

"If such is needed, Lady *Catherine*, I shall send *Maître François* with a verbal message, and now," giving young *Jean François* the indication that again I need his arm, "pray excuse me for a few minutes."

"Yes, of course," says she as I turn to leave.

Extending his arm once again, "This way, my Lady," says *Jean* quietly.

Again, placing my hand atop his forearm, *Jean François* escorts me to a nearby room with a fireplace. Before exiting to wait in the hall, he draws up the burning embers, and after placing a log on the fire, he departs.

Taking a match from the cylinder, I light the whale-oyl lamp, and picking it up in my left hand, I carry it to the far corner of the room, and setting it down atop the side table, I take a seat, but just as I am about to read the message I get a chill.

From outside, tho' unawares, I am being watched, when suddenly, knowing it to be safe, a window opens noiselessly. Feeling a slight breeze, I hear a faint voice.

"fy Arglwyddes, Aspasia."

Looking in the direction of the cool air, lips parting, mine eyes slowly close, and as they reopen amid heavier breathing, I see he whom I both adore and revere standing on the opposite side of the room, and as I slowly arise, the unread note slipping from my fingers' grasp, I am utterly motionless for several seconds. Upon regaining my senses, I lift the front of my gown slightly and run into his embrace, wherein, to my joy, he holds me tightly for several moments before releasing me a mite in order to kiss me.

Leading me to the settee, and the warmth of the fireplace, his conduct voices concern. "When thy ship made no appearance nigh the *Black Rocks* yesterday, I worried for thee."

"Yesterday's storms kept the *Willing Captive* in port, and as a result, the Governour's wife arranged yet another gala."

Rising, he stands back a few feet to look me over, "Thy ball goune, 'tis lovely."

Suddenly, "Oh lord, thou must've been caught in the storm's fury. How thoughtless thee must find me."

"Nay, my Lady, thou could not have knowne."

"And the ship and crew?" asks she.

Betwixt combating the storm and being fired upon by the harbour's cannon as wee entered port, many fine seamen were lost. Before the storm's fury ended, wee were forced to abandon the *Royal Rover*.

Showing despair, "I know I promised I wouldn't," says she, "but I cannae help worrying about thee."

Seeing her eyes tear up as she speaks, and knowing how to soothe her best, I take her within my arms and kiss her ardently.

"Provisions being short affords little time for either tears or joy. The *Good Fortune* lies nigh the point; 'twas from there I rowed to the *Willing Captive*, and by now, two of me crew have returned to the *Good Fortune* with sev'rall casks of fresh water and provisions sufficient to last sev'rall days. On the morrow, about noon, wee shall again attempt to come into port."

'Tis terribly upset, she is, as I tell her Ladyship of the events that transpired, as wee again sit on the settee, desperately wanting to helpe, she offers her services.

"Allow me, fy Arglwydd, to procure the provisions and fresh water need'd by thy crew."

Refusing her, I says, "Nay, my Lady, 'tis too dangerous, for questions as to why thou would neede such a quantity of supplies may be raised."

"But…"

Her tenderness and desire to help is a real one, and thus I inform her, "Thou oughtn't worry, the supplys being taken from the *Willing Captive*, this daye, be more than adequate."

Knowing all shall be well, she throws her head back and Laughs, and again taking her in my arms, the door opens suddenly.

Parting from him quickly, I instruct him, as I smooth the front of my gown as we both stand, "I suggest thee gives them the impression thou art French. With thine accent, a few words here and there should carry it off."

Obviously embarrassed, the Lady *Catherine* offers her apologies. "Forgive me, my Lady Aspasia, I was not aware the room was occupied."

Having to think quickly, knowing this woman as I do, and such, knowing the tale of this encounter will travel faster than the post, and within an all too brief time, the entire civilized world, including both *Philippe II*, and *King George I*, will be aware that the long suffering widow has found for herself a beau.

Knowing Captain *Roberts* speaks fluent French, and that no one else in this company does, "Lady *Catherine*, allow me to present, *Capitaine Trab Strebor*."

As the Lady *Catherine* lifts her hand, my Captain, obeying the rules of propriety, places his hand beneath hers, and bending down a mite, he places upon it, a gentle brush of his lips, whilst I tell him, "The Lady *Catherine,* our hostess, is the *Baroness Van Leemputt*, of Holland, and the wife of Lt. General," gesturing in his direction, "*Sir William Mathew*, Governour of *Saint Christophers*."[E5]

"*Madame la Baronne. Monsieur le Gouverneur.*"

"I do not remember seeing you before now, Captain," states the Baroness.

"*Capitaine Strebor* has beene ill. I hope you do not mind my inviting him."

"Not at all, my Lady."

Entering the conversation, Governour *Mathew* states, "Not to intrude, your Ladyship, but from your embrace, I am thinking this man be more than—"

Interrupting him, "Please, *Monsieur le Gouverneur, la Baronness*, I implore you. His Royal Highness, *Monseigneur le Régent*, knows nothing of *Capitaine Strebor*, as yet, and should the need arise, I would prefer to tell him myself."

"Just as you say," they both reply.

Even though the Lady *Catherine* has given the impression of allowing me any such honours, I am affearing the entire civilized world shall be whispering tall tales of this fortuitous meeting before the end of the season.

By this time, unfortunately, several others have enter'd the room. "What's this," asks the first man in uniform, "Do I perceive a blossoming romance, my Lady?"

"*Capitaine Strebor*, allow me to present *Lt. Colonel Payne*, and his brother, *Cap'n Nathaniel Payne*. They spend much of their time in the region of *Sandy Point*."

> *Feeling overwhelmed, as would any person incognito suddenly finding themselves surrounded by those who would hang him along with his lady from the nearest tree if they knew his true identity, does his best to maintain the falsehood quickly woven by his woman, and thus, bowing respectively, Captain Roberts plays his role brilliantly.*

"A pleasure to meet you gentlemen."

"The pleasure is ours, Captain."

Gesturing to the next man, "*Major Willet*, allow me to present my beau, *Capitaine Strebor*."

"Captain."

"Major."

Seizing yet another opportunity, I continue to treasonously, yet covertly, inform my beloved of the lay of the land. "The Major has the honour of commanding the guard at *Palmetto Point*. Lastly, we have *Lt McKenzie*. He's not only in command of *Fort Charles*, but also the numerous soldiers posted there."[CSP-CS6 see pages 463]

"Gentlemen, 'tis a pleasure to meet all of you," says my captain amid a cultured bow.

The sentiment is accompanied by smiles from all present, especially Mrs *Mathew*, who, taking my Captain by his arm, leads him out to the ballroom, "Do you dance, Captain?"

Believing, I am sure, that I will rescue him in my ever tactful way, he replies, "Oui, Madame," and the two of them join the others on the dance floor.

With me standing amongst the gentlemen who have gathered about, whilst each vies for their chance to dance with me, my beloved is equally sought by the ladies.

'Tis beene nigh on an hour when I am finally able to get free of the womenfolk, and just by chance, her Ladyship is able also to get clear of the gentlemen. Knowing 'twill not last if wee are not otherwise engaged, I take my woman quickly onto the ballroom floor, and blending in with the rest of those who be dancing, "Thou was quite clever in thine, introduction."

"Merci, mon Captaine," says she, smiling. "I merely pronounced thy name backwards, was all. 'Twas a game my mother and I played when I was a child."

"And 'twas a wealth of invaluable information thou supply'd as well." Adding with a look of one who is delightfully pleas'd, "Thou would'st make a first rate spy."

Giggling, "Who'd ever know that their blundering in would prove so useful."

"It could not have gone off better if it had beene planned out in detail." Wishing to be alone with my woman, "Shall wee escape out onto the verandah and into the garden?"

As the dance takes us closer to the double doors, she replys, "No time like the present, mon Captaine."

One more turn and then, as I whisk her away, passing right by William and Mrs Robles, she begins to laugh.

Having ventured beyond the realm of discovery, I asks, "Where be thy room?"

Being as hungry for me as I am for her, she takes my hand, and off wee scurry thro' an array of flowers and hedges towards her lodgings.

As wee come to a bridge with an ancient manor house on the other side, her ladyship announces, "My abode."

"Thine?"

Smiling, she says, "I just couldn't resist it; what's more, except when on duty, the entire ship's company is stopping here," adding with a laugh, "and their manner keeps life interesting for the servants."

Chuckling, "To that, I have no doubt, but then it is a holiday house, right?

Smiling, she replies, "That's right." After a moment's pause, "Well, shall wee knock, or wouldst thou prefer to play the role of a paramour and climb the trellis?"

"An amusing idea, but if it's all the same to you, I'd prefer the front door."

As her ladyship knocks, she takes command of her household.

Opening the door is stately looking fellow in livery. "Welcome home, your Ladyship. Good evening, sir. Welcome to *Finistère*."

Good evening, Chester. Entering the house, Captain *Roberts* follows closely behind me. Gesturing towards him, "Capitaine *Trab Strebor*, now and forever, is master here. So inform the rest of the staff."

"Very good, my Lady."

"Mrs Robles and William will be along later." Heading towards the stairs and my personal chamber, "Have cook warm a generous helping of both Solomon Gundie and Venison. I also want cook to prepare an assortment of tidbits, prepared fruit, bread, coffee, a pot of our best tea, and some sweets."

"I shall see to it at once, my Lady. Any special requests, Sir?"

"Onely that I want it clearly understood that her Ladyship is *Finistère's* Châtelaine, and as such, she rules the manor."

"Very good, Captain."

Proceeding up the stairs, followed by my Captain, I proceed thro' the upper vestibule and the doorway leading into a central reception area. Upon entering, Larissa, my personal maid, who has been reading whilst awaiting my return, stands and curtsies.

"Welcome home, my Lady." Curtsying again, "Good evening, sir."

"As I am Mistress, Larissa, Captain *Strebor*, is now and forever, Master here. Please inform *Mister Philips* that I wish to see him; after which, you may go to bed."

Curtsying before departing, "Thank you, my Lady. Good night, Captain."

After Larissa departs, "I thank thee for that, my Lady."

"It is as it should be, fy Arglwydd."

With a chuckle, he replies, "It's nice to know that providing they never learn my true identity, I'll always have a place on land for refuge."

"Right in the thick of it," says she, laughing. "But being it's the servants who go to town, the worst prospect would be callers. As for money, the coins in that locked chest, pointing to it, to which Chester has a key, is enough to run this household lavishly for 10 years."

Musing a moment. "Just how many servants bustle about this place?"

"About a dozen, I guess, plus, of course, those who care for the horses, farm animals, the grounds, the gamekeeper, and the kitchen crop. It helps keep the local economy going. I shall introduce thee to each of them on the morrow. In the meantime, *Mister Philips* can inform the others of both thy presence, and thine alias."

Tapping on the door, Chester enters carrying a tray filled with delectable delights that he sets on the table before us. He is accompanied by *Mister Philips*.

"Thank you, Chester. Under no circumstances am I, nor *Captain Strebor* to be disturbed before one of us rings. At that time, I expect to see a breakfast fit for a King, including cockles and fried laverbread, which is to be served on the balcony of the upper vestibule."

"Any particular time, my Lady?"

Looking at my Captain, "9ish?"

Giving me a nod, I turn, "9 in the morning, Chester."

"Very good, my Lady. "Anything else, sir?"

"Not a thing."

Bowing, "Good Night, Sir, my Lady."

After Chester departs, Captain *Roberts*, whilst enjoying his supper, tells *Mister Philips* to let the crew know of his incognito presence, after which, following him to the door, Captain *Roberts* bolts the door behind him. Turning 'round, seeing another door has been opened, my Captain, investigating, enters my, or rather, our, bedchamber.

Walking towards me slowly with his compelling eyes, our hands slowly slide over the other's body as we come together.

"I have missed thy touch."

"And I, the tenderness of thy sweet lips." As my hand moves up to caress her dark auburn hair, "I see thou hast brought with her the set of Black satin bed clothes that dons our bed on the *Willing Captive*."

"I am forever hopeful, fy Arglwydd."

Seductively inviting me onto the bed, she draws her hand upon the sheets. "Altho' they are cool to the touch, our flesh will warm them deliciously."

As I sit beside her, her Ladyship pulls on a black cord which, providing complete privacy, shrouds the bed in opulent draperies.

SOMETIME LATER ⇁

The vamp having robbed from me my strength, yet again, and thus, unable to do little else, I languish atop the comfortable feather bed.

Lifting herself up, she pulls on a white cord that furls the draperies. Looking at me intensely as her fingers comb my thick mane, "Even tho' I canne see thy wavy black hair, entrancing sable eyes, and muscular physique, engaging in daring exploits whilst wee be apart, 'tis not enough" moving into a kneeling position behind me, to rub my shoulders, "Ergo, I wish to have thy portrait to gaze upon."

"My portrait?" asks I whilst enjoying the softness of her hands as she massages my shoulders.

"*Monsieur Jean-Antoine Watteau*, the painter; he was at the ball last night."

"Well then," Whilst taking a bite of a chocolate-covered strawberry, "If he canne accomplish the feat sufficiently by noon, 2 days hence, thou shall have thy portrait."

Jumping out of bed, she robes herself as she runs out the door. Seeing her butler, she shouts, "Chester, send a courier to Governour *Mathew's* residence at once to inform *Jean-Antoine Watteau* that if he can paint a portrait and have it far enough along within 2 days to complete it in a week by memory, I shall pay him 5000 livres."

When she returns, by embracing her about her waist, I encourage her to sit beside me, and holding her close, "Ne'er again shall wee, for so long, be apart."

COME MORNING ⇁

To my amazement, *Monsieur Jean-Antoine Watteau* arrived before her Ladyship and I had finished breakfast, and over the next 36 hours, by way of a parade of services rendered and a tour of the grounds, I not onely met all the servants, but the commissioned portrait was completed.

Soon after, when the noon bell rang, it was my duty to return to my ship and crew.

When I returned to the *Good Fortune*, hoping it be otherwise, there was no news regarding Captain *Dunn*, I was, however, able to inform my officers of the intelligence provid'd by her Ladyship.

This levy of power, being the unwarranted attack on my vessels, is deem'd by me to be both unjustified and a most unnecessary evil by

the Governour of the Leeward Islands. The necessity of abandoning my flagship, and tho' she wishes to helpe, it be my charge, not that of her Ladyship, to seek justice for the ill treatment. I hope she understands that altho' wee appreciate her offer to procure provisions for us, our situation is not of such desperation that it warrants putting her at risk, especially when already wee have gleaned from her ship, sufficient supplies to keep us for a weeke of dayes.

As to my reason for going ashore, I was affrightened that Captain *Dunn*, amongst torrential persuasion, may have told of her Ladyship's presence in our company, not that he knows her true name, but her ship being unlike anny other could propose a problem, but knowing such, not to be the case, wee be free to depart.[CSP-CS5a - see page 465]

With regard to this Island's treatment, I formulate a plan. 'Tis not merely a matter of atchieving for oursefes fresh water and provisions, nor the recovery of my *Royal Rover*, and them belonging to my company, which, having beene overcome by weather, were, to my extreame dismay, left behind.

"Nay!" says I. "Here, demonstrated before us, was opprobrious oppression in the highest order, as dealt by a tyrant, and it shall be I, '*Admiral of the Leeward Islands*,'[B13] and them in my company, who shall seek the continuation of the fulfilment of our destiny, serving here our owne idea of justice for the ill treatment."

Thankfully, whilst attending the ball in incognito, I learned much about the island's extensive fortification. *Lt. General Mathew*, Governour of this here Island, is expectin' us to return, and thus, in preparing for defense, he has issued orders to despatch bands of soldiers to all parts of the island. Among them be the officers I had met: *Lt. McKenzie*, who, with his aid and thirty soldiers, is to make his way to *Fort Charles*, whilst *Major Willet* is to guard *Palmeto Point*. *Lt. Colonel Payne's* orders be to muster two companies at *Sandy Point*. His brother, *Cap'n Nathaniel Payne*, is to make his stand along the old road, and lastly, gunners be sent already to make ready the cannon which lye in 4 strategic points about the island.[CSP-CS7]

My owne plan is underway, and as wee again enter the harbour wee, once again, find ourselves fired upon.

My first observances in noting that me flagship, *Royal Rover*, has beene burnt, and belieeving those of her crew, who being unable to make the transference to the *Good Fortune*, who did not drown in the storm, have beene captured.

So furious am I, that of the two ships in the harbour, I intend to seize that one which is most to my liking whilst laying waste to the other.[CSP-CS6]

As wee near, I find both my audacious self, and me crew, taking an instant fancy to the heavily armed French Brig. Like me, such displays of force dismays them not, for no longer does me crew doubt themselves nor their capabilities when going into battle.

Sailing alongside,

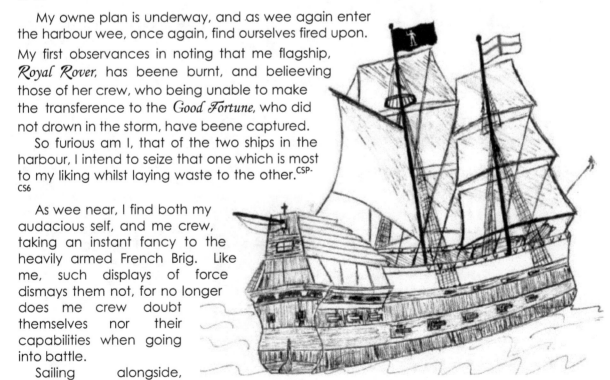

commences a fierce, yet short battle, for the Frenchies aboard 'er possess no stomach for fighting. After seizing the 22 gunn Brigantine, and finding her to be a grand ship, I re-christen her *Royal Fortune*.

The remaining ship, wee learn from the French, who are momentary being held prisoner aboard my New prize, is commanded by Captain *Gox* of *Bristol*, and for that alone wee bombard her with a hail of cannon fire long beyond the necessity, and her crew, having surrendered, me crew promptly boards her, and stripping the ship of her armament and valuables, me crew sett torches to 'er.

My crew that managed the transference, as did I, from the *Royal Rover* during the recent storm, and a few newcomers, quickly board our splendid new prize, whilst boasting proudly of her crew which numbers some 180 white men, and 48 French Creole Negroes, as well as her impressive armament. Taking command of her shall be a pleasure.

As for the *Good Fortune*, whose crew is made up mostly of undisciplined, fresh men, comprised of 100 whites and 40 French Negroes, shall henceforth be put to good use as our store ship under the command of Captain *Anstis*.

Next wee come upon the *Mary and Martha*, which wee have encountered before, but on this occasion, as a result of Captain *Thomas Willcocks'* less than cordial attitude, she is to be burnt as soon as the plundering is complete; what's more, learning that her Captain hail's from *Bristol*, the prize crew takes a particular pleasure in stripping her of armament and valuables before setting her ablaze once her crew be aboard my vessel.

In retrospect, The *Mary* of *Boston*, commanded by *Henry Fowle*, was ashore when my ships sail'd on in. Hoping a gracious attitude would be appreciated, he rowed himself to my flagship and asked if his vessel could be spared. I agreed to do so in exchange for a favour. After learning what it is that I wanted, he penned the following note.[CSP-CS9 & Page 466, 251 v.]

> To Mr. James Parsons,   27th September, 1720
>
> I shall forever be in your favour if on the morning tide you would send some sheep and some goats out to the pyrates you many see here. I am treated very civilly and promised to have my ship and cargo again, and desire Captain Henksome to send his wheel that he steers his ship with, or it may be the worse for him.
>
> Henry Fowle,
> Captain of the Mary[B3]

When our request was granted, I sent a longboat ashore at *Basseterre Road* and took from a meadow, some sheep.[CSP-CS6 & CSP-CS9]

During the questioning of *Henry Fowle*, wee learn Captain *Robert Dunn* had beene discovered by *James Dennison*, one of the gunners assigned to *Fort William, St. Christophers*, whilst unloading a canoe filled with swag, which he was to sell on our behalf; what's more, it pains me to say he has beene arrested and is imprisoned at *Sandy Point*.[CSP-CS4 & Page 465]

Whilst waiting tryal, affearing for his life, Captain *Dunn*, no doubt, amid barbaric persuasion, told 'em that if he was not released, pyrates would attack. As for *Dunn's* crew, being no news is knowne, wee must deduce they too be suffering similar imprisonment, or have beene hung already. In either case, wee belieeve this be the reason for the attack upon me ships.[CSP-CS5b & Page 465]

THE FOLLOWING NEW CLIPPING REGARDING THIS OCCURANCE WAS PREVIOUSLY PUBLISHED WITHIN APPLEBEE'S ORIGINAL WEEKLY JOURNAL LAST OCTOBER.

Journal of the Commifsioners for Trade and Plantation, PRO   *28* January *1721*

Two light men~of~war had been ordered to Newfoundland to intercept the pyrates "who continue to commit great depredation on our merchant fhip that way."

In the fame ifsue, but clearly from a different fource, was the news that the two men~of~war were the *Rofe* and the *Shark* which, having been repaired, had failed to Nantafket for "the pirates who infeft the coaft there".   CSP-CS 2

Most upset am I by what I feel is the cruellest of treatment to our persons, unseemly to be sure is anny man who would bestow such distress, and to Captain *Dunn*, a man who laboured for our benefit; ergo, shortly before sailing on, and with my usual audacity, I send forth the following letter to this English Governour, this Lieutenant-General, whom I loathe. Still, despite such feelings, I am compelled to award credit, for unlike them cowardly curds of *Trepassy*, Governour *Mathew* put forth a fight.

BLOOD and SWASH, The Unvarnished Life (& afterlife) Story of Pirate Captain, Bartholomew Roberts......pt.2 "THE WILLING CAPTIVE"

LETTER TO LIEUTENANT GENERAL WILLIAM MATHEW, GOVERNOUR OF SAINT CHRISTOPHERS
CSP-CS8 & Page 466

Royal Fortune
Sept. 27, 1720

Lieut-General Mathew,

This comes expressly from me to lett you know that had you come off as you ought to a done and drank a Glass of Wine with me and my Company I should not have harmed the least vessell in your harbour. Further it is not your Guns you fired that affrighted me or hindered our coming on shore but the wind not proveing to our expectation that hindered it. The Royal Rover you have already burnt and barbarously used some of our men, but we have now a ship as good as her and for revenge you may assure yourselves here and hereafter not to expect anything from our hands but what belongs to a Pyrate. As further Gentleman, that poor fellow you now have in prison at Sandy Point is entirely Ignorant and what he hath was give him, so they make Conscience for once let me begg you and use that man as an honest man and not as a Cr—— Without any otherwise you may expect not to have quarters to any of your Island yours

Bath. Roberts

Location: 'Saint Barthélemy to Surinam via Brava'

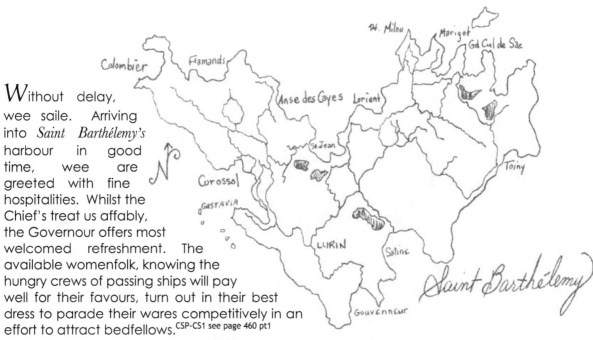

Without delay, wee saile. Arriving into *Saint Barthélemy's* harbour in good time, wee are greeted with fine hospitalities. Whilst the Chief's treat us affably, the Governour offers most welcomed refreshment. The available womenfolk, knowing the hungry crews of passing ships will pay well for their favours, turn out in their best dress to parade their wares competitively in an effort to attract bedfellows.[CSP-CS1 see page 460 pt1]

As always, when nearing land, the *Willing Captive* sailes two leagues behind, and as not to risk peril, she comes into port onely by the grace of a special greenish gold coloured rocket, which when launched, signals that all is safe for her to come forth. Should danger abound, an alternate, red-colored rocket is sent in its stead; signifying that her ladyship is to hove on the horizon. All being well, I order the firing of the greenish gold rocket. Shortly thereafter, her elegant ship, which vastly exceeds anny other in both beauty and speed, enters the harbour; even so, ne'er would I place my flag upon her and take that which her ladyship obviously prizes above all else; a place of solitude where, despite a crew complement of 18, she and I enjoy complete privacy.

Whilst a goodly store of fresh water and provisions be taken on board, all of which wee paid for generously, most of my company indulge in the pleasures offered by the locals, particularly the slatterns and drink.[CSP-CS1 see page 460 pt1]

Her ladyship prefers to handle the affairs pertaining to the *Willing Captive* herself, and she too pays for her luxurious provisions most generously. In this, she belieeves, as do I, such makes herself forever welcome. Once all ships in our company are filled to capacity, the *Willing Captive* carrying the most water; her Ladyship's sense of cleanliness being charming to say the least, keeps me in suds, and despite the added weight, the unusual ship, unlike anny other, makes 18 knots easily, for it be her outer hull, where lays a trapezoid shaped smugglers hold, four feet wide at the base which encompassing her ship, that more than compensates for the weighty cistern, keeps her riding high, as well as providing a more solid platform in the water and a thin prow, of some three feet long and razor edge sharpness, that spans out slowly below, before widening to her full breadth of 44 feet.

These elements are just some that make up her unusual design, that on a whole, creates the formula that makes her speed unequalled.

My company, now having their fill of the pleasures offered on this island, become restless, and after the voting is tallied, wee make ready to put out to sea, where, by unanimous vote, wee be bound for the coast of *Guinea*.

Ready to saile, her Ladyship and I must part for time. In parting, I kiss her long and slow, which, as always, creates for both of us, a passionate longing, nevertheless, as I step back from her, I bow. "'Twas a kiss to warm me, my Lady, till next I hold thee in my arms."

Gracefully, amid a curtsy, low to the deck, she tenderly replies, "I shall live on it until thee returns."

In the latitude of 22° North, wee met with a French ship from *Martinico*. After a brief engagement, the 32 gunn Brig with 9 swivels, was ours, and finding *M. Pomier's* French Brig to be a grand ship indeed, I re-christen her my 2nd *Royal Fortune*. CSP-CS19 & #501vi on page 472

Richly laden she be, but more important than her cargo, is the ship, for she be a handsome prize indeed, and altho' our relatively new acquisition, my 1st *Royal Fortune*, has served us well, I opt for this new prize to be my flagship, whereby not onely do I move my flag, but also her splendid name, but lett there be no talk of piracy, and as wee exchanged ships, the French Captain is pleas'd, for still he commands a fine French vessel, and once our possessions be transferred, wee, the lot of us, saile away happy.

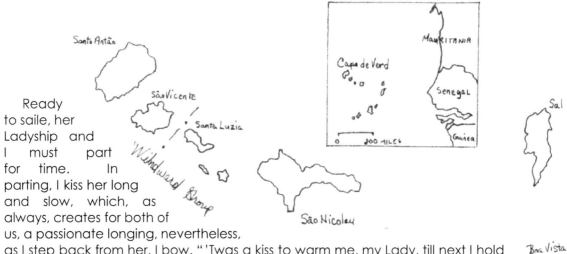

the Cape de Verd Islands 'Brava'

Once back on course to the coast of *Guinea*, I propose sailing to *Brava*, an Islet located at the Southernmost part of the *Cape de Verd Islands*, where wee will careen our grand prize.

With me crew in favour of my proposal, wee shift our course to satisfy our new heading. En route, wee find ourselves combating foul weather, once again.

The front of the massive storm, leaving not a star that canne be seene thro' the blackness that hangs above our heads like a shroud, stretches beyond the horizon, leaves onely me compass to guide us this night, and if that were not enough, despite our efforts to tack, 'tis forced wee are to return to the *West Indies*.

Surinam, now being our destination, lyes a distance of no less than 700 leagues[1], and to our dismay, there be not more than a hogshead of water betwixt the 124 men in my company. Having no recourse, I am forced to place a sentinel around our water supply. As wee continue on course, despite having rationed the precious substance to a paltry one mouthful per day, our supply; diminishes rapidly, just the same.

The going is treacherous, and whilst members of my company, enervated and sickly, be dying daily, wee who be left, altho' ourselves be as weak as possible and still be alive, push on.

Sev'rall dayes having passed, and having not the strength nor mind to write in me log, wee, by what I belieeve to be divine providence, were able to anchor, and at a mere seven fathoms in depth.

By dawn, the watch, who be up in the topmost crow's nest of the mainmast, espy'd not onely land, but also that wee had all but reached our destination, being nigh the mouth of the *Meriwinga River*, that flows just Northwest of *Brazil* within the coast of *Surinam*. Such knowledge 'twas all that be necessary to breathe a freshness into our minds and bodies.

I, together with the strongest of those who be left; however debilitated and sunken from lack of food, possessing onely modest strength in our bodies, our tongues swollen from extreme thirst, sett out upon the raft wee fashioned from wood stripped from the flooring below deck.

Altho' barely able to paddle, wee be most determined, and working together, me and eight others slowly make our way to shore. 'Twas a chore, beaching the raft, but nevertheless, weak and weary as we be, wee drag it well up on shore. Mustering our strength, wee pick up the empty water casks and baskets and venture into the interior of the island in search of fresh water and anny edibles wee canne find.

The trek, in our weakened state, takes sev'rall hours, but finally a stream lyes before us, and whilst I splash water upon my face, me men, crazed with a touch of madness; behaving like savage animals, dive into the water to refresh themselves.

After having gathered all the edibles wee could find, and having cleaned that which required such; ourselves, still quite incapacitated from our dehydrated state, gather up the casks of water and baskets, and hoping that those who were barely alive when wee sett out this morn, be breathing still, wee return to our shipmates with all speed.

Upon reaching the ship, I being the strongest, enjoying better health than most of those in me company prior to this occasion, an attribute I accredit to my fondness for tea[2], am first to climb the steep steps along the outside of me ship leading to the open deck.

Over my shoulder I be carrying both a water cask, and a pouch brimming with hotchpotch, and altho' not a great quantity, it will sustain us for sev'rall dayes.

A vast number of me crew have died, many perishing over the last daye or two by

---

[1] 700 leagues equals 2,100 nautical miles.

[2] Being one to drink tea as opposed to liquor, Cap'n Roberts was better hydrated.

drinking sea water and urine in their struggle to survive, but thus served onely to create an inextinguishable thirst which killed them.

As quickly as we be able, wee, but guarding well to be sure none is wasted, wee distribute small amounts of water to our sickly mates who had, with the helpe of our Lord God, managed to hang on long enough for our return. As the men grow more in control of their senses, the water is given to them more freely.

'Tis onely after our sufficient recovery that wee again sett out for the shore. Each man packing two water casks, and making sev'rall trips to the stream, the ship be loaded with all the fresh water wee canne stow, but finding little in the way of provisions, wee be forced to steer for the latitude of *Barbadoes*.

Certaynely not the best of choices, but 'tis there or starve. But once more, divine providence provides that which wee neede, and that me mateys, be the *Greyhound*, a fine Brigantine belonging to *Saint Christophers*,① whereby, in a further reckoning of that port's inhospitalities, refusing us the barest necessities of life, wee waste no time seizing the faire prize. With equal speed, her first mate, *James Skyrmé*,② wastes no time before putting his signature amongst those already penned beneath my articles, and I am pleas'd to state that his seamanship skills making him a highly sought after sea artist, coupled with his display of eagerness to prove himself, makes him an instant favourite, and thus, earned him the Captaincy of our new Brigantine, which wee re-christened the *Ranger*.

Aboard this prize, wee find a great haul of necessities, including a goodly supply of fresh water and provisions, as well as strong spirits.[N8]

By the end of October, 1720, news comes concerning Captain *Dunn*, the man wrongly held at *Sandy Point*. The report being that he had not onely beene treated most cruell, and afterwards hung, wee shall in consequence, as was promised within the letter I had sent to the Governour whilst there, shall enact our owne personal justice,[CSP-CS5b] as well as for a number of me crew who had beene taken prisoner who were later executed on Nevis.[E15]

Continuing on, my chief opponent be that of a Dutch interloper. No shame; however, from this battle will befall them amongst us who not be as yet members of me crew, as these Dutch be not honest seamen, nor be they pyrates; ergo, keeping to the code by which I govern myself, I am to record forthwith, the fiercest of my battles as it happened.

My opponent, the onely ship of which was of anny concern among the more than two dozen that lay before me, carry'd a formidable 42 cannon plus 7 dangerous swivel gunns, being of 2 and 3 pounders. The latter, most devastating to be sure; capable of being fired, not onely in rapid succession, but in anny direction. But this be not all, for her deadliest cannon be the four, 12 pounders that she carries,[B13] which alone, be most capable of sinking anny small craft, which be foolhardy enough to confront her, however dismayed I am not. Her lines are supreme, and for the lack of a crew such as mine, she be a fine sayler, this much I knew, and I said to myself, 'She I **Must** have!'

Royall Fortune

---

① It was later learned that the *Greyhound* was bound for Philadelphia.

② As for the *Greyhound's* mate, James Skyrmé, pirating seeming to agree with him. Not only did he join Bart's crew, he later became Captain of *Ranger*, and later, the *Great Ranger*.

Keeping her, there now be three ships within my command. The crew of me *Royal Fortune* numbers 228; 48 of whom be Negroes, and all of whom, meaning my entire crew, being highly skilled, are more than a match for anny ship who may oppose us. Those who try, shall find their Captain, however determined, to be on a fool's errand.[B8 & 9]

Despite the impressions that some may have, ne'er am I one to rush into battle, for first, as do I always, proudly, I don my Nation's colours, that being my most elegant Crimson damask coat and breeches. Once dressed, which takes mere moments, I dash out to drink a toast with me crew, and lifting our cups, I cry out, *"Damn to him who lives to wear a Halter."*[B8 & 9]

Our toast, without which me crew belieeves wee would surely hang, belieeve also that our fight against Authoritarianism is that of the Lord's bidding, and such, is always made whilst drinking onely the finest black Bohea available on the open deck.

Before us, looking over the harbour lyes a grand prize. Seeing us, she raked on canvas, and at first I thought her to be making a routine departure, but looking thro' my spyglass, it becomes obvious, as she comes about, that she plans to engage.

"Seemes the grand ship is making herself ready for battle, men," says I.

"More likely flee, she will, when the battle starts," injected Lord *Dennis*.

"Perhaps," I said. "Nonetheless, 'tis precautionary measures we'll be takin'."

Grumbling, he replied, "Aye, aye, Captain."

Still quite some distance, I ordered, "Ready the gunns!"

"Aye, Captain."

As wee near, still she does not pack on more canvas as My Lord *Dennis* and my other officers anticipated, but rather spills the wind from her sailes, and in causing them to luff, dramatically increases the speed in which wee encroached upon her.

"Look me hardies," says I, "As I said, the Dutchman intends to make a stand." Swiftly giving my first order of battle before returning to the Quarter-Deck, the ship's musicians begin to play. Leaping up the stairs, I shout, "Musketeers! Prepare to fire!" Looking over the railing I speak somewhat subdued to one of the fresh men, bestowing on him a grand honour, as I order, "Raise our colours," and as our jack was hoisted, the formidable ship sends to us her first of many fearsome broadsides. Hammering us badly with all of her larboard gunns as wee came alongside within a distance of no more than 60 feet, wee send a return bombardment, which wrecks havoc across their open deck.

"Trim 'er sails, my Lord *Main*." Pleas'd at the swiftness me *Royal Fortune* responds to the helm, but as we drew closer still, nigh 30 feet, me flagship lists to the starboard.

Rushing to me, comes my Lord *Dennis*. Speaking with great concern, "Wee be hit below the waterline, Captain, and settling fast."

Purposefully, pleased that much of our swag be aboard the *Willing Captive*, I reply, "Then spread the word quickly that wee shall be boardin' a ship that not be sinking."

Dashing off to give the order, the news spread like wildfire.

Seeing the men ready themselves, I jumped onto the railing and in this, giving them hope that the battle this daye would be ours once again, they too, with gusto, prepared to board what was to be my new flagship. Within moments, as I leapt into the shrouds, I bellowed a hearty, yet deliberately serious laugh, just before I hollered, "Into the rigging me hardies."

All of the crew, aware their ship be sinking, did not hesitate, but not one was to make the transference; untill the word be given.

Knowing the great Warship was beating us, "Our onely chance, Captain," hollers *Henry Dennis*, "is to take down her mainmast."

"Nay, my Lord, wee shan't be causing further damage to our new ship. Load instead the swivel gunns with grapeshot and reduce our opposition. After which, wee shall board 'er."

Without delay, as the swivels be fired, sent forth a volcano of fire and metal that wreaked havoc as the exploding Shells burst upon her deck. I knew at once 'twas more than grapeshot my gunner had placed within them gunns, and hurriedly, before the echo of the blast had faded, I ordered, "Over the sides men!" And as the words left my lips, the lot of them, leaving no man aboard the *Royal Fortune*, took to scrapping as they landed. Amid the fierce fighting, sev'rall of my men, knowing that the great ship would keep the *Royal Fortune* afloat, not onely throughout the battle, but long enough to transfer our personal possessions, swag, and all items deemed valuable, saw to it that the two ships were lashed together. The battle, as it raged on, was sheathed by a torrent of gunpowder, thick as fog, and as it perfumed the air as it had during previous occasions, our opponents felt the savagery of cannon from both the *Good Fortune* and the *Ranger*. This aspect of battle, being but a stench to many, was for me, a tonic, and despite the unremitting cannon fire, by not onely the opposing vessels, but also the island's fortress. When the smoak of battle cleared, wee had either sunk or plundered numerous French and English vessels that lay in these harbours belonging to *Saint Christophers* and *Dominica*, excepting the faire Dutch interloper, as she was ours for the taking and seize her wee did, [CSP-CS19 & #501 vi on page 472] making her my 3rd ship to be christened *Royal Fortune*. After which, speaking to *Henry Dennis*, "In the future, my Lord, you best be remembering that a cocky man often becomes a dead fool."

Immediately thereafter, I order a new jack be fashioned; one that blatantly, and with much contempt, thenceforth graced, with relish, the jewel of my fleet.

High from the topmost of my mizzen, yon flag shall wave, I proclaim, smugly pourtraying myself. *"The jack had a man pourtray'd on it with a flaming sword in his hand and standing on two skulls subscribed ABH and AMH,"* the initials representing: *"A BARBADIAN HEAD AND A MARTINICIAN HEAD."* [B2] A plate stamped with this singular likeness, also on the door of the Great Cabin of my flagship,[B11] shall forever remind the world of my loathing; as them skulls represent the heads of them Governours reigning over *Barbadoes* and *Martinico*, both of whom I intend to have a-swayin' beneath my jack, and after which, shall instil fear within the hearts of men for all-time, I shall look upon often whilst basking on my Quarter-Deck by day, or taking a kip beneath her when the moon is full and the air warm.

'Twas later, it was that wee heard that the Governour of the *French Leeward Islands*, seeking the aid of the British Governour of *Barbadoes*, reported our attack on *Dominica*. But my delight, worthy of a jovial celebration, was when he try'd to order *Woodes Rogers*, Captain of the British Man-O'-War, *Rose* [CSP-CS3], which had enter'd *Nassau* harbour to seeke out and destroy me, flatly refus'd, which, dare I say, is quite a complement to the skill of both me crew and that of myself.[B3]

BELOW BE A LIKENESS OF THAT LETTER.

> To the Admiralty, London,
>
> Only resolute action by Men Of War can stop the depredations of this pyrate Roberts. This day, under fire from our shore battery, he burned thirty or forty ships in the Roads, plundered several merchantmen and set fire to the town. The impudent rascal even stepped ashore to steal for his larder before he took his leave.
>
> The port is now a smouldering ruin...
>
> Lt. General William Mathew
> Governor, Saint Christopher

Sailing within sight of one of *Dominica's* peaceful harbours, wee find three ships. The first, with her Crimson Hull and Sailes, being the easily recognized, *Willing Captive*; 'tis a most welcomed surprise. None too far off, adding to my delight, lyes yet another 42-gunn Dutch interloper, with a crew of no less than 75, and if that not be enough, there is also a fine Brigantine, carrying 22-gunns, about which, I says, *"Neither of. these shall I lett go."*
CSP-CS19 & pg 472, 501 vi

Finally, being what her Ladyship craves is adventure, knowing she knows not of our new jack, nor the ships they fly upon, methinks to give her a thrill by placing her in the thick of it, and therefore wee saile in with gusto.

With my musicians playing, and upon the threatening resistance made by the Dutch ship, me crew, hungry for action, being nigh on all ships wee have encountered, have surrendered immediately following a show of our gunns as displayed by our initial cannon fire, which boorishly, as they termed it, darts across their bow. With our ports open and gunns ready, I holler, "Fire!" Pouring a broadside into the Dutchman, the battle ensues as our proposed prize, to my surprise, tho' a pleasant one, returns our fire. My gunner, and his men, be adept to their task, and upon the reloading of the starboard gunns, I again shout, "Fire!" Forthwith, all gunns pour in yet another broadside, and from my Quarter-Deck, I see sev'rall of the Dutchmen fall. As my boarding party readies themselves, and the grapnels are thrown, the Captain of the Dutch Interloper wisely strikes his colours. After our prize crew swings on over to 'er, I sett my sights on the Brigantine, who, after seeing both the power of my resolve and handiness of her well-trained crew, surrenders without incident.

The two Captains could not know that wee would not harm her Ladyship's vessel, and thus were affrightened she would be the next to fall prey to our gunns, but to our surprise, her crew having placed 28 bronze cannon, capable of spewing out 9 & 24 pounders in mere seconds within the gunn ports of the *Willing Captive's* weather deck, and as I said, neither her Ladyship, nor those of me crew aboard her knowing our new jack or ships, not onely gets underway in record speed, but opens all of her 84 ports. Having no intention of being blown out of the water on the first volley by 28 of her ladyship's 56, 36 pound bronze cannon upon her gunn decks, wee send up a greenish gold rocket to lett her ladyship know not onely that it be us, but also that I shall send over my boat with a message after night fall. In the meantime, wee saile forth to *Bennet's Key* and drop anchor.

Upon the return of my boat, which has just returned from the *Willing Captive*, I am told that she knew it was us, but having faith in the outcome, which did come to pass, she ran out her gunns to show the others that she could take care of herself, a message that I have no doubts will make the headlines throughout the civilized world.

When I thought to ask my messenger how her Ladyship knew to come here, he simply replied, "She is said to have premonitions, Captain. And seeing she be here, I cannae doubt her surprisingly accurate foresight."

Knowing that her Ladyship will be none too far behind us, and perhaps out sailing us, wee head for our destination with our two latest prizes.

Shortly following some questioning of the Brigantine's crew upon their owne vessel, I rejoice in the learning that she not onely be from *Rhode Island*, but I am sure she is the same wee gave chace to some months back, following *Baía de Todos os Santos*; the same ship that escaped the torrential weather that almost killed the lot of us; ergo, the wee take particular satisfaction in the plundering of this ship.

Looking beyond my ship's bow, hoping to catch a glimpse of the *Willing Captive*, I suddenly take notice of one of me crewman, who, whilst shedding a large overcoat, reveals a shapely figure and dark auburn tresses, and even though 'tis spellbound I be, I do my best not to appear mesmerized by her, an evident sound of shock be in me voice. "My Lady!"

As she sashays on over, wearing a most enticing outfit, one that she no doubt designed herself with the sole intention of displaying her oh so feminine frame, her attire is comprised of form fitting pants, knee high boots, and the flax linnen shirt, altho' 'tis quite large, being it belongs to me, is ty'd securely in a knot off centre at her waist. Ne'er before this moment, having seene a woman dressed in such a fashion, had I any idea that there was so much activity taking place beneath the full skirts worn by the womenfolk. In anny event, fearing her presence will create immeasurable distraction, as well as to dissuade my company from thinking her passage be that of my suggestion, I says, somewhat angrily, "I ought a clap thee in irons for stowing away upon me ship."

   To my amazement some in me crew begin to holler in protest. "She be no bother."

   Others cry out, "Lett the lass practice her seamanship skills upon this har ship for a spell."

   Still more state, "And her Ladyship canne make for us her delectable tea cakes and punch."

   Even Lord *Sympson* has a kind word, sayin', "Her presence will add a bit of luster."

   Walking up to me, my demure, yet bold woman, kisses me on the cheek, then turning, she proclaims with a smile, "I shall be delighted to help fix ye, and all of you, many fine meals, and make also your punch until your desire for such eatables is sated." Turning back to me, "And you, fy Arglwydd," tho' somewhat quieter as a devilish expression appears upon her face, "surely there is something I can do for you."

   Gazing into the eyes of the tenacious Lady of Quality, who by her owne resourcefulness, is at last sailing on board a pyrate ship, I quietly reply, "Unquestionably."

Location: 'Martinico & Saint Lucia'

Whilst stopping on the hot little island of *Tobago* to water,[CSP-CS18] wee hear tell of 2 sloops that have beene specially outfitted for the express purpose of taking me and my crew. Upon the hearing of this, I must say that in return for their gracious attitude, I decide to pay 'em a call; ergo on 18 Feb. 1721, commanding a ship of 32 gunns, and a Brigantine of 18, and some 350 men[CSP-CS10 & pg 468 #463 iii] and myself, being familiar with the Dutch Interlopers signals when coming in to trade, and having utter contempt, not onely for this Isle, but her inhabitants, I put it to my company. After counting the vote, and luring them into our grasp, wee saile in, and with the correct signal flags raised, our prey, as expected, take us for friendly traders, whereby, knowing the signals, the Frenchies, eager to trade come ahead to *Saint Lucia*, which is the usual place where the Dutch smugglers conduct their business.[CSP-CS10 continued]

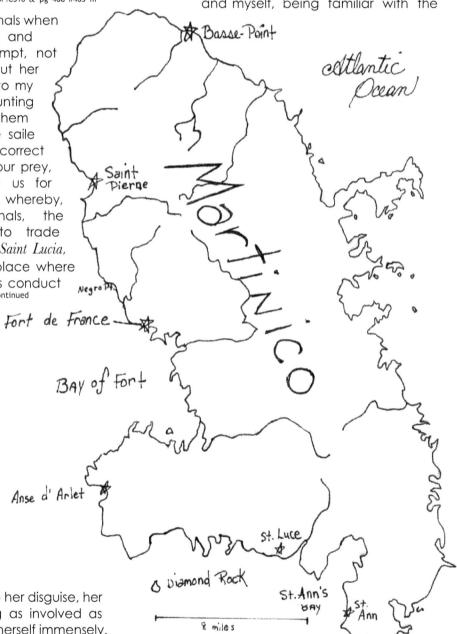

Getting back into her disguise, her Ladyship, becoming as involved as possible, is enjoying herself immensely.

As the 14 French Sloops come within boarding distance, wee heartily welcome the bargain hunters on board, and now, having 'em in my grasp, and whilst I tells them 'tis *'Gentlemen of Fortune'* wee be, and as such, I shan't have it said they came off for no purpose, Lord *Sympson* relieves them of their purse as they depart. My plan having gone off splendidly, I tells them I hope to always meet with *Martinician* traders in similar fashion; even so, knowing their Captains will take action once they learn of their fellow islanders plight, time is our enemy. As it happens, onely minutes pass after the first group depart before signal flags are raised, and we are fired upon. Having what wee came for, wee make a hasty departure, and hoisting our well-known Jolly Roger, my flotilla, using both cannon and fire as wee sally, sink all but one of the 14 ships in the harbour. The last is what wee used to sett the scurvy land lubbers still cluttering up my ships ashore.^{CSP-CS10 &} [pages 467 & 8 continued]

Now, being a willing party to the destruction of these here ships, altho' her presence aboard not be known to our adversaries, her Ladyship became a pyrate.

During the course of these events, me crew inadvertently made capture of sev'rall Frenchies, who, being disagreeable in manner, found themselves whipped in retribution for their insults. Alas, altho' I would have wished it otherwise, some of the captives, displaying an intolerable superiority, had their ears cut off as well as other similar recompense for their degrading remarks; made worse, for they themselves be smugglers. The worst of 'em being hung from the yards were used for target practice.^{CSP-CS10 & CSP-PRO3}

Altho' her Ladyship, did not witness the punishments, dealt to the worse offenders, as they did not take place aboard the *Royal Fortune*, she did demonstrate her contempt for one of the Dutch Interlopers by slapping him in the face in retaliation for the unsavoury remark he made as she walked by.

Again, altho' redundancy not be the norm for my writings, and altho' I am displeas'd by the actions of some of me crew, I nevertheless understand their feelings. 'Tis a large company, consisting of sev'rall ships and hundreds of men, and alas I cannae be aboard them all at once; however, having not witnessing most of the remarks that enraged me crew, I am not assured I would have taken steps to prevent their actions. Still, as barbaric as they were, they cannae compare in brutality to those atrocities inflicted by Naval, and Merchant ship commanders upon common seaman for minor offences, having them keelhauled or flogged untill hardly a place on their person remained unmarred, not to mention far worse tortures so unspeakable, they defy imagination.

Author's Note: As barbaric as they may seem in today's, so-called 'Civilized World,' the punishments inflicted by Naval and Merchant Commanders upon common seaman for minor offences in previous centuries did not compare in cruelty to the atrocities, e.g. flogging & keel hauling, & other tortures so unspeakable they defy imagination, e.g. Edward Collins was forced to wear a basket of shot around his neck for an hour to make him confess to the stealing of personal items [HCA 1/9/83], & Edward Abbot was lashed 40 times "furiously & violently about the face, back, head & shoulders" for asking for bread, a punishment for which he died three weeks later [HCA 1/9/137–8]; furthermore, as so said by, John Atkins, Surgeon on the H.M.S. Swallow & Scriber during the trial of Roberts' crew, some very important facts emerged among which was that of the nigh on 500 prizes, there were only 2: the Sagrada Família, off Brazil in October 1719, & El Puerto del Principe, off Dominica in January 1721 they had to fight for, and among them all, save those who fell in battle, ne'er, excepting the Governour of Martinique, & the incident regarding John Walden & Richard Harris, an act that enraged Bart, did he or his crew willfully kill a single officer, crew member, or passenger from any of the ships they encountered.[B2]

AUTHOR FURTHER STATES THAT This accounting, being exaggerated, is not quite accurate.

*To this, the author adds the following which she gleamed from Sally J. Delgado's book, "**Ship English...** Sailors' speech in the early colonial Caribbean" Published by 'languages science press'.*

Pages 94 & 95: 4.2.3 Social order and disorder
In addition to the cruel and unusual violence that sailors suffered at the hands of captors and their own tyrannous officers, they were also subject to corporal and capital punishment under the British naval law. Rules aboard ship were harsh and punishable by a range of inventive sanctions up to and including death, e.g., Edward Collins was forced to wear a basket of shot around his neck for an hour to make him confess to the stealing of personal items [HCA 1/9/83], Edward Abbot was lashed 40 times "furiously & violently….about the face, back, head & shoulders" for asking for bread, a punishment for which he died three weeks later [HCA 1/9/137–8] and an unnamed sailor accused of attempting to jump ship "was put on Shore on Some uninhabited Cape or Island [with] a Gun Some Shot a Bottle of Powder, and a bottle of Water to Subsist or Starve" [HCA 1/99/109]. Indeed, the scope of potential offenses and the energy with which punishments were administered led to a 1749 revision of the Naval Articles of War that described acceptable punishments for different types of infractions. As part of this revision process, captains were reminded that punishments should never be assigned "without sufficient cause, nor ever with the greater severity that the offence shall really deserve" (cited in Adkins & Adkins 2008: 209) which, in itself, highlights how much of a cultural phenomenon excessive and undeserved punishment had become by that time. Further testimony to this phenomenon is recoverable from the popular songs of the day, such as the 1691 ditty entitled "The Sea Martyrs or The Seamen's Sad Lamentation for Their Faithful Service, Bad Pay and Cruel Usage" which set to verse a well-known trial in which a group of common sailors organized themselves to petition for improved conditions and pay only to be accused of mutiny and put to death (cited in Palmer 1986: 58). Such cases are also evidenced in witness accounts, e.g. one case c. 1667 in which "Eleven Englishmen came together to complain to the captain that they were not allowed water enough to drink" [445f.1/510]. In this case, the captain's response was to punish the apparent ringleader by placing him in shackles with two sentinels over him until they reached port, at which time he was presumably taken to stand court martial for mutiny. Comparable events detailed in the court proceedings of March 28, 1722, describe an suspected ringleader, who was "set on Shore here by the said Capt Chaloner Ogle for his Tryal" [HCA 1/99/170]. And courts martial were not an unusual occurrence in the naval fleets of the period, e.g., the logbook of the *Albemarle* refers to four separate trials in as many months between January and April 1697 [ADM 52/1/5]. Thus, sailors were subject to ad hoc disciplinary measures determined by the captain as well as the consequences of formal legal proceedings, making harsh disciplinary measures a regular hazard of life for sailors of the early colonial period.

Following what's written above, is found within the outcome of Cap'n Roberts crew's trial.

Chapter Fourteen
Wolves in Sheep Clothing

Location: 'Bennet's Key'

Touching in *Guardaloope*, wee capture first a Sloop, and soon after, a French fly boat laden with sugar. As to the Sloop's fate, altho' she was indeed divine, wee burnt 'er, and thereafter, I plotted a new course.

Arriving nigh Moonay, our plans must change, for presently, the sea here is to high to careen; ergo, I suggest wee saile forth to *Hispaniola*, where at, *Bennet's Key*,[1] in the *Gulf of Samina*, '*Gentlemen of Fortune*,' like ourselves, given the island's proportions, being vast, grants the freedom to careen, water and provision without fear of discovery, and that being said, I am pleas'd that wee reach our destination before the month of February 1721 concludes. I am also pleas'd to find the *Willing Captive* riding peaceably at anchor, has been awaiting our arrival.^{CSP-CS11 & pages 467 & 468}

After me ship is beached and heeled over, the Bos'n aboard Lord *Main's* ship, while some be charged with provisioning and watering, others are assigned the tedious task of cleaning her hull.

Needing to reside on land during the careening, I take our ship's smale boat and escort her Ladyship to her vessel which she hath not graced since wee left *Dominico*. Afterwards, having both enjoyed a bath and donning fresh cloathes, 'tis eager I am to do a bit of exploring, and wanting her Ladyship to reside with me ashore, I tell her that her ship also be in neede of careening; ergo, she and Mrs Robles need to gather for themselves the items they'll be needin' for a weekes time ashore.

Taking but a few minutes onely, the Lady Aspasia and Mrs Robles, return, each carrying a moderate size basket, a blanket and a change of cloathes. By this, I am most pleas'd, for most women, especially the nobility, would require a great deal more just to see themselves thro' the night, yet my woman, as does her companion, no doubt at her Ladyship's insistence, brings onely those items they cannae not do without.

---

[1] See Black Bart by Stanley Richards (page 54.) Isle can be found, with extreme magnification, on Google map.

Whilst the vessels be careened, those charged with the gathering of provisions will, in an uncommonly efficient manner, help themselves to a tidy quantity of the sugar and rum stowed on the *Willing Captive*; the latter in so much quantity that the liquor aboard my flotilla will be as plentiful as fresh water. In regard to this aspect, as be the case generally, onely myself and *Harry Glasby*, who I personally chose as Master of me *Royal Fortune*, being a fellow teetotal, remains consistently sober. As Commodore of the Fleet, and I belieeve 'tis best to be stated here, that altho' the majority of my time be spent aboard my flagship by daye and the *Willing Captive* by night, I move betwixt all me ships as I see fitt; however, of late, with the ships being careened, I intend to spend my time ashore exploring with her Ladyship.

Whilst here, before setting out, the Masters of two Sloops, their names being *Tuckerman* and *Porter*, pay me a call. Their addressment of me is one displaying a good deal of honour and respect. *"Having heard of your Fame and Atchievements, we have put in here to learn your art and wisdom in the business of pyrating, since we are of the same honourable design as yourself, we hope, that with the communication of your knowledge, we shall also receive your charity as we are in want of necessaries for such adventures."* [B8&9] *

Seeing that more able-bodied hands possessing superior seamanship skills are always desirable, and their manner, being one that pleases my ears, I find myself taking most kindly to these two men, and as such, I decide to provide them with a quantity of powder and arms.

> *Whilst Captain Roberts and his Lords were in privy council, la Marquise ventured to the settlement to send a letter to d'Éperon-noire plantation, which, as far as the world is concerned, be her home.*

After 2 or 3 nights of merry activity, the two of 'em be on their way. As they depart, having their owne vessels, both adequate to accomplish their proposed task, and expecting that they ought return within a weekes time, I wish for them a prosperous new career in our service as members of my company, and as they embark on their raiding expedition, bid them, *"I hope the Lord will prosper your handy Works."* [B8&9]

For reasons of their owne, me crew holds a negativity towards those among them who do not drink themselves into a constant state of oblivion, for men of such ilk, in their eyes, excepting myself, be open to suspicion. When the aforemention'd Captains depart, *Mister Glasby*, supposedly to bid them farewell, accompanys them.

Being gone longer than the majority felt he ought, me crew belieeved him to be a deserter, and needing little justification, thinking that the two so-called pyrates came onely to aid in *Glasby's* escape, and thus being the case, a search party is sent out after them.

With that business well in hand, I take her Ladyship by the hand, and venturing off, "There is another part of the island I wish to show you, and being the night shall be upon us soon, 'tis my suggestion, seeing it be our last night here, that wee do so alone."

> ** Author's Note: During the trial,*[B2 page 74] *Harry Glaspy said, "When Roberts was cleaning at Hispaniola, two Sloops came in commanded by one Porter and one Tuckerman, to the latter of which the Prisoner (John Coleman) belonged, that these Masters came on board of Roberts, and told him, that hearing he was there, they came in to receive his Charity, being on the same account themselves, but in want of everything, at last Roberts gave them, by Agreement among themselves, eight or nine Negroes a-piece, and received the Prisoner and some others in lieu."* [sic]
>
> ~~~~~~~~~~~~~~~~~~~~~~~~~
>
> *The name of Tuckerman's sloop was, Adventure.*[B2 page 74]

Smiling, not onely from the thought of exploring, but in the knowledge that wee will be far from the others, I tells him, "I will enjoy the outing, but mostly I shall enjoy being totally alone with thee, for this is one thing wee have ne'er beene, not truly, for others have always beene close at hand."

Altho' I do not wish to alarm her, it is necessary that I tell her, "Being it could be dangerous, wee must both be well armed."

"I am most capable in the realm of outdoor activities, fy Arglwydd, as thee shall see," says she, smiling, "And now that the *Willing Captive* is boardable once again I shall go on board and don my pistols and cutlass."

Slapping her on the rump as she begins to walk off, "That be the woman I love."

Within what seemes like onely a few minutes, she returns. Toting a bundle over her shoulder, and a moderate size basket, she is again dressed in form fitting breeches, over the knee boots, and one of my shirts that she hath again ty'd off centre at the waist.

"I am ready, fy Arglwydd."

Onely twice before have I seene her dressed so, and as she approaches, I cannae helpe but ogle her, for not onely is her attire suitable to our purpose, 'tis captivating; and in addition to her frock, she hath donned not onely her carved powder horn and shot pouch, cutlash and dirk, but her pair of deeply engraved brass barrel pistols with drop down triggers and custom ivory grips, the latter of which being neatly holstered bilaterally at the point of her hips, move in an erotic fashion as she approaches. In so, my first thought was to compliment her appearance. "Thou looks delectable, my Lady Aspasia."

Blushing, "Thank thee, fy Arglwydd. It pleases me to know thee finds my outfit appetizing."

"Most assuredly," and altho' wee wish it were otherwise, being wee are in full view of me crew, which looks on, I refrain from anny public displays of affection. Being understandably curious as wee trudge off, I asks, "What dost thou tote in the basket?"

Speaking as she opens the lid, "See for thyself."

Beneath the hinged lid is found cooking equipage and food stuffs.

"As ever, my Lady, thou hast come well prepared."

Tossing me the bundle, she says, "Thee can carry the bedclothes."

With me following close behind carrying the bundle and a water bota over me shoulder, her Ladyship, clutching the basket, gallivants off.

After a few minutes, wee head into a heavily wooded area. The foliage becoming quite thick, is in neede of cutting if wee are to get thro'; ergo, pulling my cutlash from it's scabbard, I proceed to lead the way, cutting the limbs that be blocking our path, whilst her Ladyship, marking our route with her dirk, makes a small † on the bigger plants. After about an hour, when wee come to a clearing, her Ladyship, espying a stream, setts the basket on a rock and prances off.

The meadow is quite nice. Just to our right is a nice size tree that ought provide adequate shelter. Not being able to resist her frolicking, I sett down the bundle I be carrying on a fallen tree, and when I get to the stream, I find she hath removed her boots, and as she begins to wade in the cold water, she squeals with delight.

Seeing me at the water's edge, she says, "Join me, fy Arglwydd.

Quickly spreading the blanket on the grassy area onely a few feet from the stream, and having removed my shoes and silk socks, I join her.

All of a sudden, espying a water snake, she draws one of her pistols, and shooting it dead, she begins to laugh. "'Tis beene a long time since I have had such fun."

I must admit, she never ceases to amaze me.

Stepping out of the stream, she pulls out her dirk and heads for a stand of bamboo.

"Whither thou goest?"

"As thou hath no doubt noticed, the stream is full of fish. If thou maketh a lean-to, I shall see about catching our evening meal."

"And I, one delightful mermaid."

"As was aboard thy ship, fy Arglwydd?"

"How so, my Lady?"

Continuing to smile, she replies, "One woman, a band of Rovers, and a gallant so formidable that no one durst challenge him."

After some time has passed, having built for us a lean-to, I look around. First, having used her fire starter tools, her Ladyship had cleared an area for cooking, and having started the fire, and whilst the embers become right for cooking, she, again, is in the stream, this time, holding a bamboo spear in her hand, she is standing very still. Suddenly, she thrusts the spear downward. When it comes up again, I canne hardly believe mine eyes, for she hath impaled a good size fish. Removing the fish from the spear, she tosses it onto the shore. As I keep watching her, she again stands very still. After a couple minutes, to my amazement, as she again thrusts her spear, she impales another.

Walking out of the stream, she gathers up her catch, and carrying them proudly, she brings them to the campsite.

"Tea," she proclaims with a smile.

Amazed by her woodland skills, "Where did thou learn to do that?"

"My brother taught me," she replies, smiling. "He and I used to go fishing together. As it was his, cleaning critters is a man's job."

"Sounds fair," says I, nodding me head a mite, and whilst I begin to prepare the fish, her Ladyship, picking up the bedclothes, proceeds to lay them out within the lean-to.

By the time she returns, the fish be clean and ready to fry. After sliding them onto the slender metal rods her Ladyship brought in her basket, she straddles them betwixt the rocks she positioned on opposite sides of the dead tree limbs and kindling I placed twixt the rocks.

During tea, I learn that she, as do I, truly enjoys the part of *Hispaniola* wee be in. Large as this island is, the overall population is rather smale. There are no natives within this general area of the island, at least none had beene seene by my scouts.

After tea, as wee cuddle before the fire, "Some of me men have informed me that yer Ladyship takes in the sunrise most every morn since arriving at this Island. It would please me if thee will wake me at dawn, for I should like to enjoy it with you."

"Of course, fy Arglwydd."

The tone of her reply, being consistent with one who is drifting of too sleep, I knew at once that the long trek, and other activities, had worn her to a frazzle, and when I look upon her, I see she hath fallen asleep. Gently picking her up, I carry her into the lean-to where I lay her on the makeshift bed and cover her. Laying beside her, I find that I too am tired, but still, for sometime after, whilst laying on my side, knowing that on the morrow wee shall part for a spell, I gaze upon her for sometime before I too fall asleep.

As usual, since being on the island of *Hispaniola*, I wake early. 'Tis a pleasant morn indeed. The first order of business is to check on my snare. It not being far, I arrive within a few minutes. 'What luck,' thinking to myself; finding a grouse trapped inside, 'My Captain will enjoy having fresh meat to accompany the turtle eggs I toted from the ship.'

As I prepare the grouse, the sun is waking to a new day. Entering the lean-to quietly, I find my Captain sleeping peacefully, and giving the matter a couple moments thought, I am remembering that the last time I woke him was following the storm aboard our ship in the future, thus, in keeping with this déjà vu moment, I venture to awaken him by arousing his passion.

Amid his euphoric utterances, his waking moments be savouring every moment of my seamless attentions. Deeply absorbed in passion, a look of rapture begins to appear upon his swarthy face, and as his hands begin to massage the back of my neck, his fingers entangle themselves within my locks. One day perhaps, he shall understand the delight I feel in affording to him all I have to give, not only food, weapons and pleasuring, but in all things.

Finally he speaks, and in his deliciously quiet tone he whispers, "Come fy melys, Aspasia; Come kiss me."

More consumed than my Captain realizes, my heart, though heavy, rejoices also, and has been brimming ever since he called me by the same delicious pet name as in the past, or was it the future. Whichever be the case, I wish to make our last hours together, at least for a time, memorable.

Longing for his sweet love as I move up across his olive-skinned frame, he gazes into my eyes. "Why, fy melys, hast thou not waken me thusly before?"

After giving his question some thought, "Our parting always heavies my heart, fy Arglwydd, and I have observed thee to also be somewhat melancholy during these times, but for whatever the reason, I knows it must be; yet even in my sadness I am inspired by the lust that consumes me, and to those cravings, I shall always be a slave."

At the same time, knowing that I crave the tender touch of his lips, he lifts his head, and in meeting my mouth with his, sending a blanket of ever so slight chills and tingling throughout my being, his kiss enhances the very essence of my soul.

Sometime Later, with the fire going well, her Ladyship, whilst I take down the lean-to, begins to prepare our morning meal. Seeming to be onely a few minutes later, I hear her call out, "Come and get it."

Gathering up the pile of neatly folded bedcloathes, I carry 'em to the small clearing where I had built a fire to cook by.

"Sit there, fy Arglwydd," says she, motioning to the large rock nigh her.

Sitting where she suggests, being sufficiently close to the fire, I find myself pleasantly warmed. Within moments, as her Ladyship hands me my meale upon a tin plate, and a cup of tea, I says, "Thank thee, *Aspasia*."

In doing so, she flashes me a toothy grin.

"What is it," I asks her? "Whyfor art thou smiling so?"

Speaking with much happiness in her voice, "Art thou not aware of what thee just called me?"

Giving her a questioning look.

Brimming with delight, "Thee called me Aspasia. No title or pretence, just my name. For so long I have wished it."

"Titles are rather cumbersome." After a moment's pause, "Aspasia?"

"Yes, Bart?"

"May I have the extra fork held by thee?"

She was a little bewildered for a moment, and then looking at her hand, realizing she had not yet given it to me, she replies, "Yes, of course," and reaching across the fire, she hands it to me.

"Thee called me Bart?"

"Is it not a derivative of thy middle name?"

"Aye, but..."

"I wanted to hear how it sounded is all."

"And?"

"I thought it both strong and sexy, but also, thou having called me by a pet name, I felt, that with us being hear alone, only such be needed."

More content than ever, wee sit back against the rock and finish our breakfast.

She did very well I thought, cooking out here in the rough. I was supriz'd, as it was the first time I have known her to cook a full meal without the luxury of the galley on board ship, and even then Mrs Robles, and my mess crew generally do most of the cooking, her Ladyship made good use of the turtle egges and sev'rall slices of bread she had brought from her ship. Frying the latter in the egge, she served it with the grouse she snared in the open weave basket type trap she constructed out of saplings whilst sitting before the fire last evening. Altho' quite surpriz'd by her handiness in the wilderness, I could not be more pleas'd.

After breakfast, wee begin the long hike back to camp, whereupon I find quite a bit of excitement going on.

The search party having returned with Captains *Porter* and *Tuckerman*, and *Mister Glasby*, the lot have beene brought back for tryal, and to my discontent, the camp be in a state of pandemonium.

Handing the bedcloathes to her Ladyship, who is already carrying quite a load in her basket, I says, "Excuse me, Aspasia, but go I must."

Understanding completely as I dash off, she states, "Of course, fy Arglwydd."

Upon entering the camp, I focus mine eyes first on the men who have just beene chucked to the ground by those who were forced to drag 'em back after searching most of the night to locate them.

Turning my attentions to my officers, I says, "My Lords!" and whilst in a manner to gain order, I ask, "What be amiss here?"

Speaking in a gruff tone, "As you see, Captain," begins Lord *Sympson*, " 'Tis them three dogs," pointing to the men lying in the sand. "It be them alone that prompts such concerns this morn."

"Aye, that I canne see. Excellent work; however, I entrusted you with the maintenance of order, yet coming upon you, I find this ruckus."

"Having just arrived, the men are in quite an uproar. I was attempting to calm them when you arrived."

"Yes... so I see." Continuing, says I. "With the *Royal Fortune*, again afloat and fitt for service, take the prisoners on board, and on the conclusion of necessary preparations, their trial shall commence."

Diverting my attentions a mite whilst en route to her ship, her Ladyship approaches. "If I promise to be still, wouldst be possible to observe the proceedings?"

"Thou must be aware, my Lady, that should these men be found guilty, they shall suffer their punishment forthwith, and such events would not befit a lady."

"I thank thee for thine interest in my welfare, and fully understanding thy meaning, I shan't attempt to sway thee; nevertheless, let me say only that altho' thee believes me to be made of china, I am not." And after making her comment, having accepted my judgment, she turns, and without another word, she resumes her trek to the *Willing Captive*.

As she spoke, the look upon her face was one which inferred that I be overly protective, and with such in my mind, I call out to 'er. "my Lady, Aspasia."

Whereby, not presuming what I may be saying, she turns, "Yes, fy Arglwydd?"

"Thee may attend. But remember thy promise."

"I will."

Whilst handing the bundle of bed cloathes she be carrying to Mrs Robles, who had met her on the trail, she instructs her, "Please come back for these items here," and kneeling down she places the basket on the sand."

Altho' disapprovingly, Mrs Robles trudges off.

Walking the few steps to my side, and silently requesting that I escort her on board, her Ladyship holds out her hand.

Demonstrating to her that I am most honoured to do so, I place my hand beneath hers. In this manner, 'twill be clear to my company that she is not imposing, but hath beene invited to attend the proceedings.

After a short walk to the longboat, wee are rowed to the ship, whereby, in escorting her on board, her presence is to the satisfaction of me crew.

Our form of justice is honest, simple, and swift. Testimony is heard by all who wish to either bear witness, or simply voice pertinent opinions. After which, each man within the company is required to vote; the majority being the victor. With a guilty verdict, comes forth the sentence, and diktat in accordance with our laws, and whatever it may be, it is carry'd out forthwith. Ne'er does a society such as ours maintain a brig, nor delay in matters such as these; for justice served expediently allows normalcy to return without delay.

Matters such as this be held on the Quarter-Deck. Before the hearing is sett in to motion, a large bowl of punch, as well as tobacco, is made ready, the doing of which makes way for unnecessary interruptions.

During the past two hours, there has beene a great deal said regarding these here prisoners, and the proceedings thus far have lasted quite sometime. After all testimony having beene heard, and none of the prisoners being able to prove their innocence, the sentence, as declared by the majority, is that they be shot; yet, as stated, not all be in favour of this. He who objects the loudest is Lord *Valentine Ashplant*, who is not onely among those within our *'House of Lords,'* but one of the appointed judges as well.

Ever respective of our laws, he stands; as anyone canne speak for a prisoner, and having his owne feelings to offer, Lord *Ashplant* says, *"By God, Glasby shall not dye; damn me if he shall."* sic B8 & 9 Returning to his seat, he takes a puff from his pipe whilst his motion is lowdly opposed by the other judges.

"Equal terms I grant you, are for all," says one, "but—"

Angered, Lord *Ashplant* remains steadfast, and rising again, he spouts, *"God damn ye Gentlemen, I am as good a Man as the best of you; damn my Soul if ever I turned my Back to any Man in my Life, nor ever will, by God; Glasby is an honest Fellow, notwithstanding this Misfortune, and I love him,* **Devil** *damn me if I don't: I hope he'll live and repent of what he has done; but damn me if he must dye, I will dye along with him."* B8 & 9 sic

Thereupon, pulling out his pistols, he presents them to the erudite on the bench.

His speech is taken to heart by many present, and noting his high regard for *Glasby* (who knew not why B2 page 56 & 480), a new vote is taken. This time, the majority frees *Glasby*, and thus a reprieve is granted. In the case of the other two prisoners, no such pleas be offered, and as such, they are allow'd the liberty of choosing anny four from among the company to be their executioners, after which, in carrying out the sentence, they be bound to the mast and shot Dead, Dead, Dead.

Immediately following the execution, wishing this incident could 'ave beene avoided, I step onto a platform above the deck of me *Royal Fortune*, and altho' obviously fitt to be ty'd, ne'er do I stop for a moment, and hollering, "Ye, and all of you," whilst dramatically motioning to a nondescript member of me crew, "Weigh anchor, We're getting underway."

Having both the admiration compiled with a healthy respect afforded me by me crew, I wield much more power than other pyrate captains, thus I have a great deal more say in both our course direction and the actions taken. In so, I am normally given no argument, but on this day, altho' my temper be somewhat subdued, when again having to issue an order, I forcefully shove the man before me whilst shouting, "I said get underway!"

Most assuredly frightened, the men having already transferred all items of value from our discarded Sloop in favour of the Brigantine belonging to *Norton*,[CSP-CS17] who not onely being free to leave, but now in command of the Dutch built Sloop, is in a decidedly cheerful mood.

By early evening, during tea, altho' ne'er did she imply anny ill feelings to the events of the daye, sett me mind to wondering. "The tryal, and especially the punishment that followed, it ought not have beene witnessed by thine eyes."

"'Twas my decision, fy Arglwydd."

"That's just the point, my Lady. As Captain, I ought never have allowed thee to perswade me, and having done so, hath made me realize that thee, being a woman of rank, wealth and privilege, deserves much more than a life constantly shrouded in danger, hardship, and violence."

Perturbed by my remarks, she gently spouts, "Why again must thee again bring up my title and affluence when wee both agree that beyond the procurement of supplies, they are of little value, and why dost thou say I deserve more than thee can offer me? I sought thee out, and my happiness is that which I have found here with thee, and until this moment I thought—"

"For me, the time wee spend together is special indeed, and judging by thy greeting each time wee meet, I knows thee loves me; yet, even tho' the time wee share is not nigh enough, things are as they must be."

> *As the conversation continues, her Ladyship's state of bewilderment evolves into disappointment & despair.*

"The separations that lovers must bear, fy Arglwydd, is an ongoing sacrifice, no different now than from that which has existed since the beginning of time. Perhaps that is why children are so precious."

"I belieeve there is a difference. Thou art a creature of grace and beauty, who, whilst mine has beene at sea, thine hath spent thy life on God's green earth. As for children, 'tis fortunate for us thou art barren, for 'twould be unfair to press upon a child the inerasable stigma that a man of my ilk would imprint."

"A man of thine ilk? Thou art a great leader of men, one who brings forth justice when others will not; the Great Pyrate; Admiral of the *Leeward Isles*, he who possesses the honour of being called Pistol-Proof."[B8 & 9]

"I am a pyrate, my Lady. All else is lost within that reality."

It seems there are no words I can say to sway his persuasions, and needing time to consider if what I believe him to be saying is so, I bid him goodnight. " 'Tis late, fy Arglwydd, and it's beene a trying day. Wouldst thou mind if I retire early?"

Not understanding that my true concerns be grave, he bids me goodnight, "Till to-morrow, my Lady, Aspasia."

Giving him a kiss, "Goodnight." As I slowly walk towards the great cabin, I feel a tear upon my cheek.

Whilst laying beneath the bed cloathes, I am giving much consideration to the statements made by my beloved, and after many silent tears, I come to the conclusion that perhaps, in wanting to attend the tryal, I have displeased him, and that as it may, I feel that in his own way, he is saying my presence has become bothersome.

Come midnight, feeling that now is a good time to do what I believe my beloved wants, for I love him too much not to, I make my way topside, and carrying only a small candle, I lower a boat, and whilst rowing myself to *Willing Captive*, the lights having been out around the flotilla for hours, I am un noticed.

Tucking my pistols into the sash about my waist behind my back, and a carrying a candle, I enter the cabin occupied by my most trusted crew members, *Robert Crow*, young *Jean François*, and *Mister Philips*. William, my steward, sleeps here also, and altho' I know he shan't question me, the others may be a problem.

First, I approach the bunk of my trusted friend, William. Kneeling on the floor beside him, I whisper, "William." Sleeping soundly, there is not a stir. Whilst gently shaking his shoulder, I again whisper, "William."

Being confident of his position on board ship, his eyes open slowly, yet seeing me kneeling next to him, knowing that ne'er would I enter the cabin of a crewman unless the nature was of vital importance, his expression is one of grave concern.

Rising quickly to a seated position, he asks, "What be wrong, my Lady?"

"Shhh, doing so quietly, meet me on the Quarter-Deck forthwith," and rising, I depart.

Joining me in a few minutes as requested, William again asks, "What be wrong, my Lady?"

"For reasons I wish not to disclose at this time, we be getting underway, taking with us only a skeleton crew, I need you to quarter the others for a time, all but *Robert Crow*; he shall bear a message to Captain *Roberts*."

Ne'er before has William challenged me, but this time he feels I am not conducting myself within the realm of normal behaviour, as he boldly says, "my Lady, ne'er have I questioned yer motives, but this is not like you."

As a tear rolls down my cheek, "Please, William," I says to him quietly, "do not question me now. I need your help for I can not handle these men alone."

Seeing my distressed state, he obliges me without further question. "What be yer plan?"

Smiling, I says, "First, I need you to confine the crew below. After you have left on that errand, I shall awake *maître François*, *Mister Philips*, and *Robert Crow*. Once well underway, yet still within sight of the flotilla, put all but the three best seamen into a longboat. Knowing my ship makes a greater speed than the others, they shan't pursue us."

"Aye, my Lady, consider it done."

Returning to the small cabin below, and standing before his bunk and stooping slightly, I whisper, "*Mister Philips*."

In the dim light produced by the candle, I can see him rubbing his eyes whilst looking at me. "Aye, my Lady?"

"Please wake up, I need you on the Quarter-Deck, and bring the other 2 with you."

Unawares, not hearing any commotion from the lower cabin where the remainder of the crew sleep, the three of them come to me on the Quarter-Deck. "Aye, my Lady, what be the problem?"

"We're getting underway."

Seeing no one else on deck, "Where's the rest of the crew?" asks *Mister Philips*.

Noting their restless body language, I pull out my pistols, "They're quartered below."

BELOW DECK ⇁

In the main crew area, William has the men lined up, their backs against the bulkhead, letting his pistols convince them of his intent, whilst one crewman binds the hands of the others.

"What be ya meaning to do with us?" asks one of the crewman.

"There be no cause fer worry, mateys," states William, "Her Ladyship's orders are that you be sett in a longboat once wee be underway."

ON THE QUARTER DECK →

Young *Jean François* asks "And us?"

"Those still aboard shall crew the ship until my destination is reached, after which, you shall return the *Willing Captive* to Captain *Roberts*."

Speaking in a surpriz'd tone, "But surely you not be leaving, my Lady?"

"Yes, *Mister Philips*, I must."

Fearful, *Mister Crow* asks, "And what of me?"

"Before we sail, William shall place you in the *Royal Fortune's* smallest boat, bound and gagged I'm afraid, but I do not want you to be discovered until the *Willing Captive* has long since departed."

His eyes, giving me cause to suspect he might make a run for it, I cock my pistols. "Now get to the capstan, all of you, and weigh the anchor, or suffer the dire consequences of refusal."

Knowing me to be not only a crack shot, but true to my word, the lot of them follow the orders without further incident.

With the remaining crew below secured to William's satisfaction, he comes topside to assist me. "The crew, secur'd below, shan't be a problem, my Lady."

"Thank you, William," says I with a slight smile of relief, not that e'er did I doubt him. "Please take *Mister Crow* to the *Royal Fortune* and secure him within the small boat in a manner that will prevent his discovery until daybreak. After he is secure, place this note in his pocket."

"Aye, my Lady," After placing a gangplank twixt the ships, and relieving *Mister Crow* from the capstan, William ties his hands behind his back and takes him across to the *Royal Fortune's* where he secures him within a small boat.

Having weighed the anchor, the others get in position. *Jean François* goes forward to unfurl the jibs, and *Mister Philips* scurries aloft to unfurl the mainsail.

Returning, William brings in the gangplank, and with Mrs Robles at the helm, William and I brace the sheets.

With the ship underway, William, going below, releases all but three of the crew, and once topside, the lot of them climb down to the awaiting longboat and depart. Making his way back to the hold, he brings the three sea artists to me on the Quarter-Deck.

"You are here to help me return to Bermuda, after which, you three, together with *Mister Philips* and *Maître François*, will return the *Willing Captive* to Captain *Roberts*."

With the ship underway, knowing no ship upon the water can catch us, I suddenly collapse in the passageway.

Finding me doubled over in great pain, William carries me to my cabin before my misery is known to the others.

> *Come daybreak, several of the crewmen, noting the absence of the Willing Captive, rouse Captain Roberts.*

Rapping on the door I hear a man shouting, "Wake up, Captain!" but hearing no reply, the crewman, pounding again, hollers, "The *Willing Captive*, she be gone!"

Immediately, the news bringing me to full awake; I leap to my feet. "Gone?"

The crewman who had pounded on the door, along with two others, knowing I had beene sleeping, close the door upon entering. As expected, they find me in a highly agitated state. "Where the devil is she?"

Wary of my reaction, the crewman replies, "I knows not, Captain."

Quickly, the three of them move judiciously out of the way as I robe myself. Flinging open the cabin door, I rush out barefooted onto the open deck, and sure enough, the *Willing Captive* is nowhere to be seen.

Below, in a smale boat, I espy *Robert Crow* bound and gagged. Grabbing hold of a knotted rope, I leap over the side of me ship, and climbing down, I make my way to him. Entering the boat, whilst untying the gag within his mouth, "Where be the *Willing Captive*, and what of la Marquise?"

"I knows not, Captain. I onely knows that whilst her Ladyship forced us at point of pistol, she be in tears."

"And the rest of the *Willing Captive's* crew, where are they?"

"By her Ladyship's order, William was to put 'em in one of the longboats as soon as they made saile. He also shoved a paper in me pocket."

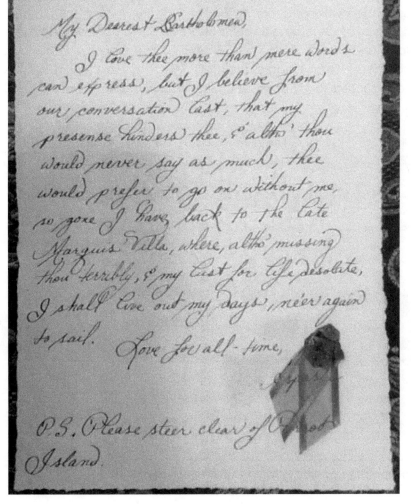

Snatching and reading the note, I holler, "All hands on deck!"

"Are wee to give chase, Captain?"

"Even under-manned, there's no other ship afloat that canne catch the *Willing Captive*," states Lord *Main*.

As me crew gathers about, it is plain to see that I be in a fearful temper.

"The crew is assembled, Captain," says Lord *Main*.

"As soon as the longboat appears and the men are aboard, make saile."

"Course direction?"

"Anywhere."

"Captain?"

Sullen, and making no reply, I aimlessly wander off.

Chapter Fifteen
Captain Anstis

Location: 'Bermuda, West Indies & Africa'

March is upon us, and once at sea it was decided to make saile Eastward from *Hispaniola* in the general direction of *Deseada* Island, and tho' most difficult, I try'd not to think of she, whom I miss terribly. En route, sailing near enough to *Martinique* and the surrounding islands, me and my crew, out of pure sport, create havoc, and in such, cause a great deal of concern for the Governour there; so much so that the British and the French join forces, building fortifications and such untill, having grown tired of the game, wee move on.^{CSP-CS see page 429}

Continuing on our way, being in neede of provisions and fresh water, I, commanding a ship of 42 guns & a Briganteen of 18 with 262 White men & 50 Negroes, with *'The Luck of a God,'* as la Marquise always call'd it, sight saile.

Upon the showing of me jack, and a single shot across their bow, Captain *Hingston*, commander of our prey, surrenders without a fuss.[CSP-CS12]

Later, Captain *Hingston* was overcome by a Spanish pirate and marooned. After being rescued by a passing ship, making landfall at *Saint Christophers*, one Captain *Whitney* was told of *Hingston's* unpleasantness. From aboard the HMS *Rose*[CSP-CS3], a Man of War, an ineffective search was conducted and after returning to *Saint Christophers*, Captain *Hingston's* letter continued thus.[CSP-CS12], ①

> I hope the ships bound from London to Jamica soon after my escape the said Roberts: for he designed to keep the station and destroy all the ships that come to these islands which may fall into his hands. They left me without any manner of clothing; and Roberts brought my brother (the chief mate) to the gears and whipped him within an inch of his life by reason he had concealed two gold rings in his pocket. This is the dismal account I am to give of this voyage.
>
> A. Hingston

---

① More relating to the incident involving Cap'n Hingston is found below on page 371.

BLOOD and SWASH, The Unvarnished Life (& afterlife) Story of Pirate Captain, Bartholomew Roberts......pt.2 "THE WILLING CAPTIVE"

MOVING ON →

My attempts to block her Ladyship from my mind, having proved unsuccessful; I canne bare her absence no longer, and whilst me crew continues to indulge themselves in the fine art of plundering Captain *Hingston's* richly laden, *Jamaica* bound ship, I give the orders for my flotilla to change course for the *Barmudas*.[B8 & 9]

Upon reaching *Castle Harbour*, I alone go ashore in a smale boat. Making my way to, my Lady Aspasia's Villa, my state of displeasure, having gotten the better of me, I kick in the door. Within moments, sev'rall servants come running into the room from all directions.

Altho' frightened by my behaviour, the chief housemaid, taking note of my fine cloathes, gives a modest curtsy. "Wha... what is it you want, Sir?"

Seeing a large painting of la Marquise hanging directly before me, and knowing without question to be in the right place, I speak as my ill temper demands. "Madame la Marquise d'Éperon-noire, in which room will I find her?"

Stepping forward, a dignified older gent says, "I am Jean Luc d'Orleans, la Marquises' great uncle. May I ask who calls for my niece?"

Wanting onely to retrieve my woman, I simply state, "I am the Lady Aspasia's, 'Special Friend.' having beene separated at sea, I am looking for her."

"You present yourself oddly for someone who makes such a claim, Monsieur."

Losing my temper, "If one of ye does not tell me where to find her, I shall, by thunder, burn this place to the ground and smoak 'er out!"

Aspasia Rebekah Jourdain, la Marquise d'Éperon-noire

A greatly terrified, little bit of a woman, speaks out. "I beseech you, Monsieur, pray do not, for her Ladyship has not graced this plantation for some 2 yeeres. When she left, 'twas aboard her ship, saying onely, 'twas adventuring she'd be and fer us not to worry."

"What she says be true, Monsieur," says the chief housemaid. "Look here." Stepping to a smale round table nigh the centre of the room, "Her Ladyship wrote to us." Opening the drawer, she takes out the letter, and 'tho' nervous as a hog in the smoak house, she walks on over to me, and stretching out her hand, she says, "This came to us a few dayes ago."

Snatching the letter from her hand, I tear it from its envelope, and seeing her signature trademark, I read it. Taking a moment to reflect, I fold the letter and return it to her. Having composed myself, I asks, "Is this the onely painting of la Marquise?"

The first maid replies, "A smaller one of the same likeness hangs in the late Marquis' bedchamber."

Demandingly, I says, "Go fetch it!"

Clambering to do as I asks, the Housemaid dashes off.

"My apologies to ye, and all of you."

More frustrated than ever before, "Where canne she be," I mutter. Within a couple of minutes, the smallish maid, accompanied by a tall black servant carrying the portrait, returns to the foyer.

Taking the portrait from him, I turn, saying, "I thank ye for the information," and leaving the great house, I begin my trek back to me *Royal Fortune*.

> *En route, Captain Roberts passes another French gentleman, who, altho' he knew the man looked familiar, could not place him; nonetheless, and hopefully unbeknownst to the finely dressed Captain Roberts, the stranger followed. The way led through a thick wooded area before reaching the beach, the stranger, from afar, watched as Bartholomew Roberts stepped into a small boat, and in minutes only, it was easy to see that he was heading towards the large ship hoving near the mouth of the harbour. Musing, knowing in his mind that the finely dressed man is more eminent than the stranger first realized, he couldn't help but wonder what manner of man, so distinguished, would row himself. Desperate to know, the stranger hurried to some men near the water's edge, but to his chagrin, none of them knew the man's identity. Dismayed, the stranger, as he began to walk off, was almost knocked down by a young boy running by him, who, displaying a great deal of enthusiasm, called out to the stranger by name.*

Shouting, the young boy cried out, "Captain *Roberts*, take me with you!"

"What's that boy?" asks the stranger with a shocked look on his face. "Who did you say that was?"

"*Bartholomew Roberts*, sir."

"The pyrate?"

"Yes, sir," shewing the stranger an artist's sketch.

"Gee," continues the boy, "I wish I was here sooner. Me dreams be filled with the stories I have heard 'bout his adventures."

Seeing the sketch, the stranger pulls a handbill from his pocket.

"By god, his face betrays him!" and finds himself in shock whilst looking at both the crinkled sketch and the rowboat for a moment longer, whilst becoming conscious of the urgency in which he must act, he begins running towards the Captains in port, hollering, "Captain *Ogle!*"

By the time the stranger stands before one of England's great sea Captains, he is breathing quite hard as he spouts, "That ship," pointing to it, "It's the *Royal Fortune!*"

"You mean the one belonging to that scourge, *Roberts*?" asks Captain *Ogle*.

Whilst awaiting the stranger's reply, the Captain's face lights brightly with the thought of hanging such a splendid trophy from his bowsprit as did *Maynard* to *Blackbeard*, and perhaps, being much more the prize, gain an admiralty in the bargain.

Showing him the handbill whilst trying to catch his breath, the stranger replies, "Yes, Captain."

With the stranger following closely upon his heels, Captain *Ogle* dashes towards his Pinnace, and having every intention of accompanying him, he continues to voice what just occurred.

En route, the stranger tells him, "He was just at d'Éperon-noire's plantation; threatened to burn the place to the ground, he did, if they did not tell him where her Ladyship is."

"How do you know this?" asks Captain *Ogle*.

"I was there, but being concealed, he did not see me. I ducked out the back door only moments before he left with la Marquise d'Éperon-noire's portrait, and seeing him leave, I followed him."

Making haste, two of the oarsmen push the Pinnace beyond the surging surf until enough freeboard is gained to allow rowing, whereby the crewmen jump into the boat. Even tho' she be a goodly distance off, 'tis easy for the trained eye to see that altho' the *Royal Fortune* is getting underway, she is doing so in a leisurely manner.

Enquiring as to a possible relationship, Captain *Ogle* asks, "Are you saying that la Marquise and that scallywag *Roberts* be acquainted?"

"I shutter at the thought, Captain," replies the Frenchman, "but given the circumstances, I must confess that it appears so. Having sailed more than 2 years ago, and except for a letter recently saying she made port in *Hispaniola*, no one knows where la Marquise has beene. You've heard, I am sure, of her yen for adventuring, and well… I suppoze she could've met him, and should he have taken a fancy to her—"

Alarmed at the notion planted in his mind, himself having copious thoughts of her, having asked for her hand some years earlier, and still having a fondness for her, Captain *Ogle* roars, "Row hard men! That ship must not escape!"

As soon as the Pinnace reaches Captain *Ogle's* Man-O'-War, he hurries aboard her, as does the stranger.

Wasting no time in issuing orders, he hollers, "Make sail!" and seeing his crew be unhurried, Captain *Ogle*, whilst pointing out to sea, rouses them to action as he exuberantly proclaims, "There, under the command of that infamous scallywag, *Bartholomew Roberts*, is the *Royal Fortune*, brimming with treasure. Will you allow her to escape?"

Knowing the legendary pyrate stows his treasure upon his ships, and visualizing their share of the infinite riches before them, the entire crew hoot and holler as they dash for action.

The Quarter-Master of His Majesty's Ship, *Swallow*,[B8 & 9] a 4th rate Ship of the Line, knowing his share, is more than double that of the rest of the crew, shouts to those who be bearing hard upon the capstan, hollers, "Slip the anchor chain and lett us be off!"

As the crew of the Man-O'-War, second only to them trained by Captain *Roberts*, scurry up the rigging to unfurl the sails whilst others on deck man the sheets and braces, the great Warship gets underway.

Hollering from his station, the gunner orders, "Make ready the gunns!"

MEANWHILE →

From upon the *Royal Fortune*, which had sail'd into *Castle Harbour* alone, underway, but not yet having rejoined the flotilla, a cry from aloft, is heard.

"Hearken on deck," yells the watch from high above in the main's crow's nest.

Looking upward, "Aye, the watch," hollers the Bos'n, "What you see?"

"There!" pointing towards the stern, "Yonder Man-O'-War is giving chace."

Immediately, Lord *Main* sent one of the crew to bring me the news, for I had retired to the great cabin. Hollering, "Captain!" amid his approach. Knocking on the door with urgency, repeating his call, "Captain!" shouts the crewman again with grave concern. "Come quick! That Man-o'-War, the one that had beene lying at anchor within *Castle Harbour*, she be in pursuit."

Turning quickly, I don my tricorne and dash out the cabin door. Rushing along the larboard side and out onto the main deck, I spot Lord *Main* along the rail of the Quarter-Deck. Touching onely, the centre tread in my haste to the rail as I traverse the steps, Lord *Main* hands me the spyglass. Looking thro', seeing the sleek ship is sailing well, I holler, "Drag on all the canvas wee canne pack."

"Aye, Captain."

Searching the ship quickly, and espying our gunner, I call out, "My Lord *Dennis*!" Seeing that he acknowledges me, I holler, "Run out the gunns."

All about my ship me crew, whilst the men aloft be actively climbing the shrouds and ratlines, slide across the yards, and finding their positions on the footropes, quickly untie the reef knots and shaking out the sailes, the deckhands work quickly to position the sailes to catch the wind. Within minutes me *Royal Fortune*, to my delight, tho' she be heavy from the stores wee had recently taken, is sailing well; nevertheless, the 4th rate Ship-Of-The-Line is slowly gaining.

Although me crew quickly hung our Topgallant Stays'ls and the Royals, the Man-O'-War gains still. ''Tis a wonder fer sure,' I thinks to myself. 'What canne be driving them so. Surely they cannae know who wee be, or why I was on their island, but chasing us they are.

Within minutes they be abreast us, and upon receiving the Warships first broadside, I knows at once their Captain has on board a crew of much skill as I holler, "Raise our colours!" and as our jack is proudly hoisted, I bellow forth, "Fire!" Whereby, wee lett go with a broadside of our owne. At that moment another broadside, bringing forth a volcano of fire and metal, wreaks havoc as it bursts upon me ship.

Lowdly, in an effort to be heard whilst speaking to *Henry Dennis*, whom I had summoned, I says, "Our onely chance, my Lord, is to take down yon ship's mainmast. Lett that be your onely task."

"Aye, aye, Captain."

To my chagrin, despite our best efforts, I knows that in order to get clear, wee must jettison not onely our anchor, and most of our water-casks, but more besides.

When the running battle begins, wee once again find ourselves having to throw over heavy stores to get clear, and tho' it pains the lot of us greatly, our burdens are being cast off with great speed, as so ordered.

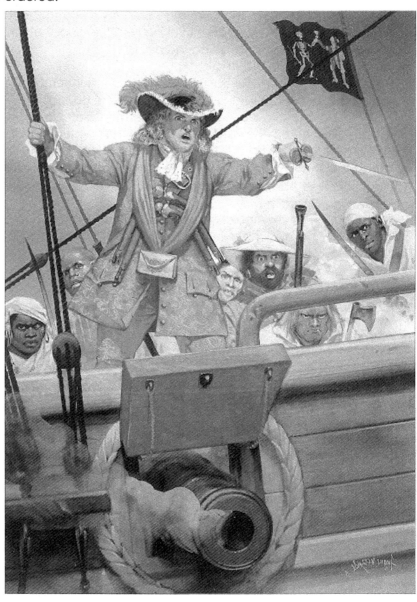

To better direct our fire, both, Lord *Dennis* and I, stand atop two of the centre cannon as he orders, "Lay to the mainmast and fire on the up roll," and as me *Royal Fortune* reaches the height of the next swell, Lord *Dennis* and I simultaneously holler, "Fire!"

With the gunns reloaded, wee again send forth a third broadside that not onely brings down both her mainmast, and mizzen, sends me crew into a chearing frenzy, but such is short-lived, for me owne ship, listing heavily, is destined to sink.

Amid the onslaught of thundering cannons, a member of the Man-O'-War's crew canne be seene swinging betwixt the ships, and as he lands on the Quarter-Deck before me, I swiftly draw my sword.

Without hesitation, the unexpected

passenger says, "I am crewman *Robert Armstrong*; and as a former member of the HMS Swallow's crew, I am at yer command, sir."[B11]

Being accustomed to new men joining me ranks on a whim, I reply, "Welcome aboard the *Royal Fortune*, *Mister Armstrong*, I am *Bartholomew Roberts*. Report to Lord *Main*, our ship's Bos'n," and whilst pointing to the man who canne be seen standing along the starboard rail, "He shall assign you your orders."[N7]

"Aye, aye, Captain," replies *Mister Armstrong*, most eagerly, as he turns to.

Having a tough time of it, the lot of us, working laboriously, get clear, but now, sinking as wee are, our onely chance, 'tho' some distance away, is to make saile for the inlet where I took her Ladyship for my woman. After a few moments, shifting my thoughts to our current dilemma, when wee arrive, providing wee canne stay afloat long enough, wee canne make repairs. Should wee make our destination, wee canne replenish our water and provisions whilst repairing our ship. If not, the supplies shan't be need'd.

As wee join up with the rest my ships, our floundering *Royal Fortune* becomes increasingly sluggish. While a few of me crew are being tended by the ship's surgeon, the majority be afraid of not reaching our destination, nevertheless, being an incurable optimist, I remain confident, and thus, do my best to provide strength and assurance.

Finally limping into the cove, wee promptly make our ship ready to undergo repairs, and sailing her nigh to the beach as possible, wee heel her over. Repairs commencing, and our provisions and water replenished in jig time, with wee sett saile for the *West Indies* by weekes end.

Plundering many a ship en route, 'tho' mostly French in design, they bear all manner of flags, and altho' keeping us well supply'd in provisions, fresh water and ammunition, the first two canne be easily gotten on shore, and for that reason, not worth the constant effort to obtain, there is however, one consolation that has made these risks worthy of our efforts, that being a French Man-O'-War, which carries not onely 52 gunns, but also the ever coveted *Governour of Martinique* himself, *Florimond Hurault de Montigny*, of whom, being the Man-O'-War, having not fired a single gunn, I hang the cowardly swine from the yardarm of his own ship[CSP-CS13 / See pg 469]; what is more, the faire prize will replace me present flagship, and again, keeping the same name, she becomes my 4th *Royal Fortune*.[B8 & 9]

Plundering 5 ships of various designs, wee burnt those who bore masters who possessed narcissist arrogance. Continuing on, wee took the Dutch ship, *Prince Eugene*, under command of Captain *Bastian Mealke*, and a smale Snow commanded by *Nicholas Hendrick*.[CSP-CS14]

Regrettably, our pyrating, being so successful, the majority of me company, becoming all too sure of themselves, and constantly in their cups, have become most unmanageable. Seeing the necessity to seeke correctment of this, I find myself taking on a magisterial carriage, whereby employing strict deportment, has sett some of me crew to grumbling, whereupon, I says, challenging each of them, *"You might join me ashore to take satisfaction of me, if you see fitt, at Sword and Pistol, for I neither value nor fear anny of you."*[B8]

LATER ⌐

Heading for *Guinea*, wee have sought to buy gold dust cheap, and thither to, take a variety of ships. From these, those who bear Captains who carry themselves wrongfully in mine eyes, for ne'er do I lett myself forget the injustice or harshness of the masters so abundantly prevalent aboard the ships I previously served on, and thus, that which I do now is my way of seeing that amid my renowned equanimity, some form of atonement, generally by way of stripping from these men their narcissistic attitude, is made. As a consequence, 'tis repeatedly voted their ships be either sunk or burnt, and even tho' no penitence by them has ever beene offered regarding their ill deeds, it leaves the ill fated Captains little else to do but reflect.

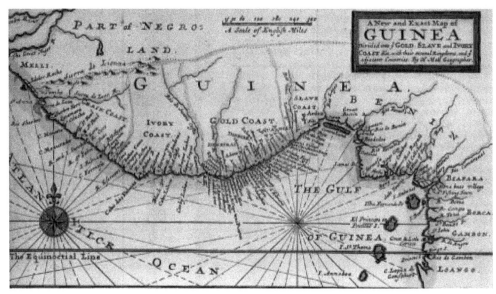

IN JUST ABOUT EVERY ASPECT, SPRING HAS BEEN VERY BUSY.

A letter dated April 24th, 1721 by Captain *Andrew Hingston* to his employers, is related to an incident that occurred the 26th day of March 1721. The original of the first part of the letter's whereabouts is unknown, but fortunately, it's contents was printed in the Weekly Journal or British Gazetteer in June 1721. Part 2 of this letter is depicted on page 363.

THE ABOVE DESCRIBED LETTER CANNE BE READ IN THE NEWS CLIPPING BELOW

Weekly Journal or Britifh Gazetteer 26 June 1721

"I am forry to give you this account of my great misfortune in my voyage. On the 26th of March I made the ifland of Defirade about eleven o'clock of noon and foon after I faw two fail ftanding the fame courfe as I did. I made the beft of my way from them but about eight at night they came alongfide me. I was then about four leagues from Antegoa. They fired at me, being pirates, one a fhip of 36 guns and 250 men and 50 Negroes; thefe I could not withftand. They had been but two day upon that ftation before they faw me, and are both under command of Captain John Roberts. They carried me into Baruba*, there they kept me five days, and what of the cargo was not fit for their purpofe they threw overboard. They took away moft of my rigging and fails, all my anchors, blocks, provifions, powder, fmall arms etc, and twelve of my men, and then carried me to the northward that I might not come into thefe iflands to give an account of them; and the firft of this inftant they left me in latitude 30° N in a very fad condition."

*corrected from Bermuda.

Watering and provisioning our ships for a voyage to *Africa*, me crew now numbers 508.[N3] Of these, 276 be aboard me *Royal Fortune*, 48 of whom be Negroes; the rest are comprised mostly of Englishmen. The balance of me company be upon our *Ranger*, the *Good Fortune*, and the *Morning Star*, and with many of the men are thinking too highly of themselves still, I knows this way of thinking will lead to the destruction of my company; therefore, in my effort to maintain order, I reprimand one of the more boisterous of the drunken crewman. Not seeing my way in these matters, he deals me a tremendous insult, and having endured enough of late, I, without hesitation or conscience thought, merely react, and impaling him upon my sword, I kill the snobbish sod on the spot.

Sometime later, his messmate, *Thomas Jones*, who had beene ashore on water detail during the incident, hears about his friend upon his return to the *Royal Fortune*. Being none too pleas'd, he seeks revenge, and in his attempt to provoke a confrontation, spouts, *"You ought be so served yerself."*[B8 & 9]

Hearing his remark, I run him thro' the body, but despite his injury, being much the stouter, he knocks me into a cannon. The impact momentarily rendering me senseless, *Mister Jones*, instigating an event that sends me company into an uproar, takes the opportunity to lay into me.[B8 & 9]

The lot of 'em, being divided over the incident, commence fighting amongst themselves, and being on the verge of Armageddon, Lord *Sympson*, ship's Quarter-Master, altho' his position precludes the necessity of a vote, but belieeving such will best serve this occurrence, he allows one to commence.

Appeesed, the majority of the company being in the opinion that the dignity of the offices, that of Captain and Commodore, being a post of Honour within our *'House of Lords,'* ought not be violated by anny person or persons, and such, 'tis decided that as soon as *Mister Jones* has recovered from his wound, he is to receive two lashes of the cat from each crewman for his offence.[B8 & 9]

TIME HAVING PASSED BY →

Thomas Jones, having received the preskrybed flogging, is not dissuaded by this punishment. Still feeling his attack was not without undue cause, he opts for revenge, but knowing he cannae exact such upon my person, he instead, as my company later discovers, held a privy meeting with Captain *Anstis*, who himself shares *Mister Jones* disaffection for me simply because I consider the *Good Fortune* to be little more than a store ship, they decide to go their own way. That same night, whilst some 400 leagues off the coast of *Africa*, on Tuesday, the 18th day of April 1721[CSP-CS5], they depart with some 70 crewmen, but before the voting, both of them mutinous conspirators lett it be known that anny man aboard the *Good Fortune* who did not see matters in the same light as they, would find themselves heaved into the shark infested water below. Consequently, in light of this coercion, the vote was unanimous.

Come daybreak, when it be discovered that both the *Good Fortune* and the *Morning Star* has gone missing, me crew is none to pleas'd. 'Tis not onely the loss of mates; or better stated, a more formidable attack force in regard to strength in numbers, but even more important to them is that of the Brigantine, for she was Yare, as well as the stores aboard her. I however, project an attitude of unconcern, for 'twas an unruly lot they were; prone to rioting and in constant neede of reprimanding. As for their thinking, they thought far too highly of themselves, and such wrong mindedness could easily bring about the ruination of my company, for a combatant, ne'er should be overconfident, as it will be his undoing. All in all, being they were the main disruptive element within my company, which be why I had assigned them such, wee be better off without 'em.

Continuing on, me crew, which now numbers 416,[N6] saile to the windward of the *River Senegal*, in *Guinea, Africa*. 'Tis within these waters that lyes the great trade area for gum. Herein, monopolizing this region, be the Frenchies, who, in an effort to dissuade the interloping trade, police these waters; however, learning they send but a mere two smale ships for this purpose, I discern that they too be rather doltish.

One of these vessels bears 10 gunns with a crew of about 65, and the second, with her 16 gunns and what appears to be some 75 in her crew, is a good deal more formidable. Not knowing the rightness of things, these vessels, upon seeing me ships, belieeving us to be engaged in the trade they be employed to thwart, drag on all the canvas possible and proceed to make chace. Naturally wee do not make a worthy effort to flee, and after allowing the two French ships to saile alongside, I order the hoisting of '*Jolly Roger*,' which be what wee call our well-known jack, whereby, the terrified Frenchies having offered onely a modicum of resistance, surrender.[B8 & 9]

More Newspaper Accounts

Applebee's Original Weekly Journal   25 March 1721

A pirate of 40 guns and 2 smaller ships cause havoc on the coast of Carthegena and St. Martha (West Indies.) They have taken several rich French ships from Petit-Guaves and 2 Dutch and about 5 English ships and sloops. But we hear since that the pirates have left for Cuba and design to go from there to Martinico. They take any nation's ship. What exploits our men-of-war have done against them we hear but little.

THE APRIL 1, 1721 EDITION OF *the London Journal*, FOLLOWING UP IN A EARLY EDITION (see page 343) COMMENTED ON THE RESULT OF THAT EXPEDITION.

On the twenty-fifth past arrived the Jeykel galley, Captain Hart, from Barbados in seven weeks. The master says that a pirate of thirty-six guns and twenty men [sic] having taken twenty-two sail of the vessel the *Rose* and the *Shark* went in pursuit of him; but the said pirate having fitted out one of the said prizes, the former thought fit not to attack them[B3].

Chapter Sixteen
Fetch and Carry

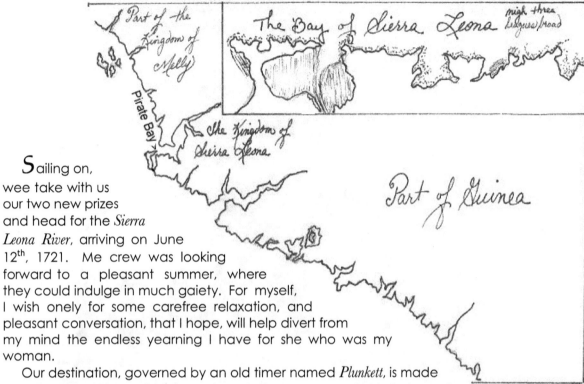

Sailing on, wee take with us our two new prizes and head for the *Sierra Leona River*, arriving on June 12th, 1721. Me crew was looking forward to a pleasant summer, where they could indulge in much gaiety. For myself, I wish onely for some carefree relaxation, and pleasant conversation, that I hope, will help divert from my mind the endless yearning I have for she who was my woman.

Our destination, governed by an old timer named *Plunkett*, is made up of about 30 Englishmen, who, during some part of their past, engaged in either privateering, buccaneering or pyrating, thereby making this the perfect place for the like to carouse, clean, and trade; what is more, the native women belonging to these here Englishmen are most eager to please, meaning their men have no qualms with regards to prostituting their womenfolk.

Of our new prizes, wee make the better of them our consort, christening her the *Great Ranger*[1] and in the doing, wee have renamed our *Ranger*, *Little Ranger*.[B8 & 9]

Finding a Trading ship in *Frenchman's Bay*, wee carry on with business, but this place not to my liking, wee take her a short distance East to a deep inlet with a narrow entrance. After rifling thro' her, wee sett her ablaze. On the following day, wishing to trade our swag for Gold-Dust, Ball and Powder, I sent a note to *Governour Plunkett*,[2] to which he replied he had no Gold to spare, but as for Powder and Ball, he had plenty; I needed onely to come for it. Irritated, I took my 3 ships on the next flood tide to the *Fort of Royal James* on *Bense Island*, and after a vigorous engagement lasting sev'rall hours, old *Mister Plunkett*, having run out of shot, made for a smale boat and rowed himself up the channel to another smale island called *Tombo*. Setting out after him, he was brought back to *Bense Island* where I was waiting.

Irritated for having expended a goodly supply of powder and shot instead of acquiring

---

[1] Altho' their ships were routinely replaced (usually upgraded or too far damaged) they, as did other ship owners, had a tendency to reuse the name.

[2] For the Entire story involving Governour Plunkett & Bense Island.[See page 475 & B7]

it, I began swearing at him, but instead of him wincing as do most, he fired right back at me. It was a pretty poor showing, the two of us cursing each other, & in sev'rall languages; me crew laughing boisterously at our little comedy, which continued untill our repulsive arguing proved fruitless. After which, conceding it to be a fair contest, I could not fault him; therefore, leaving him to make repairs to his fort, wee departed on the ebb tide, but wee did not saile too far off, for there was much plundering to do within the warehouses.

By what appeared to be by remote chance, wee happen upon the *Willing Captive*. My first thoughts, of course, be that of her Ladyship, la Marquise d'Éperon-noire.

As soon as wee are within hailing distance, my Bos'n hollers, "The Lady Aspasia, be she aboard?"

"Nay," replies the man at the helm, "nor be her companions."

In learning she not be on board, I sulk off in ill temper, belieeving that ne'er will I see her again, for I knows not where she has gone, except she not be in *Barmuda*.

During the past three months, much has taken place, but more importantly, since her

Ladyship left, it is exceedingly restless and argumentative I have become, and that not be all, for I find myself becoming autocratic, to this I attribute in part to my flotilla whose decks be swarming with countless fresh men, who are not onely unruly, but constantly laden with drink, and in no mood to reform them; methinks 'twould be best to be rid of them entirely. To add to this, when the *Willing Captive* returned without her Ladyship, even tho' the ship be mine, I have not gone aboard 'er, nor have I seene fitt to speak to the crewmen that trod her deck, who, as they relayed as her words, returned to me my ship, but neither the strain of command, nor the desire to continue, lye within my heart since her Ladyship's departure. To this, *John Walden*,[①] one of my close mates tells me how I have changed of late.

"The company, Captain, as you know, has beene most unruly, but 'tis my belief it be yer attitude of late which be the cause."

"I suggest to you, *Mister Walden*, that you take care in the manner of your words."

"You sought my opinion, Captain, but how canne I speak true if the telling proves to be my demise."

"Aye, of course. I crave yer forgiveness. Pray continue."

"'Tis a large, well-ordered company who have onely recently become uneasy, and 'tis my observances that it be yer temper of late, flaring with little provocation, is what makes them thus."

Seeing my mate harbours many deep-rooted thoughts I wish to know, I encourage him to tell me more. "Go on," says I.

"'Twas not long since that you offered a challenge to all members of the company who disagree with your usage of command, and when a man grumbled, ne'er giving him a chance to defend himself, you killed him on the spot, and then you impaled his mate, who despite his injury, dealt you a handsome beating, for which he receiv'd a whipping, unlike anny other. That episode, together with you demeanour, cost us some 70 crewmen, who by choice or not, sailed away with two ships."[CSP-CSY1]

"Well, what of it; 'twere unruly loafs, the lot of 'em."

"'Tis fortunate that the majority of the company hold you in high regard, for it makes you pistol-proof, Captain, and those who do not love you, fear you. Of the latter, most of 'em shiver and shake at the very mention of yer name."[B8 & 9]

"Would you not look upon that as an asset to our profession, *Mister Walden*?"

"la Marquise's departure created a gaping wound in yer heart, a wound for which lyes but one cure."

"Talk straight, man. What be it you suggest?"

> ① *William Smith*, (a Prisoner acquitted,) says *Walden* was known among the Pyrates mostly, by the Nick-Name of *Miss Nanney* (ironically its presumed from the Hardness of his Temper) that he
>
> For the complete passage, SEE #14 in the Reference Section-Special Notations
>
> *Author's Note: To those who not only possess minds so perverted as to believe, but go so far as to willfully spread such vile slander, especially those writers who have the responsibility to both search out & present the facts, such persons are guilty of libel. To them, I, as the Captain's Champion, with rapier in hand, shall pleased to meet you in the street.*

"It being likely her crew has knowledge that will calm yer soul, go aboard the *Willing*

Captive and speak to them. Seek out *Jean François* and *Mister Philips* specifically, for I knows that if anyone has insight on her reasons, it will be them."

Immediately doing as my friend suggests, I hail the *Willing Captive*, and having my boat hoisted out, I go aboard her.

Stepping on board, I find myself to be uneasy. 'Tis an empty feeling I have, for the Lady Aspasia, not being aboard, for she is not here to run into my arms as she did each time I return'd.

Questioning the crew, I learn they have a letter for me, but being under her Ladyship's orders, they were not to give it to me untill I came aboard seeking information.

After reading and re-folding the letter, it being almost an exact copy of the letter that William had placed in *Robert Crow's* pocket the night she left, I send my boat to me *Royal Fortune* with orders to bring *John Walden* to the *Willing Captive*. Whilst awaiting his arrivall, I speak more to the crew.

"How be it, if it was her Ladyship's wish to return to her villa in the *Barmudas*, she not be there?"

"Having gotten underway at the point of her Ladyship's pistols, wee had beene under full saile for perhaps an hour when her Ladyship took ill. Later, at the behest of Mrs Robles, wee returned, but sighting no saile, knowing it to be closer, wee sailed for *Jamaica*. Upon arrival, la Marquise being much the worse, Mrs Robles sent us to fetch a physician. Shortly after, Mrs Robles and William following, her Ladyship was toted off by stretcher bearers. After they departed, following her ladyship's orders, wee sail'd here to *Sierra Leona* and waited."

"But how..."

"She seem'd to know you would come here."

Handing *John Walden* the letter, " 'Twould please me, my friend, if you would read this. Altho' 'tis a near copy of one I have seene already, I would like your opinion."

Taking the letter, he reads it quickly, and slowly looking at me, "I have no knowledge of yer last conversation with la Marquise, Captain, but it is my feeling that something you said delivered a devastating blow to her heart, and thus, feeling she had no choice, she left."

"So to soothe what she holds to be disagreeable words, she leaves me in despair, and the company, as you have seene, thinks the less of me for it."

"Not so, Captain," *John Walden* assures me. "The company does not think less of you."

"Nor is what yer thinking about her true," adds *Jean François*.

"What our young *Jean* says be correct, Captain," spouts *John Philips*. "la Marquise, she loves you more than life itself, but in my mind there be no doubt she felt a hindrance to ya, and in order to remove the burden of her presence, she left."

" 'Tis exactly how she felt, Captain," adds *Jean François*. "Fer she be crying most of the time," and reaching into his pocket, "and being—"

"You idiot!" rebukes his shipmate, knocking him in the shoulder. "We're lost."

Their tiff, I knows, is one of grave concern, and whatever that something be, 'tis certaynely of some importance, and obviously frightening to *Mister Philips*; so much so that he be scared to reveal the information, I asks, "What lyes within your pocket *Maître François*?"

" 'Tis nothing, Captain," *Mister Philips* says, trying to explain. "Young *Jean* was just going to say that when she, um," quite tense, he clears his throat, "I mean when, her Ladyship left the ship, 'twas her wish for us to return to you what she referred to as yer ship, and being the three of 'em would find another ship to take them to the *Barmudas*, they would trouble us no more."

Jean François injecting, "That's right, and on her Ladyship's behalf, Mrs Robles took onely them items you bestowed upon her in a small case, a lighted candle, and two articles of clothing. The Lady herself had onely the Crimson gown she be wearing the daye you met, and a frilly pinkish garment draped over her arm."

Not belieeving that be all, I quickly slam the young Frenchman into the bulkhead, and pinning him with my forearm, I reach into his pocket and withdraw a small gilded edged book. Glancing at it, I read the word **DIARY**. Having seene it within her Ladyship's bureau many times, I knows it well. Demanding to know, I lowdly asks, "How did ye come by this?"

Knowing my moods of late, and noting that both of the men be shaking in their boots, *John Walden*, affearing for them, thinking these men might prefer to jump ship rather than speak another word, intervenes. "Captain, these men, they be trying to help you the best they canne, but yer manner affrightens them."

Looking at him as he speakes, taking his words to heart, and gathering my composure, I release my hold on the young man. Somewhat calmer, but obviously in control of my temper, I chuckle a mite, and whilst pourtraying a half-hearted smile, I begin again.

"*Mister Philips*, would you be so kind as to explain how you came by this book?"

Myself and *Jean* figured it must 'ave fallen from the smale bundle la Marquise was carryin' when she disembarked, but knowing not where she had beene taken, wee knew not how to return it to her.

"Then you did not search for them."

"Wee thought to search, but the presence of soldiers prevented it."

"Did ye, either of you, read what be written inside?"

"Nay, Captain," they both reply.

Knowing I do not belieeve 'em, "You canne check the signin' of the Articles," says *Mister Philips* as the shuttering of his voice begins to subside, remembering a way to prove his words. "*Jean*, and me, wee be good mates as you knows, Captain, but I canst read nor write. As for Jean, he onely reads French. See for yerself.

"*Mister Philips* speaks true, Captain," offers, *John Walden*. "I was present when he made his mark. As for *Maître François*, I be sure he speaks true as well."

Pondering the words of me crewmen, and also considering those of my trusted friend, *John Walden*, I says, "I Thank you fer yer assistance, men. You may return to your duties."

Doing his best for the company, and being a good friend, *John Walden* offers yet another suggestion. "This punishing of yerself, Captain, it be unwarranted. You knows not what she be thinkin'. Her thoughts; however," pointing to it as I clutch the leatther cover, "are no doubt written in that thar book."

Feeling intrusive just in the consideration of such an abominable idea, "You cannae seriously be suggesting I invade her privacy."

"Aye, Captain, but onely for the purpose of learning where she might be, and why."

Seeing my face; knowing how much I loathe his suggestion, "You needent read more than the last few entries. If such information exists, 'twould be found within them."

Looking at him and then at the book, I slowly turn it over. Opening the back cover, I flip to the ribbon marking the last page written on. "Scanning over the pages, it seemes there be onely two pages written since her departure. I shall read them, and them onely, and being I neede the helpe of my trusted mates, I shall read them alowd. Call for *Mister Philips* and *Maître François* to return."

Calling out as ordered, *Mister Philips* and *Maître François* return to the Quarter-Deck."

As soon as they are before me, I begin to read.

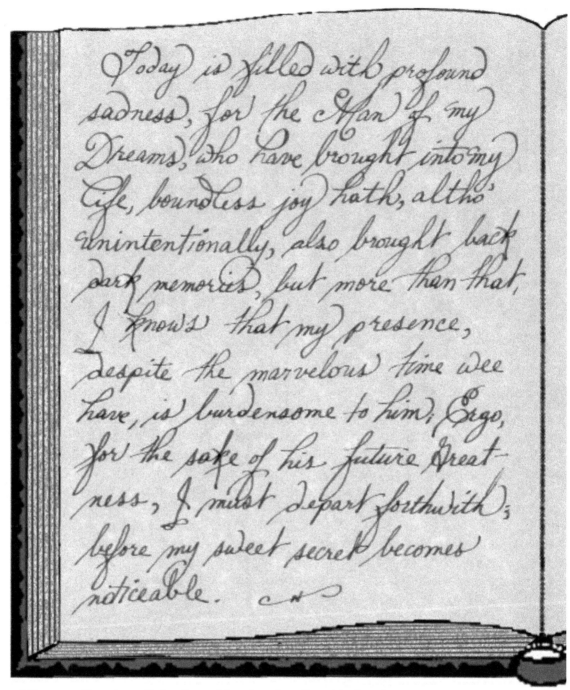

" 'Twas written in anticipation of her leaving the ship." After a moments pause, I read on. "Her Ladyship is with child." after which I left out a heavy sigh.

"Perhaps so, Captain, but surely that accounts for onely part of her decision. What bothers me is why her Ladyship suddenly felt herself a burden to you, and after discovering herself to be with child, an anchor.

"Because when she spoke of children, I told her 'twas a blessing, she being barren, for no child ought be burdened with the stigma of having beene sired by a pyrate."

Slowly turning the page.

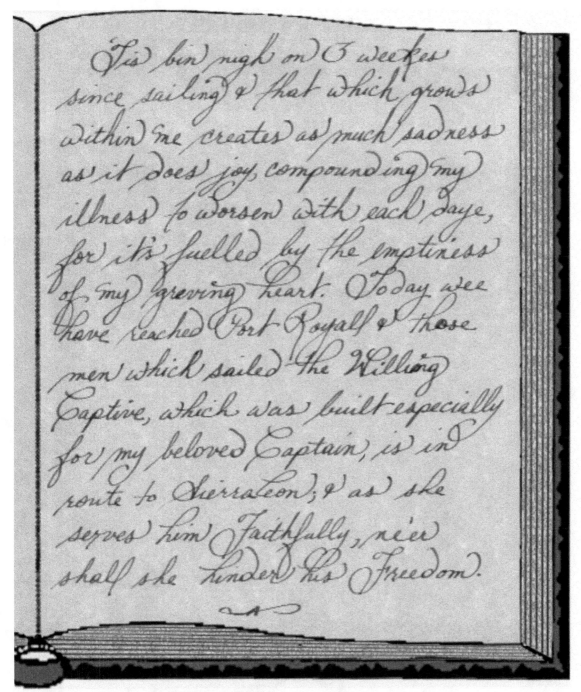

'Tis bin nigh on 3 weekes since sailing & that which grows within me creates as much sadness as it does joy, compounding my illness to worsen with each daye, for it's fuelled by the emptiness of my greving heart. Today wee have reached Port Royall & those men which sailed the Willing Captive, which was built especially for my beloved Captain, is in route to Sierraleon; & as she serves him faithfully, ne'er shall she hinder his Freedom.

"Now you knows why, Captain. Did you not tell her you love her?"

"She knows my feelings."

"Nay, Captain. Women are delicate creatures to be sure, but when it comes to the hearing of certayne things, they are no different than are wee."

"Aye, *Mister Walden*, I ought to have declared love plainly. As for her suddenly belieeving herself to be a hindrance, it must be connected to the trial. I oughtn't have allowed her to attend. Seemes I have beene both insensitive and harsh, as well as oblivious to her needes."

"And now that things have become clear, where does your heart lead you?"

"What wouldst you say should I suggest she be return'd?"

"Upon behalf of the company, I say bring 'er back."

Knowing my friend to be right, I ask young *Jean François* and *John Philips*, "Which of you spent more time with her Ladyship during her illness?"

" 'Twas I, Captain," replies young *Jean*. "As Mrs Robles had much to do, I was charged with seeing to her Ladyship's needes, and thus, I stayed by her side, day and night."

"Tell me more about la Marquise's illness and her plans to return to the *Bermudas*."

"I know onely that having taken ill shortly after wee sailed, she grew worse with each passing day."

"But such a sailing ought not to have taken no where near so long."

"Her Ladyship's illness was such that wee sailed with jibs onely, and many times wee were instructed to simply hove untill the sea was calm; what is more, in search for a physician, Mrs Robles had us put into every settlement.

"*Mister Philips*, together with her crew, you are to saile the *Willing Captive*, with all speed, back to *Port Royal*, whereby, you shall deliver to her ladyship a letter. After which, with her consent, you shall bring her back to me."

"She wont come, Captain," states *John Philips*." This much I know."

Echoing his mate, young *Jean* adds, "He cannae go in yer stead, Captain. Slam the door in his face, she will.

"They be right, Captain," states *John Walden*. " 'Tis you who must go."

Giving his words consideration, "*Mister Walden* have the, *Willing Captive's* former crew reinstated, and tell my company that whilst they careen and provision the ships, I go to fetch la Marquise."

Ships Being Careened

LATER, PORT ROYAL HARBOUR →

Having rotated 3 crews, wee arrive in *Port Royal* in just 19 dayes.

Calling to *Maître François*, "Run up la Marquise d'Éperon-noire's Pennon."

Hollering, "Aye, aye, sir," he dashes off.

Looking about with me spyglass, "Wee shall anchor on the west end."

Running to do as ordered, the young Frenchman returning in minutes onely, pennon in hand. To hoist la Marquise's banner atop the mizzen, he grabs hold of the shrouds and begins his ascent aloft.

"I shall act as cox'n."

Before going ashore, I don the suit of Crimson and Gold my woman fashioned for me. Rowing in, looking like a man of great importance, wee dock. Seeking information, I visit three of the shoppes before learnin' her ladyship is situated in the thatched cottage on the edge of town.

Not being in ill temper, as was I the last time I went in search of her, I knock moderately on the door. Moments later, 'tis Mrs Robles who opens it.

In shock, ne'er expecting to see me again, she exclaims, "Captain *Roberts!*"

"Shhh…" placing my hand over her mouth. "Speak quietly please."

In the nodding of her head, I remove my hand. "Where is her Ladyship?"

Her face, drenched in sorrow, "She's in bed, Captain."

Next to enter the foyer is William. Upon seeing me, he draws the dirk from it's sheath, barking, "You blackguard!" And lunging forward, he does his utmost to impale me.

As I block his motion with my owne blade, Mrs Robles, whilst trying to pry us apart, shrieks, "Stop it! Do you want her Ladyship to hear?"

With hateful eyes, "He'll be the death of 'er."

"No, William!" states Mrs Robles, imploring him to cease his violent attitude. "Captain *Roberts*," says she whilst looking into mine eyes, "is the onely one who can save her."

Gravely concerned, I asks, "She be ailing still?"

With a quiver in her voice, she replies, "Dreadfully, Captain."

Asking fearfully, "But there's no Danger?"

"There be no strength in 'er heart to carry on, Captain, crushing her as you have."

"William, please," pleads Mrs Robles. Turning to explain, "Since leaving the way she did, she has beene withering away."

"What sayeth the surgeon?"

"Onely that she is dying, but knows neither why, nor how to help her," replies Mrs Robles.

Explaining, William says, "'Tis a broken heart that has felled her. Not once since wee arrived has she seene her way to leave her sickbed."

"Nor has she eaten more than a few bites of gruel," adds Mrs Robles, "and less frequently, chicken broth sprinkled with bread crumbs, since the day we sailed."

"Will you be good enough to shew me to her room, William, and Mrs Robles, please make ready a plate of thinly sliced bread, one with a sprinkling of crumbled Cheese atop warmed over meate. I also want the juice from an orange, lemon or lime. Atop the other slice of bread, place the crushed remains of the fruit, and top both with a soupçon of honey. Lastly, a cup of café au lait with sugar, of which I shall see to it she eats every bite."

"At once, Captain," and off she scurries.

Venturing down the hall, William shows me to her Ladyship's door. Opening it noiselessly to peep in, I see my woman curled up facing the wall, weeping. Closing the door, I return with William to the foyer.

Within a few minutes, having prepared the food as requested, Mrs Robles approaches. "Did you see her, Captain?"

Displaying great concern, "Aye. She be facing the wall; nevertheless, I heard what sounded like muffled snivelling."

"Her every waking moment is filled with the tears of sadness, Captain. Loving you desperately as she does, I am afraid that in leaving you as she believed you wished, the all-consuming sadness has all but taken her life."

"Her Ladyship ought ne'er to have left. The *Willing Captive*, which lyes in the harbour, being her home, ought speed her recovery. Taking the tray of food from her, "You best get to packing, Mrs Robles, wee shall be leaving within the quarter hour."

"Me too, Captain?" asks William.

Replying to him, "I wouldst not saile without you."

"Bless you, Captain," says the teary-eyed Mrs Robles, adding with a sly grin, "but it shall undoubtedly require an hour to pack."

Understanding her meaning, I reply, "Aye, that it may."

Returning to her Ladyship's door, I creep in quietly, and taking no notice of my presence, I assume she hath cried herself to sleep. Noticing that her coverlet has slipped down, I sett the tray down on the table, and whilst covering her more thoroughly; my hand brushing against her bare shoulder, I find her skin cold to the touch, but what pains me more, is the squalid condition of her surroundings, for her silks and fine linnen, having beene replaced by dingy matted cotton and a tattered wool blanket, canne serve onely to lessen her spirits; nevertheless, knowing passion to be a superb method to warm an ailing body, I remove my cloathes, and being careful not to disturb her, I lye myself next to her.

With the slight motion of the bed's movement, she rolls onto her back, and even tho' she be asleep, I taste her sweet lips. As her eyes open, belieeving me to be an intruder, she begins to scream. Covering her mouth quickly, it is but seconds when thro' her tear-filled eyes she recognizes me.

"fy Arglwydd, I thought I was dreaming, but," as she wraps her arms about me, "thou art here."

Smiling upon my winsome, yet tousled woman, gently brushing her long, dark auburn tresses back off her face, "Aye, fy Arglwyddes," backing from her a mite, "and ne'er shall I again be parted from thee who be the woman I love."

> *When they touched, each moment was as fresh and new as the morning itself, their relentless passion raged with the fury of a tempest, and altho' each day has been played in the midst of Hell's Demonic Ruler, Captain Roberts, having declared his love, has brought forth a glorious promise for an undying future. V'lé has won.*

'Tis more pleas'd with our reunion than I can ever express; Captain *Roberts* loves me, and altho' there be very few occasions I think of such, I am reminded that this is a game of Lucifer's, and I have won! The relief within my soul is tremendous, and altho' I knows not when the game shall end, providing it be before noon, February 10th of the coming year, I care not, for I am basking within the best part of my life, and wherever we are, so long as we be together, makes no difference.

'Twas nigh on three-quarters of an hour before the four of us, myself cradling her Ladyship within my arms, make our way to the Pinnace, and whatever has gone on whilst wee have beene apart, I care not, for I could not be happier. I have My woman, and within three weekes wee will be back with me company within the *Sierra Leona River*.

Once on board the *Willing Captive*, William mans the helm whilst the others make saile.

A weeke later, her Ladyship joins *Mister Philips* and myself at the helm. "There be something I need to ask thee, fy Arglwydd, something that troubles me greatly."

"And that is?"

"The night I left, thee said that ne'er did thee want offspring—"

Raising my hand in a gesture to silence her, "Lett me say onely that altho' I shall ne'er wish for one, but if ever a child does come to us, I shall then have two to cherish."

Sounding greatly relieved, "The main reason I asked is because I have time and again refused my Sovereign's proposed suitors, and as thou well knows, marriages of state are expected to procreate, which altho' possible, is an unlikely event where I am concerned."

Doing my best to be tactful, "Being with child was the reason thee ran away, was it not?"

"It was amongst my reasons, but 'tis also because thou always thinks of thyself to be less than I, and what I can not seeme to make thou understand is that I would love thee, even if thee was a beggar in the street."

"But I am neither noble or beggar, I am a pyrate. This is not merely a referent, but a placement in society, and that, fy melys, is what I do not belieeve thee understands."

"I love thee for who thee be, not what thee be. The fact thou art a pyrate, the reason for it, it just makes me love thee all the more; moreover, I am very aware of what it means to be a pyrate, and I knows thou wilt be hung if taken, just as I know that I shall suffer the same fate should it become known that I saile within thy ranks freely, but methinks thee does not believe I have considered these things, so let me say to thee now that ne'er would I have come if I was not willing to risk such just to be with thee."

Observing Mrs Robles as she brings forth a tray, "Wee are to be interrupted, fy melys."

"I brought quantity enough to accommodate your appetite as well, Captain."

"Thank you, Mrs Robles."

Picking up a split Bara Maen, toasted and buttered, her ladyship, brushing it with the tip of her finger, grumbles. "Is there no jam or honey?"

Mrs Robles reminding her, "My Lady possesses a capricious temperament, onely yesterday you could not bear the sight of food."

Replying with a coy smile, my woman replies, "Perhaps, Mrs Robles, but," turning to me, "is the illusion of such, regardless of why, not be that which keeps thee interested, fy Arglwydd?"

"Mesmerized," says I, returning her smile.

Taking a letter from her silk poke, upon which lyes a gilt impression of a Fleur-de-lis, she hands it to me, saying, "This letter, written by *Monseigneur le Régent*, himself, which came to me whilst I was in *Jamaica*, 'Tis his reply to one I wrote a yeere ago last March."

Handing it back to her, "I do not read French, fy Nghariad."

"It grants me the permission to choose mine owne husband. It further states that the man I marry shall become the 2nd Marquis d'Éperon-noire, and as fy Arglwydd, thee shall enjoy the full rights and privileges thereto." Pausing a moment to sip her coffee, "It's taken many yeeres, but at last, my natural father sees things my way."

Choking on a bite of cheese, "*le Régent*, is thy natural father?"

"Yes, fy Arglwydd, duly recognized, although privately, by his brother *Louis XIV*, the late King, whose second wife, *Madame de Maintenon*, cared not that I was conceived as a result of the young duke's first illicit embrace, and such, I am, in effect, one of the Blood Royale."

I could not help but laugh.

Mrs Robles; on the other hand, befuddled, states, "I do not understand your laughter."

Obviously perturbed, "Nor do I," adds her Ladyship.

"No? Canst thou not see me as a man of distinction hobnobbing with the buffoons who occupy the French Court?"

"First of all, fy Arglwydd," her Ladyship begins, "as *'The Great Pyrate Roberts,'* thou art a man of distinction already, and pyracy suits you, thou art thine owne master, and thy ship be thy kingdom; however, as much as I would be proud to be thy wife, I did not show to thee this letter for anny purpose other than to let it be known that what I do regarding the disposition of my life is done with the blessing of *His Royal Highness Monseigneur le Régent*; moreover, thou needs no help from me, or anyone else to atchieve fame or fortune, and in either case, remembering *Sir Francis Drake*, a privateer, and *Sir Henry Morgan*, a buccaneer, such would not be a unique event, as both those men were knighted, the latter held the title of Lieutenant Governour; ergo, thou wouldst be not the first *'Gentleman Of Fortune,'* to become an aristocrat, nor, to name one, *Jean François de La Rocque, Seigneur de Roberval*, the first aristocrat to become a pyrate."

Chuckling, "What a joke it would be on the English if I were to become a wealthy Marquis, under the protection of the French government, as the Régent's owne privateer."

"Being that pyracy suits thee, methinks that would be a glorious enterprise."

"For contemplation's sake, what of me crew?"

"At my insistence, *Monseigneur le Régent* would give thy crew both a pardon and a commission under thy command. In short, excepting a portion of thy booty, which thou would be obliged to give to the crown, little else would change."

Upon finishing up that which remains on the tray, "Wouldst thou like, thenceforth to saile on the *Royal Fortune*?"

"I prefer my owne ship."

"I cannae blame thee there, Annwyl un fy, for she's nothing if not sumptuous." Taking a sip of tea, "Wouldst thou be happy if I made the *Willing Captive* my flagship?"

"I'm happy now, fy Arglwydd, and ever shall be, so long as I knows thou wilt return to me. With regard to the *Willing Captive*, if'n thee were to transfer thy flag to her, thou could lose the faith of thy company."

"How so?"

Looking rather tired, "It's not that I would not love to sail with thee, but as it is now, thou comes and goes as thy command permits, unencumbered; ergo, with thy permission, I shall continue to hove on the horizon." Musing a moment, she asks, "May I ask something about thy past."

"What would thee like to know?"

"The reason thou chose bachelorhood and the sea when thou art the eldest son of a landowner?"

"'Tis not an easie thing to tell."

Seeing the look on her face, motionless, gazing upon me with her ever loving eyes, I recount the later dayes of my youth.

"My father, *George Robert*, of *Castell-Newydd Bach*, had the honour of being the village sacristan. Come harvest time, in the Year of Our Lord, 1701, my father, feeling poorly, sent me on an errand to *Little Haven* to fetch coal. Whilst there, I met and fell in love with the daughter of a retired merchant sea captain. After courting her sev'rall months, already having asked for her hand, I made and unannounced call on my intended, and to my desolation, I espied her in dalliance with a Naval Officer."

Trying to hide her profound sadness, "Perhaps thee misunderstood."

"'Twas neither a misunderstanding, nor an isolated incident."

"How do you know for sure, he may have been a relative?"

"I too entertained that notion, and such, I stopped at the tavern. The conversations abounding within were pretty much limited to Captain *Rees'* daughter who was betrothed to a well-heeled rancher's son; what is more, they spoke of her with no more regard than they would a wanton, but the final blow came when one of them stated that the rich man's son, being too gentlemanly to bed the willing wench before he was lawfully entitled, forced her to satisfy her needes elsewhere. I was so thoroughly abashed, that I decided ne'er again would I expose myself to the treacheries of the heart."

"Thou must've been beside thyself?"

"So much so, that on the morrow, by way of no more than a note to my family, I returned to the sea where I have beene since."

As a tear fell on her cheek, "Suffering so long from unrequited love, I had no idea that so large a wound could so thoroughly befall another's heart as it did mine."

"Thy presence, fy Nghariad anwylaf, hath both healed the wound and brought joy to my inner being, but what dost thou mean by, as it did thine?"

"I have loved thee for a very long time, fy Arglwydd, and ne'er would I at anytime do anything to hurt thee, but there is something I must explain."

"Thy voice is decidedly solemn. What is it that troubles thee?"

"Things are not always as they appear, and jealous people have a way of inventing belittling stories bearing no truth."

"What art thou trying to say?"

"I am saying that Captain Rees, although he is my Godfather, is in reality, the man that most people belieeve to be my natural father, and that my middle name, and the one I used whilst visiting, *Little Haven*, is *Rebekah*."

"Backing away from her, I grow sullen."

"Please let me explain. For a short period, when my Godfather retired and left Boston, I, needing time away from Versailles, accompanied him to *Little Haven*. 'Twas he, in his attempt to use my attractiveness to acquire loans from the rich Pembrockshires, that started tongues a'waggin'; furthermore, that which thee saw was nothing more than the son of my Godfather's guest trying to free my bracelet from the lace trim on the back cushion of the settee."

"Why didst thou not come to my home in *Castell-Newydd Bach* and explain?"

"Not being a patron of the local inn, nor aware thou was dismayed, 'twasn't until thee failed to call for me a week later that I became concerned. After which, despite my Godfather's objections, I road to *Little Newcastle* the very next day, and being told thee had returned to the sea, the door was closed. Not until reading some news which mentioned your ordeal aboard the *Terrible*, was any news heard of you, nor was there any explanation as to why until now. Shortly after you had left, myself, having no choice, was escorted back to France to be married off, but ne'er hath my love for thee waned."

"18 yeeres. 18 yeeres wasted because thee not be with me."

"But I was there, fy Arglwydd, in spirit, and I hope that knowing she for whom the divine peignoir was intended, wears it at last, thine heart is filled with immeasurable joy."

"Aye, Aspasia, it is." Taking from my inside vest pocket an old yellowed paper, I read, "Beneath my breast lain an empty heart, which, since the daye I lost thee, onely sad songs weeping, shall be sung."

"Altho' very sad, 'tis also beautiful, fy Arglwydd. Who wrote it?"

"I did, the daye I lost thee, 18 yeeres ago."

"Canst thou ever forgive me?"

"For what, Aspasia. Thee was not responsible for the treachery which kept us apart, nor for my belief in't."

Darkening, she asks, "The only question that remains now is whether or not thou loves and wants me still?"

Rising to my feet, I pull her Ladyship to my breast, "I not onely love thee with a burning passion, but with all my heart, so much so that as soon as my commitment is fulfilled regarding each man having reaped £1000. by tally sheet, and that sum will be reached at *Whydah*, I shall petition, with thine helpe, thy true father for a position as a privateer, that is, should the neede for such arise. Untill then, wilt thou settle for my being onely a Marquis?"

Her face becoming alit with joy, I sweep her into mine arms and carry her to the Great Cabin to make love.

Chapter Thirty-Five
Plundering a Plenty
Location: '*Calabar*'

Upon returning, my company, still carousing about the smale village, having beene joined by *William Watts* and *William Davis* from the settlement, who be the two newest members of me crew, are currently amusing themselves with the latest mentions in the Newspapers.

FROM THE TIME OF CAPTAIN DUNN AT ST. CHRISTOPHER ISLAND (*on or about September 26th, 1720,*) WHEN SAID BECAME A REALITY, IT WAS PUBLISHED. SEE BELOW:

Applebee's Original Weekly Journal   1 July *1721*

"They write from St. Chriftopher that Captain Roberts who is the moft defperate pirate of all who range thefe feas now calls himfelf Admiral of the Leeward Iflands."

London Gazette   29 July *1721*

"Our merchants are in no little pain from the Brazilian Fleet; being apprehenfive of the famous pirate Roberts who hath of late, done fo much damage in the Weft Indies."

I find also that aside from me crew being well rested, me ships have beene not merely careened and fitted, but watered and well provisioned. After the lot of us being greeted warmly, I tells me crew of the intelligence learnt whilst in *Jamaica*, that being that His Majesty's Ships, the *Swallow*, Captained by *Chalenor Ogle*, and the *Weymouth*, by *Robert Johnson*, each being fourth rate Ships-Of-The-Line, and who just happen to be hunting us, have plans to rendezvous here, in *Sierra Leona*, late December. Nevertheless, me crew, having beene here for nigh on six weekes, and having had their fill, vote to sett saile.

As Captain, I long to return to our lively vocation of vigilantism by way of pyracy, and in cruising in the wake, as it were, of the aforementioned Warships, wee shall be provided with sufficient intelligence of their whereabouts; ergo, wee take to the sea in the beginning of August 1721.

Thus far, 'tis beene a prosperous beginning, for our adventuring along the coast en route to *Calabar*, taking every ship wee encounter, including the French slave ships, *Saint René* and the *Hermoine*, from which a goodly number of would-be slaves were freed.[B4] The next three saile wee sight, them being the *Stanwich*, a Galley commanded by Captain *Tarlton*; a Snow named *Martha*, under Captain *Lady*, and lastly, a Dutch Ship, also be plundered.

At *Sestos*, in *Liberia*, wee happen upon another grand Fregate of 26 gunns, bearing the name of *Onslow* on her hull, wee know not onely she be commanded by Captain *Michael Gee*, but also that she belongs to the *Royal African Company*. Tacking in, originally having plans to provision and water, and finding her lying peacefully at anchor, she unwittingly inviting us into her parlour. Discovering her Captain, and many of the crew being ashore, makes the Fregate an easie catch.

With one Thomas Stretton standing near, I asks William Wood, and others *"who wants to go with us, for I shall force no one."** Hearing on the quiet that the many of *Onslow's* crewmen wish to come, but are afraid of reprisals, wee oblige them by making a false show of persuasion, and in the doing, about a dozen of them readily join my company.[B2] page 50

> **Author's Note: This aspect is stated time and again. See* B2 pages 17, 31, 34, 40, 50, 63, 66 & more. Such is so testified by Thomas Stretton, who was on his 1st sea voyage, & having been acquitted early on in the trial, had no reason to lie. Also acquitted, *Harry Glaspy*, as well, many times throughout the trial, repeatedly testified that all those aboard Cap'n Roberts ships were Volunteers.

Hearing of our successful ventures, the soldiers, one *John Horn*, who advocates for them states, that they too wish to join me crew, but being landlubbers I think against it; however, after many solicitations, their chief complaint, *"Being stout fellows, We are going to starve upon a little Canky and. Plantain"* [B8 & 9] I leave the decision to me crew, who having little faith in their ability to saile, but thinking they may come in handy as members of a boarding party, take a vote, whereby the soldiers are offered one quarter of a share each. Readily accepting what wee consider a mere pittance, the soldiers sign on.[B8 & 9, & B2 page 50]

Myself, being a Sabbatarian, am most interested in recruiting the *Reverend Roger Price*, who was acting Chaplain aboard the *Onslow* during her voyage from England to *Cape Corso Castle*. There also be others in my company who be for keeping him. Accordingly, he was promised that his duties would be limited to prayer service and the making of punch, for which wee offered him a full share; but to our disappointment, he declined. Despite the loss, No ill shall befall him, and shewing him proper respect, my thoughts being not to sway him, me crew gave back to him all that he stated to be his.

In parting, the most gracious Reverend bestowed us a blessing, three prayer books, and a bottle screw, of which the lot of us be grateful.

Aside from the *Onslow's* cargo, which be valued at £9000/, the wife of a wealthy Cornish mine-captain, *Elizabeth Trengrove*,[HCA 6 & 8 & B6] was also on board. As with anny female who may be found on board a prize, she is placed under guard for her owne protection. In the case of *Mrs Trengrove*, on the advice of *John Mitchel* [HCA 6 & B2 page 34] after discovering that *William Mead* had forced off her hoop'd petticoat, she was escorted to *David Sympson* in the Gunner's Room, who, knowing she would also be a threat to the harmony aboard ship, confined her to a smale room; moreover, knowing that *Sympson's* authoritative brawn would not be challenged, I appointed him her sentinel.

The Lady Aspasia, whilst being careful not to divulge her identity, offered *Elizabeth Trengrove* a few calming words of advice. "Struggle not, *Mrs Trengrove*, for such will only serve you a dish of harsh treatment. Unlike *William Mead, Mister Sympson*, being a good man, shan't harm you, nor force himself upon you,[B6] and to this, myself being the Captain's woman should be your proof."

Befuddled, *Mrs Trengrove* asked, "How long have you been a captive?"

"Tisn't important. All that matters is that being cherished like a fine jewel and adorned in finery, as well as yearned for, I have no wish to leave." Seeing the bewildered look on *Mrs Trengrove's* face, I add, "I love Captain *Roberts* very deeply; he's a wonderful man who wants only to see that all people, men and women alike, rich or poor, serf or noble, be permitted, in keeping with their intelligence and skill, to advance within their profession, unhindered by the conventions imposed by the supercilious that maintain the social order."

"And going into battle, that does not alarm you?"

"My quarters are not located aboard either of the flagships."

> TRIAL TIDBIT: At his trial, David Simpson testified that Mrs. Trengrove, hoping that such would assure his protection, offered him sexual favors of her own volition.[HCA 6 & 8, B6 & item #6 within Bart's Articles.]

Taking the newly built Fregate as me new flagship, the grand ship is re-christened my 5th *Royal Fortune*. Not having anny use for the older French ship, altho' she served us well, wee kindly bestow her to Captain *Gee*, who, 'tho' not totally pleas'd, declines anny inclinations to object too lowdly.

Without delay wee fitt her for our purpose, making her suitable as a sea rover, which included adding 14 of the former *Royal Fortune's* gunns to her 26. After which, on or about 19 September 1721, together with the *Great Ranger* and *Little Ranger*, wee cruise leisurely down the coast towards *Jaquin*.

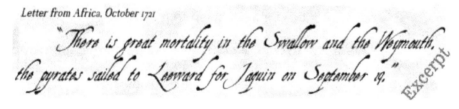

Letter from Africa, October 1721

"There is great mortality in the Swallow and the Weymouth, the pyrates sailed to Leeward for Jaquin on September 19." Excerpt

Our purpose being to careen, wee continue to make our way to a particular sandbar in *Old Calabar* where the water is a little more than two fathoms and a half more in depth. Being that it lyes within an intricate channel which is not affable to ships with a draught similar to those possessed a Man-O'-War's, such as His Majesty's Ships, *Swallow* and *Weymouth*, it is considered a relatively safe haven.

Nearing *Old Calabar*, wee meet up with Captain *Loane*, an old acquaintance, currently in command of the *Joceline*, and knowing the area well, he graciously pilots me ships into this harbour; a service for which he is well paid.[CSP-CS1 see page 460 pt1] From his crew, one *Robert Haws* joins my company. Also, whilst in these waters, wee make jovial conquests of two Galleys, the *Mercy*, and her companion vessells, the *Porcupine*, an English Interloper commanded by one Captain *Fletcher*, and the *Cornwall*, under Captain *Rolls*. From this last vessell, me crew was enlarged. Among them were two musicians, *Nicholas Bradley* & *James White*, and a Surgeon, *Peter Scudamore*, who brought with him medicines, surgical instruments, blow-pans, casters, and sev'rall Back-gammon-tables.[SP1 & B2 page 35] The three vessels, being of *Bristol* origin, made for pleasurable plundering; the booty of which, wee shall split with the crew of the *Joceline*.

The natives who inhabit this region, as compared to other places wee have seene fitt to visit, be decidedly unfriendly. The men alone number some 2000, and have beene taught, all too well, the penalties inflicted upon those tribes who trade with pyrates.

Having done my best to perswade 'em, an effort that surpassed my well-known forbearance, obliges us to use force, which I would not do if not for our extreme neede. To this, altho' far less in number, I order the soldiers within my company to march upon them; even so, and it pains me, having to relate such an incident, for it is not without cost, I order a volley fired into their ranks, but despite their losses, they refuse our patronage, still. Me crew vote to sett fire to their village, and such, knowing that an example must be made, I am constrained to shew them how ruthless this pyrate canne deal, and thus, such being an act I would never sanction if other options were open to me, I comply with me crew, who afterwards, take the provisions wee came for, leaving much gold as payment.

Losing no time, wee finish the careening and saile on to *Cabo de Lopo Gonsalves*, where wee seek to take on fresh water, and then to *Annamaboa* where wee shall gather the remaining provisions desired before sailing for the coast.

Taking some time to recoup, 'tis not untill the 14th of December, nigh *Gabone*, that wee come upon the, *Gertruycht* of Holland, captained by *Benjamin Kreeft*, wherefrom *William Church* signs me articles.[B2 page 56] About a fortnight later, on the 2 January 1722, wee came upon the *Elizabeth, John Sharp*, Master. From said vessell, 4 men, including *Adam Comry*, the vessell's Surgeon, joined me crew. That same daye, at *Cape la Hau*, wee took the *Tarlton* of *Liverpool, Joseph Trahern*, Captain. Of his crew, ten men: *Edward Tarlton, Robert Hays, Josiah Robinson, John Arnaught, John Davis, Henry Graves, Thomas Howard, John Rymer, Thomas Clyphen*, and *George Wilson* of *Bristol* (Ship's Surgeon), readily joined me crew. The latter of whom, I knew well, frequently said that should wee meet up with anny of Turnip Man's ships (the King's Ships,) wee would blow them up, and go to hell together.[B2 page 42]

On 4 January, nigh *Axim*, a Dutch Fort on the *Gold Coast*, west of *Cape Three Points*, wee come upon the Dutch ship, *Flushingham*, of whom wee kindly deprive of masts. Wee also help ourselves to her yards and vast quantity of stores, including many a fowl which shall be dressed for supper, during which time *Philip Haak*, the new crewman plays his Trumpet, during which time, me crew sings songs from a Dutch prayer book as the lot of us indulge in the wealth of long unseen culinary delights, thereby bringing to a close the long awaited end to the deprivation that wee, for so long, have yearned to quench. As a matter of course, I graciously invite the ship's master, *Geret de Haen*, to dine with us, providing he supplys the drink, which I am pleas'd to say, he agrees.[B2 page 15 & 64]

On 5 January 1722, between the Windward and *Gold Coasts*, *The Diligence*, Captained by *John Harding or Stephen Thomas*, and belonging to the *Royal African Company*, was plundered and sank. The next daye, cruising in the south region, nigh *Cape La Hou*, wee espied a fair, 12 gunn, 200 tonn slaver named *King Solomon*. Being about a league to the leeward of *Cape Apolonia*,[sic] wee encountered unfavourable winds, whereby, with the hoisting out the *Royal Fortune's* longboat. As ever, those having made the capture are allowed first choice from the cloathes on board, and such, there is no shortage of courageous men who be eager to go out for a prize. Be that as it may, the 20 men, as per my Articles, are chosen by list.

Leading the prize crew is, by custom, our Quarter-Master, a position currently held by *William Magnes*. Also among those chosen are, *William Main*, *Royal Fortune's* Bos'n; *Thomas Oughterlauney*, Ship's Pilot; *Mister Petty*, a Sail-Maker; and *Abraham Harper*, our Cooper. Afterwards, the remaining of me crew, each being permitted a new shift of cloathing, shall have it providing there be enough to go round.[B2 pg 39]

Rowing towards the ship with a great deal of enthusiasm, they are hailed by her commander, one Captain *Trahern*, but not liking the situation, he makes a futile attempt to thwart my men by firing his Musquet at them as they saile beneath his vessell's stern, who in turn, fire a volley of their owne.

Displaying their eagerness, my band of volunteers waste no time in making their intentions known as they get aboard. At that time, Captain *Trahern* puts it to his crew, asking them to stand by him in defence of the ship; he furthermore implys there is shame upon them for a-fearing a number less than half their owne. The Captain is further humiliated when his owne Bos'n, a man named, *William Philips*, takes it upon himself to speak for the ship when he states, *"I shall not!"* and 'in the King's Name,' mind you, he lays down his arms; thereafter, taking even more power unto himself, he calls for quarters. His close mates, not knowing what else to do, promptly take to heart his example, is an action which is followed forthwith by every member of the *King Solomon's* crew.[B2 page 11]

Quickly getting underway, doing their Captain proud, me brave volunteers slip the *King Solomon's* anchor cable. When the cutting of the rope takes place, Captain *Trahern* quibbles, but *John Walden* quickly informs the ship's master, *"The anchor shan't be needed."* [B8 & 9] His statement brings forth a mixed reaction. Following *John Walden's* announcement, our Noble Lord, *William Magnes*, assures the *King Solomon's* crew that, as No man is forced to sign the Articles, nor, in anny way, made to join our ranks, those who so desire, shall be sett ashore in a place where passage to whence they came canne be obtained.[B2 page 17]

Soon the *King Solomon* is alongside me flagship, and not wasting anny time, all items deem'd worthy are taken. Come evening, me crew, and most contently, merrily sing songs found within Captain *de Haen's* prayer book, and altho' written in both French and Spanish, the entire company wiles away the evening. This be an aspect that the Dutch Captain, as he looks on, finds himself to be thoroughly amazed,[B2 page 64, & B8 & 9] but; however, be his amazement, 'tis unknown whether it is that he cannae fathom how pyrates canne revel amid thievery; or canne it be that he realizes the simple knowledge of how so little canne bring such happiness, that so many rejoice in the sheer pleasure of the find.

Coming too close into *Whydah Road*, the coast obviously beset with alarm, 'tis assumed that some landlubber recognized one of me ships as wee neared the area. Later 'tis learnt that when wee were sighted, an urgent message was sent to both the English and Dutch factories. This message created such a degree of fear that the four French ships in the harbour made a hasty departure. One of them, the *Union*, wee learnt to our supreme amusement, left in such a hurry that 20 members of her crew were abandoned on shore,[B4] but 'tis of no consequence, as I, being aware of this, sought to make the best of it. Staying out of sight of *Whydah*, which be a superb port for trade ships, especially them Portageese, who purchase mostly gold, which is of course, aside from those necessities which be in constant neede, be me crews preferred plunder.

Within the *Gulf of Guinea*, as wee hove betwixt *Whydah Road*, *Axim* & the *Côte d'Ivoire*, and in the taking of six prizes, pannick ensues.

Chapter Eighteen
Whydah Road
Location: *'The West of Coast Africa'*

'Tis the 11th daye of January 1722, when, as I order, feeling the time be right, wee sailing in to *Whydah Road*, wee be flying both Saint George's ensign, and my greatly feared Jacks.

Within first sight, wee espy an array of eleven ships: 3 English, 3 French, and 5 Portageese.[B2] The French carrying some 30 gunns, and upwards of 100 men on each ship, are large. Not being a deterrence, wee saile on in, and ne'er does it cease to amaze me, for the lot of 'em strike their colours as soon as my Flotilla be within firing range, as do the remaining ships present. In placing upon each, a formidable prize crew forthwith, guarding our prizes well, and in the doing, discovering the Captains of these vessels be ashore concluding their business dealings, I send forth a messenger informing them their ships have beene seiz'd, but being the generous sort, will gladly allow them the opportunity of buying them back at a faire price, and should they wish to commence with negotiations, to send word by messenger.

In the distance be the 11 ships held for Ransom at Whydah. In the foreground, the Great Ranger, left, and on the right, proudly showing her colours, is Captain Roberts' Flagship, Royal Fortune.

After sev'rall communiqués 'twixt myself and the Captain's, I agree to ransom each ship for the sum of eight pounds of Gold-Dust. Amid these negotiations, some of me crew, altho' they did promise to return her should she not be a good sayler, absconded with a 32 gunn, French Man-O'-War. Giving assurance of this, they take with 'em some 15 of her crew for said purpose, should it be decided she is to be returned.

The sum I proposed is agreed to by all, except, Captain *Fletcher*, but to this wrinkle, I shall return. First it seemes the Captain's, hoping to justify the loss with their employers, desired a receipt for the monies paid.

Such a request, thinking, 'surely such be unprecedented;' nevertheless, amid a chuckle as I voice, "'Tis amusing, is it not?" And feeling so inclined, I wrote out the following:

> This is to certify, whom it may or doth concern, that we, GENTLEMEN OF FORTUNE, have receiv'd eight Pounds of Gold-Dust for the Ransom of the Hardey, Captain Dittwitt Commander, so that we Discharge the said Ship.
>
> Witness our Hands this 13th of January 1721-2.
>
> Batt Roberts
> Harry Gillispie

Excepting the Portageese Captains, which are signed by *David Sympson* and *Thomas Sutton*, who, in their desire to be comical, sign their names, *Aaron Whiffingpin* and *Sim. Tugmutton*. A likeness of similar issue is sent to each commander.

Returning now to the matter of Captain *Fletcher* and the English built, *Porcupine*, he and I have met before. Still possessing command, he has a new ship replacing the one wee previously seized and burnt, and carries the same name as well, but returning to the matter at hand, Captain *Fletcher*, stating that no discussions concerning such an occurrence were touched upon, nor do his ship's papers make provisions for such happenings, and thinkin' he shan't be reimbursed for his loss, refuses to pay the ransom; ergo, by setting an example by which others ought learn, 'tis my decision to burn his ship. First; however, the Negroes held hostage, whom otherwise would-be sold into slavery, Must be released. To perform this task, I have sent my trusted friend *John Walden*, and his mate, *Richard Harris*, to the *Porcupine* to unshackle the would be slaves and have them transported to my ships where they shall be given sanctuary untill such time a suitable location canne be found where they canne begin their lives anew.

Suddenly, and to my horror, Misters *Walden*, and *Harris*, altho' not without cause in their minds, claiming the Negroes were not onely wearing fetters about their wrists, but ankles as well, having barely enough time to escape into the longboats, took not the time need'd to remove the Negroes cumbersome restraints before setting fire to the ship.

As the ship became engulfed in fire, I cannae deskrybe my extreame dismay as I watched helplessly, the many who be chained, two and two together as they, in their desperation, jump ship onely to find themselves facing an equally horrific end as they be torn to pieces within the shark-infested waters. As for the many more who be trapped below in the lower holds, loosely call'd their lodgings, wherein they would not onely be fed, just barely, but forced to suffer the entire journey lying down, and within their owne excrement; what is more, many would perish in the crossing from starvation and disease; nevertheless, altho' 'tis a horrible observation, methinks such would be a light pleasantry as compared to the gruelling life that would be theirs as slaves. Unfortunately, these men, and it greaves me to say it, shan't endure either, for it be the horrific screams that be heard coming from those on board, as some 80 of these men perished within the flames.[HCA6]

As it was, onely a modicum of good came about, that being the few within longboats, and those already liberated from this wretched place. In anny case, *Mister Walden*, whatever his excuse, committed no less than that of a barbarous act, without conscience.

Altho' the hastiness that *Mister Walden* spoke of was explain'd by a message that had beene intercepted by my scouts, who, in seeing *Mister Walden*, delivered such unto him in all haste (*see excerpt below*) a message written by the, Hon. *James Phipps, Esq.*, General of the Coast, to *Mister Baldwin*, who be the agent here at *Whydah* for the *Royal African Company*. Yet, as I myself read the message, and altho' it provides support to *John Walden's* argument, explaining his haste, this fact saves him onely from the wrath of my sword, but henceforth, I choose not to be in his presence, nor shall he again trod the deck of my flagship, for if the Negroes could not be freed, all he needn't do was not sett fire to the ship.

> *Excerpt of the* '*INTERCEPTED DISPATCH: Altho' only the lower section is verbatim, this top section was taken from* **Daniel Defoe's**, '*A General History of the Pyrates.*'
>
> *To paraphrase, the dispatch stated that Captain Roberts had been seen to the Windward of Cape Three Points, and he (meaning Mr. Baldwin) might better guard against the damages to the company's ships, if he should arrive at that Road before the Man-O'-War, Swallow, which he assured him that at the time of the letter, was pursuing them to that place.*[B8&9]
>
> "*Such brave Fellows cannot be supposed to be frightned at this News, yet that it were better to avoid dry Blows, which is the best that can be expected, if overtaken.*" sic [B8&9]

Being sure the Captain's of both His Majesty's Ships, *Weymouth* and *Swallow* are hunting me, wee sett saile for *Annamaboa* with all speed, for this place in my opinion, will provide us a place of safety whilst wee careen our ships before proceeding to *Parrot Island*.

Weekly Journal   3 February *1722*

"Our merchants have advice the H.M. floop the *Shark* of *10* guns and *90* men having lately from Antegoa in queft of the pyrates on the Coaft of St. Chriftophers had the bad luck to be taken by them."

Weekly Journal   24 February *1722*

" 'Tis computed that within the five years paft, the pyrates have taken one hundred and forty Englifh veffels on the coaft of Newfoundland and Africa. The report of the taking of the Weymouth man~of~war by Roberts the pyrate proves groundlefs."

Chapter Nineteen
The Muster Sheet

Location: 'Isle of Annamaboa'

Upon our arrivall, this 1st daye of February 1722, her Ladyship, having awakened from her nap, is informed of my return, and once she presents herself on deck, my Bos'n, *Mister Main*, has orders to escort her to the Quarter-Deck of me *Royal Fortune*, but Instead, it is Mrs Robles who is brought over.

Learning her Ladyship is again under the weather, I accompany Mrs Robles to the *Willing Captive*.

Entering her ladyship's cabin, Mrs Robles, whispering, is more than fearful, yet knowing not what to do, states, "Regarding the night her Ladyship ordered the *Willing Captive* to sail, we had been gone but a few hours only when her strength failed her."

Stroking my woman's hair, "What is troubling her Ladyship? In the past, my adventurous ways have always enthralled her, bringing forth, pardon my choice of words, a lustful appetite."

"I have known la Marquise the whole of her life, Captain, and in all that time, you and the *Willing Captive* are the only things she has loved enough to fight for. Now perhaps…"

"Perhaps what?"

"I dare not tell you, Captain, but fear not, for you will know soon enough."

Two Days Later →

Her Ladyship, Mrs Robles and William, having done well by her, and no longer being cold to the touch, is recovering nicely. I, myself, check on her often, and me crew, concerned for her as well, ask after her.

On the 4th of February 1722, her Ladyship, altho' recovering still, gathers what information she canne on the pretence of updating the prize list muster sheet, accompanied by both *William Crandall*, and *William Magnes*, makes the rounds of the ships within my flotilla, and altho' most of the men be tight-lipped, her Ladyship manages to put together a fact sheet about me current crew.

TRIAL TIDBITS:

Jean Gowelt, mate aboard the *Flushing*, says *"They [the pirates] cut off all the heads of their Fowls, & later sung at Supper Spanish & French Songs out of a Dutch Prayer-Book."* an aspect, according to *Daniel Defoe*, that stupefied the Dutch Captain.[B8 & 9]

Thomas Giles testified that any man who sighted a sail was allow'd a pair of pistols.[B2]

BLOOD and SWASH, The Unvarnished Life (& afterlife) Story of Pirate Captain, Bartholomew Roberts......pt.2 "THE WILLING CAPTIVE"

CAPTAIN ROBERTS' CREW

From SHIP taken, SAIL PLAN, CAPTAIN or MASTER, WHERE, WHEN, NAME, BIRTHPLACE, POSITION, &c

Pyrate w/Davies   1718

William Magnes (35) of Minehead, Sumerset (Quarter-Master, Royal Fortune); Christopher Moody (28) (Ship's Pilot, Royal Fortune); Henry Dennis of Bidiford; & Richard Hardy (25) of Minehead (Quarter-Master, Ranger)

Pyrate w/Davies   1719

David Sympson (36) of North-Berwick (Quarter Master Royal Fortune), Valentine Ashplant (32) of Minories (Patroon of the Boat), & Thomas Sutton (23) of Berwick, Scotland (a Gunner. Cap'n of the Ranger)

Dominica, West Indies   04/1718

James Philips (35) of Antigua (tried to blow up Royal Fortune after her colors were struck [crew surrendered], but was thwarted by Glasby, Stephen Thomas & Menzies) [B2 pg 70 & 53] & Robert Birtson (30) of Ottery St.Mary, Devonshire.[B2 pg 54] These are 2 of the 13 men who were taken aboard the Revenge Sloop of Antegoa by Guarde le Coste of Martinico & marooned on Dominica.

Aura, Dutch Ship (Pyrate w/Davies)   1719

Marcus Johnson (21) of Smyrna (Greek)

Marquis del Campo, Dutch Ship (became the Rover)   1719

Michael Mare (41) of Ggent. (a Cartouch Box maker[sic]) Harry Glasby swore that Mare, having once departed the, later, whilst in a Sloop from Martinique, plundered by Roberts', States that from the sloop, only he was permitted to join Roberts' crew, because it was against their Rules to take a Foreigner.[B2 pg 38]

Princess   02/06/1719

John Stephenson (was Princess' 2nd Mate) & John Jessup #2 (20), Wisbech, Cambridgeshire[B2 pg 80]

Happy Return Sloop of St Christophers, William Taylor, Master   01/17/1720[B2 pg 40]

Robert Crow (24) of Isle Of Man

Dutch Fly-boat at Surinam   04/1720[B2 pg 37]

Agge Jacobson (30) a Dutch Man[sic]

May Flower[sic] Sloop, Guadeloupe   04/1721[B2 pg 48]

Joseph More (19) of Mere, Wilts. At his trial, this man explained the pirate punishment of Marooning. See page 118. As to his character, More, as did, William Fernon of Somersetshire, asked James Munjoy, the Cooper, after he had complained about his white hat, *"If he knew where his was, and gave him a very smart box on the Ear, and being told if it since he has been a Prisoner in Cabo Corso Castle, he impudently told him, he would do the same again."* John Sharp, being within hearing range, collaborated Munjoy's testimony.[B2 page 48]

Sloop at *St. Nicholas*, one the *Cape Verd Islands*   05/1720

Jean François (17) (became Pyrates-Ship's Boy at 15) Chiefly Yeoman of the Bos'n's stores [B2 pg 68]

Jeremiah and Ann   04/1721

Peter L' Fever, of England (Cook's Mate aboard Royal Fortune)[B2 pg 69] & William Shuren of Wapping Parish, London

York Sloop of Bristol   05/1720

William Taylor of Bristol & Thomas Owen of Bristol

Rhode Island Brigantine, Cap'n Peet   05/1720[B2 page 18]

William Main (28) (Bos'n, Royal Fortune)

Blessing, of Leamington, Robert Taylor master - Taken at Newfoundland[B2 page 31]   06/1720

John Walden (24) of Somerset shire. (Had leg shot off in battle against HMS Swallow)

Expectation Sloop of Topsham (sunk)   06//1720[B2 page 61]

Joseph Nossiter (26) of Sadbury in Devonshire

Fishing Boat, Trepassey Harbour, Newfoundland   06/1720

Thomas How, Barnstable, County Devon (a Taylor). Employ'd mostly in them mending & making the Colours (ship's flags) [B2 pg 52]

Willing Mind, of Poole, New-Found-Land[sic]   06/1720[B2 pg 38]

John Parker (22) of Winfred in Dorsetshire & Hugh Harris of Corfe-Castle, Dorsetshire

Success Sloop, Cap'n Fensilon, West Indies   06/1720[B2 pg 38]

Hercules Hankins (a Carpenter's Mate,) James Clements (20) a Jersey Man[sic]

BLOOD and SWASH, The Unvarnished Life (& afterlife) Story of Pirate Captain, Bartholomew Roberts......pt.2 "THE WILLING CAPTIVE"

Phoenix, a Snow, of Bristol, John Richards, Master   06/1720

Richard Harris (45) a Cornishman (carpenter by trade, was a sail-maker aboard Royal Fortune) [B2 pg 56]; & David Littlejohn of Bristol

Sadbury Brigantine, William Thomas, Master, New-found-land [B2 pg 46]   06/25/1720

Roger Scot; William Williams #1 (40) of nigh Plymouth; William Williams #2 (30) nigh Plymouth; William Fernon (22) of Somersetshire. 'Twas William Fernon who, at Cape la Hau on 01/02/1720, according to George Fenn during the trial, demanded to know who it was that fired the gun (it being Cap'n Joseph Trahern of the Tarlton, of Liverpool) asked them *"How they dare do it, Don't you see that Ship commanded by the famous Captain Roberts."* Later, according to Adam Comrie (surgeon) who told him that the piece of Callico[sic] that lay before him was his, Fernon, being smug as hell, replied *"Do you know where you are? Is any thing here yours?"* & concluded, that if he spoke a Word more, he would cut his ears off. [B2 pg 46]

nigh the Newfoundland Banks   07/1720

William Mackintosh (21) of Canterbury in Kent.

a Fishing Boat, Newfoundland   07/1720 [B2 pg 57]

John Philips (28) of Alloway, Scotland

Richard, a Pinque, of Biddiford; Jonathan Whitefield, Master   07/1720

James Harris & Thomas Wills (former Bos'n aboard the Richard)

Samuel, Cap'n Samuel Carey   07/14/1720

Harry Glasby (Ship's Master, Royal Fortune), Hugh Menzies: Glasby said of Menzies, *"Quarter'd in the Power-room, was a great instrument is saving her [the Royal Fortune] from being blown up."*

Little York, a Virginian, James Phillips, Master   7/18/1720

James Greenham of Marshfield, Gloucestershire

Love of Lancaster   07/18/1720 [B2 pg 47]

John Jaynson (22) of Born nigh Lancaster. (Off the Ranger)

a Dutch Interloper, El Puerto del Principe   08/1720

Daniel Harding (26) Croomsbury, Somersetshire

Grey-hound[sic] Sloop from Philadelphia belonging to St. Christophers   10/1720 [B2 pg 30]

James Skyrmé (44) of Milford Haven, Wales (Master/Commander-Little Ranger) [B2 pg 30]

Mary and Martha of St. Christophers (sunk), Thomas Willcocks, Master   11/1720 [B2 pg 57]

George Smith (25) Wales & John Wilden

Sloop from Antegoa   12/1720

Joseph Mansfield (30) Orkney Islands, nigh Dominico. Deserted from the Rose Man of War. Was looked on as a Cypher. [B2 pg 51]

Lloyd Galley, Cap'n Hyngston[sic]   03/1721

William Champnies (Formerly 2nd Mate on Lloyd Galley), George Danson, Isaac Russel (was briefly Bos'n aboard pirate) [B2 pg 74], & John du Frock (Carpenter on board Royal Fortune).

HMS Swallow, Cap'n Chaloner Ogle[sic]   03/1721

Robert Armstrong (34) of London.

Jeremiah and Ann, Captain Turner   04/1721

Robert Lilburn of Whydah; William Darling (a Caulker); William Mead; William Shuren of Wapping Parish, London; Robert Johnson (32) of Whydah; Robert Johnson (32); & Peter la Fever.

Adventure Sloop at Hispaniola, Cap'n Tuckerman   04/1721 [B2 pg 74]

John Coleman (24) of Wales

Norman Galley, nigh Cape Verd[sic]   May or June 1721 [B2 pg 73]

John Mitchel of Shadwell Parish of London (who was one of 16 aboard the boat that took the Flushingham of Holland. Was also among the 20 from the Royal Fortune who boarded the Ranger that morning she was taken. [B2 pg 64], Benjamin Jeffrys (21) of Bristol (voted Bos'n aboard Royal Fortune) [B2 pg 74], & Thomas Withstandyenot [B2 pg 69]

Onslow, Cap'n Gee at Sestos   08/08/1721 [B2 pg 48]

Abraham Harper (23) of Bristol [SEE pg 149], (a Cooper. Had 50 s./mo wages aboard Onslow); Thomas Watkins (House Carpenter, worked as a Joyner making Cartouche Boxes) [B2 pg 51]; Edward Watts (22) of Dunmore, Ireland; Peter Lashly (21) of Aberdeen; Phillip Bill (27) of St. Thomas; John Stevenson (30) of Whitby in Yorkshire. (tradesman) [E4 & B2 pg 52]; William Wood (27) of York; John Horn of Royal James' Parish, London (a Soldier); passenger on the Onslow, was a miner on Cabo Corso, [B2 pg 50]; Thomas Stretton (Carpenter) [B2 pg 75]; James Cromby, a Scot [B2 pg 41]; Thomas Gerrat (14 years a Soldier in Spain) [B2 pg 67]; Michael Lemmon (Quarter-Master aboard Onslow) [B2 pg 48];

BLOOD and SWASH, The Unvarnished Life (& afterlife) Story of Pirate Captain, Bartholomew Roberts......pt.2 "THE WILLING CAPTIVE"

George Ogle; John Jessup of Plymouth; & William Petty (30) of Deptford, (Sail-maker'.) One of the 20 from the Royal Fortune who boarded the Ranger the morning she was taken.[B2 pg 41]

Sieraleon[sic]....07/1721

William Davis (23) of Wales. Following an to Mr. Application to Mr. Plunket[sic]. Was to work for Seignrue Josseé, a black christian in Sieraleon for a year.[B2 pg 66], & William Watts (23) of Ireland. Worked for Mr. Glynn on wages of 15 $l.$ a year[B2 pg 67]

Kitty, a Dutch Snow, Nicholas Hennick, Master   07/1721[B2 pg 46]

Thomas Diggles (a Carpenter)

Semm, a Dutch Galley, at Axim   July or August 1721

Charles Bunce (26) of Exeter

Martha, a Snow, of Leverpool[sic], Cap'n Lady   08/1721[B2 pg 65]

Roger Gorsuch (a Cooper), John Watson (1st sea voyage,) Joshua Lee of Liverpool, & James Barrow

Robinson of Leverpole[sic], Cap'n Kanning   07/1721[B2 pg 71]

Robert Hartley (#1) of Liverpool, James Crane, & Benjamin Par

Stanwich Galley, out of Liverpool, Cap'n John Tarlton, Calabar   08/1721[B2 pg 70]

George Smithson (hid under his bed when taken by pirate ship approached)[B2 pg 71], Henry Graves; Roger Pye

A Dutch ship at Axim   08/1721

Andrew Ranée, a Scotsman

Thomas Brigantine (sunk), New-Found-Land[sic]   10/1721

Christopher Lang (a Sail-Maker, Ranger)[B2 pg 45]

Joceline, Cap'n Loan[sic], near Joaquin   10/1721

Robert Haws (31) of Yarmouth. Haws ingratiated himself with Roberts' & his crew by being their Pilot into Calabar, & such would deny him nothing. Later, at the Trial, Edward Evans (formerly of the Porcupine) says 'twas Haws' who was barbarous hand who both tarred the deck & after words not only set his former ship ablaze, but forced the Negroes into the dreadful choice of perishing by Fire or Water. Those who choose the latter were immediately seized by the Sharks, who tore their Limbs off. For himself, he says he was charged with the task of getting the Negroes off the Porcupine & onto Roberts' French Ship.[B2 pg 39 & 40]

Mercy Galley at Old Calabar   10/1721

John Griffin of Blackwall, Middlesex, (a Carpenter & such aboard the Royal Fortune); Thomas Giles (26) of Minehead, Somerset; Israel Hynde (30) of Bristol; Cuthbert Goss (21) of Topsham in Devon, (a Gunner) was one of the 20 from the Royal Fortune who boarded the Ranger that morning she was taken.[B2 pg 62]; & William Child (surgeon of the Mercy Galley)

Cornwall Galley at Old Calabar, Cap'n Rolls   10/1721

Peter Scudmore (35) of Bristol (a surgeon, mostly aboard the Ranger); Thomas Oughterlauney of Wisbech, Cambridgeshire [SP1]; Thomas Davis; Thomas Sever; Robert Bevins; & David Rice a Welshman from Bristol, Nicholas Bradley (a musician-hautboy) [SP1]; Christopher Granger, an Irish Man[sic] (a Carpenter's Mate) [SP1 & B2 pg 37], & James White (a musician-violin) [SP1]

Gertruycht of Holland, (a Galley) Cap'n Benjamin Kreeft   12/14/1721

William Church (a Drummer)

Elizabeth, John Sharp, Master   01/02/1722

William May, Edward Thornden, William Smith, & Adam Comrie (Ship's Surgeon aboard the Elizabeth)

Tarlton, of Liverpool, Cap'n Joseph Trahern, at Cape *la Hau*   01/02/1722

John Davis; John Arnaught; Robert Fletcher, George Wilson of Bristol, (a Surgeon); Robert Hays (20) of Liverpool; Edward Tarlton; Josiah Robinson; John Rymer (One of the 20 from the Royal Fortune who boarded the Ranger the morning she was taken.[B2 pg 41]); Thomas Clyphen, Thomas Howard; & Robert Hartley (#2) was one of the 20 from the Royal Fortune who boarded the Ranger that morning she was taken. Rec'd a musket ball in the abdomen during the action.[B2 pg 71]

Flushingham of Holland, Geret de Haen, Master, at Axim   01/04/1722

Philip Haak (a Trumpeter)

Diligence Sloop, belonging to the Royal African Company (sunk), Stephen Thomas, Master   01/05/1722

Hugh Ridley & Stephen Thomas wages being 6 l wages/month.[B2 pg 9]

King Solomon, Cap'n Trehern, *200 ton Slaver*   01/06/1722

John Lane of Lambard-Street, London; Samuel Fletcher of East-Smithfield, London; Jacob Johnson, William Smith, John Stodgill, William Phillips (29) of Lower-Shadwell; John Johnson (22) of Born nigh Lancaster (a Taylor); John King of Shadwell Parish, London; Peter devine (42) of Stepney; John Lane, Samuel Fletcher, Jacob Johnson, John King, & William Graves.

BLOOD and SWASH, The Unvarnished Life (& afterlife) Story of Pirate Captain, Bartholomew Roberts......pt.2 "THE WILLING CAPTIVE"

French Ship in Whydah Road   01/11/1722

Jacque Ardoen, Lewis Arnaut, Pierre Croissey, Jean Dugaw (a Carpenter), Jean Duplaissey, Rame Froger Gabié, Rence Frogier, Ettrien Gilliot, Jean Gittin, Peter Groffey, Jean Gumar, Jean L'Evecque, Jean Lavogue, Ranne Marraud, Jean Paquete, & Allan Pigan.

Porcupine, Cap'n Fletcher at Whydah   01/14/1722 [B2 pg 26]

William Guineys (acting Mate - Great Ranger), James Cousins, Richard Wood, Richard Scot, William Davison, Samuel Morwell, & Edward Evans (the Porcupine's Cook) [B2 page 39]

Whydah Sloop off Jacquin, Cap'n Stokes   01/13 to 15/1722

Henry Dawson & William Glass

Carlton, Cap'n Allwright at Whydah   01/1722 [B2 pg 26]

Thomas Roberts, John Cane & John Richards (Bos'n aboard the Carlton.)

ALSO: James Cousins, John Lacquet (Mate), & John Morris, 'Twas the latter, who, after the Royal Fortune surrendered to HMS Swallow, fired his pistol into the gunpowder; as well as: Richard Ashly, Clement Sloecomb, Edward Simmonds, Thomas Wincon, Henry Dyer & James Morrice who died from their wound before the trial. The latter be one of the men who shot into gunpowder (as was agreed should they ever be taken,) but the quantity of such was an insufficient amount to blow up the ship.[B2 pg 69]

Come evening, whilst making love on her black silk sheets, I discover a startling aspect. From within her breast seeps a creamish coloured fluid, from which I deduce her Ladyship is again with child which explains the weakness within her of late. Wishing to neither upset her, nor deny her, I find myself to be more gentle.

Later in the evening, I find an opportunity to speak privately with her Ladyship's companion. "Mrs Robles."

"Yes, Captain?" but in questioning the look on my face, she adds, "You appear troubled. Are you well?"

"Very well, Mrs *Robles*, but her Ladyship..." after a brief pause, "Her bosom gives every indication of, um..."

"You have discovered her secret."

"Aye, Mrs *Robles*. She is, again, with child, is she not?"

"Yes, Captain, but just as was our *Queen Elizabeth*, the Lady Aspasia was told that ne'er could she carry to term; nevertheless, since meeting you, she remains ever hopeful."

"But she does not shew."

" 'Tis always thus with her, Captain."

Shocked by her statement, "What!"

"Just a minute Captain, La Marquise, did not deceive you; she's has, however, endured much, and altho' many men had their way with her, you are the only man she has ever invited into her bed, and also, save her late husband, the only man she had physical relations with that was by choice, not force. As for le Marquis, such, by her, was regarded, as his wife, to be her duty, nothing more. His impotency was, to her, a blessing."

"Explain."

Altho' fearful of my reaction, Mrs Robles tells me about her Ladyship's life.

"la Marquise was in fact a woman of chastity, just as she presented herself; however, whilst being tutored at *Versailles* she was molested many times, and some of those attacks produced a pregnancy; her onely solace came when she learned she was prone to miscarriage, and knowing that her only means to escape the assailing was thro' marriage, is why she so rigorously devoted herself to her studies, especially after being summoned from *Little Haven* back to *Versailles*. As for the parties and gaiety for which she is famous, they served her need to escape, not merely the world she loathed, but the emptiness within her heart. Not only has she been in love you since you courted in *Little Haven*, Captain, you are the Only man she has ever loved."

Listening intently as Mrs Robles tells me of the brutality inflicted upon my woman, I am beset with great sorrow.

"In light of this, I am sure you can understand why her Ladyship cringed when men came with offers of marriage; nevertheless, having been sent by *Monseigneur le Régent*, she had no choice but to receive them, and every time, to *le Régent's* displeasure, she managed an acceptable reason that would absolve her."

"But how could she? Would such not be a Royal Command?"

"Normally yes, Captain, but her Ladyship holds a trump card."

With a chuckle, "You refer to *His Royal Highness, Monseigneur le Régent*, being her natural father."

"Yes. As a result of his guilt, and her ability to procreate being doubtful, she is granted special privilege; even so, to save face, the pretense of a possible marriage is maintained."

Finding myself some overwhelmed by such a wealth of information so suddenly thrust upon me, I find myself walking off towards the railing, and altho' keeping her distance, Mrs Robles trails behind me.

Leaning with both hands upon the railing, I look at the water below for sev'rall moments before turning to face her. "Where was her mother all this time?"

"She died from complications that arose during childbirth."

"I am just a mite confused. Considering her understandable attitude towards men, why did her Ladyship seeke me out?"

Chuckling, "Her Ladyship told me you not be in the least vain, but can it be that you are also so naïve that still you do not know the answer?"

"On the day we met she told me she craved adventure, and offered me her ship and herself in exchange for excitement, so if it is not dashing about with a cutlash, I do not understand why she…"

"Has she not told you that she loves you?"

Returning to the table and chairs to have tea, "Yes, and often, and I love her, but…"

"She not only loves you, Captain, she's in love with you. You are not only one of the few men she trusts, but also one of the few she likes. With you she feels safe, and because of you, she knows happiness, and because she knows you love her, she can be herself." As she begins to laugh, "You should've seen the faces of those Portuguese seamen in Bahía, who, not understanding her excitement, assumed the ordeal made her temporarily dotty, but then, when you were absconding with the *Sagrada Família*, when the ship's acting Captain began to make preparations for battle, she deterred them."

With great interest, I ask, "How?"

"Leaping to her feet, she made all sorts of threats against 'em, she did. As you know, Captain, her Ladyship is a powerful member of the French court, and she told 'em it would cost them their heads if they so much as sent a signal."

Speaking whilst clearly displaying grateful pride in my woman, I utter, "Did she now."

Taking a sip of her tea, "What's more, she also seemed to know all about you, and of your eccentricities."

Looking at her with a disconcerting expression, "That's an odd thing to say."

"I meant no disrespect, Captain. It just be my phrasing, but in the pirate's world, as well as those, shall we say, less fortunate, you must admit you be rather atypical."

As I take up a baked chicken leg from the tray, "Yes, I suppose I am."

Smiling at me, "In her remembrance book she drew a sketch of you right after the *Princess* sailed, but oddly enough, it looks as you do now, with your much the longer tresses and dense moustache. It also contains a horde of newspaper articles, and even copies of letters and documents, all mentioning you."

As Mrs Robles continues, 'tis a warm feeling I have, hearing from others how my woman truly feels about me.

"To her, Captain, you are not a mere man, but a God. That's why she spent months, as she no doubt told you, whilst the *Willing Captive* was being built to her specifications, traipsing up and down the coastline of the *Britannia*, and elsewhere with William, on horseback, sleeping in taverns, or when need be, in the woodland, gathering the horde that she presented to you on that little island off the coast of *Bermuda*, and interestingly enough, like a premonition, as she knew you would be in London, she knew approximately when you would be at these places."

Smiling, "Indeed. It seems her intuitiveness, as well as her outdoor skills, have served her well on many occasions."

"That they do, Captain, as have many of her unsavoury associations—"

Asking with a look of concern. "What do you mean, what unsavoury associations?"

Chuckling a bit, Mrs Robles says, "She's acquainted with just about every cut-purse and shyster throughout *Britannia* and *France*. She even knows a few in Spain, all of whom could retire after their dealings with her, and those dealings, any of which, being the goods she obtained were for you, would have been more than sufficient to get her hung if she had been caught, but alas there was no stopping her. She can be quite tenacious, Captain, and she worships the ground you walk on."

Mrs Robles telling of her Ladyship's feelings for me; not that I did not belieeve she loves me, but the depth of that love is much deeper than I realized. More than that, her Ladyship not onely understands my mind, she supports my cause. "Thank you for telling me, Mrs Robles. I shall be forever grateful."

"In lieu of her Ladyship's condition, I think it's best to take 'er ashore where she will not be subject to the motion of the water. First, however, I must tell her that I knows her Sweet Secret," and with that in mind, I return to the Great Cabin where she is resting. Upon entering, the squeak made by the door as it opens, awakens her.

Speaking tenderly, "I see thou hast awakened from thy nap, fy melys."

"Yes, fy Arglwydd. What time would it be?"

"Nigh enough six bells."

"That explains why I find myself to be famished."

"Being thou art hungry, I shall ask Mrs Robles to serve tea in a few minutes, but first, I would like to speake with thee."

Noting my somber demeanor, she props herself up into a seated position. "So serious, fy Arglwydd."

"This afternoon, amid our lovemaking, I discovered thee to be with child." The moment the words left my lips, her Ladyship turns pale.

With her words wavering, "But how?"

" 'Tis onely important that I know, and after discussing the matter with Mrs Robles, she told me of thy painful past."

As I spoke, she bowed her head, but not before I saw her eyes swell with tears. "Were thou afraid I would love thee less for it."

"I feel ashamed to have thought so, but most people tend to act strangely when they hear words like rape. I know other women who were shunned by their husbands and friends, even their own fathers after learning they had been taken by force, and I—"

"Thou needn't continue, fy melys, nor worry thyself further, for as thee knows, I am not of their ilk, and such, shan't be governed by the asinine misconceptions of others."

Hearing my words and feeling at ease, she changes the subject, and looking upon me with eagerness, wanting to know my reasons, she asks, "Why, when thou could 'ave had thine own ship, the one I offered in writing, did thee turn pyrate?"

After pausing for a moment, I begin. "Thine offer was like a drinke from heaven, and should I had not beene taken by, *Hywel Davies*, I would have returned to command thy ship, but 'twas not to be, for I was forced at point of pistol, and less than six weeks later, voted Captain. Would thou hast preferred it if I had turned down the position, and then when able, if ever, come back to thee instead?"

Looking into his eyes, knowing what I know, not only in this time, but in my own, I take a moment to consider my answer. "To be able to earn one's bread whilst performing their true niche in life is a godsend, and what could be more gratifying than to find and fulfil one's destiny. Thou were born to command, more still, thou were born to lead some sort of revolution against Tyranny. Upon this here flotilla, much like *Achilles and his Myrmidons*, resides a small, yet formidable army, and even if I could turn back time and prevent thy sailing on the *Princess*, I wouldn't, for this, fy Arglwydd, is what thou was born for."

Knowing she speaks from her heart, I kiss her hand.

Smiling moderately, she asks one more question. "I am sure that many have asked a similar question, and myself being equally curious. What is it thou tells them?"

"Who?"

"The new men who join thy company, surely others besides myself have asked whyfor thee turned pyrate."

Looking out the windows for a moment longer, I turn to her and say, "I tells them in me crew, that *what I do not like as a private man I can reconcile to my conscience as a Commander.*"[B3]

"To a seaman, not within me crew, or a landlubber, I tells 'em, *"In an honest Service, there is thin Commons, low Wages, and hard Labour; in this, Plenty and Satiety, Pleasure and Ease, Liberty and Power; and who would not ballance Creditor on this Side, when all the Hazard that is run for it, at worst, is only a sour Look or two at choaking. No! A merry Life and a short one, shall be my Motto."* [B8 & 9 sic]

Author's Note: Before The next Chapter Begins I want to point out the following facts.

Despite the report by Cap'n Ogle's having stated he espied Cap'n Robert's ships anchored beneath Cape Lopez from Princes' Island, take note also that testimony given by several crewmen from Ogle's ship, at the trial, stated he had to veer off to avoid French Man's Bank, & also that he was anchored off Parrot Island (translates to Popaguays, see Defoe's book,) this author's considerable research finds Cap'n Ogle's statement of being off Gabon, to be, not merely wrong, but a lie.

1st of all, due to the curvature of the earth, it would be impossible to see a ship anchored beneath Cape Lopez from Princes' Island which is over 100 miles away.

2nd, the places mentioned, Parrot Island & French Man's Bank, as well as several of those who mentioned escaping to Calabar, are located within the Nigerian Estuary, not at Cape Lopez, and Parrot Island being some 15-20 Nautical miles from the mouth of the Nigerian Estuary fits in with Cap'n Ogle's description, as well as the testimony given by many others. To see these places, as names have a tendency to change, you need maps from the period, which the author has.

3rd, it would help if people read what Defoe wrote correctly, within, "A General History of the Pyrates"... copyrighted 1724, on page 266, last line in 1st paragraph, the date: February 1st. wherein he then states: "The River is navigable by two Channels, & has an island about 5 Leagues up (approx 15 nautical miles); called Parrots (aka Popaguays).

4th, & especially back then when there was little more other than ever changing plant life & a bit of landscape which would be hard to discern up close, & one island pretty much looking like any other up close, & the average sailor, not being navigators, would know only what they're told with regard to their whereabouts.

Chapter Twenty
The Final Hour
Location: 'Parrot Island, Nigeria's Estuary, West Africa'*

> *Author's Note:* Even tho' this author has recently found proof that Captain Roberts was not killed in action as previously believed that 10th day of February 1722, the proof being an account of Captain Roberts being a prisoner, along with others upon pirate Captain Edward 'Ned' Low's ship in October 1722, as reported by both Low, & 2 others who knew Roberts from an earlier time when they had sailed under him, this author shall leave the ending as originally written, but in that, an alternated ending shall follow, forthwith. GOTO page 409 to read in greater detail or 410 to jump straight to the alternate ending.

Come Monday, the 5th of February 1722, a great ship, reported as being a Portageese Merchantman, was espy'd by the watch. For a time she sailed towards us, then changed her course. 'Twas my feeling the Merchantman, being wary of us, chose avoidance; ergo, her cargo most likely to be rich in sugar, for that be the main cargo within these waters, and such, being in want by the crew of the *Great Ranger*, I holler, *"Right the ship and get under sail. There is Sugar in the Offering. Bring it in, that we may have no more Mumbling."* Ordering at the same Time, the Word to be pass'd among the Crew, who would go to their Assistance, and immediately the Ranger fills with Men.[T3]

Forthwith, 20 men from me *Royal Fortune*, including my Bos'n, and many more off the *Little Ranger*, be eager to sett out after her, and as the *Great Ranger* heads for open water, I am knowing it may be dayes before she will return.

I know the great ship is in actuality His Majesty's Ship, *Swallow*. I further know her purpose is to lure the *Great Ranger* out of sight of the *Royal Fortune*; ergo, on the 8th of February: in another attempt to get, my Lord, Captain *Roberts* out of harms way, I again tell him of my foreboding feelings, whereby I beseech him to sail immediately, and later, we can rendezvous with the *Great Ranger* elsewhere, but despite his promise to heed my warning, he refuses to sail until they return.

Captain *Roberts* had no  knowledge of Captain Chaloner *Ogle's* ruthless propensities (who, lacking honour, possessed no qualms when it came to sailing, *'ruse de guerre'*, and thereby was chosen with regard to those aforementioned, ignoble specialties, so much desired by the crown,) nor that the commander of His Majesty's Ship, *Swallow* had been given a particular commission, to seek out and destroy him, and on Monday, the 5th of February 1722, whilst sailing pass an estuary off the coast of Nigeria, the *Swallow's* watch espied three vessels known to be in Captain *Roberts'* fleet: The *Royal Fortune*, the *Little Ranger* and the *Great Ranger*, all riding peacefully at anchor, off *Parrot Island*.[B8 & 9]

The above pictured ship is very similar to the 4th-rate Ship-Of-The-Line, H.M.S. Swallow.

Captain *Ogle*, a blackguard of the first water, is desperate to take my Captain and his crew, and such, will place his ship where it can hove as he lies in wait, and once the *Great Ranger* appears, ne'er giving the men upon her a fighting chance, she will be waylaid.

I feel so very torn, but still, I can not speak the truth, not without having to explain how I am to know, and I have no desire to be burnt at the stake as a witch. I know that my Lord's company will make a good fight of't for well over two hours before the *Great Ranger* will be crippled by that disreputable commander and his 50 gun Warship, and finally, when given no other option, for their ship will be unable to carry on the fight, the *Great Ranger's* crew will be forced to strike their colours. I knows also that having call'd for quarters, they shall be prisoners of one the most loathsome of men, who shan't even permit his ship's Surgeon, *John Atkins*,[①] to treat the wounded.

Not knowing what else to do, I have to put faith in Lucifer's promise, yet, my Lord Captain, already having declared his love, Lucifer's word has not yet been kept.

Come Saturday, the morning of February 10th, 1722, as the 10th hour approaches, seeing the crew is hung over from their night of carousing after the taking of the *Neptune* yesterday, I knows that His Majesty's Ship, *Swallow*, will return to the harbour momentarily. Further knowing that this time, Captain *Ogle*, being the despicable sod that he is, will hoist a French ensign, makes this a frightful time. Hoping that we will sail before the watch espies the great ship, thereby being able to change history; for having Captain *Roberts* aboard a different ship, and quite some distance away, and thereby preventing his death, I convince, my Lord Captain, by way of a lie about a grove of citrus fruits, to sail the *Little Ranger* to the other side of *Parrot Island* where the crew of the *Willing Captive* discovered them growing.

As time grows short, becoming most agitated, I am constantly searching the mouth of the estuary with my spyglass, when suddenly the Great Warship appears. Tho' I cannot speak of such, I knows at once she is His Majesty's Ship, *Swallow*. Calling to my Captain, altho' trying to sound less than grave, I make yet another plea. "fy Arglwydd, please make haste or we'll lose the entire morning."

Just as we are to depart for the *Little Ranger*, a voice from the crow's nest sings out, "Sail Ho!"

The company, unable to positively identify her as the *Great Ranger*, grows confused, whereby a debate ensues. One man suggests she be a Portuguese Merchant, whilst another, catching a glimpse of her flag, states her to be a French slaver, but at half past 10, one *Robert Armstrong*, who once sailed upon His Majesty's Ship, *Swallow*, and asserting his knowledge, positively identifies her.

Immediately upon hearing the news, Captain *Roberts*, just finishing a large plate of Solomon Gundie, dons his hat, and whilst ordering William and young *Jean François* to escort me to the *Willing Captive*, my Captain makes his way to the Quarter-Deck in haste.

The crew, still in their cups, remain doubtful of Armstrong's identification until the Warship, striking the fallacious French Ensign she'd beene flying, hoists the King's colours as she concurrently runs out her guns.[B2]

---

① Later, it was *John Atkins*, the Surgeon aboard the *H.M.S. Swallow*, who was pressed into service as a scribe at the pyrate's tryal.

Realizing the situation to be desperate; knowing that in order to escape, he will have to run the *Royal Fortune* past the Man-O'-War, Captain *Roberts* issues battle orders with boldness and spirit.

Turning; seeing I have not departed, he hollers, "Get back to thine owne ship."

Hoping that my presence can change the outcome, I holler back, "No!" And arming myself, "I too can fight!"

Returning to the open deck, "Best be so, for I haven't time to neither argue, nor put you ashore." To make a better fight of it, I call to the crew of the *Little Ranger*. "Come aboard the *Royal Fortune*." Turning to my Bos'n, I holler, "Slip the anchor." and while me flagship gets underway without delay, many of the men who normally crew the *Little Ranger* be boarding me flagship.

Directing the ship's course, knowing wee shall pass within a mere 60 feet of His Majesty's Ship, *Swallow*, 'tis the onely choice to be made.

Compounding the situation, a bolt of lightening bursts upon the deck of me ship, and without warning, wee find ourselves beset upon by a tempest of pouring Rain, Lightning, Thunder, and a smale Tornado.[B5]

With me black flags hoisted proudly, 'tis nigh 11 o'clock when the Man-O'-War, *Swallow*, being within pistol shot, gives to us, a full broadside. Wee return fire forthwith, but with me ship's mizzen top-mast, and some of her rigging disabled, our broadside does not deliver equal damage to our opponent; nevertheless, wee be sailing better than them.

Whilst they continue firing, without intermission as do wee with such gunns as both ship's canne bring to bear, wee shoot ahead, above half gunn shot when wee are suddenly becalmed, as soon as wee again catch the wind, the *Swallow*, having come about, comes alongside.[82] To better direct our fire, I leap atop a cannon, whilst hollering, "Fire!" wee hurl another broadside into the great Warship.

"Roberts himself made a gallant Figure, at the Time of the Engagement, being dressed in a rich crimson Damask Waistcoat and Breeches, a red Feather in his Hat, a Gold Chain round his Neck, with a Diamond Cross hanging to it, a Sword in his Hand, and two Pair of Pistols hanging at the End of a Silk Sling, flung over his Shoulders (according to the Fashion of the Pyrates;) is said to have given his Orders with Boldness, and Spirit." [B8&9]

About half-past one, after exchanging a few shot, Captain Bartholomew Roberts was hit by the Swallow's barrage. With his throat being torn out by grapeshot, he settled on the blocks and tackles of a gun.[B8&9] *Forthwith, his mainmast, shot away a mite below the parral, came crashing down none too far from his bleeding body to lay his Jolly Roger at his feet.*

Seeing my Captain killed;[B2 page 21] bursting into tears as I run to him, I shriek, "No!" Thwarted by Lucifer, and slumping to the ground; I cradle my beloved in my arms, yet despite being engulfed with misery, knowing he'd be listening, was shouted the hatred to end all hatreds as I stand and screech, "Lucifer, you simpering poltroon, I demand that you appear before me!"

Just then, my ever faithful William, whilst smugly replying, "You called, your Ladyship?" transforms himself into the hideous creature he is in reality right before mine eyes.

Seeing my Captain's sword lying at my feet, I reach down, and picking it up, I slowly and walk towards him.

Concurrently, John Stephenson, the ship's pilot, unaware of his Captain's fatal injuries, hollers, *"Stand up and fight like a man!"* [B8 & 9] But in rushing to him, discovering his lifeless body, he gushes into tears, saying, *"I wish for the next lot to be mine."* [B8 & 9]

Soon after, the others, discovering their loss, are overwhelmed by sadness. Nonetheless, showing both loyalty and love for their Captain, lest it fall into the hands of the enemy, the lot of them honour the request he frequently made should such come to pass by throwing his bejewelled body, properly weighted, overboard.

Turning back to face Lucifer, to his complete amazement, I punch him square in the jaw, and with great anger shrouded in tears, I challenge him to a duel. "You spiteful recreant!" and whilst pointing to the sword laying at his feet, "Pick up that weapon and fight like a man, you coward, for I shan't be satisfy'd until I have run thee thro'."

As he looks at me, "Oh my, such violence, and from a lady." Musing a moment; wondering if I really have the nerve to attack him a second time, asks, "Is it beyond thy knowledge that I could easily thrust upon thee, a bolt of lightning?"

"There is nothing thee canne do to me, for he whom I adore lies dead upon the ocean floor. 'Tis yer word thou hast broken, Lucifer; of honour, thou hast none, and I have nothing left but mine, so again I say to thee, prepare to defend thyself like a man, or by the words of my beloved, I shall run thee thro' unarmed, as thee deserves."

> *The audacity, fuelled by V'lé's loss, impresses him, and thrusting out his hands, waving them wildly in a fulgurate display of his powers, sparks emanate from his fingertips. In seconds only; as the area around her person is engulfed within an exhibition of his abilities, Lucifer's word is kept, whereby, alongside the Captain of her heart, both having the memories of the experience intact, find themselves whence they came.*

THE END

or as recounted by Charles Grey, in

PIRATES OF THE EASTERN SEAS (1618-1723): A LURID PAGE OF HISTORY.
re-Published in 1933 by S. Low, Marston & Company, Limited

Edited by Lieut.General, Sir George MacMunn

Charles Grey, is noted well for his numerous historical works, including "The Early Years of His Royal Highness the Prince Consort, (1819-1941), Compiled under the Direction of Her Majesty the Queen.

Altho' Grey's work, a continuation of Charles Johnson (aka Daniel Defoe,) on Pirates was not cited, neither were the works by Defoe, whereby, being a novelist with a great since of drama does not taint, Grey's reputation for accuracy, & this alone nullifies any credence that his work may have been, in anyway, fabricated; ergo, just as <u>this</u> author has both uncovered & collected a multitude of facts about Captain Bartholomew Roberts not generally known by other biographers, only stands to reason that Charles Grey did also, can easily place Captain Roberts, as a captive, on Captain Low's ship (aka Loe or Lowe) in October 1722, who, together with 2 others, had been freed, See pages 34-39 of the above named book *which, with other evidence, proves that in order to safeguard their much loved Captain [Roberts] from the gallows, his crew concocted the story of his body being killed in action, and being his wish, threw his body overboard. This is backed up by 2 of Low's crewmen that knew Captain Roberts 3 years earlier who had a kindly recollection of the manner in which he [Roberts] treated his crew is an attribute for which he is legendary. In lieu of these facts, & the little fact that Roberts body was reputedly thrown overboard by a crew that loved him, it is this author's contention that the crew lied to protect their captain, who had, by circumstance, managed to escape, by way of not being aboard the Royal Fortune on that fateful day; & yes, I am aware of Defoe's book,* **"The Four Voyages of Capt. George Roberts."**

If, in lieu of this, you'd prefer a different ending, abridged, of course, Read On.

BLOOD and SWASH, The Unvarnished Life (& afterlife) Story of Pirate Captain, Bartholomew Roberts......pt.2 "THE WILLING CAPTIVE"

Come the 7th day of February, already having discussed this ship and her crew becoming privateer's in the French Navy should the neede arise, "Being wee are to depart as soon as the Provisions are gathered and the ships being careened are righted, hast thou given anny thought as to where wee shall go?"

"Anywhere we want, fy Arglwydd. I shall write my Great Uncle, Jean Luc, and tell him of my decision to roam. As for those of us aboard the *Willing Captive*, we could settle down in one place, or should thee prefer, we could simply spend the rest of our lives island hopping."

"Which wouldst thou choose?"

"If thee were not so well known, I would suggest Pembrokeshire, but to stay in one place, putting down roots like a tree, doing the same thing month in and month out, such does not appeal to me. However, for your consideration, in the Pacific, some 20 miles off the West Coast, not too far off the Kingdom of California,① can be found a cluster of fertile islands, as beautiful as they are unspoiled, I know of one island in particular where the weather is perfect, and storms are rare, that would make a good home base; a place to rest and regroup, and the rest of the time, I, as does the crew aboard the *Willing Captive*, would prefer to simply go where we will at the moment, and on that note, if a war involving France, other than the on going Fox War, does break out, we shall hear of it, and your commission will go into effect. Until then, and afterwards, we can live our lives, both adventurously, and free of intrusion."

"Then that's what wee shall do. First; however, wee must travel to France where wee shall pay a call on the vicar, and afterwards accept our commission, providing the *Willing Captive* becomes my flagship, and you saile upon her always as first mate."

With a big smile, "Done!" After which, each spitting into our right hand, we shake on it.

"After wee shall collect the supplies needed, wee shall weigh anchor, and saile to what shall become our new home."

On Saturday, the morning of February 10th, 1722, I am aboard the *Royal Fortune* when the hour of 10 approaches, and altho' not yet visible, I know that His Majesty's Ship, *Swallow*, flying a French ensign, will return to the harbor momentarily. For me, as time grows short, it is a fearful time. I had hoped that by now my beloved and I would have boarded the *Willing Captive*, which, full provisioned, awaits on the opposite side of *Parrot Island*, and sail'd away.

Constantly searching the mouth of the estuary with my spyglass, I at last see the Great Warship appear. Unfortunately, most of my captain's crew be in their cups, as they celebrate, still, yesterday's capture of the *Neptune*, nor can I tell my beloved, who is just finishing a heaping plate of Solomon Gundie, of the ship's presence. Just then, as I hear the watch in the crow's nest sing out, "Sail Ho!" I knows at once the *Swallow*, has been sighted.

Running to inform his Captain, a crewman hollers, "Captain, a sail has entered the estuary, and judging from her size, it appears to be the *Great Ranger* returning."

As the company looks on, many of whom have spyglasses, are for the most part in accord with the watch, others think it be another Portuguese Merchant, whilst another, catching a glimpse of her flag, states her to be a French Guiney~man. With no one being able to positively identify her, a rousing debate ensues.

---

① Well in 18th century, with maps showing California separated from the mainland by a straight, California was thought to be an island. This was debunked via Royal Decree by King Ferdinand VI of Spain in 1747.

At half past 10, *Robert Armstrong*, a former mate aboard the 𝒮𝓌𝒶𝓁𝓁𝑜𝓌, asserting himself, positively identifies her.

Immediately, upon hearing this news, Captain *Roberts*, whilst making his way to the Quarter-Deck, gives orders to escort me to the *Willing Captive*, but before his crewmen can stop me, I draw my pistols.

"No, I shan't be put off!" and running to him, I stand at my Captain's side.

"Thou art a little fool; dost thou wish to die?"

"Nay, fy Arglwydd, but to live without thee is a fate worse than death."

Realizing the situation to be desperate, knowing that in order to make our escape wee will have to run by the Man-O'-War, I issue battle orders with boldness and spirit. With the anchor cut loose, and me ship's sailes unfurling, the *Royal Fortune* underway. Turning to her Ladyship, and with intentions of putting her ashore myself, I grab her about the waist, and carrying her over my shoulder, I descend the rope ladder affixed to the ship's hull., and when close enough to the shore, I shall lett go of her, but being ever clever, the rope, giving way under her knife, sends both of us to the ground. Getting to my feet quickly, I make a dash for my ship when, altho' injured, I find myselfe covered with blood. Turning, I see her Ladyship lying still on the beach. Running back, I am quick to see that she bleeds from a knife wound in the abdomen and is unable to travel. Knowing I cannae leave her, for if taken she would certainly hang, I scoop her into my arms, and carrying her overland, I get her aboard the *Willing Captive*.

As I dress her wound, knowing that not a ship or member of me company remains whence wee just came, for by now the *Royal Fortune* is well underway and those who be left would have escaped aboard the *Little Ranger*, there be no reason that her Ladyship and I should be parted ever again.

Later on, while I am taking sun on the Quarter-Deck, William approaches me.

Removing his hat and bowing, "Very good, my Lady. Thou art to be congratulated."

Bewildered by his statement, "Explain?"

Just then, as my ever faithful William transforms into the ghastly creature, Lucifer, he proclaims, "You have won the game!"

"You!" Rising to my feet, and slapping his face, "You son of a bitch!"

"Why be angry at me, Madame. For had it not beene for me, this reality would not have come about. Thou needed me to succeed." Sporting a jolly smile, "And what a grand adventure it was."

Sinking back down on the settee, needing much time to recover from my wound, "And my reward?"

"Thyself and Captain *Roberts*, together with thy ship, her crew, and the riches aboard her still, are free to stay or go; thou needs simply to choose a time and place and go there you shall, but choose quickly, for the British navy is all too close for comfort." Stepping back from me, "And now, Madame," as he dematerializes in a spectacular show of colored smoke and sparks, "I must depart."

Climbing the steps slowly, are Captain *Roberts*, Mrs Robles, and young *Jean François*.

"Wouldst thou care to explain that which wee just witnessed?"

"That was Lucifer, fy Arglwydd, who was, but shall never again, ride our coattails."

🯅 THE END 🯅

BLOOD and SWASH, The Unvarnished Life (& afterlife) Story of Pirate Captain, Bartholomew Roberts......pt.2 "THE WILLING CAPTIVE"

TABLE OF CONTENTS

WHAT	PAGE
REFERENCE PAGES & a BIT MORE	412
AFTERMATH	413
STATEMENT BY AUTHOR	414
NOTES ON TREPASSEY & FERRYLAND HARBOR, AND BELL TIME	416
TYPES OF SHIPS	417
COINAGE	418
LOCATIONS	419
USEFUL TERMINOLOGY	420
PERSONAL OBSERVATIONS BY THE AUTHOR	421
THE JOLLY ROGER	423
BIBLIOGRAPHY (Numbered References):	424
SPECIAL NOTATIONS (Numbered References):	425
SOLOMON GUNDIE	426
OFFICIAL PUBLIC RECORDS (Numbered References):	427
NOREWORTHY FACTS & COMMENTS (Including the final disposition of the last ROYAL FORTUNE)	433
THE ORIGIN OF THE NICKNAME BARTI DDU AKA BLACK BART	435
TIMELINE	436
DISPOSITION OF CAPTAIN ROBERTS' CREW	441
SUPPLEMENTAL INFO REGARDING CAPTAIN ROBERTS' CREW, INCLUDING THAT SOD, WALTER KENNEDY	443
WELSH & FOREIGN WORDS & MOST OF THE PHRASES IN THIS BOOK	444
A LETTER WITH REGARD TO THE TEA CAP'N ROBERTS TEA	445
SIX DOCUMENTS RE CAPTAIN ROBERTS LINEAGE & SIBLINGS	446
ORIGINAL DEATH SENTENCES	453
COPY OF A THE PARTIAL LETTER WRITTEN BY CAP'N ROBERTS	454
PAINTING OF CAP'N ROBERTS' HOME	455
PICTURES OF SAINTS PETER'S CHURCH IN LITTLE NEWCASTLE	456
PICTURES OF MONUMENT ERECTED IN CAPTAIN JOHN 'BARTHOLOMEW' ROBERTS' HONOR IN LITTLE NEWCASTLE	457
17 PAGES TAKEN FROM THE CALENDAR OF STATE PAPERS CONTAING INFOMATION ON CAP'N ROBERTS	458
A PAGE TAKEN FROM A BOOK BY REGARDING AN AMUSING INCIDENT TWIXT CAP'N ROBERTS & GOV PLUNKETT [B7]	475
ILLUSTRATIONS within BOOK 2 & ALSO within the REFERENCE SECTION	476
HISTORICAL NARRATIVES within BOOK 2	480
LIST OF TALL SHIPS & DETAILS THERETO within BOOK 2 (minus reference section & crews list)	481
SUMMING UP	484
LINEAGE: ASPASIA JOURDAIN, MARQUISE d'EPERON-NOIRE, et al.	487
THE AUTHOR'S FAMILY TREE CONTINUED FROM THE FORWARD	488
ABOUT THE AUTHOR	490
Books by V'léOnica Roberts aka V'lé Onica & Thank Yous by other authors	492

AND TRIAL TIDBITS:
PAGES: 389, 395, 480 & 486

AFTERMATH: It was apparent that although Bart's crew made a grand effort to get clear, the indomitability that Captain Roberts so fervently instilled within their hearts was gone. About half past one, off the coast of Cabo de Lopo Gonsalves, after Captain Roberts brave crew surrendered, & his beloved ship was taken, an attempt by John Philips, who was swearing very profanely, "Let's all go to Hell together," whilst en route to ignite the gunpowder in the powder magazine with a match to blow up the ship, but was thwarted by Harry Glaspy, Stephen Thomas & Hugh Menzies.[B2 pg 70 & 53] This was not the only attempt to fulfill their oath, another crewman, James Morrice, who died from his wound before the trial, shot into gunpowder, but the quantity of such was an insufficient amount to blow up the ship,[B2 pg 69] & the same was also being attempted by William Main & William Petty in Steerage, but again, there was not enough gunpowder.[B2 pg 73] As things turned out, when taken, the frigate, Royal Fortune, carried 40 guns & 150 men, 45 of whom were Negroes; the latter of whom were enslaved forthwith. Only 3 of the Royal Fortune's crew, Bart included, were killed in Action. Aboard the Frigate was found upwards of 4,000 lbs of Gold-Dust (almost $400,000 today,) & according to Captain Hill of the Neptune, who reported the incident sometime later in Barbados, the 2,000 lbs that was said to have been aboard the Little Ranger, was taken by those who remained of the ship's crew. It's interesting to note that instead of waiting for the Royal Navy to return, the Neptune made a hasty departure, as for the Little Ranger's crew, none were heard from again. That April, 1721, the largest pirate trail ever conducted was underway.

Considerable details pertaining to Captain Roberts will be found below, & each is referenced respectively in detail. For the readers pleasure, the entire trial can be found at the National Archives in Kew, England. There is also a printed copy available; see my Bibliography #B2 for the title.

STATEMENT BY AUTHOR - (RE: SBA)

THIS WORK, AS WAS HIS MEMOIRS, WAS DONE FOR THE SOLE PURPOSE OF 'SETTING THE RECORD STRAIGHT,' AND NOTHING MORE.

In addition to the author's effort to this end the author lists her own Personal Observations with regard to other works below.

AS JOHN BARTHOLOMEW ROBERTS' BIOGRAPHER, I FIND IT EXTREMELY IMPORTANT TO POINT OUT A FEW FACTS THAT HIS OTHER, SO-CALLED BIOGRAPHERS NEGLECTED TO MENTION. WHETHER IT WAS OUT OF IGNORANCE, OR JUST DIDN'T THINK IT WAS RELEVANT, I HAVEN'T A CLUE, BUT WHICHEVER IT WAS, LET ME SAY NOW THAT TO HIMSELF, & HIS DESCENDANTS, AS WELL AS MYSELF, IT HAPPENS TO BE VERY IMPORTANT. I SHALL ENDEVOUR TO KEEP IT BRIEF.

1) The first is in Total Contradiction to what many have said. George Robert was a land owner & therefore Not poor; what's more, landowners in Bart's day were 'well to do.'

2) His family has always been closely associated with the church. By this I mean a goodly number have been Reverends, Wardens, Secretaries, etc.

3) It's well known that John Robert (s) was Third mate aboard the *Princess*[B2]. What astounds me is that no one excepting myself seems to acquaint this aspect with long service, and more than that, nor do they appear to even know what a Third mate's duties are. Well, to quote Wikipedia: "Third Mate aboard a Merchant Vessel, during the period, was on a par with a Lieutenant, & is also Fourth in command, whose main responsibility was the safe Navigation of the ship, which as those of you who are already acquainted with him, are aware the he was a brilliant navigator; ergo, John Robert was hardly a newcomer. Before Sailing on the *'Princess'*, it is known that he went to sea as a ship's boy, what you may not know that he did this during the year of the Massacre of Glencoe, 1692[B3 & SEE *pg 415]. I contend that in order to have the position of navigator, he would have rose thro' the ranks reaching the position of to Sailing Master (about as far as he could in keeping with his Social Standing,) which is historically equated to a Professional Seaman & Specialist in Navigation and such, his pay was £6/month[B2], (in 1720, most working class persons earned less £20/year, & a fully staffed mansion could be rented for £30/year) And tho' not wishing to sound redundant, in the British Navy, Master was originally a warrant officer who ranked with, but after the lieutenants, this rank; however, did not become a commissioned officer until 1867, & it fell out of use in 1890.

4) WHAT MOST EVERYONE FAILS TO RECOGNISE (altho' I'm sure a great many servicemen in the same predicament [drafted] know all too well) is that once they are no longer needed, as was John Robert after the end of Queen Anne's War, they are simply out of a job after their hitch, & like today, only much worse, jobs were scarce, especially when the bulk of an individual's training, regardless of how valuable at sea, is rather useless elsewhere.

5) Many are also unaware of John Roberts placement of First Mate aboard the privateer, *'Terrible'* being how his first acquaintance with piracy (*Edward England*) came about, finding himself again in the company of pirates (this time Hywel Davies) was not a novelty.

6) As a pirate, John was quick to make captain, before that he was offered a captaincy under Commodore Hywel Davies (aka Cap'n Howell Davis) the spelling listed first is correct as documented, was found within the PRO in Haverfordwest, Pembrokeshire in 2004 by the author. Said is also cited in the book Open Secrets, located in my Bibliography.

7) And for those who are under the impression that John Robert was illiterate, they are sorely mistaken, for John could not only read & write in Welsh & English, he could, at the very least, could also read Latin, and could speak both French & Spanish, and a bit of Portuguese, all of which would be more or less a necessity for a high ranking Naval officer.

8) RE: The fact that Captain Roberts was a teetotal was never meant to imply that he never drank alcoholic beverages, but rather that he didn't indulge, and altho' it's true that he preferred tea, Bottled Beer was commonly consumed when no potable water was available, and I have no doubt that when the appropriate occasion arose, an occasional glass of wine was consumed, as was a snort of strong spirits.

In closing: The original writings which created this addition were themselves written on parchment with a quill which are entitled, "Captain Bartholomew Roberts, A Pyrates Journal," was born as a direct result of Automatic Writing (a form of dictation.) You as the reader can believe it, or not. To this, all I can say is that when it all began, having no clue what was happening or why, I was decidedly bewildered, but as my tribute to the Great Captain Roberts, of whom was the centerpiece of a high school book report containing some 70 pirate captains, which many years later (1996) became a website that I maintained for about 20 years, I sought facts, my writings are the results of those findings.

WITH REGARD TO: #1: The telling of Captain Roberts days as a young man, & Miss Rebekah, the lady of his youth… Within the town of Little Haven, which did in fact export coal, I did find info on the woman named Rebekah who came to live there when her seafaring father (or rather appointed Godfather,) a Merchant Captain from Boston Towne, who upon retiring from sea life, took up residence in the large Ivy Covered dwelling across from the car park.

#2: In the first part of this book, I accurately described a derelict house long before I ever knew of its existence, much less ever having seen it, its address is #5 and is situated along the narrow road leading down the hill into Little Haven.

#3: Regarding the picture window that Captain Roberts broke while throwing Keith out the window, it is located in the Haven Ford Hotel, Little Haven, Wales, & that edifice, again, was described long before I ever knew of its existence, or had ever seen it.

#4: For the purpose of putting an end to the discrepancy regarding the name of Cap'n Roberts' 1st ship, the *Rover,* originally named '*Marquis del Campo,*' the Dutch East~Indianman was a 3-Masted Sloop-of-War of 30 guns belonging to his Imperial Majesty, until taken by Cap'n Hywel Davies who renamed the ship, *the Rover*. Later, after Davies was dead and Cap'n Roberts, & others having been gone for 9 days, the ship's Quarter-Master, Walter Kennedy, & the rest of the *Rover's* crew who, feeling they had waited long enough, took both *the Rover* & the *Sagrada Famflia* & departed, & afterwards, 'twas them who renamed the *Rover, Royal Rover.* Later, after Trepassey, when replacing the Fortune, Cap'n Roberts', re-christened his new ship *Royal Rover*.

The following two descriptions are taken from "The American Coast Pilot, Containing Directions For The Principal Harbours, Capes and Headlands of the Coasts of North & South America." by E. & G. Blunt. 1847.

TREPASSEY HARBOR.—The entrance to this harbor is to the eastward of Cape Powles, and the direct course in will be N. E. ¼ E. Cape Powles lies from French Mistaken Point N. W. about 8 miles; from Cape Mutton W. S. W. ¾ W. one mile; and from Cape Pines N. E. by E. 5 miles. The entrance to Trepassey Harbor is three-quarters of a mile wide, and continues of that breadth full 2½ miles up; it then narrows to less than half a mile, and opens again to its former width, and there vessels commonly ride. To enter this harbor ships commonly steer over from Mistaken Point towards Cape Pine, until you fairly open the harbor; you may then safely run along the shore, for it is bold. In sailing into the harbor, you will meet with a rock on the south-eastern shore, lying about a mile from Powles Head, and one-third of a cable's length off the shore. There is, also, on the northern side, a shoal which runs along up the harbor, so far as a low green point; to clear this shoal, bring Baker's Point on with a low rocky point at the entrance of the harbor; and when you get so far up as the low green point, you may steer more westerly, and anchor either in the N. W. or N. E. arm, in 5 or 6 fathoms water. Both wood and water can be obtained with ease.

From Mistaken Point to Cape Pine the course and distance are W. N. W. ¼ W. 4 leagues and a half; and from Cape Pine to Cape Freels, west, one mile. The land about Cape Pine is barren and moderately high; from Cape Freels, the shores extend W. N. W. one mile to Black Head, and thence N. W. ¼ W. to the eastern reef, and head of St. Shot's Bay.

ST. SHOT'S BAY.—This is the fatal spot where so many vessels have been recently wrecked; the bay is about a mile deep, and from the eastern to the western head, the bearing is N. by W. ¼ W. distant two miles: it lies entirely open and exposed to the sea.

FERRYLAND HARBOR is to the northward; and its entrance is between Ferryland Head and Bois Island, being little more than half a cable's length wide. Ferryland Head has two rocks near it, called the Hare's Ears. When you have passed these and are within Bois Island, it becomes wider, having good anchorage with 8 and 10 fathoms, but north-east winds send in a heavy sea over the lower rocks, which run from Bois Island to the main.

From Bois Island to Goose Island the course is N. N. E. ¾ E. distant half a mile; and from Goose to Stone Island the course is N. N. E. ¼ N. distant half a mile.

Bell Time

Mid	Morning	Forenoon	Afternoon	Dogs*	First
0030 - 1 bell	0430 - 1 bell	0830 - 1 bell	1230 - 1 bell	1630 - 1 bell	2030 - 1 bell
0100 - 2 bells	0500 - 2 bells	0900 - 2 bells	1300 - 2 bells	1700 - 2 bells	2100 - 2 bells
0130 - 3 bells	0530 - 3 bells	0930 - 3 bells	1330 - 3 bells	1730 - 3 bells	2130 - 3 bells
0200 - 4 bells	0600 - 4 bells	1000 - 4 bells	1400 - 4 bells	1800 - 4 bells	2200 - 4 bells
0230 - 5 bells	0630 - 5 bells	1030 - 5 bells	1430 - 5 bells	1830 - 5 bells	2230 - 5 bells
0300 - 6 bells	0700 - 6 bells	1100 - 6 bells	1500 - 6 bells	1900 - 6 bells	2300 - 6 bells
0330 - 7 bells	0730 - 7 bells	1130 - 7 bells	1530 - 7 bells	1930 - 7 bells	2330 - 7 bells
0400 - 8 bells**	0800 - 8 bells	1200 - 8 bells	1600 - 8 bells	2000 - 8 bells	2400 - 8 bells

---Types of Ships---

All ships described herein are as they were built or rigged During the time of Bartholomew Roberts.

Barque (aka **Bark**): With 3 or more masts; is generally square rigged on the foremast and fore-and-aft rigged on the main, mizzen, and any other masts.

Barquentine (aka **Barkentine**): a smaller version of a Barque, is generally square-rigged on the mainmast & fore-and-aft rigged on the mizzen-mast.

Brig: a 2-masted sailing vessel of various size. The Brig, has the advantage of permitting a multitude of sail types (square &/or fore & aft) on its mail mast. Unlike the smaller brigantine which has 2, the Brig's main mast consists of 3 sections and equal to that of a fully rigged ship: a mast, topmast and topgallant mast.

Brigantine: a two-masted sailing vessel of various size, square rigged foremast and at least two sails on the main mast (the aft mast and tallest of the two): a square topsail and a gaff sail mainsail, behind the mast. The brigantine is generally larger than a sloop or schooner, but smaller than a brig.

Clipper: a very fast (averaging 18+ knots) sailing ship of the middle third of the 19th century. They were fast, yacht-like vessels, with three masts and generally narrow prow for their length, and had a large total sail area. The Clipper, generally rigged a Full Rigged Ship, she, like the Brig also had the advantage of various sail types (Square &/or Fore & Aft, & Gaff) on her Mizzen. The Clipper ship's main attribute is the ability to "clip" over the waves rather than plough through them under full sail, day and night, fair weather & foul. Meaning that whilst weather conditions forced other ships to shorten sail, dragging on every inch of canvas she could pack, the Clipper drove on, heeling so much that their lee rails were in the water. *Although not conceived until the 19th century, the Willing Captive, having been designed by la Marquise (from the future,) is an extreme Clipper with Aft raked masts, and fitments to support square, fore & aft rigging, spanker, gaff capability on her mizzen, as well as a Spinnaker.*

Frigate: A full-rigged three-masted ship, which may or may not be equipped with oars, smaller than a Ship-of-the-Line, and a single gun deck. The U.S.S. Constitution although classified as a Frigate, is a Super Frigate.

Full-rigged ship: Sometimes simply called a Ship or Frigate. capable of an array of sails (Gall, Jibs, Topsails, Topgallant, Staysails, Royals, Moonraker.)

Galley: Another name for a oar equipped Frigate.

Guiney-man (aka **Guinea-man**): A ship designed to transport slaves.

Merchant: Generally three-masted, a Merchant vessel can be any type of ship suitable to the task of carrying large quantities of cargo, generally over great distances, e.g. transatlantic voyages.

Man-of-War: A heavily armed Naval Warship.

Pinnace: A light boat, propelled by oars or sails, carried aboard merchant and war vessels. Also a small schooner-rigged vessel used a tender or a scout.

Pinque (aka **Pink**): Fast & Flexible French Vessels. Generally merchant vessels with a shallow draught and narrow stern. Can be variously rigged like a brig or a sloop. An excellent example of a French Pinque can been seen (The Seagull) in the 1998 version of Frenchman's Creek. Should you get the chance to watch this wonderful movie, & the 1943 version as well, both are the author's favourite movie, note the way the ship sails; heeling & rolling is n keeping with to her design.

Schooner: A multi-masted vessel rigged fore-and-aft on all masts. A top sail Schooner is also rigged with a square sail on the foremast, sometimes atop more of its topmasts.

Ship-of-the-Line: A Warship large enough to take a place in the line of battle, carrying from 50 to 100 cannon. Whilst the H.M.S Victory, the pride of England, is a First Rate Ship-of-the-Line, the H.M.S Swallow was a Fourth Rate Ship-of-the-Line.

Sloop: A small vessel with four to twelve cannon on her upper deck, having one, two or three masts.

Sloop-of-War: In the Royal Navy, the Sloop-of-War was a warship with a single gun deck that carried up to eighteen guns. The term *sloop-of-war* actually encompassed all of the un-rated combat vessels, including the very small gun-brigs and cutters.

Snow: Originally a 3-masted vessel, matured to be the largest of all old two-masted vessels, is similar to a brig with the addition of a trysail mast just astern the mainmast. The most visible difference between the brig and the snow is in the latter's "snow-mast," stepped directly behind the main mast. In contrast to the brig, where the gaff and boom are attached directly to the main mast, a snow's gaff, and in later times its boom, were attached to the snow-mast, permitted the gaff to be attached directly to the main mast.

--Coinage--

Piece of Eight: Spanish silver coin, aka Eight Reales or Pecos. Back when Farthings (¼ of 1 cent) were in everyday use & paper money was rare; & taking into account that whether a dollar was called a Pound, Peco, Yen, etc… the value within its own land was comparable in the manner of its purchasing power like now, only back then coins were gold or silver & were not valued only in quantities of less than a dollar like in the U.S. (Europe & Great Britain both have coins valued at 1 & 2 pound or euros.) coins, like the former $20. gold piece. Baring in mind that in 1900, roughly 180 years after the events in this book took place, a penny would buy a loaf of bread, in 1775 a pint of Beer was 6 pence, & in 1700 two Eight Reale coins would purchase a cow, an Eight Reale coin (equal to 2 weeks pay at minimum wage in the U.S. in 2015) being quite valuable, is why most people who acquired them tended to cut it into many pieces, hence the name Piece of Eight.

One Pistole (the French name given to the Spanish Double Escudo, a gold coin aka Doubloon equal to 32 reales, widely used by many countries as international currency) was worth approximately ten Livres. The Spanish dollar, 1 reale, 1/8 of what is commonly referred to as a Piece of Eight, was the coin upon which the original United States dollar was based. 250,000 Pistoles in 1718 is equal to about 7,860,000 U.S. Dollars in 2016.

Moidore: a Gold Portuguese Coin — **Doubloon**: a Spanish Coin.

Locations

Annamaboa: Now spelt Anomabu, is a fort on the coast of Ghana.

Acua: (aka Accua):, was a trading hub within the Gold Coast region on the coast of Ghana[B7]

Annobón: Is a small Island, some 7 square miles, within the Gulf of Guinea SW of São Tomö.

Antegoa: Now spelt Antigua in the Leeward Islands, lies some 30 miles east of Nevis betwixt Barbuda & Guadeloupe.

Barbados: (166 sq miles / 430 sq km) Latitude/Longitude 13° 10N, 59° 32W

Bennet's Key: Within the Gulf of Samana, is located on the east side of Hispaniola.

Brava: Lowest of the Cape Verde Islands

Carriacou Isle: is the largest island of the Grenadines.

Corvocoo Isle: is located within the Grandillos (now: Granada Islands.)

Deseada Island (aka Désirade): lies off the East coast of Guadeloupe.

Dominico: Now: Commonwealth Dominico (290 sq miles) Latitude/Longitude 15° 25N, 61° 20W.

Fernando de Noronha Isle: is situated along the East Coast of Brazil, just South of the Equator.

Grandillos: now the Granada Islands.

Guinea: (off the West coast of Africa at the Equator)

High Cameroon: (off the West coast of Africa. An estuarial inlet in the Gulf of Guinea in the Cameroon's Coast.)

Isle of Princes, The aka El Principe: Official Name Republic of São Tomë and Principe --- (371 sq miles / 960 sq km)   Latitude/Longitude 1° 30N, 8° E

La Baía de Todos os Santo: aka "Bay Of All Saints or All Saints Bay."

Santo Domingo: (18,815 sq miles / 48,730 sq km) Latitude/Longitude 19° 00N, 70° 40W (now called the Dominican Republic. In between time it was known as Hispaniola.)

Côte d'Ivoire: aka Ivory Coast.

Marygalanta: correctly spelt Marie-Galante (65.8 square miles) is an Island in Guadeloupe.

Martinique: (426 sq miles / 1,060 sq km) Latitude/Longitude 14° 40N, 61° 00W.

Montserrat: (approx 40 sq miles / 102 sq km) Latitude/Longitude 16° 45N, 62° 42W

Moonay Island: now spelt Isla Mona, lies within the straights of Mona, off the West Coast of Puerto Rico.

Parrot Island: an small island off the West coast of Africa within Nigeria's estuary.

River of Saminah: on the coast of Guiana [then-Caiana] (FR), South America, just east of Suriname and West of Brazil.

Saint Barthelémy: aka St. Bartholomew, St. Barth & St. Barts (8 sq miles/21 sq km) Latitude/Longitude 17° 50N, 62° 50W

St. Christophers: aka St. Kitts --- (68 sq miles) Latitude/Longitude 17° 20N, 62° 45W

St. Thome: Now spelt São Tomö, Lies within the Gulf of Guinea.

The Grenadines: (150 sq miles (389 sq km) Latitude/Longitude 13° 16N, 61° 23W

Surinam: also Suriname is on the N.E. Coast of South America.

Tobago and Trinidad: Latitude/Longitude 11° 00N, 61° 00W.

Zachea Island: now Isla Desocheo, lies within the straights of Mona, off the West Coast of Puerto Rico.

--- Useful Terminology ---

Aft: Toward, or near the stern.
Astern: Behind.
Avast: Halt, stop.
Bow: Front of the ship.
Boatswain/Bosun/Bos'n/Bo's'n: is responsible for duty assignments and the maintenance of the ship and its equipment.
Boot-Top: To clean the upper part of the ship's bottom of barnacles, and other marine life.
Broadside: To fire all guns (cannons) on one side simultaneously.
Cable Length: 1/10 of a nautical mile or 100 fathoms.
Careen: To heel over a ship and clean the weed and barnacles from the hull.
Colors aka Jack or Jolly Roger (aboard a pirate ship): The ship's flag.
Commodore: One who is in command of 2 or more ships.
Consort: A companion vessel.
Coxswain aka **Cox'n**: The helmsman responsible for steering a row boat.
Cutlass (Cutlash): A medium length, curved sword. Captain Roberts preferred a Medieval Sword.
Fathom: 6 feet.
Forecastle aka Fo'c's'le: Forward part of the ship.
Foremast: The foremost mast.
Heel: To lean to one side.
Hogshead: 63 gallons; 0.238 cubic meters; or 52 ½ imperial gallons.
Jack: A ship's flag that is used to indicate which country the ship comes from. Use to be flown from the Spritsail Topmast. Generally smaller than the ensign.
Knot: One Nautical mile per hour - 1 1/8 miles per hour.
Larboard: The left side of the ship when facing towards the bow.
League: About 3 miles.
Leeward: The side or direction away from the wind.
Nautical mile: 6080 feet.
Mainmast: The principal mast of a vessel: ordinarily, the second mast from the bow, of a ship having two or more masts.
Mizzenmast: The mast next aft of the mainmast, and although not relevant to this book, the mizzen is the shorter of the two masts on a Ketch or Yawl.
Moidore: An old Portuguese gold coin equal to about 27 shillings (£1. 7-)
Quarter-deck: A deck above the main deck which stretched from the stern to up and to as far as half the length of the ship. Restricted to the Captain and ship's officers and those especially invited. From whence the ship was controlled.
Ratlines: One of the small ropes fastened across the shrouds of a ship, used like rungs of a ladder for climbing aloft or descending to the open deck.
Starboard: Right side of the ship when facing towards the bow.
Stern: The rear of the ship.

Personal Observations By The Author

Said herein below is merely a means, powered by the author's determination, to correct mistakes. No disrespect is intended, nor is the author claiming perfection within her own work, but rather is making every effort to help Captain Roberts to Rest In Peace, which I have stated several times to be my main objective. My observations continue throughout the Reference Section.

A: It is thought by most that John Robert left Little Newcastle when he was around 10-13 years old, & never looked back, but I disagree. If John Robert did not return to Little Newcastle after his enlistment, and reside there for several years during his early manhood, the towns people, those living there at the time, would not have knowledge regarding his manhood Character; furthermore, I have uncovered other information telling me of one episode that took place during his late teens, Lost Love, which led to his enlistment throughout Queen Anne's War, the latter of which, coupled with his thirst for knowledge, also accounts for unparalleled seamanship, as well as proof that not only was he 10 years of age (during the year of the Massacre of Glencoe, 1692) when he went to sea the 1st time as a Ship's Boy, but also where he boarded the ship. [B3 & SEE page 415]

B: Examining the events logically, we must conclude, considering the moral feelings possessed by the brooding John Robert when taken by Hywel Davis, that he, after much contemplation, believed wholeheartedly that his life as a pirate was preordained, though he had no idea until later, just what was to be the true nature of his inescapable future, beyond the joining of their ranks, but 'tis believed, indubitably, by this author that John, once again being captured by pirates, and his quick rise to Captaincy, one can easily draw to the conclusion that those of the *Rover* knew of John Robert from his days with Edward England (unfortunately, the chapter on England's piratical career does not mention the time he spent with John Robert, nor his association with the Welsh Privateer, John Williams, Cap'n of the *Terrible*, upon which John Roberts was First Mate,) which explains his acceptance speech[c]. John, who was more than capable, yet unable to achieve his well-deserved position as Captain upon a Merchant or Naval vessel, feeling that such obtainment would be possible aboard a pirate vessel, believing it to be the long awaited fulfilment of destiny, he allowed his strong morals and character drive him into becoming the legendary pirate Captain, Bartholomew Roberts. This position, which was unlike that of any that came before him (or since,) allowed him to show to all who opposed him, and with an unmitigated passion, what a grave mistake they had made in denying him a Captaincy, and to their chagrin, he used his phenomenal talents to oppose the tyranny in which they thrived rather than being a part of it.

C: "Since I hath dipp'd my Hands in muddy water and must be a Pyrate, it is better being a Commander than a common Man."

The bloody water that Captain Roberts was referring, is the saving of the pirate crew after the demise of his friend, Captain Hywel Davies, and the force used to achieve that end, bearing in mind that up until that point in time, John Robert had not participated in any pirate acts.

As for "MUST BE A PYRATE" The quick thinking that saved the pirate crew from disaster when Hywel Davies was killed, was not the entire reason for this statement, but rather it being compiled with the fact that it was the second time he had been had involuntarily found himself in the company of pirates whilst first mate aboard the *Terrible*, where John Robert was also regarded as an exceptional mariner, seaman, and handler of men, just as Hywel Davies had when he recruited him, and the crew of the *Rover*, were quick to recognize. I believe that being twice captured, convinced John that there was no escaping piracy, and after mulling this aspect, in conjunction of the alternative, being either death or a harsh life on land, he resigned himself to a life of piracy. Lastly, I believe he was expressing, rather humbly by stepping down when the crisis was over, his desire to be a Captain, and feeling that such a position was his true calling, that it was this aspect alone that created the living legend.

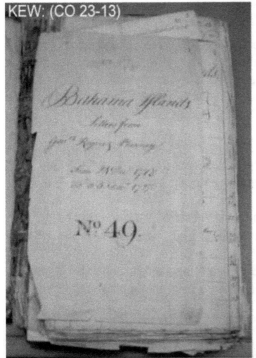

D: There seems to be some discrepancy regarding the year, but in my efforts, searching out the original documentation, 1718 is the year John Robert aka Bartholomew Roberts signed aboard, and sailed out of London on the *Princess*. In all of history no other pyrate received such notoriety, nor ever present within the newspapers and communications in the form of letters between men of state, ship's logs, nobles, others of notoriety, as well as other documents, e.g. CO 23/13, the front page of which is directly below (I have a copy of the entire document, as well as CO 31/15 (directly below.) Both of these documents are located within the National Archives in Kew, England), and thereby, providing to those who are determined in their resolve, as am I, much delicious information lies within to relish. In my case, as Bartholomew Roberts' champion, such was placed here so the world will not only be aware of, but will understand this Great Man. Both of the Documents mentioned above contain considerable information about Captain Bartholomew Roberts.

E: It makes perfect sense for John Robert to have feelings that eventually led to him embracing the life as a Pyrate. To travel as independent Captains and Crews whilst seeking the same prizes would only lead to eventual confrontations twixt the crews, especially during the division of booty; an aspect that explains why Captain Roberts limited his crew and fleet to a choice number (weeding out those who did not measure up to his personal standards,) following the philosophy, perhaps even instigating it, that a small, well equipped, highly trained attack force moves, not only more efficiently, but more successfully. One must appreciate that to train & manage a crew of 500+ pirates to move as a well greased attack force is quite a feat.

F: Description changed to a personal narrative.

G: RE: **Pirates!: Brigands, Buccaneers, and Privateers in Fact, Fiction, and Legend by** Jan Rogozinski.

I was surprised to find this book in the reference section of my local library. Nowhere within the pages written about Bartholomew Roberts, pages 292 - 294 (I can not speak of the others as I did not look at them) are there any citations, there are, however, numerous errors. In the first two paragraphs of the book alone, I found the following errors:

#1: The author states that John Roberts was born to a poor family in Pembroke County, but John Robert's family was far from poor; his father was not only a land owner, owning both horses & oxen (and perhaps the principal landowner in a village or district,) living in a large house, but John Roberts' family also had the honour of being Church Warden (St. Peter's Church, Little Newcastle) &/or Secretary, and still did until Miss Nancy Reed Davies (Church Warden) passed away in the 2007; her nephew, Richard Davies, who lives in the same house as did his illustrious ancestor, was Church Secretary until he was ordained in 2016, and, carrying on the tradition, is the Vicar in Little Newcastle.

#2: Jan Rogozinski fails to mention that Barbados sloop she mentions was Captained by the Welsh privateer, by John Williams, and before then, Captain Roberts, who had gone to sea as a Ship's Boy at the tender age of [not quite] 10, returned home, and later served in the Royal Navy throughout Queen Anne's War.

#3: John Robert signed on (in 1718) as 3rd mate, aboard the merchant slaver, *Princess*, out of London.

#4: John Robert was Never called Black Barty or Black Bart whilst he lived; that nick-named was coined by I.D. Hooson (*see page 435 below.*)

What surprises this author is that the information is all 2nd & 3rd hand. Reference material should limited to Original Source whenever possible, and should 2nd hand be necessary, such should only be cited when the original is either unobtainable or impractical.

THE INFAMOUS JOLLY ROGER

Christopher Moody, whilst he was himself Captain (1718) of a pirate vessel (later Ship's Pilot aboard the *Fortune,*) had a red flag he called the Jolie Rouge (English translation: Pretty Red) which bore an hourglass and a hand brandishing a cutlass over a skull and crossbones.[B12] A similar term, Joli Rouge, used by the French, cited Bart as a man having a hearty laugh, was uncommonly polite to his victims, and always dressed in red when going into battle. It is said to be the reason why the Welsh rugby team don red shirts. Joli Rouge translates into Nice One in Red.

According to Piet Brinton & Roger Worsley, the author's of Open Secrets[B3], 'twas the French, being so often robbed by the laughing man dressed in red, who called him Joli Rouge. Others say that Jolly Roger is a bastardization of 'Joli Rouge,' but this does not seem likely, not if one is looking at this as a French saying because the English translation for Joli is Nice One & for Jolie is Pretty Red. It's more likely that Joli or Jolie was on this occasion, not French but an archaic spelling of Jolly in English. 'Roger' was also a slang word for pirate.

Stanley Richards, author of, 'Black Bart,' (page 53): Jolly Roger, also Old Roger, was the name given to the skeleton representing death. The original Jolly Roger displayed by Bart had a white skeleton on the black flag; in one hand was held an hour-glass, and the other a dart, beneath which be a heart dripping 3 drops of blood: The chorus sung to it was: "*This flag is our Old Roger, and we shall lye under it and dye under it.*"[B4]

Whatever the case, to this day the term Jolly Roger refers Pirate flags in general. In Bart's case, his flags were flown round the clock, intentionally publicizing his presence to whomever may see them would know, without question, whose ship(s) they were observing was just one of the many ways he employed psychological warfare.

BIBLIOGRAPHY
(referenced in this book as 'B')

NOTE: *This author, will always cite the original source, of which she has read herself. Only when such is unobtainable has she cited such second hand.*

#1: CALENDAR OF STATE PAPERS, COLONIAL SERIES, AMERICA AND WEST INDIES, MARCH **1720** TO DECEMBER **1721** PRESERVED IN THE PUBLIC RECORD OFFICE.

#2: **A full and exact account, of the tryal of all the pyrates, lately taken by Captain Ogle, on board the Swallow man of war, on the coast of Guinea**: Multiple Contributors. Reproduction from Harvard University Law Library. 1723

#3: **Open Secrets** by Piet Brinton and Roger Worsley: *It's a Dilly! Most of the 'HARD TO FIND' info herein was gleaned from the PRO in Haverfordwest, Pembrokeshire, Wales.*

#4: **Black Bart** by Stanley Richards: *(Exceptionally well researched, well told, and nicely presented.)*

#5: **A Voyage To Guinea, Brazil, and the West Indies; In His Majesty's Ships, The Swallow and Weymouth** (1735) by John Atkins - Surgeon in the Royal Navy. SEE ALSO: Smith, *New Voyage,* 42-43 and Morris, "Ghost of Kidd," *N.Y. Hist.,* XIX (1938) 286.

#6: **Iron Men & Wooden Women**: Margaret S. Creighton.
Proof that Elizabeth Trengrove, altho' she did engaged in sexual relations with David Sympson, perhaps, in her own mind, to keep herself safe, such was by her own choice, not by force.

#7: **A Voyage To Guinea** by William Smith, Esq., Surveyor to Royal African Company. Second Edition - 1745 (Error: the Author, William Smith, states 1720 when in fact it was 1721. *SEE CONSEQUENTIAL INFORMATION ON PAGE ON PAGE 183.*

#8: **A General History of the Pyrates** (1972) Source: 'Yale; reprint in the original type.' by Daniel Defoe.

#9: **A General History of the Robberies & Murders of the most Notorious Pirates** (1724), by Charles Johnson.
(to this ongoing debate, I shall only state: Save a few deviations, the above 2 books are the same; ergo being generally abreast, & occasionally not, I cite both.)

Much of the information, as well as many of the quotes, come from the testimony given by Captain Roberts' crew during the Cape Corso Castle Trial, May 1722. A great deal more of the Tryal Transcript than what can be found in the 2 books above is located directly above, authored by Daniel Defoe & Capt. Charles Johnson, respectively.

The complete original transcript of the Trail is found at the PRO in Kew, England. A copy, as it was printed in the 1723 is listed above.

#10: **Ocean-Born Mary** the Truth Behind a New Hampshire Legend by Jeremy D'Entremont.

#11: **Pirates of the Eastern Seas (1618-1723;) a Lurid Page of History** by Charles Grey.

#12 **The Pirates Own Book**: Authentic Narratives of the Most Celebrated Sea Robbers by Marine Research Society: *This work, author's copy dated 1856, contains no references as to where it acquired its information.*

#13: **That Great Pirate** by Aubrey Burl: *Great info, but not written in chronological order.*

#14: **If a Pirate I must be... The True Story of "Black Bart," King of the Caribbean Pirates** by Richard Sanders.

#15: **Pirates** by David Mitchell:

#16: **The Book of Welsh Pirates & Buccaneers** by Terry Breverton.

#17: **Ship English...** Sailors' speech in the early colonial Caribbean by Sally J. Delgado. Published by 'languages science press'.

MORE SUGGESTED READING

Burke's genealogical and heraldic history of the landed gentry, Volume 2 by John Burke: *A great place to research family trees. On page 845 is stated quite a list of Governors of St. Christopher & the Leeward Islands during the time of Captain Roberts, & their families among other invaluable information of the period.*

Privateering and Piracy in Colonial America: *Contains enlightening info which is worth reading, not only in regard to Captain Roberts, but a wealth of other fascinating reading as well.*

The following Online Report, **Piracy in the Newfoundland Fishery in the Aftermath of the War of the Spanish Succession,** by Olaf Jenzen, accurately *describes the area & the goings on during the time period.*
http://www2.gredfell.mun.ca/nfld_index.htm .

---SPECIAL NOTATIONS---
(referenced in this book as 'N')

#1: Several members of Captain Roberts' crew saved the life of Thomas Grant that day, though six months had past before Mister Grant was finally successful in his repeated attempts to escape.

#2: Lle du Diable aka Devil's Island and at one time was a penal colony.

#3: A&E: "The Pirate Ships" Biography on several pirates including Captain Roberts.

#4: Pembrokeshire Snippets (official internet site) http://home.clara.net/tirbach/HelpPagepearlsPEM.html

#5: Equal to £70000.

#6: Upon the Royal Fortune there was a crew of 276; 48 of whom were Negroes and the rest of which were mostly Englishmen. On the Good Fortune were 100 white men and 40 Negroes.

#7: First encounter with H.M.S. Swallow. Robert Armstrong joins Captain Roberts crew.

#8: Discrepancy lies with in the historical records twixt this 22-gun Dutch Interloper, which also seems to be the 32-gun Dutch Slaver that was originally christened the Ranger, later becoming the Great Ranger.

#9: Incorrectly spelt Newey-bagh, by Daniel Defoe/Charles Johnson, Casnewydd Bach (also spelt Nghastell Newydd Bach; depending on which sign one is looking at) English translation "Little Newcastle," is pronounced, "Cas Newy' Bach," and is located in Pembrokeshire, SW section of Wales. During the days of Captain Roberts, Haverfordwest, which lies about 10 miles SW, was a major inlet.

#10: George Robert of Little Newcastle (see Pembrokeshire Hearth Tax list of 1670,) father of John Robert aka Bartholomew Roberts, had a total of four sons. John, Thomas, and 2 sons named William (either the 1st William had died & the name reused, or they were half brothers. I have three documents verifying such from the Haverfordwest PRO. It should be noted that the last names during the period very often varied in spelling, in this case of the Robert family, an 's' was infrequently added, a fact that is confirmed in the Last Will & Testaments left by George's sons, John & William, of which I also have copies.

#11: aka John Eshwell

#12: During the slave trade, Accra was the sight of numerous nearby forts, many of which were owned and controlled by the Dutch.   http://www.macalester.edu/courses/geog261/eskidmore/history.htm

#13: see COP5, "Letter from Placentia 194/6/83, 367" states 250 fishing boats.

A report entitled "The Problem of Piracy in the Newfoundland Fishery in the Aftermath of the War of the Spanish Succession" states 150 to 250 fishing Boats.

According to the Boston News-Letter, 22 August 1720, Roberts has only forty-five men; see extract in Jameson, Privateering and Piracy, No. 117, 317, yet the November 26th, 1720 issue of the Weekly Journal or British Gazetteer states "St. Lawrence 28 June. A pyrate in a small sloope of 12 gunns and 160 men entered Trepassy on Tuesday the 21st inst, and made himself master of the said harbour and all the ships there, being 22 sail and 250 shallops."

Captain Charles Johnson's book "General History of Pirates - 1724" (Chapter 9 - page 237 & 238) makes no mention of the number of fishing craft damaged.

Wikipedia's pages on Trepassey (https://en.wikipedia.org/wiki/Trepassey) state: "1720, on 21 June, the pirate Bartholomew Roberts approaches Trepassey, finding 172 merchant and fishing ships at anchor. Despite the ships having about forty cannons of various size between them, Roberts takes command of the harbour without opposition. Within the span of a fortnight, his crew massacre an unknown number of sailors and civilians, burns 22 of the vessels, scuttles his own sloop, the Fortune, and commandeers a Brigantine from Bristol before departing"; yet, the mysterious figure of 172 merchant and fishing ships at anchor is not cited; ergo no one but the author of said number knows from what source it originated.

All & All, 'tis probably best to take the word of Alexander Spottswoode (there a 2 or 3 different spellings of

#14: An excerpt from the Cape Coast Castle Trial: Johnson's Book. William Smith's testimony…

> *William Smith*, (a Prisoner acquitted,) says *Walden* was known among the Pyrates mostly, by the Nick-Name of *Miss Nanney* (ironically its presumed from the Hardness of his Temper) that he was one of the twenty who voluntarily came on Board the *Ranger*, in the Chace she made out after the *Swallow*, and by a Shot from that Ship, lost his Leg; his Behaviour in the Fight, till then, being bold and daring.

For a Special Treat, try:

~ ~ ~ SOLOMON GUNDIE ~ ~ ~

SPELT SOLOMONGRUNDY IN JOHNSON'S BOOK
But then the spelling of the period was anything but consistent.

Reputed as being Bart's favourite victuals, *Solomon Gundie,* is a salad that originated in early 17th century England.

Served at many restaurants within the U.K. today, *Solomon Gundie* is a hodgepodge of many disparate things: e.g. cooked meats, seafood, vegetables, fruit, leaves, nuts and flowers, dressed with oil, vinegar, and spices. Aboard ship, the recipe, providing for a nice variety, tends to be limited to whatever the cook has on hand.

And… to dispute the writings of others who call this 'Pirate Food,' the picture to the right shows that not only was this dish served in the eateries of the period, but within many fine homes & restaurants as well, including present day.

Note the controversial spelling of dish #5 on the 1760 Bill Of Fare.

You may also notice that the largest serving as a dessert.

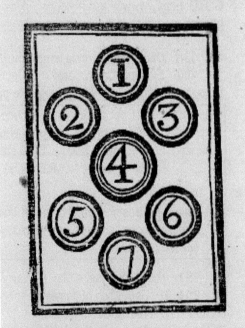

OFFICIAL PUBLIC RECORDS

High Court Admiralty Papers, PRO - (referenced in this book as 'HCA')

1: Stephenson, Second Mate; John Eshwell, ship's carpenter; William Gittus, a gunner. James Bradshaw, John Jessup, John Owen, Thomas Rogers and John Robert (aka Bartholomew Roberts).
2: Experiment. 1/54, 119 (Grant)
3: 13 Men Marooned: 1/49
4: The Fortune: 1/55, 51
5: St. Barthelemy: 1/55, 53
6: Proceedings of the Vice-Admiralty-Date: 1722-1739 (HCA 1/99) / Cape-Corso Castle Trial (HCA. 49, Bundle 104.)
7: Centre for Maritime Historical Studies: University Of Exeter - Wage Database
8 Elizabeth Trengrove: Women being aboard ship, if at all, were generally mention in general passing.
    RE #1 "Elizabeth Trengrove was a passenger in the Onslow" (HCA 1/99/80)
    RE #2 "a woman which was a passenger aboard the said shipp"^{sic} (HCA 1/101/372)
    RE #3 "an English woman, that was aboard" (HCA 1/99 in the Tyrals of Agostinho, no.4)

Calendar of State Papers - PRO (referenced in this book as 'CSP-PRO')

1: The Raid on Ferryland: WJ or BG, November 26, 1720. Newfoundland shipping: CSP (col), October 3, 1720, 165-9, no.251.

Calendar of State Papers, Colonial Series, America & West Indies
(referenced in this book as 'CSP-CS')

Requested Citation: *Calendar of State Papers Colonial Series, America and West Indies: Multiple Volumes.,* Cecil Headlam (London, 1933.)
GOTO: https://www.british-history.ac.uk/cal-state-papers/colonial/america-west-indies/vol32
https://www.british-history.ac.uk/cal-state-papers/colonial/america-west-indies/vol32/pp165-187

1: **33.1**. Cap'n Roberts paid handsomely for goods on numerous occasions.
2: **200** *Excerpt:* Cap'n Carey. Cecil Headlam (London, 1933), pp. 97-106. *British History Online.*
https://www.british-history.ac.uk/cal-state-papers/colonial/america-west-indies/vol32/pp97-106

Aug. 19. Boston, N. England.	Capt. Carey who left London 29th May was taken by a pirate ship of 26 guns and a sloop of 10 near the banks of Newfoundland who took and destroyed so much of his cargo as amounts to about £8000 sterling; and also reports that they had fallen upon and destroy'd the fishery of Newfoundland. *Signed*, Samll, Shute. Endorsed, Recd, 27th Sept 1720.
	ADDITIONALLY
	Bound for Boston with a cargo of ironware, forty-five barrels of gunpowder, and an assortment of English goods in bales and trunks. She had a crew of ten men to work the ship, and carried several passengers.

3: **251**. The HMS Rose, a Man of War; & the HMS Shark, a Sloop.
4: **251. ii**. Deposition of James Dennison, gunner of Fort Hamilton, St. Christophers, 25th Sept. 1720 RE The Arrest of Captain Dunn.
    also reported by the Weekly Journal and also within the British Gazette, December 3, 1720 (both Newspapers.) Additional information is found within the Colonial Office Papers, PRO.
5a: **251. iii**. Deposition of Robert Dunn, Master of the Sloop Relief.
    RE: Whilst Turtling in the Harbour of Curriwaccoo on 4th Sept. he was seized by Roberts the pirate, who

gave them bundles of old rigging & cloth, &c in exchange for tending the turtles. He further said Roberts told him of their immediate plans, & that they would blow up their ship if over powered.

5b: **FURTHER INFO:** Captain Dunn, under extreme duress, testified that the man the world, now known as Bartholomew Roberts, introduced himself as John Roberts. Dunn further reported the pirates had a ship of 28 guns (a ship at that time would have carried 3 masts,) & a sloop of 6 guns under his command, and that he was compelled to supply the pirates with turtles during their 3 week stay whilst careening their vessels. After which he was hung.

6: **251. i**
All officers listed & a list of the strategic points on St Christophers are as described.
Inventory of goods taken on board the Sloop Relief, as reported to Gov. Hamilton by Lt. Gov. Matthew.
Description of Lt. Gov. Matthew's substandard military plans, on St. Christophers RE Cap'n Roberts.
Cap'n Roberts seized that one which was most to his liking & burnt the other two. The one taken belonged to Henry Fowle.
Hinkston's (aka Hingston) vessel was one of the two burnt.

7: **251. iv**. Deposition of Moyse Renos, (Moses Renolds, or Renault.)
Number of ships taken along the banks of Newfoundland.
More RE Trepassey.
Aftermath RE more ships taken along the banks of Newfoundland.

8: **251. v (a)** Letter Bartholomew Roberts sent to Lt. Governor Mathew.

9: **251. v (b)** Letter by Henry Fowle, Cap'n of the Mary, to James Parsons regarding the want of sheep. Cap'n Roberts promises to return Fowle's ship if he cooperated. The promise was kept.

10: **463.iii** Knowing the usual signals used at Martinique & St. Lucia, Cap'n Roberts tricked the merchants out of the money normally use to buy slaves from the Dutch Interlopers. Was also a rare case of insubordinate merchants who paid the price for their impudence.

11: **463.iii** Captures & burns Sloop in Guadalupe, & a French fly-boat laden with sugar whilst sailing to Hispaniola to careen, water and provision without fear of discovery.

12: **463.iii** 26 March. Cap'n Andrew Hingston taken by Cap'n Roberts commanding a ship of 42 guns & a Briganteen of 18 with 262 White men & 50 Negroes.

13: **463.iii** The Hanging of the Governor of Martinique.

14: **500 iii** Deposition of Christian Mortensen. Antigua, 18th May 1721.
Royal Fortune, the briganteen, Sea King, & Nicholas Hendrick's captured snow.

15: **501** May 19, 1721 Antigua. Written by Governor Hamilton to the Council of Trade and Plantations relating to the misconduct of Capt. Thomas Whitney (cont. with 501 i); H.M.S. *Rose;* Denying Succour to Pirates, etc.

16: **501** One of several references by a high official (Ship's Capt., Governor, King, &c.) calling Bartholomew Roberts "That or The Great Pirate." SEE page 471, 2nd entry.

17: **501 iv. (a)** Disposition of Richard Simes, Master of the Sloop Fisher of Barbados. Antigua, 21st Jan., 1721.
RE: St. Lucia near Pidgeon[sic] Island, deponent's sloop & Capt. Norton's brigantine belonging to Rhode Island being seized by Captain Roberts. The taking of 4 French sloops.

18: **501 v.** Disposition of Thomas Bennett. Antigua, 24th Jan. 1721.
RE: Owner of the brigantine *Thomas,* seized by Captain Roberts 30 leagues E. of Bermudas.
Surinam to Tobago to water before encroaching on St. Lucia.

19: **501 vi.** Governor of the French Leeward Islands to Governor Hamilton. Fort Royal, Martinique. 8th Feb. 1721.
RE: Captain Roberts at St. Lucia Oct. 25th & 26th etc. regarding a letter to M. Pomier who asks that his ship be restored.
Reports that Captain Roberts, between Oct. 28th & 29th etc., burnt 15 French & English vessels at Dominica, the last, a 42 gun Dutch interloper, he took with him.
Captain Roberts sailed for St. Eustatia.
M. de Feuquières, pledging 2 good vessels & all his forces, begs Mr. Cox to send Mr. Whitney to help stop Captain Roberts.

20: **501 vii.-xviii** Governor of the French Leeward Islands to Governor Hamilton. Fort Royal, Martinique. 21 February 1721. RE: Plans being made.
Finally, His Majesty empowers Governor Hamilton with the right to suspend Naval Captains.

CALENDAR OF STATE PAPERS
AMERICA AND WEST INDIES, MARCH, 1720 to DECEMBER, 1721.

501. xxii. Governor of Martinique to Capt. Whitney. Fort Royal, Martinique, 13th March, 1721.
The pirates have left the coast of St. Domingo. I have explained to the gentlemen you sent, why I have stopped the preparation of the force I had begun to raise. *Offers* aid in case pirates return to the windward of Martinique *etc. Signed*, De Pas Feuquières.

After Considerable Planning, the French & English proceed with their Plans to Combine Forces in an Effort to Destroy the Great Pirate Roberts, 'twas to no avail, because Captain Roberts, who knew of their plan, simply left the area. After which, the following messages followed.

501. xviii. *Same* to Governor Hamilton, *Dated as preceding.* One of our ships, formerly captured by the pirates, has arrived from St. Domingo, and I do not think they are any longer likely to injure you or us. Two frigates have been sent from France to cruise off St. Domingo. I have there fore discharged the forces I was preparing *etc.*

Author's Note: The fortification beginning in 501. v. # CSP-CS18, on page 472, I have placed here the beginning and the end of this little comedy, the middle was absurd bickering that continued for sometime, throughout xix - xxv between Governor Hamilton & Capt. Whitney. As a result, this author, despite her efforts to the contrary, laughed hilariously as Bartholomew Roberts ran them in circles, just for kicks.

21: **501 xxvii.** Capt. Whitney to Governor Hamilton.
RE: H.M.S. *Rose.* goes in search of Cap'n Roberts, April 26, 1721. To cruise the Virgin Islands to search for the French pirate already taken by Captain Roberts who is thought to be cruising off Desiado[sic].

22: **277. ii** RE: Royal Rover & Good Fortune taking a ship laden with Sugar in Basseterre Road. See pg 467.

23: CITATION that mentions 4 or 5 men from the captured Royal Rover that had been hanged at Nevis following the storm after the Royal Rover had been sunk.

Calendar of State Papers, Colonial Series, America and West Indies 1722-1723
Published by His Majesty's Stationery Office 1934 (referenced in this book as 'CSP-CSY')

1: Cap'n Anstis & Thomas Jones make off with *Good Fortune* & the *Morning Star*. (333.i 1722-23)
SEE FULL ENTRY, VERBATIM, BELOW:

Calendar of State Papers, Colonial Series, America and West Indies 1722-1723
November 1722   Published by His Majesty's Stationery Office 1934 --- Located on page 161

Nov. 9. Whitehall	333. i. Petition, from the ship's companies of the *Morning Star* ship and *Good Fortune* brigantine, 14th June 1722, to Governor Sir Nicholas Lawes. Taken at sundry times by Bartholomew Roberts, the then Capt. of the above said vessels with another ship, petitioners were forced by him to serve as pirates, until on 18 April 1721, they ran away from him with above ships in hopes of obtaining H.M. pardon etc. Signed, in the form of two round robins. Copy. 2 pp. [C.O. 323, 8. Nos. 32, 32. I.]

Author's Note: After making off with the ships above on 18 April 1721, Cap'n Anstis & his scurvy crew captured a ship with a female passenger, & after 21 of the crew assaulted her successively, they broke her back & flung her into the sea.[B1&2]

These are the so-called innocents above who petitioned for a pardon claiming to have been forced.

2: Disposition of Cap'n Finn (aka Fenn, Formerly Cap'n of the *Morrice*)
    (also within the preface of CSP-CS #576 xi 1722-23)
Finn was taken by Cap'n Davies at the same time as John Robert. He later departed with Cap'n Anstis & Thomas Jones when they made off with *Good Fortune* & the *Morning Star*. SEE FULL ENTRY, VERBATIM, BELOW:

Located in the PREFACE on page vi

'Preface', in *Calendar of State Papers Colonial, America and West Indies: Volume 33, 1722-1723*, ed Cecil Headlam (London, 1934), pp. v-lix. *British History Online*
http://www.british-history.ac.uk/cal-state-papers/colonial/america-west-indies/vol33/v-lix

Captain Finn hanged at Antigua.	The Commander of the Station ships in the Leeward Islands, H.M.S. *Winchelsea* and *Hector*, being active in hunting down pirates, succeeded in capturing Captain Finn and some at Tobago. Whilst most of the men were ashore, the rest has run away with the pirate ship, *Good Fortune*. Finn had been in this Brigantine for three years, and had been "an associate of the infamous (Bartholomew) Roberts the Pyrate." Together with five of his company he was "executed at high water mark in the town of St. John's in Antegoa," and was "hung in chains on Rat Island" in the harbour (576).
June 8. St. Christophers	576. (Excerpt) On the 11th of May H.M.S. Winchelsea Capt. Orm Commander arrived at Antegoa having on board nine pyrates, which he took on the Island of Tobago, where Capt. Finn, and the greatest part of his crew, had landed, with an intention to separate, the nine mention'd being surpriz'd by a party sent by Captn. Orm in quest of thenx into the woods. Immediately on Capt. Orm's arrival at Antegoa, I went on board to take their examinations, and finding no proof against them of pyracy, I was obliged to take two persons out of the nine, who upon examination I found were forc'd into the service of the pyrates, to be evidence against the rest; the remaining seven were brought to their tryal on the 17th at the Town of St. John's, where fourteen persons named by H.M. Commission for the tryal of pyrates sate as Judges; Capt. Finn, who was an associate of the infamous Roberts the Pyrate, and the principal of these, came first upon his tryal, and the evidence was strong and plain against him, that he had been three years in the

> brigantine Good Fortune, which he commanded, and had exercis'd several notorious acts acts of pyracy, he was accordingly convicted with six more of his associates, five of which were executed at high water mark in the town of St. John's in Antegoa. One of the condemned persons being very penitent, and asserting upon his tryal, that he was forc'd from the coast of Brazil into their service where he was a pilot, he was repriev'd at the gallows; and I being thorougly convinc'd of his innocence have since pardon'd him. There was also a Portugueze one of the number taken by the pyrates at sea and prov'd to be forced on board by the evidence of two masters of ships, on which the Court of Admiralty acquitted him. Finn is hung up in chains on Rat Island in St. John's Harbour. I do not hear of any more pyrates in these seas, except the brigantine Good Fortune, who has but twelve men on board her, who run away with that vessel, whilst the rest of her crew were on the Island of Tobago.[sic]

Colonial Office Papers, PRO - (referenced in this book as 'CO')

1: Temperance. 31/15. Barbados minutes; 518
2: Philippa Sloop. 31/15. 1140
3: Benjamin. 31/15. 1175
4: Joseph Sloop. 31/15. 1140
5: Letter from Placentia 194/6/83, 367
6: Petition Of the Barbadian Merchants 31/15, 1137

Cape Coast Castle Trial. Direct Testimony, March 1722 - (referenced in this book as 'T')

1: Letters: Bundle 104; London Gazette, January 28th, 1721
2: Appleby's Original Weekly Journal, July 1, 1721
3: The Tryals of the Pyrates.

'A full and exact account, of the tryal of all the pyrates, lately taken by Captain Ogle, on board the Swallow man of war, on the coast of Guinea' is located above in the Bibliography.

Royal African Company Records (referenced in this book as 'RACR')

1: Treasury 70, 1225

Held By: The National Archives, Kew, England
(referenced in this book as 'SP')

1:
  Reference: SP 42/17/265

  Description: Printed copy of an affidavit (dated August 1722) of Charles Rowles, sworn in the presence of John Becher the Mayor of Bristol. Regards the taking of a merchant ship of that port the 'Cornwall' by a 36 gun pirate vessel [Royal Fortune] commanded by the notorious Bartholomew Roberts on the coast of [West] Africa [Gabon]. Violently carrying away nine persons of the crew including Christopher Granger the ship's carpenter, Thomas Outhertoney [Auchterloney] a 'Scotchmen', and two common sailors (Nicholas Bradley and James White) who as musicians play upon the violin and the 'hautboy' [the pipes]. viz

  Date: 1723 July 4

---Newspaper Reports not found within the body of this book---

NP1: Weekly Journal or Saturday Post (late 1719) stated the *Princess*, together with Snelgrave's *Bird*, having left London in November 1718, arrived on the Guinea coast betwixt March and April 1719.

Extras : (referenced in this book as 'E1, E2, E3, &c')

E1: Taken from the file in the possession of the **Massachusetts Historical Society**.

E2: Walter Kennedy (B: ca. 1695 - D: 19 July 1721) was hung at Execution Dock, Wapping, England.[B1&2]

E3: Defoe's, "**A General History of the Pyrates**. 1972 South Carolina. Page 67: "Kennedy, by decent an Irishman, by birth a Spaniard of Cuba."

E4: (Within the Forward): **American Maritime Units and Vessels and Their Supporters During the Revolutionary Way, 1775-1783 (including French & Spanish) E-F** by Granville W. Hough [NR: 295, LCP: 88/89] (Record 977.)

E5: Taken from "**Burke's genealogical and heraldic history of the landed gentry, Volume 2**" by John Burke, Page 845 it states that Lieutenant-General, Sir William Mathew, Governor of Saint Christopher (among his other styles.) was married to the Baroness Van Leemputt, of Holland.

E6: Captain William Kidd: (B. 22 Jan 1655 Greenock, Scotland - D. 23 May 1701 Wrapping, London, England. Found guilty, of 5 counts of Piracy, & Murder, Cap'n Kidd was hung, after which his body, having been dipped in tar, encased in a steel cage, & hung on display for 3 years as a warning to others. His last command was, the Adventure Galley. He was regarded as a brutal shipmaster. Was also reported by escaped prisoners, e.g. the trade ship, Mary, to torture captives, often by drubbing (thrashing with a drawn cutlass whilst hanging by their arms.)

E7 Captain Joseph Bradish (B. 28 Nov 1672 Sudbury, Massachusetts - D. 4 Jul 1700 Wrapping, London, England. Before he was executed for Piracy, Joseph Bradish served as Bo'sun aboard the 300 ton Pinque, Adventure, upon which, he lead a mutiny (15 Nov 1698) against Captain Thomas Gulloch, who like Kidd & Bligh, was said to also be a brutal shipmaster.[B14]

E8: HCA 1/99/29. [He] cryed out to Roberts Da_n you give the French Ship a Board : Side and board him at once.[B17]

E9: HCA 1/99/86. It was against the Pyrates (John Bartholomew Roberts) Rules to accept [Irishman], because they had been formerly cheated by one Kennedy as Irish Man who ran away with their money.[B17]

E10: HCA 1/99/120. Except for Irishmen, Captain Roberts welcomed Foreigners.[B17]

E11: HCA 1/99/124. Man was refused by Captain Roberts because he was Irish.[B17]

E12: HCA 1/99/135. Pirates swore to gain control of a captured vessel, e.g., "he returned to Roberts who Swearing said he wou'd not only have the Pump but the Mainmast too if he wanted it." [B17]

E12: HCA 1/99/135. One impressed captive who is assigned the position of carpenter's mate explains, (marked for emphasis): [he] wou'd have got clear of the Pyrates but for the Old Carpenter of the Fortune who took a liking to him, his future Behaviour was comfortable to Roberts's humour who *wth Oathes and other ill language* used to send him on Bo[ar]d of Prizes for what Carpenters Stores were wanting.[B17]

E13: CSP-CS-xxviii. Antigua. April 26, 1721 Governor Hamilton replies.

RE: Governor Hamilton reprimands Capt. Whitney; stating the failure to capture Captain Roberts was a direct result of his failing to follow orders.

E14: CSP-CS-374. (see page 467) RE: Receiving numerous complaints from the Gen. of the French Islands regarding Captain Roberts, Samuel Cox promises to send whatever forces he can. The entry, which was quite long also includes references to the HMS Rose & HMS Sharke[sic].

E15: Governor Walter Hamilton to Council of Trade, *Cal. State. Papers,* XXXII, *165; American. Weekly Mercury,* Oct. 27, 1720; *Boston Gazette.,* Oct. 24-3l, 1720.

WIKITREE: https://www.wikitree.com/wiki/Bradish-10 & https://familysearch.org/ark:/61903/1:1:F4D7-YZ6

W1: http://en.wikipedia.org/wiki/Robert_Lowther
W2: https://en.m.wikipedia.org/wiki/William_Kidd

Le Havre, France - circa 1700

Although mentioned only briefly in this work, the Harbor & Port above is pictured here because it's a fine example of how things looked during the time of The Golden Age of Piracy.

NOTEWORTHY FACTS & COMMENTS:

Captain Roberts was Multi-Lingual. Most who know of him should be aware that he could converse in both Welsh & English. As a high ranking officer, French & Spanish were generally required, & a modicum of Portuguese would have been helpful as well; how else would communication be possible, and as noted, shown below, Captain Roberts could, at the very least, read Latin. We who have truly researched him know this, was written in Greek; translated into Latin in 1515, & because it was not translated into English until the 20th Century, it becomes evident that he possessed a scholarly education, mostly self-taught, but so it is said of many. The author's father, who did not finish high school, taught at Annapolis, the U.S. Naval Academy, had an I.Q. of 198, the author, herself, also self taught, has an I.Q. of 163, was taught that a truly intelligent person is not the one who knows many things, but rather the one whose search for knowledge is never ending, & also never afraid to ask or find the answer, nor help another to do the same.

The *Royal Fortune* was taken to Port Royal, Jamaica and anchored under Salt Pond Hill, in the general vicinity of the Red marker ship. On the 28th day of August 1722, a Hurricane delivered to Captain Roberts, his pride, his *Royal Fortune*.

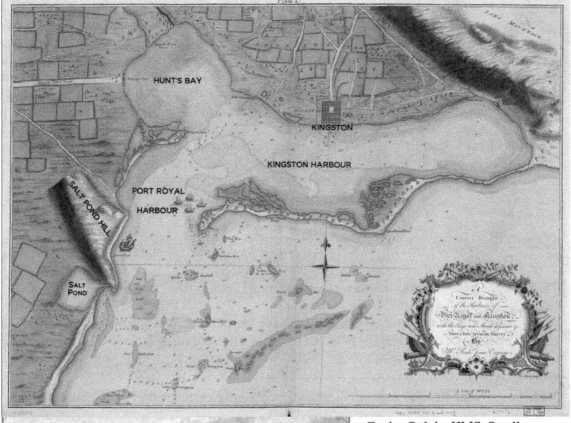

Cap'n Ogle's HMS Swallow, was anchored ff Port Royal. Governor Hamilton reported that of the 50 vessels in port (38 ships at Port Royal, 9 at Kingston, & All the Merchantmen, save one, foundered or were drove ashore,) only 4 military personnel them were spared. Some 400 lives were lost.

AT LEFT: Picture of Salt Pond Hill from across Salt Pond.

The Captain of the HMS Weymouth, companion ship of the HMS Swallow, was Captain Robert Johnson. Could Captain Charles Johnson be a pseudonym or possibly kinfolk? In either case, such could account for the vast amount of info he acquired about pirates.

The familiar pirate image being used by Morgan Spiced Rum was fashioned after the portrait of Captain Roberts located in the beginning of this book. Compare this new likeness, which coincides with the modern fitness age, to the original; which is by far more in keeping with Henry Morgan's true likeness.

There was a ship's boy, Jean François, off a French ship, who signed on the Royal Fortune when he was but 15 years of age.[B2]

Both Captain Hook & Captain Jack Sparrow are said to have some comparison to Captain Roberts, and The Dread Pirates Roberts from the film, 'The Princess Bride,' is said to be Captain Roberts.

Numerous books, websites, a song, poem, documentaries, & monument, etc. tell of, or otherwise honour Captain Roberts. Unfortunately a great deal of lies, misconceptions & derogatory comments are present as well. What is worse, and 'tis because armchair biographers restate incorrect info & propaganda, in this author's opinion, the majority of these writers can not even present simplest facts correctly. The reason for this is simply because they rely others instead of doing their own research. I, the author of this work, altho' I have cited a few biographies, have, for the most part, done my own research, providing when possible details of actual records &/or documents from within the PROs. What is needed is an honest telling, a Biodrama, & to insure its accuracy, I'd be proud to write the screenplay myself.

~ ~ ~ THE ORIGIN OF THE NICKNAME: BARTI DDU / BLACK BART ~ ~ ~

"Cerddi a Baledi," a collection of poems by I. D. Hooson (1880 – 1948), was published in 1936. The book contained a ballad in which he called pirate Captain, John 'Bartholomew' Roberts 'Barti Ddu,' [Black Bart in English].

Not only was Bart never called *Black Bart,* in any language, during his life time, its unlikely that anyone would have dared; what is more, Captain Roberts used his given name [John] throughout the first half of his Piratical activities. After he began using his middle name [Bartholomew] exclusively, he generally abbreviated it as Bart, Bath, Batt.

Note: Isaac Daniel Hooson was born in the village of Rhosllannerchrugog, Denbighshire, Wales.

Original Welsh	English Translation
"Barti Ddu o Gasnewy' Bach,	Black Bart from Little Newcastle,
Y morwr tal a'r chwerthiniad iach,	The tall sailor with the merry laugh,
Efô fydd y llyw	He'll be at the helm
Ar y llong a'r criw,	Of his ship and his men:
Barti Ddu o Gasnewy' Bach."	Black Bart from Little Newcastle.

TIMELINE

Some vessels were plundered more than once. Many that had been taken as prizes or sunk were replaced by new vessels & the name reused. Some had new Captains, & some Captains had both a new ship & employer.

WHEN	WHERE	WHAT	TOTAL
Feb 1719	Anamboe, off coast of Guinea	**Captain Davis** captures: *Princess*, *Bird*, & the *Morrice* + takes 1st two, w/Captains & crew.	
Feb/Mar 1719	En route to El Principe in the Gulf of Guinea	captures Rich Holland ship. Returns *Princess* & *Bird*, less 35 men inc. John Roberts. Lets Hollander go. Befriends Roberts.	
Feb/Mar 1719	High Cameroon	*Royal James* springs leak and is left anchored at High Cameroon.	
April 1719	Isle of Princes, Gulf of Guinea	Ship is watered and provisioned. Plans for plunder go astray. Davis ambushed & killed.	
April 1719	Isle of Princes	**Roberts is elected Captain**	
April 1719	Isle of Princes	Cap'n Davis avenged. Fort destroyed by ground assault led by Quarter-Master Kennedy. Town by ships cannon by Roberts upon a borrowed French ship within the harbour. Depart burning 2 Portuguese ships.	#2
April 1719	Near Cape Lopez	Careened Ship	
mid July 1719	Sailing Southward	Plundered: Dutch Guiney-man	#3
mid July 1719	Off Guinea Coast	*Experiment*. Cap'n Cornet. From London - Sunk	#4
1 day later	Sailing Southward	Portuguese Merchantman	#5
2 days later	Sailing Southward	*Temperance* - Bristol - Cap'n Sharman	#6
July 1719	Steering for São Tomë	Met with no sail	
July 1719	Isle of Annobón	Watered & Provisioned the ship. Sailed due West to Fernando de Noronha. off Brazil's coast. A distance of some 2,300 miles.	
Aug 1719	Arrived Fernando de Noronha	Voyage took 28 days. Watered, Provisioned & Careened the ship.	
Aug/Sept 1719	Brazilian coast	Cruised for 9 weeks. Met with no Sail.	
Sept 1719	Baía de Todos os Santos, Brazil	Espied treasure ship convey in port. 42 Merchants/2 Men-of-War. Captured heaviest laden ship, the *Sagrada Familia*. Took Portuguese Cap'n & some crew.	#7
Sept/Oct 1719	Lle du Diable, Surinam River off coast of Guiana	Place of pleasure & luxury. Stayed several weeks. Captured Rhode Island Sloop. (Lle du Diable aka Devil's Island)	#8
Oct 1719	Lle du Diable	Captured Sloop, christened the *Fortune*.	#9
Oct 1719	Lle du Diable	*Fortune* chases Rhode Island Brigantine. Cap'n Roberts & 40 others almost perish due to ill winds and currents. Upon their return to Surinam River 9 days later, Walter Kennedy, ship's Quarter-Master, & some 20 others, had absconded with both the *Rover* & the *Sagrada Familia*.	
Oct 1719	Lle du Diable	Articles Drawn.	
Jan 10, 1720	Laquary Roads, Trinidad	*Philippa* sloop, Cap'n Daniel Greaves. Took subsistence only.	#10
Jan 17, 1720	nigh Trinidad	Plundered the Sloop *Happy Return of St Christophers*. William Taylor, Master.[B2 page 40]	#11
Feb 1720	Off Barbados	Plundered 10 gun trader from Bristol.	#12
pre Feb 12, 1720	Near Barbados	*Benjamin* from Liverpool.	#13

BLOOD and SWASH, The Unvarnished Life (& afterlife) Story of Pirate Captain, Bartholomew Roberts............."REFERENCE SECTION"

Date	Location	Event	Ref
Feb 18, 1720	Near Barbados	Sloop, the *Joseph*, Cap'n Bonaventure Jelfes	#14
Feb 19, 1720	Near Barbados	pirate Cap'n Montigny la Palisse of, the *Sea King* joined Roberts.	
Feb 1720	Off Barbados	A French Pinque	#15
Feb 26, 1720	West Indies	Cap'n Roberts lets the *Philippa* go. Robert Lowther, Gov. of Barbados, specially outfits 2 ships: the *Summersett*, a Galley, Cap'n Rogers & the Sloop, *Philippa*, Daniel Greaves, Cap'n to hunt Cap'n Roberts. Majority of cargo & arms had to be jettisoned to get clear. Hatred of Barbados begins.	
Feb 1720	Dominico	Watered/Provisioned; Encountered 13 Englishmen from, the *Revenge* pirate sloop & marooned by the French Guard de la Coste, from Martinique.	
Feb/Mar 1720	Granadilloes; lagoon at Corvocoo	Careened in a weeks time. Left at night, going first to Dominico, then Corvocoo. Unknowingly avoided the 2 sloops sent by the Governor of Martinico to destroy them. Sailed down the East Coast of America. Heading, altho' not directly, to Trepassey to avenge the 13 Englishmen.	
April 1720	At Surinam	A Dutch Fly-Boat. [B2 page 37]	#16
April 1720	Off Guadeloupe	Plundered Sloop, *May Flower* [sic, B2 page 48]	#17
Apr/May 1720	En route to Trepassey	Plundered: the *Jeremiah and Ann*	#18
May 1720	New England	Watered & Sold Swag.	
May 1720	Newfoundland Banks	Plundered: a Brigantine from Teignmouth, Devon. Cap'n Peet.	#19
June 1720	En route to Trepassey nigh Deseada Island	Plundered the Sloops: *Expectation* of Topsham, & the *York* of Bristol. [B2, page 61]	#21
June 1720	Newfoundland Banks	Plundered a Galley, the *Norman*; a Pinque, the *Richard* of Bideford, Jonathan Whitfield, Master; the *Willing Mind* of Poole; plus a ship of 26 guns & its consort sloop.	#25
June 18, 1720	Newfoundland Banks	The *Blessing* from Lymington, Robert Taylor master. [B2, page 31]	#26
June 1720	Ferryland harbour	Newfoundland. Looted one ship and burned an Admiral's ship.	#28
Jun 21, 1720	Trepassey, Newfoundland. Stayed a fortnight.	Avenged 13 Englishmen, Plundered sunk &/or burnt 21 ships, inc. Admiral Babidge's merchant ship, the *Bideford* + 250 fishing. shallops. Laid waste to the hatcheries, costal sheds & machinery, & seized Cap'n Copplestone's Brigantine Galley of Bristol.	#300
June 1720	Newfoundland Banks	Roberts. Plundered the Sloop, *Success*. Cap'n Fensilon.	#301
June 1720	Newfoundland Banks	Plundered the *Phoenix*, a Snow. Cap'n J. Richards of Bristol	#302
Jun 25, 1720	Newfoundland Banks	Plundered & sank the Brigantine, *Sadbury*. Cap'n Thomas. All hands joined	#303
July 1720	St. Mary's Harbour, Newfoundland Banks	Plundered 4+ sloops and an estimated, 5 fishing shallops. [SEE illustration within]	#312
July 1720	Bound for N. Amer. coast	Plundered or sank French Fleet of 6 sail. Captured a 26 gun French ship, christened, the *Good Fortune*, left their Bristol Galley to the French.	#319
July 1720	En route to N. America	4 more French ships plundered.	#323
July 13, 1720	60 leagues East of Newfoundland	Plundered the *Samuel* of London. Cap'n Carey.	#324
July 15&16, 1720	Off New England Coast	Plundered a Bristol Snow, Cap'n Bowles; a Virginian Sloop; & the *Sidbury* also from Bristol.	#327
July 16, 1720	Off Virginia coast	The *Little York*, Bristol. James Phillips, Master	#328
July 17, 1720	Nearing New England	The *Essex*, Robert Peat, Master	#329

BLOOD and SWASH, The Unvarnished Life (& afterlife) Story of Pirate Captain, Bartholomew Roberts............."REFERENCE SECTION"

Date	Location	Event	Ref
July 18, 1720	Off Virginia coast	Plundered the Brigantine, *Love of Lancaster*. Cap'n Thomas	#330
Aug 1720	Isle of Princes	Dutch ship	#331
Aug 1720	Cariacou	Storm. Careened	
Sep 19, 1720		French Sloop	#332
Sep 19, 1720		Rhode Island Brigantine. Cap'n Cane	#333
Sep 1720		Plundered & sunk the Brigantine, *Thomas*.	#334
Sep 26, 1720	Latitude of Deseda	Supplies became dangerously short. Sailed to St. Christophers	
Sep 26, 1720	St. Christophers	Denied provisions. Gale winds hampered forced abandonment the *Royal Rover*. Roberts shelled town in retaliation after Governor hung some of his crew. Captured 1 Portuguese ship in path & burnt another whilst leaving.	#336
Sep 26-27, 1720	Basseterre, St. Christophers	Fired upon. Sent noteworthy letter to Governor. Captured 22 gun French Brig (1st *Royal Fortune*.) The *Mary & Martha*, Thomas Willcocks, Master; the *Greyhound* of Bristol, Cap'n Wilcox, re-named *Ranger*, whose Ship's mate, James Skyrmé, joined Bart's crew; the *Mary* of Boston, Cap'n Henry Fowle; Hinkston's ship (burnt), & 2 more. SEE pages 463 & 4	#343
Oct 1720	En route to Guinea. Latitude of 22°N. Tortola, Virgin Islands	Capturing M. Pomier's French Brig 32 guns + 9 Swivels from Martinique, re-christened her the 2nd *Royal Fortune*. Trading with M. Pomier, who was given the above 22 Gun Brig.	#344
Oct 1720	En route to Brava, southernmost of Cape Verde Islands.	Ill winds forced our return to the West Indies, some 700 leagues off, 124 men & only a hogshead of water. Many lives lost. Put in a the Surinam River, Guinea. Watered.	
Oct 1720	Tobago	Watered ships, learned of two sloops with designs in capturing Cap'n Roberts at Carvocoo.	
Oct 1720	Off St. Christophers	Learned of mistreatment of Cap'n Dunn at Sandy Point. Sank, burnt/seized 15 French & English ships. Captured a Dutch Brigantine the El Puerto del Principe, re-named *Great Ranger*. With the *Royal Fortune* sinking, they seized the 42-gun Dutch interloper which became their 3rd *Royal Fortune*.	#360
Oct 1720	Saint Lucia	Paid call posing as Dutch traders in the *Great Ranger*. Invited islanders to trade at Saint Lucia. Once aboard the Traders were robbed. 2 sloops fired upon them. Traders were put ashore in one ship, remaining 19 were sunk. The Martinicans with bad attitudes were punished for their insolence.	#379
Oct 31, 1720	Bermudas	Plundered & sunk the Brigantine, *Thomas*. CSP-CS18	#380
Nov 1720	A couple days later	the *Happy Return* & the *Mary and Martha*, again. Sunk CSP-PRO1 & B2 pg 57	#382
Dec 1720	Bermudas	Plundered the *Emanuel*	#383
Jan 1721		The Sloop, *Saint Anthony*. Cap'n John Rogers.	#384
Jan 1721	Basseterre Harbour	French fly-boat of cargo of sugar.	#385
Jan 13, 1721	St. Lucia harbour	Departing. burnt Sloop, took Norton's Brigantine, gave him Dutch Interloper CSP-CS17, page 472	#387
Jan 29, 1721	Dominica	The El Puerto del Principe of Flushing.B2	#388
Feb 1721	Off Martinique	Plundered *Mayflower* sloop.	#389
Feb 1721	Sailed to Moonay	Water being too high to careen, they sailed on.	
Feb 1721	Bennet's Key, in the Gulf of Saminah, Hispaniola	Careened, Watered & Provisioned. Capn's Tuckerman & Peter paid Cap'n Roberts a call. Befriended Harry Glaspy. The lot tried for treason Ashplant's speech acquitted Glaspy, other 2 were shot.	

Date	Location	Event	Ref
Feb 1721	Guadalupe	Plundered & burnt a Sloop.	#390
Feb 1721	St. Lucia & Martinique	Burnt 13 Martinican trade ships.	#403
Mar 1721	St. Barthelemy	Rested.	
Mar 26, 1721	Off Antigua	The *Lloyd*, a Galley-Cap'n Hingston.	#404
April 1721	Leeward Islands	Captured a 52 gun French Man-of-War carrying the Governor of Martinique, *Florimond Hurault de Montigny*, who Cap'n Roberts hung from the yardarm of his own ship. 4th *Royal Fortune* (estimated 5 more ships plundered here.)	#410
April 1721	Sailed for Guinea	Plundered a variety of ships. Burnt those who bore masters who possessed arrogance. *(estimated 5)*	#415
Apr 17, 1721	Antigua	Dutch ship, the *Prince Eugene* - Cap'n Bastian Meake	#416
April 1721	Antigua	A small Snow commanded by Nicholas Hendrick. CSP-CS14	#417
April 1721	West Indies	A goodly amount of ill suited Fresh men. Taking on a strict deportment, Bart, whilst giving each crewmen an ultimatum, offered each a duel.	
April 1721	The Caribbean	With shipping now at a virtual stand still in the Caribbean & Governor Spotswood of Virginia having placed a battery of 54 cannon along his coastline, Captain Roberts sought prey in Africa.	
April 1721	Sierra Leone River, Africa.	Captain Roberts crew numbers 508. Ships being: the *Royal Fortune*, the *Sea King*, the *Little Ranger*, & the *Great Ranger*. Learned the, H.M.S. *Swallow* & H.M.S. *Weymouth*, both 4th rate Ships-Of-The-Line, were hunting them.	
April 1721		Cap'n Roberts killed a man for severe insult. Attacked by Thomas Jones, the man's friend, Cap'n Roberts', defensively ran him thro'. Once recovered Jones, as was voted to receive 2 lashes of the cat from each crewman.	
Apr 18, 1721	Some 400 leagues off Africa's west coast.	Thomas Jones conspired with Thomas Anstis, Cap'n of the *Good Fortune*, who felt slighted, departed, taking both the *Good Fortune* & the, *Morning Star*, plus 70 men. Excepting the loss of the supplies, Cap'n Roberts was pleased to be rid of them.	
May 1721	River Senegal, Sierra Leone	Great trade area for gum. Area policed by 2 French warships, the *St. Agnes* & *Comte de Thoulouze*, both of which were seized.	#419
May 1721	Mid-Atlantic	A Dutch Snow, the *Christopher*. Cap'n Thomas.	#420
Jun 11, 1721	Sailed to the Sierra Leone River, Africa	Home to some 30 Englishmen, all retired Pirates, Buccaneers or Privateers. Took a French Merchant in Pirates Bay, taking it to Aberdeen Creek, she was Plundered & Burnt.	#421
Jun 12, 1721	Bense Island	Angered by Gov. Plunkett, Cap'n Roberts attacked his fort on Bense Island. During which an estimated 12 ships were destroyed. SEE Reference page regarding 'A Voyage To Guinea.'	#433
Jun 12, 1721	Returned to Sierra Leone River	Place of rest & gaiety.	
July 1721	Off Axim Coast	A Dutch Galley, the *Semm*.	#434
Aug 1721	Off Grain Coast	The *Robinson* of Liverpool. Cap'n Canning.	#435
Aug 1721	Cape Verd	*Norman* Galley.	#436
Aug 1721	En route to Calabar	Took every ship encountered, inc. the French slave ships, *Saint René*; the *Hermoine*; the *Stanwich*, a Galley, cap'n Tarlton; a Snow; the *Martha*, under Captain Lady; & a Dutch Ship. *estimated 10 total.*	#446

Date	Location	Event	Ref
Sept 1721	Sestos	Captured the *Onslow*. Cap'n Gee, a grand 26 gun Frigate belonging to the Royal African Company. Added 14 cannon. Became their 5th *Royal Fortune*. Needing major repairs, the old *Royal Fortune* was given to Cap'n Gee. Took on soldiers for ¼ share. Attempted to recruit Clergyman.	#447
Oct 5, 1721	Calabar	The *Hannibal*. Cap'n Charles Ousley of London..	#448
Oct 1721	Calabar	Plundered the *Mercy* Galley; the *Cornwall* Galley, Cap'n Rolls; the *Porcupine*, Cap'n Fletcher. Encountering 2,000 Uncooperative natives; burnt village	#451
Fall 1721	Cape Lopez	Took on fresh water.	
Fall 1721	Annobón	Provisioned	
Dec 14, 1721	Gabon	Dutch ship, the *Gertruycht* of Holland. Cap'n Benjamin Kreeft.	#452
Jan 1722	Côte d'Ivoire	Plundered 6 ships, Struck panic.	#458
Jan 2, 1722	Jacque Jacques	The *Elizabeth*. Cap'n Joseph Sharp	#459
Jan 2, 1722	Assinie	The *Tarlton* of Liverpool Cap'n Joseph Trahern.	#460
Jan 3, 1722	Calabar	The *Hannibal* - Cap'n Charles Ousley of London.	#461
Jan 4, 1722	Grand Bassam	Plundered the Dutch ship, *Flushingham*. The ship's master, Geret de Haen, amazed by the crews merriment, dined w/Cap'n Roberts.	#462
Jan 5, 1722	Cape Apollonian	Plundered & Sank the Sloop, *Diligence*. Stephen Thomas, Master	#463
Jan 6, 1722	At Whydah	Sailing in too close during chase & capture of the *King Solomon*, Bart's flotilla was spotted. Alarming the coast, the 4 ships charged with the defence of the town fled.	#464
Jan 11, 1722	At Whydah	Seized 12 slave ships. Freed 10 shiploads of slaves. 1 French ship was kept. Cap'n Roberts ordered the slaves to be released & transported to his ships. Remaining ships were ransomed for 8 lbs Gold-Dust each. Receipts were given. Cap'n Fletcher refusing to pay, the *Porcupine* was burnt. Altho' most of the slaves were transported to Roberts' ships, John Walden & his mate, Harris, failing to free all slaves before torching ship, many perished. Tally 3 English Slave Ships, 5 Portuguese & 4 French ships.	#476
Jan 11, 1722	Whydah Road	French Privateer, the *Comte de Toulouse*.	#477
Jan 1722	Set sail for Annobón	Purpose to Careen ships.	
Jan 13-15 1722	Off Jacquin nigh Whydah	*Whydah* Sloop. Cap'n Stokes of London. Burnt.	#478
Jan 17, 1722	Whydah Road	*Charlton*, Cap'n Allwright	#479
Feb 5, 1722	Parrot Island, within Nigerian estuary.	HMS *Swallow* flew Flag of a Portuguese merchant. *Great Ranger* gave chase. Crew attempted to blow up the ship but insufficient power only wounded them, some mortally. Battle lasted several hours before pirates called for quarter.	
Feb 9, 1722	Gulf of Guinea.	*The Neptune*. Cap'n Thomas Hill.	#480
Feb 10, 1722	Parrot Island	HMS *Swallow* returns. Flying a French flag. Armstrong ID's her. *Little Ranger's* crew boards *Royal Fortune*. Whilst running by H.M.S. *Swallow*, Captain Roberts was killed. With no heart to continue, the pirates called for quarter.	

NOTE: The number of ships 'estimated' above are listed within England's National Archives.

BLOOD and SWASH, The Unvarnished Life (& afterlife) Story of Pirate Captain, Bartholomew Roberts............"REFERENCE SECTION"

DISPOSITION OF CAPTAIN ROBERTS' CREW

The Following Pyrates were executed, according to their Sentence, within the Flood-Marks of Cape-Corso Castle, Africa.[B2]

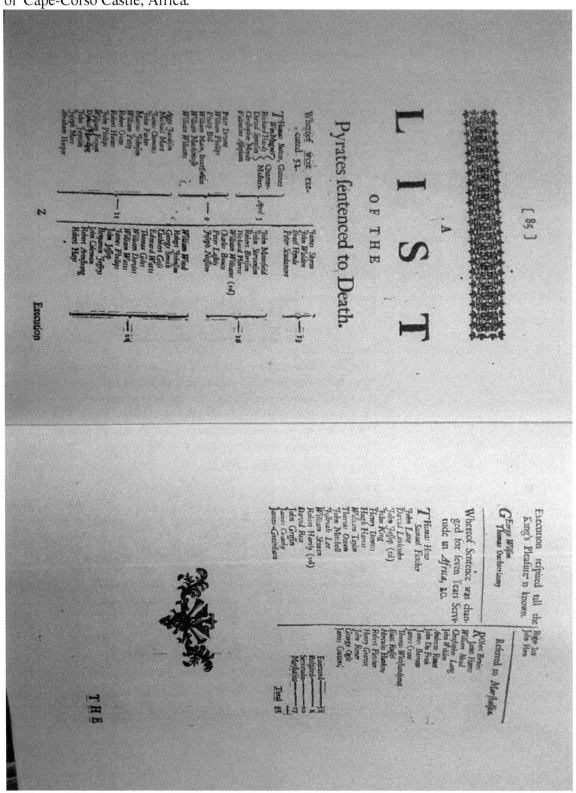

The Remainder of the Pyrates, whose Names are mentioned below, upon their humble Petition to the Court, had their Sentence changed from Death, to seven Years Servitude, conformable to our Sentence of Transportation; the Petition is as follows.

To the Honourable the President and Judges of the Court of Admiralty, for trying of Pyrates, sitting at Cape Corso Castle, Africa the 20th Day of April 1722.

The humble Petition of Thomas How, Samuel Fletches, etc. Humbly sheweth, That your Petitioners being unhappily, and unwarily drawn into that wretched and detestable Crime of Pyracy, for which they now stand justly condemned, they most humbly pray the Clemency of the Court, in the Mitigation of their Sentence, that they may be permitted to serve the Royal African Company of England, in this Country for seven Years, in such a Manner as the Court shall think proper; that by their just Punishment, being made sensible of the Error of their former Ways, they will for the future become faithful Subjects, good Servants, and useful in their Stations, if it please the Almighty to prolong their Lives. And your Petitioners, as in Duty, Etc.

The Resolution of the Court was, that the Petitioners have Leave by this Court of Admiralty, to interchange Indentures with the Captain General of the Gold Coast, for the Royal African Company's Settlements in Africa, in such Manner as he the said Captain General shall think proper.

On Thursday the 26th Day of April, the Indentures being all drawn out, according to the Grant made to the Petitioners by the Court held on Friday the 20th of this Instant; each Prisoner was send for up, signed, sealed and exchanged them in the Presence of Captain Mungo Herdman, President,

James Phipps, Esq;
Mr. Edward Hyde,
Mt. Charles Fanshaw,
And Mr. John Atkins, Register.

The following were Indentured.

Name	Prior Location	Date	Hometown
*Roger Scot	a Dutch Ship	1719	
*David Rice	Cornwall Galley at Calabar	Oct 1721	Bristol
*John Jessup 2	surrender'd up at Princes	Feb/06/1719	Wisbech, Cambridgeshire
*James Cromby	Onslow Cap'n Gee at Sestos	May 1721	London, Wapping
*John Griffin	Mercy Galley at Calabar	Oct 1721	Blackwall, Middlesex
Thomas How	Newfoundland	June 1721	Barnstable, Devon
*John Lane	King Solomon	Jan 1721	Lambard-Street, London
*Samuel Fletcher	King Solomon	Jan 1721	East-Smithfield, London
David Littlejohn	Phoenix, a Snow, Cap'n Richards	July 1721	Bristol
*John King	King Solomon	Jan 1721	Shadwell Parish, London
Henry Dennis	Pyrate w/Davies	1719	Bidiford
Hugh Harris	Willing Mind, of Poole	July 1720	Corfe-Castle, Dorsetshire
*William Taylor	York of Bristol	May 1720	Bristol
*Thomas Owen	York of Bristol	May 1720	Bristol
John Mitchel	the Norman Galley	Oct 1720	Shadwell Parish, London
Joshua Lee	the Martha, a Snow, Cap'n Lady	Aug 1721	Liverpool
William Shurin	Jeremiah and Ann	Apr 1720	Wapping Parish, London
Robert Hartley 1	Robinson of Leverpole, Cap'n Kanning	Aug 1721	Liverpool
John Griffin	the Mercy Galley at Old Calabar	Oct 1721	Blackwall, Middlesex
James Greenham	Little York, a Virginian, Phillips Master	July 1720	Marshfield, Gloucestershire
John Horn	the Onslow, Cap'n Gee at Sestos	Aug 1721	St. James' Parish, London

The following two, viz. were respited form Execution, until his Majesty's Pleasure should be known:

*Thomas Oughterlauney	Cornwall Galley at Old Calabar	Oct 1721	Wisbech, Cambridgeshire
*George Wilson	Tarlton of Liverpool at Cape la Hau	Jan 1721	of Bristol

Supplemental Information regarding Roberts' Crew

Ranger aka *Great Ranger** (32 guns: 77 Englishmen, 16 French & 10 Negroes) Most of the crew being from the *Little Ranger*; 20 of whom be off the *Royal Fortune*. The Balance below were aboard the *Royal Fortune* (40 guns: "152 of which 52 were Negroes [HCA/99/14]") when she struck.

Killed on the Royal Fortune *Royal Fortune*	3
Killed on the *Ranger*	10
Died in Passage to Cape Coast Castle	15
Died after arrival to Cape Coast Castle	4

The **70** Negroes among the Roberts' Company were sold into slavery.

The court records for 28 March 1722 saw 91 sailors stand trial, of whom: 52 were Executed, 20 were sentenced to seven-years servitude in Africa (Indentured,) 17 were sent to Marshalsea prison, and two were granted a respite. None were acquitted [HCA 1/99/181]   Of those Respited one man was eventually freed.

Conflicting information found within different Public Record Offices show discrepancies in names & the number of. To this, the author can only list those records found.

Author's Note: In an attempt to afford Captain Roberts a measure of recompense, I have added the ending of Walter Kennedy.

TAKEN FROM RICHARD SANDERS: "IF A PIRATE I MUST BE…THE TRUE STORY OF "BLACK BART," KING OF THE CARIBBEAN PIRATES

"It was a grisly spectacle. The 'drop,' which snapped the neck, was not perfected until the nineteenth century. During Cap'n Roberts' time, prisoners were simply pushed from a ladder whereby, dying via strangulation; slowly, kicking & writhing, their faces swelling, tongues protruding & eyes popping. At Execution Dock, in Wrapping, (where Kennedy was both born & hanged) friends often attended in order to pull on the legs of the hanged person to hasten the process & spare their suffering. Without this assistance, it could take as long as 45 minutes, & as death neared, prisoners would soil themselves, & their bodies were apt to spasm violently.[B15 sic"] "In the case of Kennedy, having fainted whilst standing upon the gallows, he had to be revived with water before the execution could take place.[B15 sic"]

---

* Called such by Harry Glasby during the Trials[B2].

WELSH AND FOREIGN WORDS, INC. MOST OF THE PHRASES IN THIS BOOK

The characters in this work are not only from different lands but different eras. Our chief protagonist hails from 21st Century America, and the man she loves is an early 18th Century Welshman; that being the case, this book is written in the language of both places & their respective eras; British & American English, & slang. Having several Irishmen, Irish brogue is also present.

DEAR READER, AS TRANSLATIONS ARE PROVIDED BY GOOGLE, PLEASE BE TOLERANT.

WELSH = ENGLISH:

Cymraeg = Welsh — Crymu = Wales — syr = sir — wife = gwraig — I fyny menyw = up woman
fy Anwylyd = my Beloved — fy Annwyl = my dear — un Annwyl = dear one — Hywel = Howell
Hwlffordd = Haverfordwest — Melys = Sweet — Nghariad/Cariad = Love — Dearest = Anwylaf
Mae'r olaf = The Latter — enaid = life/soul — Barti Ddu = Black Bart — Ewch â fi = Take me
Bore Da = Good Morning   Hwyl da = Good Bye   môr-lladron = Pirate/Sea Robbers
Mhwdin = Pudding/Dessert   Gwesty = Inn/Hotel   y môr-leidr mawr = the Great Pirate
Deffro = to wake up/ awake   fy Arglwyddes = my Lady   Iwon Rhobert = John Robert
fy un melys = my sweet one — Diolch yn fawr iawn, fy melys = Thank you very much, my sweet
fy Nghariad anwylaf = my dearest love — fy arglwydd, capten = my lord, captain
Diolch 'chi, fy nghariad anwylafshire (as in Pembrokeshire) = county - also Sir
Nghapten (also Capten) = Captain — am d ragwyddoldeb = For Eternity (feminine)
Ffortun Brenhinol = Royal Fortune — y môr-leidr mawr= the great sea robber (aka pirate)
rhosyn o fy mywyd = Rose of my life fy Rhosyn o nhalon = Rose of my heart   (rhosyn = rose) —
Yr olaf, Capten = The latter, Captain— fy = my (pronounced vn) showing possession
Arglwydd fy nghalon yw fy Nghapten = My captain is the lord of my heart
Diolch yn fawr = Thank you (Diolch 'chi,-NOTE the apostrope) Diolch = Thanks
Casnewydd Bach (also Nghastell Newydd Bach-this wordage, whilst printed on the village limits from one direction, the former is on the other) = Little Newcastle.
Crempogau or crempog are Welsh buttermilk pancakes
Gariad a dechreuadau newydd = love and new beginnings
fy Nghapten i = my Captain (i = possessive, e.g. showing one's love)   i = (pronounced e)
Prynhawn da, fy arglwyddes = Good afternoon, my Lady

Deffrwch fy melys -or Deffro fy melys = Wake up my sweet

Mae'd bleser eich cyfarfod chi o'r diwedd = it's a pleasure to meet you at last.

Prynhawn da, Capten. Croeso ar fwrdd Caeth Yn fodlon y = Good afternoon, Captain. Welcome to the Willing Captive.

Fy enw i yw Aspasia, Nghapten, ac er fy mod i'n hanner Ffrangeg, yrdw i, fel chithau, yn ffyrnig o falch o'm treftadaeth Gymreig. = My name is Aspasia, Captain, and although I am half French, I like you, am fiercely proud of my Welsh heritage.

☠×☠×☠×☠×☠×☠×☠

FRENCH: mon Captaine = **my Captain** — dame d'atou = **Lady-In-Waiting**
Monsieur et Madame = **Mister and Misses** — Mademoiselle = **Miss (unmarried)**
jouissance de la vie exubérante = **enjoyment of exuberant life**
ou y a-t-il une autre raison, peut-être physique, qui explique votre respiration excitée? = **Or is there another reason, perhaps physical, that explains your aroused breathing?**
Ce dernier, Capitaine = **The latter, Captain.**

FOREIGN WORDS & PHRASES WITHIN THIS BOOK - continued

SPANISH: Gracias = Thank You — Señor = Mister — Señora = Mrs — Señorita = Miss
Sí = Yes — Bueno Días = Good Day

PORTUGUESE: Vou esperar por você hoje = I shall wait upon you presently.
Você está bom, capitão? = Are you well, Captain? — Sua presença é necessária. A questão da comunicação confidencial de alguma importância. = Your presence is needed. A matter of confidential communication of some importance.
Não sacrificar-se para a gente como nós = Do not sacrifice yourself for the likes of us
Por favor Capitão, não interferem = Please Captain, do not interfere.
Mas, minha Dama = But, my lady. — Capitão-de-Mar-e-Guerra = Captain of a War Ship.
Todos os passenders deve retornar para seus quartos.= All passengers must return to their rooms. — O suficiente para sobreviver, o capitão = Enough to get by, Captain.
Sim, tripulante? = Yes, crewman? — Baía de Todos os Santos = All Saints' Bay, Brazil.
Essas ordens não me incluem!— Those orders do not include me!
Bem-vindo a bordo, minha Dama. = Welcome aboard, my Lady. — Mrs = Senhora
Têm, Tenente Garcia relatório para mim ele de uma vez = Have Lieutenant Garcia report to me at once. — Mas estou feliz aqua = But I'm happy here. — Por favor = Please
Lamento, minha Dama. Ordens do Capitão.= I'm sorry, my Lady, Captain's orders.
você deve chegar até você cabina, agora! = You must get to your cabin, now!

The letter below (used with permission,) concerns the Tea Captain Roberts was so fond of.

BLOOD and SWASH, The Unvarnished Life (& afterlife) Story of Pirate Captain, Bartholomew Roberts............."REFERENCE SECTION"

The Following Six Documents were gathered, in person, at their source, by the author.

#1: Traces one line of Captain Roberts family tree to his father, George Roberts (whose name is located in the County Hearth Tax Record.) The reader needs to keep in mind that the "s" on the end of the surname, in keeping with the time period, was added & omitted at random.

```
                George Roberts (Hearth Tax 1670).
                        |    ?
        ┌───────────────┴───────────────┐
   Cptn. John Roberts            William. (Welsh Will)
                                     ├──────────┬────────┐
                                  William    Thomas
                                  John = Martha.
                                  d. 1806
                    ┌────────────────┬─────────────┐
                   ↓              Thomas        Wllm = Jane.
                              (garden named     Reed
                               after him)        │
                                                John
                                                 ├──────↓
                                              William
                                                 ├──────↓
                                              William.
                                                 │
                             A. Vaughan    =    Harriet Mary
                              Davies              Reed.
                                   ├──────────────↓
                                 Norman
                                   │
                                 Richard

                              7 great nephew
```

446

#2: Listing of Captain Roberts siblings, shows he had 3 brothers; and that two were named William. The natural conclusion would be that the first son born William died, and when another son was born, he too was named William (a common occurrence back when childhood mortality averaged about 40%.) In this case; however, as both being alive at the same time, we must conclude that either John Bartholomew's mother had died and his father took a 2nd wife who had a son from a previous marriage also named William or that John Bartholomew was born to his father's 2nd wife. In either case, they were half brothers.

45

ABSTRACT OF WILL/ADMINISTRATION		NAME:	WILLIAM ROBERT	
EPISCOPAL CONSISTORY COURT OF ST. DAVIDS			Division (if any)	
Library Call Number 105,245	Type of Document WILL	Residence St Michael's (Presumed)		
Date 23 Mar 1743/4	Place Requested for Burial		Date of Death	
Date of Probate/Grant	Occupation			Number 45(1744)

PERSONS AND PLACE NAMES

Name	Relationship	Occupation	Residence	Properties Mentioned
John ROBERT	Son			
William ROBERT	Son			
Thomas ROBERT	Son			
William ROBERT	Bro			
Thomas ROBERT	Bro			

Executors

Bondsmen

Witnesses: John ROBERT – John THOMAS

Other Information: Will written in Welsh.

PEMBROKESHIRE RECORD OFFICE
REFERENCE Wills Abstract Fiche
DATE 29.3.04
COPYRIGHT RESERVED

PFGS1462

BLOOD and SWASH, The Unvarnished Life (& afterlife) Story of Pirate Captain, Bartholomew Roberts..............."REFERENCE SECTION"

#3: Is it well known that Bartholomew Roberts was fluent in English. The 'Last Will & Testament,' below, written by William Roberts (as referred to in the above document,) is brother of John 'Bartholomew' Roberts (aka Captain Roberts.) Such not only proves they were half brother, but also that Welsh was Captain Roberts' native tongue. Knowing also, from a particular book Captain Roberts carried, "Almagestum" by Claudius Ptolemaeus - Translated From Greek into Latin in 1515, yet not having been translated in to English until the 20th Century, we must conclude he could read Latin as well, & as a result we must deduce he possessed an excellent education.

#4: English Translation of the above Welsh Will (graciously translated by Richard Davies of Little Newcastle; now the Reverend Davies) shows more members of the Captain's family than shown within the One Line of the Family Tree. It is noteworthy that this document shows how the family name intermittently adds an "s" at the end of the name (again, a common practice during the period.)

March 23rd in the year 1744.   B.B.C.S.

This is my wish and last will of me William Robert and this is the order I put my house and possession. I give all my possessions to John Robert my son, but that John Robert is to give £40 to William Robert my son and his horse and saddle, and these possessions I give to John Roberts my son and his chest also. John Roberts is also to give from these possessions £5 to Thomas Roberts my son and John Roberts am committed to pay £40 to William Robert my brother and his horse and saddle and chest a year next Michaelmas and I John Roberts am committed to pay £5 to Thomas Roberts my brother a year next Michaelmas. I commit William Robert my son to stay with John Roberts my son 2 years for his food, his drink, his clothes and some money in his pocket, unless he marries beforehand, an if he does marry he is free to go where he pleases and I William Robert in this my last will do give two year heifer to William Robert my son in addition

---

A true + perfect inventory of all the goods, cattles and chattels of William Robert of the parish of Newcastle in the county of Pembroke - yeoman, lately deceased viewed and apprized by us whose names are hereunto subscribed the 13 day of April 1744 as followeth.

8 oxen + all other the particulars in the schedule hereunto mentioned amounting in the whole to the sum of £19 .. 17s .. 5d.

#5: PRO listing of Wills of the period depicting William Robert's as a Landowner (inherited from his father, was the eldest living son.) In former times, yeoman meant he was free and cultivated his own land. For those of you tracing your family tree please note the number families in Pembrokeshire having the surname Robert/Roberts. Remember also that this list only contains those who had actually had written Wills, & also that this is ONLY one page among several.

#6: Below, graciously made available by Richard Davies of Little Newcastle; now the Reverend Davies, is a copy of one of the pages from the record book within Saint Peter's Parish in Little Newcastle. It lists the last person carrying the family surname who was buried in Little Newcastle's Churchyard.

BLOOD and SWASH, The Unvarnished Life (& afterlife) Story of Pirate Captain, Bartholomew Roberts............"REFERENCE SECTION"

THE FOLLOWING DOCUMENT IS A COPY OF THE TRIAL PROCEEDINGS. Until it was pinched, I had a copy of the entire, original document, and with MANY THANKS TO MARK KEHOE (www.pirate surgeon.com) I now have a typed copy.

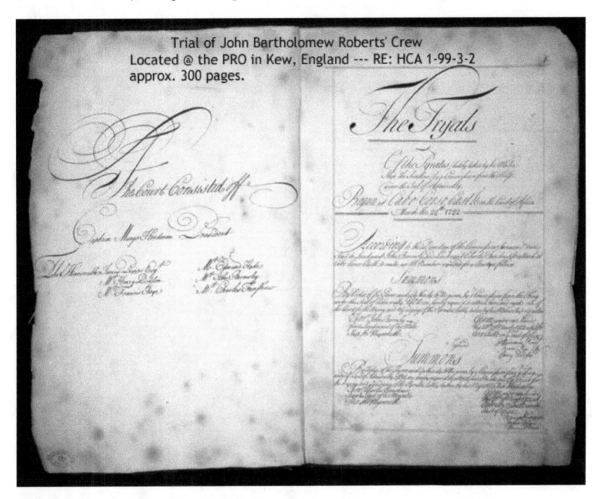

Whilst at the Pubic Record Office 'PRO' in Kew, which is located not to far from London, England, I was able to make photographic copies of a wealth of information. The Tryals, front page, as shown above, is among the multitude of pictures I took with a digital camera, which were fairly new at the time. I also have copies of ALL of the letters written by Woodes Rogers containing pertinent info; both are loaded with invaluable information concerning Captain Roberts.

V'léOnica Roberts

*It's my intention to put out a copy of the Original Tryals transcript in 2023/24. Look for it on Amazon.

BLOOD and SWASH, The Unvarnished Life (& afterlife) Story of Pirate Captain, Bartholomew Roberts............."REFERENCE SECTION"

Below are copies of two of the ORIGINAL DEATH SENTENCES prescribed to some of those belonging to Captain Roberts' crew who where hung for piracy.

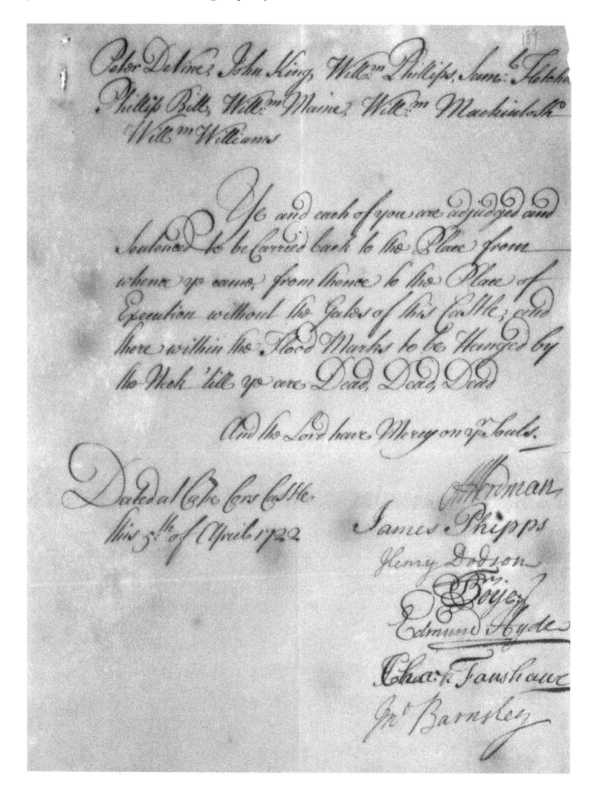

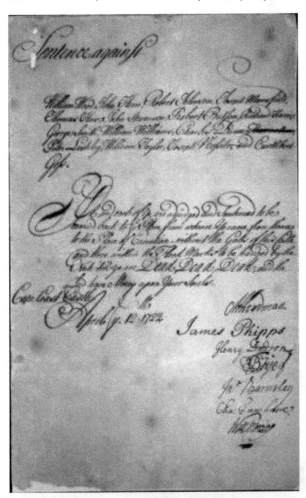

This picture below, which pre-dates digital cameras, is a portion of a letter written by Captain Roberts. This document is/was held at the Haslemere Museum Public Record Office[B3]. It is said that Cap'n Roberts, who wrote in a fine hand, wrote a lot[B3], and the above named PRO has many of his writings.

The author has hope of acquiring a copy of the entire document below, as wells as other documents written by Cap'n Roberts.

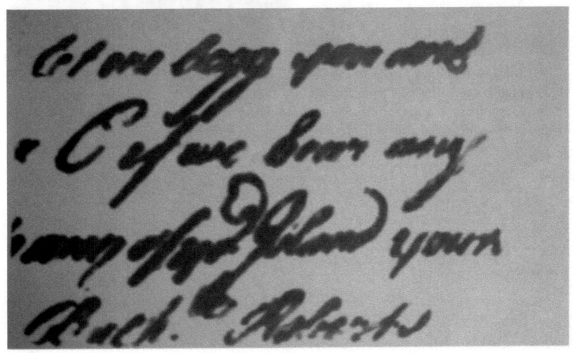

Mrs Reese of Little Newcastle, (well into her 80s in 2004 whose husband was 85, told the Author that the painting below depicts Captain Roberts' home as a boy. The house, which lies in the background with the red brick chimney was the main house. It is still occupied by descendants of the Roberts' family. The smaller house in the foreground on the left (3 bedrooms) also belonged to the family, which was a rental in 2005, has since been sold.

Of the two buildings in the foreground, one on each side of the tree, the house on the left, which is situated across from the village green upon which rests the monument (shown below) honouring Captain Bartholomew Roberts, sits across the green from St. Peter's, Little Newcastle's own charming church.

Saint Peter's Church, Little Newcastle.

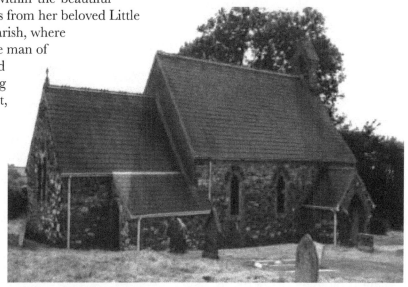

Altho' it is the author's pride to say that while she had the good fortune to live within the beautiful country of Wales, only 10 miles from her beloved Little Newcastle, and its charming parish, where she was not only married to the man of her dreams, & so much looked forward to not only attending the only church she cares about, but to also be able to help out there wherever she was able, it is too her great dismay & sadness, despite her many efforts, that she has yet been able to return; will never she quit trying, even if all she achieves is to be buried there, where, knowing she is home, & safe, at last, she can, at least, Rest in Peace.

The Medieval building, once partially demolished (repaired during the 18th century restorations,) retains the 12th century Baptismal Font, as well as a beautiful memorial plaque honouring the Symmons family who are also relations to the Roberts' family line.

This monument (right,) which stands on the village green where a Castle once stood, was erected in Captain Roberts' honour by those residing in and around the village of Little Newcastle.

Little Newcastle Parish can be seen in the background at the far side of the village green.

The road that rounds the green is surrounded by homes, both farmland & grazing land, & a Racing Stable comprises the gist of the ever charming village.

The Author wishes the monument stated the pirate Captain's name, John Bartholomew Roberts, & <u>NOT</u> Barti Ddu (Black Bart,) which was merely an invention for a poem.

CALENDAR OF STATE PAPERS,

COLONIAL SERIES,

AMERICA AND WEST INDIES,

MARCH, 1720 to DECEMBER, 1721.

PRESERVED IN THE

PUBLIC RECORD OFFICE.

EDITED BY

CECIL HEADLAM, M.A.

ISSUED BY THE AUTHORITY OF THE LORDS COMMISSIONERS OF HIS MAJESTY'S TREASURY
UNDER THE DIRECTION OF THE MASTER OF THE ROLLS.

LONDON:
PUBLISHED BY HIS MAJESTY'S STATIONERY OFFICE.

1933.

> *Author's Note:* The following page has been placed here for the express purpose of putting an end to the discrepancy regarding the name of Cap'n Roberts' 1st ship, the Rover. Originally named Marquis del Campo, the Dutch East~Indianman was a 3-Masted Sloop-of-War of 30 guns belonging to his Imperial Majesty taken by Cap'n Hywel Davies, who added 2 Cannon & 7 Swivel Guns, renamed the ship, the Rover. Later, after Davies was dead, and after Bahía, Cap'n Roberts, & others having been gone for 9 days on a chase, the ship's Quarter-Master, Walter Kennedy, & the rest of the Rover's crew who, feeling they had waited long enough, took both the Rover & the Sagrada Familia & departed. Afterwards, Kennedy renamed the Rover, Royal Rover. Cap'n Roberts', Royal Rover, was the name given to the ship that replaced the Fortune, immediately after Trepassey.

Facsimile

CALENDAR OF STATE PAPERS,
AMERICA AND WEST INDIES, MARCH, 1720 to DECEMBER, 1721.

11

Excerpt

March 28. Nevis. 28. Governor Hamilton to the Council of Trade and Plantations. *Refers to* his orders to Capt. Rose, *v.* 16th Feb. Proving calm he left [*the pirate ship*] at an anchor at St. Christopher's and came up himself [*to me at Nevis*]. She was called amongst the pirates by the name of the *Royal Rover*, and has committed a great many depredations upon the coast ship they called the *King James* which they sunk and betook themselves to this. She is a ship of force capable of mounting 30 guns and had once near 200 men (and as far as I can learn) was in the service of His Imperial Majesty when she was taken but she is now much out of order for which reason I suppose they quitted her. As I have met with a vast deal of trouble and opposition from some persons who would have disputed with me the power I had of seizing her I think it my duty to lay before your Lordships a distinct account of the manner in which the ship was taken, and the measures that were took to prevent my securing of her either for H.M. or for the Right Honourable the Lord High Admiral *etc.* The crew that belonged to her came to a separation some betook themselves to a snow and some to the sloop mentioned in Mr. Popple's letter the rest (to what number I cannot discover) either being weary of that sort of life or thinking they had got booty enough resolved to steal ashore in such places as they thought they were most likely to escape undiscovered in, or where they might pass unquestioned according the six mentioned (16*th Feb.*) were landed upon Anguilla pretending to be shipwreckt but being detected and brought up here have since been tried, found guilty and received sentence of death, the residue carried the ship down to St. Thomas's (an Island the Danes are settled upon) brought her to an anchor there out of the reach of their cannon and went themselves on shoar and passed publickly (as I am informed) as Pirates, and were so far from being questioned for it that the Governor himself was in treaty with them for the ship, as the persons who brought her away have represented to me. Major Holmes etc. seized her as a pirate, what men were then in her quitting her and making their escape on shoar, *etc. as* 16*th Feb.* Signed, W. Hamilton. *Enclosed* Recd. 16th May, 1720, Read 27th June, 1721. 3½ *pp.*

BLOOD and SWASH, The Unvarnished Life (& afterlife) Story of Pirate Captain, Bartholomew Roberts............"REFERENCE SECTION"

ONE OF MANY EXAMPLES OF CAP'N ROBERTS TAKING ONLY SUBSISTENCE

pg 18

Facsimile

CALENDAR OF
STATE PAPERS
AMERICA AND WEST INDIES,
MARCH, 1720 to DECEMBER, 1721.

March 31. 33. Lt. Governor Bennett to Mr. Popple. *Refers to* triplicate enclosure
Bermuda of proceedings of Court of Admiralty *etc. Signed* Ben. Bennett.
Endorsed, Recd. 10th May, Read 7th July, 1720. 1p.

part 1: 33. i. Bermuda. May 31st, 1720. A Newspaper. By the master of a sloop that arrived here 21st Jan. from Virginia I am informed, that about the middle of the same month on (*e*) Capt. Knott bound to that place from London in the latitude 27 was come up with and taken by a pirate ship of 36 guns and above 160 men who took what they wanted out of the merchantman and gave him money and goods of a very considerable value for the same and sent him about his business several of the pirates being on board him, whom when the ship arrived in Virginia dispersed themselves but being discovered were taken up, also the ship seized, and the Capt. in custody; the pirate came last from Brazile and had been on the coast of Guinea.---

**MORE REGARDING AFTERMATH FOLLOWING KENNEDY ABSCONDING WITH ROVER
SEE 251. iv. below for more info**

part 3: I hear of several British and French sloops that have been taken to windward amongst the French and the Islands inhabited by the Indians, but what certainty there is in it I know not; but this is confirmed [that] seized, and the Capt. in custody; the pirate came last from Brazile and a pirate ship that took some time since a Portugueze ship upon the coast of Brazile which he carried to Cayon a French Island, and there

pg 19 plundered her, and there took also a Rhode Island sloop, and after detaining the master for some days, he gave him the Portugueze ship with which he is arrived at Antigua, the pirate went afterwards to the windward of Barbadoes, where he took two New York snows, the one he plundered and afterwards gave the vessel to the master and men again, the other they have fitted out of the pirate ship she being a much better sailor, and are gone to the northward with, and gave the the ship to the master of the snow; his men and some others that pre- to have been forced, of which they landed five white men and one black upon Anguilla, of which number there are now two in goal at Antigua and the rest are sent for they say the Quartermaster of the pirate and one more were on board the said ship, from whence, and their haveing divided their plunder to the windward of Barbadoes (as these men say) it is concluded they have broke up and are shifting for themselves by dropping some in one place, some in another, for they had a great booty in the Brazile ship, at least 15,000 moidores besides a vast quantity of dust gold they had got upon the coast of Guinea, where they had taken many prizes. Same endorsement. 1*pp.*

AMERICA AND WEST INDIES.   105

1720.

Aug. 17.
Treasury Chambers.
198. Mr. Tilson to Mr. Popple. When Mr. West was appointed *etc.* (*v.* 6th May), it was intended that the standing fee of £100 guineas pr. annum apeice to the Attorney and Sollicitor General and 10 guineas pr. annum to each of their Clerks should cease, and that the Board of Trade should (as often as they might have occasion to apply for the opinion of either of them) give the usual fee for such their opinion, and bring the expence thereof into the Contingent bill of their Office. The Lords Commrs. of H.M. Treasury desire that their Lordships may take their measures accordingly *etc. Signed,* Chris. Tilson. *Endorsed,* Recd. 25th, Read 26th Aug. 1720. *Addressed.* 1 *p.* [*C.O.* 388, 77. *No.* 84; *and* 389, 37. *pp.* 188, 189.]

Aug. 18.
Whitehall.
199. Mr. Delafaye to the Council of Trade and Plantations. Upon your representation of 16th inst. *etc.*, the Lords Justices direct that you give all possible dispatch to the report you are to lay before them of what is further necessary to be done for the safety of Carolina, *etc. Signed,* Ch. Delafaye. *Endorsed,* Recd. Read 19th Aug., 1720. 1 *p.* [*C.O.* 5, 358. *ff.* 11, 12*v.*]

Aug. 19.
Boston,
N. England.
200. Governor Shute to the Council of Trade and Plantations. *Encloses following.* I shall by the next ship send an account of the stores of New Hampshire. Since I sent an answer to the Query relating to the manufactures of this country I have been informed that there are some camblets and druggets made in the country and sent to some of the shops in Boston, but I don't observe that they are worn by any but the ordinary people. I hope I shall quickly receive some answer relating to the affair of the Speaker mentioned 1st June *etc.* For tho' in the next Assembly they chose another Speaker, I find they still persist in the opinion that the King's Govr. has no negative upon the Speaker. Capt. Carey who left London 29th May was taken by a pirate ship of 26 guns and a sloop of 10 near the banks of Newfoundland who took and destroyed so much of his cargo as amounts to about £8000 sterling; and also reports that they had fallen upon and destroy'd the fishery of Newfoundland. *Signed,* Samll. Shute. *Endorsed,* Recd. 27th Sept. 1720, Read 7th March, 17$\frac{20}{21}$. 2 *pp. Enclosed,*

> 200. i, ii. Accounts of the stores of war expended and remaining at H.M. Castle William, Boston, June 24th, 1720. *Signed,* Zec. Tuthill, Lt. *Endorsed as preceding.* 2 *pp.* [*C.O.* 5, 868. *ff.* 5–6, 7*v.*–9 (*with abstract*).]

Aug. 20.
Whitehall.
201. Mr. Secretary Craggs to the Council of Trade and Plantations. Enclosed I transmit a Memorial setting forth the reasons why a Comptroller should be appointed over the King's Woods in New England, and as H.M. is inclined to confer

AMERICA AND WEST INDIES. 165

1720.

Sept. 29. **250.** Office accounts of the Board of Trade, June 24–Sept. 29, 1720. *v.* Journal of Council. [*C.O.* 388, 77. *Nos.* 94, 96, 98.]

Oct. 3. **251.** Governor Hamilton to the Council of Trade and
Antigua. Plantations. *Refers to enclosures. Continues:* By which you will perceive that these seas are again infested with pirates of considerable force *etc.*, who on the 27th and 28th of the last month openly and in the daytime burnt and destroyed our vessels in the Road of Basseterre, and had the audaciousness to insult H.M. Fort *etc.* (*v.* encl. i.) *Continues:* The *Rose* man of war and *Sharke* sloop arrived here some time in June last, but so much shattered with beating the seas, that the Capt. told me soon after his arrival that the ship was almost unfit for service very foul, and her upper works so tender that he durst not heave her down: and there being no place of hauling her ashore here, nor conveniencies to refit her, and the hurricane time coming on I thought it necessary and for H.M. service to condescend to the Captain's request which was to let him go to the Northward to refit upon promise that he would return about the middle of this month. I hear by a ship arrived from Boston that she is safe arrived there but that he cannot be with me till the latter end of November next and indeed had he been here 'tis much to be feared he would not have been able to have coped with them, tho' on my part he should have had all the assistance possible. In my letters of the 15th March 1717 the 6th of Jan. 17|⅞ and the 19th Dec. following I humbly desired your Lordships to represent to H.M. how uncapable so small a ship as the *Seaford* was (or indeed any ship of that force as this towitt the *Rose* is) was to protect the Trade from the insults of these vermine, and that such ship would be in danger of being overpowered even when she went out to cruise on them and at the same time I desired that your Lordships would represent to H.M. that a fifth rate or at least a ship of 36 or 40 guns, might be appointed *etc.*, to which your Lordships were pleased to answer that you had been informed several of the pirates had surrendered *etc.*, and that you hoped the rest would follow *etc.* upon H.M. Proclamation of pardon, but your Lordsships may now plainly perceive how little Acts of Grace and Mercy work on these vermine (several of these present pirates have, as I have been informed, surrendered more than once upon H.M. said Proclamation) and that nothing but force will subdue them; and I daresay had we a ship of that force we should not only drive them out of these seas, but in some measure prevent their doing further mischief, for they come among these Islands not so much for gain, but to pick up straglers, and victual their ships for other enterprises. I come now once more as it is my duty to lay these matters

166   COLONIAL PAPERS.

1720.

before your Lordships, and humbly hope you will agree with me in opinion how necessary it will be for H.M. service, and the protection of our Trade that such a ship as I before mentioned should be sent on this station, and that your Lordships will represent this matter to H.M. and use your good offices towards procuring such a one *etc.* We are small Colonies and subsist chiefly on trade; if our homeward bound vessels are taken and plundered and our provision ships intercepted, what have we that lyes not at the mercy of these villains? *Signed,* W. Hamilton. *Endorsed,* Recd. 5th, Read 9th Dec., 1720. 2¾ pp. *Enclosed,*

    251. i. Extract of letter from Lt. General Mathew to Governor Hamilton, 29th Sept. 1720. [*St. Christophers*]. Upon the information of James Dennison (*encl. ii*), I had the sloop *referred to* examined, an inventory made, and refer Mr. Thomas Otley's claim to the goods to your Excellency *etc. Continues:* Tuesday about one of the clock Lt. Isaac Thomas sent me an express with notice that these pirates were actually coming into Basse Terre Road. I immediately ordered Lt. McKenzie to Charles Fort and put a subaltern and 30 of the Militia therein. Ordered Lt. Coll. Payne to get the two companys under arms at Sandy Point Town, Capt. Nat. Paine to do the like at Old Road, Major Willet at Palmeto Point, with orders to the gunners at these four places to be in readiness, and then rode to Basse Terre. I gat there by two found the pirates ship and sloop with black flaggs *etc*, had cut out one ship that was under sail actually then, and had set two more on fire, and our Battery without powder or ball rammer or gun (except two) fit for any service, and everything in confusion. I took from Mr. Hare's store by force 7½ barrels of powder, Mr. Parsons furnished a half barril pickt up about town, some shot big and little got four small three pounders from Mr. Peter Thomas mounted on the beach with some shot for them, and two more of the guns on the battery in order, and we had then a small cannonading for about an hour, but what with bad gunners unsizable shot *etc.* we did them no hurt and they went out of reach for that afternoon and night, this gave me some time to remedy our confusons *etc.* The ship they had taken belonged to one Fowls consigned to Mr. Parsons. Fowls with two of his men goes off to them just before I gat to town, and was kept on board. One Hinkston (whose behaviour savored much of knave or coward) had a ship in the Road which they set on fire, tho' there were 500 barrels of beef in, he had it seems sent his boat on board them of his own

1720.

accord, which with his men they also detained, as they went out of the Road I perceived she burned but slowly *etc*. *With the aid of William Panton gets her ashore and puts out fire. Continues:* By the time the night was closed and every man had got his post along the Bay *etc*. Capt. Hinkston's men came on shoar from the Pirate, and brought me the letters (*enclosed*) *etc*. In the morning [*the pirates still*] lay off Basse Terre, waiting for these sheep. We got by this time 13 great guns in good order among them a 24 pounder, and had got shot from Palmeto Point and cartridge paper from Old Road, about 9 the pirate sloop stood directly in, and just about gun shot off a boat put off from her, and she stood out again, the boat brought on shore Capt. Fowles and one of his men and another man whom they would have forced, but his unwillingness and being troubled with fits made them put him on shore, this man is under a guard, and I wait the Sollicitor General's opinion about him having sent to him to examine him close. About 11 the sloop stood in again for these sheep *etc*. (for Capt. Fowl's forsooth could hardly be kept from going to them again hoping to have his ship *etc*.) The sloop came close in almost among our sloops, and we had time to give her two rounds of all our guns of which 7 hit her tore her gibb setled her made [= ? *main*] sail by cutting the hallyards 'tis supposed, and we believe one of the 24 pd. ball. took her in the bow. She made no return but got out as well as she could and shee and the ship ran into the Grand Golett and there turned Fowls ship adrift. I wish they may not have got some of your Excellency's mutton for their boat went on shoar *etc*. They stretched for Nevis, could not fetch hardly Morton's Bay; so stood away westward along shore. We brought Fowls' ship in again and found this fine distich in chalk on the companion

    For our words sake we let thee go
    But to Creoles we are a foe—

or something of remembering Creoles as a foe, and a Death's head and arm with a Cutlace, and on board Hinkston they had versifyed in chalk

        In thee I find
        Content of mind.

They standing along shore I got on horseback leaving the care of all at Basse Terre to Col. McDowal, and with about 70 horse and dragoons waited on them as far as Old Road, *etc*. This morning at 10 they were seen for the last time to the N. ward and E. of St. Bartholomews *etc*. Col. McDowal, Major Milliken,

168   COLONIAL PAPERS.

1720.

Mr. Spooner, Mr. Hunt and Mr. Thos. Otley gave me all imaginable assistance *etc. Recommends* Peter Thomas to command the troop of horse of Basse Terre. *Continues:* These villains are certainly going to windward of Antego and Barbados *etc.* They want bread and will wait some New England vessels coming. They offer any price for Mr. Pinney, Spooner and Brown for condemning their comrades at Nevis, threaten and bluster much and have intelligences off this island in particular that I am surprised at. *Same endorsement. Copy.* 3¾ *pp.*

251. ii. Deposition of James Dennison, gunner of Fort Hamilton, St. Christophers, 25th Sept. 1720. Deponent arrested Robert Dunn (*v. following*) whom he found landing goods out of a canoe. Dunn endeavoured to prevent him from examining the sloop *etc. Signed,* James Dennison. *Same endorsement. Copy.* 2 *pp.*

251. iii. Deposition of Robert Dunn, Master of the Sloop *Relief*, Jeremiah Burroughs owner, of Bermuda. Turtling in the harbour of Curriwaccoo on 4th Sept., he was seized by a pirate ship and sloop, commanded by one Roberts, of Barbados, about 130 men all told. The remnant of the *Royal Rover's* crew are in this gang. The ship they took on the banks of Newfoundland, French-built, and one of 21 they took there *etc.* The pirates dismissed deponent after putting on board his sloop some bundles of old rigging and cloth *etc.* in return for his tending them with turtles *etc.* which they made him do. They said they intended to take Marygalante. They intend to take their revenge off Antego and Barbados and then go on the coast of Brazil or the East Indies. They would blow up rather than be taken. Every man double armed, and mostly Englishmen. Say they will when they leave these coasts take none but Spanish and Portuguese *etc. Signed,* Robert Dunn. *Dated and endorsed as preceding. Copy.* 2 *pp.*

251. iv. Deposition of Moyse Renos, (Moses Renolds, or Renault,) of Dartmouth, Mariner. St. Christophers, 26th Sept., 1720. Was taken by a pirate sloop when on a fishing voyage on the Banks of Newfoundland in a pink belonging to William Cane of St. Johns. Within five or six days they took four or five prizes amongst them a vessell of Bristol one Thomas Commander who formerly used to trade to Barbados they intended to use him ill but he giving them an account that a ship and sloop was fitted out of Barbados to pursue them (for they had been in the *Royall Rover* in these seas)

AMERICA AND WEST INDIES. 169

1720.

and that it was reported at Barbados they had sunk the said pyrates, they in their merriments hereon returned him his ship and dismissed him but took two or three of his men by force who made their escape afterwards. Thence they went to Trepassi, and found in the harbour 22 sail of English bankers and fishers, of these they took one and in 10 days fitted her out with 18 guns for their own use oblidgeing the crews of all the ships to work and of the severall crews five or six took on willingly with them *etc*. They forced three or four more but only took provisions and left all the rest of the vessells there except one they burnt *etc*. They next took 5 or 6 sail of French bankers, among them the ship they are now in, putting the Frenchmen on board the ship they took at Trepassi, for they would not force or permit any of any nation to be with them only English *etc*. *Corroborates preceding. Signed,* Moyse Renos. *Endorsed as preceding. Copy.* 2¼ *pp.*

251. v. Inventory of goods taken on board the sloop *Relief*. (v. *Nos.* i. and iii.) *Same endorsement. Copy.* 2 *pp.*

(a) Bartholomew Roberts, the Pirate, to Lt. General Mathew. *Royall Fortune,* Sept. 27th, 1720. This comes expressly from me to lett you know that had you come off as you ought to a done and drank a glass of wine with me and my company I should not harmed the least vessell in your harbour. Farther it is not your gunns you fired yt. affrighted me or hindred our coming on shore but the wind not proving to our expectation that hindred it. The *Royall Rover* you have already burnt and barbarously used some of our men but we have now a ship as good as her and for revenge you may assure yourselves here and hereafter not to expect anything from our hands but what belongs to a pirate as farther Gentlemen that poor fellow you now have in prison at Sandy point is entirely ignorant and what he hath was gave him and so pray make conscience for onee let me begg you and use that man as an honest man and not as a C if we hear any otherwise you may expect not to have quarters to any of your Island yours, *Signed,* Bathll. Roberts. *Copy.* ½ p.

(b) Henry Fowle to James Parsons. Sept. 27, 1720. *Requests him* to send in the morning some sheep goats *etc.* in a boat to the pirates. "I am treated very civilly and promised to have my ship and cargo again and desire Capt. Henksone to send his wheel that he stears his ship with, or it may be the worse for him" *etc. Signed,* Henry Fowle. *Copy.* ½ p. *The whole endorsed as preceding.* [*C.O.* 152, 13. *ff.* 20–21v., 23–24v., 25v.–26v., 27v.–28v., 29v.–32v., 33v., 34, 35v.]

EXTRAS FROM THE CALENDAR STATE PAPERS REGARDING CAPTAIN ROBERTS.

CALENDAR OF STATE PAPERS,
AMERICA AND WEST INDIES, MARCH, 1720 to DECEMBER, 1721

Facsimile

Oct. 31. **277. ii.** Lt. Governor Bennett to the Council of Trade and Plantations. St. Christophers. Two private vessels, one a ship of 34 guns, the other a sloop of 6 guns, haveing on board them both 130 men cut out of Bassetere road a loaded ship and burnt another that had begun to take in sugar, that cut out they kept two days and then gave her to the Capt. without doeing much damage : these pirates have been at Newfoundland and and had burnt, sunk and taken above 20 sail *etc. Signed,* Ben. Bennett. *Endorsed,* Reed. 20th March, 172$\frac{0}{1}$, Read 13th June, 1722. 1*p*. [*C.O.* 37,10. *Nos.* 25, 25. i., ii.]
Barbados.

Excerpt

281. i. Lt Governor Gledhill to Mr. Secretary Craggs. Placentia, July 3, 1720. If what these proclamations suggests that H.M. intentions are to destroy or remove the fishery, the pyrates are doing it effectually. There are many ships drove in here by the pyrates who infest our coast *etc. Refers to his* scheme for making roads *etc. v.* 1st Oct. 1719. *Continues :—*These Pyrates have now destroyed near 150 boats and 26 ships at Trepassy and St. Maryes, wch. if a communication had been cut o're land, had not been above two days march to have rescued those harbours where the pyrates have been repairing their ships for 14 days past. Asks for particular instructions on these points *etc. Signed,* S. Gladhill. *Copy.* 3½ *pp.* [*C.O.* 194, 6. *Nos.* 83, 83.i.]

CALENDAR OF STATE PAPERS,
AMERICA AND WEST INDIES, MARCH, 1720 to DECEMBER, 1721

Facsimile

Feb. 4. **374.** Samuel Cox to the Council of Trade and Plantations. I have lately received intelligence upon oath from severalls, and an express from the Generall of the French Islands, giving an account of a pyrate in that neighborhood who is become very formidable exercising thereabouts the vilest cruelties on the subjects of all Nations, and very earnestly solliciting me "to send what force I can to join with such as he can raise," in order to exterminate that race of robbers. Common humanity would determine what should be done in such an exigence, but we had this consideration to add, that we may we may soon expect him to windward of this Island, which might be attended with fatall consequences. *Signed,* Saml. Cox. *Endorsed*, Reed 30th March, 1721. Includes referrences to H.M.S. *Rose* & *Sharke.*
Barbados.

Excerpt

CALENDAR OF
STATE PAPERS
AMERICA AND WEST INDIES,
MARCH, 1720 to DECEMBER, 1721.

February 18. 463 iii
Martinique & Sta. Lucea

News from Barbadoes, Antigua and Jamaica. Bermuda. Feb. 18, 1721, a pirate ship of 32 guns, comanded by one Jon. Roberts, and a brigantine of 18 with 350 men in both, had lately come up with a Dutch interloper of 30 guns and about 90 men as she lay at an anchor with her yards and top-masts down at Sta. Lucea. The pirates at first endeavoured to board her but she running out her booms or fenders prevented them, and then began to engage, the interloper mantaining an obstinate defence for four hours and killed a great many of the pirates, but being overpower'd was forced to submit and what men the pirates found alive on board they put to death after several cruel methods. The Dutch interloper has the character of a handsome warlike vessell and was extraordinary well fitted in every respect, in which the pirates have now 36 guns mounted : When the pirates had refitted after the battle, they went with their prize under Dutch colours close along the harbor's mouths on Martinique shoar, and made the usual signals that the Dutch interlopers were accustomed to do to give notice to the inhabitants when they came off from the coast of Guiny with negroes, and then went again to Sta. Lucea the place for tradeing on such occasions with the interlopers. In two or three days several sloops were fitted out of Martinique and went down in order to purchase slaves which vessells the pirates secur'd as the were actually tradeing; soe those that came latest in knew not the others were taken till they were sensible of their own misfortune, and by this way of manageing they took 14 sail of French sloops, in each of which was a considerable summe of money for that trade. The men they took they barbarously abused some they almost whip't to death others had their ears cut off others they fixed to the yards arms and fired at them as a mark and all their actions look'd like practiceing of cruelty, and at last they sunk and burnt 13 of the 14 sail and let the other return with the poor tormented men to Martinique to tell the storie. After this tragical scene was over they (the pirates) stretched along amongst the French Islands and passing by Guardalupa they saw a large ship at an anchor in the Road, which they cut of haveing 600 hogsheads of sugar on board, from thence they went to Domonico where they intended to carcin - - - On 26th March Capt. Hingston Commander of a ship belonging to London in her way to Jamaica was taken about 4 leagues S. of Antigua by John Roberts Commander of a pirate ship of 42 and a briganteen of 18 with 262 white men and 50 negroes in both carryed to Burbuda, and there kept 5 or 6 days having in that time thrown over severall stills coppers saddles bails of dry goods *etc.* and stript their masts of some running rigging and sails and took forceably 12 of his sailors and then discharged him

Facsimile

CALENDAR OF
STATE PAPERS
AMERICA AND WEST INDIES,
MARCH, 1720 to DECEMBER, 1721.

463 iii continued   with his ship ; The pirate ship had been a French man of war some small time before taken by Roberts in her way from Martinique to France with the Governor of Martinique on board who the pirates hanged at the yard arm *etc*. The pirate run on board the French ship in the night. 2*pp.* [*C.O.*37, 10, *Nos.*17, 17. i-iii.]

Faxsimile

CALENDAR OF
STATE PAPERS,
AMERICA AND WEST INDIES,

May 19.   500. ii.   Address of the Lt. Governor and Council of Antigua to Governor Hamilton. *Urge* his assent to the Powder Act, without the clause for suspending its execution until confirmed by H.M. By the exp. iration of the last Powder Act, there is scarce powder sufficient remaining to protect us against the insults of the Pirates, much less against any sudden invasion *etc. Signed*, Gilbert Fleming D. Cl. Councill. *Endorsed*, Reed. 24th, Read 25th July, 1721.
Antigua.

~~~~~~~~~~~~

500. iii.   Deposition of Christian Mortensen. Antigua, 18th May, 1721. Was taken in April on a Dutch ship by a pirate ship the *Royal Fortune* (described) commanded by one Roberts *etc*. A briganteen, the *Sea King*, accompanied her, and having taken a snow commanded by Nicholas Hendrick, put deponent on board, *etc. Signed*, Gilbert Fleming D. Cl. Councill. *Endorsed*, Reed. 24th, Read 25th July, 1721. [*C.O.* 152, 13. *ff.* 276-277v., 278v.–282v., 283v.]

~~~~~~~~~~~~

May 19.   501.   Governor Hamilton to the Council of Trade and Plantations. Refers to enclosures, relating to the misconduct of Capt. Thomas Capt. Thomas Whitney, H.M.S. *Rose etc.*
Antigua.

The references pertaining to Captain Roberts within the #501. entry are written below.
Excerpts from 501.

...Refers to enclosures. Continues: I doubt not but your Lordships I doubt not but your Lordships will for the service of H.M. and the preservation of these Colonies make such a representation to H.M. as that the transgressor may be taken notice of, for if Captains attending this Station are at their own disposal, and not under the command of the Governour in Chief for the time being it is not in the power of the best Governour to perform his duty, these Islands lying so far asunder that in case they should in time of peace be insulted by pirates, or in time of war be attack'd by the enemy it would wholy out of the power of any Governour to succour or relieve them, except he has the command of the vessels, at least those that attend the Station...

...an account by affidavits of some persons that had been taken and kept for some time on board the pirate Roberts, as also from the General of the French Islands, that the pirates were hovering about these Islands, and had done a great deal of damage as well to several of H.M. subjects, as to the subjects of the French King, and that the French General sent one Monsr. de Malherbe, with proposals and credentials farther to agree upon any method that should be taken to go in quest of the said pirates, I immediately acquainted Capt. Whitney, to witt on Saturday the 19 of february with with what I had received...

Excerpts from 501. cont.

...had Capt. Whitney after this followed the remaining part of the orders then sent him (which was in case he did not get intelligences of the pirates there) to cruise for some days to the windward of this Island, he might in all probability have prevented their taking of a ship after that bound for Jamaica which was taken, within two or three leagues of this Island, which they carried to the Island of Barbouda, and there kept her for several days, plundered her for part of her cargoe, and then let her go after having forced twelve of her men to go with them, which ship was after that taken again by a pirate sloop, that run away some time since (as I have been informed) from Martinique, just to the windward of Spanish Town, one of the Virgin Islands...

...he thought proper to sail the very day the London ship arrived for for St. Christophers, and returned not till the 26 April, and then would not come into the Road or Harbour of Saint Johns as usual, but anchored in a more remote place from thence he sent me a letter by Capt. Pomcroy with an information that he believed the Great Pirate Roberts was cruising off Desseada and that so soon a the Shark joyned him he would cruise in quest of said Roberts in in the tract of Barbados... *Signed,* W. Hamilton. *Endorsed,* Reed. 28th July, Read 14th Sept., 1721.

Facsimile

501. i. Remonstrance of the Lt. Govemour and Council of Antigua to the the Council of Trade and Plantations. Capt. Whitney (*v. preceding*) upon a motion from H.E. for his going in quest of some pirates peremptorily declared to H.E. that he had no power to give him orders altho' he then saw H.M. Instructions to H.E. impowering him so to do etc. During Capt. Whitney's absence in North America (*v. preceding*) the Islands were insulted by pirates, vessels taken, others cut out of the Roads and trade greatly discouraged by that hazard attending it. Refer to enclosures. It may be of very fatall consequence should succeeding Capts. govern themselves with the like independency *etc.* There is not the least room for him to suspect H.E.'s loyalty, who hath on all occasions given the most convincing evidences of his zeal for the service of H.M. *etc. Signed,* Edw. Byam, Jno. Hamilton, Thomas Morris, Will. Byam, John Gamble, Natha. Crump, Jno. Frye, Archd. Cochran. *Endorsed,* Reed. 28th July, Read 14th Sept., 1721. 5½ *pp.*

Facsimile

CALENDAR OF
STATE PAPERS,
AMERICA AND WEST INDIES,
MARCH, 1720 to DECEMBER, 1721

Dec. 8. 739. Lt. Governor Bennett to the Council of Trade and Planta-
Bermuda. tions. From Barbados I understand that that coast and Martinique whom have taken several vessels, and that their place of randevouz was att Sta. Lucea, and that the Govemour of Martinique had sent up to the Presidt. of Barbados for the assistance of a man of war *etc. Refers to enclosure. Signed,* Ben. Bennett. *Endorsed,* Reed. 24th Jan., 172½, Read 13th June, 1722.

Excerpt

AMERICA AND WEST INDIES.

1721.

501. iv (a). Deposition of Richard Simes, Master of the Sloop *Fisher* of Barbados. Antigua, 21st Jan., 1721. On Jan. 13th lying at an anchor in Sta. Lucia near Pidgeon Island, deponent's sloop and Capt. Norton's brigantine belonging to Rhode Island, were seized by the Pirate Roberts *etc.*, who afterwards sailed for the windward of Barbados, to cruise for provisions of which they seemed to be in great want. They took 4 French sloops, three of which they sunk, and the other they gave to deponent. They forced Capt. Norton and all his men to remain with them, using his mate very barbarously. John Smith, an Irishman, went voluntarily. *Described. Signed,* Richard Simes. *Same endorsement.* 1½ pp.

501. v. Deposition of Thomas Bennett. Antigua, 24th Jan., 1721. Owner of the brigantine *Thomas,* on 31st Oct. last, he was seized by the Pirate Roberts 30 leagues E. of Bermudas. They went from Surinam to Tobago to water and thence stood for Sta. Lucia. *Corroborates preceding.* Names and description of 8 sailors still detained by the pirates against their will. *Signed,* Thomas Bennett. *Same endorsement.* 2½ pp.

501. vi. Governor of the French Leeward Islands to Governor Hamilton. Fort Royal, Martinique. 8th Feb., 1721 (N.S.) *Alludes* to depredations of the pirate Roberts off Sta. Lucia 25th and 26th Oct. *etc,* who gave to the master of a Barbados brigantine the vessel of a poor inhabitant of Martinique the bearer of this letter, M. Pomier, which he had seized. This vessel has been brought into Antigua. *Asks that* it may be restored. Between 28th and 31st of Oct. these pirates seized, burned or sank 15 French and English vessels and one Dutch interloper of 42 guns at Dominica. The pirate has the latter vessel with him, besides his own, taken at Tortola, a brigantine of 22 guns and two boats. This squadron of pirates has sailed for St. Eustatia in order to seize another interloper there. Having no man of war now at his disposal, M. de Feuquières wrote to Mr. Cox begging him to send Mr. Whitney who had recently passed Martinique, to return thither, when he would help him with two good vessels and all his forces to seek out the pirates *etc. Signed,* De Pas Feuquières. Bénard. *Same endorsement. French.* 2 pp.

501. vii. *Same* to *Same.* Fort Royal, Martinique. 21st Feb., 1721. N.S. Sends French Artillery officer, M. le Malherbe, to concert measures against the pirates. *Signed and endorsed as preceding. French.* 1¼ pp.

501. xxvii. Capt. Whitney to Governor Hamilton. H.M.S. *Rose.* Five Islands April 26, 1721. I have been cruising among the Virgin Islands in quest of a French pirate that had taken a ship bound to Jamaica, who was so unlucky to be taken just before by Roberts in sight of this Island, and carried to Barbuda where he staid five days. I put the master on shoar at St. Xphers and by his information believe Roberts to be cruising off Desiado. I design when the *Shark* joins me to go in quest of him, and cruise in the tract of Barbados where I design to victual. I should be glad to know if your Excellency has any commands that way. *Signed,* Thomas Whitney. *Same endorsement. Copy.* ¾ *p.*

501. xxviii. Governor Hamilton to Capt. Whitney. Antigua, April 26th, 1721. *Reply to preceding.* If you had followed my orders at your return from Martinique to cruize for some days to windward of these Islands, you might in all probability have come up with the pirate Roberts and prevented the misfortune to the ship bound to Jamaica. *Encloses* following order and requests him to return after his cruise to carry him to Leeward to visit the other Islands of his Government *etc. Signed,* W. Hamilton. *Same endorsement.* 1¼ *pp.*

727. i. Memorial to the Envoy of the States General. The ship *El Puerto del Principe* of Flushing was taken by Roberts the Pirate at Dominica, 29th Jan., 1721, and afterwards brought into Tarpaulin Cove, N.E., by Benjamin Norton of Newport, R.I., who pretends that Roberts took a brigantine from him, and gave him this ship instead. Norton broke bulk at Tarpaulin Cove (a byplace fit for roguery), and in a clandestine manner put a considerable part of her cargo into small vessels, and sent them to sundry ports therewith; some of the cargo he hid in the woods, and some part he left on board.

COLONIAL PAPERS.

1721.

Treaty is on foot, the Board will so represent this growing evil as that it may be restrained *etc.* The depredations committed by the Spaniards on this coast has cost the Government nearly £1000 *etc.* (A ship, lately arrived here from the Isle of May, was taken in her passage by Roberts a pirate (50 guns, 240 men) who said he expected to be joined by another ship and would then visit Virginia, and avenge the pirates who have been executed here. "Considering the boldness of this fellow, who last year with no more than a sloop of 10 guns and 60 men, ventured into Trepassy in Newfoundland where there were a great number of merchant ships, upwards of 1200 men and 40 ps. of cannon, and yet for want of courage in this headless multitude, plundered and burnt divers ships there, and made such as he pleased prisoners, I thought it prudence to make use of this opportunity to put the countrey in a better posture of defence and have got the Council unanimously to consent to the erecting of batterys at the mouth of James River, York and Rappahanock where I shall in a few days have 54 pieces of canon mounted and hope when these batterys are finished according to the plan I have laid, the country will have no occasion to be under any alarm at what the pyrates may be able to do, and the ships in our rivers may ly in safety, but in order to prevent the danger to the trade of these Plantations, I am humbly of opinion that ships of greater force than those now stationed here, are necessary to be sent to guard the coasts; for there is not one of the guardships on this coast fitt to encounter such a one as this Roberts has now under his command, and 'tis no easy matter for two or more of the men of war to joine of a sudden so remote as their stations are from one another for suppressing any great force of the pyrates appearing on these coasts. Certainly a 40 or 50 gun ship is absolutely necessary to convoy our merchant ships out to sea, and a smaller vessel such as a sloop or brigantine to pursue little pickeroons in shoal water, where a great ship cannot come at them, would be very serviceable towards the security of our trade, and driving the pyrates from this coast, where they frequently resort to furnish themselves with provisions, as well as to wait for good ships when their own are grown out of repair, and if last year there had been two men of war here, the one to have cruised while the other cleaned, the great loss this Colony and the trade of Great Britain in generall suffered here from the Spanish privateers had been prevented.") *Encloses* accounts of Revenue and Journals of Council *etc.*) *Continues:*—Your Lordships will observe by the many petitions for leave to take up land how much the frontiers of this country are likely to be extended, and principally upon the hopes of H.M. gracious approbation of the Act pass'd this last Session, and the Address of the Assembly for encouraging the possessing the passes of the Great Mountains, both which I hope by your Lordsps. favourable interposition are by this

A Voyage to Guinea. 41

ON *Monday*, the Seventh, I began my Survey, but here I met with no such Opposition as at *Gambia*, the Inhabitants of this Country being more us'd to the Customs and Manners of the *Europeans*. Nevertheless, there are several Things in these Parts worth our Observation, of which I shall make Mention as I proceed. And first, I shall give a short Description of the Country in general.

SIERRALEONE was first discover'd by the *Portuguese*, but I cannot be rightly inform'd at what Time the *English* became Masters of it, nor indeed is it very material, since they have had it a Number of Years in their Possession unmolested, till *Roberts*, the famous Pirate took it in the Year 1720, when Old *Plunkett*, who was blown up in *Gambia* Castle, was Governor, which he effected in the following Manner: *Roberts* having then three good stout Ships under his Command, put into *Sierraleone* for fresh Water, and finding a Trading Ship in *Frenchman's* Bay, he took her from thence and carried her into ano-

42 A Voyage to Guinea.

ther Bay, with a long narrow Enterance near the Cape, and where there was a great Depth of Water. This, in my Survey, I have call'd *Pirates-Bay*, because when *Roberts* had rifled her, he set Fire to her: Part of her Bottom was to be seen at Low Water when I was there. The next Day, he sent up a Boat well mann'd and arm'd, with his humble Service to *Governor Plunkett* desiring to know if he could spare him any Gold Dust, or Powder and Ball. Old *Plunkett* return'd him Word, that he had no Gold to spare; but as for Powder and Ball, he had some at Mr. *Roberts's* Service, if he would come for it. *Roberts*, having receiv'd this Answer, brought up his three Ships next Flood before *Bense* Island, and a smart Engagement soon follow'd between him and the Governor, which lasted several Hours, till *Plunkett* had fir'd away all his Shot and Iron Bars; upon which, he betook himself to his Boat, row'd up the back Channel to a small Island call'd *Tombo*; but they quickly follow'd, took him, and brought him back again to *Bense*, where *Roberts* was, who upon the first Sight of *Plunkett* swore at him like any Devil, for

A Voyage to Guinea. 43

his *Irish* Impudence in daring to resist him. Old *Plunkett*, finding he had got into bad Company, fell a swearing and cursing as fast or faster than *Roberts*; which made the rest of the Pirates laugh heartily, desiring *Roberts* to fit down and hold his Peace, for he had no Share in the Pallaver with *Plunkett* at all. So that by meer Dint of Cursing and Damning, Old *Plunkett*, as I am told, sav'd his Life.

WHEN they had rifled the Warehouses, they went aboard their Ships, and sail'd out of the River the next Ebb, leaving Old *Plunkett* once more in the quiet Possession of his Fort, which the Pirates had not damag'd greatly.

THIS is a mountainous, barren Country, especially towards the Cape, where the Hills are exceeding high and rocky, but nevertheless they are cover'd with Trees which harbour many wild Beasts; such as Tigers, Leopards and Lions; from whence it was first call'd by the *Portuguese*, SIERRA DE LEONE; or, *The Mountain of Lions*. And the Country gives its Name to the River, which

BLOOD and SWASH, The Unvarnished Life (& afterlife) Story of Pirate Captain, Bartholomew Roberts............."REFERENCE SECTION"

WHAT	ILLUSTRATIONS within BOOK 2	PAGE
Author's Book Cover on Captain Bartholomew Roberts, A Pyrate Journal		188**
Picture of la Marquise d'Éperon-noire's Diary		189*
Page From la Marquise d'Éperon-noire's Diary		190*
Page From la Marquise d'Éperon-noire's Diary		191*
Versailles, France		194
Woodcut of Captain Edward England		195
Color Drawing Courtesy of TheFairyGodgather.com		198
Captain Bartholomew Roberts		199
The Pelican Inn, London (circa 1720)		201
Map of London (circa 1720)		201
Painting of London Docks (circa 1720)		203
Leather Letter Pouch		208*
Letter from la Marquise d'Éperon-noir to John Robert		209*
Antique Map of Pembrokeshire		211
Page From la Marquise d'Éperon-noire's Diary		217*
Page From la Marquise d'Éperon-noire's Diary		218*
Page From la Marquise d'Éperon-noire's Diary		229*
Page From la Marquise d'Éperon-noire's Diary		230*
Map of West Coast of Africa		232*
Cape Coast Castle on the coast of Guinea		232*
Woodcut of Captain Hywel Davies		234
Map of West Coast of Africa Depicting Cameroon		236*
Sea Level View Entering Santo Antoinio Principe		236
The Opposite side of Annamaboa Fort		237
The Ambush & Murder of Captain Hywel Davies & several of his crew		239
Snippet from Daniel Defoe's book: Speech made by, Lord Henry Dennis, Rover's Master Gunner, that got John Robert elected Captain.		240
Newspaper Clipping		243*
Map depicting the location of Fernando de Noronha Island within the Atlantic		243*
Drawing of the Rover being Careened		244*
Depiction of, la Marquise d'Éperon-noire Carriage Riding in Bermuda		247
Map of La Baía de Todos os Santos		248
The Portuguese Treasure Fleet, including the *Sagrada Família*		251
Captain Roberts. First Flag he designed		251
Captain Roberts at Whydah (armed with a Saber & 4 Pistols)		258
This skilled artist drew not only an outstanding depiction of the Captain's Coat, Necklace, Ponytail, Mustache & Royale, but, look sharp at the captain's right forearm. The picture also contains what the author believes is a true likeness of his magnificent Cross.		
Map depicting the location of Îles du Salut, nigh off Surinam (aka Devil's Island.)		262*
Painting of Îles du Salut, nigh off Surinam (aka Devil's Island.)		263
Page From la Marquise d'Éperon-noire's Diary		264*

WHAT	PAGE
Page From la Marquise d'Éperon-noire's Diary	265*
Newspaper Clipping	266*
Newspaper Clippings	267*
Drawing of a Tall Ship	268
Map of the Island of Antigua	269*
Reproduction of the Letter Written by the Governor of the Leeward Islands to Mr. Popple, the Secretary of the Commissioner of Trade and Plantations in London.	269*
Post Script to the above letter	270*
The Articles of Captain Bartholomew Roberts	271*
Map of Tobago Isle	272*
Map of the Islands of Saint Christophers	274*
Map of the Island Barbados	275*
Sea Battle	277
Newspaper Clipping	278*
Map of Corvocoo Isle (aka Carriacou)	279*
Captain Roberts (Holding a Medieval Sword)	280
Newspaper Clipping	280*
Map of the Island of Guadeloupe	300*
Map of Ferryland	300
Map of Trepassey Bay	301
A typical French fishing shallop of the period	302
The Port of Trepassey	302
Newspaper Clipping	304*
Reproduction of the Letter Written by Alexander Spottswood (Lt. Governor of the Colony of Virginia, 1710-1722) to the Board of Trade.	307*
Reproduction of the Letter written by a Secretary of Placentia, near Trepassey	308*
Newspaper Clippings	308*
Reproduction of # 281.i. Calendar State Papers. RE: Trepassey	309*
Map of the Newfoundland Region, including Trepassey Bay	310*
Reproduction of the 'Cross Of George' flag with 4 cannon ball holes.	310*
Reproduction of Letter Written by Cap'n Bartholomew Roberts to King George I	311*
A recreation of an article within the author's Oct 15th, 1720 antique newspaper	313*
Newspaper Clipping RE the Brigantine Essex & Ocean Born Mary	316*
Essex County Court Records from August 31st, 1720	317*
Another Newspaper Clipping RE the Brigantine Essex & Ocean Born Mary	317*
Another Newspaper Clipping RE the Brigantine Essex & Ocean Born Mary	318*
John Leverett, President of Harvard College, wrote a letter in regard to the *Samuel*	318*
Map of Carriacou Isle (aka Corvocoo)	319*
Picture depicting Storm of coast of St. Christophers which forced the abandoning of the *Royal Rover*.	320*
Letter to Governor Mathew, of the Leeward Isles from, la Marquise d'Éperon-noire	323*
Map showing the Black Rocks where Cap'n Dunn was to meet Cap'n Roberts at Saint Christophers Island.	326*

What	Page
Woodcut of Captain Roberts	327
Depiction of la Marquise d'Éperon-noir's vacation home on Saint Christophers	333
Oil Portrait of Captain Roberts	335
Representation of the ship *Royal Rover*	336*
Drawing of Captain Roberts (Holding a Medieval Sword)	337
Reproduction of the Letter Written by Henry Fowle (Cap'n of the ship Mary) to James Parsons regarding sheep & Cap'n Henksome's ship's Wheel.	338*
Newspaper Clippings	338*
Letter to Lt. General William Mathew, Governor of Saint Christophers Island	339*
Map of Saint Barthélemy's Island	340*
Map of the Cape de Verd Islands, specifically the Isle of Brava	341*
Map depicting the location of Surinam	342*
Drawing depicting the *Royal Fortune*	343*
Second flag designed by Captain Roberts	345
Letter to the Admiralty, London, from Lt. General William Mathew, Governor of Saint Christophers Island.	346*
Map of Dominico Isle	346*
Drawing depicting the *Royal Fortune*	347*
Map of Martinique	349*
Map of Saint Lucia	350*
Map of The Leeward Islands, specifically depicting Bennet's Key	352*
Letter from la Marquise d'Éperon-noire to Bartholomew Roberts	362*
Recreation of a Letter from Captain A. Hingston to Captain Whitney	363*
Map of Bermuda	364*
Oil Painting depicting the likeness of Madame Aspasia Jourdain, la Marquise d'Éperon-noire.	364*
Letter from la Marquise d'Éperon-noire to her household in Bermuda	365*
Pencil sketch of Bartholomew Roberts by the Author	366
Painting of a Sea Battle, presumable of the *Royal Fortune* & *H.M.S. Swallow*	368
Picture of Bartholomew Roberts & crew members during battle	369
Antique Map of Guinea	371
Newspaper Clipping	371*
Newspaper Clippings	373*
Map of the Port of Guinea	374*
Picture of Bartholomew Roberts (Holding a Saber)	375
Page From la Marquise d'Éperon-noire's Diary	379*
Page From la Marquise d'Éperon-noire's Diary	380*
Ships being Careened	381
Newspaper Clippings	387*
Drawing of the frigate, Onslow (aka Royal Fortune)	387*
Reproduction of the Letter excerpt from Africa regarding *H.M.S. Swallow* & Weymouth en route to Joaquin.	389*
Map of the locations of towns on the Ghana coast	390*

What	Page
Drawing depicting some of Bartholomew Roberts' crew	390
Picture of Bartholomew Roberts at Whydah (Holding a Medieval Sword)	392
Reproduction of the Ransom letter written by Bartholomew Roberts at Whydah	393*
Newspaper Clippings	394
List of Captain Roberts' Crew	395
Map of the Nigerian Estuary depicting Parrot Island & Frenchmen's Bank where Captain Roberts was killed.	403*
Captain Chaloner Ogle	404
The Weymouth. a 4th-rate Ship-Of-The-Line. Very similar to the , H.M.S. Swallow	404
Picture depicting the *Royal Fortune* with a tornado at sea during her final Battle against HMS Swallow.	406
Drawing of Captain Roberts in his final battle	407
Painting depicting the death of Captain Bartholomew Roberts	408

What	ILLUSTRATIONS - Reference Section	Page
Snippets RE Trepassey Harbor, St. Shots Bay & Ferryland Harbor taken from "The American Coast Pilot, Containing Directions For The Principal Harbours, Capes and Headlands of the Coasts of North & South America" by E. & G. Blunt. 1847.		416
Bell Time		416
Front page of CO 23/13, Bahama Islands, Letter from Gov. Rogers Phenney dated Dec 1718 - Dec 1727 PRO, Kew, England which was photographed by author.		422
Front page of CO 31/15, A Representation of the Miserable State of Barbados, PRO, Kew, England which was photographed by author.		422
First flag used by Captain Bartholomew Roberts		423
Snippet: excerpt of William Smith's testimony during the Cape Coast Castle Trial		426
1760 Bill Of Fare. Referencing Solomon Gundie		426
Snippet (Colonial State Papers): His Majesty empowers Governor Hamilton the right to suspend Naval Captains (#501 xxvi, 21 February 1721)		429
Snippet (Colonial State Papers): the French & English proceed with their Plans to Combine Forces in a Effort to Destroy Cap'n Roberts (#501 xxvii & xxviii, 13 March 1721)		429
Map of Le Havre, France. Depicted as an excellent reference of ports of the day.		433
Map of Port Royal in Jamaica depicting Salt Pan Hill & Picture of Salt Pond.		
The Hanging of that Loathsome Scalawag, Walter Kennedy		443
Letter regarding the Tea, of which, Captain Roberts was so fond.		445
One line of Captain Roberts family tree		446
Abstract of Will/Administration RE William Roberts, Cap'n Roberts' brother Pembrokeshire Record Office.		447
Copy of the 'Last Will & Testament' written by the aforementioned William Roberts		448

BLOOD and SWASH, The Unvarnished Life (& afterlife) Story of Pirate Captain, Bartholomew Roberts............"REFERENCE SECTION"

What	Page
English translation of the aforementioned 'Last Will & Testament'	449
Pembrokeshire Record Office listing of Wills depicting the aforementioned, William Robert as a Landowner.	450
Page taken from record book within Saint Peter's Parrish in Little Newcastle	451
Front page of Transcript of the Tryals of Cap'n Roberts' crew. Located in The National Archives Kew, England. Full Document in Possession of the Author.	452
Copies of 2 the Original Death Sentences for some of Cap'n Roberts' crew	453
Copy of a portion of the Original letter written by Cap'n Roberts' to the Governor of Saint Christophers' Island. Letter is located in The National Archives Kew, England.	454
Painting containing Captain Roberts' ancestral home. Courtesy of Mrs Reese of Little Newcastle, Wales	455
2 Pictures of Saint Peter's Church in Little Newcastle.	456
Monument erected in Captain Roberts' honor	457
Close Up of the plaque on the aforementioned Monument	457
16 Pages From: Calendar of State Papers, Colonial Series referencing Cap'n Roberts	458
Page From: from 'A Voyage to Guinea' referencing an expletive filled Argument twixt Cap'n Roberts & Governor Plunkett which took place at Bense Island, as well as other invaluable information.	475
Clipping from The Western Telegraph (2005) of the Author & her late husband Bart Roberts (succumbed of Lung Cancer, 05 Oct 2015.)	488

*Drawn or otherwise created or reproduced by the author.
**Drawn by the author & arranged Katrina Henson.

Regarding **HISTORICAL NARRATIVES within BOOK 2**	Page
The Dutch East~Indiaman Ship, Marquis del Campo.	231
Captain Hywel Davies takes the Guiney-man entitled, Princess, et al.	233
Captain Hywel Davies.	238
Vague reports regarding Kennedy & the fate of the Rover & the Sagrada Família.	269
The ship's, Phillipa & Summersett Galley, & the birth of ever-lasting hatred.	276

More Trial Tidbits

John Sharp said that like an Officer[*], *Abraham Harper* always carried a Rattan (aka Baston; a weapon similar to a Baton or Billy Club.) in his hand, directing about the Provisions, & what else related to his office.[B6, page 48]

[*] was referring to the officers aboard Navy & Merchant vessels.

According to *Harry Glasby*, it was one of *Roberts'* rules to take All Englishmen out of foreign ships [B6 pg 56]

Harry Glasby testified: "**Richard Harris** *was one of the jury at* **Dominico**, *when himself, another white man & a Negro, were for Deserting, sentenced to death over a bowl; that the 2 latter were finally shot, & he escaped only by a Fancy* **Valentine Ashplant** *(a Leading Man about them) took to him.*" [B6 pg 56]

TALL SHIPS within BOOK 2 (minus Crews List & Timeline)

Name of Ship & Captain etc	Configuration, if known	Page (s)
Benjamin	Launched 1716 - Full Rigged Ship	275
HMS Bideford, after which, a Merchant Admiral Babridge's ship at Trepassey	24 gun, 6th Rate Ship of the Line -	305

    Launched 14 Mar 1721 - Foundered in 14 Mar 1736 due to a leak.
    Member of the Gibraltar Group. After commissioning, she spent her career West Indies, Morocco & Portugal on trade duties.
    24 guns: Upper Deck: 20# 6 pounders, Quarterdeck: 4# 4 pounders.
    Length: 94 ft 3 in, Beam: 26 ft 3 in, Depth of Hold 11 ft 6 in. Tons: 281 burthen.

Bird		208, 232, 432
Blessing		310, 376
Cornwall, Rolls, Cap'n	Galley. Peter Scudamore, Surgeon	389

    and 2 musicians, Nicholas Bradley (hautboy) & James White (violin), signed Articles.[SP1]

Diligence, John Harding or Stephen Thomas, Cap'n a 69 ft., 3-Masted English Slaver		390
Eagle	Snow	270
Elizabeth, John Sharp, Master	Adam Comry, Surgeon, signed Articles	390
Expectation, of Topsham	Sloop	300
Experiment	English Ship, Cap'n Cornet	242, 277, 280, 427
Essex, Robert Peat, Cap'n	some say Brig, other say Brigantine	316, 317, 318
Fisher, Richard Simes, Master	Barbados Sloop (Antigua, 21 Jan 1721)	472. SEE #501 iv
Flushingham (aka Vlissingen), Dutch ship. Geret de Haen, Master. Philip Haak, trumpeter, signed Articles		390
Fortune	Sloop of 10 guns SEE page 307	263, 268, 272, 274, 278, 279, 282, 283, 285, 293, 294, 300, 301, 303, 306, 459

    Described by Alexander Spotswood (Lt-Gov. of Virginia, 1710-1722) also described as a ship of 38 Carriage & 12 Swivel Guns, & 240 men, & a Brigantine of 18 Guns, also well mann'd. He told the Master of this Ship that he expected speedily to be joined by a Ship of 46 Guns.

Gertruycht, of Holland. Benjamin Kreeft, Cap'n		390
Good Fortune (Thomas Anstis, Commander)	80 ton Brigantine - 16 guns	303, 310, 316, 320, 321, 327, 328, 329, 331, 335, 336, 337, 345, 372
Great Ranger, 32-gun. Brig., Former Dutch Slaver 'El Puerto del Príncipe' Cap'n Thomas Sutton		343, 345, 374, 389, 404, 410
Greyhound, of Saint Christophers - Cap'n Cox	Brigantine	343
Happy Return, William Taylor, Master	Sloop belonging to St. Christophers	275, 300
Hardey, Cap'n Dittwitt		393 (See Ransom note)
Hermoine	French slave ship	387
HMS Rose, Woodes Rogers, Cap'n Launched: 25 Apr 1712	6th Rate Ship of the Line - (a Man-O'-War) (338 & 373 News Clipping)	247, 338, 345, 363, 373, 427, 462, 467, 473

    Member of the Gibraltar Group. After commissioning, she spent her career in Home waters & N. America on trade duties.
    24 guns: Upper Deck: 20# 6 pounders, Quarterdeck: 4# 4 pounders.
    Length: 94 ft, Beam: 26 ft, Depth of Hold 11 ft 6 in. Tons: $273\,^{26}/_{94}$ burthen.

HMS Swallow, Chaloner Ogle, Cap'n Launched: 10 Feb 1703, Rebuilt & Re-launched 25 Mar 1719 - Broken up, 1728	4th Rate Ship of the Line - (a Man of War)	351, 367, 387, 389, 404-407, 410, 426, 424, 433, 434

    50 guns: Gundeck: 22# 18 pounders, Upper Gundeck: 22# 9 pounders, Quarterdeck: 4# 6 pounders, & Forecastle: 2# 6 pounders.
    3 decks. Length: 130 ft, Beam: 35 ft, Depth of Hold 14 ft. Tons: 711 burthen.

HMS Shark (also Sharke) Launched: 20 Apr 1711	Sloop of War (338 & 373 News Clippings)	338, 373, 427, 462, 467, 473
HMS Weymouth Launched: 8 Aug 1683	4th Rate Ship of the Line - (a Man of War)	387, 389*, 394, 424, 433

    50 guns: Gundeck: 22# 18 pounders, Upper Gundeck: 22# 9 pounders, Quarterdeck: 4# 6 pounders, & Forecastle: 2# 6 pounders.
    3 decks. Length: 130 ft, Beam: 35 ft, Depth of Hold 14 ft. Tons: 715 burthen.

Jeremiah and Ann	Dutch Guiney~man (aka Slave Ship)	280

BLOOD and SWASH, The Unvarnished Life (& afterlife) Story of Pirate Captain, Bartholomew Roberts.............."REFERENCE SECTION"

Ship	Description	Pages
Joceline, Loane, Cap'n		389
Joseph	Cap'n Bonaventure Jelfes	276
King Solomon, Trahern, Cap'n	200 ton Slaver, 12 guns	390, 391
Little York, a Virginian. James Phillips, Master		316
Little Ranger (was the Ranger) (formerly the Privateer, Comte de Toulouse)	French Brigantine, James Skyrmé, Cap'n	374, 389, 403-406, 411
Love, of Lancaster		316
Marquis del Campo, a 3-masted Sloop of War Renamed, the Rover, by Cap'n Howel Davies[B2] (See page 186 of the reference book)	Dutch East~Indiaman, 30 guns	231, 233, 459
Mary, of Boston - Cap'n Henry Fowle		337
Mary and Martha, of St. Christopher	Thomas Willcocks, Master	200, 212, 300, 337
Martha, of Leverpool	Snow, Cap'n Lady	387
Mayflower	Sloop	275
Mercy	Galley	389
Morning Star		372, 430
Morrice	Sloop	232-234, 430
Neptune. Hill, Cap'n		410, 413
Norman	Galley	310
Norton's Brigantine (Cap'n Roberts took 4 French sloops sinking 3. The 4th they gave to deponent)	belonging to Rhode Island (13 Jan 1721)	472. SEE #501 iv
Onslow, Cap'n Gee	Frigate of 26 guns	387
Pearl		195
Philippa, Cap'n Daniel Greaves (aka Graves)	Sloop - 6 guns	274-277
Phoenix. from Bristol, John Richards, Master	Snow	316
Porcupine, Cap'n Fletcher, an English Interloper		389, 393
Prince Eugene, Cap'n Bastian Mealke		370
Princess, of London, Cap'n Abraham Plumb	Guiney~man (aka Slave Ship)	186, 195-198, 200-203, 205, 207, 208, 231-234, 252, 287, 289, 400, 402, 414, 422, 423, 432
Ranger		343, 345, 372, 374, 426
Relief, Cap'n Dunn - Smuggler	Sloop	319, 320, 326, 427
Revenge, of Antigua	Sloop	279
Richard, of Bideford	Pinque (aka Pink)	310
Rover (formerly the, Marquis del Campo. Beefed up by Davies[B2. see page 187])	Dutch East~Indiaman, 32 guns & 27 Swivels	210, 231-234, 236-238, 240, 241, 244, 248, 252, 253, 255, 256, 258, 260, 261, 263, 267-270, 272, 283, 287, 421, 459
Royal Fortune #1	Brig - 22 guns	337
Royal Fortune #2	French Brig of 32 carriage guns & 9 Swivels	341, 344
Royal Fortune #3		345, 350, 353, 357, 358, 361, 365-370
Royal Fortune #4		372, 377, 385
Royal Fortune #5 (formerly the Onslow)	Frigate - 40 guns	389, 390, 392, 395, 403-405, 406, 410, 411, 428
Royal James (aka King James)		231-236, 238, 459
Royal Rover	3 Masted, 220 ton French Ship - 28 guns	306, 310, 315, 320, 321, 328, 329, 331, 336, 337, 429, 459
Royal Hynde	French Pinque (aka Pink)	232-234
Sadbury (perhaps Sidbury), Captain Thomas	Brigantine	319

BLOOD and SWASH, The Unvarnished Life (& afterlife) Story of Pirate Captain, Bartholomew Roberts............"REFERENCE SECTION"

Sagrada Família		251, 260, 261, 263, 268, 269, 351, 400, 459
Saint René	French slave ship	387
Samuel	6 guns	310-313
Sea King	Cap'n Montigny le Palisse	276, 277, 428
Sea Nymph	Snow	269
Stanwich, commanded by Captain Tarlton	Galley	387
Summersett, Owen Rogers, Commodore	Galley - 16 guns	276, 278
Tarlton, of Liverpool, Joseph Trahern, Cap'n	George Wilson, Surgeon, Signed Articles	390
Temperance Ship kept by Roberts, former Cap'n	Sharman was give a Portuguese craft in trade.	243
Terrible		185, 195, 414, 421
Thomas (30 leagues E. of Bermudas)	Brigantine (31 Oct 1720)	472. SEE #501 v
Union		391
Victory		195
Willing Mind		310
York, of Bristol	Sloop	300, 310

Author's Note: The ideal method to cover the crew requirements of a vessel was by voluntary recruits, and this method was most successful for enlisting commissioned officers during the Anglo-Dutch wars of the seventeenth century. Privileged second and third sons of the landed gentry not eligible to inherit titles often sought commissions and favor from family members to help them advance in the navy whilst at the same time fulfilling their desires to travel and build a reputation (Brown 2011: 53). In contrast, efforts to encourage volunteers for lower-ranked positions in the fleet was often less productive. The men needed for these positions would not enjoy the financial rewards and status associated with the ranks reserved for "gentlemen,"[1] and their work was often hard and considered menial. Yet, popular broadsheet ballads commonly pandered to the working classes in order to motivate voluntary recruitment.

[1] "Gentleman" in this context refers to landed gentry and the adult males of wealthy families of the period without the intention of suggesting any personal respectability or strength of character. [B4]

SUMMING UP: During Bartholomew Roberts', almost four year career, he had not only plundered, burnt or sank nigh on 500 vessels, beaten garrisons of fully trained troops, armadas of foreign shipping, freed hundreds of would be slaves, and obliterated well-armed shorelines and harbors, all of which brought shipping to a standstill, he managed to make off with more than £50 million in swag. The authorities of the period were mortally afraid of him, crediting him with the courage and capacity to carry out any piratical feat. Fortunately, all he did is not lost, for despite the efforts of the English crown to conceal one of what they consider(ed) to be their main embarrassment, Bart is well remembered. and to that end, it'll be a better day when all of those who think of others in the role of the greatest and/or most famous pirate, e.g. Morgan, Kidd, and Blackbeard, come to realize who it is that is truly worthy of the title; being some others may be better known, greater they are not. The Honor of the Greatest and Most Successful pirate; and yet, this be only one facet of this man's persona (being known also for both his quiet demeanor, & patient endurance) belongs to pirate Captain, John 'Bartholomew' Roberts, & having had the honor of being dubbed, "That Great Pyrate," during his lifetime, shall be, for **ALL TIME** his! This aside, what needs to be most remembered, is that Bart was a man of courage who defied those in power; the ultimate 'WHITE KNIGHT,' though it was Crimson he wore; having pride in his homeland being the reason. Bartholomew Roberts, together with his morals, and sense of right and justice, were all part of that which made up this incomparable man; it was through piratical methods, aided by his reputation (that he took great care to nurture) which always preceded him, that provided the means to achieve his goal, which was to help alleviate suffering, and remember, he was attacking the Government's right to abuse the populace, the Merchant Captains & their Employers, and the Slavers, the latter being anyone who captured, sold, or kept a human being as a slave. To begin, Captain Roberts, to intentionally publicize his presence to whomever may see them know, unquestionably, whose ship (s) they were observing, flew his flags around the clock, he also had a audacity to announce his arrival, either in writing by special messenger, or with the aid of boisterous musicians and cannon fire when entering a harbor. This was just a few of the many ways Bart employed his own brand of psychological warfare. Another was through intimidation. Bart, having had his fill of men who achieved their high ranking positions by means of birth or wealth as opposed to knowledge & skill which was his fate, had a point to make. Bart was also against slavery, & he was equally opposed to the thousands of white men dying at the pleasure of a ruler, who, for the sole purpose to obtain more wealth; land and the people who live there pay taxes being the principle wealth for every country, did their utmost to obtain more land by way of establishing new colonies on foreign soil. Bart's remedy was to embarked on a crusade, one method being to free as many captured slaves as possible from slave ships, another was to enlist from other ships as many recruits as possible, this way robbing the Sea Captains of their manpower whilst at the same time increasing his own. He was so efficient in his methods, that by Spring of 1721, Merchant Shipping came to a virtual standstill; no shipping meant no new men would ship out, & in turn put an end to those who would've died in both the established & upstart colonies along the African coast, & in addition to the countless single men, as well as entire families, who would've been sent forth to establish new colonies, this, as par for the course, also meant no plunder, & Bart being interested in little beyond sustenance, cared little about it.

When you examine his methods & the reasons for his actions with an open mind, it's easy to see that Bart was at war with Tyranny, and the greatest perpetrators at the time just happened to be the major Powers, the wealthy merchants, & the Sea Captains in their employ.

TRIAL TIDBIT: **MAROONING** as Defined by *Joseph More*. [B2 page 48]
"It was a Punishment among them for something notoriously villainous, such they accounted Desertion, and whenever it was carry'd against an Offender, he was put on shore on some uninhabited Cape or Island, with a Gun, some Shot, a Bottle of Powder, and a Bottle of Water, to subsist of starve."

LINEAGE REFERENCES WITHIN THIS BOOK

H1: Mme Aspasia Rebekah Jourdain, Marquise d'Eperon-noire. Died Childless.
Born: Summer of 1686. Pembrokeshire, Wales - Married in 1705. Falling into obscurity, when and where she died is unknown.
Mother: Marie Hywel.
Father (in the eyes of the law): Herbert Joseph Smith Rees.
Married: Sir Guillaume Jourdain, marquis d'Éperon-noire (1702) by Arrangement*.
*After rather extensive bargaining betwixt Mme de Maintenon and the Marquis d'Éperon-noire, Aspasia became Sir Guillaume's 2nd wife.

Humble Beginnings: In 1685, about a year before Aspasia was born, her mother, Marie, travelled to Versailles with her husband on court business. Presumed barren following the miscarriage of her first child some years earlier, she was threatened with divorce if she did not conceive before they were to return to Boston. Fearful of this impending action, Marie, in dalliance with the 11 year old Philippe-Charles d'Orléans, became pregnant by design. At that same time, the court physician determined that her husband's bout with the pox years earlier had rendered him sterile. To preserve her husband's honour, and win Louis XIV's favour, Marie, at the Queen's request, journeyed to Wales. Having died in childbirth, Marie's husband, wishing to hide from polite society, his late wife's indiscretion, opened negotiations with the Mme de Maintenon, Queen Consort & la duc d'Orléans, Philippe de France. After Aspasia's true birthright was acknowledged, she, although never raised to the high position of *Princess du Sang*, she was made a *légitimée of France* by king Louis XIV. Arrangements having been made, Aspasia, in the care of her Nursery Governess, Mrs Robles, journeyed to France in 1693.

H2: the Honourable Mrs Neville Robles, also known as **Mme Robles, Baroness de Rhoslyn**; so styled by Special Arrangement so she may be privileged to be the personal nursery governess of Aspasia within the confines of the French court, was answerable only to her benefactor, la Marquise de Maintenon. As time went on, the Baroness' position, in keeping with the needs of her charge, changed. Her final honor was that of Lady's Maid, Companion, Confident & Personal Cook to Marquise d'peron-noire. *Was also a Kinsman, the companion, and midwife to Marie Hywel.*

H3: Sir Guillaume Jourdain, marquis d'Éperon-noire (b. 1648 - d. 1715.) Married in 1705
A paternal grandson of François de la Béraudière, marquis de l'Ile-Jourdain, seigneur de Rouhet, Chevalier par ordre du Roi, was a courtier of Louis XIV of France. Sir Guillaumes' Bermudian Estate, located in Paget Parish, raised Mulberries and Silk Worms, from which was produced not only an enormous supply of silk cocoons, as well as an immense quantity of yard goods there from, but also a vast amount of Mulberry Wine.

H4: Queen Consort aka Françoise d'Aubigné, la Marquise de Maintenon: 2nd wife of Louis XIV.

H5: Marie Hywel, an American Colonist (Boston Towne, MA) of Welsh/Germanic & French decent, was born in Pembrokeshire, Wales. **Spouse:** Herbert Joseph Smith Rees. Issue: 1 child, a daughter: Mme Aspasia Rebekah Jourdain, Marquise d'Eperon-noire. Died from Childbed Fever (complications following childbirth.)

H6: Herbert Joseph Smith Rees: A sea Captain, who was born in Pembrokeshire, Wales &

later retired in Little Haven, Wales, was an American Colonist (Boston, MA) of English, Welsh, French, and German decent with great wealth. A direct descendant of a Welsh Nobleman who accompanied Sir Walter Raleigh, an act that helped to colonize Massachusetts Bay. Spouse: Marie Hywel, an American Colonist. Issue: 1 natural child, Trilby, a daughter. Trilby married the 6th Viscount of Dragonwood, Dragonwood Plantation, São Salvador, Brazil, by arrangement. No issue. ALSO: Although believed to be Aspasia's natural father in the eyes of the world, he was, in reality, her Godfather.

H7: Philippe, duc de Chartres, nephew of Louis XIV, who rose to the position of Philippe II, Monseigneur le Régent, was, after having been seduced by the much older Marie Hywel, Aspasia's Natural Father.

The d'Éperon-noire plantation in Bermuda raised Silk Cocoons & Mulberries. The leaves of Mulberry plant provided the food that silkworms feasted, & the Cocoons were transformed into the finest silk fabrics of various weaves. As a secondary industry, the fruit of the Mulberry plant, was made into wine.

Although Mme Aspasia Rebekah Jourdain, marquise d'Éperon-noire, did in fact have full rights to her late husband's (Sir Guillaume Jourdain, marquis d'Éperon-noire) title, afforded her by her uncle, Louis XIV of France whilst she lived, her estate, being childless, & a widow, still, reverted to the crown upon her death.

The Author's Family Tree continued from the FORWARD

Returning to those of whom the author is particularly proud, rests Wladislaus Dragwlya, vaivoda partium Transalpinarum[Latin] (aka Vlad Drăculea) of whom she is a Direct Descendant, as well as the House of Spencer. Hugh Howell is a direct decendant of Henry VIII, and his wife, Margaret Howell (née Middleton) is a direct decendant both of Baron Robert de Vere (1164-1221) one of the 25 Barons who were surety for the Magna Carte (1215) and ancestor of Kate Middleton, Princess of Wales.

On the author's Paternal side, altho' that research has been limited, the author is a Direct Descendant of Felix Mendelssohn, and has a line within Joan of Arc's ancestral family tree, she is also proud to boast to having a Privateer during the American Revolution as well. As an extra tidbit regarding the latter, Micajah Smith, whilst guarding New Jersey's Little Egg Harbor; having been appointed Captain of the LM PA Fly, a 3 gun Schooner[E4], with a crew of 20, and utilizing the harbor's shifting sandbars effectively, captured 3 British merchant ships, 2 of which (the Venus, & the Jupiter,) their name plaques can be seen just under the water at low tide. As a reward for his efforts, Captain Smith was awarded a Land Grant consisting of 28.5 acres on the South side of Little Egg Harbor River, N.J. 16 Dec. 1784, and a Griskmill.

Of a more recent vintage lies two notable inventors: Albert Summers Howell of Bell & Howell (the author's great grandfather,) & her own father, Richard J. Smith, whose main in preoccupation was 'steam engines,' was a highly respected inventor & aeronautic engineer (aka rocket scientist;) moreover, the majority of the amusement rides today run on the bearings he invented that are so perfectly round, they are measured with light beams. Mr.

Smith not only taught at Annapolis, he worked on the Lunar Moon Rover, and was one of those offered a contract by the U.S. Government, General Motors & Lear with regard to the production of Steam Engines for automobiles. Over the years, both sides of the author's family were joined in marriage at least twice. The first time was a Howell, then spelt Hywel, specifically, Marie Hywel of Pembrokeshire who married Herbert Joseph Smith Rees (a Bostonian Sea Captain who retired in Little Haven.) Marie Hywel is the mother of Madame Aspasia Rebekah Jourdain, la Marquise d'Éperon-noire.

Both sides of the author's family tree is lined with creators/artists/designers of some sort, be them Innovators, Inventors, Builders, Mechanical Engineers, Writers, Painters, Sketch Artists, Crafters, Animal Trainers, an Architect, a Teacher, etc., as well as numerous First Responders, e.g. Firemen, as well as an amateur Composer, & several amateur Keyboardists; moreover, both families have taken part in every war involving France, Great Britain, & the United States; sometimes as rivals. e.g., In 1066, while her Smith line was amongst those in William the Conqueror's army, the author's Howell line was Welsh Saxon and was living in & around Letterston, Wales; what's more, as far as can be determined, up until the 21st century, with the exception of 1 member in the Smith line of the author's ancestral tree has produced at least one Seaman in each generation as far back as 1580 (Roanoke Expedition).

An interesting note: Both the Robert & Howell families within the author's family tree, et al., had a habit of inconsistency with regard to the spelling. In the case of Robert, an s was intermittently added making it Roberts, often by the same person &/or immediate family. The Howell surname was interchangeable with Hywel (sometimes Hwyel,) and All the spellings, still widely used today, have been standardized.

Without question, the 18th century part of the author's lineage (altho' the whole of which inspires her to measure up,) is no proof in itself that the rest of Book Two, beyond that pertaining to Captain Roberts is factual, when you couple it with her knowledge without fore study of the territory, places, people & happenings within Captain Roberts' lifetime, and adding to that her understanding of the period, sense of belonging (deep feeling of being home,) and the knowledge of places she'd never been; not just names, but facts concerning the people, what they did, and how they lived, the geographical layout of the town & buildings, statistical data regarding their chief imports & exports with regard to agriculture, mining & trade, not to mention that she knew her way around Pembrokeshire, Wales (but only when traveling on the 'older' B roads, etc.) from the moment she arrived like she had lived there before. All in all, these give the author honest cause to believe it's much more than mere fiction whilst at the same time, dispelling her prior disbelief regarding life renewing itself, now believes that in some cases, people can live more than one corporeal life, and if they are very lucky, that which never was, can one day be.

ABOUT THE AUTHOR

Having revered Bartholomew Roberts since her formative years, V'léOnica, not only made, 'The Great Pirate,' the centerpiece when she created her pirate website in 1996 *(taken down due to lack of resources in 2015)* was taken from a book report she wrote as a Freshman in High School,) she took it upon herself to become his Champion. In dedicating her life to the task of, 'Setting the Record Straight,' she moved to Pembrokeshire, Wales, where she met his Mirror Image, who, incidentally, asked her to marry him the next day, & believing him to be the reincarnation of he whom she had been in love much of her life, they were married in her beloved Little Newcastle Church.

Unfortunately, whilst residing in the USA for the purpose of selling their property, the real estate market crashed & they got stuck. A few years later, after a mere 10 years, the happy couple's blissful relationship, at the corporal level, ended when her beloved Bart succumbed to metastatic lung cancer; an event V'lé holds the United State directly responsible[*]. Since that time, altho' pining for him endlessly, V'lé, in hopes such would provide her the means to return home to her cherished Pembrokeshire, endeavored to finish the two books she had begun whilst he lived. Afterwards, should she be so fortunate as to succeed, her only desire is to reside as close as possible to the village of Little Newcastle so she may help care for, & preserve, the Little Church & Village both she & Captain Roberts shall forever hold dear.

---

[*] To read why the author holds the U.S. responsible for Bart's death, turn to page 491.

WHY THE AUTHOR HOLDS THE U.S. ACCOUNTABLE FOR HER HUSBAND'S DEATH.

When Bart applied for his Green Card, the U.S. required him to have a chest X-ray & take a TB test. For American Citizens a result of 15 or less is acceptable, but in Bart's case, even though his test was rated a 5, he was required to take some medication for 9 months. We later discovered this medication could cause Liver Cancer, & that's exactly what it did. In late 2012, Bart, required by his new employer, had another chest X-ray & fitness exam. In late September, while on a break, Bart, as did 2 other immigrants, who neither new each other or worked in the same department, stepped outside within the same few minutes, & altho' they could see one another, were not within close proximity. Each complained of droplets landing on their arm from a chem trail. A couple days later, all 3 were sick for a week, causing us to cancel out vacation, which also prevented V'lé from taking her dying mother (who died the following March) on what would've been her only vacation in a several years. By mid summer, 2014, Bart was having trouble breathing, having both a X-ray & a Cat Scan, he was told that it appeared the illness in September had left some scar tissue in his lungs, & the Doctors suspected he had acquired Valley Fever, but not to worry cause it should clear up in a couple months, adding that the valley fever would fair better in a damper climate, & they lived in the Mojave desert. The need for continued employment, & owing a home which would need to be sold, not to mention lacking the means, prevented us from relocating right away. Getting increasing worse, Bart had more tests in late 2014. He was told basically the same thing. In November, the house was sold for 20% of market value, & they bought a motorhome & started hunting for Camp Host jobs where the weather was more humid. V'lé being disabled, as well as a sufferer of chronic Bronchitis, which would be far worse in humid weather, did not help our situation. Finally, several months later in the spring of 2015, a camp host job would be available that fall at an RV Park in California, & while making plans to go Bart, took another turn for the worse, & after have more tests they could ill afford, the Doctors continued to tell us that Bart had Valley Fever. For reasons unknown, they were contacted by a hospice who offered their assistance, & being grateful for any help she could get, V'lé gladly accepted. About a month later she asked the caregiver if he had seen Bart's medical records. He told her Bart had Lung Cancer that had evolved from metastatic Liver Cancer. Bart, who was listless & unable to work, as well as showing signs of depression, spent all of his time in bed, & knowing it was already too late, V'lé opted not to tell him, at least not then & needing some sort of income that would pay for the only medicines that eased his cough, continued to get things situated so they could get that job in California, but on 03 October 2015, just days before they were to leave, Bart was rushed to the hospital where he died 2 days later. If not for the Cancer giving drug the government made him take, & the Chemtrail the government sprayed into the air, V'lé's beloved Bart would not have become ill; to say nothing of the fact that if the 'so-called' Doctors had told them the truth in the beginning, they could've returned to Wales forthwith where Bart would've received decent medical care.

Books by V'léOnica Roberts *aka* V'lé Onica
ALL OF THIS AUTHOR'S WORKS ARE EPISTOLARY STRUCTURED.

1) **THE TRUE & COMPLETE MEMOIRS OF THE PYRATE CAPTAIN, EXTRAORDINAIRE! THE ILLUSTRIOUS CAPTAIN, JOHN 'BARTHOLOMEW' ROBERTS THE MOST SUCCESSFUL PYRATE OF ALL TIME!**
'Limited to 1000 copies, this work is Out Of Print'

2) **CAPTAIN BARTHOLOMEW ROBERTS, THE MOST SUCCESSFUL PIRATE OF ALL TIME! A PYRATE'S JOURNAL** are scanned prints of the original Memoirs. Presented in cursive. Altho not currently available, the author intends to re-release it later in 2023.

3) **THE TRUE ADVENTURES OF THAT GREAT PIRATE, BARTHOLOMEW ROBERTS** is more or less a reprint of the Memoirs transformed form Diary form to Prose.

4) **BLOOD & SWASH: THE UNVARNISHED LIFE (& AFTER-LIFE) STORY OF A PIRATE CAPTAIN, BARTHOLOMEW ROBERTS**. A 2-part series; an Epistolary Structured Narrative presented in First Person. CONTAINS OVER 150 PICTURES, MAPS, LETTERS, NEWS ARTICLES, ETC. + NIGH ON 80 PAGES OF REFERENCE MATERIAL, MOST OF WHICH IS IN COLOR. Available in both B&W & Full Color.
A Sizzling biographical Adventure Romance with the Greatest of ALL Pirates, personifying the essence of a Stalwart man; even though to some, he may only be a pirate!
SYNOPSIS: For the love of a man long since past, our heroine searches for a way to include romance in their otherwise perfect relationship, but there's another, who in vying for the soul of the Great Pirate, enlists the aids of an old flame, believed dead, who will stop at nothing to achieve his objective, but when Lucifer's henchman fails at the corporeal level, our fervent duo, as they are besieged by maniacal devilry, struggle for their very existence.

Following a storm at sea, our heroine is thrust back in time to the days of her beloved, where (now a Lady of Rank, Power, & Considerable Means) she must battle outside her element if she is to have any chance to save the pirate captain she loves from his already known fate.

5) **LUCIFER'S RESURGENCE.** Except for the Bibliography & Lineage references, the majority of the historical references, together with the nigh on 80 reference pages, have been omitted. Otherwise, with it's over 150 pictures, maps, letters, news articles, etc., most of which are in color, this book is effectively the same as #4. Available in both B&W & Full Color.

<u>Thank Yous by other authors</u>

Ocean-Born Mary: The Truth Behind a New Hampshire Legend
by Jeremy D'Entremont   See Pages 9, 110 & 111.

The Historie of Pirates pages   (as V'léOnica Evans)

Plus a multitude of online references.

Note: On May 17th, 2005, Captain Roberts' Birthday, V'lé Onica was married to James Bartholomew Roberts[*] of Milford Haven, in Saint Peter's Parish, Little Newcastle, Wales. It was the happiest day of her life. Since his passing, V'léOnica Roberts (missing him terribly) wearing widow weeds, still, prays each day that one day they will be together again.

---

* On October 5, 2015, almost 11 years to the day the author & Bart met, Bart died.

Printed in the USA
CPSIA information can be obtained
at www.ICGtesting.com
LVHW081555260124
769959LV00005B/725